THIS SIDE OF PARADISE

&

THE BEAUTIFUL AND DAMNED

This Side of Paradise
&
The Beautiful and Damned

◆

F. Scott Fitzgerald

with an Introduction and Notes by
LIONEL KELLY

WORDSWORTH CLASSICS

For my husband
ANTHONY JOHN RANSON
with love from your wife, the publisher.
Eternally grateful for your unconditional love.

Readers who are interested in other titles from
Wordsworth Editions are invited to visit our website at
www.wordsworth-editions.com

This edition first published in 2011 by
Wordsworth Editions Limited
8B East Street, Ware, Hertfordshire SG12 9HJ

ISBN 978 1 84022 662 1

Text © Wordsworth Editions Limited 2011
Introduction and Notes © Lionel Kelly 2011

Wordsworth® is a registered trade mark of
Wordsworth Editions Limited

Wordsworth Editions
is the company founded in 1987 by
MICHAEL TRAYLER

Typeset in Great Britain by Antony Gray
Printed and bound by Clays Ltd, St Ives plc

Contents

GENERAL INTRODUCTION

Wordsworth Classics are inexpensive editions designed to appeal to the general reader and students. We commissioned teachers and specialists to write wide-ranging, jargon-free Introductions and to provide Notes that would assist the understanding of our readers rather than interpret the stories for them. In the same spirit, because the pleasures of reading are inseparable from the surprises, secrets and revelations that all narratives contain, we strongly advise you to enjoy this book before turning to the Introduction.

General Adviser: KEITH CARABINE
Rutherford College, University of Kent at Canterbury

INTRODUCTION TO
THIS SIDE OF PARADISE

This Side of Paradise, though often neglected today, was an instant success on first publication in 1920. However, when the manuscript was originally submitted to the publishers, Scribner's, they rejected it. In spite of this, Fitzgerald felt sufficiently encouraged to work on revisions, and when he took it to them again, they accepted it. After the first edition there were eight reprints in 1920, and by 1921 some forty-nine thousand copies had been sold. Fitzgerald was transformed from a struggling author of a few short stories, earning less than a thousand dollars in 1919, to the most celebrated young novelist of the day whose earnings in 1920 had reached almost nineteen thousand dollars, comparable to a hundred and ninety thousand dollars at the present time. Rich and famous overnight, Fitzgerald became the figure that his central character in the novel, Amory Blaine, failed to be.

This Side of Paradise is one of those novels that serves to mark a moment in American cultural history, appearing out of nowhere yet speaking to and widely read by an audience it discovered, like the

equally successful J. D. Salinger's *The Catcher in the Rye* (1951) and
Jack Kerouac's *On the Road* (1957). Two features of the novel under-
line its impact on the reading public. First, *This Side of Paradise*
appealed to the society it described, the generation of late-teenage
and early-twenties men and women who saw in it a reflection of
their own lives, with its celebration of party-going, dances, nights at
the theatre, and the rituals of the mating game shown here at their
most ardent and comic, and set at a point in time when conventional
sexual mores were changing into something distinctively modern
and daring. Second, Amory Blaine is a brilliantly imagined figure,
one whose rampant egotism is at the mercy of his own and his
author's capacity for irony as we follow him through prep school,
university and beyond. His story is a history of how his early
romantic egotism is transformed into the cynical idealism he
acknowledges as his condition at the end of the novel.

Fitzgerald's early novels and short stories, especially his collection
Tales of the Jazz Age (1922), are held to describe and define a period
in American history known as 'the Jazz Age', the decade of the 1920s,
a period of sustained economic buoyancy in America brought to an
end by the Wall Street Crash of 1929. In a retrospective essay of
1931, 'Echoes of the Jazz Age',[1] Fitzgerald specifies its origins,
decline and defining quality. In his account it lasted from the May
Day riots of 1919 to the Wall Street Crash in October 1929, though
its essence was over by 1923. It was driven by the generation who
were adolescent during the First World War and relieved from the
anxieties of war in 1918, and their revolt from the established order
of things seemed focused entirely on the pursuit of pleasure. The
frenzied impetus of the young to enjoy life to the full was soon to be
shared by an older generation, so that by 1923 'their elders, tired of
watching the carnival with ill-concealed envy, had discovered that
young liquor will take the place of young blood, and with a whoop
the orgy began. The younger generation was starred no longer.' As
the noun 'jazz' is the defining term here, we might expect some
account of the nature and variety of its musical idioms from its
origins in the southern black American community into mainstream
American life, but this complex history is not part of Fitzgerald's
enterprise. 'Jazz' he writes means 'first sex, then dancing, then music',
and his only comment on jazz music in this essay is the sentence:

1   F. Scott Fitzgerald, *The Crack-Up*, edited by Edmund Wilson, 1931, pp.
13–22

'For a while bootleg Negro records with their phallic euphemisms made everything suggestive . . . '[2] The Jazz Age was also the time of Prohibition in America, and the consequent appearance of the speakeasy. Prohibition against the sale, manufacture and distribution of alcohol throughout the United States became law in 1920, though the Federal Government did little to enforce the law. The effect was to drive the manufacture and sale of alcohol underground, a trade that rapidly came under the control of gangsters. The notorious St Valentine's Day massacre in 1929 led to widespread disenchantment with the consequences of the act and it was revoked in 1933. The term 'speakeasy' refers to low-class bars where alcohol was sold, where customers were asked to 'speak easy', quietly, when ordering alcohol. Speakeasy clubs proliferated in the major cities, especially in New York City.

Fitzgerald prefaces his novel with quotations from Rupert Brooke and Oscar Wilde. They were not casually chosen. First are two lines from Brooke's poem 'Tiare Tahiti', which provides Fitzgerald with his title, a poem about a love affair between Brooke and a Tahitian woman during his stay on Tahiti. The second is a quotation from Oscar Wilde's play *Lady Windermere's Fan*. These two passages alert us to the paradoxical fusion of the romantic imperative with the ironic deflationary impulse central to Fitzgerald's presentation of character, scene, and situation throughout. If Brooke, like Swinburne and Keats, represents the literary appeal of romance in the quotations from them in the novel, it is Wilde the ironist who exposes the gap between appearance and reality in his characters, and of course, the audiences he wrote for. While this alternation between romance and irony is transparent in the novel, it shows that in revising early drafts Fitzgerald achieved a critical distance between the autobiographical material he was calling on and his grasp of those materials and how to present them. The most significant difference between the early manuscripts of *This Side of Paradise* and the final version was Fitzgerald's change from a first- to a third-person narrator.

2   For a recent expert account of the emergence of jazz and its musicians, see Jed Rasula, 'Jazz and American Modernism', in *The Cambridge Companion to American Modernism*, edited by Walter Kalaidjian, Cambridge University Press, 2005, pp. 157–76

For readers who come to this novel having previously read Fitzgerald's *The Great Gatsby* (1925), *This Side of Paradise* may well seem a somewhat chaotic apprentice work, without the formal control of all the elements manifestly evident in the later novel. However, if we turn to the structure of the novel, the distinguished Fitzgerald scholar Jackson R. Bryer reminds us of Northrop Frye's *Anatomy of Criticism* (1957) and the tradition Frye gives of the 'anatomy' form of narrative where the customary logic of narrative progression is subject to violent dislocations that give the appearance of carelessness. These dislocations include inset digressions, catalogues, the stylising of characters in a comedic vein, disruptive dialogues, a pervading tone of contemplative irony, verse interludes, a display of erudition, a mixture of prose and verse, and symposium discussions, as in the example of Joyce's *Finnegan's Wake*, Sterne's *Tristram Shandy* and Burton's *Anatomy of Melancholy*. It may seem inappropriate to put *This Side of Paradise* in this company, but it is a way of arguing for Fitzgerald's unorthodox narrative practice in this novel. For example, the comedic stylising of character is evident in the first chapter, which is developed through a series of capitalised headings itemising Amory's progress. The son of a mother who embodies 'a culture rich in all arts and traditions, barren of all ideas' (p. 44), he is nurtured in a view of himself as 'particularly superior' to all the other boys at school, even though he knows 'this conviction was built upon shifting sands' (p. 47). His letter responding to Myra St Claire's invitation to her 'bobbing party' shows his grasp of grammar and spelling to be poor. In the 'Snapshots of the Young Egotist' sequence we learn that school ruined his French and that '[h]is masters considered him idle, unreliable and superficially clever', but his egotism survives as he 'wondered how people could fail to notice that he was a boy marked for glory' (p. 54). In bed at night he dreams of great accomplishments but 'It was always the becoming he dreamed of, never the being. This, too, was quite characteristic of Amory' (p. 54). He thinks of himself as intellectually not marked for 'a mechanical or scientific genius' but as being debarred 'from no other heights'; sees himself physically as 'exceedingly handsome', and believes that socially he possesses 'personality, charm, magnetism, poise, the power of dominating all contemporary males, the gift of fascinating all women' (p. 55). This analysis of Amory's egotism is exacting yet engages our interest in him as a charismatic figure. At the end of the first chapter there is a kind of double-entry bookkeeping passage itemising the distinction between 'The Slicker' and 'The Big Man', following a conversation at prep school between Amory and Rahill, the president of the sixth form, a pair of philosophers as they think of themselves. Such conversations are modest versions of the symposium debate, where ideas are thrashed out in discourse. Here, as elsewhere in the novel, Amory feels 'the need of conversation to formulate his own ideas'. If on this occasion, the issue is trivial, whether 'a fellow slicks his hair back with water' or not, it evolves into a formula distinguishing the self-confident boy who understands his social place and role from the one who does not. We may think of this passage as an example of the puerile anxieties that preoccupy the adolescent mind, but these late-night questionings of self-identity are true to this moment in Amory's career, and are never wholly quieted. It is an unconscious irony that in the final paragraph of the first chapter he decides on Princeton as the university of his choice, because it 'drew him most, with its atmosphere of bright colours and its alluring reputation as the pleasantest country club in America' (p. 69). Amory's ambition to achieve high social status at Princeton must not be stridently pursued, not 'running it out' as the expression went, but achieved through natural aptitude in the flourishing of his social, creative and sporting gifts within the undergraduate community. His ultimate failure at Princeton is due to neglect of his studies and he never graduates. He returns briefly in 1917, then enlists in the army with his Princeton contemporaries, some of whom see action in the war and are killed. Another example of unorthodox narrative practice comes in the first section of Book Two, 'The Débutante', where his pursuit of Rosalind Connage is presented as the text of a drama, with stage directions setting time and place. The context is Rosalind's 'début' into society, for she is now eighteen and positioned as an object in the market economy of marriage. A beautiful, sharp-witted young woman, she must marry well, and though Mrs Connage has not yet met Amory, she already thinks Rosalind won't care for him because ' "He doesn't sound like a money-maker" ', to which Rosalind replies, ' "Mother, I never *think* about money" ', where that word 'think' is finely positioned because she knows it is in her power to ensure that money will come with a wealthy suitor. The keynote of her relationship with Amory is given in response to his suggestion, ' "Suppose – we fell in love" ', when she replies, ' "I've suggested pretending." ' Later, when Amory urges they should get married instantly she says they can't because,

' "I'd be your squaw – in some horrible place" ', and to Amory's urging that, ' "We'll have two hundred and seventy-five dollars a month all told" ', she replies, ' "Darling, I don't even do my own hair, usually" ', a wonderfully measured put-down in all that it implies of her needs. What she wants is made clear as she finishes with Amory, and says, ' "I'm just a little girl. I like sunshine and pretty things and cheerfulness – and I dread responsibility. I don't want to think about pots and kitchens and brooms. I want to worry whether my legs will get slick and brown when I swim in the summer" ' (p. 193). Her affair with Amory amounts to little more than kisses, and her cultivated despair when he is dismissed and she cries out, ' "Oh, Amory, what have I done to you?" ' is shown for all it shallowness in this stage aside (*And deep under the aching sadness that will pass in time, Rosalind feels that she has lost something, she knows not what, she knows not why.*)

2

This Side of Paradise can also be read as an autobiographical novel in the tradition of Joyce's *A Portrait of the Artist as a Young Man* (1916), a book that 'puzzled and depressed' Amory (p. 203), though we are not told why. It is possible that Fitzgerald wished to obscure the impact of Joyce's work on him, for Stephen Dedalus is another who oscillates between moods of romantic idealism and bitter irony. There is certainly one notable echo of Joyce's novel in *This Side of Paradise*. Joyce ends with Stephen's eloquent, if ironic, words affirming his sense of his destiny, 'I go to encounter for the millionth time the reality of experience and to forge in the smithy of my soul the uncreated conscience of my race.' In the final chapter of *This Side of Paradise*, we read of Amory that, 'He was his own best example – sitting in the rain, a human creature of sex and pride, foiled by chance and his own temperament of the balm of love and children, preserved to help in building up the living consciousness of the race' (p. 248). The story of Amory Blaine's life and times follows Fitzgerald own history, not only in the Princeton episodes, but also in Amory's failed love affairs. However, Fitzgerald invests Amory Blaine with a start in life quite different from his own circumstances as the child of much-loved but materially unsuccessful parents. Like Anthony Patch in *The Beautiful and Damned*, Amory Blaine is a scion of an aristocracy 'founded sheerly on money', and inherits from his mother 'every trait, except the stray inexpressible few, that made him worth while'.

The trajectory of the novel is to take Amory from his beginnings as spoilt little rich boy – a figure of pervasive interest in Fitzgerald's work – to the end where, with the Blaine fortune gone, the love of his life married to someone else, in a spirit of resigned stoicism, he acknowledges that 'I know myself . . . but that is all', a redemptive expression honouring the classical injunction to 'know thyself'.

Two sequences in the first chapter are of particular interest. The first is where Amory, a teenager, withdraws in horror from Myra St Claire in the car after a kiss on her cheek because 'Then, their lips brushed like young wild flowers in the wind'. This sentence, in the romance idiom Fitzgerald was always called to, is undercut not by irony on this occasion but by Amory's 'disgust, loathing for the whole incident. He desired frantically to be away, never to see Myra again, never to kiss anyone . . . and he wanted to creep out of his body and hide somewhere safe out of sight, up in the corner of his mind' (p. 52). It is an extraordinary moment, a revolt from human intimacy, and he stares at Myra 'as though she were a new animal of whose presence on the earth he had not heretofore been aware'. It is a proleptic moment, anticipating other occasions in the novel where Amory's relationships with young women are fraught with something devilish he senses in them, something inauthentic that repels him. The second sequence is Amory's visit to Monsignor Darcy, the fictionalised version of Monsignor Sigourney Fay to whom the novel is dedicated. Fay's impact on Fitzgerald is represented in the novel as a union of sympathies in which Darcy, 'the jovial, impressive prelate who could dazzle an embassy ball, and the green-eyed, intent youth, in his first long trousers, accepted in their own minds a relation of father and son within a half-hour's conversation'. Darcy encourages Amory's naïve sympathy for lost causes – Bonnie Prince Charlie, Hannibal, the Southern Confederacy – and assures the boy that sympathy with Irish patriotism 'should, by all means, be one of his principal biases'. If the paternal idiom of this relationship is central, as a Catholic priest committed to celibacy Darcy represents a relationship in which the sexual agenda is neutralised. In his letter of January 1918 to Amory, Darcy writes: ' "I've enjoyed imagining that you were my son, that perhaps when I was young I went into a state of coma and begat you, and when I came to, had no recollection of it . . . it's the paternal instinct, Amory – celibacy goes deeper than the flesh . . . " ' (p. 166). The extent to which Fitzgerald subscribed to this notion may be tested by reading his brilliant short story of 1924, 'Absolution', precisely located in the confessional box where a young boy's admission of a sin – he has lied to his father about not earlier attending confession – closes with the priest, Father Schwartz, collapsing in the box under the oppression of his own sensory feelings for 'the heat and the sweat and the life' out there in the world denied to him through his calling.

In 'Spires and Gargoyles', the longest chapter in the novel, Amory Blaine's time at Princeton follows Fitzgerald's own preoccupations there, with an abiding passion for American football, girls and the art of writing – poems, plays and journalism – nurtured in the intense collegiate atmosphere, while doing as little academic study as possible. The outlets for writing include the undergraduate newspaper, the *Daily Princetonian*, the *Nassau Literary Magazine*, and material for the Triangle Club, which staged and toured with a new musical comedy each year. Amory's literary ambitions and publications in these contexts are based on Fitzgerald's. The index to the *Nassau Literary Magazine*, for example, shows fifteen entries by Fitzgerald during his Princeton days including an entry in February 1917 under the title 'Spires and Gargoyles'. Amory's intellectual life is enhanced by his friendship with Tom D'Invilliers, a figure modelled on the poet John Peale Bishop, who introduces him to the poetry of Stephen Phillips, and the work of Oscar Wilde. The friendship between Tom and Amory is said to cause 'mild titters among the other freshmen, who called them ' "Dr Johnson and Boswell" ' (p. 82). It is Tom who persuades Amory to publish his satire on popular professors in the *Nassau Lit* (p. 126). Under Tom's influence Amory's enthusiasm for the poetry of Rupert Brooke and Algernon Swinburne flourishes, though at the end of the novel Amory sees a fatal link in them between beauty and evil over the problem of sex. This Catholic tendency reflects back to the way in which Amory's affairs with women are attended by a sense of something devilish or evil. While D'Invilliers is shown to be a serious aesthete, Amory's interest in girls is writ large and he is drawn to desirable young women from privileged backgrounds.

There are then two issues which dog Amory's love affairs as the novel progresses, money and sex. While his largely adolescent affair with Isabelle Borge is easily disposed of in the bitter acknowledgement ' "Damn her! . . . she's spoiled my year!" ', the love affairs with Rosalind Connage and Eleanor Savage come to grief over money. With the Blaine family resources in decline he cannot compete with the rich suitors for either girl. It is Eleanor who tells Amory, ' "Every year that I don't marry I've got less chance of a first-class man. At the best I can have my choice from one or two cities and, of course, I have to marry into a dinner-coat"' (p. 225). This follows Fitzgerald's own experiences with Ginevra King, the teenage Chicago socialite he first fell in love with, and then with Zelda Sayre, who married him in 1920 following the successful appearance of *This Side of Paradise* but who had earlier rejected him because of his impoverished circumstances. The association of women, sex and a sense of evil, present in almost all Amory's affairs, features in Fitzgerald's later novels and short stories. In *Tender is the Night*, for example, Nicole Diver is the victim of paternal incest, a situation reflected with a kind of savage irony in the title of the film *Daddy's Girl*, which is to star the other female lead in the novel, Rosemary Hoyt. In 'The Egoist Considers' chapter of *This Side of Paradise* there is a section called 'The Devil', where Amory runs from the apartment of Phoebe Column and her friend Axia when 'temptation crept over him like a warm wind' and he sees an apparition he thinks to be the devil. In the hotel room in Atlantic City when Amory is rescuing his friend Alec Connage from the embarrassment of being caught there with a woman he has picked up for sex, the apparition is there again as Amory sees 'over by the window . . . something else, featureless and indistinguishable, yet strangely familiar' (p. 233). And there is the earlier incident of the girl he sits with in a limousine outside the Country Club in Louisville, where he has been on tour with the Triangle Club. In response to his question, ' "Why on earth are we here" ', the girl replies, ' "I don't know. I'm just full of the devil" ' (p. 88). Similarly, though Eleanor Savage is an entrancing figure who nurtures in him 'a sense of coming home' (p. 218), when he thinks about her later we are told that 'Eleanor was, say, the last time that evil crept close to Amory under the mask of beauty, the last weird mystery that held him with wild fascination and pounded his soul to flakes' (p. 213). The Eleanor sequence in the 'Young Irony' chapter shows Amory's courtship of her as a kind of literary performance in the manner of Rupert Brooke, in which his attitudes to life, to her and to himself are said to be 'reflexes of the dead Englishman's literary moods' as his sits listening to her reading Brooke's poems 'up and down the scale from Granchester to Waikiki' (p. 220).

How are we to account for this preoccupation with sex and evil in a novel said to celebrate the Jazz Age? Is it simply a neurosis Amory cannot overcome? As I have indicated, it is eventually identified with 'the strong phallic worship in Brooke and the early Wells', where he finds evil with beauty inseparably linked. Beauty is 'still a constant rising tumult; soft in Eleanor's voice, in an old song at night, rioting deliriously through life like superimposed waterfalls, half rhythm, half darkness. Amory knew that every time he had reached towards it longingly it had leered out at him with the grotesque face of evil' (p. 260). Beauty, he decides, is too associated with licence and indulgence, with weakness, and 'weak things were never good'. From this he comes to the conclusion that while his disillusion is complete he has arrived at a point where he is leaving behind 'his chance of being a certain type of artist' and now it 'seemed so much more important to be a certain sort of man'. He thinks about religion and considers that on the one hand 'there was a certain intrinsic lack in those to whom orthodox religion was necessary' and that commitment to the Catholic faith was 'conceivably . . . an empty ritual', but that, on the other, 'it was seemingly the only assimilative, traditionary bulwark against the decay of morals'. But he cannot commit himself to acceptance yet, and wants 'to keep the tree without ornaments' (p. 260), to have the bulwark of faith without the duties of obedience that go with it. The insecurity of his religious convictions has been shown in the culminating parts of the Eleanor Savage sequence in 'Young Irony', where she denies his panacea of ' "The Catholic Church or the maxims of Confucius" ' and argues that ' "It's just all cloaks, sentiment and spiritual rouge and panaceas. I'll tell you there *is* no God, not even a definite abstract goodness" '; and despite his challenge to her that she is merely ' "Talking about God again after the manner of atheists" ', 'His materialism, always a thin cloak, was torn to shreds by Eleanor's blasphemy . . . She knew it and it angered him that she knew it' (p. 226).

As we follow Amory's sense that it is now 'important to be a certain sort of man', what sense of him are we left with as the novel ends? Throughout, his social views fluctuate between resentment of 'social barriers as artificial distinctions made by the strong' (p. 75), and his admiration for a figure such as Dick Humbird who 'seemed to Amory

---

3   Arthur Mizener, Fitzgerald's first biographer, and editor of *F. Scott Fitzgerald: Afternoon of an Author* (Bodley Head, 1958), a collection of fourteen short stories and six essays by Fitzgerald, in his Introduction to Fitzgerald's essay 'Princeton' of 1927, writes: 'Fitzgerald does not criticize Princeton for being undemocratic, but for being snobbish instead of aristocratic. This is a very precise representation of the attitude of a time and a place . . . ' Mizener was himself a graduate of Princeton.

a perfect type of aristocrat . . . the eternal example of what the upper class tries to be' (p. 102).[3] In the America of the 1920s, it was acceptable for Amory to further define Humbird as someone who 'could have lunched at Sherry's with a coloured man, yet people would have somehow known that it was all right'. Humbird's subsequent death in a car accident is seen as 'so horrible and unaristocratic'. Tom D'Invilliers, who is ' "sick of adapting myself to the local snobbishness of this corner of the world" ' (p. 107), reads Amory as a ' "rubber ball" ' who bounces from one social clique to another in his attempts to shine in the society of Princeton. In 'Narcissus Off Duty', a wonderfully comic title and appropriate here, where it is as though the author of self-love has turned from his own reflection to find that there are other charming and intelligent people in the world, Amory is briefly attracted to Burne Holiday whose 'keen enthusiasm' for socialism, economics and pacifism, and for Tolstoy, Edward Carpenter and Walt Whitman, has 'in it no quality of dilettantism' (p. 138). They discuss the hypothetical relationship between physical bearing and moral nature in the belief that 'light-haired men' are generally more successful and morally sound, a debate fed by the interest in the social science of eugenics in the 1920s.[4]

As the heading of Book One indicates, Amory is defined at the outset as a Romantic Egotist, whilst the last chapter of Book Two is titled 'The Egotist Becomes a Personage', and he now defines himself as a 'cynical idealist', a condition he shares with his creator. It was John Peale Bishop who said Fitzgerald 'had the rare faculty of being able to experience romantic and ingenuous emotions and half an hour later regard them with satiric detachment'. It is a faculty Amory shares to a considerable degree in the way he plunges wholeheartedly into all his enterprises, with his peers at Princeton, his love affairs, his literary ambitions, and retains that ability to mock himself and others in the process. In 'A Damp Symbolic Interlude' – itself an irony – Amory walks the grounds of the university at night, inspired

4 In *The Great Gatsby* Fitzgerald has Tom Buchanan say that 'Civilisation's going to pieces', and recommends '*The Rise of the Coloured Empires* by this man Goddard'. It is characteristic of Buchanan to get the title of the book and the author's name wrong. What he refers to is Lothrop Stoddard's *The Rising Tide of Color Against World Supremacy* (1920). Stoddard's eugenicist theory was that the population explosion among coloured peoples in the twentieth century would erase white supremacy and lead to the collapse of colonialism.

by its Gothic architecture, whose 'dreaming peaks were still in lofty aspiration towards the sky', and he 'felt a nervous excitement that might have been the very throb of its slow heart'. This is an example of the over-active imagination of a young man out late at night thinking of where he is and what his future is to be in this almost sacred place until the mood of the passage is undercut by the concluding lines, ' "I'm very damn wet!" he said aloud to the sundial.' His poems in a romance idiom and his satires show a telling sense of what is fitting for the figure addressed in them. With his cousin Clara, who refuses to indulge him in a love affair, he writes a poem called 'St Cecilia', which manages a chaste tone. He answers Eleanor's poem sent to him long after their time together with his own 'Summer Storm', with this poignant recall of her:

> And now *you* pass me in the mist . . . your hair
> Rain-blown about you, damp lips curved once more
> In that wild irony, that gay despair
> That made you old when we have met before;

His satire on a Princeton professor is an accomplished piece (pp. 126–7), and a memory of Isabelle combines a lyrical recall of her –

> there was an idle day
> Of ours, when happy endings didn't bore
> Our unfermented souls; I could adore
> Your eager face beside me, wide-eyed, gay,

with this bitter ending –

> You wept a bit, and I grew sad for you
> Right here! Where Mr X defends divorce
> And What's-Her-Name falls fainting in his arms.

This double-edged quality of showing the ardour of youth and the painful checks that follow the arc of Amory's experiences appealed and spoke to the young generation of the 1920s. It is the distinguishing feature of the novel's style, and underlies its enduring appeal.

In the final pages there is a long scene where Amory is given a lift by the father of his former classmate Jesse Ferrenby, killed in action in France. Thinking of his friend, 'the man who in college had borne off the crown that he had aspired to', he now thinks of that Princeton time as 'What little boys they had been, working for blue ribbons – ', a late, telling perspective on his own history (p. 259). With Ferrenby's father, Amory airs his recent interest in socialism, and while it is always hazardous to take any of Amory's pronouncements as settled statements of a considered point of view, it is difficult to relate his view of social poverty with his claims on socialist ideology. ' "I detest poor people," ' thought Amory suddenly. ' "I hate them for being poor. Poverty may have been beautiful once, but it's rotten now . . . It's essentially cleaner to be corrupt and rich than it is to be innocent and poor" ' (p. 241). He acknowledges that 'he was lacking in all human sympathy' and saw in poverty 'only coarseness, physical filth, and stupidity'. Critics have not found this conversion from the would-be aristocrat to the left-wing theorist very convincing. It is best I think to see him poised at the end on the cusp of a new beginning which is as yet indeterminate: if 'the waters of disillusion had left a deposit on his soul, responsibility and a love of life, the faint stirring of old ambitions and unrealised dreams' suggest there is that within him still to fashion a role and place in the world.

3

I end with quotations from two of Fitzgerald's contemporaries. In an obituary essay written just after Fitzgerald's death in 1940, the poet and novelist Glenway Wescott (1901–87) wrote:

> *This Side of Paradise* haunted the decade like a song, popular but perfect. It hung over an entire youth-movement like a banner, somewhat discoloured and wind-worn now; the wind has lapsed out of it. But a book which college boys really read is a rare thing, not to be dismissed idly or in a moment of severe sophistication.

Gertrude Stein (1874–1946), the most audacious theorist of literary fiction in the twentieth century, writes in a letter acknowledging Fitzgerald's gift to her of a copy of *The Great Gatsby* in 1925:

> You are creating the contemporary world much as Thackeray did his in *Pendennis* and *Vanity Fair* and this isn't a bad compliment. You make a modern world and a modern orgy strangely enough it was never done until you did it in *This Side of Paradise*. My belief in *This Side of Paradise* was alright. This is as good a book and different and older and that is what one does, one does not get better but different and older and that is always a pleasure.[5]

5   F. Scott Fitzgerald, *The Crack-Up*, New Directions, 1956, edited by Edmund Wilson. See herein Glenway Westcott's essay 'The Moral of Scott Fitzgerald', p. 326, and the letter from Gertrude Stein, p. 308.

INTRODUCTION TO
THE BEAUTIFUL AND DAMNED

The Beautiful and Damned is a novel about failure, one of Fitzgerald's central subjects. It was itself a modest success in terms of sales on publication in 1922 but contemporary reviews of it were lukewarm, and over the years it has come to be regarded as Fitzgerald's least accomplished novel. However, it is a compelling representation of Anthony Patch's long decline and fall. The problem is perhaps structural and stylistic. The novel has fewer of the structural idiosyncrasies of *This Side of Paradise*, though Fitzgerald retained the use of section headings in each chapter of the novel's three books as they deal sequentially with Anthony Patch's early history in Book One, his courtship and marriage to Gloria Gilbert in Book Two, and his alcoholic decline in Book Three. These headings are used as a tonal preface to the incidents that follow, and there are three sections presented in drama form, of which the second, 'A Flashback in Paradise', a dialogue between 'The Voice' and 'Beauty', is the least satisfactory example of this mixture of fictional and dramatic modes, and he abandoned these devices in his three later novels. A major difference in narrative practice between the later and earlier novels is in his use of emotionally involved narrators in *The Great Gatsby* and *The Last Tycoon*, and an impersonal narrative voice in *Tender is the Night*. In *The Beautiful and Damned* there are many occasions when it is difficult precisely to locate the narrative voice, to know whether what we are reading is what his characters think and believe, or whether the voice is authorial, and I shall return to this issue.

The Beautiful and Damned opens with an equivocal description of its central character, Anthony Patch. At the age of twenty-five, he is introduced as a man whom 'irony, the Holy Ghost of this later day, had, theoretically at least, descended upon'. If, as Fitzgerald puts it, 'Irony was the final polish of the shoe, the ultimate dab of the clothes-brush, a sort of intellectual "There!" ', Anthony has 'as yet gone no further than the conscious stage'. The ambivalence entailed in the word 'theoretically' is enlarged as Anthony is said to fluctuate between a sense of himself as wondering 'whether he is not without honour and slightly mad, a shameful and obscene thinness glistening on the surface of the world like oil on a clean pond', and those occasions when he thinks himself 'rather an exceptional young man, thoroughly sophisticated, well adjusted to his environment, and somewhat more significant than anyone else he knows'. Both these views, the detrimental and the honorific, show that at this stage he has not achieved a secure sense of himself and his world. If the rhetorical figure of irony is foregrounded in this opening passage, it is soon accompanied by the figuring of romance in the way we saw as endemic to Fitzgerald's practice in *This Side of Paradise*

In 1913 Anthony is living in self-indulgent luxury in a fashionable district of New York on an unearned income of seven thousand dollars a year inherited from his mother, a sum about seven times the average salary of a schoolteacher at that time. In addition he receives an annual Christmas gift of a five-hundred-dollar bond from his multimillionaire grandfather, Adam J. Patch. Though he is often 'hard up' he has 'great expectations' of his grandfather's millions, until that moment when he discovers he has been cut out of the grandfather's will. Arthur Mizener, in the earliest critical biography of Fitzgerald, argued that Fitzgerald had failed to give Anthony that quality of character which would make him 'a man more sinned against than sinning', and that in the portrait of the marriage of Anthony and Gloria, there is 'no adequate cause for their suffering nor for the importance he gives it', points of view shared by most critics of the novel thereafter. It is difficult to resist this collective view of Anthony. If he is not a perfect example of what Fitzgerald calls 'the Aryan ideal', the first example of racial stereotyping, he is handsome with 'that especial cleanness borrowed from beauty', a conjunction thereafter pointedly used of Gloria. The problem with Anthony is that he does not do anything of social value, and enjoys nothing so much as his bathroom with its luxurious fittings, its walls decorated with photographs of 'four celebrated thespian beauties of the day'. A necessary visit to his grandfather, who naturally wants him to '*do* something' after years of idle travel in Europe, means 'that work had come into his life as a permanent idea' (p. 276), and that is how it remains thereafter. His idea of work is 'the theoretical creation of essays on the popes of the Renaissance' (p. 274), an enterprise for which he seems ill equipped, and which results in only one minor publication some years later, though the idea of this collection as a mode of work becomes a fall-back position for him throughout. Married and spending way beyond his means, he 'lingered over pleasant fancies of himself either as editor of a brilliant weekly of opinion' or a 'scintillant producer of satiric comedy and

Parisian musical revue' (p. 425). Eventually he takes a job in that 'Sanctum Americanum', the New York Stock Exchange, arranged for him by his grandfather, but quits after a few weeks because 'he considered himself ill adapted to the work' (p. 430). In Book Three, at a point where the need to earn money has become critical, he pursues the possibility of work as a door-to-door salesmen paid on a commission basis, but this too is swiftly abandoned. The effect of all this is to show Anthony as little more than a privileged idler waiting to collect his inheritance. During his army service, enraged by not achieving officer status on entry, he loses what promotion he gains through carelessness, and spends his time in an illicit love affair with a working-class girl who foolishly believes in his vows of love.

If he lacks any notable intellectual gifts he none the less comes across as a figure of charm and elegance, with a certain capacity for wit, as we see him in company with his Harvard friends Maury Noble and Dick Caramel. With Noble we should note the significance of his surname, for nobility is what he lacks, an early instance of the practice of ironic naming in this novel, like Patch which implies a covering over of something worn and threadbare, as though Anthony is the tacked-on remnant of his grandfather's line. Shuttleworth is another indicative naming, described as a 'former gambler, saloon-keeper, and general reprobate', a worthless figure whose interest in the grandfather's wealth is as keen as Anthony's. The ironic resonance of Caramel's surname is clear too, and Fitzgerald takes some risks with this figure of the young novelist who, after winning public acclaim with his first novel, *The Demon Lover*, fritters away his gifts in writing popular romance stories for magazines, a situation not unlike Fitzgerald's own history in the 1920s. Anthony, Noble and Caramel are together in the first dramatised section (pp. 279–82) as they meet to dine. Caramel is the butt of their apolitical nihilism as Noble boasts that he will ' "go on shining as a brilliantly meaningless figure in a meaningless world" ', and sees art as meaningless in itself, even if it ' "isn't in that it tries to make life less so" '. His argument about ' "moral freedom" ' impoverished by the want of intelligence in those who argue for it is a kind of aristocratic hauteur, as is so much of what he represents throughout.

One mode of work does feature repeatedly, the film industry, initially through Gloria Gilbert's father who is said to have 'entered the celluloid business, and as this required only the minute measure of intelligence he brought to it, he did well for several years' (p. 293).

The attempt here is to show Gilbert as an unimportant lackey of the movie business, but the unavoidable implication is of an industry that does not require much intelligence, and similarly affects the first presentation of Joseph Bloeckman, one of Gloria's unsuccessful suitors. What is at issue here is whose view is this of the film industry – that of the characters in the novel, or Fitzgerald's? Anthony and Maury Noble make a pose that all work is risible, because fundamentally pointless in a meaningless world. It is a question of voice here, and I think that in the early 1920s, as an ambitious young writer, Fitzgerald could afford to be cavalier about that other art form, the movies.

He was to work in it himself as a scriptwriter in the 1930s, and though his relations with the studios he worked for were always difficult, he came to a much greater understanding of what was involved in making films, and of the relationship between a film director, his actors, scriptwriters, and the money men who controlled the industry, a knowledge which bore fruit in his final and unfinished novel *The Last Tycoon* (1941) and *The Pat Hobby Stories* (1962). Gloria's attempts to enter the movies are bolstered by her sense that she is beautiful enough to succeed despite the fact that she has no experience of acting, and her one screen-test, arranged by Bloeckman, is a humiliating failure.

The treatment of Bloeckman raises another issue of point of view, and who is responsible for the way he is described. In the 'Sunlight and Moonlight' section of chapter three he 'was a stoutening, ruddy Jew of about thirty-five, with an expressive face under smooth sandy hair – and, no doubt, in most business gatherings his personality would have been considered ingratiating' (p. 332). He is treated with polite disdain by Maury and Anthony, the Harvard men whose cultural signifiers he does not share and cannot understand. A few pages later we have a résumé of his history, and though he is 'a dignified man and a proud one', find he was 'born in Munich . . . had begun his American career as a peanut vender with a travelling circus . . . ' and from these beginnings had flourished in the film industry which 'had borne him up with it where it threw off dozens of men with more financial ability, more imagination and more practical ideas . . . ' (p. 334). There is so much ambivalence in all this, and of course this history is one that Fitzgerald has made for him, not a history Anthony or Maury know of. The issue here is Bloeckman's ethnic identity, his Jewishness; elsewhere we read of Gloria being entranced as 'her eyes rested upon a Semitic violinist who swayed his shoulders to the rhythm of the year's mellowest foxtrot' (p. 316), where 'Semitic' seems gratuitous. When Bloeckman learns that Anthony is related to Adam J. Patch, and describes the grandfather as ' "a fine man" ', ' "a fine example of an American" ', Anthony agrees with this but, within himself, 'I detest these underdone men, he thought coldly. Boiled looking! Ought to be shoved back in the oven; just one more minute would do it' (p. 332) Of course, this novel dates from 1922, not 1942, when it would have been impossible to write that last sentence attributed to Anthony. It remains seriously offensive, though the oven it refers to is the 'melting pot' of cultural absorption immigrants to the United States underwent in the process of becoming 'American'. In the two later books of the novel Bloeckman is shown as a well-disposed friend to both Gloria and Anthony up to the point towards the end of the novel where Anthony in a drunken stupor charges Bloeckman with keeping Gloria out of the movies, calls him a ' "goddam Jew" ' and Bloeckman beats him up, one in a sequence of moments showing the ultimate degradation of Anthony.

Gloria Gilbert is given a kind of mythic origin in this novel in 'A Flashback in Paradise', in the dialogue between 'Beauty' and 'the Voice', and the association of her with classical myth is emphasised in the heading of the second chapter of Book One, 'Portrait of a Siren', where 'siren' stands for the archetypal seductive woman. Later, as Anthony and Gloria sit together at the Marathon cabaret, 'the freshness of her cheeks was a gossamer projection from a land of delicate and undiscovered shades; her hand gleaming on the stained tablecloth was a shell from some far and wildly virginal sea . . . ' (p. 315), a figuring of her which calls on the myth of the birth of Aphrodite. However, Gloria's view of herself in this scene seems blasphemous to Anthony as she says, ' "I've got a streak of what you'd call cheapness. I don't know where I get it but it's – oh, things like this and bright colours and gaudy vulgarity. I seem to belong here. These people could appreciate me and take me for granted, and these men would fall in love with me and admire me, whereas the clever men I meet would just analyse me and tell me I'm this because of this or that . . . " ' (p. 316). Anthony disagrees, and against her view of herself says, ' "I'm not a realist," ' and adds, ' "No, only the romanticist preserves the things worth preserving." ' Driven by a romantic compulsion deep within himself, 'as she talked and caught his eyes and turned her lovely head, she moved him as he had never been moved before. The sheath that held her soul had assumed significance – that was all. She was a sun, radiant, growing, gathering light and storing it – then after an eternity pouring it forth in a glance, the fragment of a sentence, to that part of him that cherished all beauty and all illusion' (pp. 316–17). This eloquent passage is characteristic of Fitzgerald's capacity for a poetic and symbolic vocabulary and shows the moment of Anthony's deep bonding with Gloria. The whole scene is redolent with significance, especially in the conclusion that he 'cherished all beauty and all illusion'. One of the illusions they both have to face is that mortal beauty is not invulnerable to time, and it is noticeable as the novel develops how much attention is given to their ages, particularly Gloria's, as she advances into her thirties and sees the dimming of her physical beauty.

It is worth noting that Anthony is brought up without any maternal or feminine influence, his mother having died when he was five. Indeed, in Fitzgerald's early novels mothers are maligned figures, despite the warmth of his feelings for his own mother, nor do women in general fare much better. In 'A Flashback in Paradise', when Beauty asks the Voice about this ' "new country" ' to which she is being sent to spend the next fifteen years, the answer is that not only is it ' "the most opulent, most gorgeous land on earth" ', but it is also a place ' "where ugly women control strong men" ' – and that ' "all men, even those of great wealth, obey implicitly their women" '. Beauty is told she will be a ' " 'susciety gurl' " ', ' "a sort of bogus aristocrat" ', and that she will be known as a ' "ragtime kid, a flapper, a jazz-baby, and a baby vamp" ', all those terms used of the young women in Fitzgerald's short stories of the 1920s. If there is an element of slapstick comedy in this, 'A Flashback in Paradise' ends with a deliberate irony on Fitzgerald's part as the stage direction shows Anthony seven years later sitting by the front windows of his apartment listening to 'the chimes of St Anne's', for St Anne is the mother of Mary, in the Christian world the mother of the most hallowed of all mothers. After his years at Harvard, Anthony spends time in Italy where his experience of women, in the company of Maury Noble, includes 'the peculiar charm of Latin women and had a delightful sense of being very young and free in a civilisation that was very old and free', where 'free' implies without moral restraints. Against this there is that bizarre moment in his apartment when he sees a girl in a red négligé drying her hair on the roof of a house, and 'felt persistently that the girl was beautiful – then of a sudden he understood: it was her distance' from him that had brought him 'nearer to adoration than in the deepest kiss he had ever known' (p. 278) and he knows the object of desire will only remain so while distant from him. A moment later when he sees her clearly he sees she 'was fat, full thirty-five, utterly undistinguished'. There are other moments of this kind, as for example where Gloria is imagined hurrying 'along Fifth Avenue, a Nordic Ganymede', whose effect on masculine eyes would give 'back forgotten dreams to the husbands of many obese and comic women' (p. 341). In bed at night in his apartment and thinking of the 'union of his soul with Gloria's' and the sound of the city 'promising that, in a little while, life would be beautiful as a story, promising happiness . . . a new note separated itself jarringly from the soft crying of the night', the noise of a woman's laughter which soon becomes hysterical with 'some animal quality . . . that . . . grasped at his imagination, and for the first time in four months aroused his old aversion and horror towards all the business of life' (pp. 371–2).

The issue of ethnic identity I have noted in the presentation of Bloeckman occurs variously as in Gloria as a 'Nordic Ganymede', and the earlier notion of the 'Aryan ideal'. A view of the swelling population of New York notes that 'Jewesses were coming out into a society of Jewish men and women, from Riverside to the Bronx, and looking forward to a rising young broker or jeweller and a kosher wedding; Irish girls were casting their eyes, with licence at last to do so, upon a society of young Tammany politicians, pious undertakers and grown-up choirboys' (p. 287). After graduation Dick Caramel works in the slums of New York 'to muck about with bewildered Italians as secretary to an "Alien Young Men's Rescue Association", to work with immigrant 'Italians, Poles, Scandinavians, Czechs, Armenians – with the same wrongs, the same exceptionally ugly faces and very much the same smells', a constituency identified as 'the débris of Europe', a role he abandons to take up writing fiction. We might think that this view of 'the débris of Europe' is one that Anthony naturally assumes, given his inherited status as a scion of American moneyed aristocracy. In the 'Symposium' chapter of Book Two, Maury Noble attributes a crude Darwinianism to nature as the agency which ' "had invented ways to rid the race of the inferior and thus give the remainder strength to fill her higher . . . intentions" ', and complains, ' "In this republic I saw the black beginning to mingle with the white – in Europe there was taking place an economic catastrophe to save three or four diseased and wretchedly governed races from the one mastery that might organise them for material prosperity"' (p. 448), a view of German ambitions in the First World War. While these attitudes are in character with Maury Noble, that earlier view of the 'débris of Europe' is more difficult to locate or dissociate from Fitzgerald. In a letter to Edmund Wilson of May 1921, after his first visit to Europe, he writes: 'God damn the continent of Europe . . . The negroid streak creeps northward to defile the Nordic race. Already the Italians have the souls of black-amoors. Raise the bars of immigration and permit only Scandin-avians, Teutons, Anglo-Saxons and Celts to enter . . . I think it's a shame that England and America didn't let Germany conquer Europe. It's the only thing that would have saved the fleet of tottering old wrecks.'[1] After this outburst Fitzgerald quickly adds an apology for these views and writes: 'My reactions were all philistine, anti-socialistic, provincial and racially snobbish. I believe at last in the white man's burden.' However, it is difficult to resist the view that this racial antagonism enters *The Beautiful and Damned* in a damaging way, not only through Maury Noble but also through the authorial voice.

In an essay about immigration and acculturation relative to the sense of American national identity in the early years of the twentieth century, Lawrence Levine debates the opposed notions of progress and nostalgia.[2] From the 'gilded age' of the post-Civil War years of the 1870s and 1880s through the Progressive Era of the 1890s to the 1920s, industrial and economic buoyancy in the United States seemed to underwrite the prospect of material and social well-being for all its citizens in a progressive modern imperative. Against this notion of progress associated particularly with the urban com-munities of large cities such as New York and Chicago, with their populations swollen by European immigrants, there went a nostalgic yearning for an American identity defined by the sociological concept of 'Gemeinschaft' which refers to an ideal type or model of a society where social bonds are personal and direct, with strong shared values and beliefs within an ethnically unified community. In America this notion relates to the small town rural agricultural communities of

1   *The Letters of F. Scott Fitzgerald*, edited with an Introduction by Andrew Turnbull, Bodley Head, London, 1963, pp. 326–7
2   'Progress and Nostalgia: The Self-Image of the Nineteen Twenties' by Lawrence W. Levine, in *The American Novel and the Nineteen Twenties*, Stratford-upon-Avon Studies 13, Edward Arnold, London, 1971, pp. 37–58

the nineteenth century, bonded together by common economic and moral principles, with their centres of worship clustered in and around the town square. It is precisely in such a community that Anthony and Gloria settle for part of each year in the Grey House near Marietta in which they transgress every one of such a community's values. Marietta, we are told, 'itself offered little social life', surrounded as it was by '[h]alf a dozen farm-estates', and the townspeople 'were a particularly uninteresting type – unmarried females were predominant for the most part – with school-festival horizons and souls bleak as the forbidding white architecture of the three churches' (p. 399). As Levine points out these communities supported Prohibition and other moral reform movements in the late years of the nineteenth and early years of the twentieth century, and in the Southern United States it was from such communities that the Ku Klux Klan was formed, not only in its support for white supremacy, but in its call for a return to what were construed as the moral values of the original white settlers. Here we should remember that Anthony is named after Anthony Comstock (1844–1915), who sought and enforced laws regulating morality with fanatical zeal, a man so admired by Adam Patch that his grandson is named after him, though Anthony drops Comstock from his name when he enters Harvard. But Comstock's reformist principles hang over Anthony through his grandfather, and affect the issue of the will once Adam Patch turns up without warning at the Grey House to find Anthony and Gloria with their friends in a riotously drunken party, immediately leaves, and refuses to see Anthony thereafter. If *The Beautiful and Damned* provides a close-focus view of Anthony's alcoholic decline, its social ambience is bounded by these issues of ethnicity on the one hand and on the other by the intimacies of a family narrative where the inheritance of wealth provides an ironic gloss on the materialist identity of the American Dream.

The marriage of Gloria and Anthony is authentic in that they are presented as clearly in love, though they see marriage through a romantic lens. In her diary she writes that her marriage will be a 'live, lovely, glamorous performance, and the world shall be the scenery'; and it will be childless, for the conception of children would cause her to 'grow rotund and unseemly, to lose my self-love, to think in terms of milk, oatmeal, nurse, diapers . . . ' (p. 370). There is a moment when she thinks she is pregnant but that turns out to be a false alarm. She prefers 'dream children . . . dazzling little creatures . . . on golden, golden wings', a sentimentalism echoed in Anthony's view that his marriage was the 'union of his soul with Gloria's, whose radiant fire and freshness was the living material of which the dead beauty of books was made' (pp. 371–2). It is of course a marriage whose economy is run on the expectation of inheriting Adam Patch's millions. Individually and together they lack any sense of responsibility, beyond the pursuit of pleasure. She cannot do the simplest domestic tasks such as sorting out the laundry for someone else to deal with. They nurture the idea that 'on some misty day he would enter a sort of glorified diplomatic service and be envied by princes and prime ministers for his beautiful wife', an unreality which makes Gloria appeal at one point, ' "I wish somebody'd take care of us" ', long before Anthony's alcoholism becomes the dominant reality of their life. If marriage brings him 'responsibility and possession', he discovers that management of her temper becomes 'almost the primary duty' of his day, and this soon leads him to a profound sense of failure: 'He was ineffectual and vaguely helpless here as he had always been. One of those personalities who, in spite of all their words, are inarticulate, he seemed to have inherited only the vast tradition of human failure – that, and the sense of death' (p. 421). They follow the routine of the 'simple healthy leisure class' to which they belong, and return to Marietta for the summer months after a 'restive and lazily extravagant' trip along the California coast 'drifting from Pasadena to Coronado, from Coronado to Santa Barbara, with no purpose more apparent than Gloria's desire to dance by different music or catch some infinitesimal variant along the changing colours of the sea', a hedonistic life that is finally brought to a halt by Anthony's declining financial resources. An incident on their first approach to Marietta is significant in the way it becomes a recurrent motif in Fitzgerald's later novels. Gloria is 'a driver of many eccentricities and of infinite carelessness' (p. 391), persistently breaking the speed limit, and she wrecks their 'cheap but sparkling new roadster' by driving over a fire-hydrant 'and ripp[ing] the transmission violently from the car' (p. 392). In *The Great Gatsby*, Jordan Baker is a careless driver who leaves responsibility on the roads to others, and when Myrtle Wilson is hit and killed by Gatsby's car Daisy Buchanan was driving. In *Tender is the Night*, Nicole risks the lives of Dick and their children by wilful reckless driving.

In the 'Symposium' chapter of Book Two Gloria flees the Grey House to the bridge above the railway station of Marietta pursued by Anthony, Maury and Dick Caramel, and there they debate the meaninglessness of life. Maury has a sense now of ' "the fading radiance of existence" ', a phrase that unconsciously typifies the subsequent representation of Anthony and Gloria's life together. In affirmation of this the next chapter is ironically called 'The Broken Lute', for the lute is the instrument traditionally associated with the art of the love song. The 'broken lute' motif goes with all the other moments from this point on where the romance of Anthony and Gloria's marriage is challenged, and goes with the pervasive attention to their ageing and diminishing beauty. Book Three with its depiction of Anthony's alcoholic degeneration is therefore replete with ironic reversals. For example, in 'The Sinister Summer' chapter of Book Two, Gloria airs her views on women and cleanliness, that ' "Women soil easily" ' and associates them with ' "a certain hysterical animality, the cunning, dirty sort of animality" ', thinks men are different and that ' "one of the commonest characters of romance is a man going gallantly to the devil" ' (p. 433), a comment that goes with Anthony's risible story of the Chevalier O'Keefe. In the final pages, Gloria's view of women and cleanliness is turned against her on the deck of the *Berengaria*, when a 'pretty girl in yellow' says to her companion of Gloria, ' "I can't stand her, you know. She seems sort of – sort of dyed and *unclean*, if you know what I mean" ' (p. 583). In this scene Gloria is wearing the Russian-sable coat that Anthony had to deny her earlier: as the pretty girl in yellow notes, it ' "must have cost a small fortune" '. This is the dominant irony, that Anthony the broken man now has Adam Patch's millions, a reversal of expectation following the long and expensive legal challenge to Adam Patch's will. As he sits in a wheelchair gazing out to sea, reflecting bitterly on the way his 'craving for romance had been punished', he is comforted by the notion that, ' "It was a hard fight, but I didn't give up and I came through!" ' (p. 584). But I think the dominant image of Anthony in Book Three comes a little earlier: 'He was heavier now, his stomach was a limp weight against his belt; his flesh had softened and expanded. He was thirty-two and his mind was a bleak and disordered wreck' (pp. 553–4). I share Arthur Mizener's view that Gloria is a more successful character than Anthony 'because the trivial things she believes in she does so with courage, and when forced to recognise it, takes her defeat with something like dignity'.

There is a view that *The Beautiful and Damned* is to some degree a naturalist novel in the manner of Stephen Crane's *Maggie: A Girl of the Streets* (1893), Frank Norris's *McTeage* (1899) and Theodore

Dreiser's *Sister Carrie* (1900). In a letter to his editor Maxwell Perkins of February 1920, Fitzgerald wrote: 'I've fallen lately under the influence of an author who's quite changed my point of view – Frank Norris. I think *McTeage* & *Vandover* are both excellent . . . There are things in *Paradise* that might have been written by Norris – those drunken scenes for instance – in fact all the realism.'[3] Naturalistic fiction in the latter half of the nineteenth century was influenced by the biological determinism of Darwin or the economic determinism of Marx, and conceived of humankind as controlled by instincts or passions, or by social and economic environment and circumstances, having no free will. Naturalist fictions commonly emphasise the animal nature of human beings and the struggle for survival. There is evidence of such a point of view in *The Beautiful and Damned*, largely in the representation of the poor, and relative to the urge to procreation. In the second chapter of Book One detailing the invitations Anthony receives to meet young women available in the marriage market, New York is seen as a vast emporium-like venue for breeding, stratified according to social levels of status: at the bottom are 'the working girls, poor ugly souls, wrapping soap in the factories and showing finery in the big stores, dream[ing] that perhaps in the spectacular excitement of this winter they might obtain for themselves the coveted male – as in a muddled carnival crowd an inefficient pickpocket may consider his chances increased' (p. 287). This goes with a reiterated association Fitzgerald makes between women and animality, that women are more predatory than men in sexual matters, and Anthony is disturbed by his premonition of what will follow his own marriage ceremony, 'his old aversion and horror towards all the business of life . . . Life was that sound out there, that ghastly reiterated female sound' (p. 372). One of the most reductive and mechanistic views of the human condition in this novel, and characteristic of naturalism, comes later in the view of the poorer areas of New York as the 'city of luxury and mystery, of preposterous hopes and exotic dreams' which becomes the site of the

> sweating streets of the upper East Side, each one passing the car window like the space between the spokes of a gigantic wheel, each one with its vigorous colourful revelation of poor children swarming in feverish activity like vivid ants in alleys of red sand. From the tenement windows leaned rotund, moon-shaped

3   Turnbull, *The Letters of F. Scott Fitzgerald*, op. cit., p. 144

mothers, as constellations of this sordid heaven; women like dark imperfect jewels, women like vegetables, women like great bags of abominably dirty laundry.   [pp. 466–7]

Anthony's sexually opportunistic relationship with Dorothy Raycroft while on army service, her emotional dependence on him and his final repudiation of her when she follows him to New York are also in this naturalist idiom. In the passages I have quoted above about women and the sexual imperative, it is difficult to dissociate Fitzgerald's point of view from that of his characters. However, I take the view that naturalism is an incidental feature of *The Beautiful and Damned*, and that the novel's momentum is determined by Fitzgerald's understanding of the power of material wealth and its identification with the concept of the American Dream in the early years of the twentieth century. If the idea of the 'American Dream' is now little more than a rhetorical cliché, Fitzgerald gives a version of its original impetus at the end of *The Great Gatsby*, through his narrator, Nick Carraway, when he writes:

I became aware of the old island here that flowered once for Dutch sailors' eyes – a fresh, green breast of the new world. Its vanished trees, the trees that had made way for Gatsby's house, had once pandered in whispers to the last and greatest of all human dreams; for a transitory enchanted moment man must have held his breath in the presence of this continent, compelled into an aesthetic contemplation he neither understood nor desired, face to face for the last time in history with something commensurate to his capacity for wonder.

If the early European settlers into America from the sixteenth century onwards imagined this 'New World' as the location of a new beginning in human history, the ideology of this world was enshrined in the Declaration of Independence of 1776, with its most cherished affirmation that 'All men are created equal'. It is in the fall from these ideals that the American Dream became tarnished, especially in its latter day association with the pursuit of wealth.

In an essay on Fitzgerald's brilliant short story *The Diamond as Big as the Ritz* (1922) and *The Great Gatsby*, the distinguished critic Marius Bewley argues that 'More than with any other writer in the American tradition, Scott Fitzgerald's novels have been based on a concept of class', and that the 'class role of Fitzgerald's characters is possible because he instinctively realised the part that money played in creating and supporting a way of life focused in the Ivy League universities, country clubs, trips to the Riviera, and the homes of the wealthy', and that he is the first American writer who 'seems to have discovered that such a thing as American class *really* existed'.[4] Bewley disputes the view that Fitzgerald was 'taken in' by wealth and the monied class, and that 'some of his gaudiest celebrations of it are simultaneously the most annihilating criticisms'.

The Beautiful and Damned, as the novel's title implies, should be seen as a part of that annihilating criticism.

LIONEL KELLY
University of Reading

EDITORIAL NOTE

I am indebted to Professor Jackson R. Bryer's edition of *This Side of Paradise* (2009), and to Professor Alan Margolies's edition of *The Beautiful and Damned* (1998, reissued 2009), in the Oxford World Classics series, especially for their expertise in identifying American locations and social and cultural allusions in these novels.

---

4   Marius Bewley, *The Eccentric Design: Form in the Classic American Novel*, Chatto and Windus, London, 1959, pp. 259–87

BIBLIOGRAPHY

Letters

The Letters of F. Scott Fitzgerald, ed. Andrew Turnbull, Bodley Head, London, 1963

Dear Scott/Dear Max: The Fitzgerald-Perkins Correspondence, ed. John Kuehl and Jackson R. Bryer, New York, 1971

As Ever, Scott Fitz—: Letters Between F. Scott Fitzgerald and His Literary Agent, Harold Ober, 1919–40, ed. Matthew J. Bruccoli, with the assistance of Jennifer McCabe Atkinson, Philadelphia, 1972

Correspondence of F. Scott Fitzgerald, ed. Matthew J. Bruccoli and Margaret M. Duggan, with the assistance of Susan Walker, New York, 1980

F. Scott Fitzgerald: A Life in Letters, ed. Matthew J. Bruccoli, with the assistance of Judith S. Baughman, New York, 1994

Dear Scott, Dearest Zelda: The Love Letters of F. Scott Fitzgerald, ed. Jackson R. Bryer and Cathy W. Barks, New York, 2002

Biography

Bruccoli, Matthew J., *Some Sort of Epic Grandeur: The Life of F. Scott Fitzgerald*, 2nd rev. edn, Columbia, South Carolina, 2002

Donaldson, Scott, *Fool for Love: F. Scott Fitzgerald*, New York, 1983

Le Vot, André, *F. Scott Fitzgerald: A Biography*, translated by William Byron, Garden City, New York, 1983

Mellow, James R., *Invented Lives: F. Scott & Zelda Fitzgerald*, Boston, 1984

Mizener, Arthur, *The Far Side of Paradise: A Biography of F. Scott Fitzgerald*, rev. edn., New York, 1965

Piper, Henry Dan, *F. Scott Fitzgerald: A Critical Portrait*, New York, 1965

Turnbull, Andrew, *Scott Fitzgerald*, New York, 1962

Criticism

Allen, Joan M., *Candles and Carnival Lights: The Catholic Sensibility of F. Scott Fitzgerald*, New York, 1978

Astro, Richard, '*Vandover and the Brute* and *The Beautiful and Damned*: A Search for Thematic and Stylistic Reinterpretations', *Modern Fiction Studies*, 14, Winter 1968–9, pp. 397–413

Burhans, Clinton S., Jr, 'Structure and Theme in *This Side of Paradise*', *Journal of English and Germanic Philology*, 68, October 1969, pp. 605–24

Bruccoli, Matthew J. and Baughman, Judith S. (eds), *Conversations with F. Scott Fitzgerald*, Jackson, Miss., 2004

—— and Bryer, Jackson R. (eds), *F. Scott Fitzgerald in His Own Time: A Miscellany*, Kent, Ohio, 1971

—— and Smith, Scottie Fitzgerald and Kerr, Joan P. (eds), *The Romantic Egoists: A Pictorial Autobiography from the Scrapbooks and Albums of Scott and Zelda Fitzgerald*, New York, 1974

Bryer, Jackson R. (ed.), *F. Scott Fitzgerald: The Critical Reception*, New York, 1978

—— and Margolies, Alan and Prigozy, Ruth (eds), *F. Scott Fitzgerald: New Perspectives*, Athens, Georgia, 2000

Claridge, Henry (ed.), *F. Scott Fitzgerald: Critical Assessments*, 4 vols., Robertsbridge, 1991

Curnutt, Kirk, 'Youth Culture and the Spectacle of Waste: *This Side of Paradise* and *The Beautiful and Damned*', in Jackson R. Bryer, Ruth Prigozy and Milton R. Stern (eds), *F. Scott Fitzgerald in the Twenty-First Century*, Tuscaloosa, Alabama and London, 2003, pp. 79–103

Elias, Amy J., 'The Composition and Revision of Fitzgerald's *The Beautiful and Damned*', *Princeton University Library Chronicle*, 51, 1990, pp. 245–66

Fryer, Sarah Beebe, *Fitzgerald's New Women: Harbingers of Change*, Ann Arbor, 1988

Gervais, Ronald J., ' "Sleepy Hollow's Gone": Pastoral Myth and Artifice in Fitzgerald's *The Beautiful and Damned*', *Ball State University Forum*, 22, 1981, pp. 75–9

Gross, Barry, 'The Dark Side of Twenty-Five: Fitzgerald and *The Beautiful and Damned*', *Bucknell Review*, 16, 1968, pp. 40–52

—— '*This Side of Paradise*: The Dominating Intention', *Studies in the Novel*, 1, Spring 1969, 51–9

Hendriksen, Jack, '*This Side of Paradise* as a Bildungsroman', New York, 1991

Hoffman, Madelyn, 'This Side of Paradise: A Study of Pathological Narcissism', Literature and Psychology, 28, 3–4, 1978, pp. 178–85

James, Pearl, 'History and Masculinity in F. Scott Fitzgerald's This Side of Paradise', Modern Fiction Studies, 51, Spring 2005, pp. 1–33

Kahn, Sy, 'This Side of Paradise: The Pageantry of Disillusion', Midwest Quarterly, 7, Winter 1966, 177–94

Kazin, Alfred (ed.), F. Scott Fitzgerald: The Man and His Work, Cleveland, 1951

Kennedy, J. Gerald and Bryer, Jackson R. (eds), French Connections: Hemingway and Fitzgerald Abroad, New York, 1998

Lee, A. Robert (ed.), Scott Fitzgerald: The Promises of Life, London and New York, 1989

Marquand, John P., 'Looking Backwards. Fitzgerald: This Side of Paradise', Saturday Review of Literature, 22, 6 August 1949, 30–1

Mizener, Arthur (ed.), F, Scott Fitzgerald: A Collection of Critical Essays, Englewood Cliffs, NJ, 1968

Monk, Craig, 'The Political F. Scott Fitzgerald: Liberal Illusion and Disillusion in This Side of Paradise and The Beautiful and Damned', American Studies International, 33, October 1995, 60–70

Podis, Leonard A., 'The Beautiful and Damned: Fitzgerald's Test of Youth', Fitzgerald/Hemingway Annual, 5, 1973, 141–7

Prigozy, Ruth, (ed.), The Cambridge Companion to F. Scott Fitzgerald, Cambridge and New York, 2002

Raubicheck, Walter, 'The Catholic Romanticism of This Side of Paradise', in Jackson R. Bryer, Ruth Prigozy and Milton R. Stern (eds), F. Scott Fitzgerald in the Twenty-First Century, Tuscaloosa, Alabama, and London, 2003, 54–65

Roulston, Robert, 'This Side of Paradise: The Ghost of Rupert Brooke', Fitzgerald/Hemingway Annual, 7, 1975, 117–30

—— 'The Beautiful and Damned: The Alcoholic's Revenge', Literature and Psychology, 27/3, 1977, 156–63

Searles, George J., 'The Symbolic Function of Food and Eating in F. Scott Fitzgerald's The Beautiful and Damned', Ball State University Forum, 22, Summer 1981, 14–19

Sklar, Robert, F. Scott Fitzgerald: The Last Laocoön, New York, 1967

Smith, Susan Harris, 'Some Biographical Aspects of This Side of Paradise', Fitzgerald/Hemingway Annual, 2, 1970, 96–101

Stavola, Thomas J., *Scott Fitzgerald: Crisis in an American Identity*, New York and London, 1979

Tanner, Stephen L., 'The Devil and F. Scott Fitzgerald', in Jackson R. Bryer, Ruth Prigozy and Milton R. Stern (eds), *F. Scott Fitzgerald in the Twenty-First Century*, Tuscaloosa, Alabama, and London, 2003, 66–78

Tuttleton, James W., 'The Presence of Poe in *This Side of Paradise*', *English Language Notes*, 3, June 1966, 384–9

Ulrich, David W., 'Reconstructing Fitzgerald's "Twice-Told Tales": Intertextuality in *This Side of Paradise* and *Tender is the Night*', *F. Scott Fitzgerald Review*, 3, 2004, 43–71

Van Arsdale, Nancy P., 'Princeton as Modernist's Hermeneutics: Rereading *This Side of Paradise*', in Jackson R. Bryer, Alan Margolies and Ruth Prigozy (eds), *F. Scott Fitzgerald: New Perspectives*, Athens, Georgia, 2000, 39–50

Way, Brian, *F. Scott Fitzgerald and the Art of Social Fiction*, London and New York, 1980

West, James L. W., III, *The Making of 'This Side of Paradise'*, Philadelphia, 1983

—— 'The Question of Vocation in *This Side of Paradise* and *The Beautiful and Damned*', in Ruth Prigozy (ed.), *The Cambridge Companion to F. Scott Fitzgerald*, Cambridge and New York, 2002, 48–56

Wilson, Edmund (ed.), *The Crack-Up*, New York, 1945

This Side of Paradise

◆

F. Scott Fitzgerald

. . . Well this side of Paradise!
There's little comfort in the wise.

RUPERT BROOKE

Experience is the name so many
people give to their mistakes.

OSCAR WILDE[1]

Contents

To Sigourney Fay[2]

BOOK ONE

THE ROMANTIC EGOTIST

CHAPTER I

Amory, Son of Beatrice

Amory Blaine inherited from his mother every trait, except the stray inexpressible few, that made him worth while. His father, an ineffectual, inarticulate man with a taste for Byron and a habit of drowsing over the *Encyclopaedia Britannica*, grew wealthy at thirty through the death of two elder brothers, successful Chicago brokers, and in the first flush of feeling that the world was his, went to Bar Harbor[3] and met Beatrice O'Hara. In consequence, Stephen Blaine handed down to posterity his height of just under six feet and his tendency to waver at crucial moments, these two abstractions appearing in his son Amory. For many years he hovered in the background of his family's life, an unassertive figure with a face half-obliterated by lifeless, silky hair, continually occupied in 'taking care' of his wife, continually harassed by the idea that he didn't and couldn't understand her.

But Beatrice Blaine! There was a woman! Early pictures taken on her father's estate at Lake Geneva, Wisconsin, or in Rome at the Sacred Heart Convent – an educational extravagance that in her youth was only for the daughters of the exceptionally wealthy – showed the exquisite delicacy of her features, the consummate art and simplicity of her clothes. A brilliant education she had – her youth passed in Renaissance glory, she was versed in the latest gossip of the Older Roman Families; known by name as a fabulously wealthy American girl to Cardinal Vitori and Queen Margherita[4] and more subtle celebrities that one must have had some culture even to have heard of. She learned in England to prefer whisky-and-soda to wine, and her small talk was broadened in two senses during a winter in Vienna. All in all Beatrice O'Hara absorbed the sort of education that will be quite impossible ever again; a tutelage measured by the number of things and people one could be contemptuous of and charming about; a culture rich in all arts and traditions, barren of all ideas, in the last of those days when the great gardener clipped the inferior roses to produce one perfect bud.

In her less important moments she returned to America, met Stephen Blaine and married him – this almost entirely because she was a little bit weary, a little bit sad. Her only child was carried through a tiresome season and brought into the world on a spring day in ninety-six.

When Amory was five he was already a delightful companion for her. He was an auburn-haired boy, with great, handsome eyes which he would grow up to in time, a facile imaginative mind and a taste for fancy dress. From his fourth to his tenth year he *did* the country with his mother in her father's private car, from Coronado,[5] where his mother became so bored that she had a nervous breakdown in a fashionable hotel, down to Mexico City, where she took a mild, almost epidemic consumption. This trouble pleased her, and later she made use of it as an intrinsic part of her atmosphere – especially after several astounding bracers.

So, while more or less fortunate little rich boys were defying governesses on the beach at Newport,[6] or being spanked or tutored or read to from *Do and Dare* or *Frank on the Mississippi*,[7] Amory was biting acquiescent bellboys in the Waldorf,[8] outgrowing a natural repugnance to chamber music and symphonies, and deriving a highly specialised education from his mother.

'Amory.'

'Yes, Beatrice.' (Such a quaint name for his mother; she encouraged it.)

'Dear, don't *think* of getting out of bed yet. I've always suspected that early rising in early life makes one nervous. Clothilde is having your breakfast brought up.'

'All right.'

'I am feeling very old today, Amory,' she would sigh, her face a rare cameo of pathos, her voice exquisitely modulated, her hands as facile as Bernhardt's.[9] 'My nerves are on edge – on edge. We must leave this terrifying place tomorrow and go searching for sunshine.'

Amory's penetrating green eyes would look out through tangled hair at his mother. Even at this age he had no illusions about her.

'Amory.'

'Oh, *yes*.'

'I want you to take a red-hot bath – as hot as you can bear it, and just relax your nerves. You can read in the tub if you wish.'

She fed him sections of the *Fêtes Galantes*[10] before he was ten; at eleven he could talk glibly, if rather reminiscently, of Brahms and Mozart and Beethoven. One afternoon, when left alone in the hotel at Hot Springs,[11] he sampled his mother's apricot cordial, and as the taste pleased him, he became quite tipsy. This was fun for a while, but he essayed a cigarette in his exaltation, and succumbed to a vulgar, plebeian reaction. Though this incident horrified Beatrice, it also secretly amused her and became part of what in a later generation would have been termed her 'line'.

'This son of mine,' he heard her tell a room full of awestruck, admiring women one day, 'is entirely sophisticated and quite charming – but delicate – we're all delicate; *here*, you know.' Her hand was radiantly outlined against her beautiful bosom; then sinking her voice to a whisper, she told them of the apricot cordial. They rejoiced, for she was a brave *raconteuse*, but many were the keys turned in sideboard locks that night against the possible defection of little Bobby or Barbara . . .

These domestic pilgrimages were invariably in state; two maids, the private car, or Mr Blaine when available, and very often a physician. When Amory had the whooping-cough four disgusted specialists glared at each other hunched around his bed; when he took scarlet fever the number of attendants, including physicians and nurses, totalled fourteen. However, blood being thicker than broth, he was pulled through.

The Blaines were attached to no city. They were the Blaines of Lake Geneva; they had quite enough relatives to serve in place of friends, and an enviable standing from Pasadena to Cape Cod.[12] But Beatrice grew more and more prone to like only new acquaintances, as there were certain stories, such as the history of her constitution and its many amendments, memories of her years abroad, that it was necessary for her to repeat at regular intervals. Like Freudian dreams, they must be thrown off, else they would sweep in and lay siege to her nerves. But Beatrice was critical about American women, especially the floating population of ex-Westerners.

'They have accents, my dear,' she told Amory, 'not Southern accents or Boston accents, not an accent attached to any locality, just an accent' – she became dreamy. 'They pick up old, moth-eaten London accents that are down on their luck and have to be used by someone. They talk as an English butler might after several years in a Chicago grand-opera company.' She became almost incoherent – 'Suppose – time in every Western woman's life – she feels her husband is prosperous enough for her to have – accent – they try to impress *me*, my dear – '

Though she thought of her body as a mass of frailties, she considered her soul quite as ill, and therefore important in her life. She had once been a Catholic, but discovering that priests were infinitely more attentive when she was in process of losing or regaining faith in Mother Church, she maintained an enchantingly wavering attitude. Often she deplored the bourgeois quality of the American Catholic clergy, and was quite sure that had she lived in the shadow of the great Continental cathedrals her soul would still be a thin flame on the mighty altar of Rome. Still, next to doctors, priests were her favourite sport.

'Ah, Bishop Wiston,' she would declare, 'I do not *want* to talk of myself. I can imagine the stream of hysterical women fluttering at your doors, beseeching you to be *simpatico*' – then after an interlude filled by the clergyman – 'but my mood – is – oddly dissimilar.'

Only to bishops and above did she divulge her clerical romance. When she had first returned to her country there had been a pagan, Swinburnian young man in Asheville,[13] for whose passionate kisses and unsentimental conversations she had taken a decided penchant – they had discussed the matter pro and con with an intellectual romancing quite devoid of sappiness. Eventually she had decided to marry for background, and the young pagan from Asheville had gone through a spiritual crisis, joined the Catholic Church, and was now – Monsignor Darcy.

'Indeed, Mrs Blaine, he is still delightful company – quite the cardinal's right-hand man.'

'Amory will go to him one day, I know,' breathed the beautiful lady, 'and Monsignor Darcy will understand him as he understood me.'

Amory became thirteen, rather tall and slender, and more than ever on to his Celtic mother. He had tutored occasionally – the idea being that he was to 'keep up', at each place 'taking up the work where he left off', yet as no tutor ever found the place he left off, his mind was still in very good shape. What a few more years of this life would have made of him is problematical. However, four hours out from land, Italy bound, with Beatrice, his appendix burst, probably from too many meals in bed, and after a series of frantic telegrams to Europe and America, to the amazement of the passengers the great ship slowly wheeled around and returned to New York to deposit Amory at the pier. You will admit that if it was not life it was magnificent.

After the operation Beatrice had a nervous breakdown that bore a suspicious resemblance to delirium tremens, and Amory was left in Minneapolis, destined to spend the ensuing two years with his aunt and uncle. There the crude, vulgar air of Western civilisation first catches him – in his underwear, so to speak.

A KISS FOR AMORY

His lip curled when he read it.

I am going to have a bobbing party [it said] on Thursday, December the seventeenth, at five o'clock, and I would like it very much if you could come.

Yours truly,

MYRA ST CLAIRE

RSVP

He had been two months in Minneapolis, and his chief struggle had been the concealing from 'the other guys at school' how particularly superior he felt himself to be, yet this conviction was built upon shifting sands. He had shown off one day in French class (he was in senior French class) to the utter confusion of Mr Reardon, whose accent Amory damned contemptuously, and to the delight of the class. Mr Reardon, who had spent several weeks in Paris ten years before, took his revenge on the verbs, whenever he had his book open. But another time Amory showed off in history class with quite disastrous results, for the boys there were his own age, and they shrilled innuendoes at each other all the following week: 'Aw – I b'lieve, doncherknow, the Umuricun revolution was *lawgely* an affair of the middul *clawses*,' or 'Washington came of very good blood – aw, quite good – I b'lieve.'

Amory ingeniously tried to retrieve himself by blundering on purpose. Two years before he had commenced a history of the United States which, though it only got as far as the Colonial Wars, had been pronounced by his mother completely enchanting.

His chief disadvantage lay in athletics, but as soon as he discovered that it was the touchstone of power and popularity at school, he began to make furious, persistent efforts to excel in the winter sports, and with his ankles aching and bending in spite of his efforts, he skated valiantly around the Lorelie rink every afternoon, wondering how soon he would be able to carry a hockey-stick without getting it inexplicably tangled in his skates.

The invitation to Miss Myra St Claire's bobbing party spent the morning in his coat pocket, where it had an intense physical affair with a dusty piece of peanut brittle. During the afternoon he brought it to light with a sigh, and after some consideration and a preliminary draft in the back of Collar and Daniell's *First-Year Latin*, composed an answer:

MY DEAR MISS ST CLAIRE – Your truly charming envitation for the evening of next Thursday evening was truly delightful to receive this morning. I will be charm and inchanted indeed to present my compliments on next Thursday evening.
   Faithfully,

AMORY BLAINE

On Thursday, therefore, he walked pensively along the slippery, shovel-scraped sidewalks, and came in sight of Myra's house, on the half-hour after five, a lateness which he fancied his mother would have favoured. He waited on the doorstep with his eyes nonchalantly half-closed, and planned his entrance with precision. He would cross the floor, not too hastily, to Mrs St Claire, and say with exactly the correct modulation: 'My *dear* Mrs St Claire, I'm *frightfully* sorry to be late, but my maid' – he paused there and realised he would be quoting – 'but my uncle and I had to see a fella – Yes, I've met your enchanting daughter at dancing-school.' Then he would shake hands, using that slight, half-foreign bow, with all the starchy little females, and nod to the fellas who would be standing round, paralysed into rigid groups for mutual protection.

A butler (one of the three in Minneapolis) swung open the door. Amory stepped inside and divested himself of cap and coat. He was mildly surprised not to hear the shrill squawk of conversation from the next room, and he decided it must be quite formal. He approved of that – as he approved of the butler.

'Miss Myra,' he said.

To his surprise the butler grinned horribly. 'Oh, yeah,' he declared, 'she's here.'

He was unaware that his failure to be cockney was ruining his standing. Amory considered him coldly.

'But,' continued the butler, his voice rising unnecessarily, 'she's the only one what *is* here. The party's gone.'

Amory gasped in sudden horror. 'What?'

'She's been waitin' for Amory Blaine. That's you, ain't it? Her mother says that if you showed up by five-thirty you two was to go after 'em in the Packard.'

Amory's despair was crystallised by the appearance of Myra herself, bundled to the ears in a polo coat, her face plainly sulky, her voice pleasant only with difficulty.

' 'Lo, Amory.'

' 'Lo, Myra.' He had described the state of his vitality.

'Well – you *got* here, *any*ways.'

'Well – I'll tell you. I guess you don't know about the auto accident,' he romanced.

Myra's eyes opened wide.

'Who was it to?'

'Well,' he continued desperately, 'uncle 'n aunt 'n I.'

'Was anyone *killed*?'

Amory paused and then nodded.

'Your uncle?' – alarm.

'Oh, no – just a horse – a sorta grey horse.'

At this point the Erse butler snickered.

'Probably killed the engine,' he suggested. Amory would have put him on the rack without a scruple.

'We'll go now,' said Myra coolly. 'You see, Amory, the bobs were ordered for five and everybody was here, so we couldn't wait – '

'Well, I couldn't help it, could I?'

'So mama said for me to wait till ha'past five. We'll catch the bob before it gets to the Minnehaha Club, Amory.'

Amory's shredded poise dropped from him. He pictured the happy party jingling along snowy streets, the appearance of the limousine, the horrible public descent of him and Myra before sixty reproachful eyes, his apology – a real one this time. He sighed aloud.

'What?' enquired Myra.

'Nothing. I was just yawning. Are we *surely* going to catch up with 'em before they get there?' He was encouraging a faint hope that they might slip into the Minnehaha Club and meet the others there, be found in blasé seclusion before the fire and quite regain his lost attitude.

'Oh, sure Mike, we'll catch 'em all right – let's hurry.'

He became conscious of his stomach. As they stepped into the machine he hurriedly slapped the paint of diplomacy over a rather boxlike plan he had conceived. It was based upon some 'trade-lasts'[14] gleaned at dancing-school, to the effect that he was 'awful good-looking and *English*, sort of'.

'Myra,' he said, lowering his voice and choosing his words carefully, 'I beg a thousand pardons. Can you ever forgive me?' She regarded him gravely, his intent green eyes, his mouth, that to her thirteen-year-old, Arrow-collar[15] taste was the quintessence of romance. Yes, Myra could forgive him very easily.

'Why – yes – sure.'

He looked at her again, and then dropped his eyes. He had lashes.

'I'm awful,' he said sadly. 'I'm diff'runt. I don't know why I make *faux pas*. 'Cause I don't care, I s'pose.' Then, recklessly: 'I been smoking too much. I've got t'bacca heart.'

Myra pictured an all-night tobacco debauch, with Amory pale and reeling from the effect of nicotined lungs. She gave a little gasp.

'Oh, *Amory*, don't smoke. You'll stunt your *growth*!'

'I don't care,' he persisted gloomily. 'I gotta. I got the habit. I've done a lot of things that if my fambly knew' – he hesitated, giving her imagination time to picture dark horrors – 'I went to the burlesque show last week.'

Myra was quite overcome. He turned the green eyes on her again. 'You're the only girl in town I like much,' he exclaimed in a rush of sentiment. 'You're *simpatico*.'

Myra was not sure that she was, but it sounded stylish though vaguely improper.

Thick dusk had descended outside, and as the limousine made a sudden turn she was jolted against him; their hands touched.

'You shouldn't smoke, Amory,' she whispered. 'Don't you know that?'

He shook his head.

'Nobody cares.'

Myra hesitated.

'*I* care.'

Something stirred within Amory.

'Oh, yes, you do! You got a crush on Froggy Parker. I guess everybody knows that.'

'No, I haven't,' very slowly.

A silence, while Amory thrilled. There was something fascinating about Myra, shut away here cosily from the dim, chill air. Myra, a little bundle of clothes, with strands of yellow hair curling out from under her skating cap.

'Because I've got a crush, too – ' He paused, for he heard in the distance the sound of young laughter, and, peering through the frosted glass along the lamp-lit street, he made out the dark outline of the bobbing party. He must act quickly. He reached over with a violent, jerky effort, and clutched Myra's hand – her thumb, to be exact.

'Tell him to go to the Minnehaha straight,' he whispered. 'I wanta talk to you – I *got* to talk to you.'

Myra made out the party ahead, had an instant vision of her mother, and then – alas for convention – glanced into the eyes beside her. 'Turn down this side street, Richard, and drive straight to the Minnehaha Club!' she cried through the speaking tube. Amory sank back against the cushions with a sigh of relief.

'I can kiss her,' he thought. 'I'll bet I can. I'll *bet* I can!'

Overhead the sky was half crystalline, half misty, and the night around was chill and vibrant with rich tension. From the Country Club steps the roads stretched away, dark creases on the white blanket; huge heaps of snow lining the sides like the tracks of giant moles. They lingered for a moment on the steps, and watched the white holiday moon.

'Pale moons like that one' – Amory made a vague gesture – 'make people *mystérieuse*. You look like a young witch with her cap off and her hair sorta mussed' – her hands clutched at her hair – 'Oh, leave it, it looks *good*.'

They drifted up the stairs and Myra led the way into the little den of his dreams, where a cosy fire was burning before a big sink-down couch. A few years later this was to be a great stage for Amory, a cradle for many an emotional crisis. Now they talked for a moment about bobbing parties.

'There's always a bunch of shy fellas,' he commented, 'sitting at the tail of the bob, sorta lurkin' an' whisperin' an' pushin' each other off. Then there's always some crazy cross-eyed girl' – he gave a terrifying imitation – 'she's always talkin' *hard*, sorta, to the chaperone.'

'You're such a funny boy,' puzzled Myra.

'How d'y' mean?' Amory gave immediate attention, on his own ground at last.

'Oh – always talking about crazy things. Why don't you come skiing with Marylyn and me tomorrow?'

'I don't like girls in the daytime,' he said shortly, and then, thinking this a bit abrupt, he added: 'But I like you.' He cleared his throat. 'I like you first and second and third.'

Myra's eyes became dreamy. What a story this would make to tell Marylyn! Here on the couch with this *wonderful*-looking boy –

the little fire – the sense that they were alone in the great building –

Myra capitulated. The atmosphere was too appropriate.

'I like you the first twenty-five,' she confessed, her voice trembling, 'and Froggy Parker twenty-sixth.'

Froggy had fallen twenty-five places in one hour. As yet he had not even noticed it.

But Amory, being on the spot, leaned over quickly and kissed Myra's cheek. He had never kissed a girl before, and he tasted his lips curiously, as if he had munched some new fruit. Then their lips brushed like young wild flowers in the wind.

'We're awful,' rejoiced Myra gently. She slipped her hand into his, her head drooped against his shoulder. Sudden revulsion seized Amory, disgust, loathing for the whole incident. He desired frantic-ally to be away, never to see Myra again, never to kiss anyone; he became conscious of his face and hers, of their clinging hands, and he wanted to creep out of his body and hide somewhere safe out of sight, up in the corner of his mind.

'Kiss me again.' Her voice came out of a great void.

'I don't want to,' he heard himself saying. There was another pause.

'I don't want to!' he repeated passionately.

Myra sprang up, her cheeks pink with bruised vanity, the great bow on the back of her head trembling sympathetically.

'I hate you!' she cried. 'Don't you ever dare to speak to me again!'

'What?' stammered Amory.

'I'll tell mama you kissed me! I will too! I will too! I'll tell mama, and she won't let me play with you!'

Amory rose and stared at her helplessly, as though she were a new animal of whose presence on the earth he had not heretofore been aware.

The door opened suddenly, and Myra's mother appeared on the threshold, fumbling with her lorgnette.

'Well,' she began, adjusting it benignantly, 'the man at the desk told me you two children were up here – How do you do, Amory.'

Amory watched Myra and waited for the crash – but none came. The pout faded, the high pink subsided, and Myra's voice was placid as a summer lake when she answered her mother.

'Oh, we started so late, mama, that I thought we might as *well* – '

He heard from below the shrieks of laughter, and smelled the vapid odour of hot chocolate and teacakes as he silently followed mother and daughter downstairs. The sound of the graphophone[16]

mingled with the voices of many girls humming the air, and a faint
glow was born and spread over him:

> 'Casey-Jones – mounted to the cab-un
> Casey-Jones – 'th his orders in his hand.
> Casey-Jones – mounted to the cab-un
> Took his farewell journey to the prom-ised land.'

SNAPSHOTS OF THE YOUNG EGOTIST

Amory spent nearly two years in Minneapolis. The first winter he
wore moccasins that were born yellow, but after many applications
of oil and dirt assumed their mature colour, a dirty, greenish brown;
he wore a grey plaid mackinaw coat, and a red toboggan cap. His
dog, Count Del Monte, ate the red cap, so his uncle gave him a grey
one that pulled down over his face. The trouble with this one was
that you breathed into it and your breath froze; one day the darn
thing froze his cheek. He rubbed snow on his cheek, but it turned
bluish-black just the same.

The Count Del Monte ate a box of bluing once, but it didn't hurt
him. Later, however, he lost his mind and ran madly up the street,
bumping into fences, rolling in gutters, and pursuing his eccentric
course out of Amory's life. Amory cried on his bed.

'Poor little Count,' he cried. 'Oh, *poor* little *Count!*'

After several months he suspected Count of a fine piece of
emotional acting.

Amory and Frog Parker considered that the greatest line in literature
occurred in Act III of *Arsène Lupin.*[17]

They sat in the first row at the Wednesday and Saturday matinées.
The line was: 'If one can't be a great artist or a great soldier, the next
best thing is to be a great criminal.'

Amory fell in love again, and wrote a poem. This was it:

> Marylyn and Sall*ee*,
> Those are the girls for me.
> Marylyn stands above
> Sall*ee* in that sweet, deep love.

He was interested in whether McGovern of Minnesota[18] would make the first or second All-American, how to do the card-pass, how to do the coin-pass, chameleon ties, how babies were born, and whether Three-fingered Brown was really a better pitcher than Christy Mathewson.[19]

Among other things he read: *For the Honor of the School, Little Women* (twice), *The Common Law, Sappho, Dangerous Dan McGrew, The Broad Highway* (three times), *The Fall of the House of Usher, Three Weeks, Mary Ware, The Little Colonel's Chum, Gunga Din,*[20] the *Police Gazette* and *Jim-Jam Jems.*[21]

He had all the Henty biases in history, and was particularly fond of the cheerful murder stories of Mary Roberts Rinehart.[22]

School rubined his French and gave him a distaste for standard authors. His masters considered him idle, unreliable and superficially clever.

He collected locks of hair from many girls. He wore the rings of several. Finally he could borrow no more rings, owing to his nervous habit of chewing them out of shape. This, it seemed, usually aroused the jealous suspicions of the next borrower.

All through the summer months Amory and Frog Parker went each week to the Stock Company. Afterwards they would stroll home in the balmy air of August night, dreaming along Hennepin and Nicollet Avenues, through the gay crowd. Amory wondered how people could fail to notice that he was a boy marked for glory, and when faces of the throng turned towards him and ambiguous eyes stared into his, he assumed the most romantic of expressions and walked on the air cushions that lie on the asphalts of fourteen.

Always, after he was in bed, there were voices – indefinite, fading, enchanting – just outside his window, and before he fell asleep he would dream one of his favourite waking dreams, the one about becoming a great half-back, or the one about the Japanese invasion, when he was rewarded by being made the youngest general in the world. It was always the becoming he dreamed of, never the being. This, too, was quite characteristic of Amory.

CODE OF THE YOUNG EGOTIST

Before he was summoned back to Lake Geneva, he had appeared, shy but inwardly glowing, in his first long trousers, set off by a purple accordion tie and a 'Belmont' collar with the edges unassailably meeting, purple socks and handkerchief with a purple border peeping from his breast pocket. But more than that, he had formulated his first philosophy, a code to live by, which, as near as it can be named, was a sort of aristocratic egotism.

He had realised that his best interests were bound up with those of a certain variant, changing person, whose label, in order that his past might always be identified with him, was Amory Blaine. Amory marked himself a fortunate youth, capable of infinite expansion for good or evil. He did not consider himself a 'strong char'c'ter', but relied on his facility (learn things sorta quick) and his superior mentality (read a lotta deep books). He was proud of the fact that he could never become a mechanical or scientific genius. From no other heights was he debarred.

Physically: Amory thought that he was exceedingly handsome. He was. He fancied himself an athlete of possibilities and a supple dancer.

Socially: Here his condition was, perhaps, most dangerous. He granted himself personality, charm, magnetism, poise, the power of dominating all contemporary males, the gift of fascinating all women.

Mentally: Complete, unquestioned superiority.

Now a confession will have to be made. Amory had rather a Puritan conscience. Not that he yielded to it – later in life he almost completely slew it – but at fifteen it made him consider himself a great deal worse than other boys . . . unscrupulousness . . . the desire to influence people in almost every way, even for evil . . . a certain coldness and lack of affection, amounting sometimes to cruelty . . . a shifting sense of honour . . . an unholy selfishness . . . a puzzled, furtive interest in everything concerning sex.

There was, also, a curious strain of weakness running crosswise through his make-up . . . a harsh phrase from the lips of an older boy (older boys usually detested him) was liable to sweep him off his poise into surly sensitiveness or timid stupidity . . . he was a slave to his own moods and he felt that though he was capable of recklessness and audacity, he possessed neither courage, perseverance, nor self-respect.

Vanity, tempered with self-suspicion if not self-knowledge, a sense of people as automatons to his will, a desire to 'pass' as many boys as possible and get to a vague top of the world . . . with this background did Amory drift into adolescence.

PREPARATORY TO THE GREAT ADVENTURE

The train slowed up with midsummer languor at Lake Geneva, and Amory caught sight of his mother waiting in her electric on the gravelled station drive. It was an ancient electric, one of the early types, and painted grey. The sight of her sitting there, slenderly erect, and of her face, where beauty and dignity combined, melting to a dreamy recollected smile, filled him with a sudden great pride of her. As they kissed coolly and he stepped into the electric, he felt a quick fear lest he had lost the requisite charm to measure up to her.

'Dear boy – you're *so* tall . . . look behind and see if there's anything coming . . .'

She looked left and right, she slipped cautiously into a speed of two miles an hour, beseeching Amory to act as sentinel; and at one busy crossing she made him get out and run ahead to signal her forward like a traffic policeman. Beatrice was what might be termed a careful driver.

'You *are* tall – but you're still very handsome – you've skipped the awkward age, or is that sixteen; perhaps it's fourteen or fifteen; I can never remember; but you've skipped it.'

'Don't embarrass me,' murmured Amory.

'But, my dear boy, what odd clothes! They look as if they were a *set* – don't they? Is your underwear purple, too?'

Amory grunted impolitely.

'You must go to Brooks[23] and get some really nice suits. Oh, we'll have a talk tonight or perhaps tomorrow night. I want to tell you about your heart – you've probably been neglecting your heart – and you don't *know*.'

Amory thought how superficial was the recent overlay of his own generation. Aside from a minute shyness, he felt that the old cynical kinship with his mother had not been one bit broken. Yet for the first few days he wandered about the gardens and along the shore in a state of superloneliness, finding a lethargic content in smoking 'Bull'[24] at the garage with one of the chauffeurs.

The sixty acres of the estate were dotted with old and new summer houses and many fountains and white benches that came suddenly into sight from foliage-hung hiding-places; there was a great and constantly increasing family of white cats that prowled the many flower-beds and were silhouetted suddenly at night against the darkening trees. It was on one of the shadowy paths that Beatrice at last captured Amory, after Mr Blaine had, as usual, retired for the evening to his private library. After reproving him for avoiding her, she took him for a long tête-à-tête in the moonlight. He could not reconcile himself to her beauty, that was mother to his own, the exquisite neck and shoulders, the grace of a fortunate woman of thirty.

'Amory, dear,' she crooned softly, 'I had such a strange, weird time after I left you.'

'Did you, Beatrice?'

'When I had my last breakdown' – she spoke of it as a sturdy, gallant feat – 'the doctors told me' – her voice sang on a confidential note – 'that if any man alive had done the consistent drinking that I have, he would have been physically *shattered*, my dear, and in his *grave* – long in his grave.'

Amory winced, and wondered how this would have sounded to Froggy Parker.

'Yes,' continued Beatrice tragically, 'I had dreams – wonderful visions.' She pressed the palms of her hands into her eyes. 'I saw bronze rivers lapping marble shores, and great birds that soared through the air, parti-coloured birds with iridescent plumage. I heard strange music and the flare of barbaric trumpets – what?'

Amory had snickered.

'What, Amory?'

'I said go on, Beatrice.'

'That was all – it merely recurred and recurred – gardens that flaunted colouring against which this would be quite dull, moons that whirled and swayed, paler than winter moons, more golden than harvest moons – '

'Are you quite well now, Beatrice?'

'Quite well – as well as I will ever be. I am not understood, Amory. I know that can't express it to you, Amory, but – I am not understood.'

Amory was quite moved. He put his arm around his mother, rubbing his head gently against her shoulder.

'Poor Beatrice – poor Beatrice.'

'Tell me about *you*, Amory. Did you have two *horrible* years?'

Amory considered lying, and then decided against it.

'No, Beatrice. I enjoyed them. I adapted myself to the bourgeoisie. I became conventional.' He surprised himself by saying that, and he pictured how Froggy would have gaped.

'Beatrice,' he said suddenly, 'I want to go away to school. Everybody in Minneapolis is going to go away to school.'

Beatrice showed some alarm.

'But you're only fifteen.'

'Yes, but everybody goes away to school at fifteen, and I *want* to, Beatrice.'

On Beatrice's suggestion the subject was dropped for the rest of the walk, but a week later she delighted him by saying: 'Amory, I have decided to let you have your way. If you still want to, you can go to school.'

'Yes?'

'To St Regis's in Connecticut.'

Amory felt a quick excitement.

'It's being arranged,' continued Beatrice. 'It's better that you should go away. I'd have preferred you to have gone to Eton, and then to Christ Church, Oxford, but it seems impracticable now – and for the present we'll let the university question take care of itself.'

'What are you going to do, Beatrice?'

'Heaven knows. It seems my fate to fret away my years in this country. Not for a second do I regret being American – indeed, I think that a regret typical of very vulgar people, and I feel sure we are the great coming nation – yet' – and she sighed – 'I feel my life should have drowsed away close to an older, mellower civilisation, a land of greens and autumnal browns – '

Amory did not answer, so his mother continued: 'My regret is that you haven't been abroad, but still, as you are a man, it's better that you should grow up here under the snarling eagle – is that the right term?'

Amory agreed that it was. She would not have appreciated the Japanese invasion.

'When do I go to school?'

'Next month. You'll have to start East a little early to take your examinations. After that you'll have a free week, so I want you to go up the Hudson and pay a visit.'

'To who?'

'To Monsignor Darcy, Amory. He wants to see you. He went to Harrow and then to Yale – became a Catholic. I want him to talk to you – I feel he can be such a help – ' She stroked his auburn hair gently. 'Dear Amory, dear Amory – '

'Dear Beatrice – '

So early in September Amory, provided with 'six suits summer under-wear, six suits winter underwear, one sweater or T-shirt, one jersey, one overcoat, winter, etc.', set out for New England, the land of schools.

There were Andover and Exeter with their memories of New England dead – large, college-like democracies; St Mark's, Groton, St Regis's – recruited from Boston and the Knickerbocker families of New York; St Paul's, with its great rinks; Pomfret and St George's, prosperous and well-dressed; Taft and Hotchkiss, which prepared the wealth of the Middle West for social success at Yale; Pawling, Westminster, Choate, Kent, and a hundred others; all milling out their well-set-up, conventional, impressive type, year after year; their mental stimulus the college entrance exams; their vague purpose set forth in a hundred circulars as 'To impart a Thorough Mental, Moral and Physical Training as a Christian Gentleman, to fit the boy *for meeting the problems of his day and generation*, and to give a solid foundation in the Arts and Sciences'.

At St Regis's Amory stayed three days and took his exams with a scoffing confidence, then doubled back to New York to pay his tutelary visit. The metropolis, barely glimpsed, made little impression on him, except for the sense of cleanliness he drew from the tall white buildings seen from a Hudson River steamboat in the early morning. Indeed, his mind was so crowded with dreams of athletic prowess at school that he considered this visit only as a rather tiresome prelude to the great adventure. This, however, it did not prove to be.

Monsignor Darcy's house was an ancient, rambling structure set on a hill overlooking the river, and there lived its owner, between his trips to all parts of the Roman-Catholic world, rather like an exiled Stuart king waiting to be called to the rule of his land. Monsignor was forty-four then, and bustling – a trifle too stout for symmetry, with hair the colour of spun gold, and a brilliant, enveloping personality. When he came into a room clad in his full purple regalia from thatch to toe, he resembled a Turner sunset,[25] and attracted both admiration and attention. He had written two novels: one of them violently anti-Catholic, just before his conversion, and five years later another, in which he had attempted to turn all his clever jibes against Catholics into even cleverer innuendoes against Episcopalians. He was intensely ritualistic, startlingly dramatic, loved the idea of God enough to be a celibate, and rather liked his neighbour.

Children adored him because he was like a child; youth revelled in his company because he was still a youth, and couldn't be shocked. In the proper land and century he might have been a Richelieu – at present he was a very moral, very religious (if not particularly pious) clergyman, making a great mystery about pulling rusty wires, and appreciating life to the fullest, if not entirely enjoying it.

He and Amory took to each other at first sight – the jovial, impressive prelate who could dazzle an embassy ball, and the green-eyed, intent youth, in his first long trousers, accepted in their own minds a relation of father and son within a half-hour's conversation.

'My dear boy, I've been waiting to see you for years. Take a big chair and we'll have a chat.'

'I've just come from school – St Regis's, you know.'

'So your mother says – a remarkable woman; have a cigarette – I'm sure you smoke. Well, if you're like me, you loathe all science and mathematics – '

Amory nodded vehemently.

'Hate 'em all. Like English and history.'

'Of course. You'll hate school for a while, too, but I'm glad you're going to St Regis's.'

'Why?'

'Because it's a gentleman's school, and democracy won't hit you so early. You'll find plenty of that in college.'

'I want to go to Princeton,' said Amory. 'I don't know why, but I think of all Harvard men as sissies, like I used to be, and all Yale men as wearing big blue sweaters and smoking pipes.'

Monsignor chuckled. 'I'm one, you know.'

'Oh, you're different – I think of Princeton as being lazy and good-looking and aristocratic – you know, like a spring day. Harvard seems sort of indoors – '

'And Yale is November, crisp and energetic,' finished Monsignor. 'That's it.'

They slipped briskly into an intimacy from which they never recovered. 'I was for Bonnie Prince Charlie,' announced Amory.

'Of course you were – and for Hannibal – '26

'Yes, and for the Southern Confederacy.' He was rather sceptical about being an Irish patriot – he suspected that being Irish was being somewhat common – but Monsignor assured him that Ireland was a romantic lost cause and Irish people quite charming, and that it should, by all means, be one of his principal biases.

After a crowded hour which included several more cigarettes, and during which Monsignor learned, to his surprise but not to his horror, that Amory had not been brought up a Catholic, he announced that he had another guest. This turned out to be the Honourable Thornton Hancock, of Boston, ex-minister to The Hague, author of an erudite history of the Middle Ages and the last of a distinguished, patriotic, and brilliant family.

'He comes here for a rest,' said Monsignor confidentially, treating Amory as a contemporary. 'I act as an escape from the weariness of agnosticism, and I think I'm the only man who knows how his staid old mind is really at sea and longs for a sturdy spar like the Church to cling to.'

Their first luncheon was one of the memorable events of Amory's early life. He was quite radiant and gave off a peculiar brightness and charm. Monsignor called out the best that he had thought by question and suggestion, and Amory talked with an ingenuous brilliance of a thousand impulses and desires and repulsions and faiths and fears. He and Monsignor held the floor, and the older man, with his less receptive, less accepting, yet certainly not colder mentality, seemed content to listen and bask in the mellow sunshine that played between these two. Monsignor gave the effect of sunlight to many people; Amory gave it in his youth and, to some extent, when he was very much older, but never again was it quite so mutually spontaneous.

'He's a radiant boy,' thought Thornton Hancock, who had seen the splendour of two continents and talked with Parnell and Gladstone and Bismarck[27] – and afterwards he added to Monsignor: 'But his education ought not to be entrusted to a school or college.'

But for the next four years the best of Amory's intellect was concentrated on matters of popularity, the intricacies of a university social system and American Society as represented by Biltmore teas and Hot Springs golf-links.[28]

. . . In all, a wonderful week, that saw Amory's mind turned inside out, a hundred of his theories confirmed, and his joy of life crystallised to a thousand ambitions. Not that the conversation was scholastic – heaven forbid! Amory had only the vaguest idea as to what Bernard Shaw was – but Monsignor made quite as much out of *The Beloved Vagabond* and *Sir Nigel*,[29] taking good care that Amory never once felt out of his depth.

But the trumpets were sounding for Amory's preliminary skirmish with his own generation.

'You're not sorry to go, of course. With people like us our home is where we are not,' said Monsignor.

'I *am* sorry – '

'No, you're not. No one person in the world is necessary to you or to me.'

'Well – '

'Goodbye.'

THE EGOTIST DOWN

Amory's two years at St Regis's, though in turn painful and triumphant, had as little real significance in his own life as the American 'prep' school, crushed as it is under the heel of the universities, has to American life in general. We have no Eton to create the self-consciousness of a governing class; we have, instead, clean, flaccid and innocuous preparatory schools.

He went all wrong at the start, was generally considered both conceited and arrogant, and universally detested. He played football intensely, alternating a reckless brilliancy with a tendency to keep himself as safe from hazard as decency would permit. In a wild panic he backed out of a fight with a boy his own size, to a chorus of scorn, and a week later, in desperation, picked a battle with another boy very much bigger, from which he emerged badly beaten, but rather proud of himself.

He was resentful against all those in authority over him, and this, combined with a lazy indifference towards his work, exasperated every master in school. He grew discouraged and imagined himself a pariah; took to sulking in corners and reading after lights. With a dread of being alone he attached a few friends, but since they were not among the élite of the school, he used them simply as mirrors of himself, audiences before which he might do that posing absolutely essential to him. He was unbearably lonely, desperately unhappy.

There were some few grains of comfort. Whenever Amory was submerged, his vanity was the last part to go below the surface, so he could still enjoy a comfortable glow when 'Wookey-wookey', the deaf old housekeeper, told him that he was the best-looking boy she had ever seen. It had pleased him to be the lightest and youngest man on the first football squad; it pleased him when Dr Dougall told him at the end of a heated conference that he could, if he wished, get the best marks in school. But Dr Dougall was wrong. It was temperamentally impossible for Amory to get the best marks in school.

Miserable, confined to bounds, unpopular with both faculty and students – that was Amory's first term. But at Christmas he had returned to Minneapolis, tight-lipped and strangely jubilant.

'Oh, I was sort of fresh at first,' he told Frog Parker patronisingly, 'but I got along fine – lightest man on the squad. You ought to go away to school, Froggy. It's great stuff.'

INCIDENT OF THE WELL-MEANING PROFESSOR

On the last night of his first term, Mr Margotson, the senior master, sent word to study hall that Amory was to come to his room at nine. Amory suspected that advice was forthcoming, but he determined to be courteous, because this Mr Margotson had been kindly disposed towards him.

His summoner received him gravely, and motioned him to a chair. He hemmed several times and looked consciously kind, as a man will when he knows he's on delicate ground.

'Amory,' he began. 'I've sent for you on a personal matter.'

'Yes, sir.'

'I've noticed you this year and I – I like you. I think you have in you the makings of a – a very good man.'

'Yes, sir,' Amory managed to articulate. He hated having people talk as if he were an admitted failure.

'But I've noticed,' continued the older man blindly, 'that you're not very popular with the boys.'

'No, sir.' Amory licked his lips.

'Ah – I thought you might not understand exactly what it was they – ah – objected to. I'm going to tell you, because I believe – ah – that when a boy knows his difficulties he's better able to cope with them – to conform to what others expect of him.' He a-hemmed again with delicate reticence, and continued: 'They seem to think that you're – ah – rather too fresh – '

Amory could stand no more. He rose from his chair, scarcely controlling his voice when he spoke.

'I know – oh, *don't* you s'pose I know.' His voice rose. 'I know what they think; do you s'pose you have to *tell* me!' He paused. 'I'm – I've got to go back now – hope I'm not rude – '

He left the room hurriedly. In the cool air outside, as he walked to his house, he exulted in his refusal to be helped.

'That *damn* old fool!' he cried wildly. 'As if I didn't *know*!'

He decided, however, that this was a good excuse not to go back to study hall that night, so, comfortably couched up in his room, he munched Nabiscos and finished *The White Company*.[30]

INCIDENT OF THE WONDERFUL GIRL

There was a bright star in February. New York burst upon him on Washington's Birthday with the brilliance of a long-anticipated event. His glimpse of it as a vivid whiteness against a deep-blue sky had left a picture of splendour that rivalled the dream cities in the *Arabian Nights*; but this time he saw it by electric light, and romance gleamed from the chariot-race sign on Broadway[31] and from the women's eyes at the Astor, where he and young Paskert from St Regis's had dinner. When they walked down the aisle of the theatre, greeted by the nervous twanging and discord of untuned violins and the sensuous, heavy fragrance of paint and powder, he moved in a sphere of epicurean delight. Everything enchanted him. The play was *The Little Millionaire*,[32] with George M. Cohan, and there was one stunning young brunette who made him sit with brimming eyes in the ecstasy of watching her dance.

> 'Oh – you – wonderful girl,
>   What a wonderful girl you are – '

sang the tenor, and Amory agreed silently, but passionately.

> 'All – your – wonderful words
>   Thrill me through – '

The violins swelled and quavered on the last notes, the girl sank to a crumpled butterfly on the stage, a great burst of clapping filled the house. Oh, to fall in love like that, to the languorous magic melody of such a tune!

The last scene was laid on a roof-garden, and the cellos sighed to the musical moon, while light adventure and facile froth-like comedy flitted back and forth in the calcium. Amory was on fire to be an *habitué* of roof-gardens, to meet a girl who should look like that – better, that very girl; whose hair would be drenched with golden moonlight, while at his elbow sparkling wine was poured by an unintelligible waiter.

When the curtain fell for the last time he gave such a long sigh that the people in front of him twisted around and stared and said loud enough for him to hear: 'What a *remarkable*-looking boy!'

This took his mind off the play, and he wondered if he really did seem handsome to the population of New York.

Paskert and he walked in silence towards their hotel. The former was the first to speak. His uncertain fifteen-year-old voice broke in in a melancholy strain on Amory's musings: 'I'd marry that girl tonight.'

There was no need to ask what girl he referred to.

'I'd be proud to take her home and introduce her to my people,' continued Paskert.

Amory was distinctly impressed. He wished he had said it instead of Paskert. It sounded so mature.

'I wonder about actresses; are they all pretty bad?'

'No, *sir*, not by a darn sight,' said the worldly youth with emphasis, 'and I know that girl's as good as gold. I can tell.'

They wandered on, mixing in the Broadway crowd, dreaming on the music that eddied out of the cafés. New faces flashed on and off like myriad lights, pale or rouged faces, tired, yet sustained by a weary excitement. Amory watched them in fascination. He was planning his life. He was going to live in New York, and be known at every restaurant and café, wearing a dress-suit from early evening to early morning, sleeping away the dull hours of the forenoon.

'Yes, *sir*, I'd marry that girl tonight!'

HEROIC IN GENERAL TONE

October of his second and last year at St Regis's was a high point in Amory's memory. The game with Groton was played from three of a snappy, exhilarating afternoon far into the crisp autumnal twilight, and Amory at quarter-back, exhorting in wild despair, making impossible tackles, calling signals in a voice that had diminished to a hoarse, furious whisper, yet found time to revel in the blood-stained bandage around his head, and the straining, glorious heroism of plunging, crashing bodies and aching limbs. For those minutes courage flowed like wine out of the November dusk, and he was the eternal hero, one with the sea-rover on the prow of a Norse galley, one with Roland and Horatius, Sir Nigel and Ted Coy,[33] scraped and stripped into trim and then flung by his own will into the breach, beating back the tide, hearing from afar the thunder of cheers . . .

finally bruised and weary, but still elusive, circling an end, twisting, changing pace, straight-arming . . . falling behind the Groton goal with two men on his legs, in the only touchdown of the game.

THE PHILOSOPHY OF THE SLICKER

From the scoffing superiority of sixth-form year and success Amory looked back with cynical wonder on his status of the year before. He was changed as completely as Amory Blaine could ever be changed. Amory plus Beatrice plus two years in Minneapolis – these had been his ingredients when he entered St Regis's. But the Minneapolis years were not a thick enough overlay to conceal the 'Amory plus Beatrice' from the ferreting eyes of a boarding-school, so St Regis's had very painfully drilled Beatrice out of him, and begun to lay down new and more conventional planking on the fundamental Amory. But both St Regis's and Amory were unconscious of the fact that this fundamental Amory had not in himself changed. Those qualities for which he had suffered, his moodiness, his tendency to pose, his laziness, and his love of playing the fool, were now taken as a matter of course, recognised eccentricities in a star quarter-back, a clever actor, and the editor of the *St Regis Tatler*: it puzzled him to see impressionable small boys imitating the very vanities that had not long ago been contemptible weaknesses.

After the football season he slumped into dreamy content. The night of the pre-holiday dance he slipped away and went early to bed for the pleasure of hearing the violin music cross the grass and come surging in at his window. Many nights he lay there dreaming awake of secret cafés in Montmartre, where ivory women delved in romantic mysteries with diplomats and soldiers of fortune, while orchestras played Hungarian waltzes and the air was thick and exotic with intrigue and moonlight and adventure. In the spring he read *L'Allegro*,[34] by request, and was inspired to lyrical outpourings on the subject of Arcady and the pipes of Pan. He moved his bed so that the sun would wake him at dawn that he might dress and go out to the archaic swing that hung from an apple tree near the sixth-form house. Seating himself in this he would pump higher and higher until he got the effect of swinging into the wide air, into a fairyland of piping satyrs and nymphs with the faces of fair-haired girls he passed in the streets of Eastchester. As the swing reached its highest point, Arcady really lay just over the brow of a certain hill, where the brown road dwindled out of sight in a golden dot.

He read voluminously all spring, the beginning of his eighteenth year: *The Gentleman from Indiana*, *The New Arabian Nights*, *The Morals of Marcus Ordeyne*, *The Man Who Was Thursday*,[35] which he liked without understanding; *Stover at Yale*, that became somewhat of a textbook; *Dombey and Son*, because he thought he really should read better stuff; Robert Chambers, David Graham Phillips and E. Phillips Oppenheim[36] complete, and a scattering of Tennyson and Kipling. Of all his class work only *L'Allegro* and some quality of rigid clarity in solid geometry stirred his languid interest.

As June drew near, he felt the need of conversation to formulate his own ideas, and, to his surprise, found a co-philosopher in Rahill, the president of the sixth form. In many a talk, on the highroad or lying belly-down along the edge of the baseball diamond, or late at night with their cigarettes glowing in the dark, they threshed out the questions of school, and there was developed the term 'slicker'.

'Got tobacco?' whispered Rahill one night, putting his head inside the door five minutes after lights.

'Sure.'

'I'm coming in.'

'Take a couple of pillows and lie in the window-seat, why don't you.'

Amory sat up in bed and lit a cigarette while Rahill settled for a conversation. Rahill's favourite subject was the respective futures of the sixth form, and Amory never tired of outlining them for his benefit.

'Ted Converse? 'At's easy. He'll fail his exams, tutor all summer at Harstrum's,[37] get into Sheff[38] with about four conditions, and flunk out in the middle of the freshman year. Then he'll go back West and raise hell for a year or so; finally his father will make him go into the paint business. He'll marry and have four sons, all boneheads. He'll always think St Regis's spoiled him, so he'll send his sons to day school in Portland. He'll die of locomotor ataxia[39] when he's forty-one, and his wife will give a baptising stand or whatever you call it to the Presbyterian Church, with his name on it – '

'Hold up, Amory. That's too darned gloomy. How about yourself?'

'I'm in a superior class. You are, too. We're philosophers.'

'I'm not.'

'Sure you are. You've got a darn good head on you.' But Amory knew that nothing in the abstract, no theory or generality, ever moved Rahill until he stubbed his toe upon the concrete minutiae of it.

'Haven't,' insisted Rahill. 'I let people impose on me here and don't get anything out of it. I'm the prey of my friends, damn it – do their lessons, get 'em out of trouble, pay 'em stupid summer visits, and always entertain their kid sisters; keep my temper when they get selfish and then they think they pay me back by voting for me and telling me I'm the "big man" of St Regis's. I want to get where everybody does their own work and I can tell people where to go. I'm tired of being nice to every poor fish in school.'

'You're not a slicker,' said Amory suddenly.

'A what?'

'A slicker.'

'What the devil's that?'

'Well, it's something that – that – there's a lot of them. You're not one, and neither am I, though I am more than you are.'

'Who is one? What makes you one?'

Amory considered.

'Why – why, I suppose that the *sign* of it is when a fellow slicks his hair back with water.'

'Like Carstairs?'

'Yes – sure. He's a slicker.'

They spent two evenings getting an exact definition. The slicker was good-looking or clean-looking; he had brains, social brains, that is, and he used all means on the broad path of honesty to get ahead, be popular, admired, and never in trouble. He dressed well, was particularly neat in appearance, and derived his name from the fact that his hair was inevitably worn short, soaked in water or tonic, parted in the middle, and slicked back as the current of fashion dictated. The slickers of that year had adopted tortoiseshell spectacles as badges of their slickerhood, and this made them so easy to recognise that Amory and Rahill never missed one. The slicker seemed distributed through school, always a little wiser and shrewder than his contemporaries, managing some team or other, and keeping his cleverness carefully concealed.

Amory found the slicker a most valuable classification until his junior year in college, when the outline became so blurred and indeterminate that it had to be subdivided many times, and became only a quality. Amory's secret ideal had all the slicker qualifications, but, in addition, courage and tremendous brains and talents – also Amory conceded him a bizarre streak that was quite irreconcilable to the slicker proper.

This was a first real break from the hypocrisy of school tradition.

The slicker was a definite element of success, differing intrinsically from the prep-school 'big man'.

THE SLICKER	THE BIG MAN
1 Clever sense of social values.	1 Inclined to stupidity and unconscious of social values.
2 Dresses well. Pretends that dress is superficial – but knows that it isn't.	2 Thinks dress is superficial, and is inclined to be careless about it.
3 Goes into such activities as he can shine in.	3 Goes out for everything from a sense of duty.
4 Gets to college and is, in a worldly way, successful.	4 Gets to college and has a problematical future. Feels lost without his circle, and always says that schooldays were happiest, after all. Goes back to school and makes speeches about what St Regis's boys are doing.
5 Hair slicked.	5 Hair not slicked.

Amory had decided definitely on Princeton, even though he would be the only boy entering that year from St Regis's. Yale had a romance and glamour from the tales of Minneapolis, and St Regis's men who had been 'tapped for Skull and Bones',[40] but Princeton drew him most, with its atmosphere of bright colours and its alluring reputation as the pleasantest country club in America. Dwarfed by the menacing college exams, Amory's schooldays drifted into the past. Years afterwards, when he went back to St Regis's, he seemed to have forgotten the successes of sixth-form year, and to be able to picture himself only as the unadjustable boy who had hurried down corridors, jeered at by his rabid contemporaries mad with common sense.

CHAPTER 2

Spires and Gargoyles

At first Amory noticed only the wealth of sunshine creeping across the long, green swards, dancing on the leaded window-panes, and swimming around the tops of spires and towers and battlemented walls. Gradually he realised that he was really walking up University Place, self-conscious about his suitcase, developing a new tendency to glare straight ahead when he passed anyone. Several times he could have sworn that men turned to look at him critically. He wondered vaguely if there was something the matter with his clothes, and wished he had shaved that morning on the train. He felt unnecessarily stiff and awkward among these white-flannelled, bareheaded youths, who must be juniors and seniors, judging from the *savoir faire* with which they strolled.

He found that 12 University Place was a large, dilapidated mansion, at present apparently uninhabited, though he knew it housed usually a dozen freshmen. After a hurried skirmish with his landlady he sallied out on a tour of exploration, but he had gone scarcely a block when he became horribly conscious that he must be the only man in town who was wearing a hat. He returned hurriedly to 12 University, left his derby, and, emerging bareheaded, loitered down Nassau Street, stopping to investigate a display of athletic photographs in a store window, including a large one of Allenby, the football captain, and next attracted by the sign 'Jigger Shop'[41] over a confectionary window. This sounded familiar, so he sauntered in and took a seat on a high stool.

'Chocolate sundae,' he told a coloured person.

'Double-chocolate jiggah? Anything else?'

'Why – yes.'

'Bacon bun?'

'Why – yes.'

He munched four of these, finding them of pleasing savour, and then consumed another double-chocolate jigger before ease descended upon him. After a cursory inspection of the pillowcases, leather pennants and Gibson girls[42] that lined the walls, he left, and continued along Nassau Street with his hands in his pockets. Gradually he was learning to distinguish between upperclassmen and entering men, even though the freshman cap[43] would not appear until the following Monday. Those who were too obviously, too nervously at home were freshmen, for as each train brought a new contingent it was immediately absorbed into the hatless, white-shod, book-laden throng, whose function seemed to be to drift endlessly up and down the street, emitting great clouds of smoke from brand-new pipes. By afternoon Amory realised that now the newest arrivals were taking him for an upperclassman, and he tried conscientiously to look both pleasantly blasé and casually critical, which was as near as he could analyse the prevalent facial expression.

At five o'clock he felt the need of hearing his own voice, so he retreated to his house to see if anyone else had arrived. Having climbed the rickety stairs he scrutinised his room resignedly, concluding that it was hopeless to attempt any more inspired decoration than class banners and Tiger pictures.[44] There was a tap at the door.

'Come in!'

A slim face with grey eyes and a humorous smile appeared in the doorway.

'Got a hammer?'

'No – sorry. Maybe Mrs Twelve, or whatever she goes by, has one.'

The stranger advanced into the room.

'You an inmate of this asylum?'

Amory nodded.

'Awful barn for the rent we pay.'

Amory had to agree that it was.

'I thought of the campus,' he said, 'but they say there's so few freshmen that they're lost. Have to sit around and study for something to do.'

The grey-eyed man decided to introduce himself.

'My name's Holiday.'

'Blaine's my name.'

They shook hands with the fashionable low swoop. Amory grinned.

'Where'd you prep?'

'Andover – where did you?'

'St Regis's.'

'Oh, did you? I had a cousin there.'

They discussed the cousin thoroughly, and then Holiday announced that he was to meet his brother for dinner at six.

'Come along and have a bite with us.'

'All right.'

At the Kenilworth, Amory met Burne Holiday – he of the grey eyes was Kerry – and during a limpid meal of thin soup and anaemic vegetables they stared at the other freshmen, who sat either in small groups looking very ill at ease, or in large groups seeming very much at home.

'I hear Commons is pretty bad,' said Amory.

'That's the rumour. But you've got to eat there – or pay anyways.'

'Crime!'

'Imposition!'

'Oh, at Princeton you've got to swallow everything the first year. It's like a damned prep school.'

Amory agreed.

'Lot of pep, though,' he insisted. 'I wouldn't have gone to Yale for a million.'

'Me either.'

'You going out for anything?' enquired Amory of the elder brother.

'Not me – Burne here is going out for the *Prince* – the *Daily Princetonian*, you know.'

'Yes, I know.'

'You going out for anything?'

'Why – yes. I'm going to take a whack at freshman football.'

'Play at St Regis's?'

'Some,' admitted Amory depreciatingly, 'but I'm getting so damned thin.'

'You're not thin.'

'Well, I used to be stocky last fall.'

'Oh!'

After supper they attended the movies, where Amory was fascinated by the glib comments of a man in front of him, as well as by the wild yelling and shouting.

'*Yoho!*'

'Oh, honey-*baby* – you're so big and strong, but oh, so *gentle*!'

'Clinch!'

'Oh, *clinch*!'

'Kiss her, kiss 'at lady, *quick*!'

'Oh-h-h – !'

A group began whistling 'By The Sea',[45] and the audience took it up noisily. This was followed by an indistinguishable song that included much stamping and then by an endless, incoherent dirge.

'Oh-h-h-h-h
She works in a Jam Factoree
And – that-may-be-all-right
But you can't-fool-me
For I know – DAMN – WELL
That she DON'T-make-jam-all-night!
Oh-h-h-h!'

As they pushed out, giving and receiving curious impersonal glances, Amory decided that he liked the movies, wanted to enjoy them as the row of upperclassmen in front had enjoyed them, with their arms along the backs of the seats, their comments Gaelic and caustic, their attitude a mixture of critical wit and tolerant amusement.

'Want a sundae – I mean a jigger?' asked Kerry.

'Sure.'

They suppered heavily and then, still sauntering, eased back to 12.

'Wonderful night.'

'It's a whiz.'

'You men going to unpack?'

'Guess so. Come on, Burne.'

Amory decided to sit for a while on the front steps, so he bade them good-night.

The great tapestries of trees had darkened to ghosts back at the last edge of twilight. The early moon had drenched the arches with pale blue, and, weaving over the night, in and out of the gossamer rifts of moon, swept a song, a song with more than a hint of sadness, infinitely transient, infinitely regretful.

He remembered that an alumnus of the nineties had told him of one of Booth Tarkington's amusements: standing in mid-campus in the small hours and singing tenor songs to the stars, arousing mingled emotions in the couched undergraduates according to the sentiment of their moods.

Now, far down the shadowy line of University Place a white-clad phalanx broke the gloom, and marching figures, white-shirted, white-trousered, swung rhythmically up the street, with linked arms and heads thrown back:

'Going back – going back,
Going – back – to – Nas-sau – Hall,
Going back – going back –
To the – Best – Old – Place – of – All.

Going back – going back,
From all – this – earth-ly – ball,
We'll – clear – the – track – as – we – go – back –
Going – back – to – Nas-sau – Hall!'

Amory closed his eyes as the ghostly procession drew near. The song soared so high that all dropped out except the tenors, who bore the melody triumphantly past the danger-point and relinquished it to the fantastic chorus. Then Amory opened his eyes, half afraid that sight would spoil the rich illusion of harmony.

He sighed eagerly. There at the head of the white platoon marched Allenby, the football captain, slim and defiant, as if aware that this year the hopes of the college rested on him, that his hundred-and-sixty pounds were expected to dodge to victory through the heavy blue and crimson lines.[46]

Fascinated, Amory watched each rank of linked arms as it came abreast, the faces indistinct above the polo shirts, the voices blended in a paean of triumph – and then the procession passed through shadowy Campbell Arch, and the voices grew fainter as it wound eastward over the campus.

The minutes passed and Amory sat there very quietly. He regretted the rule that would forbid freshmen to be outdoors after curfew, for he wanted to ramble through the shadowy scented lanes, where Witherspoon brooded like a dark mother over Whig and Clio, her Attic children, where the black Gothic snake of Little curled down to Cuyler and Patton, these in turn flinging the mystery out over the placid slope rolling to the lake.

Princeton of the daytime filtered slowly into his consciousness – West and Reunion, redolent of the sixties, Seventy-nine Hall, brick-red and arrogant, Upper and Lower Pyne, aristocratic Elizabethan ladies not quite content to live among shopkeepers, and, topping all, climbing with clear blue aspiration, the great dreaming spires of Holder and Cleveland towers.

From the first he loved Princeton – its lazy beauty, its half-grasped significance, the wild moonlight revel of the rushes, the handsome, prosperous big-game crowds, and under it all the air of struggle that pervaded his class. From the day when, wild-eyed and exhausted, the jerseyed freshmen sat in the gymnasium and elected someone from Hill School class president, a Lawrenceville celebrity vice-president, a hockey star from St Paul's secretary, up until the end of sophomore year it never ceased, that breathless social system, that worship, seldom named, never really admitted, of the bogey 'big man'.

First it was schools, and Amory, alone from St Regis's, watched the crowds form and widen and form again; St Paul's, Hill, Pomfret, eating at certain tacitly reserved tables in Commons, dressing in their own corners of the gymnasium, and drawing unconsciously about them a barrier of the slightly less important but socially ambitious to protect them from the friendly, rather puzzled high-school element. From the moment he realised this Amory resented social barriers as artificial distinctions made by the strong to bolster up their weak retainers and keep out the almost strong.

Having decided to be one of the gods of the class, he reported for freshman football practice, but in the second week, playing quarter-back, already paragraphed in corners of the *Princetonian*, he wrenched his knee seriously enough to put him out for the rest of the season. This forced him to retire and consider the situation.

'12 Univee' housed a dozen miscellaneous question-marks. There were three or four inconspicuous and quite startled boys from Lawrenceville, two amateur wild men from a New York private school (Kerry Holiday christened them the 'plebeian drunks'), a Jewish youth, also from New York, and, as compensation for Amory, the two Holidays, to whom he took an instant fancy.

The Holidays were rumoured twins, but really the dark-haired one, Kerry, was a year older than his blond brother, Burne. Kerry was tall, with humorous grey eyes, and a sudden, attractive smile; he became at once the mentor of the house, reaper of ears that grew too high, censor of conceit, vendor of rare, satirical humour. Amory spread the table of their future friendship with all his ideas of what college should and did mean. Kerry, not inclined as yet to take things seriously, chided him gently for being curious at this in-opportune time about the intricacies of the social system, but liked him and was both interested and amused.

Burne, fair-haired, silent and intent, appeared in the house only as a busy apparition, gliding in quietly at night and off again in the early morning to get up his work in the library – he was out for the *Princetonian*, competing furiously against forty others for the coveted first place. In December he came down with diphtheria, and someone else won the competition, but, returning to college in February, he dauntlessly went after the prize again. Necessarily, Amory's acquaintance with him was in the way of three-minute chats, walking to and from lectures, so he failed to penetrate Burne's one absorbing interest and find what lay beneath it.

Amory was far from contented. He missed the place he had won at St Regis's, the being known and admired, yet Princeton stimulated him, and there were many things ahead calculated to arouse the Machiavelli latent in him, could he but insert a wedge. The upper-class clubs, concerning which he had pumped a reluctant graduate during the previous summer, excited his curiosity: Ivy, detached and breathlessly aristocratic; Cottage, an impressive *mélange* of brilliant adventurers and well-dressed philanderers; Tiger Inn, broad-shouldered and athletic, vitalised by an honest elaboration of prep-school standards; Cap and Gown, anti-alcoholic, faintly religious and politically powerful; flamboyant Colonial; literary Quadrangle; and the dozen others, varying in age and position.

Anything which brought an under classman into too glaring a light was labelled with the damning brand of 'running it out'. The movies thrived on caustic comments, but the men who made them were generally running it out; talking of clubs was running it out; standing for anything very strongly, as, for instance, drinking parties or teetotalling, was running it out; in short, being personally conspicuous was not tolerated, and the influential man was the non-committal man, until at club elections in sophomore year everyone should be sewed up in some bag for the rest of his college career.

Amory found that writing for the *Nassau Literary Magazine* would get him nothing, but that being on the board of the *Daily Princetonian* would get anyone a good deal. His vague desire to do immortal acting with the English Dramatic Association faded out when he found that the most ingenious brains and talents were concentrated upon the Triangle Club, a musical-comedy organisation that every year took a great Christmas trip. In the meanwhile, feeling strangely alone and restless in Commons, with new desires and ambitions stirring in his mind, he let the first term go by between an envy of the embryo successes and a puzzled fretting with Kerry as to why they were not accepted immediately among the élite of the class.

Many afternoons they lounged in the windows of 12 Univee and watched the class pass to and from Commons, noting satellites already attaching themselves to the more prominent, watching the lonely grind with his hurried step and downcast eye, envying the happy security of the big school groups.

'We're the damned middle class, that's what!' he complained to

Kerry one day as he lay stretched out on the sofa, consuming a family of Fatimas[47] with contemplative precision.

'Well, why not? We came to Princeton so we could feel that way towards the small colleges – have it on 'em, more self-confidence, dress better, cut a swathe – '

'Oh, it isn't that I mind the glittering caste system,' admitted Amory. 'I like having a bunch of hot cats on top, but gosh, Kerry, I've got to be one of them.'

'But just now, Amory, you're only a sweaty bourgeois.'

Amory lay for a moment without speaking.

'I won't be – long,' he said finally. 'But I hate to get anywhere by working for it. I'll show the marks, don't you know.'

'Honourable scars.' Kerry craned his neck suddenly at the street. 'There's Langueduc, if you want to see what he looks like – and Humbird just behind.'

Amory rose dynamically and sought the windows.

'Oh,' he said, scrutinising these worthies, 'Humbird looks like a knock-out, but this Langueduc – he's the rugged type, isn't he? I distrust that sort. All diamonds look big in the rough.'

'Well,' said Kerry, as the excitement subsided, 'you're a literary genius. It's up to you.'

'I wonder' – Amory paused – 'if I could be. I honestly think so sometimes. That sounds like the devil, and I wouldn't say it to anybody except you.'

'Well – go ahead. Let your hair grow and write poems like this guy D'Invilliers in the *Lit.*'

Amory reached lazily at a pile of magazines on the table.

'Read his latest effort?'

'Never miss 'em. They're rare.'

Amory glanced through the issue.

'Hello!' he said in surprise, 'he's a freshman, isn't he?'

'Yeah.'

'Listen to this! My God!

> "A serving lady speaks:
>   Black velvet trails its folds over the day,
>   White tapers, prisoned in their silver frames,
>   Wave their thin flames like shadows in the wind,
>   Pia, Pompia, come – come away – "

Now, what the devil does that mean?'

'It's a pantry scene.'

' "Her toes are stiffened like a stork's in flight;
        She's laid upon her bed, on the white sheets,
        Her hands pressed on her smooth bust like a saint,
        Bella Cunizza, come into the light!"

My gosh, Kerry, what in hell is it all about? I swear I don't get him at
all, and I'm a literary bird myself.'

'It's pretty tricky,' said Kerry, 'only you've got to think of hearses
and stale milk when you read it. That isn't as pash as some of them.'

Amory tossed the magazine on the table.

'Well,' he sighed, 'I sure am up in the air. I know I'm not a regular
fellow, yet I loathe anybody else that isn't. I can't decide whether to
cultivate my mind and be a great dramatist, or to thumb my nose at
the *Golden Treasury*[48] and be a Princeton slicker.'

'Why decide?' suggested Kerry. 'Better drift, like me. I'm going to
sail into prominence on Burne's coat-tails.'

'I can't drift – I want to be interested. I want to pull strings,
even for somebody else, or be Princetonian chairman or Triangle
president. I want to be admired, Kerry.'

'You're thinking too much about yourself.'

Amory sat up at this.

'No. I'm thinking about you, too. We've got to get out and mix
around the class right now, when it's fun to be a snob. I'd like to
bring a sardine to the prom in June, for instance, but I wouldn't do it
unless I could be damn debonaire about it – introduce her to all the
prize parlour-snakes, and the football captain, and all that simple
stuff.'

'Amory,' said Kerry impatiently, 'you're just going around in a
circle. If you want to be prominent, get out and try for something; if
you don't, just take it easy.' He yawned. 'Come on, let's let the
smoke drift off. We'll go down and watch football practice.'

Amory gradually accepted this point of view, decided that next fall
would inaugurate his career, and relinquished himself to watching
Kerry extract joy from 12 Univee.

They filled the Jewish youth's bed with lemon pie; they put out
the gas all over the house every night by blowing into the jet in
Amory's room, to the bewilderment of Mrs Twelve and the local
plumber; they set up the effects of the plebeian drunks – pictures,
books and furniture – in the bathroom, to the confusion of the pair,
who hazily discovered the transposition on their return from a

Trenton spree; they were disappointed beyond measure when the plebeian drunks decided to take it as a joke; they played red-dog and twenty-one and jackpot from dinner to dawn, and on the occasion of one man's birthday persuaded him to buy sufficient champagne for a hilarious celebration. The donor of the party having remained sober, Kerry and Amory accidentally dropped him down two flights of stairs and called, shamefaced and penitent, at the infirmary all the following week.

'Say, who are all these women?' demanded Kerry one day, protesting at the size of Amory's mail. 'I've been looking at the postmarks lately – Farmington and Dobbs and Westover and Dana Hall[49] – what's the idea?'

Amory grinned.

'All from the Twin Cities.'[50] He named them off. 'There's Marylyn De Witt – she's pretty, got a car of her own and that's damn convenient; there's Sally Weatherby – she's getting too fat; there's Myra St Claire, she's an old flame, easy to kiss if you like it – '

'What line do you throw 'em?' demanded Kerry. 'I've tried everything, and the mad wags aren't even afraid of me.'

'You're the "nice boy" type,' suggested Amory.

'That's just it. Mother always feels the girl is safe if she's with me. Honestly, it's annoying. If I start to hold somebody's hand, they laugh at me, and *let* me, just as if it wasn't part of them. As soon as I get hold of a hand they sort of disconnect it from the rest of them.'

'Sulk,' suggested Amory. 'Tell 'em you're wild and have 'em reform you – go home furious – come back in half an hour – startle 'em.'

Kerry shook his head.

'No chance. I wrote a St Timothy[51] girl a really loving letter last year. In one place I got rattled and said: "My God, how I love you!" She took some nail scissors, clipped out the "My God" and showed the rest of the letter all over school. Doesn't work at all. I'm just "good old Kerry" and all that rot.'

Amory smiled and tried to picture himself as 'good old Amory'. He failed completely.

February dripped snow and rain, the cyclonic freshman midyears passed, and life in 12 Univee continued interesting if not purposeful. Once a day Amory indulged in a club sandwich, cornflakes and Julienne potatoes at 'Joe's', accompanied usually by Kerry or Alec Connage. The latter was a quiet, rather aloof slicker from Hotchkiss, who lived next door and shared the same enforced singleness as Amory, due to the fact that his entire class had gone to

Yale. 'Joe's' was unaesthetic and faintly unsanitary, but a limitless charge account could be opened there, a convenience that Amory appreciated. His father had been experimenting with mining stocks and, in consequence, his allowance, while liberal, was not at all what he had expected.

'Joe's' had the additional advantage of seclusion from curious upper-class eyes, so at four each afternoon Amory, accompanied by friend or book, went up to experiment with his digestion. One day in March, finding that all the tables were occupied, he slipped into a chair opposite a freshman who bent intently over a book at the last table. They nodded briefly. For twenty minutes Amory sat consuming bacon buns and reading *Mrs Warren's Profession*[52] (he had discovered Shaw quite by accident while browsing in the library during mid-years); the other freshman, also intent on his volume, meanwhile did away with a trio of chocolate malted milks.

By and by Amory's eyes wandered curiously to his fellow-luncher's book. He spelled out the name and title upside down – *Marpessa* by Stephen Phillips.[53] This meant nothing to him, his metrical education having been confined to such Sunday classics as 'Come into the Garden, Maude',[54] and what morsels of Shakespeare and Milton had been recently forced upon him.

Moved to address his *vis-à-vis*, he simulated interest in his book for a moment, and then exclaimed aloud as if involuntarily: 'Ha! Great stuff!'

The other freshman looked up and Amory registered artificial embarrassment.

'Are you referring to your bacon buns?' His cracked, kindly voice went well with the large spectacles and the impression of a voluminous keenness that he gave.

'No,' Amory answered. 'I was referring to Bernard Shaw.' He turned the book around in explanation.

'I've never read any Shaw. I've always meant to.' The boy paused and then continued: 'Did you ever read Stephen Phillips, or do you like poetry?'

'Yes, indeed,' Amory affirmed eagerly. 'I've never read much of Phillips, though.' (He had never heard of any Phillips except the late David Graham Phillips.)

'It's pretty fair, I think. Of course he's a Victorian.' They sallied into a discussion of poetry, in the course of which they introduced themselves, and Amory's companion proved to be none other than 'that awful highbrow, Thomas Parke D'Invilliers', who signed the passionate love-poems in the *Lit*. He was, perhaps, nineteen, with stooped shoulders, pale blue eyes, and, as Amory could tell from his general appearance, without much conception of social competition and such phenomena of absorbing interest. Still, he liked books, and it seemed for ever since Amory had met anyone who did; if only that St Paul's crowd at the next table would not mistake *him* for a bird, too, he would enjoy the encounter tremendously. They didn't seem to be noticing, so he let himself go, discussed books by the dozens – books he had read, read about, books he had never heard of, rattling off lists of titles with the facility of a Brentano's clerk.[55] D'Invilliers was partially taken in and wholly delighted. In a good-natured way he had almost decided that Princeton was one part deadly Philistines and one part deadly grinds, and to find a person who could mention Keats without stammering, yet evidently washed his hands, was rather a treat.

'Ever read any Oscar Wilde?' he asked.

'No. Who wrote it?'

'It's a man – don't you know?'

'Oh, surely.' A faint chord was struck in Amory's memory. 'Wasn't the comic opera, *Patience*,[56] written about him?'

'Yes, that's the fella. I've just finished a book of his, *The Picture of Dorian Gray*,[57] and I certainly wish you'd read it. You'd like it. You can borrow it if you want to.'

'Why, I'd like it a lot – thanks.'

'Don't you want to come up to the room? I've got a few other books.'

Amory hesitated, glanced at the St Paul's group – one of them was the magnificent, exquisite Humbird – and he considered how determinate the addition of this friend would be. He never got to the stage of making them and getting rid of them – he was not hard enough for that – so he measured Thomas Parke D'Invilliers' undoubted attractions and value against the menace of cold eyes behind tortoise-rimmed spectacles that he fancied glared from the next table.

'Yes, I'll go.'

So he found *Dorian Gray* and the 'Mystic and Sombre Dolores' and the 'Belle Dame Sans Merci';[58] for a month was keen on naught else. The world became pale and interesting, and he tried hard to look at Princeton through the satiated eyes of Oscar Wilde and Swinburne – or 'Fingal O'Flahertie'[59] and 'Algernon Charles', as he called them in *précieuse* jest. He read enormously every night –

Shaw, Chesterton, Barrie, Pinero, Yeats, Synge, Ernest Dowson, Arthur Symons, Keats, Sudermann, Robert Hugh Benson,[60] the Savoy Operas[61] – just a heterogeneous mixture, for he suddenly discovered that he had read nothing for years.

Tom D'Invilliers became at first an occasion rather than a friend. Amory saw him about once a week, and together they gilded the ceiling of Tom's room and decorated the walls with imitation tapestry, bought at an auction, tall candlesticks and figured curtains. Amory liked him for being clever and literary without effeminacy or affectation. In fact, Amory did most of the strutting and tried painfully to make every remark an epigram, than which, if one is content with ostensible epigrams, there are many feats harder. 12 Univee was amused. Kerry read *Dorian Gray* and simulated Lord Henry, following Amory about, addressing him as 'Dorian' and pretending to encourage in him wicked fancies and attenuated tendencies to ennui. When he carried it into Commons, to the amazement of the others at table, Amory became furiously embarrassed, and after that made epigrams only before D'Invilliers or a convenient mirror.

One day Tom and Amory tried reciting their own and Lord Dunsany's poems[62] to the music of Kerry's graphophone.

'Chant!' cried Tom. 'Don't recite! *Chant!*'

Amory, who was performing, looked annoyed, and claimed that he needed a record with less piano in it. Kerry thereupon rolled on the floor in stifled laughter.

'Put on "Hearts and Flowers"!'[63] he howled. 'Oh, my Lord, I'm going to cast a kitten.'

'Shut off the damn graphophone,' Amory cried, rather red in the face. 'I'm not giving an exhibition.'

In the meanwhile Amory delicately kept trying to awaken a sense of the social system in D'Invilliers, for he knew that this poet was really more conventional than he, and needed merely watered hair, a smaller range of conversation, and a darker brown hat to become quite regular. But the liturgy of Livingstone collars and dark ties fell on heedless ears; in fact D'Invilliers faintly resented his efforts; so Amory confined himself to calls once a week, and brought him occasionally to 12 Univee. This caused mild titters among the other freshmen, who called them 'Dr Johnson and Boswell'.[64]

Alec Connage, another frequent visitor, liked him in a vague way, but was afraid of him as a highbrow. Kerry, who saw through his poetic patter to the solid, almost respectable depths within, was immensely amused and would have him recite poetry by the hour, while he lay with closed eyes on Amory's sofa and listened:

> 'Asleep or waking is it? for her neck
> Kissed over close, wears yet a purple speck
> Wherein the pained blood falters and goes out;
> Soft and stung softly – fairer for a fleck . . . '[65]

'That's good,' Kerry would say softly. 'It pleases the elder Holiday. That's a great poet, I guess.' Tom, delighted at an audience, would ramble through the *Poems and Ballads* until Kerry and Amory knew them almost as well as he.

Amory took to writing poetry on spring afternoons, in the gardens of the big estates near Princeton, while swans made effective atmosphere in the artificial pools, and slow clouds sailed harmoniously above the willows. May came too soon, and suddenly unable to bear walls, he wandered the campus at all hours through starlight and rain.

A DAMP SYMBOLIC INTERLUDE

The night mist fell. From the moon it rolled, clustered about the spires and towers, and then settled below them, so that the dreaming peaks were still in lofty aspiration towards the sky. Figures that dotted the day like ants now brushed along as shadowy ghosts, in and out of the foreground. The Gothic halls and cloisters were infinitely more mysterious as they loomed suddenly out of the darkness, outlined each by myriad faint squares of yellow light. Indefinitely from somewhere a bell boomed the quarter-hour, and Amory, pausing by the sun-dial, stretched himself out full length on the damp grass. The cool bathed his eyes and slowed the flight of time – time that had crept so insidiously through the lazy April afternoons, seemed so intangible in the long spring twilights. Evening after evening the senior singing had drifted over the campus in melancholy beauty, and through the shell of his undergraduate consciousness had broken a deep and reverent devotion to the grey walls and Gothic peaks and all they symbolised as warehouses of dead ages.

The tower that in view of his window sprang upward, grew into a spire, yearning higher until its uppermost tip was half invisible against the morning skies, gave him the first sense of the transiency and unimportance of the campus figures except as holders of the apostolic succession. He liked knowing that Gothic architecture, with its upward trend, was peculiarly appropriate to universities, and the idea became personal to him. The silent stretches of green, the quiet halls with an occasional late-burning scholastic light held his imagination in a strong grasp, and the chastity of the spire became a symbol of this perception.

'Damn it all,' he whispered aloud, wetting his hands in the damp and running them through his hair. 'Next year I work!' Yet he knew that where now the spirit of spires and towers made him dreamily acquiescent, it would then overawe him. Where now he realised only his own inconsequence, effort would make him aware of his own impotency and insufficiency.

The college dreamed on – awake. He felt a nervous excitement that might have been the very throb of its slow heart. It was a stream where he was to throw a stone whose faint ripple would be vanishing almost as it left his hand. As yet he had given nothing, he had taken nothing.

A belated freshman, his oilskin slicker rasping loudly, slushed along the soft path. A voice from somewhere called the inevitable formula, 'Stick out your head!' below an unseen window. A hundred little sounds of the current drifting on under the fog pressed in finally on his consciousness.

'Oh, God!' he cried suddenly, and started at the sound of his voice in the stillness. The rain dripped on. A minute longer he lay without moving, his hands clenched. Then he sprang to his feet and gave his clothes a tentative pat.

'I'm very damn wet!' he said aloud to the sundial.

HISTORICAL

The war began in the summer following his freshman year. Beyond a sporting interest in the German dash for Paris the whole affair failed either to thrill or interest him. With the attitude he might have held towards an amusing melodrama he hoped it would be long and bloody. If it had not continued he would have felt like an irate ticket-holder at a prizefight where the principals refused to mix it up.

That was his total reaction.

'All right, *ponies*!'

'Shake it up!'

'Hey, ponies – how about easing up on that crap game and shaking a mean hip?'

'Hey, *ponies*!'

The coach fumed helplessly, the Triangle Club president, glowering with anxiety, varied between furious bursts of authority and fits of temperamental lassitude, when he sat spiritless and wondered how the devil the show was ever going on tour by Christmas.

'All right. We'll take the pirate song.'

The ponies took last drags at their cigarettes and slumped into place; the leading lady rushed into the foreground, setting his hands and feet in an atmospheric mince; and as the coach clapped and stamped and tumped and da-da'd, they hashed out a dance.

A great, seething ant-hill was the Triangle Club. It gave a musical comedy every year, travelling with cast, chorus, orchestra and scenery all through Christmas vacation. The play and music were the work of undergraduates, and the club itself was the most influential of institutions, over three hundred men competing for it every year.

Amory, after an easy victory in the first sophomore Princetonian competition, stepped into a vacancy of the cast as Boiling Oil, a Pirate Lieutenant. Every night for the last week they had rehearsed *Ha-Ha Hortense!* in the Casino, from two in the afternoon until eight in the morning, sustained by dark and powerful coffee, and sleeping in lectures through the interim. A rare scene, the Casino. A big, barnlike auditorium, dotted with boys as girls, boys as pirates, boys as babies; the scenery in course of being violently set up; the spotlight man rehearsing by throwing weird shafts into angry eyes; over all the constant tuning of the orchestra or the cheerful tumpty-tump of a Triangle tune. The boy who writes the lyrics stands in the corner, biting a pencil, with twenty minutes to think of an encore; the business manager argues with the secretary as to how much money can be spent on 'those damn milkmaid costumes'; the old graduate, president in ninety-eight, perches on a box and thinks how much simpler it was in his day.

How a Triangle show ever got off was a mystery, but it was a riotous mystery, anyway, whether or not one did enough service to wear a little gold Triangle on his watch-chain. *Ha-Ha Hortense!* was written over six times and had the names of nine collaborators on the programme. All Triangle shows started by being 'something different – not just a regular musical comedy', but when the several authors, the president, the coach and the faculty committee finished with it, there remained just the old reliable Triangle show with the old reliable jokes and the star comedian who got expelled or sick or something just before the trip, and the dark-whiskered man in the pony-ballet, who 'absolutely won't shave twice a day, doggone it!'

There was one brilliant place in *Ha-Ha Hortense!* It is a Princeton tradition that whenever a Yale man who is a member of the widely advertised 'Skull and Bones' hears the sacred name mentioned, he must leave the room. It is also a tradition that the members are invariably successful in later life, amassing fortunes or votes or coupons or whatever they choose to amass. Therefore, at each performance of *Ha-Ha Hortense!* half a dozen seats were kept from sale and occupied by six of the worst-looking vagabonds that could be hired from the streets, further touched up by the Triangle make-up man. At the moment in the show where Firebrand, the Pirate Chief, pointed at his black flag and said, 'I am a Yale graduate – note my Skull and Bones!' – at this very moment the six vagabonds were instructed to rise *conspicuously* and leave the theatre with looks of deep melancholy and an injured dignity. It was claimed though never proved that on one occasion the hired Elis [66] were swelled by one of the real thing.

They played through vacation to the fashionable of eight cities. Amory liked Louisville and Memphis best: these knew how to meet strangers, furnished extraordinary punch, and flaunted an astonishing array of feminine beauty. Chicago he approved for a certain verve that transcended its loud accent – however, it was a Yale town, and as the Yale Glee Club was expected in a week, the Triangle received only divided homage. In Baltimore, Princeton was at home, and everyone fell in love. There was a proper consumption of strong waters all along the line; one man invariably went on the stage highly stimulated, claiming that his particular interpretation of the part required it. There were three private cars; however, no one slept except in the third car, which was called the 'animal car', and where were herded the spectacled wind-jammers of the orchestra. Everything was so hurried that there was no time to be bored, but when they arrived in Philadelphia, with vacation nearly over, there was rest in getting out of the heavy atmosphere of flowers and grease-paint, and the ponies took off their corsets with abdominal pains and sighs of relief.

When the disbanding came, Amory set out post haste for Minneapolis, for Sally Weatherby's cousin, Isabelle Borge, was coming to spend the winter in Minneapolis while her parents went abroad. He remembered Isabelle only as a little girl with whom he had played sometimes when he first went to Minneapolis. She had gone to Baltimore to live – but since then she had developed a past.

Amory was in full stride, confident, nervous and jubilant. Scurrying back to Minneapolis to see a girl he had known as a child seemed the interesting and romantic thing to do, so without compunction he wired his mother not to expect him . . . sat in the train, and thought about himself for thirty-six hours.

'PETTING'

On the Triangle trip Amory had come into constant contact with that great current American phenomenon, the 'petting party'.

None of the Victorian mothers – and most of the mothers were Victorian – had any idea how casually their daughters were accustomed to be kissed. '*Servant*-girls are that way,' says Mrs Huston-Carmelite to her popular daughter. 'They kissed first and proposed to afterwards.'

But the Popular Daughter becomes engaged every six months between sixteen and twenty-two, when she arranges a match with young Hambell, of Cambell & Hambell, who fatuously considers himself her first love, and between engagements the PD (she is selected by the cut-in system at dances, which favours the survival of the fittest) has other sentimental last kisses in the moonlight, or the firelight, or the outer darkness.

Amory saw girls doing things that even in his memory would have been impossible: eating three-o'clock, after-dance suppers in impossible cafés, talking of every side of life with an air half of earnestness, half of mockery, yet with a furtive excitement that Amory considered stood for a real moral let-down. But he never realised how widespread it was until he saw the cities between New York and Chicago as one vast juvenile intrigue.

Afternoon at the Plaza, with winter twilight hovering outside and faint drums downstairs . . . they strut and fret in the lobby, taking another cocktail, scrupulously attired and waiting. Then the swinging doors revolve and three bundles of fur mince in. The theatre comes afterwards; then a table at the Midnight Frolic[67] – of course, mother will be along there, but she will serve only to make things more secretive and brilliant as she sits in solitary state at the deserted table and thinks such entertainments as this are not half so bad as they are painted, only rather wearying. But the PD is in love again . . . it was odd, wasn't it? – that though there was so much room left in the taxi the PD and the boy from Williams[68] were somehow crowded out and had to go in a separate car. Odd! Didn't you notice how flushed the PD was when she arrived just seven minutes late? But the PD 'gets away with it'.

The 'belle' had become the 'flirt', the 'flirt' had become the 'baby vamp'. The 'belle' had five or six callers every afternoon. If the PD, by some strange accident, has two, it is made pretty uncomfortable for the one who hasn't a date with her. The 'belle' was surrounded by a dozen men in the intermissions between dances. Try to find the PD between dances, just *try* to find her.

The same girl . . . deep in an atmosphere of jungle music and the questioning of moral codes. Amory found it rather fascinating to feel that any popular girl he met before eight he might quite possibly kiss before twelve.

'Why on earth are we here?' he asked the girl with the green combs one night as they sat in someone's limousine, outside the Country Club in Louisville.

'I don't know. I'm just full of the devil.'

'Let's be frank – we'll never see each other again. I wanted to come out here with you because I thought you were the best-looking girl in sight. You really don't care whether you ever see me again, do you?'

'No – but is this your line for every girl? What have I done to deserve it?'

'And you didn't feel tired dancing or want a cigarette or any of the things you said? You just wanted to be – '

'Oh, let's go in,' she interrupted, 'if you want to *analyse*. Let's not *talk* about it.'

When the hand-knit, sleeveless jerseys were stylish, Amory, in a burst of inspiration, named them 'petting shirts'. The name travelled from coast to coast on the lips of parlour-snakes and PDs.

DESCRIPTIVE

Amory was now eighteen years old, just under six feet tall and exceptionally, but not conventionally, handsome. He had rather a young face, the ingenuousness of which was marred by the penetrating green eyes, fringed with long dark eyelashes. He lacked somehow that intense animal magnetism that so often accompanies beauty in men or women; his personality seemed rather a mental thing, and it was not in his power to turn it on and off like a water-faucet. But people never forgot his face.

ISABELLE

She paused at the top of the staircase. The sensations attributed to divers on springboards, leading ladies on opening nights, and lumpy, husky young men on the day of the Big Game, crowded through her. She should have descended to a burst of drums or a discordant blend of themes from *Thaïs* and *Carmen*.[69] She had never been so curious about her appearance, she had never been so satisfied with it. She had been sixteen years old for six months.

'Isabelle!' called her cousin Sally from the doorway of the dressing-room.

'I'm ready.' She caught a slight lump of nervousness in her throat.

'I had to send back to the house for another pair of slippers. It'll be just a minute.'

Isabelle started towards the dressing-room for a last peek in the mirror, but something decided her to stand there and gaze down the broad stairs of the Minnehaha Club. They curved tantalisingly, and she could catch just a glimpse of two pairs of masculine feet in the hall below. Pump-shod in uniform black, they gave no hint of identity, but she wondered eagerly if one pair were attached to Amory Blaine. This young man, not as yet encountered, had nevertheless taken up a considerable part of her day – the first day of her arrival.

Coming up in the machine from the station, Sally had volunteered, amid a rain of question, comment, revelation and exaggeration: 'You remember Amory Blaine, of *course*. Well, he's simply mad to see you again. He's stayed over a day from college, and he's coming tonight. He's heard so much about you – says he remembers your eyes.'

This had pleased Isabelle. It put them on equal terms, although she was quite capable of staging her own romances, with or without advance advertising. But following her happy tremble of anticipation, came a sinking sensation that made her ask: 'How do you mean he's heard about me? What sort of things?'

Sally smiled. She felt rather in the capacity of a showman with her more exotic cousin.

'He knows you're – you're considered beautiful and all that' – she paused – 'and I guess he knows you've been kissed.'

At this Isabelle's little fist had clenched suddenly under the fur robe. She was accustomed to be thus followed by her desperate past, and it never failed to rouse in her the same feeling of resentment; yet – in a strange town it was an advantageous reputation. She was a 'Speed', was she? Well – let them find out.

Out of the window Isabelle watched the snow glide by in the frosty morning. It was ever so much colder here than in Baltimore; she had not remembered; the glass of the side door was iced, the windows were shirred with snow in the corners. Her mind played still with one subject. Did *he* dress like that boy there, who walked calmly down a bustling business street, in moccasins and winter-carnival costume? How very *Western*! Of course he wasn't that way: he went to Princeton, was a sophomore or something. Really she had no distinct idea of him. An ancient snapshot she had preserved in an old Kodak book had impressed her by the big eyes (which he had probably grown up to by now). However, in the last month, when her winter visit to Sally had been decided on, he had assumed the proportions of a worthy adversary. Children, most astute of matchmakers, plot their campaigns quickly, and Sally had played a clever correspondence sonata to Isabelle's excitable temperament. Isabelle had been for some time capable of very strong, if very transient emotions . . .

They drew up at a spreading, white-stone building, set back from the snowy street. Mrs Weatherby greeted her warmly and her various younger cousins were produced from the corners where they skulked politely. Isabelle met them tactfully. At her best she allied all with whom she came in contact – except older girls and some women. All the impressions she made were conscious. The half-dozen girls she renewed acquaintance with that morning were all rather impressed and as much by her direct personality as by her reputation. Amory Blaine was an open subject. Evidently a bit light of love, neither popular nor unpopular – every girl there seemed to have had an affair with him at sometime or other, but no one volunteered any really useful information. He was going to fall for her . . . Sally had published that information to her young set and they were retailing it back to Sally as fast as they set eyes on Isabelle. Isabelle resolved secretly that she would, if necessary, *force* herself to like him – she owed it to Sally. Suppose she were terribly disappointed. Sally had painted him in such glowing colours – he was good-looking, 'sort of distinguished, when he wants to be', had a line, and was properly inconstant. In fact, he summed up all the romance that her age and environment led her to desire. She wondered if those were his dancing-shoes that fox-trotted tentatively around the soft rug below.

All impressions and, in fact, all ideas were extremely kaleidoscopic to Isabelle. She had that curious mixture of the social and the artistic temperaments found often in two classes, society women and actresses. Her education or, rather, her sophistication, had been absorbed from the boys who had dangled on her favour; her tact was instinctive, and her capacity for love-affairs was limited only by the number of the susceptible within telephone distance. Flirt smiled from her large black-brown eyes and shone through her intense physical magnetism.

So she waited at the head of the stairs that evening while slippers were fetched. Just as she was growing impatient, Sally came out of the dressing-room, beaming with her accustomed good nature and high spirits, and together they descended to the floor below, while the shifting searchlight of Isabelle's mind flashed on two ideas: she was glad she had high colour tonight, and she wondered if he danced well.

Downstairs, in the club's great room, she was surrounded for a moment by the girls she had met in the afternoon, then she heard Sally's voice repeating a cycle of names, and found herself bowing to a sextet of black and white, terribly stiff, vaguely familiar figures. The name Blaine figured somewhere, but at first she could not place him. A very confused, very juvenile moment of awkward backings and bumpings followed, and everyone found himself talking to the person he least desired to. Isabelle manoeuvred herself and Froggy Parker, freshman at Harvard, with whom she had once played hopscotch, to a seat on the stairs. A humorous reference to the past was all she needed. The things Isabelle could do socially with one idea were remarkable. First, she repeated it rapturously in an enthusiastic contralto with a soupçon of Southern accent; then she held it off at a distance and smiled at it – her wonderful smile; then she delivered it in variations and played a sort of mental catch with it, all this in the nominal form of dialogue. Froggy was fascinated and quite unconscious that this was being done, not for him, but for the green eyes that glistened under the shining carefully watered hair, a little to her left, for Isabelle had discovered Amory. As an actress even in the fullest flush of her own conscious magnetism gets a deep impression of most of the people in the front row, so Isabelle sized up her antagonist. First, he had auburn hair, and from her feeling of disappointment she knew that she had expected him to be dark and of garter-advertisement slenderness . . . For the rest, a faint flush and a straight, romantic profile; the effect set off by a close-fitting dress suit and a silk ruffled shirt of the kind that women still delight to see men wear, but men were just beginning to get tired of.

During this inspection Amory was quietly watching.

'Don't *you* think so?' she said suddenly, turning to him, innocent-eyed.

There was a stir, and Sally led the way over to their table. Amory struggled to Isabelle's side, and whispered: 'You're my dinner partner, you know. We're all coached for each other.'

Isabelle gasped – this was rather right in line. But really she felt as if a good speech had been taken from the star and given to a minor character . . . She mustn't lose the leadership a bit. The dinner-table glittered with laughter at the confusion of getting places and then curious eyes were turned on her, sitting near the head. She was enjoying this immensely, and Froggy Parker was so engrossed with the added sparkle of her rising colour that he forgot to pull out Sally's chair, and fell into a dim confusion. Amory was on the other side, full of confidence and vanity, gazing at her in open admiration. He began directly, and so did Froggy:

'I've heard a lot about you since you wore braids – '

'Wasn't it funny this afternoon – '

Both stopped. Isabelle turned to Amory shyly. Her face was always enough answer for anyone, but she decided to speak.

'How – from whom?'

'From everybody – for all the years since you've been away.' She blushed appropriately. On her right Froggy was *hors de combat* already, although he hadn't quite realised it.

'I'll tell you what I remembered about you all these years,' Amory continued. She leaned slightly towards him and looked modestly at the celery before her. Froggy sighed – he knew Amory, and the situations that Amory seemed born to handle. He turned to Sally and asked her if she was going away to school next year. Amory opened with grapeshot.

'I've got an adjective that just fits you.' This was one of his favourite starts – he seldom had a word in mind, but it was a curiosity provoker, and he could always produce something complimentary if he got in a tight corner.

'Oh – what?' Isabelle's face was a study in enraptured curiosity.

Amory shook his head.

'I don't know you very well yet.'

'Will you tell me – afterwards?' she half whispered.

He nodded.

'We'll sit out.'

Isabelle nodded.

'Did anyone ever tell you, you have keen eyes?' she said.

Amory attempted to make them look even keener. He fancied, but he was not sure, that her foot had just touched his under the table. But it might possibly have been only the table leg. It was so hard to tell. Still it thrilled him. He wondered quickly if there would be any difficulty in securing the little den upstairs.

BABES IN THE WOODS

Isabelle and Amory were distinctly not innocent, nor were they particularly brazen. Moreover, amateur standing had very little value in the game they were playing, a game that would presumably be her principal study for years to come. She had begun as he had, with good looks and an excitable temperament, and the rest was the result of accessible popular novels and dressing-room conversation culled from a slightly older set. Isabelle had walked with an artificial gait at nine and a half, and when her eyes, wide and starry, proclaimed the ingenue most. Amory was proportionately less deceived. He waited for the mask to drop off, but at the same time he did not question her right to wear it. She, on her part, was not impressed by his studied air of blasé sophistication. She had lived in a larger city and had slightly an advantage in range. But she accepted his pose – it was one of the dozen little conventions of this kind of affair. He was aware that he was getting this particular favour now because she had been coached; he knew that he stood for merely the best game in sight, and that he would have to improve his opportunity before he lost his advantage. So they proceeded with an infinite guile that would have horrified her parents.

After the dinner the dance began . . . smoothly. Smoothly? – boys cut in on Isabelle every few feet and then squabbled in the corners with: 'You might let me get more than an inch!' and, 'She didn't like it either – she told me so next time I cut in.' It was true – she told everyone so, and gave every hand a parting pressure that said: 'You know that your dances are *making* my evening.'

But time passed, two hours of it, and the less subtle beaux had better learned to focus their pseudo-passionate glances elsewhere, for eleven o'clock found Isabelle and Amory sitting on the couch in the little den off the reading-room upstairs. She was conscious that they were a handsome pair, and seemed to belong distinctively in this seclusion, while lesser lights fluttered and chattered downstairs.

Boys who passed the door looked in enviously – girls who passed only laughed and frowned and grew wise within themselves.

They had now reached a very definite stage. They had traded accounts of their progress since they had met last, and she had listened to much she had heard before. He was a sophomore, was on the *Princetonian* board, hoped to be chairman in senior year. He learned that some of the boys she went with in Baltimore were 'terrible speeds' and came to dances in states of artificial stimulation; most of them were twenty or so, and drove alluring red Stutzes.[70] A good half seemed already to have flunked out of various schools and colleges, but some of them bore athletic names that made him look at her admiringly. As a matter of fact, Isabelle's closer acquaintance with the universities was just commencing. She had bowing acquaintance with a lot of young men who thought she was a 'pretty kid – worth keeping an eye on'. But Isabelle strung the names into a fabrication of gaiety that would have dazzled a Viennese nobleman. Such is the power of young contralto voices on sink-down sofas.

He asked her if she thought he was conceited. She said there was a difference between conceit and self-confidence. She adored self-confidence in men.

'Is Froggy a good friend of yours?' she asked.

'Rather – why?'

'He's a bum dancer.'

Amory laughed.

'He dances as if the girl were on his back instead of in his arms.'

She appreciated this.

'You're awfully good at sizing people up.'

Amory denied this painfully. However, he sized up several people for her. Then they talked about hands.

'You've got awfully nice hands,' she said. 'They look as if you played the piano. Do you?'

I have said they had reached a very definite stage – nay, more, a very critical stage. Amory had stayed over a day to see her, and his train left at twelve-eighteen that night. His trunk and suitcase awaited him at the station; his watch was beginning to hang heavy in his pocket.

'Isabelle,' he said suddenly, 'I want to tell you something.' They had been talking lightly about 'that funny look in her eyes', and Isabelle knew from the change in his manner what was coming – indeed, she had been wondering how soon it would come. Amory reached above their heads and turned out the electric light, so that they were in the dark, except for the red glow that fell through the door from the reading-room lamps.

Then he began: 'I don't know whether or not you know what you – what I'm going to say. Lordy, Isabelle – this *sounds* like a line, but it isn't.'

'I know,' said Isabelle softly.

'Maybe we'll never meet again like this – I have darned hard luck sometimes.' He was leaning away from her on the other arm of the lounge, but she could see his eyes plainly in the dark.

'You'll meet me again – silly.' There was just the slightest emphasis on the last word – so that it became almost a term of endearment. He continued a bit huskily: 'I've fallen for a lot of people – girls – and I guess you have, too – boys, I mean, but, honestly, you – ' he broke off suddenly and leaned forward, chin on his hands: 'Oh, what's the use – you'll go your way and I suppose I'll go mine.'

Silence for a moment. Isabelle was quite stirred; she wound her handkerchief into a tight ball, and by the faint light that streamed over her, dropped it deliberately on the floor. Their hands touched for an instant, but neither spoke. Silences were becoming more frequent and more delicious. Outside another stray couple had come up and were experimenting on the piano in the next room. After the usual preliminary of 'Chopsticks', one of them started 'Babes In The Woods'[71] and a light tenor carried the words into the den:

> 'Give me your hand –
> I'll understand
> We're off to slumberland.'

Isabelle hummed it softly and trembled as she felt Amory's hand close over hers.

'Isabelle,' he whispered. 'You know I'm mad about you. You *do* give a darn about me.'

'Yes.'

'How much do you care – do you like anyone better?'

'No.' He could scarcely hear her, although he bent so near that he felt her breath against his cheek.

'Isabelle, I'm going back to college for six long months, and why shouldn't we – if I could only just have one thing to remember you by – '

'Close the door . . . ' Her voice had just stirred so that he half wondered whether she had spoken at all. As he swung the door softly shut, the music seemed quivering just outside.

'Moonlight is bright,
Kiss me good-night.'

What a wonderful song, she thought – everything was wonderful tonight, most of all this romantic scene in the den, with their hands clinging and the inevitable looming charmingly close. The future vista of her life seemed an unending succession of scenes like this: under moonlight and pale starlight, and in the backs of warm limousines and in low, cosy roadsters stopped under sheltering trees – only the boy might change, and this one was *so* nice. He took her hand softly. With a sudden movement he turned it and, holding it to his lips, kissed the palm.

'Isabelle!' His whisper blended in the music, and they seemed to float nearer together. Her breath came faster. 'Can't I kiss you, Isabelle – Isabelle?' Lips half parted, she turned her head to him in the dark. Suddenly the ring of voices, the sound of running footsteps surged towards them. Quick as a flash Amory reached up and turned on the light, and when the door opened and three boys, the wrathy and dance-craving Froggy among them, rushed in, he was turning over the magazines on the table, while she sat without moving, serene and unembarrassed, and even greeted them with a welcoming smile. But her heart was beating wildly, and she felt somehow as if she had been deprived.

It was evidently over. There was a clamour for a dance, there was a glance that passed between them – on his side despair, on hers regret, and then the evening went on, with the reassured beaux and the eternal cutting in.

At quarter to twelve Amory shook hands with her gravely, in the midst of a small crowd assembled to wish him good-speed. For an instant he lost his poise, and she felt a bit rattled when a satirical voice from a concealed wit cried: 'Take her outside, Amory!' As he took her hand he pressed it a little, and she returned the pressure as she had done to twenty hands that evening – that was all.

At two o'clock back at the Weatherbys' Sally asked her if she and

Amory had had a 'time' in the den. Isabelle turned to her quietly. In her eyes was the light of the idealist, the inviolate dreamer of Joan-like dreams.

'No,' she answered. 'I don't do that sort of thing any more; he asked me to, but I said no.'

As she crept into bed she wondered what he'd say in his special delivery tomorrow. He had such a good-looking mouth – would she ever – ?

'Fourteen angels were watching o'er them,' sang Sally sleepily from the next room.

'Damn!' muttered Isabelle, punching the pillow into a luxurious lump and exploring the cold sheets cautiously. 'Damn!'

CARNIVAL

Amory, by way of the *Princetonian*, had arrived. The minor snobs, finely balanced thermometers of success, warmed to him as the club elections grew nigh, and he and Tom were visited by groups of upperclassmen who arrived awkwardly, balanced on the edges of the furniture and talked of all subjects except the one of absorbing interest. Amory was amused at the intent eyes upon him, and, in case the visitors represented some club in which he was not interested, took great pleasure in shocking them with unorthodox remarks.

'Oh, let me see – ' he said one night to a flabbergasted delegation, 'what club do you represent?'

With visitors from Ivy and Cottage and Tiger Inn he played the 'nice, unspoilt, ingenuous boy' very much at ease and quite unaware of the object of the call.

When the fatal morning arrived, early in March, and the campus became a document in hysteria, he slid smoothly into Cottage with Alec Connage and watched his suddenly neurotic class with much wonder.

There were fickle groups that jumped from club to club; there were friends of two or three days who announced tearfully and wildly that they must join the same club, nothing should separate them; there were snarling disclosures of long-hidden grudges as the Suddenly Prominent remembered snubs of freshman year. Unknown men were elevated into importance when they received certain coveted bids; others who were considered 'all set' found that they had made unexpected enemies, felt themselves stranded and deserted, talked wildly of leaving college.

In his own crowd Amory saw men kept out for wearing green hats, for being 'a damn tailor's dummy', for having 'too much pull in heaven', for getting drunk one night 'not like a gentleman, by God', or for unfathomable secret reasons known to no one but the wielders of the black balls.[72]

This orgy of sociability culminated in a gigantic party at the Nassau Inn, where punch was dispensed from immense bowls, and the whole downstairs became a delirious, circulating, shouting pattern of faces and voices.

'Hi, Dibby – 'gratulations!'

'Goo' boy, Tom, you got a good bunch in Cap.'

'Say, Kerry – '

'Oh, Kerry – I hear you went Tiger with all the weight-lifters!'

'Well, I didn't go Cottage – the parlour-snakes' delight.'

'They say Overton fainted when he got his Ivy bid – Did he sign up the first day? – oh, *no*. Tore over to Murray-Dodge on a bicycle – afraid it was a mistake.'

'How'd you get into Cap – you old roué?'

' 'Gratulations!'

' 'Gratulations yourself. Hear you got a good crowd.'

When the bar closed, the party broke up into groups and streamed, singing, over the snow-clad campus, in a weird delusion that snobbishness and strain were over at last, and that they could do what they pleased for the next two years.

Long afterwards Amory thought of sophomore spring as the happiest time of his life. His ideas were in tune with life as he found it; he wanted no more than to drift and dream and enjoy a dozen new-found friendships through the April afternoons.

Alec Connage came into his room one morning and woke him up into the sunshine and peculiar glory of Campbell Hall shining in the window.

'Wake up, Original Sin, and scrape yourself together. Be in front of Renwick's in half an hour. Somebody's got a car.' He took the bureau cover and carefully deposited it, with its load of small articles, upon the bed.

'Where'd you get the car?' demanded Amory cynically.

'Sacred trust, but don't be a critical goopher or you can't go!'

'I think I'll sleep,' Amory said calmly, resettling himself and reaching beside the bed for a cigarette.

'Sleep!'

'Why not? I've got a class at eleven-thirty.'

'You damned gloom! Of course, if you don't want to go to the coast – '

With a bound Amory was out of bed, scattering the bureau cover's burden on the floor. The coast . . . he hadn't seen it for years, since he and his mother were on their pilgrimage.

'Who's going?' he demanded as he wriggled into his BVD's.

'Oh, Dick Humbird and Kerry Holiday and Jesse Ferrenby and – oh about five or six. Speed it up, kid!'

In ten minutes Amory was devouring cornflakes in Renwick's, and at nine-thirty they bowled happily out of town, headed for the sands of Deal Beach.

'You see,' said Kerry, 'the car belongs down there. In fact, it was stolen from Asbury Park[73] by persons unknown, who deserted it in Princeton and left for the West. Heartless Humbird here got permission from the city council to deliver it.'

'Anybody got any money?' suggested Ferrenby, turning around from the front seat.

There was an emphatic negative chorus.

'That makes it interesting.'

'Money – what's money? We can sell the car.'

'Charge him salvage or something.'

'How're we going to get food?' asked Amory.

'Honestly,' answered Kerry, eying him reprovingly, 'do you doubt Kerry's ability for three short days? Some people have lived on nothing for years at a time. Read the *Boy Scout Monthly*.'

'Three days,' Amory mused, 'and I've got classes.'

'One of the days is the Sabbath.'

'Just the same, I can only cut six more classes, with over a month and a half to go.'

'Throw him out!'

'It's a long walk back.'

'Amory, you're running it out, if I may coin a new phrase.'

'Hadn't you better get some dope on yourself, Amory?'

Amory subsided resignedly and drooped into a contemplation of the scenery. Swinburne seemed to fit in somehow.

> Oh, winter's rains and ruins are over,
>   And all the seasons of snows and sins;
> The days dividing lover and lover,
>   The light that loses, the night that wins;
> And time remembered is grief forgotten,

And frosts are slain and flowers begotten,
And in green underwood and cover,
  Blossom by blossom the spring begins.

The full streams feed on flower of – [74]

'What's the matter, Amory? Amory's thinking about poetry, about the pretty birds and flowers. I can see it in his eye.'

'No, I'm not,' he lied. 'I'm thinking about the *Princetonian*. I ought to make up tonight; but I can telephone back, I suppose.'

'Oh,' said Kerry respectfully, 'these important men – '

Amory flushed and it seemed to him that Ferrenby, a defeated competitor, winced a little. Of course, Kerry was only kidding, but he really mustn't mention the *Princetonian*.

It was a halcyon day, and as they neared the shore and the salt breezes scurried by, he began to picture the ocean and long, level stretches of sand and red roofs over blue sea. Then they hurried through the little town and it all flashed upon his consciousness to a mighty paean of emotion . . .

'Oh, good Lord! *Look* at it!' he cried.

'What?'

'Let me out, quick – I haven't seen it for eight years! Oh, gentlefolk, stop the car!'

'What an odd child!' remarked Alec.

'I do believe he's a bit eccentric.'

The car was obligingly drawn up at a curb, and Amory ran for the boardwalk. First, he realised that the sea was blue and that there was an enormous quantity of it, and that it roared and roared – really all the banalities about the ocean that one could realise, but if anyone had told him then that these things were banalities, he would have gaped in wonder.

'Now we'll get lunch,' ordered Kerry, wandering up with the crowd. 'Come on, Amory, tear yourself away and get practical.'

'We'll try the best hotel first,' he went on, 'and thence and so forth.'

They strolled along the boardwalk to the most imposing hostelry in sight, and, entering the dining-room, scattered about a table.

'Eight Bronxes,' commanded Alec, 'and a club sandwich and Juliennes. The food for one. Hand the rest around.'

Amory ate little, having seized a chair where he could watch the sea and feel the rock of it. When luncheon was over they sat and smoked quietly.

'What's the bill?'

Someone scanned it.

'Eight twenty-five.'

'Rotten overcharge. We'll give them two dollars and one for the waiter. Kerry, collect the small change.'

The waiter approached, and Kerry gravely handed him a dollar, tossed two dollars on the check, and turned away. They sauntered leisurely towards the door, pursued in a moment by the suspicious Ganymede.[75]

'Some mistake, sir.'

Kerry took the bill and examined it critically.

'No mistake!' he said, shaking his head gravely, and, tearing it into four pieces, he handed the scraps to the waiter, who was so dumfounded that he stood motionless and expressionless while they walked out.

'Won't he send after us?'

'No,' said Kerry; 'for a minute he'll think we're the proprietor's sons or something; then he'll look at the check again and call the manager, and in the meantime – '

They left the car at Asbury and street-car'd to Allenhurst, where they investigated the crowded pavilions for beauty. At four there were refreshments in a lunch-room, and this time they paid an even smaller per cent on the total cost; something about the appearance and *savoir-faire* of the crowd made the thing go, and they were not pursued.

'You see, Amory, we're Marxian Socialists,' explained Kerry. 'We don't believe in property and we're putting it to the great test.'

'Night will descend,' Amory suggested.

'Watch, and put your trust in Holiday.'

They became jovial about five-thirty and, linking arms, strolled up and down the boardwalk in a row, chanting a monotonous ditty about the sad sea waves. Then Kerry saw a face in the crowd that attracted him and, rushing off, reappeared in a moment with one of the homeliest girls Amory had ever set eyes on. Her pale mouth extended from ear to ear, her teeth projected in a solid wedge, and she had little, squinty eyes that peeped ingratiatingly over the side sweep of her nose. Kerry presented them formally.

'Name of Kaluka, Hawaiian queen! Let me present Messrs Connage, Sloane, Humbird, Ferrenby and Blaine.'

The girl bobbed courtesies all around. Poor creature; Amory supposed she had never before been noticed in her life – possibly she was half-witted. While she accompanied them (Kerry had invited her to supper) she said nothing which could discountenance such a belief.

'She prefers her native dishes,' said Alec gravely to the waiter, 'but any coarse food will do.'

All through supper he addressed her in the most respectful language, while Kerry made idiotic love to her on the other side, and she giggled and grinned. Amory was content to sit and watch the by-play, thinking what a light touch Kerry had, and how he could transform the barest incident into a thing of curve and contour. They all seemed to have the spirit of it more or less, and it was a relaxation to be with them. Amory usually liked men individually, yet feared them in crowds unless the crowd was around him. He wondered how much each one contributed to the party, for there was somewhat of a spiritual tax levied. Alec and Kerry were the life of it, but not quite the centre. Somehow the quiet Humbird and Sloane, with his impatient superciliousness, were the centre.

Dick Humbird had, ever since freshman year, seemed to Amory a perfect type of aristocrat. He was slender but well-built – black curly hair, straight features, and rather a dark skin. Everything he said sounded intangibly appropriate. He possessed infinite courage, an averagely good mind, and a sense of honour with a clear charm and *noblesse oblige* that varied it from righteousness. He could dissipate without going to pieces, and even his most bohemian adventures never seemed 'running it out'. People dressed like him, tried to talk as he did . . . Amory decided that he probably held the world back, but he wouldn't have changed him . . .

He differed from the healthy type that was essentially middle class – he never seemed to perspire. Some people couldn't be familiar with a chauffeur without having it returned; Humbird could have lunched at Sherry's with a coloured man, yet people would have somehow known that it was all right. He was not a snob, though he knew only half his class. His friends ranged from the highest to the lowest, but it was impossible to 'cultivate' him. Servants worshipped him, and treated him like a god. He seemed the eternal example of what the upper class tries to be.

'He's like those pictures in the *Illustrated London News* of the English officers who have been killed,' Amory had said to Alec. 'Well,' Alec had answered, 'if you want to know the shocking truth, his father was a grocery clerk who made a fortune in Tacoma real estate and came to New York ten years ago.'

Amory had felt a curious sinking sensation.

This present type of party was made possible by the surging together of the class after club elections – as if to make a last desperate attempt to know itself, to keep together, to fight off the tightening spirit of the clubs. It was a let-down from the conventional heights they had all walked so rigidly.

After supper they saw Kaluka to the boardwalk, and then strolled back along the beach to Asbury. The evening sea was a new sensation, for all its colour and mellow age was gone, and it seemed the bleak waste that made the Norse sagas sad; Amory thought of Kipling's 'Beaches of Lukannon before the sealers came'.[76]

It was still a music, though infinitely sorrowful.

Ten o'clock found them penniless. They had suppered greatly on their last eleven cents and, singing, strolled up through the casinos and lighted arches on the boardwalk, stopping to listen approvingly to all band concerts. In one place Kerry took up a collection for the French War Orphans which netted a dollar and twenty cents, and with this they bought some brandy in case they caught cold in the night. They finished the day in a moving-picture show and went into solemn systematic roars of laughter at an ancient comedy, to the startled annoyance of the rest of the audience. Their entrance was distinctly strategic, for each man as he entered pointed reproachfully at the one just behind him. Sloane, bringing up the rear, disclaimed all knowledge and responsibility as soon as the others were scattered inside; then as the irate ticket-taker rushed in he followed nonchalantly.

They reassembled later by the Casino and made arrangements for the night. Kerry wormed permission from the watchman to sleep on the platform and, having collected a huge pile of rugs from the booths to serve as mattresses and blankets, they talked until midnight, and then fell into a dreamless sleep, though Amory tried hard to stay awake and watch that marvellous moon settle on the sea.

So they progressed for two happy days, up and down the shore by street-car or machine, or by shoe-leather on the crowded boardwalk; sometimes eating with the wealthy, more frequently dining frugally at the expense of an unsuspecting restaurateur. They had their photos taken, eight poses, in a quick-development store. Kerry insisted on grouping them as a 'varsity' football team, and then as a tough gang from the East Side, with their coats inside out, and himself sitting in the middle on a cardboard moon. The photographer probably has them yet – at least, they never called for them. The weather was perfect, and again they slept outside, and again Amory fell unwillingly asleep.

Sunday broke stolid and respectable, and even the sea seemed to mumble and complain, so they returned to Princeton via the Fords of transient farmers, and broke up with colds in their heads, but otherwise none the worse for wandering.

Even more than in the year before, Amory neglected his work, not deliberately but lazily and through a multitude of other interests. Co-ordinate geometry and the melancholy hexameters of Corneille and Racine[77] held forth small allurements, and even psychology, which he had eagerly awaited, proved to be a dull subject full of muscular reactions and biological phrases rather than the study of personality and influence. That was a noon class, and it always sent him dozing. Having found that, 'Subjective and objective, sir,' answered most of the questions, he used the phrase on all occasions, and it became the class joke when, on a query being levelled at him, he was nudged awake by Ferrenby or Sloane to gasp it out.

Mostly there were parties – to Orange or the Shore, more rarely to New York and Philadelphia, though one night they marshalled fourteen waitresses out of Childs' and took them to ride down Fifth Avenue on top of an auto bus. They all cut more classes than were allowed, which meant an additional course the following year, but spring was too rare to let anything interfere with their colourful ramblings. In May Amory was elected to the Sophomore Prom Committee, and when after a long evening's discussion with Alec they made out a tentative list of class probabilities for the Senior Council, they placed themselves among the surest. The Senior Council was composed presumably of the eighteen most representative seniors, and in view of Alec's football managership and Amory's chance of nosing out Burne Holiday as *Princetonian* chairman, they seemed fairly justified in this presumption. Oddly enough, they both placed D'Invilliers as among the possibilities, a guess that a year before the class would have gaped at.

All through the spring Amory had kept up an intermittent correspondence with Isabelle Borgé, punctuated by violent squabbles and chiefly enlivened by his attempts to find new words for love. He discovered Isabelle to be discreetly and aggravatingly unsentimental in letters, but he hoped against hope that she would prove not too exotic a bloom to fit the large spaces of spring as she had fitted the den in the Minnehaha Club. During May he wrote thirty-page documents almost nightly, and sent them to her in bulky envelopes exteriorly labelled 'Part I' and 'Part II'.

'Oh, Alec, I believe I'm tired of college,' he said sadly, as they walked the dusk together.

'I think I am, too, in a way.'

'All I'd like would be a little home in the country, some warm country, and a wife, and just enough to do to keep from rotting.'

'Me, too.'

'I'd like to quit.'

'What does your girl say?'

'Oh!' Amory gasped in horror. 'She wouldn't *think* of marrying . . . that is, not now. I mean the future, you know.'

'My girl would. I'm engaged.'

'Are you really?'

'Yes. Don't say a word to anybody, please, but I am. I may not come back next year.'

'But you're only twenty! Give up college?'

'Why, Amory, you were saying a minute ago – '

'Yes,' Amory interrupted, 'but I was just wishing. I wouldn't think of leaving college. It's just that I feel so sad these wonderful nights. I sort of feel they're never coming again, and I'm not really getting all I could out of them. I wish my girl lived here. But marry – not a chance. Especially as father says the money isn't forthcoming as it used to be.'

'What a waste these nights are!' agreed Alec.

But Amory sighed and made use of the nights. He had a snapshot of Isabelle, enshrined in an old watch, and at eight almost every night he would turn off all the lights except the desk lamp and, sitting by the open windows with the picture before him, write her rapturous letters.

. . . Oh it's so hard to write you what I really *feel* when I think about you so much; you've gotten to mean to me a *dream* that I can't put on paper any more. Your last letter came and it was wonderful! I read it over about six times, especially the *last* part, but I do wish, sometimes, you'd be more *frank* and tell me what you really do think of me, yet your last letter was too good to be true, and I can hardly wait until June! Be sure and be able to come to the prom. It'll be fine, I think, and I want to bring *you* just at the end of a wonderful year. I often think over what you said on that night and wonder how much you meant. If it were anyone but you – but you see I *thought* you were fickle the first time I saw you and you are so popular and everything that I can't imagine you really liking me *best*.

Oh, Isabelle, dear – it's a wonderful night. Somebody is playing 'Love Moon' on a mandolin far across the campus, and the music seems to bring you into the window. Now he's playing 'Goodbye, Boys, I'm Through',[78] and how well it suits me. For I *am* through with everything. I have decided never to take a cocktail again, and I know I'll never again fall in love – I couldn't – you've been too much a part of my days and nights to ever let me think of another girl. I meet them all the time and they don't interest me. I'm not pretending to be blasé, because it's not that. It's just that I'm in love. Oh, *dearest* Isabelle (somehow I can't call you just Isabelle, and I'm afraid I'll come out with the 'dearest' before your family this June), you've got to come to the prom, and then I'll come up to your house for a day and everything'll be perfect . . .

And so on in an eternal monotone that seemed to both of them infinitely charming, infinitely new.

June came and the days grew so hot and lazy that they could not worry even about exams, but spent dreamy evenings on the court of Cottage, talking of long subjects until the sweep of country towards Stony Brook became a blue haze and the lilacs were white around tennis-courts, and words gave way to silent cigarettes . . . Then down deserted Prospect and along McCosh with song everywhere around them, up to the hot joviality of Nassau Street.

Tom D'Invilliers and Amory walked late in those days. A gambling fever swept through the sophomore class and they bent over the bones till three o'clock many a sultry night. After one session they came out of Sloane's room to find the dew fallen and the stars old in the sky.

'Let's borrow bicycles and take a ride,' Amory suggested.

'All right. I'm not a bit tired and this is almost the last night of the year, really, because the prom stuff starts Monday.'

They found two unlocked bicycles in Holder Court and rode out about half-past three along the Lawrenceville Road.

'What are you going to do this summer, Amory?'

'Don't ask me – same old things, I suppose. A month or two in Lake Geneva – I'm counting on you to be there in July, you know – then there'll be Minneapolis, and that means hundreds of summer hops, parlour-snaking, getting bored – But oh, Tom,' he added suddenly, 'hasn't this year been slick!'

'No,' declared Tom emphatically, a new Tom, clothed by Brooks, shod by Franks,[79] 'I've won this game, but I feel as if I never want to play another. You're all right – you're a rubber ball, and somehow it suits you, but I'm sick of adapting myself to the local snobbishness of this corner of the world. I want to go where people aren't barred because of the colour of their neckties and the roll of their coats.'

'You can't, Tom,' argued Amory, as they rolled along through the scattering night; 'wherever you go now you'll always unconsciously apply these standards of "having it" or "lacking it". For better or worse we've stamped you; you're a Princeton type!'

'Well, then,' complained Tom, his cracked voice rising plaintively, 'why do I have to come back at all? I've learned all that Princeton has to offer. Two years more of mere pedantry and lying around a club aren't going to help. They're just going to disorganise me, conventionalise me completely. Even now I'm so spineless that I wonder how I get away with it.'

'Oh, but you're missing the real point, Tom,' Amory interrupted. 'You've just had your eyes opened to the snobbishness of the world in a rather abrupt manner. Princeton invariably gives the thoughtful man a social sense.'

'You consider you taught me that, don't you?' he asked quizzically, eying Amory in the half dark.

Amory laughed quietly.

'Didn't I?'

'Sometimes,' he said slowly, 'I think you're my bad angel. I might have been a pretty fair poet.'

'Come on, that's rather hard. You chose to come to an Eastern college. Either your eyes were opened to the mean scrambling quality of people, or you'd have gone through blind, and you'd hate to have done that – been like Marty Kaye.'

'Yes,' he agreed, 'you're right. I wouldn't have liked it. Still, it's hard to be made a cynic at twenty.'

'I was born one,' Amory murmured. 'I'm a cynical idealist.' He paused and wondered if that meant anything.

They reached the sleeping school of Lawrenceville, and turned to ride back.

'It's good, this ride, isn't it?' Tom said presently.

'Yes; it's a good finish, it's knock-out; everything's good tonight. Oh, for a hot, languorous summer and Isabelle!'

'Oh, you and your Isabelle! I'll bet she's a simple one . . . let's say some poetry.'

So Amory declaimed the 'Ode to a Nightingale' to the bushes they passed.

'I'll never be a poet,' said Amory as he finished. 'I'm not enough of a sensualist really; there are only a few obvious things that I notice as primarily beautiful: women, spring evenings, music at night, the sea; I don't catch the subtle things like "silver-snarling trumpets".[80] I may turn out an intellectual, but I'll never write anything but mediocre poetry.'

They rode into Princeton as the sun was making coloured maps of the sky behind the graduate school, and hurried to the refreshment of a shower that would have to serve in place of sleep. By noon the bright-costumed alumni crowded the streets with their bands and choruses, and in the tents there was great reunion under the orange-and-black banners that curled and strained in the wind. Amory looked long at one house which bore the legend 'Sixty-nine'. There a few grey-haired men sat and talked quietly while the classes swept by in panorama of life.

UNDER THE ARC-LIGHT

Then tragedy's emerald eyes glared suddenly at Amory over the edge of June. On the night after his ride to Lawrenceville a crowd sallied to New York in quest of adventure, and started back to Princeton about twelve o'clock in two machines. It had been a gay party and different stages of sobriety were represented. Amory was in the car behind; they had taken the wrong road and lost the way, and so were hurrying to catch up.

It was a clear night and the exhilaration of the road went to Amory's head. He had the ghost of two stanzas of a poem forming in his mind . . .

So the grey car crept nightwards in the dark and there was no life stirred as it went by . . . As the still ocean paths before the shark in starred and glittering waterways, beauty-high, the moon-swathed trees divided, pair on pair, while flapping nightbirds cried across the air . . .

A moment by an inn of lamps and shades, a yellow inn under a yellow moon – then silence, where crescendo laughter fades . . . the car swung out again to the winds of June, mellowed the shadows where the distance grew, then crushed the yellow shadows into blue . . .

They jolted to a stop, and Amory peered up, startled. A woman was standing beside the road, talking to Alec at the wheel. Afterwards he remembered the harpy effect that her old kimono gave her, and the cracked hollowness of her voice as she spoke: 'You Princeton boys?'

'Yes.'

'Well, there's one of you killed here, and two others about dead.'

'*My God!*'

'Look!' She pointed and they gazed in horror. Under the full light of a roadside arc-light lay a form, face downward in a widening circle of blood.

They sprang from the car. Amory thought of the back of that head – that hair – that hair . . . and then they turned the form over.

'It's Dick – Dick Humbird!'

'Oh, Christ!'

'Feel his heart!'

Then the insistent voice of the old crone in a sort of croaking triumph: 'He's quite dead, all right. The car turned over. Two of the men that weren't hurt just carried the others in, but this one's no use.'

Amory rushed into the house and the rest followed with a limp mass that they laid on the sofa in the shoddy little front parlour. Sloane, with his shoulder punctured, was on another lounge. He was half delirious, and kept calling something about a chemistry lecture at 8:10.

'I don't know what happened,' said Ferrenby in a strained voice. 'Dick was driving and he wouldn't give up the wheel; we told him he'd been drinking too much – then there was this damn curve – oh, my *God*! . . . ' He threw himself face downwards on the floor and broke into dry sobs.

The doctor had arrived, and Amory went over to the couch, where someone handed him a sheet to put over the body. With a sudden hardness, he raised one of the hands and let it fall back inertly. The brow was cold but the face not expressionless. He looked at the shoe-laces – Dick had tied them that morning. *He* had tied them – and now he was this heavy white mass. All that remained of the charm and personality of the Dick Humbird he had known – oh, it was all so horrible and unaristocratic and close to the earth. All tragedy has that strain of the grotesque and squalid – so useless, futile . . . the way animals die . . . Amory was reminded of a cat that had lain horribly mangled in some alley of his childhood.

'Someone go to Princeton with Ferrenby.'

Amory stepped outside the door and shivered slightly at the late night wind – a wind that stirred a broken fender on the mass of bent metal to a plaintive, tinny sound.

CRESCENDO!

Next day, by a merciful chance, passed in a whirl. When Amory was by himself his thoughts zigzagged inevitably to the picture of that red mouth yawning incongruously in the white face, but with a determined effort he piled present excitement upon the memory of it and shut it coldly away from his mind.

Isabelle and her mother drove into town at four, and they rode up smiling Prospect Avenue, through the gay crowd, to have tea at Cottage. The clubs had their annual dinners that night, so at seven he loaned her to a freshman and arranged to meet her in the gymnasium at eleven, when the upperclassmen were admitted to the freshman dance. She was all he had expected, and he was happy and eager to make that night the centre of every dream. At nine the upper classes stood in front of the clubs as the freshman torchlight parade rioted past, and Amory wondered if the dress-suited groups against the dark, stately backgrounds and under the flare of the torches made the night as brilliant to the staring, cheering freshmen as it had been to him the year before.

The next day was another whirl. They lunched in a gay party of six in a private dining-room at the club, while Isabelle and Amory looked at each other tenderly over the fried chicken and knew that their love was to be eternal. They danced away the prom until five, and the stags cut in on Isabelle with joyous abandon, which grew more and more enthusiastic as the hour grew late, and their wines, stored in overcoat pockets in the coat room, made old weariness wait until another day. The stag line is a most homogeneous mass of men. It fairly sways with a single soul. A dark-haired beauty dances by and there is a half-gasping sound as the ripple surges forward and someone sleeker than the rest darts out and cuts in. Then when the six-foot girl (brought by Kaye in your class, and to whom he has been trying to introduce you all evening) gallops by, the line surges back and the groups face about and become intent on far corners of the hall, for Kaye, anxious and perspiring, appears elbowing through the crowd in search of familiar faces.

'I say, old man, I've got an awfully nice – '

'Sorry, Kaye, but I'm set for this one. I've got to cut in on a fella.'

'Well, the next one?'

'What – ah – er – I swear I've got to go cut in – look me up when she's got a dance free.'

It delighted Amory when Isabelle suggested that they leave for a while and drive around in her car. For a delicious hour that passed too soon they glided the silent roads about Princeton and talked from the surface of their hearts in shy excitement. Amory felt strangely ingenuous and made no attempt to kiss her.

Next day they rode up through the Jersey country, had luncheon in New York, and in the afternoon went to see a problem play at which Isabelle wept all through the second act, rather to Amory's embarrassment – though it filled him with tenderness to watch her. He was tempted to lean over and kiss away her tears, and she slipped her hand into his under cover of darkness to be pressed softly.

Then at six they arrived at the Borges' summer place on Long Island, and Amory rushed upstairs to change into a dinner coat. As he put in his studs he realised that he was enjoying life as he would probably never enjoy it again. Everything was hallowed by the haze of his own youth. He had arrived, abreast of the best in his generation at Princeton. He was in love and his love was returned. Turning on all the lights, he looked at himself in the mirror, trying to find in his own face the qualities that made him see clearer than the great crowd of people, that made him decide firmly, and able to influence and follow his own will. There was little in his life now that he would have changed . . . Oxford might have been a bigger field.

Silently he admired himself. How conveniently well he looked, and how well a dinner coat became him. He stepped into the hall and then waited at the top of the stairs, for he heard footsteps coming. It was Isabelle, and from the top of her shining hair to her little golden slippers she had never seemed so beautiful.

'Isabelle!' he cried, half involuntarily, and held out his arms. As in the storybooks, she ran into them, and on that half-minute, as their lips first touched, rested the high point of vanity, the crest of his young egotism.

CHAPTER 3

The Egotist Considers

'Ouch! Let me go!'

He dropped his arms to his sides.

'What's the matter?'

'Your shirt stud – it hurt me – look!' She was looking down at her neck, where a little blue spot about the size of a pea marred its pallor.

'Oh, Isabelle,' he reproached himself, 'I'm a goopher. Really, I'm sorry – I shouldn't have held you so close.'

She looked up impatiently.

'Oh, Amory, of course you couldn't help it, and it didn't hurt much; but what *are* we going to do about it?'

'*Do* about it?' he asked. 'Oh – that spot; it'll disappear in a second.'

'It isn't,' she said, after a moment of concentrated gazing, 'it's still there – and it looks like Old Nick – oh, Amory, what'll we do! It's *just* the height of your shoulder.'

'Massage it,' he suggested, repressing the faintest inclination to laugh.

She rubbed it delicately with the tips of her fingers, and then a tear gathered in the corner of her eye, and slid down her cheek.

'Oh, Amory,' she said despairingly, lifting up a most pathetic face, 'I'll just make my whole neck *flame* if I rub it. What'll I do?'

A quotation sailed into his head and he couldn't resist repeating it aloud.

'All the perfumes of Arabia will not whiten this little hand.'[81]

She looked up and the sparkle of the tear in her eye was like ice.

'You're not very sympathetic.'

Amory mistook her meaning.

'Isabelle, darling, I think it'll – '

'Don't touch me!' she cried. 'Haven't I enough on my mind and you stand there and *laugh*!'

Then he slipped again.

'Well, it *is* funny, Isabelle, and we were talking the other day about a sense of humour being – '

She was looking at him with something that was not a smile, rather the faint, mirthless echo of a smile, in the corners of her mouth.

'Oh, shut up!' she cried suddenly, and fled down the hallway towards her room. Amory stood there, covered with remorseful confusion.

'Damn!'

When Isabelle reappeared she had thrown a light wrap about her shoulders, and they descended the stairs in a silence that endured through dinner.

'Isabelle,' he began rather testily, as they arranged themselves in the car, bound for a dance at the Greenwich Country Club, 'you're angry, and I'll be, too, in a minute. Let's kiss and make up.'

Isabelle considered glumly.

'I hate to be laughed at,' she said finally.

'I won't laugh any more. I'm not laughing now, am I?'

'You did.'

'Oh, don't be so darned feminine.'

Her lips curled slightly. 'I'll be anything I want.'

Amory kept his temper with difficulty. He became aware that he had not an ounce of real affection for Isabelle, but her coldness piqued him. He wanted to kiss her, kiss her a lot, because then he knew he could leave in the morning and not care. On the contrary, if he didn't kiss her, it would worry him . . . It would interfere vaguely with his idea of himself as a conqueror. It wasn't dignified to come off second best, *pleading*, with a doughty warrior like Isabelle.

Perhaps she suspected this. At any rate, Amory watched the night that should have been the consummation of romance glide by with great moths overhead and the heavy fragrance of roadside gardens, but without those broken words, those little sighs . . .

Afterwards they supped on ginger ale and devil's food in the pantry, and Amory announced a decision.

'I'm leaving early in the morning.'

'Why?'

'Why not?' he countered.

'There's no need.'

'However, I'm going.'

'Well, if you insist on being ridiculous – '

'Oh, don't put it that way,' he objected.

' – just because I won't let you kiss me. Do you think – '

'Now, Isabelle,' he interrupted, 'you know it's not that – even suppose it is. We've reached the stage where we either ought to kiss – or – or – nothing. It isn't as if you were refusing on moral grounds.'

She hesitated.

'I really don't know what to think about you,' she began, in a feeble, perverse attempt at conciliation. 'You're so funny.'

'How?'

'Well, I thought you had a lot of self-confidence and all that; remember you told me the other day that you could do anything you wanted, or get anything you wanted?'

Amory flushed. He *had* told her a lot of things.

'Yes.'

'Well, you didn't seem to feel so self-confident tonight. Maybe you're just plain conceited.'

'No, I'm not,' he hesitated. 'At Princeton – '

'Oh, you and Princeton! You'd think that was the world, the way you talk! Perhaps you *can* write better than anybody else on your old *Princetonian*; maybe the freshmen *do* think you're important – '

'You don't understand – '

'Yes, I do,' she interrupted. 'I *do*, because you're always talking about yourself and I used to like it; now I don't.'

'Have I tonight?'

'That's just the point,' insisted Isabelle. 'You got all upset tonight. You just sat and watched my eyes. Besides, I have to think all the time I'm talking to you – you're so critical.'

'I make you think, do I?' Amory repeated with a touch of vanity.

'You're a nervous strain' – this emphatically – 'and when you analyse every little emotion and instinct I just don't have 'em.'

'I know.' Amory admitted her point and shook his head helplessly.

'Let's go.' She stood up.

He rose abstractedly and they walked to the foot of the stairs.

'What train can I get?'

'There's one about 9:11 if you really must go.'

'Yes, I've got to go, really. Good-night.'

'Good-night.'

They were at the head of the stairs, and as Amory turned into his room he thought he caught just the faintest cloud of discontent in her face. He lay awake in the darkness and wondered how much he cared – how much of his sudden unhappiness was hurt vanity – whether he was, after all, temperamentally unfitted for romance.

When he awoke, it was with a glad flood of consciousness. The early wind stirred the chintz curtains at the windows and he was idly puzzled not to be in his room at Princeton with his school football picture over the bureau and the Triangle Club on the wall opposite.

Then the grandfather's clock in the hall outside struck eight, and the memory of the night before came to him. He was out of bed, dressing, like the wind; he must get out of the house before he saw Isabelle. What had seemed a melancholy happening, now seemed a tiresome anticlimax. He was dressed at half-past, so he sat down by the window; felt that the sinews of his heart were twisted somewhat more than he had thought. What an ironic mockery the morning seemed! – bright and sunny, and full of the smell of the garden; hearing Mrs Borge's voice in the sun-parlour below, he wondered where was Isabelle.

There was a knock at the door.

'The car will be around at ten minutes of nine, sir.'

He returned to his contemplation of the outdoors, and began repeating over and over, mechanically, a verse from Browning, which he had once quoted to Isabelle in a letter:

> 'Each life unfulfilled, you see,
>   It hangs still, patchy and scrappy;
> We have not sighed deep, laughed free,
>   Starved, feasted, despaired – been happy.'[82]

But his life would not be unfulfilled. He took a sombre satisfaction in thinking that perhaps all along she had been nothing except what he had read into her; that this was her high point, that no one else would ever make her think. Yet that was what she had objected to in him; and Amory was suddenly tired of thinking, thinking!

'Damn her!' he said bitterly, 'she's spoiled my year!'

THE SUPERMAN GROWS CARELESS

On a dusty day in September Amory arrived in Princeton and joined the sweltering crowd of conditioned men who thronged the streets. It seemed a stupid way to commence his upper-class years, to spend four hours a morning in the stuffy room of a tutoring school, imbibing the infinite boredom of conic sections. Mr Rooney, pander to the dull, conducted the class and smoked innumerable Pall Malls as he drew diagrams and worked equations from six in the morning until midnight.

'Now, Langueduc, if I used that formula, where would my A point be?'

Langueduc lazily shifts his six-foot-three of football material and tries to concentrate.

'Oh – ah – I'm damned if I know, Mr Rooney.'

'Oh, why of course, of course you can't *use* that formula. *That's* what I wanted you to say.'

'Why, sure, of course.'

'Do you see why?'

'You bet – I suppose so.'

'If you don't see, tell me. I'm here to show you.'

'Well, Mr Rooney, if you don't mind, I wish you'd go over that again.'

'Gladly. Now here's *A* . . . '

The room was a study in stupidity – two huge stands for paper, Mr Rooney in his shirt-sleeves in front of them, and slouched around on chairs, a dozen men: Fred Sloane, the pitcher, who absolutely *had* to get eligible; 'Slim' Langueduc, who would beat Yale this fall, if only he could master a poor fifty per cent; McDowell, gay young sophomore, who thought it was quite a sporting thing to be tutoring here with all these prominent athletes.

'Those poor birds who haven't a cent to tutor, and have to study during the term are the ones I pity,' he announced to Amory one day, with a flaccid camaraderie in the droop of the cigarette from his pale lips. 'I should think it would be such a bore, there's so much else to do in New York during the term. I suppose they don't know what they miss, anyhow.' There was such an air of 'you and I' about Mr McDowell that Amory very nearly pushed him out of the open window when he said this . . . Next February his mother would wonder why he didn't make a club and increase his allowance . . . simple little nut . . .

Through the smoke and the air of solemn, dense earnestness that filled the room would come the inevitable helpless cry: 'I don't get it! Repeat that, Mr Rooney!' Most of them were so stupid or careless that they wouldn't admit when they didn't understand, and Amory was of the latter. He found it impossible to study conic sections; something in their calm and tantalising respectability breathing defiantly through Mr Rooney's fetid parlours distorted their equations into insoluble anagrams. He made a last night's effort with the proverbial wet towel, and then blissfully took the exam, wondering unhappily why all the colour and ambition of the spring before had faded out. Somehow, with the defection of Isabelle the idea of undergraduate success had loosed its grasp on his imagination, and he contemplated a possible failure to pass off his condition with equanimity, even though it would arbitrarily mean his removal from the *Princetonian* board and the slaughter of his chances for the Senior Council.

There was always his luck.

He yawned, scribbled his honour pledge on the cover, and sauntered from the room.

'If you don't pass it,' said the newly arrived Alec as they sat on the window-seat of Amory's room and mused upon a scheme of wall decoration, 'you're the world's worst goopher. Your stock will go down like an elevator at the club and on the campus.'

'Oh, hell, I know it. Why rub it in?'

' 'Cause you deserve it. Anybody that'd risk what you were in line for *ought* to be ineligible for *Princetonian* chairman.'

'Oh, drop the subject,' Amory protested. 'Watch and wait and shut up. I don't want everyone at the club asking me about it, as if I were a prize potato being fattened for a vegetable show.' One evening a week later Amory stopped below his own window on the way to Renwick's, and, seeing a light, called up: 'Oh, Tom, any mail?'

Alec's head appeared against the yellow square of light.

'Yes, your result's here.'

His heart clamoured violently.

'What is it, blue or pink?'

'Don't know. Better come up.'

He walked into the room and straight over to the table, and then suddenly noticed that there were other people in the room.

' 'Lo, Kerry.' He was most polite. 'Ah, men of Princeton.' They seemed to be mostly friends, so he picked up the envelope marked 'Registrar's Office', and weighed it nervously.

'We have here quite a slip of paper.'

'Open it, Amory.'

'Just to be dramatic, I'll let you know that if it's blue, my name is withdrawn from the editorial board of the *Prince*, and my short career is over.'

He paused, and then saw for the first time Ferrenby's eyes, wearing a hungry look and watching him eagerly. Amory returned the gaze pointedly.

'Watch my face, gentlemen, for the primitive emotions.'

He tore it open and held the slip up to the light.

'Well?'

'Pink or blue?'

'Say what it is.'

'We're all ears, Amory.'

'Smile or swear – or something.'

There was a pause . . . a small crowd of seconds swept by . . . then he looked again and another crowd went on into time.

'Blue as the sky, gentlemen . . . '

AFTERMATH

What Amory did that year from early September to late in the spring was so purposeless and inconsecutive that it seems scarcely worth recording. He was, of course, immediately sorry for what he had lost. His philosophy of success had tumbled down upon him, and he looked for the reasons.

'Your own laziness,' said Alec later.

'No – something deeper than that. I've begun to feel that I was meant to lose this chance.'

'They're rather off you at the club, you know; every man that doesn't come through makes our crowd just so much weaker.'

'I hate that point of view.'

'Of course, with a little effort you could still stage a comeback.'

'No – I'm through – as far as ever being a power in college is concerned.'

'But, Amory, honestly, what makes me the angriest isn't the fact that you won't be chairman of the *Prince* and on the Senior Council, but just that you didn't get down and pass that exam.'

'Not me,' said Amory slowly; 'I'm mad at the concrete thing. My own idleness was quite in accord with my system, but the luck broke.'

'Your system broke, you mean.'

'Maybe.'

'Well, what are you going to do? Get a better one quick, or just bum around for two more years as a has-been?'

'I don't know yet . . . '

'Oh, Amory, buck up!'

'Maybe.'

Amory's point of view, though dangerous, was not far from the true one. If his reactions to his environment could be tabulated, the chart would have appeared like this, beginning with his earliest years:

1 The fundamental Amory.
2 Amory plus Beatrice.
3 Amory plus Beatrice plus Minneapolis.

Then St Regis's had pulled him to pieces and started him over again:

4   Amory plus St Regis's.
5   Amory plus St Regis's plus Princeton.

That had been his nearest approach to success through conformity. The fundamental Amory, idle, imaginative, rebellious, had been nearly snowed under. He had conformed, he had succeeded, but as his imagination was neither satisfied nor grasped by his own success, he had listlessly, half-accidentally chucked the whole thing and become again:

6   The fundamental Amory.

FINANCIAL

His father died quietly and inconspicuously at Thanksgiving. The incongruity of death with either the beauties of Lake Geneva or with his mother's dignified, reticent attitude diverted him, and he looked at the funeral with an amused tolerance. He decided that burial was after all preferable to cremation, and he smiled at his old boyhood choice, slow oxidation in the top of a tree. The day after the ceremony he was amusing himself in the great library by sinking back on a couch in graceful mortuary attitudes, trying to determine whether he would, when his day came, be found with his arms crossed piously over his chest (Monsignor Darcy had once advocated this posture as being the most distinguished) or with his hands clasped behind his head, a more pagan and Byronic attitude.

What interested him much more than the final departure of his father from things mundane was a tri-cornered conversation between Beatrice, Mr Barton, of Barton and Krogman, their lawyers, and himself that took place several days after the funeral. For the first time he came into actual cognisance of the family finances, and realised what a tidy fortune had once been under his father's management. He took a ledger labelled '1906' and ran through it rather carefully. The total expenditure that year had come to something over one hundred and ten thousand dollars. Forty thousand of this had been Beatrice's own income, and there had been no attempt to account for it: it was all under the heading, 'Drafts, cheques and letters of credit forwarded to Beatrice Blaine'. The dispersal of the rest was rather minutely itemised: the taxes and improvements on the Lake Geneva estate had come to almost nine thousand dollars; the general upkeep, including Beatrice's electric and a French car, bought that year, was over thirty-five thousand dollars. The rest was fully taken care of, and there were invariably items which failed to balance on the right side of the ledger.

In the volume for 1912 Amory was shocked to discover the decrease in the number of bond holdings and the great drop in the income. In the case of Beatrice's money this was not so pronounced, but it was obvious that his father had devoted the previous year to several unfortunate gambles in oil. Very little of the oil had been burned, but Stephen Blaine had been rather badly singed. The next year and the next and the next showed similar decreases, and Beatrice had for the first time begun using her own money for keeping up the house. Yet her doctor's bill for 1913 had been over nine thousand dollars.

About the exact state of things Mr Barton was quite vague and confused. There had been recent investments, the outcome of which was for the present problematical, and he had an idea there were further speculations and exchanges concerning which he had not been consulted.

It was not for several months that Beatrice wrote Amory the full situation. The entire residue of the Blaine and O'Hara fortunes consisted of the place at Lake Geneva and approximately a half million dollars, invested now in fairly conservative six-per-cent holdings. In fact, Beatrice wrote that she was putting the money into railroad and street-car bonds as fast as she could conveniently transfer it.

I am quite sure [she wrote to Amory] that if there is one thing we can be positive of, it is that people will not stay in one place. This Ford person has certainly made the most of that idea. So I am instructing Mr Barton to specialise on such things as Northern Pacific and these Rapid Transit Companies, as they call the street-cars. I shall never forgive myself for not buying Bethlehem Steel. I've heard the most *fascinating* stories. You must go into finance, Amory. I'm sure you would revel in it. You start as a messenger or a teller, I believe, and from that you go up – almost indefinitely. I'm sure if I were a man I'd love the handling of money; it has become quite a senile passion with me. Before I get any farther I want to discuss something. A Mrs Bispam, an over-cordial little lady whom I met at a tea the other day, told me that her son, he is at Yale, wrote her that all the boys there wore their summer underwear *all during the winter*, and also went about with their heads wet and in low shoes on the *coldest days*. Now, Amory, I don't know whether that is a fad at Princeton too, but I don't want you to be so foolish. It not only inclines a young man to *pneumonia* and *infantile paralysis*, but to all forms of lung trouble, to which you are particularly *inclined*. You cannot experiment with your health. I have found that out. I will not make myself ridiculous, as some mothers no doubt do, by insisting that you wear overshoes, though I remember one Christmas you wore them around *constantly* without a single buckle latched, making such a curious swishing sound, and you refused to buckle them because it was not the thing to do. The very *next* Christmas you would not wear even *rubbers*, though I begged you. You are nearly twenty years old now, dear, and I can't be with you constantly to find whether you are doing the sensible thing.

This has been a very *practical* letter. I warned you in my last that the lack of money to do the things one wants to makes one quite prosy and domestic, but there is still plenty for everything if we are not too extravagant. Take care of yourself, my dear boy, and do try to write at least *once* a week, because I imagine all sorts of horrible things if I don't hear from you.

Affectionately,

MOTHER

FIRST APPEARANCE OF THE TERM 'PERSONAGE'

Monsignor Darcy invited Amory up to the Stuart palace on the Hudson for a week at Christmas, and they had enormous conversations around the open fire. Monsignor was growing a trifle stouter and his personality had expanded even with that, and Amory felt both rest and security in sinking into a squat, cushioned chair and joining him in the middle-aged sanity of a cigar.

'I've felt like leaving college, Monsignor.'

'Why?'

'All my career's gone up in smoke; you think it's petty and all that, but – '

'Not at all petty. I think it's most important. I want to hear the whole thing. Everything you've been doing since I saw you last.'

Amory talked; he went thoroughly into the destruction of his egotistic highways, and in a half-hour the listless quality had left his voice.

'What would you do if you left college?' asked Monsignor.

'Don't know. I'd like to travel, but of course this tiresome war prevents that. Anyways, mother would hate not having me graduate. I'm just at sea. Kerry Holiday wants me to go over with him and join the Lafayette Escadrille.'[83]

'You know you wouldn't like to go.'

'Sometimes I would – tonight I'd go in a second.'

'Well, you'd have to be very much more tired of life than I think you are. I know you.'

'I'm afraid you do,' agreed Amory reluctantly. 'It just seemed an easy way out of everything – when I think of another useless, draggy year.'

'Yes, I know; but to tell you the truth, I'm not worried about you; you seem to me to be progressing perfectly naturally.'

'No,' Amory objected. 'I've lost half my personality in a year.'

'Not a bit of it!' scoffed Monsignor. 'You've lost a great amount of vanity and that's all.'

'Lordy! I feel, anyway, as if I'd gone through another fifth form at St Regis's.'

'No.' Monsignor shook his head. 'That was a misfortune; this has been a good thing. Whatever worth while comes to you won't be through the channels you were searching last year.'

'What could be more unprofitable than my present lack of pep?'

'Perhaps in itself . . . but you're developing. This has given you time to think and you're casting off a lot of your old luggage about success and the superman and all. People like us can't adopt whole theories, as you did. If we can do the next thing, and have an hour a day to think in, we can accomplish marvels, but as far as any high-handed scheme of blind dominance is concerned – we'd just make asses of ourselves.'

'But, Monsignor, I can't do the next thing.'

'Amory, between you and me, I have only just learned to do it myself. I can do the one hundred things beyond the next thing, but I stub my toe on that, just as you stubbed your toe on mathematics this fall.'

'Why do we have to do the next thing? It never seems the sort of thing I should do.'

'We have to do it because we're not personalities, but personages.'

'That's a good line – what do you mean?'

'A personality is what you thought you were, what this Kerry and Sloane you tell me of evidently are. Personality is a physical matter almost entirely; it lowers the people it acts on – I've seen it vanish in a long sickness. But while a personality is active, it overrides "the next thing". Now a personage, on the other hand, gathers. He is never thought of apart from what he's done. He's a bar on which a thousand things have been hung – glittering things sometimes, as ours are; but he uses those things with a cold mentality back of them.'

'And several of my most glittering possessions had fallen off when I needed them.' Amory continued the metaphor eagerly.

'Yes, that's it; when you feel that your garnered prestige and talents and all that are hung out, you need never bother about anybody; you can cope with them without difficulty.'

'But, on the other hand, if I haven't my possessions, I'm helpless!'

'Absolutely.'

'That's certainly an idea.'

'Now you've a clean start – a start Kerry or Sloane can constitutionally never have. You brushed three or four ornaments down, and, in a fit of pique, knocked off the rest of them. The thing now is to collect some new ones, and the farther you look ahead in the collecting the better. But remember, do the next thing!'

'How clear you can make things!'

So they talked, often about themselves, sometimes of philosophy and religion, and life as respectively a game or a mystery. The priest seemed to guess Amory's thoughts before they were clear in his own head, so closely related were their minds in form and groove.

'Why do I make lists?' Amory asked him one night. 'Lists of all sorts of things?'

'Because you're a mediaevalist,' Monsignor answered. 'We both are. It's the passion for classifying and finding a type.'

'It's a desire to get something definite.'

'It's the nucleus of scholastic philosophy.'

'I was beginning to think I was growing eccentric till I came up here. It was a pose, I guess.'

'Don't worry about that; for you not posing may be the biggest pose of all. Pose – '

'Yes?'

'But do the next thing.'

After Amory returned to college he received several letters from Monsignor which gave him more egotistic food for consumption.

I am afraid that I gave you too much assurance of your inevitable safety, and you must remember that I did that through faith in your springs of effort; not in the silly conviction that you will arrive without struggle. Some nuances of character you will have to take for granted in yourself, though you must be careful in confessing them to others. You are unsentimental, almost incapable of affection, astute without being cunning and vain without being proud.

Don't let yourself feel worthless; often through life you will really be at your worst when you seem to think best of yourself; and don't worry about losing your 'personality', as you persist in calling it; at fifteen you had the radiance of early morning, at twenty you will begin to have the melancholy brilliance of the moon, and when you are my age you will give out, as I do, the genial golden warmth of 4 p.m.

If you write me letters, please let them be natural ones. Your last, that dissertation on architecture, was perfectly awful – so 'highbrow' that I picture you living in an intellectual and emotional vacuum; and beware of trying to classify people too definitely into types; you will find that all through their youth they will persist annoyingly in jumping from class to class, and by pasting a supercilious label on everyone you meet you are merely packing a Jack-in-the-box that will spring up and leer at you when you begin to come into really antagonistic contact with the world. An idealisation of some such a man as Leonardo da Vinci would be a more valuable beacon to you at present.

You are bound to go up and down, just as I did in my youth, but do keep your clarity of mind, and if fools or sages dare to criticise don't blame yourself too much.

You say that convention is all that really keeps you straight in this 'woman proposition'; but it's more than that, Amory; it's the fear that what you begin you can't stop; you would run amuck, and I know whereof I speak; it's that half-miraculous sixth sense by which you detect evil, it's the half-realised fear of God in your heart.

Whatever your *métier* proves to be – religion, architecture, literature – I'm sure you would be much safer anchored to the Church, but I won't risk my influence by arguing with you even though I am secretly sure that the 'black chasm of Romanism' yawns beneath you. Do write me soon.

With affectionate regards,

THAYER DARCY

Even Amory's reading paled during this period; he delved further into the misty side streets of literature: Huysmans, Walter Pater, Théophile Gautier, and the racier sections of Rabelais, Boccaccio, Petronius and Suetonius. One week, through general curiosity, he inspected the private libraries of his classmates and found Sloane's as typical as any: sets of Kipling, O. Henry, John Fox Jr [84] and Richard Harding Davis; *What Every Middle-Aged Woman Ought to Know*, *The Spell of the Yukon*;[85] a 'gift' copy of James Whitcomb Riley, an assortment of battered, annotated schoolbooks, and, finally, to his surprise, one of his own late discoveries, the collected poems of Rupert Brooke.

Together with Tom D'Invilliers, he sought among the lights of Princeton for someone who might found the Great American Poetic Tradition.

The undergraduate body itself was rather more interesting that year than had been the entirely Philistine Princeton of two years before. Things had livened surprisingly, though at the sacrifice of much of the spontaneous charm of freshman year. In the old Princeton they would never have discovered Tanaduke Wylie. Tanaduke was a sophomore, with tremendous ears and a way of saying, 'The earth swirls down through the ominous moons of preconsidered generations!' that made them vaguely wonder why it did not sound quite clear but never question that it was the utterance of a super-soul. At least so Tom and Amory took him. They told him in all earnestness that he had a mind like Shelley's, and featured his ultrafree free verse and prose poetry in the *Nassau Literary Magazine*. But Tanaduke's genius absorbed the many colours of the age, and he took to the Bohemian life, to their great disappointment. He talked of Greenwich Village now instead of 'noon-swirled moons', and met winter muses, unacademic and cloistered by Forty-Second Street and Broadway, instead of the Shelleyan dream-children with whom he had regaled their expectant appreciation. So they surrendered Tanaduke to the futurists, deciding that he and his flaming ties would do better there. Tom gave him the final advice that he should stop writing for two years and read the complete works of Alexander Pope four times, but on Amory's suggestion that Pope for Tanaduke was like foot-ease for stomach trouble, they withdrew in laughter, and called it a coin's toss whether this genius was too big or too petty for them.

Amory rather scornfully avoided the popular professors who dispensed easy epigrams and thimblefuls of Chartreuse to groups of admirers every night. He was disappointed, too, at the air of general uncertainty on every subject that seemed linked with the pedantic temperament; his opinions took shape in a miniature satire called 'In a Lecture-Room', which he persuaded Tom to print in the *Nassau Lit.*

Good-morning, Fool . . .
    Three times a week
You hold us helpless while you speak,
Teasing our thirsty souls with the
Sleek 'yeas' of your philosophy . . .
Well, here we are, your hundred sheep,
Tune up, play on, pour forth . . . we sleep . . .
You are a student, so they say;
You hammered out the other day
A syllabus, from what we know
Of some forgotten folio;
You'd sniffled through an era's must,
Filling your nostrils up with dust,
And then, arising from your knees,
Published, in one gigantic sneeze . . .
But here's a neighbour on my right,
An *Eager Ass*, considered bright;
Asker of questions . . . How he'll stand,
With earnest air and fidgy hand,
After this hour, telling you
He sat all night and burrowed through
Your book . . . Oh, you'll be coy and he
Will simulate precosity,
And pedants both, you'll smile and smirk,
And leer, and hasten back to work . . .

'Twas this day week, sir, you returned
A theme of mine, from which I learned
(Through various comment on the side
Which you had scrawled) that I defied
The *highest rules of criticism*
For *cheap* and *careless* witticism . . .
  'Are you quite sure that this could be?'
And
  'Shaw is no authority!'
But *Eager Ass*, with what he's sent,
Plays havoc with your best per cent.

Still – still I meet you here and there . . .
When Shakespeare's played you hold a chair,
And some defunct, moth-eaten star
Enchants the mental prig you are . . .
A radical comes down and shocks
The *atheistic orthodox*?
You're representing *Common Sense*,
Mouth open, in the audience.

And, sometimes, even chapel lures
That conscious tolerance of yours,
That broad and beaming view of truth
(Including *Kant* and *General Booth*[86] . . .)
And so from shock to shock you live,
A hollow, pale affirmative . . .

The hour's up . . . and roused from rest
One hundred children of the blest
Cheat you a word or two with feet
That down the noisy aisle-ways beat . . .
Forget on *narrow-minded earth*
The Mighty Yawn that gave you birth.

In April, Kerry Holiday left college and sailed for France to enroll in the Lafayette Escadrille. Amory's envy and admiration of this step was drowned in an experience of his own to which he never succeeded in giving an appropriate value, but which, nevertheless, haunted him for three years afterwards.

THE DEVIL

Healy's they left at twelve and taxied to Bistolary's. There were Axia Marlowe and Phoebe Column, from the Summer Garden show, Fred Sloane and Amory. The evening was so very young that they felt ridiculous with surplus energy, and burst into the café like Dionysian revellers.

'Table for four in the middle of the floor,' yelled Phoebe. 'Hurry, old dear, tell 'em we're here!'

'Tell 'em to play "Admiration"!' shouted Sloane. 'You two order; Phoebe and I are going to shake a wicked calf,' and they sailed off in the muddled crowd. Axia and Amory, acquaintances of an hour, jostled behind a waiter to a table at a point of vantage; there they took seats and watched.

'There's Findle Margotson, from New Haven!' she cried above the uproar. ' 'Lo, Findle! Whoo-ee!'

'Oh, Axia!' he shouted in salutation. 'C'mon over to our table.'

'No!' Amory whispered.

'Can't do it, Findle; I'm with somebody else! Call me up tomorrow about one o'clock!'

Findle, a nondescript man-about-Bisty's, answered incoherently and turned back to the brilliant blonde whom he was endeavouring to steer around the room.

'There's a natural damn fool,' commented Amory.

'Oh, he's all right. Here's the old jitney waiter.[87] If you ask me, I want a double daiquiri.'

'Make it four.'

The crowd whirled and changed and shifted. They were mostly from the colleges, with a scattering of the male refuse of Broadway, and women of two types, the higher of which was the chorus girl. On the whole it was a typical crowd, and their party as typical as any. About three-fourths of the whole business was for effect and therefore, harmless, ended at the door of the café soon enough for the five-o'clock train back to Yale or Princeton; about one-fourth continued on into the dimmer hours and gathered strange dust from strange places. Their party was scheduled to be one of the harmless kind. Fred Sloane and Phoebe Column were old friends; Axia and Amory new ones. But strange things are prepared even in the dead of night, and the unusual, which lurks least in the café, home of the prosaic and inevitable, was preparing to spoil for him the waning romance of Broadway. The way it took was so inexpressibly terrible, so unbelievable, that afterwards he never thought of it as experience; but it was a scene from a misty tragedy, played far behind the veil, and that it meant something definite he knew.

About one o'clock they moved to Maxim's, and two found them in Devinière's. Sloane had been drinking consecutively and was in a state of unsteady exhilaration, but Amory was quite tiresomely sober; they had run across none of those ancient, corrupt buyers of champagne who usually assisted their New York parties. They were just through dancing and were making their way back to their chairs when Amory became aware that someone at a nearby table was looking at him. He turned and glanced casually . . . a middle-aged man dressed in a brown sack suit, it was, sitting a little apart at a table by himself and watching their party intently. At Amory's glance he smiled faintly. Amory turned to Fred, who was just sitting down.

'Who's that pale fool watching us?' he complained indignantly.

'Where?' cried Sloane. 'We'll have him thrown out!' He rose to his feet and swayed back and forth, clinging to his chair. 'Where is he?'

Axia and Phoebe suddenly leaned and whispered to each other across the table, and before Amory realised it they found themselves on their way to the door.

'Where now?'

'Up to the flat,' suggested Phoebe. 'We've got brandy and fizz – and everything's slow down here tonight.'

Amory considered quickly. He hadn't been drinking, and decided that if he took no more, it would be reasonably discreet for him to trot along in the party. In fact, it would be, perhaps, the thing to do in order to keep an eye on Sloane, who was not in a state to do his own thinking. So he took Axia's arm, and piling intimately into a taxicab, they drove out over the Hundreds and drew up at a tall, white-stone apartment-house . . . Never would he forget that street . . . It was a broad street, lined on both sides with just such tall, white-stone buildings, dotted with dark windows; they stretched along as far as the eye could see, flooded with a bright moonlight that gave them a calcium pallor. He imagined each one to have an elevator and a coloured hall-boy and a key-rack; each one to be eight storeys high and full of three- and four-room suites. He was rather glad to walk into the cheeriness of Phoebe's living-room and sink on to a sofa, while the girls went rummaging for food.

'Phoebe's great stuff,' confided Sloane, *sotto voce*.

'I'm only going to stay half an hour,' Amory said sternly. He wondered if it sounded priggish.

'Hell y' say,' protested Sloane. 'We're here now – don't le's rush.'

'I don't like this place,' Amory said sulkily, 'and I don't want any food.'

Phoebe reappeared with sandwiches, brandy bottle, siphon and four glasses.

'Amory, pour 'em out,' she said, 'and we'll drink to Fred Sloane, who has a rare, distinguished edge.'

'Yes,' said Axia, coming in, 'and Amory. I like Amory.' She sat down beside him and laid her yellow head on his shoulder.

'I'll pour,' said Sloane; 'you use siphon, Phoebe.'

They filled the tray with glasses.

'Ready, here she goes!'

Amory hesitated, glass in hand.

There was a minute while temptation crept over him like a warm wind, and his imagination turned to fire, and he took the glass from Phoebe's hand. That was all; for at the second that his decision came, he looked up and saw, ten yards from him, the man who had been in the café, and with his jump of astonishment the glass fell from his uplifted hand. There the man half sat, half leaned against a pile of pillows on the corner divan. His face was cast in the same yellow wax as in the café, neither the dull, pasty colour of a dead man – rather a sort of virile pallor – nor unhealthy, you'd have called it; but like a strong man who'd worked in a mine or done night shifts in a damp climate. Amory looked him over carefully and later he could have drawn him after a fashion, down to the merest details. His mouth was the kind that is called frank, and he had steady grey eyes that moved slowly from one to the other of their group, with just the shade of a questioning expression. Amory noticed his hands; they weren't fine at all, but they had versatility and a tenuous strength . . . they were nervous hands that sat lightly along the cushions and moved constantly with little jerky openings and closings. Then, suddenly, Amory perceived the feet, and with a rush of blood to the head he realised he was afraid. The feet were all wrong . . . with a sort of wrongness that he felt rather than knew . . . It was like weakness in a good woman, or blood on satin; one of those terrible incongruities that shake little things in the back of the brain. He wore no shoes, but, instead, a sort of half moccasin, pointed, though, like the shoes they wore in the fourteenth century, and with the little ends curling up. They were a darkish brown and his toes seemed to fill them to the end . . . They were unutterably terrible . . .

He must have said something, or looked something, for Axia's voice came out of the void with a strange goodness.

'Well, look at Amory! Poor old Amory's sick – old head going round?'

'Look at that man!' cried Amory, pointing towards the corner divan.

'You mean that purple zebra!' shrieked Axia facetiously. 'Ooo-ee! Amory's got a purple zebra watching him!'

Sloane laughed vacantly.

'Ole zebra gotcha, Amory?'

There was a silence . . . The man regarded Amory quizzically . . . Then the human voices fell faintly on his ear: 'Thought you weren't drinking,' remarked Axia sardonically, but her voice was good to hear; the whole divan that held the man was alive; alive like heat waves over asphalt, like wriggling worms . . .

'Come back! Come back!' Axia's arm fell on his. 'Amory, dear, you aren't going, Amory!' He was halfway to the door.

'Come on, Amory, stick 'th us!'

'Sick, are you?'

'Sit down a second!'

'Take some water.'

'Take a little brandy . . . '

The elevator was close, and the coloured boy was half asleep, paled to a livid bronze . . . Axia's beseeching voice floated down the shaft. Those feet . . . those feet . . .

As they settled to the lower floor the feet came into view in the sickly electric light of the paved hall.

IN THE ALLEY

Down the long street came the moon, and Amory turned his back on it and walked. Ten, fifteen steps away sounded the footsteps. They were like a slow dripping, with just the slightest insistence in their fall. Amory's shadow lay perhaps ten feet ahead of him, and soft shoes was presumably that far behind. With the instinct of a child Amory edged in under the blue darkness of the white buildings, cleaving the moonlight for haggard seconds, once bursting into a slow run with clumsy stumblings. After that he stopped suddenly; he must keep hold, he thought. His lips were dry and he licked them.

If he met anyone good – were there any good people left in the world or did they all live in white apartment-houses now? Was everyone followed in the moonlight? But if he met someone good who'd know what he meant and hear this damned scuffle . . . then the scuffling grew suddenly nearer, and a black cloud settled over the moon. When again the pale sheen skimmed the cornices, it was almost beside him, and Amory thought he heard a quiet breathing. Suddenly he realised that the footsteps were not behind, had never been behind, they were ahead and he was not eluding but following . . . following. He began to run, blindly, his heart knocking heavily, his hands clenched. Far ahead a black dot showed itself, resolved slowly into a human shape. But Amory was beyond that now; he turned off the street and darted into an alley, narrow and dark and smelling of old rottenness. He twisted down a long, sinuous blackness, where the moonlight was shut away except for tiny glints and patches . . . then suddenly sank panting into a corner by a fence, exhausted. The steps ahead stopped, and he could hear them shift slightly with a continuous motion, like waves around a dock.

He put his face in his hands and covered eyes and ears as well as he could. During all this time it never occurred to him that he was delirious or drunk. He had a sense of reality such as material things could never give him. His intellectual content seemed to submit passively to it, and it fitted like a glove everything that had ever preceded it in his life. It did not muddle him. It was like a problem whose answer he knew on paper, yet whose solution he was unable to grasp. He was far beyond horror. He had sunk through the thin surface of that, now moved in a region where the feet and the fear of white walls were real, living things, things he must accept. Only far inside his soul a little fire leaped and cried that something was pulling him down, trying to get him inside a door and slam it behind him. After that door was slammed there would be only footfalls and white buildings in the moonlight, and perhaps he would be one of the footfalls.

During the five or ten minutes he waited in the shadow of the fence, there was somehow this fire . . . that was as near as he could name it afterwards. He remembered calling aloud: 'I want someone stupid. Oh, send someone stupid!' This to the black fence opposite him, in whose shadows the footsteps shuffled . . . shuffled. He supposed 'stupid' and 'good' had become somehow intermingled through previous association. When he called thus it was not an act of will at all – will had turned him away from the moving figure in the street; it was almost instinct that called, just the pile on pile of inherent tradition or some wild prayer from way over the night. Then something clanged like a low gong struck at a distance, and before his eyes a face flashed over the two feet, a face pale and distorted with a sort of infinite evil that twisted it like flame in the wind; *but he knew, for the half instant that the gong tanged and hummed, that it was the face of Dick Humbird.*

Minutes later he sprang to his feet, realising dimly that there was no more sound, and that he was alone in the greying alley. It was cold, and he started on a steady run for the light that showed the street at the other end.

AT THE WINDOW

It was late morning when he woke and found the telephone beside his bed in the hotel tolling frantically, and remembered that he had left word to be called at eleven. Sloane was snoring heavily, his clothes in a pile by his bed. They dressed and ate breakfast in silence, and then sauntered out to get some air. Amory's mind was working slowly, trying to assimilate what had happened and separate from the chaotic imagery that stacked his memory the bare shreds of truth. If the morning had been cold and grey he could have grasped the reins of the past in an instant, but it was one of those days that New York gets sometimes in May, when the air on Fifth Avenue is a soft, light wine. How much or how little Sloane remembered Amory did not care to know; he apparently had none of the nervous tension that was gripping Amory and forcing his mind back and forth like a shrieking saw.

Then Broadway broke upon them, and with the babel of noise and the painted faces a sudden sickness rushed over Amory.

'For God's sake, let's go back! Let's get off of this – this place!'

Sloane looked at him in amazement.

'What do you mean?'

'This street, it's ghastly! Come on! let's get back to the Avenue!'

'Do you mean to say,' said Sloane stolidly, 'that 'cause you had some sort of indigestion that made you act like a maniac last night, you're never coming on Broadway again?'

Simultaneously Amory classed him with the crowd, and he seemed no longer Sloane of the debonair humour and the happy personality, but only one of the evil faces that whirled along the turbid stream.

'Man!' he shouted so loud that the people on the corner turned and followed them with their eyes, 'it's filthy, and if you can't see it, you're filthy, too!'

'I can't help it,' said Sloane doggedly. 'What's the matter with you? Old remorse getting you? You'd be in a fine state if you'd gone through with our little party.'

'I'm going, Fred,' said Amory slowly. His knees were shaking under him, and he knew that if he stayed another minute on this street he would keel over where he stood. 'I'll be at the Vanderbilt for lunch.' And he strode rapidly off and turned over to Fifth Avenue. Back at the hotel he felt better, but as he walked into the barbershop, intending to get a head massage, the smell of the powders and tonics brought back Axia's sidelong, suggestive smile, and he left hurriedly.

In the doorway of his room a sudden blackness flowed around him like a divided river.

When he came to himself he knew that several hours had passed. He pitched on to the bed and rolled over on his face with a deadly fear that he was going mad. He wanted people, someone sane and stupid and good. He lay for he knew not how long without moving. He could feel the little hot veins on his forehead standing out, and his terror had hardened on him like plaster. He felt he was passing up again through the thin crust of horror, and now only could he distinguish the shadowy twilight he was leaving. He must have fallen asleep again, for when he next recollected himself he had paid the hotel bill and was stepping into a taxi at the door. It was raining torrents.

On the train for Princeton he saw no one he knew, only a crowd of fagged-looking Philadelphians. The presence of a painted woman across the aisle filled him with a fresh burst of sickness and he changed to another car, tried to concentrate on an article in a popular magazine. He found himself reading the same paragraphs over and over, so he abandoned this attempt and leaning over wearily pressed his hot forehead against the damp window-pane. The car, a smoker, was hot and stuffy with most of the smells of the state's alien population; he opened a window and shivered against the cloud of fog that drifted in over him. The two hours' ride was like days, and he nearly cried aloud with joy when the towers of Princeton loomed up beside him and the yellow squares of light filtered through the blue rain.

Tom was standing in the centre of the room, pensively relighting a cigar-stub. Amory fancied he looked rather relieved on seeing him.

'Had a hell of a dream about you last night,' came in the cracked voice through the cigar smoke. 'I had an idea you were in some trouble.'

'Don't tell me about it!' Amory almost shrieked. 'Don't say a word; I'm tired and pepped out.'

Tom looked at him queerly and then sank into a chair and opened his Italian notebook. Amory threw his coat and hat on the floor, loosened his collar, and took a Wells novel at random from the shelf. 'Wells is sane,' he thought, 'and if he won't do I'll read Rupert Brooke.'

Half an hour passed. Outside the wind came up, and Amory started as the wet branches moved and clawed with their fingernails at the window-pane. Tom was deep in his work, and inside the room only the occasional scratch of a match or the rustle of leather as they shifted in their chairs broke the stillness. Then like a zigzag of lightning came the change. Amory sat bolt upright, frozen cold in his chair. Tom was looking at him with his mouth drooping, eyes fixed.

'God help us!' Amory cried.

'Oh, my heavens!' shouted Tom, 'look behind!' Quick as a flash Amory whirled around. He saw nothing but the dark window-pane. 'It's gone now,' came Tom's voice after a second in a still terror. 'Something was looking at you.'

Trembling violently, Amory dropped into his chair again.

'I've got to tell you,' he said. 'I've had one hell of an experience. I think I've – I've seen the devil or – something like him. What face did you just see? – or no,' he added quickly, 'don't tell me!'

And he gave Tom the story. It was midnight when he finished, and after that, with all lights burning, two sleepy, shivering boys read to each other from *The New Machiavelli*,[88] until dawn came up out of Witherspoon Hall, and the *Princetonian* fell against the door, and the May birds hailed the sun on last night's rain.

CHAPTER 4

Narcissus Off Duty

During Princeton's transition period, that is, during Amory's last two years there, while he saw it change and broaden and live up to its Gothic beauty by better means than night parades, certain individuals arrived who stirred it to its plethoric depths. Some of them had been freshmen, and wild freshmen, with Amory; some were in the class below; and it was in the beginning of his last year and around small tables at the Nassau Inn that they began questioning aloud the institutions that Amory and countless others before him had questioned so long in secret. First, and partly by accident, they struck on certain books, a definite type of biographical novel that Amory christened 'quest' books. In the 'quest' book the hero set off in life armed with the best weapons and avowedly intending to use them as such weapons are usually used, to push their possessors ahead as selfishly and blindly as possible, but the heroes of the 'quest' books discovered that there might be a more magnificent use for them. *None Other Gods, Sinister Street* and *The Research Magnificent* [89] were examples of such books; it was the latter of these three that gripped Burne Holiday and made him wonder in the beginning of senior year how much it was worth while being a diplomatic autocrat around his club on Prospect Avenue and basking in the highlights of class office. It was distinctly through the channels of aristocracy that Burne found his way. Amory, through Kerry, had had a vague drifting acquaintance with him, but not until January of senior year did their friendship commence.

'Heard the latest?' said Tom, coming in late one drizzly evening with that triumphant air he always wore after a successful conversational bout.

'No. Somebody flunked out? Or another ship sunk?'

'Worse than that. About one-third of the junior class are going to resign from their clubs.'

'What!'

'Actual fact!'

'Why!'

'Spirit of reform and all that. Burne Holiday is behind it. The club presidents are holding a meeting tonight to see if they can find a joint means of combating it.'

'Well, what's the idea of the thing?'

'Oh, clubs injurious to Princeton democracy; cost a lot; draw social lines, take time; the regular line you get sometimes from disappointed sophomores. Woodrow [90] thought they should be abolished and all that.'

'But this is the real thing?'

'Absolutely. I think it'll go through.'

'For Pete's sake, tell me more about it.'

'Well,' began Tom, 'it seems that the idea developed simultaneously in several heads. I was talking to Burne awhile ago, and he claims that it's a logical result if an intelligent person thinks long enough about the social system. They had a "discussion crowd" and the point of abolishing the clubs was brought up by someone – everybody there leaped at it – it had been in each one's mind, more or less, and it just needed a spark to bring it out.'

'Fine! I swear I think it'll be most entertaining. How do they feel up at Cap and Gown?'

'Wild, of course. Everyone's been sitting and arguing and swearing and getting mad and getting sentimental and getting brutal. It's the same at all the clubs; I've been the rounds. They get one of the radicals in the corner and fire questions at him.'

'How do the radicals stand up?'

'Oh, moderately well. Burne's a damn good talker, and so obviously sincere that you can't get anywhere with him. It's so evident that resigning from his club means so much more to him than preventing it does to us that I felt futile when I argued; finally took a position that was brilliantly neutral. In fact, I believe Burne thought for a while that he'd converted me.'

'And you say almost a third of the junior class are going to resign?'

'Call it a fourth and be safe.'

'Lord – who'd have thought it possible!'

There was a brisk knock at the door, and Burne himself came in. 'Hello, Amory – hello, Tom.'

Amory rose.

' 'Evening, Burne. Don't mind if I seem to rush; I'm going to Renwick's.'

Burne turned to him quickly.

'You probably know what I want to talk to Tom about, and it isn't a bit private. I wish you'd stay.'

'I'd be glad to.' Amory sat down again, and as Burne perched on a table and launched into argument with Tom, he looked at this revolutionary more carefully than he ever had before. Broad-browed and strong-chinned, with a fineness in the honest grey eyes that were like Kerry's, Burne was a man who gave an immediate impression of bigness and security – stubborn, that was evident, but his stubbornness wore no stolidity, and when he had talked for five minutes Amory knew that this keen enthusiasm had in it no quality of dilettantism.

The intense power Amory felt later in Burne Holiday differed from the admiration he had had for Humbird. This time it began as purely a mental interest. With other men whom he had thought of as primarily first-class, he had been attracted first by their personalities, and in Burne he missed that immediate magnetism to which he usually swore allegiance. But that night Amory was struck by Burne's intense earnestness, a quality he was accustomed to associate only with the dread stupidity, and by the great enthusiasm that struck dead chords in his heart. Burne stood vaguely for a land Amory hoped he was drifting towards – and it was almost time that land was in sight. Tom and Amory and Alec had reached an impasse; never did they seem to have new experiences in common, for Tom and Alec had been as blindly busy with their committees and boards as Amory had been blindly idling, and the things they had for dissection – college, contemporary personality and the like – they had hashed and rehashed for many a frugal conversational meal.

That night they discussed the clubs until twelve, and, in the main, they agreed with Burne. To the roommates it did not seem such a vital subject as it had in the two years before, but the logic of Burne's objections to the social system dovetailed so completely with everything they had thought, that they questioned rather than argued, and envied the sanity that enabled this man to stand out so against all traditions.

Then Amory branched off and found that Burne was deep in other things as well. Economics had interested him and he was turning socialist. Pacifism played in the back of his mind, and he read the *Masses* [91] and Lyof Tolstoy faithfully.

'How about religion?' Amory asked him.

'Don't know. I'm in a muddle about a lot of things – I've just discovered that I've a mind, and I'm starting to read.'

'Read what?'

'Everything. I have to pick and choose, of course, but mostly things to make me think. I'm reading the four gospels now, and *The Varieties of Religious Experience.*' [92]

'What chiefly started you?'

'Wells, I guess, and Tolstoy, and a man named Edward Carpenter.[93] I've been reading for over a year now – on a few lines, on what I consider the essential lines.'

'Poetry?'

'Well, frankly, not what you call poetry, or for your reasons – you two write, of course, and look at things differently. Whitman is the man that attracts me.'

'Whitman?'

'Yes; he's a definite ethical force.'

'Well, I'm ashamed to say that I'm a blank on the subject of Whitman. How about you, Tom?'

Tom nodded sheepishly.

'Well,' continued Burne, 'you may strike a few poems that are tiresome, but I mean the mass of his work. He's tremendous – like Tolstoy. They both look things in the face, and, somehow, different as they are, stand for somewhat the same things.'

'You have me stumped, Burne,' Amory admitted. 'I've read *Anna Karenina* and *The Kreutzer Sonata* [94] of course, but Tolstoy is mostly in the original Russian as far as I'm concerned.'

'He's the greatest man in hundreds of years,' cried Burne enthusiastically. 'Did you ever see a picture of that shaggy old head of his?'

They talked until three, from biology to organised religion, and when Amory crept shivering into bed it was with his mind aglow with ideas and a sense of shock that someone else had discovered the path he might have followed. Burne Holiday was so evidently developing – and Amory had considered that he was doing the same. He had fallen into a deep cynicism over what had crossed his path, plotted the imperfectability of man and read Shaw and Chesterton enough to keep his mind from the edges of decadence – now suddenly all his mental processes of the last year and a half seemed stale and futile – a petty consummation of himself . . . and like a sombre background lay that incident of the spring before, that filled half his nights with a dreary terror and made him unable to pray. He was not even a Catholic, yet that was the only ghost of a code that he had, the gaudy, ritualistic, paradoxical Catholicism whose prophet was Chesterton, whose claqueurs[95] were such reformed rakes of literature as Huysmans and Bourget,[96] whose American sponsor was Ralph Adams Cram,[97] with his adulation of thirteenth-century cathedrals – a Catholicism which Amory found convenient and ready-made, without priest or sacraments or sacrifice.

He could not sleep, so he turned on his reading-lamp and, taking down *The Kreutzer Sonata*, searched it carefully for the germs of Burne's enthusiasm. Being Burne was suddenly so much realler than being clever. Yet he sighed . . . here were other possible clay feet.

He thought back through two years, of Burne as a hurried, nervous freshman, quite submerged in his brother's personality. Then he remembered an incident of sophomore year, in which Burne had been suspected of the leading role.

Dean Hollister had been heard by a large group arguing with a taxi-driver, who had driven him from the junction. In the course of the altercation the dean remarked that he 'might as well buy the taxicab'. He paid and walked off, but next morning he entered his private office to find the taxicab itself in the space usually occupied by his desk, bearing a sign which read 'Property of Dean Hollister. Bought and Paid for' . . . It took two expert mechanics half a day to disassemble it into its minutest parts and remove it, which only goes to prove the rare energy of sophomore humour under efficient leadership.

Then again, that very fall, Burne had caused a sensation. A certain Phyllis Styles, an intercollegiate prom-trotter, had failed to get her yearly invitation to the Harvard-Princeton game.

Jesse Ferrenby had brought her to a smaller game a few weeks before, and had pressed Burne into service – to the ruination of the latter's misogyny.

'Are you coming to the Harvard game?' Burne had asked indiscreetly, merely to make conversation.

'If you ask me,' cried Phyllis quickly.

'Of course I do,' said Burne feebly. He was unversed in the arts of Phyllis, and was sure that this was merely a vapid form of kidding. Before an hour had passed he knew that he was indeed involved. Phyllis had pinned him down and served him up, informed him the train she was arriving by, and depressed him thoroughly. Aside from loathing Phyllis, he had particularly wanted to stag that game and entertain some Harvard friends.

'She'll see,' he informed a delegation who arrived in his room to josh him. 'This will be the last game she ever persuades any young innocent to take her to!'

'But, Burne – why did you *invite* her if you didn't want her?'

'Burne, you *know* you're secretly mad about her – that's the *real* trouble.'

'What can *you* do, Burne? What can *you* do against Phyllis?'

But Burne only shook his head and muttered threats which consisted largely of the phrase: 'She'll see, she'll see!'

The blithesome Phyllis bore her twenty-five summers gayly from the train, but on the platform a ghastly sight met her eyes. There were Burne and Fred Sloane arrayed to the last dot like the lurid figures on college posters. They had bought flaring suits with huge peg-top trousers and gigantic padded shoulders. On their heads were rakish college hats, pinned up in front and sporting bright orange-and-black bands, while from their celluloid collars blossomed flaming orange ties. They wore black armbands with orange 'Ps', and carried canes flying Princeton pennants, the effect completed by socks and peeping handkerchiefs in the same colour motifs. On a clanking chain they led a large, angry tomcat, painted to represent a tiger.

A good half of the station crowd was already staring at them, torn between horrified pity and riotous mirth, and as Phyllis, with her svelte jaw dropping, approached, the pair bent over and emitted a college cheer in loud, far-carrying voices, thoughtfully adding the name 'Phyllis' to the end. She was vociferously greeted and escorted enthusiastically across the campus, followed by half a hundred village urchins – to the stifled laughter of hundreds of alumni and visitors, half of whom had no idea that this was a practical joke, but thought that Burne and Fred were two varsity sports showing their girl a collegiate time.

Phyllis's feelings as she was paraded by the Harvard and Princeton stands, where sat dozens of her former devotees, can be imagined. She tried to walk a little ahead, she tried to walk a little behind – but they stayed close, that there should be no doubt whom she was with, talking in loud voices of their friends on the football team, until she could almost hear her acquaintances whispering: 'Phyllis Styles must be *awfully hard up* to have to come with *those two*.'

That had been Burne, dynamically humorous, fundamentally serious. From that root had blossomed the energy that he was now trying to orient with progress . . .

So the weeks passed and March came and the clay feet that Amory looked for failed to appear. About a hundred juniors and seniors resigned from their clubs in a final fury of righteousness, and the clubs in helplessness turned upon Burne their finest weapon: ridicule. Everyone who knew him liked him – but what he stood for (and he began to stand for more all the time) came under the lash of many tongues, until a frailer man than he would have been snowed under.

'Don't you mind losing prestige?' asked Amory one night. They had taken to exchanging calls several times a week.

'Of course I don't. What's prestige, at best?'

'Some people say that you're just a rather original politician.'

He roared with laughter.

'That's what Fred Sloane told me today. I suppose I have it coming.'

One afternoon they dipped into a subject that had interested Amory for a long time – the matter of the bearing of physical attributes on a man's make-up. Burne had gone into the biology of this, and then: 'Of course health counts – a healthy man has twice the chance of being good,' he said.

'I don't agree with you – I don't believe in "muscular Christianity".'

'I do – I believe Christ had great physical vigour.'

'Oh, no,' Amory protested. 'He worked too hard for that. I imagine that when he died he was a broken-down man – and the great saints haven't been strong.'

'Half of them have.'

'Well, even granting that, I don't think health has anything to do with goodness; of course, it's valuable to a great saint to be able to stand enormous strains, but this fad of popular preachers rising on their toes in simulated virility, bellowing that calisthenics will save the world – no, Burne, I can't go that.'

'Well, let's waive it – we won't get anywhere, and besides I haven't quite made up my mind about it myself. Now, here's something I *do* know – personal appearance has a lot to do with it.'

'Colouring?' Amory asked eagerly.

'Yes.'

'That's what Tom and I figured,' Amory agreed. 'We took the year-books for the last ten years and looked at the pictures of the Senior Council. I know you don't think much of that august body, but it does represent success here in a general way. Well, I suppose only about thirty-five per cent of every class here are blonds, are really light – yet *two-thirds* of every Senior Council are light. We looked at pictures of ten years of them, mind you; that means that out of every *fifteen* light-haired men in the senior class *one* is on the Senior Council, and of the dark-haired men it's only one in *fifty*.'

'It's true,' Burne agreed. 'The light-haired man *is* a higher type, generally speaking. I worked the thing out with the Presidents of the United States once, and found that way over half of them were light-haired – yet think of the preponderant number of brunettes in the race.'

'People unconsciously admit it,' said Amory. 'You'll notice a blond person is *expected* to talk. If a blonde girl doesn't talk we call her a "doll"; if a light-haired man is silent he's considered stupid. Yet the world is full of "dark silent men" and "languorous brunettes" who haven't a brain in their heads, but somehow are never accused of the dearth.'

'And the large mouth and broad chin and rather big nose undoubtedly make the superior face.'

'I'm not so sure.' Amory was all for classical features.

'Oh, yes – I'll show you,' and Burne pulled out of his desk a photographic collection of heavily bearded, shaggy celebrities – Tolstoy, Whitman, Carpenter, and others.

'Aren't they wonderful?'

Amory tried politely to appreciate them, and gave up laughingly.

'Burne, I think they're the ugliest-looking crowd I ever came across. They look like an old men's home.'

'Oh, Amory, look at that forehead on Emerson; look at Tolstoy's eyes.' His tone was reproachful.

Amory shook his head.

'No! Call them remarkable-looking or anything you want – but ugly they certainly are.'

Unabashed, Burne ran his hand lovingly across the spacious foreheads, and piling up the pictures put them back in his desk.

Walking at night was one of his favourite pursuits, and one night he persuaded Amory to accompany him.

'I hate the dark,' Amory objected. 'I didn't use to – except when I was particularly imaginative, but now, I really do – I'm a regular fool about it.'

'That's useless, you know.'

'Quite possibly.'

'We'll go east,' Burne suggested, 'and down that string of roads through the woods.'

'Doesn't sound very appealing to me,' admitted Amory reluctantly, 'but let's go.'

They set off at a good gait, and for an hour swung along in a brisk argument until the lights of Princeton were luminous white blots behind them.

'Any person with any imagination is bound to be afraid,' said Burne earnestly. 'And this very walking at night is one of the things I was afraid about. I'm going to tell you why I can walk anywhere now and not be afraid.'

'Go on,' Amory urged eagerly. They were striding towards the woods, Burne's nervous, enthusiastic voice warming to his subject.

'I used to come out here alone at night, oh, three months ago, and I always stopped at that crossroads we just passed. There were the woods looming up ahead, just as they do now, there were dogs howling and the shadows and no human sound. Of course, I peopled the woods with everything ghastly, just like you do; don't you?'

'I do,' Amory admitted.

'Well, I began analysing it – my imagination persisted in sticking horrors into the dark – so I stuck my imagination into the dark instead, and let it look out at me – I let it play stray dog or escaped convict or ghost, and then saw myself coming along the road. That made it all right – as it always makes everything all right to project yourself completely into another's place. I knew that if I were the dog or the convict or the ghost I wouldn't be a menace to Burne Holiday any more than he was a menace to me. Then I thought of my watch. I'd better go back and leave it and then essay the woods. No; I decided, it's better on the whole that I should lose a watch than that I should turn back – and I did go into them – not only followed the road through them, but walked into them until I wasn't frightened any more – did it until one night I sat down and dozed off in there; then I knew I was through being afraid of the dark.'

'Lordy,' Amory breathed. 'I couldn't have done that. I'd have come out halfway, and the first time an automobile passed and made the dark thicker when its lamps disappeared, I'd have come in.'

'Well,' Burne said suddenly, after a few moments' silence, 'we're halfway through, let's turn back.'

On the return he launched into a discussion of will.

'It's the whole thing,' he asserted. 'It's the one dividing line between good and evil. I've never met a man who led a rotten life and didn't have a weak will.'

'How about great criminals?'

'They're usually insane. If not, they're weak. There is no such thing as a strong, sane criminal.'

'Burne, I disagree with you altogether; how about the superman?'

'Well?'

'He's evil, I think, yet he's strong and sane.'

'I've never met him. I'll bet, though, that he's stupid or insane.'

'I've met him over and over and he's neither. That's why I think you're wrong.'

'I'm sure I'm not – and so I don't believe in imprisonment except for the insane.'

On this point Amory could not agree. It seemed to him that life and history were rife with the strong criminal, keen, but often self-deluding; in politics and business one found him and among the old statesmen and kings and generals; but Burne never agreed and their courses began to split on that point.

Burne was drawing further and further away from the world about him. He resigned the vice-presidency of the senior class and took to reading and walking as almost his only pursuits. He voluntarily attended graduate lectures in philosophy and biology, and sat in all of them with a rather pathetically intent look in his eyes, as if waiting for something the lecturer would never quite come to. Sometimes Amory would see him squirm in his seat; and his face would light up; he was on fire to debate a point.

He grew more abstracted on the street and was even accused of becoming a snob, but Amory knew it was nothing of the sort, and once when Burne passed him four feet off, absolutely unseeingly, his mind a thousand miles away, Amory almost choked with the romantic joy of watching him. Burne seemed to be climbing heights where others would be forever unable to get a foothold.

'I tell you,' Amory declared to Tom, 'he's the first contemporary I've ever met whom I'll admit is my superior in mental capacity.'

'It's a bad time to admit it – people are beginning to think he's odd.'

'He's way over their heads – you know you think so yourself when you talk to him – Good Lord, Tom, you *used* to stand out against "people". Success has completely conventionalised you.'

Tom grew rather annoyed.

'What's he trying to do – be excessively holy?'

'No! not like anybody you've ever seen. Never enters the Philadelphian Society.[98] He has no faith in that rot. He doesn't believe that public swimming-pools and a kind word in time will right the wrongs of the world; moreover, he takes a drink whenever he feels like it.'

'He certainly is getting in wrong.'

'Have you talked to him lately?'

'No.'

'Then you haven't any conception of him.'

The argument ended nowhere, but Amory noticed more than ever how the sentiment towards Burne had changed on the campus.

'It's odd,' Amory said to Tom one night when they had grown more amicable on the subject, 'that the people who violently disapprove of

Burne's radicalism are distinctly the Pharisee class – I mean they're the best-educated men in college – the editors of the papers, like yourself and Ferrenby, the younger professors . . . The illiterate athletes like Langueduc think he's getting eccentric, but they just say, "Good old Burne has got some queer ideas in his head," and pass on – the Pharisee class – Gee! they ridicule him unmercifully.'

The next morning he met Burne hurrying along McCosh walk after a recitation.

'Whither bound, Tsar?'

'Over to the *Prince* office to see Ferrenby,' he waved a copy of the morning's *Princetonian* at Amory. 'He wrote this editorial.'

'Going to flay him alive?'

'No – but he's got me all balled up. Either I've misjudged him or he's suddenly become the world's worst radical.'

Burne hurried on, and it was several days before Amory heard an account of the ensuing conversation. Burne had come into the editor's sanctum displaying the paper cheerfully.

'Hello, Jesse.'

'Hello there, Savonarola.'[99]

'I just read your editorial.'

'Good boy – didn't know you stooped that low.'

'Jesse, you startled me.'

'How so?'

'Aren't you afraid the faculty'll get after you if you pull this irreligious stuff?'

'What?'

'Like this morning.'

'What the devil – that editorial was on the coaching system.'

'Yes, but that quotation – '

Jesse sat up.

'What quotation?'

'You know: "He who is not with me is against me." '[100]

'Well – what about it?'

Jesse was puzzled but not alarmed.

'Well, you say here – let me see.' Burne opened the paper and read: ' "*He who is not with me is against me*, as that gentleman said who was notoriously capable of only coarse distinctions and puerile generalities." '

'What of it?' Ferrenby began to look alarmed. 'Oliver Cromwell said it, didn't he? or was it Washington, or one of the saints? Good Lord, I've forgotten.'

Burne roared with laughter.

'Oh, Jesse, oh, good, kind Jesse.'

'Who said it, for Pete's sake?'

'Well,' said Burne, recovering his voice, 'St Matthew attributes it to Christ.'

'My God!' cried Jesse, and collapsed backwards into the waste-basket.

AMORY WRITES A POEM

The weeks tore by. Amory wandered occasionally to New York on the chance of finding a new shining green auto-bus, that its stick-of-candy glamour might penetrate his disposition. One day he ventured into a stock-company revival of a play whose name was faintly familiar. The curtain rose – he watched casually as a girl entered. A few phrases rang in his ear and touched a faint chord of memory. Where – ? When – ?

Then he seemed to hear a voice whispering beside him, a very soft, vibrant voice: 'Oh, I'm such a poor little fool; *do* tell me when I do wrong.'

The solution came in a flash and he had a quick, glad memory of Isabelle.

He found a blank space on his programme, and began to scribble rapidly:

> 'Here in the figured dark I watch once more,
>   There, with the curtain, roll the years away;
>   Two years of years – there was an idle day
> Of ours, when happy endings didn't bore
> Our unfermented souls; I could adore
>   Your eager face beside me, wide-eyed, gay,
>   Smiling a repertoire while the poor play
> Reached me as a faint ripple reaches shore.
>   Yawning and wondering an evening through,
>   I watch alone . . . and chatterings, of course,
>   Spoil the one scene which, somehow, *did* have charms;
> You wept a bit, and I grew sad for you
>   Right here! Where Mr X defends divorce
>   And What's-Her-Name falls fainting in his arms.'

'Ghosts are such dumb things,' said Alec, 'they're slow-witted. I can always out-guess a ghost.'

'How?' asked Tom.

'Well, it depends where. Take a bedroom, for example. If you use *any* discretion a ghost can never get you in a bedroom.'

'Go on, s'pose you think there's maybe a ghost in your bedroom – what measures do you take on getting home at night?' demanded Amory, interested.

'Take a stick,' answered Alec, with ponderous reverence, 'one about the length of a broom-handle. Now, the first thing to do is to get the room *cleared* – to do this you rush with your eyes closed into your study and turn on the lights – next, approaching the closet, carefully run the stick in the door three or four times. Then, if nothing happens, you can look in. *Always, always* run the stick in viciously first – *never* look first!'

'Of course, that's the ancient Celtic school,' said Tom gravely.

'Yes – but they usually pray first. Anyway, you use this method to clear the closets and also for behind all doors – '

'And the bed,' Amory suggested.

'Oh, Amory, no!' cried Alec in horror. 'That isn't the way – the bed requires different tactics – let the bed alone, as you value your reason – if there is a ghost in the room and that's only about a third of the time, it is *almost always* under the bed.'

'Well – ' Amory began.

Alec waved him into silence.

'Of *course* you never look. You stand in the middle of the floor and before he knows what you're going to do make a sudden leap for the bed – never walk near the bed; to a ghost your ankle is your most vulnerable part – once in bed, you're safe; he may lie around under the bed all night, but you're safe as daylight. If you still have doubts pull the blanket over your head.'

'All that's very interesting, Alec.'

'Isn't it?' Alec beamed proudly. 'All my own, too – the Sir Oliver Lodge[101] of the new world.'

Amory was enjoying college immensely again. The sense of going forward in a direct, determined line had come back; youth was stirring and shaking out a few new feathers. He had even stored enough surplus energy to sally into a new pose.

'What's the idea of all this "distracted" stuff, Amory?' asked Alec one day, and then as Amory pretended to be cramped over his book in a daze: 'Oh, don't try to act Burne, the mystic, to me.'

Amory looked up innocently.

'What?'

'What?' mimicked Alec. 'Are you trying to read yourself into a rhapsody with – let's see the book.'

He snatched it; regarded it derisively.

'Well?' said Amory a little stiffly.

' "*The Life of St Teresa*",' read Alec aloud. 'Oh, my gosh!'

'Say, Alec.'

'What?'

'Does it bother you?'

'Does what bother me?'

'My acting dazed and all that?'

'Why, no – of course it doesn't *bother* me.'

'Well, then, don't spoil it. If I enjoy going around telling people guilelessly that I think I'm a genius, let me do it.'

'You're getting a reputation for being eccentric,' said Alec, laughing, 'if that's what you mean.'

Amory finally prevailed, and Alec agreed to accept his face value in the presence of others if he was allowed rest periods when they were alone; so Amory 'ran it out' at a great rate, bringing the most eccentric characters to dinner, wild-eyed grad students, preceptors[102] with strange theories of God and government, to the cynical amazement of the supercilious Cottage Club.

As February became slashed by sun and moved cheerfully into March, Amory went several times to spend weekends with Monsignor; once he took Burne, with great success, for he took equal pride and delight in displaying them to each other. Monsignor took him several times to see Thornton Hancock, and once or twice to the house of a Mrs Lawrence, a type of Rome-haunting American whom Amory liked immediately.

Then one day came a letter from Monsignor, which appended an interesting postscript:

Do you know [it ran] that your third cousin, Clara Page, widowed six months and very poor, is living in Philadelphia? I don't think you've ever met her, but I wish, as a favour to me, you'd go to see her. To my mind, she's rather a remarkable woman, and just about your age.

Amory sighed and decided to go, as a favour . . .

CLARA

She was immemorial . . . Amory wasn't good enough for Clara, Clara of ripply golden hair, but then no man was. Her goodness was above the proxy morals of the husband-seeker, apart from the dull literature of female virtue.

Sorrow lay lightly around her, and when Amory found her in Philadelphia he thought her steely blue eyes held only happiness; a latent strength, a realism, was brought to its fullest development by the facts that she was compelled to face. She was alone in the world, with two small children, little money, and, worst of all, a host of friends. He saw her that winter in Philadelphia entertaining a houseful of men for an evening, when he knew she had not a servant in the house except the little coloured girl guarding the babies overhead. He saw one of the greatest libertines in that city, a man who was habitually drunk and notorious at home and abroad, sitting opposite her for an evening, discussing *girls' boarding-schools* with a sort of innocent excitement. What a twist Clara had to her mind! She could make fascinating and almost brilliant conversation out of the thinnest air that ever floated through a drawing-room.

The idea that the girl was poverty-stricken had appealed to Amory's sense of situation. He arrived in Philadelphia expecting to be told that 921 Ark Street was in a miserable lane of hovels. He was even disappointed when it proved to be nothing of the sort. It was an old house that had been in her husband's family for years. An elderly aunt, who objected to having it sold, had put ten years' taxes with a lawyer and pranced off to Honolulu, leaving Clara to struggle with the heating-problem as best she could. So no wild-haired woman with a hungry baby at her breast and a sad Amelia-like[103] look greeted him. Instead, Amory would have thought from his reception that she had not a care in the world.

A calm virility and a dreamy humour, marked contrasts to her level-headedness – into these moods she slipped sometimes as a refuge. She could do the most prosy things (though she was wise enough never to stultify herself with such 'household arts' as *knitting* and *embroidery*), yet immediately afterwards pick up a book and let her imagination rove as a formless cloud with the wind. Deepest of all in her personality was the golden radiance that she diffused around her. As an open fire in a dark room throws romance and pathos into the quiet faces at its edge, so she cast her lights and shadows around the rooms that held her, until she made of her prosy old uncle a man of quaint and meditative charm, metamorphosed the stray telegraph boy into a Puck-like creature of delightful originality. At first this quality of hers somehow irritated Amory. He considered his own uniqueness sufficient, and it rather embarrassed him when she tried to read new interests into him for the benefit of what other adorers were present. He felt as if a polite but insistent stage-manager were attempting to make him give a new interpretation of a part he had conned for years.

But Clara talking, Clara telling a slender tale of a hatpin and an inebriated man and herself . . . People tried afterwards to repeat her anecdotes but for the life of them they could make them sound like nothing whatever. They gave her a sort of innocent attention and the best smiles many of them had smiled for long; there were few tears in Clara, but people smiled misty-eyed at her.

Very occasionally Amory stayed for little half-hours after the rest of the court had gone, and they would have bread and jam and tea late in the afternoon or 'maple-sugar lunches', as she called them, at night.

'You *are* remarkable, aren't you!' Amory was becoming trite from where he perched in the centre of the dining-room table one six o'clock.

'Not a bit,' she answered. She was searching out napkins in the sideboard. 'I'm really most humdrum and commonplace. One of those people who have no interest in anything but their children.'

'Tell that to somebody else,' scoffed Amory. 'You know you're perfectly effulgent.' He asked her the one thing that he knew might embarrass her. It was the remark that the first bore made to Adam.

'Tell me about yourself.'

And she gave the answer that Adam must have given.

'There's nothing to tell.'

But eventually Adam probably told the bore all the things he thought about at night when the locusts sang in the sandy grass, and he must have remarked patronisingly how *different* he was from Eve, forgetting how different she was from him . . . at any rate, Clara told Amory much about herself that evening. She had had a harried life from sixteen on, and her education had stopped sharply with her leisure. Browsing in her library, Amory found a tattered grey book out of which fell a yellow sheet that he impudently opened. It was a poem that she had written at school about a grey convent wall on a grey day, and a girl with her cloak blown by the wind sitting atop it and thinking about the many-coloured world.

As a rule such sentiment bored him, but this was done with so much simplicity and atmosphere, that it brought a picture of Clara to his mind, of Clara on such a cool, grey day with her keen blue eyes staring out, trying to see her tragedies come marching over the gardens outside. He envied that poem. How he would have loved to have come along and seen her on the wall and talked nonsense or romance to her, perched above him in the air. He began to be frightfully jealous of everything about Clara: of her past, of her babies, of the men and women who flocked to drink deep of her cool kindness and rest their tired minds as at an absorbing play.

'*Nobody* seems to bore you,' he objected.

'About half the world do,' she admitted, 'but I think that's a pretty good average, don't you?' and she turned to find something in Browning that bore on the subject. She was the only person he ever met who could look up passages and quotations to show him in the middle of the conversation, and yet not be irritating to distraction. She did it constantly, with such a serious enthusiasm that he grew fond of watching her golden hair bent over a book, brow wrinkled ever so little at hunting her sentence.

Through early March he took to going to Philadelphia for weekends. Almost always there was someone else there and she seemed not anxious to see him alone, for many occasions presented themselves when a word from her would have given him another delicious half-hour of adoration. But he fell gradually in love and began to speculate wildly on marriage. Though this design flowed through his brain even to his lips, still he knew afterwards that the desire had not been deeply rooted. Once he dreamt that it had come true and woke up in a cold panic, for in his dream she had been a silly, flaxen Clara, with the gold gone out of her hair and platitudes falling insipidly from her changeling tongue. But she was the first fine woman he ever knew and one of the few good people who ever interested him. She made her goodness such an asset. Amory had decided that most good people either dragged theirs after them as a liability, or else distorted it to artificial geniality, and of course there were the ever-present prig and Pharisee – (but Amory never included *them* as being among the saved).

ST CECILIA

Over her grey and velvet dress,
      Under her molten, beaten hair,
Colour of rose in mock distress
      Flushes and fades and makes her fair;
Fills the air from her to him
      With light and languor and little sighs,
Just so subtly he scarcely knows . . .
      Laughing, lightning, colour of rose.

'Do you like me?'

'Of course I do,' said Clara seriously.

'Why?'

'Well, we have some qualities in common. Things that are spontaneous in each of us – or were originally.'

'You're implying that I haven't used myself very well?'

Clara hesitated.

'Well, I can't judge. A man, of course, has to go through a lot more, and I've been sheltered.'

'Oh, don't stall, please, Clara,' Amory interrupted; 'but do talk about me a little, won't you?'

'Surely, I'd adore to.' She didn't smile.

'That's sweet of you. First answer some questions. Am I painfully conceited?'

'Well – no, you have tremendous vanity, but it'll amuse the people who notice its preponderance.'

'I see.'

'You're really humble at heart. You sink to the third hell of depression when you think you've been slighted. In fact, you haven't much self-respect.'

'Centre of target twice, Clara. How do you do it? You never let me say a word.'

'Of course not – I can never judge a man while he's talking. But I'm not through; the reason you have so little real self-confidence, even though you gravely announce to the occasional philistine that you think you're a genius, is that you've attributed all sorts of atrocious faults to yourself and are trying to live up to them. For instance, you're always saying that you are a slave to highballs.'

'But I am, potentially.'

'And you say you're a weak character, that you've no will.'

'Not a bit of will – I'm a slave to my emotions, to my likes, to my hatred of boredom, to most of my desires – '

'You are not!' She brought one little fist down on to the other. 'You're a slave, a bound helpless slave to one thing in the world, your imagination.'

'You certainly interest me. If this isn't boring you, go on.'

'I notice that when you want to stay over an extra day from college you go about it in a sure way. You never decide at first while the merits of going or staying are fairly clear in your mind. You let your imagination shinny on the side of your desires for a few hours, and then you decide. Naturally your imagination, after a little freedom, thinks up a million reasons why you should stay, so your decision when it comes isn't true. It's biassed.'

'Yes,' objected Amory, 'but isn't it lack of willpower to let my imagination shinny on the wrong side?'

'My dear boy, there's your big mistake. This has nothing to do with willpower; that's a crazy, useless word, anyway; you lack judgement – the judgement to decide at once when you know your imagination will play you false, given half a chance.'

'Well, I'll be darned!' exclaimed Amory in surprise, 'that's the last thing I expected.'

Clara didn't gloat. She changed the subject immediately. But she had started him thinking and he believed she was partly right. He felt like a factory-owner who after accusing a clerk of dishonesty finds that his own son, in the office, is changing the books once a week. His poor, mistreated will that he had been holding up to the scorn of himself and his friends, stood before him innocent, and his judgement walked off to prison with the unconfinable imp, imagination, dancing in mocking glee beside him. Clara's was the only advice he ever asked without dictating the answer himself – except, perhaps, in his talks with Monsignor Darcy.

How he loved to do any sort of thing with Clara! Shopping with her was a rare, epicurean dream. In every store where she had ever traded she was whispered about as the beautiful Mrs Page.

'I'll bet she won't stay single long.'

'Well, don't scream it out. She ain't lookin' for no advice.'

'*Ain't* she beautiful!'

(*Enter a floor-walker – silence till he moves forward, smirking.*)

'Society person, ain't she?'

'Yeah, but poor now, I guess; so they say.'

'Gee! girls, *ain't* she some kid!'

And Clara beamed on all alike. Amory believed that tradespeople gave her discounts, sometimes to her knowledge and sometimes without it. He knew she dressed very well, had always the best of everything in the house, and was inevitably waited upon by the head floor-walker at the very least.

Sometimes they would go to church together on Sunday and he would walk beside her and revel in her cheeks moist from the soft water in the new air. She was very devout, always had been, and God knows what heights she attained and what strength she drew down to herself when she knelt and bent her golden hair into the stained-glass light.

'St Cecelia,' he cried aloud one day, quite involuntarily, and the people turned and peered, and the priest paused in his sermon and Clara and Amory turned to fiery red.

That was the last Sunday they had, for he spoiled it all that night. He couldn't help it.

They were walking through the March twilight where it was as warm as June, and the joy of youth filled his soul so that he felt he must speak.

'I think,' he said and his voice trembled, 'that if I lost faith in you I'd lose faith in God.'

She looked at him with such a startled face that he asked her the matter.

'Nothing,' she said slowly, 'only this: five men have said that to me before, and it frightens me.'

'Oh, Clara, is that your fate!'

She did not answer.

'I suppose love to you is – ' he began.

She turned like a flash.

'I have never been in love.'

They walked along, and he realised slowly how much she had told him . . . never in love . . . She seemed suddenly a daughter of light alone. His entity dropped out of her plane and he longed only to touch her dress with almost the realisation that Joseph must have had of Mary's eternal significance. But quite mechanically he heard himself saying: 'And I love you – any latent greatness that I've got is . . . oh, I can't talk, but Clara, if I come back in two years in a position to marry you – '

She shook her head.

'No,' she said; 'I'd never marry again. I've got my two children and I want myself for them. I like you – I like all clever men, you more than any – but you know me well enough to know that I'd never marry a clever man – '

She broke off suddenly.

'Amory.'

'What?'

'You're not in love with me. You never wanted to marry me, did you?'

'It was the twilight,' he said wonderingly. 'I didn't feel as though I were speaking aloud. But I love you – or adore you – or worship you – '

'There you go – running through your catalogue of emotions in five seconds.'

He smiled unwillingly.

'Don't make me out such a lightweight, Clara; you *are* depressing sometimes.'

'You're not a lightweight, of all things,' she said intently, taking his arm and opening wide her eyes – he could see their kindliness in the fading dusk. 'A lightweight is an eternal nay.'

'There's so much spring in the air – there's so much lazy sweetness in your heart.'

She dropped his arm.

'You're all fine now, and I feel glorious. Give me a cigarette. You've never seen me smoke, have you? Well, I do, about once a month.'

And then that wonderful girl and Amory raced to the corner like two mad children gone wild with pale-blue twilight.

'I'm going to the country for tomorrow,' she announced, as she stood panting, safe beyond the flare of the corner lamp-post. 'These days are too magnificent to miss, though perhaps I feel them more in the city.'

'Oh, Clara!' Amory said; 'what a devil you could have been if the Lord had just bent your soul a little the other way!'

'Maybe,' she answered; 'but I think not. I'm never really wild and never have been. That little outburst was pure spring.'

'And you are, too,' said he.

They were walking along now.

'No – you're wrong again, how can a person of your own self-reputed brains be so constantly wrong about me? I'm the opposite of everything spring ever stood for. It's unfortunate, if I happen to look like what pleased some soppy old Greek sculptor, but I assure you that if it weren't for my face I'd be a quiet nun in the convent

without' – then she broke into a run and her raised voice floated back
to him as he followed – 'my precious babies, which I must go back
and see.'

She was the only girl he ever knew with whom he could understand
how another man might be preferred. Often Amory met wives whom
he had known as débutantes, and looking intently at them imagined
that he found something in their faces which said: 'Oh, if I could
only have gotten *you!*' Oh, the enormous conceit of the man!

But that night seemed a night of stars and singing and Clara's
bright soul still gleamed on the ways they had trod.

'Golden, golden is the air – ' he chanted to the little pools of water .
. . *'Golden is the air, golden notes from golden mandolins, golden frets of
golden violins, fair, oh, wearily fair . . . Skeins from braided baskets
mortals may not hold; oh, what young extravagant God, who would know
or ask it? . . . who could give such gold . . .* '

AMORY IS RESENTFUL

Slowly and inevitably, yet with a sudden surge at the last, while
Amory talked and dreamed, war rolled swiftly up the beach and
washed the sands where Princeton played. Every night the gymnasium echoed as platoon after platoon swept over the floor and
shuffled out the basketball markings. When Amory went to Washington the next weekend he caught some of the spirit of crisis which
changed to repulsion in the Pullman car coming back, for the berths
across from him were occupied by stinking aliens – Greeks, he
guessed, or Russians. He thought how much easier patriotism had
been to a homogeneous race, how much easier it would have been to
fight as the Colonies fought, or as the Confederacy fought. And he
did no sleeping that night, but listened to the aliens guffaw and
snore while they filled the car with the heavy scent of latest America.

In Princeton everyone bantered in public and told themselves
privately that their deaths at least would be heroic. The literary
students read Rupert Brooke passionately; the lounge-lizards worried
over whether the government would permit the English-cut uniform
for officers; a few of the hopelessly lazy wrote to the obscure branches
of the War Department, seeking an easy commission and a soft
berth.

Then, after a week, Amory saw Burne and knew at once that
argument would be futile – Burne had come out as a pacifist. The
socialist magazines, a great smattering of Tolstoy, and his own

intense longing for a cause that would bring out whatever strength lay in him, had finally decided him to preach peace as a subjective ideal.

'When the German army entered Belgium,' he began, 'if the inhabitants had gone peaceably about their business, the German army would have been disorganised in – '

'I know,' Amory interrupted, 'I've heard it all. But I'm not going to talk propaganda with you. There's a chance that you're right – but even so we're hundreds of years before the time when non-resistance can touch us as a reality.'

'But, Amory, listen – '

'Burne, we'd just argue – '

'Very well.'

'Just one thing – I don't ask you to think of your family or friends, because I know they don't count a picayune with you beside your sense of duty – but, Burne, how do you know that the magazines you read and the societies you join and these idealists you meet aren't just plain *German*?'

'Some of them are, of course.'

'How do you know they aren't *all* pro-German – just a lot of weak ones – with German-Jewish names.'

'That's the chance, of course,' he said slowly. 'How much or how little I'm taking this stand because of propaganda I've heard, I don't know; naturally I think that it's my most innermost conviction – it seems a path spread before me just now.'

Amory's heart sank.

'But think of the cheapness of it – no one's really going to martyr you for being a pacifist – it's just going to throw you in with the worst – '

'I doubt it,' he interrupted.

'Well, it all smells of Bohemian New York to me.'

'I know what you mean, and that's why I'm not sure I'll agitate.'

'You're one man, Burne – going to talk to people who won't listen – with all God's given you.'

'That's what Stephen[104] must have thought many years ago. But he preached his sermon and they killed him. He probably thought as he was dying what a waste it all was. But you see, I've always felt that Stephen's death was the thing that occurred to Paul on the road to Damascus, and sent him to preach the word of Christ all over the world.'

'Go on.'

'That's all – this is my particular duty. Even if right now I'm just a pawn – just sacrificed. God! Amory – you don't think I like the Germans!'

'Well, I can't say anything else – I get to the end of all the logic about non-resistance, and there, like an excluded middle, stands the huge spectre of man as he is and always will be. And this spectre stands right beside the one logical necessity of Tolstoy's, and the other logical necessity of Nietzsche's – ' Amory broke off suddenly. 'When are you going?'

'I'm going next week.'

'I'll see you, of course.'

As he walked away it seemed to Amory that the look in his face bore a great resemblance to that in Kerry's when he had said goodbye under Blair Arch two years before. Amory wondered unhappily why he could never go into anything with the primal honesty of those two.

'Burne's a fanatic,' he said to Tom, 'and he's dead wrong and, I'm inclined to think, just an unconscious pawn in the hands of anarchistic publishers and German-paid rag wavers – but he haunts me – just leaving everything worth while – '

Burne left in a quietly dramatic manner a week later. He sold all his possessions and came down to the room to say goodbye, with a battered old bicycle, on which he intended to ride to his home in Pennsylvania.

'Peter the Hermit[105] bidding farewell to Cardinal Richelieu,' suggested Alec, who was lounging in the window-seat as Burne and Amory shook hands.

But Amory was not in a mood for that, and as he saw Burne's long legs propel his ridiculous bicycle out of sight beyond Alexander Hall, he knew he was going to have a bad week. Not that he doubted the war – Germany stood for everything repugnant to him; for materialism and the direction of tremendous licentious force; it was just that Burne's face stayed in his memory and he was sick of the hysteria he was beginning to hear.

'What on earth is the use of suddenly running down Goethe,' he declared to Alec and Tom. 'Why write books to prove he started the war – or that that stupid, overestimated Schiller is a demon in disguise?'

'Have you ever read anything of theirs?' asked Tom shrewdly.

'No,' Amory admitted.

'Neither have I,' he said laughing.

'People will shout,' said Alec quietly, 'but Goethe's on his same old shelf in the library – to bore anyone that wants to read him!'

Amory subsided, and the subject dropped.

'What are you going to do, Amory?'

'Infantry or aviation, I can't make up my mind – I hate mechanics, but then of course aviation's the thing for me – '

'I feel as Amory does,' said Tom. 'Infantry or aviation – aviation sounds like the romantic side of the war, of course – like cavalry used to be, you know; but like Amory I don't know a horsepower from a piston-rod.'

Somehow Amory's dissatisfaction with his lack of enthusiasm culminated in an attempt to put the blame for the whole war on the ancestors of his generation . . . all the people who cheered for Germany in 1870[106] . . . All the materialists rampant, all the idolisers of German science and efficiency. So he sat one day in an English lecture and heard *Locksley Hall* quoted and fell into a brown study with contempt for Tennyson and all he stood for – for he took him as a representative of the Victorians.

> 'Victorians, Victorians, who never learned to weep,
>   Who sowed the bitter harvest that your children go to reap – '

scribbled Amory in his notebook. The lecturer was saying something about Tennyson's solidity and fifty heads were bent to take notes. Amory turned over to a fresh page and began scrawling again.

> 'They shuddered when they found what Mr Darwin was about,
>   They shuddered when the waltz came in and Newman
>   hurried out – '

But the waltz came in much earlier; he crossed that out.

'And entitled "A Song in Time of Order",' came the professor's voice, droning far away. 'Time of Order' – Good Lord! Everything crammed in the box and the Victorians sitting on the lid smiling serenely . . . With Browning in his Italian villa crying bravely: 'All's for the best.' Amory scribbled again.

> 'You knelt up in the temple and he bent to hear you pray,
>   You thanked him for your "glorious gains" – reproached
>   him for "Cathay".'

Why could he never get more than a couplet at a time?

Now he needed something to rhyme with:

'You would keep Him straight with science, tho' He had
                                    gone wrong before . . . '

Well, anyway . . .

'You met your children in your home – "I've fixed it up!" you
    cried,
        Took your fifty years of Europe, and then virtuously – died.'

'That was to a great extent Tennyson's idea,' came the lecturer's
voice. 'Swinburne's "Song in Time of Order" might well have been
Tennyson's title. He idealised order against chaos, against waste.'

At last Amory had it. He turned over another page and scrawled
vigorously for the twenty minutes that were left of the hour. Then
he walked up to the desk and deposited a page torn out of his
notebook.

'Here's a poem to the Victorians, sir,' he said coldly.

The professor picked it up curiously while Amory backed rapidly
through the door.

Here is what he had written:

                'Songs in the time of order
                    You left for us to sing,
                        Proofs with excluded middles,
                            Answers to life in rhyme,

                Keys of the prison warder
                And ancient bells to ring,
                    Time was the end of riddles,
                        We were the end of time . . .

                Here were domestic oceans
                And a sky that we might reach,
                    Guns and a guarded border,
                        Gauntlets – but not to fling,

                Thousands of old emotions
                    And a platitude for each,
                        Songs in the time of order –
                            And tongues, that we might sing.'

Early April slipped by in a haze – a haze of long evenings on the club veranda with the graphophone playing 'Poor Butterfly'[107] inside . . . for 'Poor Butterfly' had been the song of that last year. The war seemed scarcely to touch them and it might have been one of the senior springs of the past, except for the drilling every other afternoon, yet Amory realised poignantly that this was the last spring under the old regime.

'This is the great protest against the superman,' said Amory.

'I suppose so,' Alec agreed.

'He's absolutely irreconcilable with any Utopia. As long as he occurs, there's trouble and all the latent evil that makes a crowd list and sway when he talks.'

'And of course all that he is is a gifted man without a moral sense.'

'That's all. I think the worst thing to contemplate is this – it's all happened before, how soon will it happen again? Fifty years after Waterloo, Napoleon was as much a hero to English schoolchildren as Wellington. How do we know our grandchildren won't idolise von Hindenburg[108] the same way?'

'What brings it about?'

'Time, damn it, and the historian. If we could only learn to look on evil as evil, whether it's clothed in filth or monotony or magnificence.'

'God! Haven't we raked the universe over the coals for four years?'

Then the night came that was to be the last. Tom and Amory, bound in the morning for different training-camps, paced the shadowy walks as usual and seemed still to see around them the faces of the men they knew.

'The grass is full of ghosts tonight.'

'The whole campus is alive with them.'

They paused by Little and watched the moon rise, to make silver of the slate roof of Dodd and blue the rustling trees.

'You know,' whispered Tom, 'what we feel now is the sense of all the gorgeous youth that has rioted through here in two hundred years.'

A last burst of singing flooded up from Blair Arch – broken voices for some long parting.

'And what we leave here is more than this class; it's the whole heritage of youth. We're just one generation – we're breaking all the links that seemed to bind us here to top-booted and high-stocked generations. We've walked arm and arm with Burr and Light-Horse Harry Lee[109] through half these deep-blue nights.'

'That's what they are,' Tom tangented off, 'deep blue – a bit of colour would spoil them, make them exotic. Spires, against a sky that's a promise of dawn, and blue light on the slate roofs – it hurts . . . rather – '

'Goodbye, Aaron Burr,' Amory called towards deserted Nassau Hall, 'you and I knew strange corners of life.'

His voice echoed in the stillness.

'The torches are out,' whispered Tom. 'Ah, Messalina,[110] the long shadows are building minarets on the stadium – '

For an instant the voices of freshman year surged around them and then they looked at each other with faint tears in their eyes.

'Damn!'

'Damn!'

The last light fades and drifts across the land – the low, long land, the sunny land of spires; the ghosts of evening tune again their lyres and wander singing in a plaintive band down the long corridors of trees; pale fires echo the night from tower top to tower: Oh, sleep that dreams, and dream that never tires, press from the petals of the lotus flower something of this to keep, the essence of an hour.

No more to wait the twilight of the moon in this sequestered vale of star and spire, for one eternal morning of desire passes to time and earthy afternoon. Here, Heraclitus,[111] did you find in fire and shifting things the prophecy you hurled down the dead years; this midnight my desire will see, shadowed among the embers, furled in flame, the splendour and the sadness of the world.

MAY 1917–FEBRUARY 1919

A letter dated January 1918, written by Monsignor Darcy to Amory, who is a second lieutenant in the 171st Infantry, Port of Embarkation, Camp Mills, Long Island.

My Dear Boy – All you need tell me of yourself is that you still are; for the rest I merely search back in a restive memory, a thermometer that records only fevers, and match you with what I was at your age. But men will chatter and you and I will still shout our futilities to each other across the stage until the last silly curtain falls *plump!* upon our bobbing heads. But you are starting the spluttering magic-lantern show of life with much the same array of slides as I had, so I need to write you if only to shriek the colossal stupidity of *people* . . .

This is the end of one thing: for better or worse you will never again be quite the Amory Blaine that I knew, never again will we meet as we have met, because your generation is growing hard, much harder than mine ever grew, nourished as they were on the stuff of the nineties.

Amory, lately I reread Aeschylus and there in the divine irony of the *Agamemnon* I find the only answer to this bitter age – all the world tumbled about our ears, and the closest parallel ages back in that hopeless resignation. There are times when I think of the men out there as Roman legionaries, miles from their corrupt city, stemming back the hordes . . . hordes a little more menacing, after all, than the corrupt city . . . another blind blow at the race, furies that we passed with ovations years ago, over whose corpses we bleated triumphantly all through the Victorian era . . .

And afterwards an out-and-out materialistic world – and the Catholic Church. I wonder where you'll fit in. Of one thing I'm sure – Celtic you'll live and Celtic you'll die; so if you don't use heaven as a continual referendum for your ideas you'll find earth a continual recall to your ambitions.

Amory, I've discovered suddenly that I'm an old man. Like all old men, I've had dreams sometimes and I'm going to tell you of them. I've enjoyed imagining that you were my son, that perhaps when I was young I went into a state of coma and begat you, and when I came to, had no recollection of it . . . it's the paternal instinct, Amory – celibacy goes deeper than the flesh . . .

Sometimes I think that the explanation of our deep resemblance is some common ancestor, and I find that the only blood that the Darcys and the O'Haras have in common is that of the O'Donahues . . . Stephen was his name, I think . . .

When the lightning strikes one of us it strikes both: you had hardly arrived at the port of embarkation when I got my papers to start for Rome, and I am waiting every moment to be told where to take ship. Even before you get this letter I shall be on the ocean; then will come your turn. You went to war as a gentleman should, just as you went to school and college, because it was the thing to do. It's better to leave the blustering and tremulo-heroism to the middle classes; they do it so much better.

Do you remember that weekend last March when you brought Burne Holiday from Princeton to see me? What a magnificent boy he is! It gave me a frightful shock afterwards when you wrote that he thought me splendid; how could he be so deceived? Splendid is the one thing that neither you nor I are. We are many other things – we're extraordinary, we're clever, we could be said, I suppose, to be brilliant. We can attract people, we can make atmosphere, we can almost lose our Celtic souls in Celtic subtleties, we can almost always have our own way; but splendid – rather not!

I am going to Rome with a wonderful dossier and letters of introduction that cover every capital in Europe, and there will be 'no small stir' when I get there. How I wish you were with me! This sounds like a rather cynical paragraph, not at all the sort of thing that a middle-aged clergyman should write to a youth about to depart for the war; the only excuse is that the middle-aged clergyman is talking to himself. There are deep things in us and you know what they are as well as I do. We have great faith, though yours at present is uncrystallised; we have a terrible honesty that all our sophistry cannot destroy and, above all, a childlike simplicity that keeps us from ever being really malicious.

I have written a keen for you which follows. I am sorry your cheeks are not up to the description I have written of them, but you *will* smoke and read all night –

At any rate here it is:

> *A Lament for a Foster Son, and He going to the War*
> *against the King of Foreign*

Ochone
He is gone from me the son of my mind
   And he in his golden youth like Angus Oge
Angus of the bright birds
   And his mind strong and subtle like the mind of Cuchulin
                                        on Muirtheme.

Awirra sthrue
His brow is as white as the milk of the cows of Maeve
   And his cheeks like the cherries of the tree
And it bending down to Mary and she feeding the Son
                                        of God.

Aveelia Vrone
His hair is like the golden collar of the Kings at Tara
   And his eyes like the four grey seas of Erin.
And they swept with the mists of rain.

Mavrone go Gudyo
He to be in the joyful and red battle
   Amongst the chieftains and they doing great deeds
                                        of valour
His life to go from him
   It is the chords of my own soul would be loosed.

A Vich Deelish
My heart is in the heart of my son
   And my life is in his life surely
A man can be twice young
   In the life of his sons only.

Jia du Vaha Alanav
May the Son of God be above him and beneath him, before
                                        him and behind him
   May the King of the elements cast a mist over the eyes
                                        of the King of Foreign,

May the Queen of the Graces lead him by the hand the
way he can go through the midst of his enemies and they
not seeing him
May Patrick of the Gael and Collumb of the Churches
and the five thousand Saints of Erin be better than a
shield to him

And he got into the fight.
Och Ochone.

Amory – Amory – I feel, somehow, that this is all; one or both of us
is not going to last out this war . . . I've been trying to tell you how
much this reincarnation of myself in you has meant in the last few
years . . . curiously alike we are . . . curiously unlike.

Goodbye, dear boy, and God be with you.

THAYER DARCY

EMBARKING AT NIGHT

Amory moved forward on the deck until he found a stool under an
electric light. He searched in his pocket for notebook and pencil and
then began to write, slowly, laboriously:

We leave tonight . . .
    Silent, we filled the still, deserted street,
        A column of dim grey,

And ghosts rose startled at the muffled beat
    Along the moonless way;
The shadowy shipyards echoed to the feet
    That turned from night and day.

And so we linger on the windless decks,
    See on the spectre shore
Shades of a thousand days, poor grey-ribbed wrecks . . .
    Oh, shall we then deplore
Those futile years!
            See how the sea is white!
The clouds have broken and the heavens burn
To hollow highways, paved with gravelled light
The churning of the waves about the stern
    Rises to one voluminous nocturne,
                . . . We leave tonight.'

A letter from Amory, headed 'Brest, March 11th, 1919', to Lieutenant
T. P. D'Invilliers, Camp Gordon, Ga.

DEAR BAUDELAIRE – We meet in Manhattan on the 30th of this
very mo.; we then proceed to take a very sporty apartment, you
and I and Alec, who is at my elbow as I write. I don't know what
I'm going to do but I have a vague dream of going into politics.
Why is it that the pick of the young Englishmen from Oxford and
Cambridge go into politics and in the USA we leave it to the
muckers? – raised in the ward, educated in the assembly and sent
to Congress, fat-paunched bundles of corruption, devoid of 'both
ideas and ideals' as the debaters used to say. Even forty years ago
we had good men in politics, but we, we are brought up to pile up
a million and 'show what we are made of'. Sometimes I wish I'd
been an Englishman; American life is so damned dumb and stupid
and healthy.

Since poor Beatrice died I'll probably have a little money, but
very darn little. I can forgive mother almost everything except the
fact that in a sudden burst of religiosity towards the end, she left
half of what remained to be spent in stained-glass windows and
seminary endowments. Mr Barton, my lawyer, writes me that my
thousands are mostly in street railways and that the said Street
R.R.s are losing money because of the five-cent fares. Imagine a
salary list that gives $350 a month to a man that can't read and
write! – yet I believe in it, even though I've seen what was once a
sizable fortune melt away between speculation, extravagance, the
democratic administration, and the income tax – modern, that's
me all over, Mabel.

At any rate we'll have really knock-out rooms – you can get a
job on some fashion magazine, and Alec can go into the Zinc
Company or whatever it is that his people own – he's looking over
my shoulder and he says it's a brass company, but I don't think it
matters much, do you? There's probably as much corruption in
zinc-made money as brass-made money. As for the well-known
Amory, he would write immortal literature if he were sure enough
about anything to risk telling anyone else about it. There is no
more dangerous gift to posterity than a few cleverly turned
platitudes.

Tom, why don't you become a Catholic? Of course to be a
good one you'd have to give up those violent intrigues you used to
tell me about, but you'd write better poetry if you were linked up

to tall golden candlesticks and long, even chants, and even if the American priests are rather burgeois, as Beatrice used to say, still you need only go to the sporty churches, and I'll introduce you to Monsignor Darcy who really is a wonder.

Kerry's death was a blow, so was Jesse's to a certain extent. And I have a great curiosity to know what queer corner of the world has swallowed Burne. Do you suppose he's in prison under some false name? I confess that the war instead of making me orthodox, which is the correct reaction, has made me a passionate agnostic. The Catholic Church has had its wings clipped so often lately that its part was timidly negligible, and they haven't any good writers any more. I'm sick of Chesterton.

I've only discovered one soldier who passed through the much-advertised spiritual crisis, like this fellow, Donald Hankey,[112] and the one I knew was already studying for the ministry, so he was ripe for it. I honestly think that's all pretty much rot, though it seemed to give sentimental comfort to those at home; and may make fathers and mothers appreciate their children. This crisis-inspired religion is rather valueless and fleeting at best. I think four men have discovered Paris to one that discovered God.

But us – you and me and Alec – oh, we'll get a Jap butler and dress for dinner and have wine on the table and lead a contemplative, emotionless life until we decide to use machine-guns with the property owners – or throw bombs with the Bolshevik. God! Tom, I hope something happens. I'm restless as the devil and have a horror of getting fat or falling in love and growing domestic.

The place at Lake Geneva is now for rent but when I land I'm going West to see Mr Barton and get some details. Write me care of the Blackstone, Chicago.

S'ever, dear Boswell,

SAMUEL JOHNSON

BOOK TWO

THE EDUCATION OF A PERSONAGE

CHAPTER I

The Débutante

The time is February. The place is a large, dainty bedroom in the Connage house on Sixty-Eighth Street, New York. A girl's room: pink walls and curtains and a pink bedspread on a cream-coloured bed. Pink and cream are the motifs of the room, but the only article of furniture in full view is a luxurious dressing-table with a glass top and a three-sided mirror. On the walls there is an expensive print of Cherry Ripe, *a few polite dogs by Landseer, and the* King of the Black Isles *by Maxfield Parrish.*[113]

(Great disorder consisting of the following items: (1) seven or eight empty cardboard boxes, with tissue-paper tongues hanging panting from their mouths; (2) an assortment of street dresses mingled with their sisters of the evening, all upon the table, all evidently new; (3) a roll of tulle, which has lost its dignity and wound itself tortuously around everything in sight, and (4) upon the two small chairs, a collection of lingerie that beggars description. One would enjoy seeing the bill called forth by the finery displayed and one is possessed by a desire to see the princess for whose benefit – Look! There's someone! Disappointment! This is only a maid hunting for something. She lifts a heap from a chair – not there; another heap, the dressing-table, the chiffonier drawers. She brings to light several beautiful chemises and an amazing pair of pyjamas but this does not satisfy her – she goes out.

An indistinguishable mumble from the next room.

Now, we are getting warm. This is Alec's mother, MRS CONNAGE, *ample, dignified, rouged to the dowager point and quite worn out. Her lips move significantly as she looks for* IT. *Her search is less thorough than the maid's but there is a touch of fury in it that quite makes up for its sketchiness. She stumbles on the tulle and her 'damn' is quite audible. She retires, empty-handed.*

More chatter outside and a girl's voice, a very spoiled voice, says: 'Of all the stupid people – '

After a pause a third seeker enters, not she of the spoiled voice, but a younger edition. This is CECILIA CONNAGE, *sixteen, pretty, shrewd, and constitutionally good-humoured. She is dressed for the evening in a gown the obvious simplicity of which probably bores her. She goes to the nearest pile, selects a small pink garment and holds it up appraisingly.*

CECILIA: Pink?

ROSALIND (*outside*): Yes!

CECILIA: *Very* snappy?

ROSALIND: Yes!

CECILIA: I've got it!

(*She sees herself in the mirror of the dressing-table and commences to shimmy enthusiastically.*)

ROSALIND (*outside*): What are you doing – trying it on?

(CECILIA *ceases and goes out carrying the garment at the right shoulder. From the other door, enters* ALEC CONNAGE. *He looks around quickly and in a huge voice shouts:* 'Mama!' *There is a chorus of protest from next door and encouraged he starts towards it, but is repelled by another chorus.*)

ALEC: So *that's* where you all are! Amory Blaine is here.

CECILIA (*quickly*): Take him downstairs.

ALEC: Oh, he *is* downstairs.

MRS CONNAGE: Well, you can show him where his room is. Tell him I'm sorry that I can't meet him now.

ALEC: He's heard a lot about you all. I wish you'd hurry. Father's telling him all about the war and he's restless. He's sort of temperamental.

(*This last suffices to draw* CECILIA *into the room.*)

CECILIA (*seating herself high upon lingerie*): How do you mean – temperamental? You used to say that about him in letters.

ALEC: Oh, he writes stuff.

CECILIA: Does he play the piano?

ALEC: Don't think so.

CECILIA (*speculatively*): Drink?

ALEC: Yes – nothing queer about him.

CECILIA: Money?

ALEC: Good Lord – ask him, he used to have a lot, and he's got some income now.

(MRS CONNAGE *appears.*)

MRS CONNAGE: Alec, of course we're glad to have any friend of yours –

ALEC: You certainly ought to meet Amory.

MRS CONNAGE: Of course, I want to. But I think it's so childish of you to leave a perfectly good home to go and live with two other boys in some impossible apartment. I hope it isn't in order that you can all drink as much as you want. (*She pauses.*) He'll be a little neglected tonight. This is Rosalind's week, you see. When a girl comes out, she needs *all* the attention.

ROSALIND (*outside*): Well, then, prove it by coming here and hooking me.

(MRS CONNAGE *goes.*)

ALEC: Rosalind hasn't changed a bit.

CECILIA (*in a lower tone*): She's awfully spoiled.

ALEC: She'll meet her match tonight.

CECILIA: Who – Mr Amory Blaine?

(ALEC *nods.*)

CECILIA: Well, Rosalind has still to meet the man she can't out-distance. Honestly, Alec, she treats men terribly. She abuses them and cuts them and breaks dates with them and yawns in their faces – and they come back for more.

ALEC: They love it.

CECILIA: They hate it. She's a – she's a sort of vampire, I think – and she can make girls do what she wants usually – only she hates girls.

ALEC: Personality runs in our family.

CECILIA (*resignedly*): I guess it ran out before it got to me.

ALEC: Does Rosalind behave herself?

CECILIA: Not particularly well. Oh, she's average – smokes sometimes, drinks punch, frequently kissed – Oh, yes – common knowledge – one of the effects of the war, you know.

(MRS CONNAGE *emerges.*)

MRS CONNAGE: Rosalind's almost finished so I can go down and meet your friend.

(ALEC *and his mother go out.*)

ROSALIND (*outside*): Oh, mother –

CECILIA: Mother's gone down.

(*And now* ROSALIND *enters.* ROSALIND *is – utterly* ROSALIND. *She is one of those girls who need never make the slightest effort to have men fall in love with them. Two types of men seldom do: dull men are usually afraid of her cleverness and intellectual men are usually afraid of her beauty. All others are hers by natural prerogative.*

If ROSALIND *could be spoiled the process would have been complete by this time, and as a matter of fact, her disposition is not all it should be;*

*she wants what she wants when she wants it and she is prone to make
everyone around her pretty miserable when she doesn't get it – but in the
true sense she is not spoiled. Her fresh enthusiasm, her will to grow and
learn, her endless faith in the inexhaustibility of romance, her courage
and fundamental honesty – these things are not spoiled.*

*There are long periods when she cordially loathes her whole family.
She is quite unprincipled; her philosophy is* carpe diem *for herself and*
laissez-faire *for others. She loves shocking stories: she has that coarse
streak that usually goes with natures that are both fine and big. She
wants people to like her, but if they do not it never worries her or
changes her. She is by no means a model character.*

The education of all beautiful women is the knowledge of men.
ROSALIND *had been disappointed in man after man as individuals, but
she had great faith in man as a sex. Women she detested. They
represented qualities that she felt and despised in herself – incipient
meanness, conceit, cowardice, and petty dishonesty. She once told a
roomful of her mother's friends that the only excuse for women was the
necessity for a disturbing element among men. She danced exceptionally
well, drew cleverly but hastily, and had a startling facility with words,
which she used only in love-letters.*

But all criticism of ROSALIND *ends in her beauty. There was that
shade of glorious yellow hair, the desire to imitate which supports the dye
industry. There was the eternal kissable mouth, small, slightly sensual
and utterly disturbing. There were grey eyes and an unimpeachable skin
with two spots of vanishing colour. She was slender and athletic, without
underdevelopment, and it was a delight to watch her move about a
room, walk along a street, swing a golf club or turn a 'cartwheel'.*

*A last qualification – her vivid, instant personality escaped that
conscious, theatrical quality that* AMORY *had found in* ISABELLE.
MONSIGNOR DARCY *would have been quite up a tree whether to call her
a personality or a personage. She was perhaps the delicious, inexpressible,
once-in-a-century blend.*

*On the night of her début she is, for all her strange, stray wisdom,
quite like a happy little girl. Her mother's maid has just done her hair,
but she has decided impatiently that she can do a better job herself. She
is too nervous just now to stay in one place. To that we owe her presence
in this littered room. She is going to speak.* ISABELLE's *alto tones had
been like a violin, but if you could hear* ROSALIND, *you would say her
voice was musical as a waterfall.)*

ROSALIND: Honestly, there are only two costumes in the world that I
really enjoy being in – (*combing her hair at the dressing-table.*) One's

a hoop skirt with pantaloons; the other's a one-piece bathing-suit. I'm quite charming in both of them.

CECILIA: Glad you're coming out?

ROSALIND: Yes; aren't you?

CECILIA (*cynically*): You're glad so you can get married and live on Long Island with the *fast younger married set*. You want life to be a chain of flirtation with a man for every link.

ROSALIND: *Want* it to be one! You mean I've *found* it one.

CECILIA: Ha!

ROSALIND: Cecelia, darling, you don't know what a trial it is to be – like me. I've got to keep my face like steel in the street to keep men from winking at me. If I laugh hard from a front row in the theatre, the comedian plays to me for the rest of the evening. If I drop my voice, my eyes, my handkerchief at a dance, my partner calls me up on the phone every day for a week.

CECILIA: It must be an awful strain.

ROSALIND: The unfortunate part is that the only men who interest me at all are the totally ineligible ones. Now – if I were poor I'd go on the stage.

CECILIA: Yes, you might as well get paid for the amount of acting you do.

ROSALIND: Sometimes when I've felt particularly radiant I've thought, why should this be wasted on one man?

CECILIA: Often when you're particularly sulky, I've wondered why it should all be wasted on just one family. (*getting up*) I think I'll go down and meet Mr Amory Blaine. I like temperamental men.

ROSALIND: There aren't any. Men don't know how to be really angry or really happy – and the ones that do, go to pieces.

CECILIA: Well, I'm glad I don't have all your worries. I'm engaged.

ROSALIND (*with a scornful smile*): Engaged? Why, you little lunatic! If mother heard you talking like that she'd send you off to boarding-school, where you belong.

CECILIA: You won't tell her, though, because I know things I could tell – and you're too selfish!

ROSALIND (*a little annoyed*): Run along, little girl! Who are you engaged to, the iceman? The man that keeps the candy-store?

CECILIA: Cheap wit – goodbye, darling, I'll see you later.

ROSALIND: Oh, be *sure* and do that – you're such a help.

(*Exit* CECILIA. ROSALIND *finishes her hair and rises, humming. She goes up to the mirror and starts to dance in front of it on the soft carpet. She watches not her feet, but her eyes – never casually but always intently, even when she smiles. The door suddenly opens and then slams behind* AMORY, *very cool and handsome as usual. He melts into instant confusion.*)

HE: Oh, I'm sorry. I thought –

SHE (*smiling radiantly*): Oh, you're Amory Blaine, aren't you?

HE (*regarding her closely*): And you're Rosalind?

SHE: I'm going to call you Amory – oh, come in – it's all right – mother'll be right in – (*under her breath*) unfortunately.

HE (*gazing around*): This is sort of a new wrinkle for me.

SHE: This is no man's land.

HE: This is where you – you – (*pause*)

SHE: Yes – all those things. (*She crosses to the bureau.*) See, here's my rouge – eye pencils.

HE: I didn't know you were that way.

SHE: What did you expect?

HE: I thought you'd be sort of – sort of – sexless; you know, swim and play golf.

SHE: Oh, I do – but not in business hours.

HE: Business?

SHE: Six to two – strictly.

HE: I'd like to have some stock in the corporation.

SHE: Oh, it's not a corporation – it's just 'Rosalind, Unlimited'. Fifty-one shares, name, goodwill and everything goes at $25,000 a year.

HE (*disapprovingly*): Sort of a chilly proposition.

SHE: Well, Amory, you don't mind – do you? When I meet a man that doesn't bore me to death after two weeks, perhaps it'll be different.

HE: Odd, you have the same point of view on men that I have on women.

SHE: I'm not really feminine, you know – in my mind.

HE (*interested*): Go on.

SHE: No, you – you go on – you've made me talk about myself. That's against the rules.

HE: Rules?

SHE: My own rules – but you – Oh, Amory, I hear you're brilliant. The family expects *so* much of you.

HE: How encouraging!

SHE: Alec said you'd taught him to think. Did you? I didn't believe anyone could.

HE: No. I'm really quite dull.

(*He evidently doesn't intend this to be taken seriously.*)

SHE: Liar.

HE: I'm – I'm religious – I'm literary. I've – I've even written poems.

SHE: *Vers libre* – splendid! (*She declaims.*)

> The trees are green,
> The birds are singing in the trees,
> The girl sips her poison,
> The bird flies away the girl dies.

HE (*laughing*): No, not that kind.

SHE: (*suddenly*): I like you.

HE: Don't.

SHE: Modest too –

HE: I'm afraid of you. I'm always afraid of a girl – until I've kissed her.

SHE (*emphatically*): My dear boy, the war is over.

HE: So I'll always be afraid of you.

SHE (*rather sadly*): I suppose you will.

(*a slight hesitation on both their parts*)

HE (*after due consideration*): Listen. This is a frightful thing to ask.

SHE (*knowing what's coming*): After five minutes.

HE: But will you – kiss me? Or are you afraid?

SHE: I'm never afraid – but your reasons are so poor.

HE: Rosalind, I really *want* to kiss you.

SHE: So do I.

(*They kiss – definitely and thoroughly.*)

HE (*after a breathless second*): Well, is your curiosity satisfied?

SHE: Is yours?

HE: No, it's only aroused.

(*He looks it.*)

SHE (*dreamily*): I've kissed dozens of men. I suppose I'll kiss dozens more.

HE (*abstractedly*): Yes, I suppose you could – like that.

SHE: Most people like the way I kiss.

HE (*remembering himself*): Good Lord, yes. Kiss me once more, Rosalind.

SHE: No – my curiosity is generally satisfied at one.

HE: (*discouraged*): Is that a rule?

SHE: I make rules to fit the cases.

HE: You and I are somewhat alike – except that I'm years older in experience.

SHE: How old are you?

HE: Almost twenty-three. You?

SHE: Nineteen – just.

HE: I suppose you're the product of a fashionable school.

SHE: No – I'm fairly raw material. I was expelled from Spence[114] – I've forgotten why.

HE: What's your general trend?

SHE: Oh, I'm bright, quite selfish, emotional when aroused, fond of admiration –

HE (*suddenly*): I don't want to fall in love with you –

SHE (*raising her eyebrows*): Nobody asked you to.

HE (*continuing coldly*): But I probably will. I love your mouth.

SHE: Hush! Please don't fall in love with my mouth – hair, eyes, shoulders, slippers – but *not* my mouth. Everybody falls in love with my mouth.

HE: It's quite beautiful.

SHE: It's too small.

HE: No it isn't – let's see.

(*He kisses her again with the same thoroughness.*)

SHE (*rather moved*): Say something sweet.

HE (*frightened*): Lord help me.

SHE (*drawing away*): Well, don't – if it's so hard.

HE: Shall we pretend? So soon?

SHE: We haven't the same standards of time as other people.

HE: Already it's – other people.

SHE: Let's pretend.

HE: No – I can't – it's sentiment.

SHE: You're not sentimental?

HE: No, I'm romantic – a sentimental person thinks things will last – a romantic person hopes against hope that they won't. Sentiment is emotional.

SHE: And you're not? (*with her eyes half-closed*) You probably flatter yourself that that's a superior attitude.

HE: Well – Rosalind, Rosalind, don't argue – kiss me again.

SHE (*quite chilly now*): No – I have no desire to kiss you.

HE (*openly taken aback*): You wanted to kiss me a minute ago.

SHE: This is now.

HE: I'd better go.

SHE: I suppose so.

(*He goes towards the door.*)

SHE: Oh!

(*He turns.*)

SHE (*laughing*): Score – Home Team: One hundred; Opponents: Zero.

(*He starts back.*)

SHE (*quickly*): Rain – no game.

(*He goes out. She goes quietly to the chiffonier, takes out a cigarette-case and hides it in the side drawer of a desk. Her mother enters, notebook in hand.*)

MRS CONNAGE: Good – I've been wanting to speak to you alone before we go downstairs.

ROSALIND: Heavens! you frighten me!

MRS CONNAGE: Rosalind, you've been a very expensive proposition.

ROSALIND (*resignedly*): Yes.

MRS CONNAGE: And you know your father hasn't what he once had.

ROSALIND (*making a wry face*): Oh, please don't talk about money.

MRS CONNAGE: You can't do anything without it. This is our last year in this house – and unless things change Cecelia won't have the advantages you've had.

ROSALIND (*impatiently*): Well – what is it?

MRS CONNAGE: So I ask you to please mind me in several things I've put down in my notebook. The first one is: don't disappear with young men. There may be a time when it's valuable, but at present I want you on the dance-floor where I can find you. There are certain men I want to have you meet and I don't like finding you in some corner of the conservatory exchanging silliness with any-one – or listening to it.

ROSALIND (*sarcastically*): Yes, listening to it *is* better.

MRS CONNAGE: And don't waste a lot of time with the college set – little boys nineteen and twenty years old. I don't mind a prom or a football game, but staying away from advantageous parties to eat in little cafés downtown with Tom, Dick and Harry –

ROSALIND (*offering her code, which is, in its way, quite as high as her mother's*): Mother, it's done – you can't run everything now the way you did in the early nineties.

MRS CONNAGE (*paying no attention*): There are several bachelor friends of your father's that I want you to meet tonight – youngish men.

ROSALIND (*nodding wisely*): About forty-five?

MRS CONNAGE (*sharply*): Why not?

ROSALIND: Oh, *quite* all right – they know life and are so adorably tired looking (*shakes her head*) – but they *will* dance.

MRS CONNAGE: I haven't met Mr Blaine – but I don't think you'll care for him. He doesn't sound like a money-maker.

ROSALIND: Mother, I never *think* about money.

MRS CONNAGE: You never keep it long enough to think about it.

ROSALIND (*sighs*): Yes, I suppose someday I'll marry a ton of it – out of sheer boredom.

MRS CONNAGE (*referring to notebook*): I had a wire from Hartford. Dawson Ryder is coming up. Now there's a young man I like, and he's floating in money. It seems to me that since you seem tired of Howard Gillespie you might give Mr Ryder some encouragement. This is the third time he's been up in a month.

ROSALIND: How did you know I was tired of Howard Gillespie?

MRS CONNAGE: The poor boy looks so miserable every time he comes.

ROSALIND: That was one of those romantic, pre-battle affairs. They're all wrong.

MRS CONNAGE (*having said her say*): At any rate, make us proud of you tonight.

ROSALIND: Don't you think I'm beautiful?

MRS CONNAGE: You know you are.

(*From downstairs is heard the moan of a violin being tuned, the roll of a drum.* MRS CONNAGE *turns quickly to her daughter.*)

MRS CONNAGE: Come!

ROSALIND: One minute!

(*Her mother leaves.* ROSALIND *goes to the glass where she gazes at herself with great satisfaction. She kisses her hand and touches her mirrored mouth with it. Then she turns out the lights and leaves the room. Silence for a moment. A few chords from the piano, the discreet patter of faint drums, the rustle of new silk, all blend on the staircase outside and drift in through the partly opened door. Bundled figures pass in the lighted hall. The laughter heard below becomes doubled and multiplied. Then someone comes in, closes the door, and switches on the lights. It is* CECILIA. *She goes to the chiffonier, looks in the drawers, hesitates – then to the desk whence she takes the cigarette-case and extracts one. She lights it and then, puffing and blowing, walks towards the mirror.*)

CECILIA (*in tremendously sophisticated accents*): Oh, yes, coming out is *such* a farce nowadays, you know. One really plays around so much before one is seventeen that it's positively an anticlimax. (*She shakes hands with a visionary middle-aged nobleman.*) Yes, your grace – I b'lieve I've heard my sister speak of you. Have a puff – they're very good. They're – they're Coronas.[115] You don't smoke? What a pity! The king doesn't allow it, I suppose. Yes, I'll dance.

(*So she dances around the room to a tune from downstairs, her arms outstretched to an imaginary partner, the cigarette waving in her hand.*)

The corner of a den downstairs, filled by a very comfortable leather lounge. A small light is on each side above, and in the middle, over the couch hangs a painting of a very old, very dignified gentleman, period 1860. Outside the music is heard in a fox-trot.

ROSALIND *is seated on the lounge and on her left is* HOWARD GILLESPIE, *a vapid youth of about twenty-four. He is obviously very unhappy, and she is quite bored.*

GILLESPIE (*feebly*): What do you mean I've changed. I feel the same towards you.

ROSALIND: But you don't look the same to me.

GILLESPIE: Three weeks ago you used to say that you liked me because I was so blasé, so indifferent – I still am.

ROSALIND: But not about me. I used to like you because you had brown eyes and thin legs.

GILLESPIE (*helplessly*): They're still thin and brown. You're a vampire, that's all.

ROSALIND: The only thing I know about vamping is what's on the piano score. What confuses men is that I'm perfectly natural. I used to think you were never jealous. Now you follow me with your eyes wherever I go.

GILLESPIE: I love you.

ROSALIND (*coldly*): I know it.

GILLESPIE: And you haven't kissed me for two weeks. I had an idea that after a girl was kissed she was – was – won.

ROSALIND: Those days are over. I have to be won all over again every time you see me.

GILLESPIE: Are you serious?

ROSALIND: About as usual. There used to be two kinds of kisses: first when girls were kissed and deserted; second, when they were engaged. Now there's a third kind, where the man is kissed and deserted. If Mr Jones of the nineties bragged he'd kissed a girl, everyone knew he was through with her. If Mr Jones of 1919 brags the same everyone knows it's because he can't kiss her any more. Given a decent start any girl can beat a man nowadays.

GILLESPIE: Then why do you play with men?

ROSALIND (*leaning forward confidentially*): For that first moment, when he's interested. There is a moment – oh, just before the first kiss, a whispered word – something that makes it worth while.

GILLESPIE: And then?

ROSALIND: Then after that you make him talk about himself. Pretty soon he thinks of nothing but being alone with you – he sulks, he won't fight, he doesn't want to play – Victory!

(*Enter* DAWSON RYDER, *twenty-six, handsome, wealthy, faithful to his own; a bore perhaps, but steady and sure of success.*)

RYDER: I believe this is my dance, Rosalind.

ROSALIND: Well, Dawson, so you recognise me. Now I know I haven't got too much paint on. Mr Ryder, this is Mr Gillespie.

(*They shake hands and* GILLESPIE *leaves, tremendously downcast.*)

RYDER: Your party is certainly a success.

ROSALIND: Is it – I haven't seen it lately. I'm weary – Do you mind sitting out a minute?

RYDER: Mind – I'm delighted. You know I loathe this 'rushing' idea. See a girl yesterday, today, tomorrow.

ROSALIND: Dawson!

RYDER: What?

ROSALIND: I wonder if you know you love me.

RYDER (*startled*): What? Oh – you know you're remarkable!

ROSALIND: Because you know I'm an awful proposition. Anyone who marries me will have his hands full. I'm mean – mighty mean.

RYDER: Oh, I wouldn't say that.

ROSALIND: Oh, yes, I am – especially to the people nearest to me. (*She rises.*) Come, let's go. I've changed my mind and I want to dance. Mother is probably having a fit.

(*Exeunt. Enter* ALEC *and* CECILIA.)

CECILIA: Just my luck to get my own brother for an intermission.

ALEC (*gloomily*): I'll go if you want me to.

CECILIA: Good heavens, no – with whom would I begin the next dance? (*sighs*) There's no colour in a dance since the French officers went back.[116]

ALEC (*thoughtfully*): I don't want Amory to fall in love with Rosalind.

CECILIA: Why, I had an idea that that was just what you did want.

ALEC: I did, but since seeing these girls – I don't know. I'm awfully attached to Amory. He's sensitive and I don't want him to break his heart over somebody who doesn't care about him.

CECILIA: He's very good looking.

ALEC (*still thoughtfully*): She won't marry him, but a girl doesn't have to marry a man to break his heart.

CECILIA: What does it? I wish I knew the secret.

ALEC: Why, you cold-blooded little kitty. It's lucky for some that the Lord gave you a pug nose.

(*Enter* MRS CONNAGE.)

MRS CONNAGE: Where on earth is Rosalind?

ALEC (*brilliantly*): Of course you've come to the best people to find out. She'd naturally be with us.

MRS CONNAGE: Her father has marshalled eight bachelor millionaires to meet her.

ALEC: You might form a squad and march through the halls.

MRS CONNAGE: I'm perfectly serious – for all I know she may be at the Cocoanut Grove[117] with some football player on the night of her début. You look left and I'll –

ALEC (*flippantly*): Hadn't you better send the butler through the cellar?

MRS CONNAGE (*perfectly serious*): Oh, you don't think she'd be there?

CECILIA: He's only joking, mother.

ALEC: Mother had a picture of her tapping a keg of beer with some high hurdler.

MRS CONNAGE: Let's look right away.

(*They go out.* ROSALIND *comes in with* GILLESPIE.)

GILLESPIE: Rosalind – Once more I ask you. Don't you care a blessed thing about me?

(AMORY *walks in briskly.*)

AMORY: My dance.

ROSALIND : Mr Gillespie, this is Mr Blaine.

GILLESPIE: I've met Mr Blaine. From Lake Geneva, aren't you?

AMORY: Yes.

GILLESPIE (*desperately*): I've been there. It's in the – the Middle West, isn't it?

AMORY (*spicily*): Approximately. But I always felt that I'd rather be provincial hot-tamale than soup without seasoning.

GILLESPIE: What!

AMORY: Oh, no offence.

(GILLESPIE *bows and leaves.*)

ROSALIND: He's too much *people*.

AMORY: I was in love with a *people* once.

ROSALIND: So?

AMORY: Oh, yes – her name was Isabelle – nothing at all to her except what I read into her.

ROSALIND: What happened?

AMORY: Finally I convinced her that she was smarter than I was – then she threw me over. Said I was critical and impractical, you know.

ROSALIND: What do you mean impractical?

AMORY: Oh – drive a car, but can't change a tyre.

ROSALIND: What are you going to do?

AMORY: Can't say – run for President, write –

ROSALIND: Greenwich Village?

AMORY: Good heavens, no – I said write – not drink.

ROSALIND: I like businessmen. Clever men are usually so homely.

AMORY: I feel as if I'd known you for ages.

ROSALIND: Oh, are you going to commence the 'pyramid' story?

AMORY: No – I was going to make it French. I was Louis XIV and you were one of my – my – (*changing his tone*) Suppose – we fell in love.

ROSALIND: I've suggested pretending.

AMORY: If we did it would be very big.

ROSALIND: Why?

AMORY: Because selfish people are in a way terribly capable of great loves.

ROSALIND (*turning her lips up*): Pretend.
   (*Very deliberately they kiss.*)

AMORY: I can't say sweet things. But you *are* beautiful.

ROSALIND: Not that.

AMORY: What then?

ROSALIND (*sadly*): Oh, nothing – only I want sentiment, real sentiment – and I never find it.

AMORY: I never find anything else in the world – and I loathe it.

ROSALIND: It's so hard to find a male to gratify one's artistic taste.
   (*Someone has opened a door and the music of a waltz surges into the room.* ROSALIND *rises.*)

ROSALIND: Listen! they're playing 'Kiss Me Again'.[118]
   (*He looks at her.*)

AMORY: Well?

ROSALIND: Well?

AMORY (*softly – the battle lost*): I love you.

ROSALIND: I love you – now.
   (*They kiss.*)

AMORY: Oh, God, what have I done?

ROSALIND: Nothing. Oh, don't talk. Kiss me again.

AMORY: I don't know why or how, but I love you – from the moment I saw you.

ROSALIND: Me too – I – I – oh, tonight's tonight.
   (*Her brother strolls in, starts and then in a loud voice says:* 'Oh, excuse me,' *and goes.*)

ROSALIND (*her lips scarcely stirring*): Don't let me go – I don't care who knows what I do.

AMORY: Say it!

ROSALIND: I love you – now. (*They part.*) Oh – I am very youthful, thank God – and rather beautiful, thank God – and happy, thank God, thank God – (*She pauses and then, in an odd burst of prophecy, adds*) Poor Amory!

(*He kisses her again.*)

KISMET

Within two weeks Amory and Rosalind were deeply and passionately in love. The critical qualities which had spoiled for each of them a dozen romances were dulled by the great wave of emotion that washed over them.

'It may be an insane love-affair,' she told her anxious mother, 'but it's not inane.'

The wave swept Amory into an advertising agency early in March, where he alternated between astonishing bursts of rather exceptional work and wild dreams of becoming suddenly rich and touring Italy with Rosalind.

They were together constantly, for lunch, for dinner, and nearly every evening – always in a sort of breathless hush, as if they feared that any minute the spell would break and drop them out of this paradise of rose and flame. But the spell became a trance, seemed to increase from day to day; they began to talk of marrying in July – in June. All life was transmitted into terms of their love, all experience, all desires, all ambitions, were nullified – their senses of humour crawled into corners to sleep; their former love-affairs seemed faintly laughable and scarcely regretted juvenilia.

For the second time in his life Amory had had a complete boule-versement and was hurrying into line with his generation.

A LITTLE INTERLUDE

Amory wandered slowly up the avenue and thought of the night as inevitably his – the pageantry and carnival of rich dusk and dim streets . . . it seemed that he had closed the book of fading harmonies at last and stepped into the sensuous vibrant walks of life. Everywhere these countless lights, this promise of a night of streets and singing – he moved in a half-dream through the crowd as if expecting to meet

Rosalind hurrying towards him with eager feet from every corner . . . How the unforgettable faces of dusk would blend to her, the myriad footsteps, a thousand overtures, would blend to her footsteps; and there would be more drunkenness than wine in the softness of her eyes on his. Even his dreams now were faint violins drifting like summer sounds upon the summer air.

The room was in darkness except for the faint glow of Tom's cigarette where he lounged by the open window. As the door shut behind him, Amory stood a moment with his back against it.

'Hello, Benvenuto Blaine.[119] How went the advertising business today?'

Amory sprawled on a couch.

'I loathed it as usual!' The momentary vision of the bustling agency was displaced quickly by another picture. 'My God! She's wonderful!'

Tom sighed.

'I can't tell you,' repeated Amory, 'just how wonderful she is. I don't want you to know. I don't want anyone to know.'

Another sigh came from the window – quite a resigned sigh.

'She's life and hope and happiness, my whole world now.'

He felt the quiver of a tear on his eyelid.

'Oh, *golly*, Tom!'

BITTER SWEET

'Sit like we do,' she whispered.

He sat in the big chair and held out his arms so that she could nestle inside them.

'I knew you'd come tonight,' she said softly, 'like summer, just when I needed you most . . . darling . . . darling . . . '

His lips moved lazily over her face.

'You *taste* so good,' he sighed.

'How do you mean, lover?'

'Oh, just sweet, just sweet . . . ' he held her closer.

'Amory,' she whispered, 'when you're ready for me I'll marry you.'

'We won't have much at first.'

'Don't!' she cried. 'It hurts when you reproach yourself for what you can't give me. I've got your precious self – and that's enough for me.'

'Tell me . . . '

'You know, don't you? Oh, you know.'

'Yes, but I want to hear you say it.'

'I love you, Amory, with all my heart.'

'Always, will you?'

'All my life – Oh, Amory – '

'What?'

'I want to belong to you. I want your people to be my people. I want to have your babies.'

'But I haven't any people.'

'Don't laugh at me, Amory. Just kiss me.'

'I'll do what you want,' he said.

'No, I'll do what *you* want. We're *you* – not me. Oh, you're so much a part, so much all of me . . . '

He closed his eyes.

'I'm so happy that I'm frightened. Wouldn't it be awful if this was – was the high point? . . . '

She looked at him dreamily.

'Beauty and love pass, I know . . . Oh, there's sadness, too. I suppose all great happiness is a little sad. Beauty means the scent of roses and then the death of roses – '

'Beauty means the agony of sacrifice and the end of agony . . . '

'And, Amory, we're beautiful, I know. I'm sure God loves us – '

'He loves you. You're his most precious possession.'

'I'm not his, I'm yours. Amory, I belong to you. For the first time I regret all the other kisses; now I know how much a kiss can mean.'

Then they would smoke and he would tell her about his day at the office – and where they might live. Sometimes, when he was particularly loquacious, she went to sleep in his arms, but he loved that Rosalind – all Rosalinds – as he had never in the world loved anyone else. Intangibly fleeting, unrememberable hours.

AQUATIC INCIDENT

One day Amory and Howard Gillespie meeting by accident downtown took lunch together, and Amory heard a story that delighted him. Gillespie after several cocktails was in a talkative mood; he began by telling Amory that he was sure Rosalind was slightly eccentric.

He had gone with her on a swimming party up in Westchester County, and someone mentioned that Annette Kellerman[120] had been there one day on a visit and had dived from the top of a rickety, thirty-foot summer-house. Immediately Rosalind insisted that Howard should climb up with her to see what it looked like.

A minute later, as he sat and dangled his feet on the edge, a form shot by him; Rosalind, her arms spread in a beautiful swan dive, had sailed through the air into the clear water.

'Of course, *I* had to go, after that – and I nearly killed myself. I thought I was pretty good to even try it. Nobody else in the party tried it. Well, afterwards Rosalind had the nerve to ask me why I stooped over when I dived. "It didn't make it any easier," she said, "it just took all the courage out of it." I ask you, what can a man do with a girl like that? Unnecessary, I call it.'

Gillespie failed to understand why Amory was smiling delightedly all through lunch. He thought perhaps he was one of these hollow optimists.

FIVE WEEKS LATER

Again the library of the Connage house.

(ROSALIND *is alone, sitting on the lounge staring very moodily and unhappily at nothing. She has changed perceptibly – she is a trifle thinner for one thing; the light in her eyes is not so bright; she looks easily a year older. Her mother comes in, muffled in an opera-cloak. She takes in* ROSALIND *with a nervous glance.*)

MRS CONNAGE: Who is coming tonight?

(ROSALIND *fails to hear her, at least takes no notice.*)

MRS CONNAGE: Alec is coming up to take me to this Barrie play, *Et tu, Brutus.*[121] (*She perceives that she is talking to herself.*) Rosalind! I asked you who is coming tonight?

ROSALIND (*starting*): Oh – what – oh – Amory –

MRS CONNAGE (*sarcastically*): You have so *many* admirers lately that I couldn't imagine *which* one. (ROSALIND *doesn't answer.*) Dawson Ryder is more patient than I thought he'd be. You haven't given him an evening this week.

ROSALIND (*with a very weary expression that is quite new to her face*): Mother – please –

MRS CONNAGE: Oh, *I* won't interfere. You've already wasted over two months on a theoretical genius who hasn't a penny to his name, but *go* ahead, waste your life on him. *I* won't interfere.

ROSALIND (*as if repeating a tiresome lesson*): You know he has a little income – and you know he's earning thirty-five dollars a week in advertising –

MRS CONNAGE: And it wouldn't buy your clothes. (*She pauses but* ROSALIND *makes no reply.*) I have your best interests at heart when

I tell you not to take a step you'll spend your days regretting. It's not as if your father could help you. Things have been hard for him lately and he's an old man. You'd be dependent absolutely on a dreamer, a nice, well-born boy, but a dreamer – merely *clever*. (*She implies that this quality in itself is rather vicious.*)

ROSALIND: For heaven's sake, mother –

(*A maid appears, announces Mr Blaine who follows immediately. AMORY's friends have been telling him for ten days that he 'looks like the wrath of God', and he does. As a matter of fact he has not been able to eat a mouthful in the last thirty-six hours.*)

AMORY: Good-evening, Mrs Connage.

MRS CONNAGE (*not unkindly*): Good-evening, Amory.

(*AMORY and ROSALIND exchange glances – and ALEC comes in. ALEC's attitude throughout has been neutral. He believes in his heart that the marriage would make AMORY mediocre and ROSALIND miserable, but he feels a great sympathy for both of them.*)

ALEC: Hi, Amory!

AMORY: Hi, Alec! Tom said he'd meet you at the theatre.

ALEC: Yeah, just saw him. How's the advertising today? Write some brilliant copy?

AMORY: Oh, it's about the same. I got a rise – (*Everyone looks at him rather eagerly*) – of two dollars a week. (*general collapse*)

MRS CONNAGE: Come, Alec, I hear the car.

(*A good-night, rather chilly in sections. After MRS CONNAGE and ALEC go out there is a pause. ROSALIND still stares moodily at the fireplace. AMORY goes to her and puts his arm around her.*)

AMORY: Darling girl.

(*They kiss. Another pause and then she seizes his hand, covers it with kisses and holds it to her breast.*)

ROSALIND (*sadly*): I love your hands, more than anything. I see them often when you're away from me – so tired; I know every line of them. Dear hands!

(*Their eyes meet for a second and then she begins to cry – a tearless sobbing.*)

AMORY: Rosalind!

ROSALIND: Oh, we're so darned pitiful!

AMORY: Rosalind!

ROSALIND: Oh, I want to die!

AMORY: Rosalind, another night of this and I'll go to pieces. You've been this way four days now. You've got to be more encouraging or I can't work or eat or sleep. (*He looks around helplessly as if searching for new words to clothe an old, shopworn phrase.*) We'll have to make a start. I *like* having to make a start together. (*His forced hopefulness fades as he sees her unresponsive.*) What's the matter? (*He gets up suddenly and starts to pace the floor.*) It's Dawson Ryder, that's what it is. He's been working on your nerves. You've been with him every afternoon for a week. People come and tell me they've seen you together, and I have to smile and nod and pretend it hasn't the slightest significance for me. And you won't tell me anything as it develops.

ROSALIND: Amory, if you don't sit down I'll scream.

AMORY (*sitting down suddenly beside her*): Oh, Lord.

ROSALIND (*taking his hand gently*): You know I love you, don't you?

AMORY: Yes.

ROSALIND: You know I'll always love you –

AMORY: Don't talk that way; you frighten me. It sounds as if we weren't going to have each other. (*She cries a little and rising from the couch goes to the armchair.*) I've felt all afternoon that things were worse. I nearly went wild down at the office – couldn't write a line. Tell me everything.

ROSALIND: There's nothing to tell, I say. I'm just nervous.

AMORY: Rosalind, you're playing with the idea of marrying Dawson Ryder.

ROSALIND (*after a pause*): He's been asking me to all day.

AMORY: Well, he's got his nerve!

ROSALIND (*after another pause*): I like him.

AMORY: Don't say that. It hurts me.

ROSALIND: Don't be a silly idiot. You know you're the only man I've ever loved, ever will love.

AMORY (*quickly*): Rosalind, let's get married – next week.

ROSALIND: We can't.

AMORY: Why not?

ROSALIND: Oh, we can't. I'd be your squaw – in some horrible place.

AMORY: We'll have two hundred and seventy-five dollars a month all told.

ROSALIND: Darling, I don't even do my own hair, usually.

AMORY: I'll do it for you.

ROSALIND (*between a laugh and a sob*): Thanks.

AMORY: Rosalind, you *can't* be thinking of marrying someone else. Tell me! You leave me in the dark. I can help you fight it out if you'll only tell me.

ROSALIND: It's just – us. We're pitiful, that's all. The very qualities I love you for are the ones that will always make you a failure.

AMORY (*grimly*): Go on.

ROSALIND: Oh – it *is* Dawson Ryder. He's so reliable, I almost feel that he'd be a – a background.

AMORY: You don't love him.

ROSALIND: I know, but I respect him, and he's a good man and a strong one.

AMORY (*grudgingly*): Yes – he's that.

ROSALIND: Well – here's one little thing. There was a little poor boy we met in Rye on Tuesday afternoon – and, oh, Dawson took him on his lap and talked to him and promised him an Indian suit – and next day he remembered and bought it – and, oh, it was so sweet and I couldn't help thinking he'd be so nice to – to our children – take care of them – and I wouldn't have to worry.

AMORY (*in despair*): Rosalind! Rosalind!

ROSALIND (*with a faint roguishness*): Don't look so consciously suffering.

AMORY: What power we have of hurting each other!

ROSALIND (*commencing to sob again*): It's been so perfect – you and I. So like a dream that I'd longed for and never thought I'd find. The first real unselfishness I've ever felt in my life. And I can't see it fade out in a colourless atmosphere!

AMORY: It won't – it won't!

ROSALIND: I'd rather keep it as a beautiful memory – tucked away in my heart.

AMORY: Yes, women can do that – but not men. I'd remember always, not the beauty of it while it lasted, but just the bitterness, the long bitterness.

ROSALIND: Don't!

AMORY: All the years never to see you, never to kiss you, just a gate shut and barred – you don't dare be my wife.

ROSALIND: No – no – I'm taking the hardest course, the strongest course. Marrying you would be a failure and I never fail – if you don't stop walking up and down I'll scream!

(*Again he sinks despairingly on to the lounge.*)

AMORY: Come over here and kiss me.

ROSALIND: No.

AMORY: Don't you *want* to kiss me?

ROSALIND: Tonight I want you to love me calmly and coolly.

AMORY: The beginning of the end.

ROSALIND (*with a burst of insight*): Amory, you're young. I'm young. People excuse us now for our poses and vanities, for treating people like Sancho[122] and yet getting away with it. They excuse us now. But you've got a lot of knocks coming to you –

AMORY: And you're afraid to take them with me.

ROSALIND: No, not that. There was a poem I read somewhere – you'll say Ella Wheeler Wilcox[123] and laugh – but listen:

> For this is wisdom – to love and live,
> To take what fate or the gods may give,
> To ask no question, to make no prayer,
> To kiss the lips and caress the hair,
> Speed passion's ebb as we greet its flow,
> To have and to hold and in time – let go.[124]

AMORY: But we haven't had.

ROSALIND: Amory, I'm yours – you know it. There have been times in the last month I'd have been completely yours if you'd said so. But I can't marry you and ruin both our lives.

AMORY: We've got to take our chance for happiness.

ROSALIND: Dawson says I'd learn to love him.

(AMORY *with his head sunk in his hands does not move. The life seems suddenly gone out of him.*)

ROSALIND: Lover! Lover! I can't do with you, and I can't imagine life without you.

AMORY: Rosalind, we're on each other's nerves. It's just that we're both high-strung, and this week –

(*His voice is curiously old. She crosses to him and taking his face in her hands, kisses him.*)

ROSALIND: I can't, Amory. I can't be shut away from the trees and flowers, cooped up in a little flat, waiting for you. You'd hate me in a narrow atmosphere. I'd make you hate me.

(*Again she is blinded by sudden uncontrolled tears.*)

AMORY: Rosalind –

ROSALIND: Oh, darling, go – Don't make it harder! I can't stand it –

AMORY (*his face drawn, his voice strained*): Do you know what you're saying? Do you mean for ever?

(*There is a difference somehow in the quality of their suffering.*)

ROSALIND: Can't you see –

AMORY: I'm afraid I can't if you love me. You're afraid of taking two years' knocks with me.

ROSALIND: I wouldn't be the Rosalind you love.

AMORY (*a little hysterically*): I can't give you up! I can't, that's all! I've got to have you!

ROSALIND (*a hard note in her voice*): You're being a baby now.

AMORY (*wildly*): I don't care! You're spoiling our lives!

ROSALIND: I'm doing the wise thing, the only thing.

AMORY: Are you going to marry Dawson Ryder?

ROSALIND: Oh, don't ask me. You know I'm old in some ways – in others – well, I'm just a little girl. I like sunshine and pretty things and cheerfulness – and I dread responsibility. I don't want to think about pots and kitchens and brooms. I want to worry whether my legs will get slick and brown when I swim in the summer.

AMORY: And you love me.

ROSALIND: That's just why it has to end. Drifting hurts too much. We can't have any more scenes like this.

(*She draws his ring from her finger and hands it to him. Their eyes are blind again with tears.*)

AMORY (*his lips against her wet cheek*): Don't! Keep it, please – oh, don't break my heart!

(*She presses the ring softly into his hand.*)

ROSALIND (*brokenly*): You'd better go.

AMORY: Goodbye –

(*She looks at him once more, with infinite longing, infinite sadness.*)

ROSALIND: Don't ever forget me, Amory –

AMORY: Goodbye –

(*He goes to the door, fumbles for the knob, finds it – she sees him throw back his head – and he is gone. Gone – she half starts from the lounge and then sinks forward on her face into the pillows.*)

ROSALIND: Oh, God, I want to die! (*After a moment she rises and with her eyes closed feels her way to the door. Then she turns and looks once more at the room. Here they had sat and dreamed: that tray she had so often filled with matches for him; that shade that they had discreetly lowered one long Sunday afternoon. Misty-eyed she stands and remembers; she speaks aloud.*)

Oh, Amory, what have I done to you?

(*And deep under the aching sadness that will pass in time, Rosalind feels that she has lost something, she knows not what, she knows not why.*)

CHAPTER 2

Experiments in Convalescence

The Knickerbocker Bar, beamed upon by Maxfield Parrish's jovial, colourful *Old King Cole*, was well crowded. Amory stopped in the entrance and looked at his wristwatch; he wanted particularly to know the time, for something in his mind that catalogued and classified liked to chip things off cleanly. Later it would satisfy him in a vague way to be able to think, 'That thing ended at exactly twenty minutes after eight on Thursday, June 10, 1919.' This was allowing for the walk from her house – a walk concerning which he had afterwards not the faintest recollection.

He was in rather grotesque condition: two days of worry and nervousness, of sleepless nights, of untouched meals, culminating in the emotional crisis and Rosalind's abrupt decision – the strain of it had drugged the foreground of his mind into a merciful coma. As he fumbled clumsily with the olives at the free-lunch table, a man approached and spoke to him, and the olives dropped from his nervous hands.

'Well, Amory . . . '

It was someone he had known at Princeton; he had no idea of the name.

'Hello, old boy – ' he heard himself saying.

'Name's Jim Wilson – you've forgotten.'

'Sure, you bet, Jim. I remember.'

'Going to reunion?'

'You know!' Simultaneously he realised that he was not going to reunion.

'Get overseas?'

Amory nodded, his eyes staring oddly. Stepping back to let someone pass, he knocked the dish of olives to a crash on the floor. 'Too bad,' he muttered. 'Have a drink?'

Wilson, ponderously diplomatic, reached over and slapped him on the back. 'You've had plenty, old boy.'

Amory eyed him dumbly until Wilson grew embarrassed under the scrutiny.

'Plenty, hell!' said Amory finally. 'I haven't had a drink today.'

Wilson looked incredulous.

'Have a drink or not?' cried Amory rudely.

Together they sought the bar.

'Rye high.'

'I'll just take a Bronx.'[125]

Wilson had another; Amory had several more. They decided to sit down. At ten o'clock Wilson was displaced by Carling, class of '15. Amory, his head spinning gorgeously, layer upon layer of soft satisfaction setting over the bruised spots of his spirit, was discoursing volubly on the war.

' 'S a mental was'e,' he insisted with owl-like wisdom. 'Two years my life spent inalleshual vacuity. Los' idealism, got be physcal anmal,' he shook his fist expressively at Old King Cole, 'got be Prussian 'bout ev'thing, women 'specially. Use' be straight 'bout women college. Now don'givadam.' He expressed his lack of principle by sweeping a seltzer bottle with a broad gesture to noisy extinction on the floor, but this did not interrupt his speech. 'Seek pleasure where find it for tomorrow die. 'At's philos'phy for me now on.'

Carling yawned, but Amory, waxing brilliant, continued: 'Use' wonder 'bout things – people satisfied compromise, fif'y-fif'y att'tude on life. Now don' wonder, don' wonder – ' He became so emphatic in impressing on Carling the fact that he didn't wonder that he lost the thread of his discourse and concluded by announcing to the bar at large that he was a 'physcal anmal'.

'What are you celebrating, Amory?'

Amory leaned forward confidentially.

'Cel'brating blowmylife. Great moment blow my life. Can't tell you 'bout it – '

He heard Carling addressing a remark to the bartender: 'Give him a bromo-seltzer.'

Amory shook his head indignantly.

'None that stuff!'

'But listen, Amory, you're making yourself sick. You're white as a ghost.'

Amory considered the question. He tried to look at himself in the mirror but even by squinting up one eye could only see as far as the row of bottles behind the bar.

'Like som'n solid. We go get some – some salad.'

He settled his coat with an attempt at nonchalance, but letting go of the bar was too much for him, and he slumped against a chair.

'We'll go over to Shanley's,' suggested Carling, offering an elbow.

With this assistance Amory managed to get his legs in motion enough to propel him across Forty-Second Street.

Shanley's was very dim. He was conscious that he was talking in a loud voice, very succinctly and convincingly, he thought, about a desire to crush people under his heel. He consumed three club sandwiches, devouring each as though it were no larger than a chocolate-drop. Then Rosalind began popping into his mind again, and he found his lips forming her name over and over. Next he was sleepy, and he had a hazy, listless sense of people in dress suits, probably waiters, gathering around the table . . .

. . . He was in a room and Carling was saying something about a knot in his shoelace.

'Nemmine,' he managed to articulate drowsily. 'Sleep in 'em . . . '

STILL ALCOHOLIC

He awoke laughing and his eyes lazily roamed his surroundings, evidently a bedroom and bath in a good hotel. His head was whirring and picture after picture was forming and blurring and melting before his eyes, but beyond the desire to laugh he had no entirely conscious reaction. He reached for the phone beside his bed.

'Hello – what hotel is this – ? Knickerbocker? All right, send up two rye highballs – '

He lay for a moment and wondered idly whether they'd send up a bottle or just two of those little glass containers. Then, with an effort, he struggled out of bed and ambled into the bathroom.

When he emerged, rubbing himself lazily with a towel, he found the bar boy with the drinks and had a sudden desire to kid him. On reflection he decided that this would be undignified, so he waved him away.

As the new alcohol tumbled into his stomach and warmed him, the isolated pictures began slowly to form a cinema reel of the day before. Again he saw Rosalind curled weeping among the pillows, again he felt her tears against his cheek. Her words began ringing in his ears: 'Don't ever forget me, Amory – don't ever forget me – '

'Hell!' he faltered aloud, and then he choked and collapsed on the bed in a shaken spasm of grief. After a minute he opened his eyes and regarded the ceiling.

'Damned fool!' he exclaimed in disgust, and with a voluminous sigh rose and approached the bottle. After another glass he gave way loosely to the luxury of tears. Purposely he called up into his mind little incidents of the vanished spring, phrased to himself emotions that would make him react even more strongly to sorrow.

'We were so happy,' he intoned dramatically, 'so very happy.' Then he gave way again and knelt beside the bed, his head half-buried in the pillow.

'My own girl – my own – Oh – '

He clenched his teeth so that the tears streamed in a flood from his eyes.

'Oh . . . my baby girl, all I had, all I wanted! . . . Oh, my girl, come back, come back! I need you . . . need you . . . we're so pitiful . . . just misery we brought each other . . . She'll be shut away from me . . . I can't see her; I can't be her friend. It's got to be that way – it's got to be – '

And then again: 'We've been so happy, so very happy . . . '

He rose to his feet and threw himself on the bed in an ecstasy of sentiment, and then lay exhausted while he realised slowly that he had been very drunk the night before, and that his head was spinning again wildly. He laughed, rose, and crossed again to Lethe . . .

At noon he ran into a crowd in the Biltmore bar, and the riot began again. He had a vague recollection afterwards of discussing French poetry with a British officer who was introduced to him as 'Captain Corn, of His Majesty's Foot', and he remembered attempting to recite 'Clair de Lune'[126] at luncheon; then he slept in a big, soft chair until almost five o'clock when another crowd found and woke him; there followed an alcoholic dressing of several temperaments for the ordeal of dinner. They selected theatre tickets at Tyson's for a play that had a four-drink programme – a play with two monotonous voices, with turbid, gloomy scenes, and lighting effects that were hard to follow when his eyes behaved so amazingly. He imagined afterwards that it must have been *The Jest* . . .[127]

. . . Then the Cocoanut Grove, where Amory slept again on a little balcony outside. Out in Shanley's, Yonkers, he became almost logical, and by a careful control of the number of highballs he drank, grew quite lucid and garrulous. He found that the party consisted of five men, two of whom he knew slightly; he became righteous about paying his share of the expense and insisted in a loud voice on arranging everything then and there, to the amusement of the tables around him . . .

Someone mentioned that a famous cabaret star was at the next table, so Amory rose and, approaching gallantly, introduced himself . . . this involved him in an argument, first with her escort and then with the head waiter – Amory's attitude being a lofty and exaggerated courtesy . . . he consented, after being confronted with irrefutable logic, to being led back to his own table.

'Decided to commit suicide,' he announced suddenly.

'When? Next year?'

'Now. Tomorrow morning. Going to take a room at the Commodore, get into a hot bath and open a vein.'

'He's getting morbid!'

'You need another rye, old boy!'

'We'll all talk it over tomorrow.'

But Amory was not to be dissuaded, from argument at least.

'Did you ever get that way?' he demanded confidentially *fortaccio*.

'Sure!'

'Often?'

'My chronic state.'

This provoked discussion. One man said that he got so depressed sometimes that he seriously considered it. Another agreed that there was nothing to live for. 'Captain Corn', who had somehow rejoined the party, said that in his opinion it was when one's health was bad that one felt that way most. Amory's suggestion was that they should each order a Bronx, mix broken glass in it, and drink it off. To his relief no one applauded the idea, so having finished his highball, he balanced his chin in his hand and his elbow on the table – a most delicate, scarcely noticeable sleeping position, he assured himself – and went into a deep stupor . . .

He was awakened by a woman clinging to him, a pretty woman, with brown, disarranged hair and dark blue eyes.

'Take me home!' she cried.

'Hello!' said Amory, blinking.

'I like you,' she announced tenderly.

'I like you too.'

He noticed that there was a noisy man in the background and that one of his party was arguing with him.

'Fella I was with's a damn fool,' confided the blue-eyed woman. 'I hate him. I want to go home with you.'

'You drunk?' queried Amory with intense wisdom.

She nodded coyly.

'Go home with him,' he advised gravely. 'He brought you.'

At this point the noisy man in the background broke away from his detainers and approached.

'Say!' he said fiercely. 'I brought this girl out here and you're butting in!'

Amory regarded him coldly, while the girl clung to him closer.

'You let go that girl!' cried the noisy man.

Amory tried to make his eyes threatening.

'You go to hell!' he directed finally, and turned his attention to the girl. 'Love first sight,' he suggested.

'I love you,' she breathed and nestled close to him. She *did* have beautiful eyes.

Someone leaned over and spoke in Amory's ear.

'That's just Margaret Diamond. She's drunk and this fellow here brought her. Better let her go.'

'Let him take care of her, then!' shouted Amory furiously. 'I'm no WYCA worker, am I? – am I?'

'Let her go!'

'It's *her* hanging on, damn it! Let her hang!'

The crowd around the table thickened. For an instant a brawl threatened, but a sleek waiter bent back Margaret Diamond's fingers until she released her hold on Amory, whereupon she slapped the waiter furiously in the face and flung her arms about her raging original escort.

'Oh, Lord!' cried Amory.

'Let's go!'

'Come on, the taxis are getting scarce!'

'Check, waiter.'

'C'mon, Amory. Your romance is over.'

Amory laughed.

'You don't know how true you spoke. No idea. 'At's the whole trouble.'

AMORY ON THE LABOUR QUESTION

Two mornings later he knocked at the president's door at Bascome and Barlow's Advertising Agency.

'Come in!'

Amory entered unsteadily.

' 'Morning, Mr Barlow.'

Mr Barlow brought his glasses to the inspection and set his mouth slightly ajar that he might better listen.

'Well, Mr Blaine. We haven't seen you for several days.'

'No,' said Amory. 'I'm quitting.'

'Well – well – this is – '

'I don't like it here.'

'I'm sorry. I thought our relations had been quite – ah – pleasant. You seemed to be a hard worker – a little inclined perhaps to write fancy copy – '

'I just got tired of it,' interrupted Amory rudely. 'It didn't matter a damn to me whether Harebell's flour was any better than anyone else's. In fact, I never ate any of it. So I got tired of telling people about it – oh, I know I've been drinking – '

Mr Barlow's face steeled by several ingots of expression.

'You asked for a position – '

Amory waved him to silence.

'And I think I was rottenly underpaid. Thirty-five dollars a week – less than a good carpenter.'

'You had just started. You'd never worked before,' said Mr Barlow coolly.

'But it took about ten thousand dollars to educate me where I could write your darned stuff for you. Anyway, as far as length of service goes, you've got stenographers here you've paid fifteen a week for five years.'

'I'm not going to argue with you, sir,' said Mr Barlow rising.

'Neither am I. I just wanted to tell you I'm quitting.'

They stood for a moment looking at each other impassively and then Amory turned and left the office.

A LITTLE LULL

Four days after that he returned at last to the apartment. Tom was engaged on a book review for the *New Democracy* on the staff of which he was employed. They regarded each other for a moment in silence.

'Well?'

'Well?'

'Good Lord, Amory, where'd you get the black eye – and the jaw?'

Amory laughed.

'That's a mere nothing.'

He peeled off his coat and bared his shoulders.

'Look here!'

Tom emitted a low whistle.

'What hit you?'

Amory laughed again.

'Oh, a lot of people. I got beaten up. Fact.' He slowly replaced his shirt. 'It was bound to come sooner or later and I wouldn't have missed it for anything.'

'Who was it?'

'Well, there were some waiters and a couple of sailors and a few stray pedestrians, I guess. It's the strangest feeling. You ought to get beaten up just for the experience of it. You fall down after a while and everybody sort of slashes in at you before you hit the ground – then they kick you.'

Tom lighted a cigarette.

'I spent a day chasing you all over town, Amory. But you always kept a little ahead of me. I'd say you've been on some party.'

Amory tumbled into a chair and asked for a cigarette.

'You sober now?' asked Tom quizzically.

'Pretty sober. Why?'

'Well, Alec has left. His family had been after him to go home and live, so he – '

A spasm of pain shook Amory.

'Too bad.'

'Yes, it is too bad. We'll have to get someone else if we're going to stay here. The rent's going up.'

'Sure. Get anybody. I'll leave it to you, Tom.'

Amory walked into his bedroom. The first thing that met his glance was a photograph of Rosalind that he had intended to have framed, propped up against a mirror on his dresser. He looked at it unmoved. After the vivid mental pictures of her that were his portion at present, the portrait was curiously unreal. He went back into the study.

'Got a cardboard box?'

'No,' answered Tom, puzzled. 'Why should I have? Oh, yes – there may be one in Alec's room.'

Eventually Amory found what he was looking for and, returning to his dresser, opened a drawer full of letters, notes, part of a chain, two little handkerchiefs and some snapshots. As he transferred them carefully to the box his mind wandered to some place in a book where the hero, after preserving for a year a cake of his lost love's soap, finally washed his hands with it. He laughed and began to hum 'After You've Gone'[128] . . . ceased abruptly . . .

The string broke twice, and then he managed to secure it, dropped the package into the bottom of his trunk, and having slammed the lid returned to the study.

'Going out?' Tom's voice held an undertone of anxiety.

'Uh-huh.'

'Where?'

'Couldn't say, old keed.'

'Let's have dinner together.'

'Sorry. I told Sukey Brett I'd eat with him.'

'Oh.'

'Bye-bye.'

Amory crossed the street and had a highball; then he walked to Washington Square and found a top seat on a bus. He disembarked at Forty-Third Street and strolled to the Biltmore bar.

'Hi, Amory!'

'What'll you have?'

'Yo-ho! Waiter!'

TEMPERATURE NORMAL

The advent of Prohibition with the 'thirsty-first' put a sudden stop to the submerging of Amory's sorrows, and when he awoke one morning to find that the old bar-to-bar days were over, he had neither remorse for the past three weeks nor regret that their repetition was impossible. He had taken the most violent, if the weakest, method to shield himself from the stabs of memory, and while it was not a course he would have prescribed for others, he found in the end that it had done its business: he was over the first flush of pain.

Don't misunderstand! Amory had loved Rosalind as he would never love another living person. She had taken the first flush of his youth and brought from his unplumbed depths tenderness that had surprised him, gentleness and unselfishness that he had never given to another creature. He had later love-affairs, but of a different sort: in those he went back to that, perhaps, more typical frame of mind, in which the girl became the mirror of a mood in him. Rosalind had drawn out what was more than passionate admiration; he had a deep, undying affection for Rosalind.

But there had been, near the end, so much dramatic tragedy, culminating in the arabesque nightmare of his three weeks' spree, that he was emotionally worn out. The people and surroundings that he remembered as being cool or delicately artificial, seemed to promise him a refuge. He wrote a cynical story which featured his father's funeral and dispatched it to a magazine, receiving in return a cheque for sixty dollars and a request for more of the same tone. This tickled his vanity, but inspired him to no further effort.

He read enormously. He was puzzled and depressed by *A Portrait of the Artist as a Young Man*, intensely interested by *Joan and Peter* and *The Undying Fire*,[129] and rather surprised by his discovery through a critic named Mencken of several excellent American novels: *Vandover and the Brute*, *The Damnation of Theron Ware* and *Jennie Gerhardt*.[130] Mackenzie, Chesterton, Galsworthy, Bennett,[131] had sunk in his appreciation from sagacious, life-saturated geniuses to merely diverting contemporaries. Shaw's aloof clarity and brilliant consistency and the gloriously intoxicated efforts of H. G. Wells to fit the key of romantic symmetry into the elusive lock of truth alone won his rapt attention.

He wanted to see Monsignor Darcy, to whom he had written when he landed, but he had not heard from him; besides he knew that a visit to Monsignor would entail the story of Rosalind, and the thought of repeating it turned him cold with horror.

In his search for cool people he remembered Mrs Lawrence, a very intelligent, very dignified lady, a convert to the Church, and a great devotee of Monsignor's.

He called her on the phone one day. Yes, she remembered him perfectly; no, Monsignor wasn't in town, was in Boston she thought; he'd promised to come to dinner when he returned. Couldn't Amory take luncheon with her?

'I thought I'd better catch up, Mrs Lawrence,' he said rather ambiguously when he arrived.

'Monsignor was here just last week,' said Mrs Lawrence regretfully. 'He was very anxious to see you, but he'd left your address at home.'

'Did he think I'd plunged into Bolshevism?' asked Amory, interested.

'Oh, he's having a frightful time.'

'Why?'

'About the Irish Republic. He thinks it lacks dignity.'

'So?'

'He went to Boston when the Irish President[132] arrived and he was greatly distressed because the receiving committee, when they rode in an automobile, *would* put their arms around the President.'

'I don't blame him.'

'Well, what impressed you more than anything while you were in the army? You look a great deal older.'

'That's from another, more disastrous battle,' he answered, smiling in spite of himself. 'But the army – let me see – well, I discovered that physical courage depends to a great extent on the physical shape a man is in. I found that I was as brave as the next man – it used to worry me before.'

'What else?'

'Well, the idea that men can stand anything if they get used to it, and the fact that I got a high mark in the psychological examination.'

Mrs Lawrence laughed. Amory was finding it a great relief to be in this cool house on Riverside Drive, away from more condensed New York and the sense of people expelling great quantities of breath into a little space. Mrs Lawrence reminded him vaguely of Beatrice, not in temperament, but in her perfect grace and dignity. The house, its furnishings, the manner in which dinner was served, were in immense contrast to what he had met in the great places on Long Island, where the servants were so obtrusive that they had positively to be bumped out of the way, or even in the houses of more conservative 'Union Club' families. He wondered if this air of symmetrical restraint, this grace, which he felt was continental, was distilled through Mrs Lawrence's New England ancestry or acquired in long residence in Italy and Spain.

Two glasses of sauterne at luncheon loosened his tongue, and he talked, with what he felt was something of his old charm, of religion and literature and the menacing phenomena of the social order. Mrs Lawrence was ostensibly pleased with him, and her interest was especially in his mind; he wanted people to like his mind again – after a while it might be such a nice place in which to live.

'Monsignor Darcy still thinks that you're his reincarnation, that your faith will eventually clarify.'

'Perhaps,' he assented. 'I'm rather pagan at present. It's just that religion doesn't seem to have the slightest bearing on life at my age.'

When he left her house he walked down Riverside Drive with a feeling of satisfaction. It was amusing to discuss again such subjects as this young poet, Stephen Vincent Benét,[133] or the Irish Republic. Between the rancid accusations of Edward Carson and Justice Cohalan[134] he had completely tired of the Irish question; yet there had been a time when his own Celtic traits were pillars of his personal philosophy.

There seemed suddenly to be much left in life, if only this revival of old interests did not mean that he was backing away from it again – backing away from life itself.

RESTLESSNESS

'I'm tres old and tres bored, Tom,' said Amory one day, stretching himself at ease in the comfortable window-seat. He always felt most natural in a recumbent position.

'You used to be entertaining before you started to write,' he continued. 'Now you save any idea that you think would do to print.'

Existence had settled back to an ambitionless normality. They had decided that with economy they could still afford the apartment, which Tom, with the domesticity of an elderly cat, had grown fond of. The old English hunting prints on the wall were Tom's, and the large tapestry by courtesy, a relic of decadent days in college, and the great profusion of orphaned candlesticks and the carved Louis XIV chair in which no one could sit more than a minute without acute spinal disorders – Tom claimed that this was because one was sitting in the lap of Montespan's wraith[135] – at any rate, it was Tom's furniture that decided them to stay.

They went out very little: to an occasional play, or to dinner at the Ritz or the Princeton Club. With Prohibition the great rendezvous had received their death wounds; no longer could one wander to the Biltmore bar at twelve or five and find congenial spirits, and both Tom and Amory had outgrown the passion for dancing with Midwestern or New Jersey debbies at the Club-de-Vingt (surnamed the 'Club de Gink') or the Plaza Rose Room – besides even that required several cocktails 'to come down to the intellectual level of the women present', as Amory had once put it to a horrified matron.

Amory had lately received several alarming letters from Mr Barton – the Lake Geneva house was too large to be easily rented; the best rent obtainable at present would serve this year to do little more than pay for the taxes and necessary improvements; in fact, the lawyer suggested that the whole property was simply a white elephant on Amory's hands. Nevertheless, even though it might not yield a cent for the next three years, Amory decided with a vague sentimentality that for the present, at any rate, he would not sell the house.

This particular day on which he announced his ennui to Tom had been quite typical. He had risen at noon, lunched with Mrs Lawrence, and then ridden abstractedly homeward atop one of his beloved buses.

'Why shouldn't you be bored,' yawned Tom. 'Isn't that the conventional frame of mind for the young man of your age and condition?'

'Yes,' said Amory speculatively, 'but I'm more than bored; I am restless.'

'Love and war did for you.'

'Well,' Amory considered, 'I'm not sure that the war itself had any great effect on either you or me – but it certainly ruined the old backgrounds, sort of killed individualism out of our generation.'

Tom looked up in surprise.

'Yes it did,' insisted Amory. 'I'm not sure it didn't kill it out of the whole world. Oh, Lord, what a pleasure it used to be to dream I might be a really great dictator or writer or religious or political leader – and now even a Leonardo da Vinci or Lorenzo de Medici couldn't be a real old-fashioned bolt in the world. Life is too huge and complex. The world is so overgrown that it can't lift its own fingers, and I was planning to be such an important finger – '

'I don't agree with you,' Tom interrupted. 'There never were men placed in such egotistic positions since – oh, since the French Revolution.'

Amory disagreed violently.

'You're mistaking this period when every nut is an individualist for a period of individualism. Wilson has only been powerful when he has represented; he's had to compromise over and over again. Just as soon as Trotsky and Lenin take a definite, consistent stand they'll become merely two-minute figures like Kerensky. Even Foch[136] hasn't half the significance of Stonewall Jackson. War used to be the most individualistic pursuit of man, and yet the popular heroes of the war had neither authority nor responsibility: Guynemer and Sergeant York. How could a schoolboy make a hero of Pershing?[137] A big man has no time really to do anything but just sit and be big.'

'Then you don't think there will be any more permanent world heroes?'

'Yes – in history – not in life. Carlyle would have difficulty getting material for a new chapter on *The Hero as a Big Man*.'[138]

'Go on. I'm a good listener today.'

'People try so hard to believe in leaders now, pitifully hard. But we no sooner get a popular reformer or politician or soldier or writer or philosopher – a Roosevelt, a Tolstoy, a Wood,[139] a Shaw, a Nietzsche – than the cross-currents of criticism wash him away. My Lord, no man can stand prominence these days. It's the surest path to obscurity. People get sick of hearing the same name over and over.'

'Then you blame it on the press?'

'Absolutely. Look at you; you're on the *New Democracy*, considered the most brilliant weekly in the country, read by the men who do things and all that. What's your business? Why, to be as clever, as interesting, and as brilliantly cynical as possible about every man, doctrine, book, or policy that is assigned you to deal with. The more strong lights, the more spiritual scandal you can throw on the matter, the more money they pay you, the more the people buy the issue. You, Tom d'Invilliers, a blighted Shelley, changing, shifting, clever, unscrupulous, represent the critical consciousness of the race – Oh, don't protest, I know the stuff. I used to write book reviews in college; I considered it rare sport to refer to the latest honest, conscientious effort to propound a theory or a remedy as a "welcome addition to our light summer reading". Come on now, admit it.'

Tom laughed, and Amory continued triumphantly.

'We *want* to believe. Young students try to believe in older authors, constituents try to believe in their Congressmen, countries try to believe in their statesmen, but they *can't*. Too many voices, too much scattered, illogical, ill-considered criticism. It's worse in the case of newspapers. Any rich, unprogressive old party with that particularly grasping, acquisitive form of mentality known as financial genius can own a paper that is the intellectual meat and drink of thousands of tired, hurried men, men too involved in the business of modern living to swallow anything but predigested food. For two cents the voter buys his politics, prejudices and philosophy. A year later there is a new political ring or a change in the paper's ownership, consequence: more confusion, more contradiction, a sudden inrush of new ideas, their tempering, their distillation, the reaction against them – '

He paused only to get his breath.

'And that is why I have sworn not to put pen to paper until my ideas either clarify or depart entirely; I have quite enough sins on my soul without putting dangerous, shallow epigrams into people's heads; I might cause a poor, inoffensive capitalist to have a vulgar liaison with a bomb, or get some innocent little Bolshevik tangled up with a machine-gun bullet – '

Tom was growing restless under this lampooning of his connection with the *New Democracy*.

'What's all this got to do with your being bored?'

Amory considered that it had much to do with it.

'How'll I fit in?' he demanded. 'What am I for? To propagate the race? According to the American novels we are led to believe that the "healthy American boy" from nineteen to twenty-five is an entirely sexless animal. As a matter of fact, the healthier he is the less that's true. The only alternative to letting it get you is some violent interest. Well, the war is over; I believe too much in the responsibilities of authorship to write just now; and business, well, business speaks for itself. It has no connection with anything in the world that I've ever been interested in, except a slim, utilitarian connection with economics. What I'd see of it, lost in a clerkship, for the next and best ten years of my life would have the intellectual content of an industrial movie.'

'Try fiction,' suggested Tom.

'Trouble is I get distracted when I start to write stories – get afraid I'm doing it instead of living – get thinking maybe life is waiting for me in the Japanese Gardens at the Ritz or at Atlantic City or on the lower East Side.

'Anyway,' he continued, 'I haven't the vital urge. I wanted to be a regular human being but the girl couldn't see it that way.'

'You'll find another.'

'God! Banish the thought. Why don't you tell me that "if the girl had been worth having she'd have waited for you"? No, sir, the girl really worth having won't wait for anybody. If I thought there'd be another I'd lose my remaining faith in human nature. Maybe I'll play – but Rosalind was the only girl in the wide world that could have held me.'

'Well,' yawned Tom, 'I've played confidant a good hour by the clock. Still, I'm glad to see you're beginning to have violent views again on something.'

'I am,' agreed Amory reluctantly. 'Yet when I see a happy family it makes me sick at my stomach – '

'Happy families try to make people feel that way,' said Tom cynically.

TOM THE CENSOR

There were days when Amory listened. These were when Tom, wreathed in smoke, indulged in the slaughter of American literature. Words failed him.

'Fifty thousand dollars a year,' he would cry. 'My God! Look at them, look at them – Edna Ferber, Gouverneur Morris,[140] Fannie Hurst,[141] Mary Roberts Rinehart – not producing among 'em one story or novel that will last ten years. This man Cobb[142] – I don't think he's either clever or amusing – and what's more, I don't think very many people do, except the editors. He's just groggy with advertising. And – oh Harold Bell Wright[143] – oh Zane Grey – '

'They try.'

'No, they don't even try. Some of them *can* write, but they won't sit down and do one honest novel. Most of them *can't* write, I'll admit. I believe Rupert Hughes[144] tries to give a real, comprehensive picture of American life, but his style and perspective are barbarous. Ernest Poole and Dorothy Canfield[145] try but they're hindered by their absolute lack of any sense of humour; but at least they crowd their work instead of spreading it thin. Every author ought to write every book as if he were going to be beheaded the day he finished it.'

'Is that *double entente*?'

'Don't slow me up! Now there's a few of 'em that seem to have some cultural background, some intelligence and a good deal of literary felicity but they just simply won't write honestly; they'd all claim there was no public for good stuff. Then why the devil is it that Wells, Conrad, Galsworthy, Shaw, Bennett, and the rest depend on America for over half their sales?'

'How does little Tommy like the poets?'

Tom was overcome. He dropped his arms until they swung loosely beside the chair and emitted faint grunts.

'I'm writing a satire on 'em now, calling it "Boston Bards and Hearst Reviewers".'[146]

'Let's hear it,' said Amory eagerly.

'I've only got the last few lines done.'

'That's very modern. Let's hear 'em, if they're funny.'

Tom produced a folded paper from his pocket and read aloud, pausing at intervals so that Amory could see that it was free verse:

> 'So
> Walter Arensberg,
> Alfred Kreymborg,
> Carl Sandburg,
> Louis Untermeyer,
> Eunice Tietjens,
> Clara Shanafelt,
> James Oppenheim,
> Maxwell Bodenheim,
> Richard Glaenzer,
> Scharmel Iris,

Conrad Aiken,
I place your names here
So that you may live
If only as names,
Sinuous, mauve-coloured names,
In the Juvenilia
Of my collected editions.'[147]

Amory roared.

'You win the iron pansy. I'll buy you a meal on the arrogance of the last two lines.'

Amory did not entirely agree with Tom's sweeping damnation of American novelists and poets. He enjoyed both Vachel Lindsay and Booth Tarkington, and admired the conscientious, if slender, artistry of Edgar Lee Masters.

'What I hate is this idiotic drivel about "I am God – I am man – I ride the winds – I look through the smoke – I am the life sense".'

'It's ghastly!'

'And I wish American novelists would give up trying to make business romantically interesting. Nobody wants to read about it, unless it's crooked business. If it was an entertaining subject they'd buy the life of James J. Hill[148] and not one of these long office tragedies that harp along on the significance of smoke – '

'And gloom,' said Tom. 'That's another favourite, though I'll admit the Russians have the monopoly. Our speciality is stories about little girls who break their spines and get adopted by grouchy old men because they smile so much. You'd think we were a race of cheerful cripples and that the common end of the Russian peasant was suicide – '

'Six o'clock,' said Amory, glancing at his wristwatch. 'I'll buy you a grea' big dinner on the strength of the Juvenilia of your collected editions.'

LOOKING BACKWARD

July sweltered out with a last hot week, and Amory in another surge of unrest realised that it was just five months since he and Rosalind had met. Yet it was already hard for him to visualise the heart-whole boy who had stepped off the transport, passionately desiring the adventure of life. One night while the heat, overpowering and enervating, poured into the windows of his room he struggled for several hours in a vague effort to immortalise the poignancy of that time.

The February streets, wind-washed by night, blow full of strange half-intermittent damps, bearing on wasted walks in shining sight wet snow plashed into gleams under the lamps, like golden oil from some divine machine, in an hour of thaw and stars.

Strange damps – full of the eyes of many men, crowded with life borne in upon a lull . . . Oh, I was young, for I could turn again to you, most finite and most beautiful, and taste the stuff of half-remembered dreams, sweet and new on your mouth.

. . . There was a tanging in the midnight air – silence was dead and sound not yet awoken – Life cracked like ice! – one brilliant note and there, radiant and pale, you stood . . . and spring had broken. (The icicles were short upon the roofs and the changeling city swooned.)

Our thoughts were frosty mist along the eaves; our two ghosts kissed, high on the long, mazed wires – eerie half-laughter echoes here and leaves only a fatuous sigh for young desires; regret has followed after things she loved, leaving the great husk.

ANOTHER ENDING

In mid-August came a letter from Monsignor Darcy, who had evidently just stumbled on his address:

MY DEAR BOY – Your last letter was quite enough to make me worry about you. It was not a bit like yourself. Reading between the lines I should imagine that your engagement to this girl is making you rather unhappy, and I see you have lost all the feeling of romance that you had before the war. You make a great mistake if you think you can be romantic without religion. Sometimes I think that with both of us the secret of success, when we find it, is the mystical element in us: something flows into us that enlarges our personalities, and when it ebbs out our personalities shrink; I should call your last two letters rather shrivelled. Beware of losing yourself in the personality of another being, man or woman.

His Eminence Cardinal O'Neill and the Bishop of Boston are staying with me at present, so it is hard for me to get a moment to write, but I wish you would come up here later if only for a weekend. I go to Washington this week.

What I shall do in the future is hanging in the balance. Absolutely between ourselves I should not be surprised to see the red hat of a cardinal descend upon my unworthy head within the next eight months. In any event, I should like to have a house in New York or Washington where you could drop in for weekends.

Amory, I'm very glad we're both alive; this war could easily have been the end of a brilliant family. But in regard to matrimony, you are now at the most dangerous period of your life. You might marry in haste and repent at leisure, but I think you won't. From what you write me about the present calamitous state of your finances, what you want is naturally impossible. However, if I judge you by the means I usually choose, I should say that there will be something of an emotional crisis within the next year.

Do write me. I feel annoyingly out of date on you.

With greatest affection,

THAYER DARCY

Within a week after the receipt of this letter their little household fell precipitously to pieces. The immediate cause was the serious and probably chronic illness of Tom's mother. So they stored the furniture, gave instructions to sublet and shook hands gloomily in the Pennsylvania Station. Amory and Tom seemed always to be saying goodbye.

Feeling very much alone, Amory yielded to an impulse and set off southward, intending to join Monsignor in Washington. They missed connections by two hours, and, deciding to spend a few days with an ancient, remembered uncle, Amory journeyed up through the luxuriant fields of Maryland into Ramilly County. But instead of two days his stay lasted from mid-August nearly through September, for in Maryland he met Eleanor.

CHAPTER 3

Young Irony

For years afterwards when Amory thought of Eleanor he seemed still to hear the wind sobbing around him and sending little chills into the places beside his heart. The night when they rode up the slope and watched the cold moon float through the clouds, he lost a further part of him that nothing could restore; and when he lost it he lost also the power of regretting it. Eleanor was, say, the last time that evil crept close to Amory under the mask of beauty, the last weird mystery that held him with wild fascination and pounded his soul to flakes.

With her his imagination ran riot and that is why they rode to the highest hill and watched an evil moon ride high, for they knew then that they could see the devil in each other. But Eleanor – did Amory dream her? Afterwards their ghosts played, yet both of them hoped from their souls never to meet. Was it the infinite sadness of her eyes that drew him or the mirror of himself that he found in the gorgeous clarity of her mind? She will have no other adventure like Amory, and if she reads this she will say: 'And Amory will have no other adventure like me.'

Nor will she sigh, any more than he would sigh.

Eleanor tried to put it on paper once:

> The fading things we only know
> > We'll have forgotten . . .
> > > Put away . . .
> Desires that melted with the snow,
> > And dreams begotten
> > > This today:
> The sudden dawns we laughed to greet,
> > That all could see, that none could share,
> Will be but dawns . . . and if we meet
> > We shall not care.
>
> Dear . . . not one tear will rise for this . . .
> > A little while hence
> > > No regret
> Will stir for a remembered kiss –

> Not even silence,
>   When we've met,
> Will give old ghosts a waste to roam,
>   Or stir the surface of the sea . . .
> If grey shapes drift beneath the foam
>   We shall not see.

They quarrelled dangerously because Amory maintained that *sea* and *see* couldn't possibly be used as a rhyme. And then Eleanor had part of another verse that she couldn't find a beginning for:

> . . . But wisdom passes . . . still the years
> Will feed us wisdom . . . Age will go
> Back to the old – For all our tears
>   We shall not know.

Eleanor hated Maryland passionately. She belonged to the oldest of the old families of Ramilly County and lived in a big, gloomy house with her grandfather. She had been born and brought up in France . . . I see I am starting wrong. Let me begin again.

Amory was bored, as he usually was in the country. He used to go for far walks by himself – and wander along reciting 'Ulalume' to the cornfields, and congratulating Poe for drinking himself to death in that atmosphere of smiling complacency. One afternoon he had strolled for several miles along a road that was new to him, and then through a wood on bad advice from a coloured woman . . . losing himself entirely. A passing storm decided to break out, and to his great impatience the sky grew black as pitch and the rain began to splatter down through the trees, become suddenly furtive and ghostly. Thunder rolled with menacing crashes up the valley and scattered through the woods in intermittent batteries. He stumbled blindly on, hunting for a way out, and finally, through webs of twisted branches, caught sight of a rift in the trees where the unbroken lightning showed open country. He rushed to the edge of the woods and then hesitated whether or not to cross the fields and try to reach the shelter of the little house marked by a light far down the valley. It was only half-past five, but he could see scarcely ten steps before him, except when the lightning made everything vivid and grotesque for great sweeps around.

Suddenly a strange sound fell on his ears. It was a song, in a low, husky voice, a girl's voice, and whoever was singing was very close to him. A year before he might have laughed, or trembled; but in his restless mood he only stood and listened while the words sank into his consciousness:

> 'Les sanglots longs
> Des violons
>   De l'automne
> Blessent mon coeur
> D'une langueur
>   Monotone.'

The lightning split the sky, but the song went on without a quaver. The girl was evidently in the field and the voice seemed to come vaguely from a haystack about twenty feet in front of him.

Then it ceased: ceased and began again in a weird chant that soared and hung and fell and blended with the rain:

> 'Tout suffocant
> Et blême quand
>   Sonne l'heure
> Je me souviens
> Des jours anciens
>   Et je pleure . . . '[149]

'Who the devil is there in Ramilly County,' muttered Amory aloud, 'who would deliver Verlaine in an extemporaneous tune to a soaking haystack?'

'Somebody's there!' cried the voice unalarmed. 'Who are you? – Manfred,[150] St Christopher or Queen Victoria?'

'I'm Don Juan!' Amory shouted on impulse, raising his voice above the noise of the rain and the wind.

A delighted shriek came from the haystack.

'I know who you are – you're the blond boy that likes "Ulalume" – I recognise your voice.'

'How do I get up?' he cried from the foot of the haystack, whither he had arrived, dripping wet. A head appeared over the edge – it was so dark that Amory could just make out a patch of damp hair and two eyes that gleamed like a cat's.

'Run back!' came the voice, 'and jump and I'll catch your hand – no, not there – on the other side.'

He followed directions and as he sprawled up the side, knee-deep in hay, a small, white hand reached out, gripped his, and helped him on to the top.

'Here you are, Juan,' cried she of the damp hair. 'Do you mind if I drop the Don?'

'You've got a thumb like mine!' he exclaimed.

'And you're holding my hand, which is dangerous without seeing my face.' He dropped it quickly.

As if in answer to his prayers came a flash of lightning and he looked eagerly at her who stood beside him on the soggy haystack, ten feet above the ground. But she had covered her face and he saw nothing but a slender figure, dark, damp, bobbed hair, and the small white hands with the thumbs that bent back like his.

'Sit down,' she suggested politely, as the dark closed in on them. 'If you'll sit opposite me in this hollow you can have half of the raincoat, which I was using as a waterproof tent until you so rudely interrupted me.'

'I was asked,' Amory said joyfully; 'you asked me – you know you did.'

'Don Juan always manages that,' she said, laughing, 'but I shan't call you that any more, because you've got reddish hair. Instead you can recite "Ulalume" and I'll be Psyche, your soul.'

Amory flushed, happily invisible under the curtain of wind and rain. They were sitting opposite each other in a slight hollow in the hay with the raincoat spread over most of them, and the rain doing for the rest. Amory was trying desperately to see Psyche, but the lightning refused to flash again, and he waited impatiently. Good Lord! supposing she wasn't beautiful – supposing she was forty and pedantic – heavens! Suppose, only suppose, she was mad. But he knew the last was unworthy. Here had Providence sent a girl to amuse him, just as it sent Benvenuto Cellini men to murder, and he was wondering if she was mad, just because she exactly filled his mood.

'I'm not,' she said.

'Not what?'

'Not mad. I didn't think you were mad when I first saw you, so it isn't fair that you should think so of me.'

'How on earth – '

As long as they knew each other Eleanor and Amory could be 'on a subject' and stop talking with the definite thought of it in their heads, yet ten minutes later speak aloud and find that their minds had followed the same channels and led them each to a parallel idea, an idea that others would have found absolutely unconnected with the first.

'Tell me,' he demanded, leaning forward eagerly, 'how do you know about "Ulalume" – how did you know the colour of my hair? What's your name? What were you doing here? Tell me all at once!'

Suddenly the lightning flashed in with a leap of overreaching light and he saw Eleanor, and looked for the first time into those eyes of hers. Oh, she was magnificent – pale skin, the colour of marble in starlight, slender brows, and eyes that glittered green as emeralds in the blinding glare. She was a witch, of perhaps nineteen, he judged, alert and dreamy and with the tell-tale white line over her upper lip that was a weakness and a delight. He sank back with a gasp against the wall of hay.

'Now you've seen me,' she said calmly, 'and I suppose you're about to say that my green eyes are burning into your brain.'

'What colour is your hair?' he asked intently. 'It's bobbed, isn't it?'

'Yes, it's bobbed. I don't know what colour it is,' she answered, musing, 'so many men have asked me. It's medium, I suppose – No one ever looks long at my hair. I've got beautiful eyes, though, haven't I? I don't care what you say, I have beautiful eyes.'

'Answer my question, Madeline.'[151]

'Don't remember them all – besides my name isn't Madeline, it's Eleanor.'

'I might have guessed it. You *look* like Eleanor – you have that Eleanor look. You know what I mean.'

There was a silence as they listened to the rain.

'It's going down my neck, fellow lunatic,' she offered finally.

'Answer my questions.'

'Well – name of Savage, Eleanor; live in big old house mile down road; nearest living relation to be notified, grandfather – Ramilly Savage; height, five feet four inches; number on watch-case, 3077 W; nose, delicate aquiline; temperament, uncanny – '

'And me,' Amory interrupted, 'where did you see me?'

'Oh, you're one of *those* men,' she answered haughtily, 'must lug old self into conversation. Well, my boy, I was behind a hedge sunning myself one day last week, and along comes a man saying in a pleasant, conceited way of talking:

> "And now when the night was senescent"

(says he)

> "And the star dials pointed to morn,
> At the end of the path a liquescent"

(says he)

> "And nebulous lustre was born."[152]

'So I poked my eyes up over the hedge, but you had started to run, for some unknown reason, and so I saw but the back of your beautiful head. "Oh!" says I, "there's a man for whom many of us might sigh," and I continued in my best Irish – '

'All right,' Amory interrupted. 'Now go back to yourself.'

'Well, I will. I'm one of those people who go through the world giving other people thrills, but getting few myself except those I read into men on such nights as these. I have the social courage to go on the stage, but not the energy; I haven't the patience to write books; and I never met a man I'd marry. However, I'm only eighteen.'

The storm was dying down softly and only the wind kept up its ghostly surge and made the stack lean and gravely settle from side to side. Amory was in a trance. He felt that every moment was precious. He had never met a girl like this before – she would never seem quite the same again. He didn't at all feel like a character in a play, the appropriate feeling in an unconventional situation – instead, he had a sense of coming home.

'I have just made a great decision,' said Eleanor after another pause, 'and that is why I'm here, to answer another of your questions. I have just decided that I don't believe in immortality.'

'Really! how banal!'

'Frightfully so,' she answered, 'but depressing with a stale, sickly depression, nevertheless. I came out here to get wet – like a wet hen; wet hens always have great clarity of mind,' she concluded.

'Go on,' Amory said politely.

'Well – I'm not afraid of the dark, so I put on my slicker and rubber boots and came out. You see I was always afraid, before, to say I didn't believe in God – because the lightning might strike me – but here I am and it hasn't, of course, but the main point is that this time I wasn't any more afraid of it than I had been when I was a Christian Scientist, like I was last year. So now I know I'm a materialist and I was fraternising with the hay when you came out and stood by the woods, scared to death.'

'Why, you little wretch – ' cried Amory indignantly. 'Scared of what?'

'*Yourself!*' she shouted, and he jumped. She clapped her hands and laughed. 'See – see! Conscience – kill it like me! Eleanor Savage, materiologist – no jumping, no starting, come early – '

'But I *have* to have a soul,' he objected. 'I can't be rational – and I won't be molecular.'

She leaned towards him, her burning eyes never leaving his own, and whispered with a sort of romantic finality: 'I thought so, Juan, I feared so – you're sentimental. You're not like me. I'm a romantic little materialist.'

'I'm not sentimental – I'm as romantic as you are. The idea, you know, is that the sentimental person thinks things will last – the romantic person has a desperate confidence that they won't.' (This was an ancient distinction of Amory's.)

'Epigrams. I'm going home,' she said sadly. 'Let's get off the haystack and walk to the crossroads.'

They slowly descended from their perch. She would not let him help her down and motioning him away arrived in a graceful lump in the soft mud where she sat for an instant, laughing at herself. Then she jumped to her feet and slipped her hand into his, and they tiptoed across the fields, jumping and swinging from dry spot to dry spot. A transcendent delight seemed to sparkle in every pool of water, for the moon had risen and the storm had scurried away into western Maryland. When Eleanor's arm touched his he felt his hands grow cold with deadly fear lest he should lose the shadow brush with which his imagination was painting wonders of her. He watched her from the corners of his eyes as ever he did when he walked with her – she was a feast and a folly and he wished it had been his destiny to sit for ever on a haystack and see life through her green eyes. His paganism soared that night and when she faded out like a grey ghost down the road, a deep singing came out of the fields and filled his way homeward. All night the summer moths flitted in and out of Amory's window; all night large looming sounds swayed in mystic reverie through the silver grain – and he lay awake in the clear darkness.

SEPTEMBER

Amory selected a blade of grass and nibbled at it scientifically.

'I never fall in love in August or September,' he proffered.

'When then?'

'Christmas or Easter. I'm a liturgist.'

'Easter!' She turned up her nose. 'Huh! Spring in corsets!'

'Easter *would* bore spring, wouldn't she? Easter has her hair braided, wears a tailored suit.'

> 'Bind on thy sandals, oh, thou most fleet.
> Over the splendour and speed of thy feet – '[153]

quoted Eleanor softly, and then added: 'I suppose Hallowe'en is a better day for autumn than Thanksgiving.'

'Much better – and Christmas Eve does very well for winter, but summer . . . '

'Summer has no day,' she said. 'We can't possibly have a summer love. So many people have tried that the name's become proverbial. Summer is only the unfulfilled promise of spring, a charlatan in place of the warm balmy nights I dream of in April. It's a sad season of life without growth . . . It has no day.'

'Fourth of July,' Amory suggested facetiously.

'Don't be funny!' she said, raking him with her eyes.

'Well, what could fulfil the promise of spring?'

She thought a moment.

'Oh, I suppose heaven would, if there was one,' she said finally, 'a sort of pagan heaven – you ought to be a materialist,' she continued irrelevantly.

'Why?'

'Because you look a good deal like the pictures of Rupert Brooke.'

To some extent Amory tried to play Rupert Brooke as long as he knew Eleanor. What he said, his attitude towards life, towards her, towards himself, were all reflexes of the dead Englishman's literary moods. Often she sat in the grass, a lazy wind playing with her short hair, her voice husky as she ran up and down the scale from Granchester to Waikiki.[154] There was something most passionate in Eleanor's reading aloud. They seemed nearer, not only mentally, but physically, when they read, than when she was in his arms, and this was often, for they fell half into love almost from the first. Yet was Amory capable of love now? He could, as always, run through the emotions in a half-hour, but even while they revelled in their imaginations, he knew that neither of them could care as he had cared once before – I suppose that was why they turned to Brooke, and Swinburne, and Shelley. Their chance was to make everything fine and finished and rich and imaginative; they must bend tiny golden tentacles from his imagination to hers, that would take the place of the great, deep love that was never so near, yet never so much of a dream.

One poem they read over and over, Swinburne's 'Triumph of Time', and four lines of it rang in his memory afterwards on warm nights when he saw the fireflies among dusky tree trunks and heard the low drone of many frogs. Then Eleanor seemed to come out of the night and stand by him, and he heard her throaty voice, with its tone of a fleecy-headed drum, repeating:

'Is it worth a tear, is it worth an hour,
  To think of things that are well outworn;
Of fruitless husk and fugitive flower,
  The dream forgone and the deed forborne?'[155]

They were formally introduced two days later, and his aunt told him her history. The Ramillys were two: old Mr Ramilly and his granddaughter, Eleanor. She had lived in France with a restless mother whom Amory imagined to have been very like his own, on whose death she had come to America, to live in Maryland. She had gone to Baltimore first, to stay with a bachelor uncle, and there she insisted on being a débutante at the age of seventeen. She had a wild winter and arrived in the country in March, having quarrelled frantically with all her Baltimore relatives, and shocked them into fiery protest. A rather fast crowd had come out, who drank cocktails in limousines and were promiscuously condescending and patronising towards older people, and Eleanor with an *esprit* that hinted strongly of the boulevards, led many innocents, still redolent of St Timothy's and Farmington, into paths of Bohemian naughtiness. When the story came to her uncle, a forgetful cavalier of a more hypocritical era, there was a scene, from which Eleanor emerged, subdued but rebellious and indignant, to seek haven with her grandfather who hovered in the country on the near side of senility. That's as far as her story went; she told him the rest herself, but that was later.

Often they swam and as Amory floated lazily in the water he shut his mind to all thoughts except those of hazy soap-bubble lands where the sun splattered through wind-drunk trees. How could anyone possibly think or worry, or do anything except splash and dive and loll there on the edge of time while the flower months failed. Let the days move over – sadness and memory and pain recurred outside, and here, once more, before he went on to meet them, he wanted to drift and be young.

There were days when Amory resented that life had changed from an even progress along a road stretching ever in sight, with the scenery merging and blending, into a succession of quick, unrelated scenes – two years of sweat and blood; that sudden absurd instinct for paternity that Rosalind had stirred; the half-sensual, half-neurotic quality of this autumn with Eleanor. He felt that it would take all time, more than he could ever spare, to glue these strange cumbersome pictures into the scrapbook of his life. It was all like a banquet where he sat for this half-hour of his youth and tried to enjoy brilliant epicurean courses.

Dimly he promised himself a time where all should be welded together. For months it seemed that he had alternated between being borne along a stream of love or fascination, or left in an eddy, and in the eddies he had not desired to think, rather to be picked up on a wave's top and swept along again.

'The despairing, dying autumn and our love – how well they harmonise!' said Eleanor sadly one day as they lay dripping by the water.

'The Indian summer of our hearts – ' he ceased.

'Tell me,' she said finally, 'was she light or dark?'

'Light.'

'Was she more beautiful than I am?'

'I don't know,' said Amory shortly.

One night they walked while the moon rose and poured a great burden of glory over the garden until it seemed fairyland with Amory and Eleanor, dim phantasmal shapes, expressing eternal beauty in curious elfin love moods. Then they turned out of the moonlight into the trellised darkness of a vine-hung pagoda, where there were scents so plaintive as to be nearly musical.

'Light a match,' she whispered. 'I want to see you.'

Scratch! Flare!

The night and the scarred trees were like scenery in a play, and to be there with Eleanor, shadowy and unreal, seemed somehow oddly familiar. Amory thought how it was only the past that ever seemed strange and unbelievable. The match went out.

'It's black as pitch.'

'We're just voices now,' murmured Eleanor, 'little lonesome voices. Light another.'

'That was my last match.'

Suddenly he caught her in his arms.

'You *are* mine – you know you're mine!' he cried wildly . . . the moonlight twisted in through the vines and listened . . . the fireflies hung upon their whispers as if to win his glance from the glory of her eyes.

THE END OF SUMMER

'No wind is stirring in the grass; not one wind stirs . . . the water in the hidden pools, as glass, fronts the full moon and so inters the golden token in its icy mass,' chanted Eleanor to the trees that skeletoned the body of the night. 'Isn't it ghostly here? If you can hold your horse's feet up, let's cut through the woods and find the hidden pools.'

'It's after one, and you'll get the devil,' he objected, 'and I don't know enough about horses to put one away in the pitch dark.'

'Shut up, you old fool,' she whispered irrelevantly, and, leaning over, she patted him lazily with her riding-crop. 'You can leave your old plug in our stable and I'll send him over tomorrow.'

'But my uncle has got to drive me to the station with this old plug at seven o'clock.'

'Don't be a spoil-sport – remember, you have a tendency towards wavering that prevents you from being the entire light of my life.'

Amory drew his horse up close beside, and, leaning towards her, grasped her hand.

'Say I am – *quick*, or I'll pull you over and make you ride behind me.'

She looked up and smiled and shook her head excitedly.

'Oh, do! – or rather, don't! Why are all the exciting things so uncomfortable, like fighting and exploring and skiing in Canada? By the way, we're going to ride up Harper's Hill. I think that comes in our programme about five o'clock.'

'You little devil,' Amory growled. 'You're going to make me stay up all night and sleep in the train like an immigrant all day tomorrow, going back to New York.'

'Hush! someone's coming along the road – let's go! *Whoo-ee-oop!*' And with a shout that probably gave the belated traveller a series of shivers, she turned her horse into the woods and Amory followed slowly, as he had followed her all day for three weeks.

The summer was over, but he had spent the days in watching Eleanor, a graceful, facile Manfred, build herself intellectual and imaginative pyramids while she revelled in the artificialities of the temperamental teens and they wrote poetry at the dinner-table.

When Vanity kissed Vanity, a hundred happy Junes ago, he pondered o'er her breathlessly, and, that all men might ever know, he rhymed her eyes with life and death: 'Thru Time I'll save my love!' he said . . . yet Beauty vanished with his breath, and, with her lovers, she was dead . . .

    – Ever his wit and not her eyes, ever his art and not her hair:

'Who'd learn a trick in rhyme, be wise and pause before his sonnet there' . . . So all my words, however true, might sing you to a thousandth June, and no one ever *know* that you were Beauty for an afternoon.

So he wrote one day, when he pondered how coldly we thought of the 'Dark Lady of the Sonnets', and how little we remembered her as the great man wanted her remembered. For what Shakespeare *must* have desired, to have been able to write with such divine despair, was that the lady should live . . . and now we have no real interest in her . . . The irony of it is that if he had cared *more* for the poem than for the lady the sonnet would be only obvious, imitative rhetoric and no one would ever have read it after twenty years . . .

This was the last night Amory ever saw Eleanor. He was leaving in the morning and they had agreed to take a long farewell trot by the cold moonlight. She wanted to talk, she said – perhaps the last time in her life that she could be rational (she meant pose with comfort). So they had turned into the woods and rode for half an hour with scarcely a word, except when she whispered, 'Damn!' at a bothersome branch – whispered it as no other girl was ever able to whisper it. Then they started up Harper's Hill, walking their tired horses.

'Good Lord! It's quiet here!' whispered Eleanor; 'much more lonesome than the woods.'

'I hate woods,' Amory said, shuddering. 'Any kind of foliage or underbrush at night. Out here it's so broad and easy on the spirit.'

'The long slope of a long hill.'

'And the cold moon rolling moonlight down it.'

'And thee and me, last and most important.'

It was quiet that night – the straight road they followed up to the edge of the cliff knew few footsteps at any time. Only an occasional Negro cabin, silver-grey in the rock-ribbed moonlight, broke the long line of bare ground; behind lay the black edge of the woods like a dark frosting on white cake, and ahead the sharp, high horizon. It was much colder – so cold that it settled on them and drove all the warm nights from their minds.

'The end of summer,' said Eleanor softly. 'Listen to the beat of our horses' hoofs – tump-tump-tump-a-tump.' Have you ever been feverish and had all noises divide into "tump-tump-tump" until you could swear eternity was divisible into so many tumps? That's the way I feel – old horses go tump-tump . . . I guess that's the only thing that separates horses and clocks from us. Human beings can't go "tump-tump-tump" without going crazy.'

The breeze freshened and Eleanor pulled her cape around her and shivered.

'Are you very cold?' asked Amory.

'No, I'm thinking about myself – my black old inside self, the real one, with the fundamental honesty that keeps me from being absolutely wicked by making me realise my own sins.'

They were riding up close by the cliff and Amory gazed over. Where the fall met the ground a hundred feet below, a black stream made a sharp line, broken by tiny glints in the swift water.

'Rotten, rotten old world,' broke out Eleanor suddenly, 'and the wretchedest thing of all is me – oh, *why* am I a girl? Why am I not a stupid – ? Look at you; you're stupider than I am, not much, but some, and you can lope about and get bored and then lope somewhere else, and you can play around with girls without being involved in meshes of sentiment, and you can do anything and be justified – and here am I with the brains to do everything, yet tied to the sinking ship of future matrimony. If I were born a hundred years from now, well and good, but now what's in store for me – I have to marry, that goes without saying. Who? I'm too bright for most men, and yet I have to descend to their level and let them patronise my intellect in order to get their attention. Every year that I don't marry I've got less chance of a first-class man. At the best I can have my choice from one or two cities and, of course, I have to marry into a dinner-coat.

'Listen,' she leaned close again, 'I like clever men and good-looking men, and, of course, no one cares more for personality than I do. Oh, just one person in fifty has any glimmer of what sex is. I'm hipped on Freud and all that, but it's rotten that every bit of *real* love in the world is ninety-nine per cent passion and one little soupçon of jealousy.' She finished as suddenly as she began.

'Of course, you're right,' Amory agreed. 'It's a rather unpleasant overpowering force that's part of the machinery under everything. It's like an actor that lets you see his mechanics! Wait a minute till I think this out . . . '

He paused and tried to get a metaphor. They had turned from the cliff and were riding along the road about fifty feet to the left.

'You see everyone's got to have some cloak to throw around it. The mediocre intellects, Plato's second class, use the remnants of romantic chivalry diluted with Victorian sentiment – and we who consider ourselves the intellectuals cover it up by pretending that it's another side of us, has nothing to do with our shining brains; we pretend that the fact that we realise it is really absolving us from being a prey to it. But the truth is that sex is right in the middle of our purest abstractions, so close that it obscures vision . . . I can kiss you now and will . . . ' He leaned towards her in his saddle, but she drew away.

'I can't – I can't kiss you now – I'm more sensitive.'

'You're more stupid then,' he declared rather impatiently. 'Intellect is no protection from sex any more than convention is . . . '

'What is?' she fired up. 'The Catholic Church or the maxims of Confucius?'

Amory looked up, rather taken aback.

'That's your panacea, isn't it?' she cried. 'Oh, you're just an old hypocrite, too. Thousands of scowling priests keeping the degenerate Italians and illiterate Irish repentant with gabble-gabble about the sixth and ninth commandments.[156] It's just all cloaks, sentiment and spiritual rouge and panaceas. I'll tell you there *is* no God, not even a definite abstract goodness; so it's all got to be worked out for the individual by the individual here in high white foreheads like mine, and you're too much the prig to admit it.' She let go her reins and shook her little fists at the stars.

'If there's a God let him strike me – strike me!'

'Talking about God again after the manner of atheists,' Amory said sharply. His materialism, always a thin cloak, was torn to shreds by Eleanor's blasphemy . . . She knew it and it angered him that she knew it.

'And like most intellectuals who don't find faith convenient,' he continued coldly, 'like Napoleon and Oscar Wilde and the rest of your type, you'll yell loudly for a priest on your deathbed.'

Eleanor drew her horse up sharply and he reined in beside her.

'Will I?' she said in a queer voice that scared him. 'Will I? Watch! *I'm going over the cliff!*' And before he could interfere she had turned and was riding breakneck for the end of the plateau.

He wheeled and started after her, his body like ice, his nerves in a vast clangour. There was no chance of stopping her. The moon was under a cloud and her horse would step blindly over. Then some ten feet from the edge of the cliff she gave a sudden shriek and flung herself sideways – plunged from her horse and, rolling over twice, landed in a pile of brush five feet from the edge. The horse went over with a frantic whinny. In a minute he was by Eleanor's side and saw that her eyes were open.

'Eleanor!' he cried.

She did not answer, but her lips moved and her eyes filled with sudden tears.

'Eleanor, are you hurt?'

'No; I don't think so,' she said faintly, and then began weeping.

'My horse dead?'

'Good God – Yes!'

'Oh!' she wailed. 'I thought I was going over. I didn't know – '

He helped her gently to her feet and boosted her on to his saddle. So they started homeward; Amory walking and she bent forward on the pommel, sobbing bitterly.

'I've got a crazy streak,' she faltered, 'twice before I've done things like that. When I was eleven mother went – went mad – stark raving crazy. We were in Vienna – '

All the way back she talked haltingly about herself, and Amory's love waned slowly with the moon. At her door they started from habit to kiss good-night, but she could not run into his arms, nor were they stretched to meet her as in the week before. For a minute they stood there, hating each other with a bitter sadness. But as Amory had loved himself in Eleanor, so now what he hated was only a mirror. Their poses were strewn about the pale dawn like broken glass. The stars were long gone and there were left only the little sighing gusts of wind and the silences between . . . but naked souls are poor things ever, and soon he turned homeward and let new lights come in with the sun.

A POEM THAT ELEANOR SENT AMORY
SEVERAL YEARS LATER

Here, Earth-born, over the lilt of the water,
    Lisping its music and bearing a burden of light,
Bosoming day as a laughing and radiant daughter . . .
    Here we may whisper unheard, unafraid of the night.
Walking alone . . . was it splendour, or what, we were bound with,
    Deep in the time when summer lets down her hair?
Shadows we loved and the patterns they covered the ground with,
    Tapestries, mystical, faint in the breathless air.

That was the day . . . and the night for another story,
    Pale as a dream and shadowed with pencilled trees –
Ghosts of the stars came by who had sought for glory,

Whispered to us of peace in the plaintive breeze,
Whispered of old dead faiths that the day had shattered,
  Youth the penny that bought delight of the moon;
That was the urge that we knew and the language that mattered
  That was the debt that we paid to the usurer June.

Here, deepest of dreams, by the waters that bring not
  Anything back of the past that we need not know,
What if the light is but sun and the little streams sing not,
  We are together, it seems . . . I have loved you so . . .
What did the last night hold, with the summer over,
  Drawing us back to the home in the changing glade?
What leered out of the dark in the ghostly clover?

God! . . . till you stirred in your sleep . . . and were wild
                                        afraid . . .
Well . . . we have passed . . . we are chronicle now to the eerie.
  Curious metal from meteors that failed in the sky;
Earth-born the tireless is stretched by the water, quite weary,
  Close to this ununderstandable changeling that's I . . .
Fear is an echo we traced to Security's daughter;
  Now we are faces and voices . . . and less, too soon,
Whispering half-love over the lilt of the water . . .
  Youth the penny that bought delight of the moon.

A POEM AMORY SENT TO ELEANOR AND
WHICH HE CALLED 'SUMMER STORM'

Faint winds, and a song fading and leaves falling,
Faint winds, and far away a fading laughter . . .
And the rain and over the fields a voice calling . . .

Our grey blown cloud scurries and lifts above,
Slides on the sun and flutters there to waft her
Sisters on. The shadow of a dove
Falls on the cote, the trees are filled with wings;
And down the valley through the crying trees
The body of the darker storm flies; brings
With its new air the breath of sunken seas
And slender tenuous thunder . . .
But I wait . . .

Wait for the mists and for the blacker rain –
Heavier winds that stir the veil of fate,
Happier winds that pile her hair;
                                    Again
They tear me, teach me, strew the heavy air
Upon me, winds that I know, and storm.

There was a summer every rain was rare;
There was a season every wind was warm . . .
And now *you* pass me in the mist . . . your hair
Rain-blown about you, damp lips curved once more
In that wild irony, that gay despair
That made you old when we have met before;
Wraith-like you drift on out before the rain,
Across the fields, blown with the stemless flowers,
With your old hopes, dead leaves and loves again –
Dim as a dream and wan with all old hours
(Whispers will creep into the growing dark . . .
Tumult will die over the trees)
                                    Now night
Tears from her wetted breast the splattered blouse
Of day, glides down the dreaming hills, tear-bright,
To cover with her hair the eerie green . . .
Love for the dusk . . . Love for the glistening after;
Quiet the trees to their last tops . . . serene . . .

Faint winds, and far away a fading laughter . . .

CHAPTER 4

The Supercilious Sacrifice

Atlantic City. Amory paced the boardwalk at day's end, lulled by the everlasting surge of changing waves, smelling the half-mournful odour of the salt breeze. The sea, he thought, had treasured its memories deeper than the faithless land. It seemed still to whisper of Norse galleys ploughing the water world under raven-figured flags, of the British dreadnoughts, grey bulwarks of civilisation, steaming up through the fog of one dark July into the North Sea.

'Well – Amory Blaine!'

Amory looked down into the street below. A low racing car had drawn to a stop and a familiar cheerful face protruded from the driver's seat.

'Come on down, goopher!' cried Alec.

Amory called a greeting and descending a flight of wooden steps approached the car. He and Alec had been meeting intermittently, but the barrier of Rosalind lay always between them. He was sorry for this; he hated to lose Alec.

'Mr Blaine, this is Miss Waterson, Miss Wayne and Mr Tully.'

'How d'y do?'

'Amory,' said Alec exuberantly, 'if you'll jump in we'll take you to some secluded nook and give you a wee jolt of Bourbon.'

Amory considered.

'That's an idea.'

'Step in – move over, Jill, and Amory will smile very handsomely at you.'

Amory squeezed into the back seat beside a gaudy, vermilion-lipped blonde.

'Hello, Doug Fairbanks,' she said flippantly. 'Walking for exercise or hunting for company?'

'I was counting the waves,' replied Amory gravely. 'I'm going in for statistics.'

'Don't kid me, Doug.'

When they reached an unfrequented side street Alec stopped the car among deep shadows.

'What you doing down here these cold days, Amory?' he demanded, as he produced a quart of Bourbon from under the fur rug.

Amory avoided the question. Indeed, he had had no definite reason for coming to the coast.

'Do you remember that party of ours, sophomore year?' he asked instead.

'Do I? When we slept in the pavilions up in Asbury Park – '

'Lord, Alec! It's hard to think that Jesse and Dick and Kerry are all three dead.'

Alec shivered.

'Don't talk about it. These dreary fall days depress me enough.'

Jill seemed to agree.

'Doug here is sorta gloomy anyways,' she commented. 'Tell him to drink deep – it's good and scarce these days.'

'What I really want to ask you, Amory, is where you are – '

'Why, New York, I suppose – '

'I mean tonight, because if you haven't got a room yet you'd better help me out.'

'Glad to.'

'You see, Tully and I have two rooms with bath between at the Ranier, and he's got to go back to New York. I don't want to have to move. Question is, will you occupy one of the rooms?'

Amory was willing, if he could get in right away.

'You'll find the key in the office; the rooms are in my name.'

Declining further locomotion or further stimulation, Amory left the car and sauntered back along the boardwalk to the hotel.

He was in an eddy again, a deep, lethargic gulf, without desire to work or write, love or dissipate. For the first time in his life he rather longed for death to roll over his generation, obliterating their petty fevers and struggles and exultations. His youth seemed never so vanished as now in the contrast between the utter loneliness of this visit and that riotous, joyful party of four years before. Things that had been the merest commonplaces of his life then, deep sleep, the sense of beauty around him, all desire, had flown away and the gaps they left were filled only with the great listlessness of his disillusion.

'To hold a man a woman has to appeal to the worst in him.' This sentence was the thesis of most of his bad nights, of which he felt this was to be one. His mind had already started to play variations on the subject. Tireless passion, fierce jealousy, longing to possess and crush – these alone were left of all his love for Rosalind; these remained to him as payment for the loss of his youth – bitter calomel under the thin sugar of love's exaltation.

In his room he undressed and wrapping himself in blankets to keep out the chill October air drowsed in an armchair by the open window.

He remembered a poem he had read months before:

> Oh staunch old heart who toiled so long for me,
> I waste my years sailing along the sea –

Yet he had no sense of waste, no sense of the present hope that waste implied. He felt that life had rejected him.

'Rosalind! Rosalind!' He poured the words softly into the half-darkness until she seemed to permeate the room; the wet salt breeze filled his hair with moisture, the rim of a moon seared the sky and made the curtains dim and ghostly. He fell asleep.

When he awoke it was very late and quiet. The blanket had slipped partly off his shoulders and he touched his skin to find it damp and cold.

Then he became aware of a tense whispering not ten feet away.

He became rigid.

'*Don't make a sound!*' It was Alec's voice. '*Jill – do you hear me?*'

'Yes – ' breathed very low, very frightened. They were in the bathroom.

Then his ears caught a louder sound from somewhere along the corridor outside. It was a mumbling of men's voices and a repeated muffled rapping. Amory threw off the blankets and moved close to the bathroom door.

'My God!' came the girl's voice again. 'You'll have to let them in.'

'*Sh!*'

Suddenly a steady, insistent knocking began at Amory's hall door and simultaneously out of the bathroom came Alec, followed by the vermilion-lipped girl. They were both clad in pyjamas.

'Amory!' an anxious whisper.

'What's the trouble?'

'It's house detectives. My God, Amory – they're just looking for a test-case – '

'Well, better let them in.'

'You don't understand. They can get me under the Mann Act.'[157]

The girl followed him slowly, a rather miserable, pathetic figure in the darkness.

Amory tried to plan quickly.

'You make a racket and let them in your room,' he suggested anxiously, 'and I'll get her out by this door.'

'They're here too, though. They'll watch this door.'

'Can't you give a wrong name?'

'No chance. I registered under my own name; besides, they'd trail the auto licence number.'

'Say you're married.'

'Jill says one of the house detectives knows her.'

The girl had stolen to the bed and tumbled upon it; lay there listening wretchedly to the knocking which had grown gradually to a pounding. Then came a man's voice, angry and imperative: 'Open up or we'll break the door in!'

In the silence when this voice ceased Amory realised that there were other things in the room besides people . . . over and around the figure crouched on the bed there hung an aura, gossamer as a moonbeam, tainted as stale, weak wine, yet a horror, diffusively brooding already over the three of them . . . and over by the window among the stirring curtains stood something else, featureless and indistinguishable, yet strangely familiar . . . Simultaneously two great cases presented themselves side by side to Amory; all that took place in his mind, then, occupied in actual time less than ten seconds.

The first fact that flashed radiantly on his comprehension was the great impersonality of sacrifice – he perceived that what we call love and hate, reward and punishment, had no more to do with it than the date of the month. He quickly recapitulated the story of a sacrifice he had heard of in college: a man had cheated in an examination; his roommate in a gust of sentiment had taken the entire blame and due to the shame of it the innocent one's entire future seemed shrouded in regret and failure, capped by the ingratitude of the real culprit. He had finally taken his own life – years afterwards the facts had come out. At the time the story had both puzzled and worried Amory. Now he realised the truth; that sacrifice was no purchase of freedom. It was like a great elective office, it was like an inheritance of power – to certain people at certain times an essential luxury, carrying with it not a guarantee but a responsibility, not a security but an infinite risk. Its very momentum might drag him down to ruin – the passing of the emotional wave that made it possible might leave the one who made it high and dry for ever on an island of despair.

. . . Amory knew that afterwards Alec would secretly hate him for having done so much for him . . .

. . . All this was flung before Amory like an opened scroll, while ulterior to him and speculating upon him were those two breathless, listening forces: the gossamer aura that hung over and about the girl and that familiar thing by the window.

Sacrifice by its very nature was arrogant and impersonal; sacrifice should be eternally supercilious.

Weep not for me but for thy children.[158]

That – thought Amory – would be somehow the way God would talk to me.

Amory felt a sudden surge of joy and then like a face in a motion-picture the aura over the bed faded out; the dynamic shadow by the window, that was as near as he could name it, remained for the fraction of a moment and then the breeze seemed to lift it swiftly out of the room. He clenched his hands in quick ecstatic excitement . . . the ten seconds were up . . .

'Do what I say, Alec – do what I say. Do you understand?'

Alec looked at him dumbly – his face a tableau of anguish.

'You have a family,' continued Amory slowly. 'You have a family and it's important that you should get out of this. Do you hear me?' He repeated clearly what he had said. 'Do you hear me?'

'I hear you.' The voice was curiously strained, the eyes never for a second left Amory's.

'Alec, you're going to lie down here. If anyone comes in you act drunk. You do what I say – if you don't I'll probably kill you.'

There was another moment while they stared at each other. Then Amory went briskly to the bureau and, taking his pocketbook, beckoned peremptorily to the girl. He heard one word from Alec that sounded like 'penitentiary', then he and Jill were in the bathroom with the door bolted behind them.

'You're here with me,' he said sternly. 'You've been with me all evening.'

She nodded, gave a little half cry.

In a second he had the door of the other room open and three men entered. There was an immediate flood of electric light and he stood there blinking.

'You've been playing a little too dangerous a game, young man!'

Amory laughed.

'Well?'

The leader of the trio nodded authoritatively at a burly man in a check suit.

'All right, Olson.'

'I got you, Mr O'May,' said Olson, nodding. The other two took a curious glance at their quarry and then withdrew, closing the door angrily behind them.

The burly man regarded Amory contemptuously.

'Didn't you ever hear of the Mann Act? Coming down here with her,' he indicated the girl with his thumb, 'with a New York licence on your car – to a hotel like *this*.' He shook his head implying that he had struggled over Amory but now gave him up.

'Well,' said Amory rather impatiently, 'what do you want us to do?'

'Get dressed, quick – and tell your friend not to make such a racket.' Jill was sobbing noisily on the bed, but at these words she subsided sulkily and, gathering up her clothes, retired to the bathroom. As Amory slipped into Alec's BVDs he found that his attitude towards the situation was agreeably humorous. The aggrieved virtue of the burly man made him want to laugh.

'Anybody else here?' demanded Olson, trying to look keen and ferret-like.

'Fellow who had the rooms,' said Amory carelessly. 'He's drunk as an owl, though. Been in there asleep since six o'clock.'

'I'll take a look at him presently.'

'How did you find out?' asked Amory curiously.

'Night clerk saw you go upstairs with this woman.'

Amory nodded; Jill reappeared from the bathroom, completely if rather untidily arrayed.

'Now then,' began Olson, producing a notebook, 'I want your real names – no damn John Smith or Mary Brown.'

'Wait a minute,' said Amory quietly. 'Just drop that big-bully stuff. We merely got caught, that's all.'

Olson glared at him.

'Name?' he snapped.

Amory gave his name and New York address.

'And the lady?'

'Miss Jill – '

'Say,' cried Olson indignantly, 'just ease up on the nursery rhymes. What's your name? Sarah Murphy? Minnie Jackson?'

'Oh, my God!' cried the girl cupping her tear-stained face in her hands. 'I don't want my mother to know. I don't want my mother to know.'

'Come on now!'

'Shut up!' cried Amory at Olson.

An instant's pause.

'Stella Robbins,' she faltered finally. 'General Delivery, Rugway, New Hampshire.'

Olson snapped his notebook shut and looked at them very ponderously.

'By rights the hotel could turn the evidence over to the police and you'd go to penitentiary, you would, for bringin' a girl from one state to 'nother f'r immoral purp'ses – ' He paused to let the majesty of his words sink in. 'But – the hotel is going to let you off.'

'It doesn't want to get in the papers,' cried Jill fiercely. 'Let us off! Huh!'

A great lightness surrounded Amory. He realised that he was safe and only then did he appreciate the full enormity of what he might have incurred.

'However,' continued Olson, 'there's a protective association among the hotels. There's been too much of this stuff, and we got a 'rangement with the newspapers so that you get a little free publicity. Not the name of the hotel, but just a line sayin' that you had a little trouble in 'lantic City. See?'

'I see.'

'You're gettin' off light – damn light – but – '

'Come on,' said Amory briskly. 'Let's get out of here. We don't need a valedictory.'

Olson walked through the bathroom and took a cursory glance at Alec's still form. Then he extinguished the lights and motioned them to follow him. As they walked into the elevator Amory considered a piece of bravado – yielded finally. He reached out and tapped Olson on the arm.

'Would you mind taking off your hat? There's a lady in the elevator.'

Olson's hat came off slowly. There was a rather embarrassing two minutes under the lights of the lobby while the night clerk and a few belated guests stared at them curiously; the loudly dressed girl with bent head, the handsome young man with his chin several points aloft; the inference was quite obvious. Then the chill outdoors – where the salt air was fresher and keener still with the first hints of morning.

'You can get one of those taxis and beat it,' said Olson, pointing to the blurred outline of two machines whose drivers were presumably asleep inside.

'Goodbye,' said Olson. He reached in his pocket suggestively, but Amory snorted, and, taking the girl's arm, turned away.

'Where did you tell the driver to go?' she asked as they whirled along the dim street.

'The station.'

'If that guy writes my mother – '

'He won't. Nobody'll ever know about this – except our friends and enemies.'

Dawn was breaking over the sea.

'It's getting blue,' she said.

'It does very well,' agreed Amory critically, and then as an after-thought: 'It's almost breakfast-time – do you want something to eat?'

'Food – ' she said with a cheerful laugh. 'Food is what queered the party. We ordered a big supper to be sent up to the room about two o'clock. Alec didn't give the waiter a tip, so I guess the little bastard snitched.'

Jill's low spirits seemed to have gone faster than the scattering night. 'Let me tell you,' she said emphatically, 'when you want to stage that sorta party stay away from liquor, and when you want to get tight stay away from bedrooms.'

'I'll remember.'

He tapped suddenly at the glass and they drew up at the door of an all-night restaurant.

'Is Alec a great friend of yours?' asked Jill as they perched them-selves on high stools inside, and set their elbows on the dingy counter.

'He used to be. He probably won't want to be any more – and never understand why.'

'It was sorta crazy you takin' all that blame. Is he pretty important? Kinda more important than you are?'

Amory laughed.

'That remains to be seen,' he answered. 'That's the question.'

THE COLLAPSE OF SEVERAL PILLARS

Two days later back in New York Amory found in a newspaper what he had been searching for – a dozen lines which announced to whom it might concern that Mr Amory Blaine, who 'gave his address' as, etc., had been requested to leave his hotel in Atlantic City because of entertaining in his room a lady *not* his wife.

Then he started, and his fingers trembled, for directly above was a longer paragraph of which the first words were: 'Mr and Mrs Leland R. Connage are announcing the engagement of their daughter, Rosalind, to Mr J. Dawson Ryder, of Hartford, Connecticut – '

He dropped the paper and lay down on his bed with a frightened, sinking sensation in the pit of his stomach. She was gone, definitely, finally gone. Until now he had half unconsciously cherished the hope deep in his heart that someday she would need him and send for him, cry that it had been a mistake, that her heart ached only for the pain she had caused him. Never again could he find even the sombre luxury of wanting her – not this Rosalind, harder, older – nor any beaten, broken woman that his imagination brought to the door of his forties; Amory had wanted her youth, the fresh radiance of her mind and body, the stuff that she was selling now once and for all. So far as he was concerned, young Rosalind was dead.

A day later came a crisp, terse letter from Mr Barton in Chicago, which informed him that as three more street-car companies had gone into the hands of receivers he could expect for the present no further remittances. Last of all, on a dazed Sunday night, a telegram told him of Monsignor Darcy's sudden death in Philadelphia five days before.

He knew then what it was that he had perceived among the curtains of the room in Atlantic City.

CHAPTER 5

The Egotist Becomes a Personage

A fathom deep in sleep I lie
　　With old desires, restrained before,
To clamour lifeward with a cry,
　　As dark flies out the greying door;
And so in quest of creeds to share
　　I seek assertive day again . . .
But old monotony is there:
　　Endless avenues of rain.

Oh, might I rise again! Might I
　　Throw off the heat of that old wine,
See the new morning mass the sky
　　With fairy towers, line on line;
Find each mirage in the high air
　　A symbol, not a dream again . . .
But old monotony is there:
　　Endless avenues of rain.

Under the glass porte-cochère[159] of a theatre Amory stood, watching the first great drops of rain splatter down and flatten to dark stains on the sidewalk. The air became grey and opalescent; a solitary light suddenly outlined a window over the way; then another light; then a hundred more danced and glimmered into vision. Under his feet a thick, iron-studded skylight turned yellow; in the street the lamps of the taxicabs sent out glistening sheens along the already black pavement. The unwelcome November rain had perversely stolen the day's last hour and pawned it with that ancient fence, the night.

The silence of the theatre behind him ended with a curious snapping sound, followed by the heavy roaring of a rising crowd and the interlaced clatter of many voices. The matinée was over.

He stood aside, edged a little into the rain to let the throng pass. A small boy rushed out, sniffed in the damp, fresh air and turned up the collar of his coat; came three or four couples in a great hurry; came a further scattering of people whose eyes as they emerged glanced invariably, first at the wet street, then at the rain-filled air, finally at the dismal sky; last a dense, strolling mass that depressed him with its heavy odour compounded of the tobacco smell of the men and the fetid sensuousness of stale powder on women. After the thick crowd came another scattering; a stray half-dozen; a man on crutches; finally the rattling bang of folding seats inside announced that the ushers were at work.

New York seemed not so much awakening as turning over in its bed. Pallid men rushed by, pinching together their coat-collars; a great swarm of tired, magpie girls from a department-store crowded along with shrieks of strident laughter, three to an umbrella; a squad of marching policemen passed, already miraculously protected by oilskin capes.

The rain gave Amory a feeling of detachment, and the numerous unpleasant aspects of city life without money occurred to him in threatening procession. There was the ghastly, stinking crush of the subway – the car cards[160] thrusting themselves at one, leering out like dull bores who grab your arm with another story; the querulous worry as to whether someone isn't leaning on you; a man deciding not to give his seat to a woman, hating her for it; the woman hating him for not doing it; at worst a squalid phantasmagoria of breath, and old cloth on human bodies and the smells of the food men ate – at best just people – too hot or too cold, tired, worried.

He pictured the rooms where these people lived – where the patterns of the blistered wallpapers were heavy reiterated sun-flowers on green and yellow backgrounds, where there were tin bathtubs and gloomy hallways and verdureless, unnamable spaces in back of the buildings; where even love dressed as seduction – a sordid murder around the corner, illicit motherhood in the flat above. And always there was the economical stuffiness of indoor winter, and the long summers, nightmares of perspiration between sticky enveloping walls . . . dirty restaurants where careless, tired people helped themselves to sugar with their own used coffee-spoons, leaving hard brown deposits in the bowl.

It was not so bad where there were only men or else only women; it was when they were vilely herded that it all seemed so rotten. It was some shame that women gave off at having men see them tired and poor – it was some disgust that men had for women who were tired and poor. It was dirtier than any battlefield he had seen, harder to contemplate than any actual hardship moulded of mire and sweat and danger, it was an atmosphere wherein birth and marriage and death were loathsome, secret things.

He remembered one day in the subway when a delivery boy had brought in a great funeral wreath of fresh flowers, how the smell of it had suddenly cleared the air and given everyone in the car a momentary glow.

'I detest poor people,' thought Amory suddenly. 'I hate them for being poor. Poverty may have been beautiful once, but it's rotten now. It's the ugliest thing in the world. It's essentially cleaner to be corrupt and rich than it is to be innocent and poor.' He seemed to see again a figure whose significance had once impressed him – a well-dressed young man gazing from a club window on Fifth Avenue and saying something to his companion with a look of utter disgust. Probably, thought Amory, what he said was: 'My God! Aren't people horrible!'

Never before in his life had Amory considered poor people. He thought cynically how completely he was lacking in all human sympathy. O. Henry had found in these people romance, pathos, love, hate – Amory saw only coarseness, physical filth and stupidity. He made no self-accusations: never any more did he reproach himself for feelings that were natural and sincere. He accepted all his reactions as a part of him, unchangeable, unmoral. This problem of poverty transformed, magnified, attached to some grander, more dignified attitude might someday even be his problem; at present it roused only his profound distaste.

He walked over to Fifth Avenue, dodging the blind, black menace of umbrellas, and standing in front of Delmonico's hailed an autobus. Buttoning his coat closely around him he climbed to the roof, where he rode in solitary state through the thin, persistent rain, stung into alertness by the cool moisture perpetually reborn on his cheek. Somewhere in his mind a conversation began, rather resumed its place in his attention. It was composed not of two voices, but of one, which acted alike as questioner and answerer:

Q. – Well – what's the situation?
A. – That I have about twenty-four dollars to my name.
Q. – You have the Lake Geneva estate.
A. – But I intend to keep it.
Q. – Can you live?
A. – I can't imagine not being able to. People make money in books and I've found that I can always do the things that people do in books. Really they are the only things I can do.
Q. – Be definite.
A. – I don't know what I'll do – nor have I much curiosity.

Tomorrow I'm going to leave New York for good. It's a bad town unless you're on top of it.

Q. – Do you want a lot of money?

A. – No. I am merely afraid of being poor.

Q. – Very afraid?

A. – Just passively afraid.

Q. – Where are you drifting?

A. – Don't ask *me*!

Q. – Don't you care?

A. – Rather. I don't want to commit moral suicide.

Q. – Have you no interests left?

A. – None. I've no more virtue to lose. Just as a cooling pot gives off heat, so all through youth and adolescence we give off calories of virtue. That's what's called ingenuousness.

Q. – An interesting idea.

A. – That's why a 'good man going wrong' attracts people. They stand around and literally *warm themselves* at the calories of virtue he gives off. Sarah makes an unsophisticated remark and the faces simper in delight – 'How *innocent* the poor child is!' They're warming themselves at her virtue. But Sarah sees the simper and never makes that remark again. Only she feels a little colder after that.

Q. – All your calories gone?

A. – All of them. I'm beginning to warm myself at other people's virtue.

Q. – Are you corrupt?

A. – I think so. I'm not sure. I'm not sure about good and evil at all any more.

Q. – Is that a bad sign in itself?

A. – Not necessarily.

Q. – What would be the test of corruption?

A. – Becoming really insincere – calling myself 'not such a bad fellow', thinking I regretted my lost youth when I only envy the delights of losing it. Youth is like having a big plate of candy. Sentimentalists think they want to be in the pure, simple state they were in before they ate the candy. They don't. They just want the fun of eating it all over again. The matron doesn't want to repeat her girlhood – she wants to repeat her honeymoon. I don't want to repeat my innocence. I want the pleasure of losing it again.

Q. – Where are you drifting?

This dialogue merged grotesquely into his mind's most familiar state – a grotesque blending of desires, worries, exterior impressions and physical reactions.

One Hundred and Twenty-Seventh Street – or One Hundred and Thirty-Seventh Street . . . Two and three look alike – no, not much. Seat damp . . . are clothes absorbing wetness from seat, or seat absorbing dryness from clothes? . . . Sitting on wet substance gave appendicitis, so Froggy Parker's mother said. Well, he'd had it – I'll sue the steamboat company, Beatrice said, and my uncle has a quarter interest – did Beatrice go to heaven? . . . probably not. He represented Beatrice's immortality, also love-affairs of numerous dead men who surely had never thought of him . . . if it wasn't appendicitis, influenza maybe. What? One Hundred and Twentieth Street? That must have been One Hundred and Twelfth back there. One One Two instead of One Two Seven. Rosalind not like Beatrice, Eleanor like Beatrice, only wilder and brainier. Apartments along here expensive – probably hundred and fifty a month – maybe two hundred. Uncle had only paid hundred a month for whole great big house in Minneapolis. Question – were the stairs on the left or right as you came in? Anyway, in 12 Univee they were straight back and to the left. What a dirty river – want to go down there and see if it's dirty – French rivers all brown or black, so were Southern rivers. Twenty-four dollars meant four hundred and eighty doughnuts. He could live on it three months and sleep in the park. Wonder where Jill was – Jill Bayne, Fayne, Sayne – what the devil – neck hurts, darned uncomfortable seat. No desire to sleep with Jill, what could Alec see in her? Alec had a coarse taste in women. Own taste the best; Isabelle, Clara, Rosalind, Eleanor, were all-American. Eleanor would pitch, probably southpaw. Rosalind was outfield, wonderful hitter. Clara first base, maybe. Wonder what Humbird's body looked like now. If he himself hadn't been bayonet instructor he'd have gone up to line three months sooner, probably been killed. Where's the darned bell –

The street numbers of Riverside Drive were obscured by the mist and dripping trees from anything but the swiftest scrutiny, but Amory had finally caught sight of one – One Hundred and Twenty-Seventh Street. He got off and with no distinct destination followed a winding, descending sidewalk and came out facing the river, in particular a long pier and a partitioned litter of shipyards for miniature craft: small launches, canoes, rowboats and catboats. He turned northward and followed the shore, jumped a small wire fence and found himself in a great disorderly yard adjoining a dock. The hulls of many boats in various stages of repair were around him; he smelled sawdust and paint and the scarcely distinguishable flat odour of the Hudson. A man approached through the heavy gloom.

'Hello,' said Amory.

'Got a pass?'

'No. Is this private?'

'This is the Hudson River Sporting and Yacht Club.'

'Oh! I didn't know. I'm just resting.'

'Well – ' began the man dubiously.

'I'll go if you want me to.'

The man made non-committal noises in his throat and passed on. Amory seated himself on an overturned boat and leaned forward thoughtfully until his chin rested in his hand.

'Misfortune is liable to make me a damn bad man,' he said slowly.

IN THE DROOPING HOURS

While the rain drizzled on Amory looked futilely back at the stream of his life, all its glitterings and dirty shallows. To begin with, he was still afraid – not physically afraid any more, but afraid of people and prejudice and misery and monotony. Yet, deep in his bitter heart, he wondered if he was after all worse than this man or the next. He knew that he could sophisticate himself finally into saying that his own weakness was just the result of circumstances and environment; that often when he raged at himself as an egotist something would whisper ingratiatingly: 'No. Genius!' That was one manifestation of fear, that voice which whispered that he could not be both great and good, that genius was the exact combination of those inexplicable grooves and twists in his mind, that any discipline would curb it to mediocrity. Probably more than any concrete vice or failing Amory despised his own personality – he loathed knowing that tomorrow and the thousand days after he would swell pompously at a compliment and sulk at an ill word like a third-rate musician or a first-class actor. He was ashamed of the fact that very simple and honest people usually distrusted him; that he had been cruel, often, to those who had sunk their personalities in him – several girls, and a man here and there through college, that he had been an evil influence on; people who had followed him here and there into mental adventures from which he alone rebounded unscathed.

Usually, on nights like this, for there had been many lately, he could escape from this consuming introspection by thinking of children and the infinite possibilities of children – he leaned and listened and he heard a startled baby awake in a house across the street and lend a tiny whimper to the still night. Quick as a flash he turned away, wondering with a touch of panic whether something in the brooding despair of his mood had made a darkness in its tiny soul. He shivered. What if some day the balance was overturned, and he became a thing that frightened children and crept into rooms in the dark, approached dim communion with those phantoms who whispered shadowy secrets to the mad of that dark continent upon the moon . . .

Amory smiled a bit.

'You're too much wrapped up in yourself,' he heard someone say. And again – 'Get out and do some real work – '

'Stop worrying – '

He fancied a possible future comment of his own.

'Yes – I was perhaps an egotist in youth, but I soon found it made me morbid to think too much about myself.'

Suddenly he felt an overwhelming desire to let himself go to the devil – not to go violently as a gentleman should, but to sink safely and sensuously out of sight. He pictured himself in an adobe house in Mexico, half-reclining on a rug-covered couch, his slender, artistic fingers closed on a cigarette while he listened to guitars strumming melancholy undertones to an age-old dirge of Castile and an olive-skinned, carmine-lipped girl caressed his hair. Here he might live a strange litany, delivered from right and wrong and from the hound of heaven and from every God (except the exotic Mexican one who was pretty slack himself and rather addicted to Oriental scents) – delivered from success and hope and poverty into that long chute of indulgence which led, after all, only to the artificial lake of death.

There were so many places where one might deteriorate pleasantly: Port Said, Shanghai, parts of Turkestan, Constantinople, the South Seas – all lands of sad, haunting music and many odours, where lust could be a mode and expression of life, where the shades of night skies and sunsets would seem to reflect only moods of passion: the colours of lips and poppies.

Once he had been miraculously able to scent evil as a horse detects a broken bridge at night, but the man with the queer feet in Phoebe's room had diminished to the aura over Jill. His instinct perceived the fetidness of poverty, but no longer ferreted out the deeper evils in pride and sensuality.

There were no more wise men; there were no more heroes; Burne Holiday was sunk from sight as though he had never lived; Monsignor was dead. Amory had grown up to a thousand books, a thousand lies; he had listened eagerly to people who pretended to know, who knew nothing. The mystical reveries of saints that had once filled him with awe in the still hours of night, now vaguely repelled him. The Byrons and Brookes who had defied life from mountain tops were in the end but *flâneurs* and poseurs, at best mistaking the shadow of courage for the substance of wisdom. The pageantry of his disillusion took shape in a world-old procession of Prophets, Athenians, Martyrs, Saints, Scientists, Don Juans, Jesuits, Puritans, Fausts, Poets, Pacifists; like costumed alumni at a college reunion they streamed before him as their dreams, personalities and creeds had in turn thrown coloured lights on his soul; each had tried to express the glory of life and the tremendous significance of man; each had boasted of synchronising what had gone before into his own rickety generalities; each had depended after all on the set stage and the convention of the theatre, which is that man in his hunger for faith will feed his mind with the nearest and most convenient food.

Women – of whom he had expected so much; whose beauty he had hoped to transmute into modes of art; whose unfathomable instincts, marvellously incoherent and inarticulate, he had thought to perpetuate in terms of experience – had become merely consecrations to their own posterity. Isabelle, Clara, Rosalind, Eleanor, were all removed by their very beauty, around which men had swarmed, from the possibility of contributing anything but a sick heart and a page of puzzled words to write.

Amory based his loss of faith in help from others on several sweeping syllogisms. Granted that his generation, however bruised and decimated from this Victorian war, were the heirs of progress. Waving aside petty differences of conclusions which, although they might occasionally cause the deaths of several millions of young men, might be explained away – supposing that after all Bernard Shaw and Bernhardi, Bonar Law and Bethmann-Hollweg[161] were mutual heirs of progress if only in agreeing against the ducking of witches – waiving the antitheses and approaching individually these men who seemed to be the leaders, he was repelled by the discrepancies and contradictions in the men themselves.

There was, for example, Thornton Hancock, respected by half the intellectual world as an authority on life, a man who had verified and believed the code he lived by, an educator of educators, an adviser to Presidents – yet Amory knew that this man had, in his heart, leaned on the priest of another religion.

And Monsignor, upon whom a cardinal rested, had moments of strange and horrible insecurity – inexplicable in a religion that explained even disbelief in terms of its own faith: if you doubted the devil it was the devil that made you doubt him. Amory had seen Monsignor go to the houses of stolid philistines, read popular novels furiously, saturate himself in routine, to escape from that horror.

And this priest, a little wiser, somewhat purer, had been, Amory knew, not essentially older than he.

Amory was alone – he had escaped from a small enclosure into a great labyrinth. He was where Goethe was when he began *Faust*; he was where Conrad was when he wrote *Almayer's Folly*.

Amory said to himself that there were essentially two sorts of people who through natural clarity or disillusion left the enclosure and sought the labyrinth. There were men like Wells and Plato, who had, half unconsciously, a strange, hidden orthodoxy, who would accept for themselves only what could be accepted for all men – incurable romanticists who never, for all their efforts, could enter the labyrinth as stark souls; there were on the other hand sword-like pioneering personalities, Samuel Butler, Renan,[162] Voltaire, who progressed much slower, yet eventually much further, not in the direct pessimistic line of speculative philosophy but concerned in the eternal attempt to attach a positive value to life . . .

Amory stopped. He began for the first time in his life to have a strong distrust of all generalities and epigrams. They were too easy, too dangerous to the public mind. Yet all thought usually reached the public after thirty years in some such form: Benson and Chesterton had popularised Huysmans and Newman; Shaw had sugar-coated Nietzsche and Ibsen and Schopenhauer. The man in the street heard the conclusions of dead genius through someone else's clever paradoxes and didactic epigrams.

Life was a damned muddle . . . a football game with everyone off-side and the referee got rid of – everyone claiming the referee would have been on his side . . .

Progress was a labyrinth . . . people plunging blindly in and then rushing wildly back, shouting that they had found it . . . the invisible king – the *élan vital* – the principle of evolution . . . writing a book, starting a war, founding a school . . .

Amory, even had he not been a selfish man, would have started all enquiries with himself. He was his own best example – sitting in the rain, a human creature of sex and pride, foiled by chance and his own temperament of the balm of love and children, preserved to help in building up the living consciousness of the race.

In self-reproach and loneliness and disillusion he came to the entrance of the labyrinth.

Another dawn flung itself across the river, a belated taxi hurried along the street, its lamps still shining like burning eyes in a face white from a night's carouse. A melancholy siren sounded far down the river.

MONSIGNOR

Amory kept thinking how Monsignor would have enjoyed his own funeral. It was magnificently Catholic and liturgical. Bishop O'Neill sang solemn high mass and the cardinal gave the final absolutions. Thornton Hancock, Mrs Lawrence, the British and Italian ambassadors, the papal delegate, and a host of friends and priests were there – yet the inexorable shears had cut through all these threads that Monsignor had gathered into his hands. To Amory it was a haunting grief to see him lying in his coffin, with closed hands upon his purple vestments. His face had not changed, and, as he never knew he was dying, it showed no pain or fear. It was Amory's dear old friend, his and the others' – for the church was full of people with daft, staring faces, the most exalted seeming the most stricken.

The cardinal, like an archangel in cope and mitre, sprinkled the holy water; the organ broke into sound; the choir began to sing the *Requiem aeternam*.[163]

All these people grieved because they had to some extent depended upon Monsignor. Their grief was more than sentiment for the 'crack in his voice or a certain break in his walk', as Wells put it. These people had leaned on Monsignor's faith, his way of finding cheer, of making religion a thing of lights and shadows, making all light and shadow merely aspects of God. People felt safe when he was near.

Of Amory's attempted sacrifice had been born merely the full realisation of his disillusion, but of Monsignor's funeral was born the romantic elf who was to enter the labyrinth with him. He found something that he wanted, had always wanted and always would want – not to be admired, as he had feared; not to be loved, as he had made himself believe; but to be necessary to people, to be indispensable; he remembered the sense of security he had found in Burne.

Life opened up in one of its amazing bursts of radiance and Amory suddenly and permanently rejected an old epigram that had been playing listlessly in his mind: 'Very few things matter and nothing matters very much.'

On the contrary, Amory felt an immense desire to give people a sense of security.

THE BIG MAN WITH GOGGLES

On the day that Amory started on his walk to Princeton the sky was a colourless vault, cool, high and barren of the threat of rain. It was a grey day, that least fleshly of all weathers; a day of dreams and far hopes and clear visions. It was a day easily associated with those abstract truths and purities that dissolve in the sunshine or fade out in mocking laughter by the light of the moon. The trees and clouds were carved in classical severity; the sounds of the countryside had harmonised to a monotone, metallic as a trumpet, breathless as the Grecian urn.

The day had put Amory in such a contemplative mood that he caused much annoyance to several motorists who were forced to slow up considerably or else run him down. So engrossed in his thoughts was he that he was scarcely surprised at that strange phenomenon – cordiality manifested within fifty miles of Manhattan – when a passing car slowed down beside him and a voice hailed him. He looked up and saw a magnificent Locomobile[164] in which sat two middle-aged men, one of them small and anxious looking, apparently an artificial growth on the other, who was large and begoggled and imposing.

'Do you want a lift?' asked the apparently artificial growth, glancing from the corner of his eye at the imposing man as if for some habitual, silent corroboration.

'You bet I do. Thanks.'

The chauffeur swung open the door, and, climbing in, Amory settled himself in the middle of the back seat. He took in his companions curiously. The chief characteristic of the big man seemed to be a great confidence in himself set off against a tremendous boredom with everything around him. That part of his face which protruded under the goggles was what is generally termed 'strong'; rolls of not undignified fat had collected near his chin; somewhere above was a wide thin mouth and the rough model for a Roman nose, and, below, his shoulders collapsed without a struggle into the powerful bulk of his chest and belly. He was excellently and quietly dressed. Amory noticed that he was inclined to stare straight at the back of the chauffeur's head as if speculating steadily but hopelessly some baffling hirsute problem.

The smaller man was remarkable only for his complete submersion in the personality of the other. He was of that lower secretarial type who at forty have engraved upon their business cards: 'Assistant to the President', and without a sigh consecrate the rest of their lives to second-hand mannerisms.

'Going far?' asked the smaller man in a pleasant disinterested way.

'Quite a stretch.'

'Hiking for exercise?'

'No,' responded Amory succinctly, 'I'm walking because I can't afford to ride.'

'Oh.'

Then again: 'Are you looking for work? Because there's lots of work,' he continued rather testily. 'All this talk of lack of work. The West is especially short of labour.' He expressed the West with a sweeping, lateral gesture.

Amory nodded politely.

'Have you a trade?'

No – Amory had no trade.

'Clerk, eh?'

No – Amory was not a clerk.

'Whatever your line is,' said the little man, seeming to agree wisely with something Amory had said, 'now is the time of opportunity and business openings.' He glanced again towards the big man, as a lawyer grilling a witness glances involuntarily at the jury.

Amory decided that he must say something and for the life of him could think of only one thing to say.

'Of course I want a great lot of money – '

The little man laughed mirthlessly but conscientiously.

'That's what everyone wants nowadays, but they don't want to work for it.'

'A very natural, healthy desire. Almost all normal people want to be rich without great effort – except the financiers in problem plays, who want to "crash their way through". Don't you want easy money?'

'Of course not,' said the secretary indignantly.

'But,' continued Amory disregarding him, 'being very poor at present I am contemplating socialism as possibly my forte.'

Both men glanced at him curiously.

'These bomb throwers – ' The little man ceased as words lurched ponderously from the big man's chest. 'If I thought you were a bomb thrower I'd run you over to the Newark jail. That's what I think of Socialists.'

Amory laughed.

'What are you,' asked the big man, 'one of these parlour Bolsheviks, one of these idealists? I must say I fail to see the difference. The idealists loaf around and write the stuff that stirs up the poor immigrants.'

'Well,' said Amory, 'if being an idealist is both safe and lucrative, I might try it.'

'What's your difficulty? Lost your job?'

'Not exactly, but – well, call it that.'

'What was it?'

'Writing copy for an advertising agency.'

'Lots of money in advertising.'

Amory smiled discreetly.

'Oh, I'll admit there's money in it eventually. Talent doesn't starve any more. Even art gets enough to eat these days. Artists draw your magazine covers, write your advertisements, hash out ragtime for your theatres. By the great commercialising of printing you've found a harmless, polite occupation for every genius who might have carved his own niche. But beware the artist who's an intellectual also. The artist who doesn't fit – the Rousseau, the Tolstoy, the Samuel Butler, the Amory Blaine – '

'Who's he?' demanded the little man suspiciously.

'Well,' said Amory, 'he's a – he's an intellectual personage not very well known at present.'

The little man laughed his conscientious laugh, and stopped rather suddenly as Amory's burning eyes turned on him.

'What are you laughing at?'

'These *intellectual* people – '

'Do you know what it means?'

The little man's eyes twitched nervously.

'Why, it *usually* means – '

'It *always* means brainy and well educated,' interrupted Amory. 'It means having an active knowledge of the race's experience.' Amory decided to be very rude. He turned to the big man. 'The young man,' he indicated the secretary with his thumb, and said young man as one says bellboy, with no implication of youth, 'has the usual muddled connotation of all popular words.'

'You object to the fact that capital controls printing?' said the big man, fixing him with his goggles.

'Yes – and I object to doing their mental work for them. It seemed to me that the root of all the business I saw around me consisted in overworking and underpaying a bunch of dubs who submitted to it.'

'Here now,' said the big man, 'you'll have to admit that the labouring man is certainly highly paid – five- and six-hour days – it's ridiculous. You can't buy an honest day's work from a man in the trade unions.'

'You've brought it on yourselves,' insisted Amory. 'You people never make concessions until they're wrung out of you.'

'What people?'

'Your class; the class I belonged to until recently; those who by inheritance or industry or brains or dishonesty have become the moneyed class.'

'Do you imagine that if that road-mender over there had the money he'd be any more willing to give it up?'

'No, but what's that got to do with it?'

The older man considered.

'No, I'll admit it hasn't. It rather sounds as if it had though.'

'In fact,' continued Amory, 'he'd be worse. The lower classes are narrower, less pleasant and personally more selfish – certainly more stupid. But all that has nothing to do with the question.'

'Just exactly what is the question?'

Here Amory had to pause to consider exactly what the question was.

AMORY COINS A PHRASE

'When life gets hold of a brainy man of fair education,' began Amory slowly, 'that is, when he marries he becomes, nine times out of ten, a conservative as far as existing social conditions are concerned. He may be unselfish, kind-hearted, even just in his own way, but his first job is to provide and to hold fast. His wife shoos him on, from ten thousand a year to twenty thousand a year, on and on, in an enclosed treadmill that hasn't any windows. He's done! Life's got him! He's no help! He's a spiritually married man.'

Amory paused and decided that it wasn't such a bad phrase.

'Some men,' he continued, 'escape the grip. Maybe their wives have no social ambitions; maybe they've hit a sentence or two in a "dangerous book" that pleased them; maybe they started on the tread-mill as I did and were knocked off. Anyway, they're the congressmen you can't bribe, the Presidents who aren't politicians, the writers, speakers, scientists, statesmen who aren't just popular grab-bags for a half-dozen women and children.'

'He's the natural radical?'

'Yes,' said Amory. 'He may vary from the disillusioned critic, like old Thornton Hancock, all the way to Trotsky. Now this spiritually unmarried man hasn't direct power, for unfortunately the spiritually married man, as a by-product of his money chase, has garnered in the great newspaper, the popular magazine, the influential weekly – so that Mrs Newspaper, Mrs Magazine, Mrs Weekly can have a better limousine than those oil people across the street or those cement people round the corner.

'Why not?'

'It makes wealthy men the keepers of the world's intellectual con-science and, of course, a man who has money under one set of social institutions quite naturally can't risk his family's happiness by letting the clamour for another appear in his newspaper.'

'But it appears,' said the big man.

'Where? – in the discredited mediums. Rotten cheap-papered weeklies.'

'All right – go on.'

'Well, my first point is that through a mixture of conditions of which the family is the first, there are these two sorts of brains. One sort takes human nature as it finds it, uses its timidity, its weakness and its strength for its own ends. Opposed is the man who, being spiritually unmarried, continually seeks for new systems that will control or counteract human nature. His problem is harder. It is not life that's complicated, it's the struggle to guide and control life. That is his struggle. He is a part of progress – the spiritually married man is not.'

The big man produced three big cigars, and proffered them on his huge palm. The little man took one, Amory shook his head and reached for a cigarette.

'Go on talking,' said the big man. 'I've been wanting to hear one of you fellows.'

GOING FASTER

'Modern life,' began Amory again, 'changes no longer century by century, but year by year, ten times faster than it ever has before – populations doubling, civilisations unified more closely with other civilisations, economic interdependence, racial questions, and – we're *dawdling* along. My idea is that we've got to go very much faster.' He slightly emphasised the last words and the chauffeur unconsciously increased the speed of the car. Amory and the big man laughed; the little man laughed, too, after a pause.

'Every child,' said Amory, 'should have an equal start. If his father can endow him with a good physique and his mother with some common sense in his early education, that should be his heritage. If the father can't give him a good physique, if the mother has spent in chasing men the years in which she should have been preparing herself to educate her children, so much the worse for the child. He shouldn't be artificially bolstered up with money, sent to these horrible tutoring schools, dragged through college . . . Every boy ought to have an equal start.'

'All right,' said the big man, his goggles indicating neither approval nor objection.

'Next I'd have a fair trial of government ownership of all industries.'

'That's been proved a failure.'

'No – it merely failed. If we had government ownership we'd have the best analytical business minds in the government working for something besides themselves. We'd have Mackays instead of Burlesons;[165] we'd have Morgans in the Treasury Department; we'd have Hills running interstate commerce. We'd have the best lawyers in the Senate.'

'They wouldn't give their best efforts for nothing. McAdoo – '[166]

'No,' said Amory, shaking his head. 'Money isn't the only stimulus that brings out the best that's in a man, even in America.'

'You said a while ago that it was.'

'It is, right now. But if it were made illegal to have more than a certain amount the best men would all flock for the one other reward which attracts humanity – honour.'

The big man made a sound that was very like *boo*. 'That's the silliest thing you've said yet.'

'No, it isn't silly. It's quite plausible. If you'd gone to college you'd have been struck by the fact that the men there would work twice as hard for any one of a hundred petty honours as those other men did who were earning their way through.'

'Kid's – child's play!' scoffed his antagonist.

'Not by a darned sight – unless we're all children. Did you ever see a grown man when he's trying for a secret society – or a rising family whose name is up at some club? They'll jump when they hear the sound of the word. The idea that to make a man work you've got to hold gold in front of his eyes is a growth, not an axiom. We've done that for so long that we've forgotten there's any other way. We've made a world where that's necessary. Let me tell you' – Amory became emphatic – 'if there were ten men insured against either wealth or starvation, and offered a green ribbon for five hours' work a day and a blue ribbon for ten hours' work a day nine out of ten of them would be trying for the blue ribbon. That competitive instinct only wants a badge. If the size of their house is the badge they'll sweat their heads off for that. If it's only a blue ribbon, I damn near believe they'll work just as hard. They have in other ages.'

'I don't agree with you.'

'I know it,' said Amory nodding sadly. 'It doesn't matter any more though. I think these people are going to come and take what they want pretty soon.'

A fierce hiss came from the little man.

'*Machine-guns!*'

'Ah, but you've taught them their use.'

The big man shook his head.

'In this country there are enough property owners not to permit that sort of thing.'

Amory wished he knew the statistics of property owners and non-property owners; he decided to change the subject.

But the big man was aroused.

'When you talk of "taking things away", you're on dangerous ground.'

'How can they get it without taking it? For years people have been stalled off with promises. Socialism may not be progress, but the threat of the red flag is certainly the inspiring force of all reform. You've got to be sensational to get attention.'

'Russia is your example of a beneficent violence, I suppose?'

'Quite possibly,' admitted Amory. 'Of course, it's overflowing just as the French Revolution did, but I've no doubt that it's really a great experiment and well worth while.'

'Don't you believe in moderation?'

'You won't listen to the moderates, and it's almost too late. The truth is that the public has done one of those startling and amazing things that they do about once in a hundred years. They've seized an idea.'

'What is it?'

'That however the brains and abilities of men may differ, their stomachs are essentially the same.'

THE LITTLE MAN GETS HIS

'If you took all the money in the world,' said the little man with much profundity, 'and divided it up in equ – '

'Oh, shut up!' said Amory briskly and, paying no attention to the little man's enraged stare, he went on with his argument.

'The human stomach – ' he began; but the big man interrupted rather impatiently.

'I'm letting you talk, you know,' he said, 'but please avoid stomachs. I've been feeling mine all day. Anyway, I don't agree with one- half you've said. Government ownership is the basis of your whole argument, and it's invariably a beehive of corruption. Men won't work for blue ribbons, that's all rot.'

When he ceased the little man spoke up with a determined nod, as if resolved this time to have his say out.

'There are certain things which are human nature,' he asserted with an owl-like look, 'which always have been and always will be, which can't be changed.'

Amory looked from the small man to the big man helplessly.

'Listen to that! *That's* what makes me discouraged with progress. *Listen* to that! I can name offhand over one hundred natural phenomena that have been changed by the will of man – a hundred instincts in man that have been wiped out or are now held in check by civilisation. What this man here just said has been for thousands of years the last refuge of the associated mutton-heads of the world. It negates the efforts of every scientist, statesman, moralist, reformer, doctor and philosopher that ever gave his life to humanity's service. It's a flat impeachment of all that's worth while in human nature.

Every person over twenty-five years old who makes that statement in cold blood ought to be deprived of the franchise.'

The little man leaned back against the seat, his face purple with rage. Amory continued, addressing his remarks to the big man.

'These quarter-educated, stale-minded men such as your friend here, who *think* they think, every question that comes up, you'll find his type in the usual ghastly muddle. One minute it's "the brutality and inhumanity of these Prussians" – the next it's "we ought to exterminate the whole German people". They always believe that "things are in a bad way now", but they "haven't any faith in these idealists". One minute they call Wilson "just a dreamer, not practical" – a year later they rail at him for making his dreams realities. They haven't clear logical ideas on one single subject except a sturdy, stolid opposition to all change. They don't think uneducated people should be highly paid, but they won't see that if they don't pay the uneducated people their children are going to be uneducated too, and we're going round and round in a circle. That – is the great middle class!'

The big man with a broad grin on his face leaned over and smiled at the little man.

'You're catching it pretty heavy, Garvin; how do you feel?'

The little man made an attempt to smile and act as if the whole matter were so ridiculous as to be beneath notice. But Amory was not through.

'The theory that people are fit to govern themselves rests on this man. If he can be educated to think clearly, concisely and logically, freed of his habit of taking refuge in platitudes and prejudices and sentimentalisms, then I'm a militant Socialist. If he can't, then I don't think it matters much what happens to man or his systems, now or hereafter.'

'I am both interested and amused,' said the big man. 'You are very young.'

'Which may only mean that I have neither been corrupted nor made timid by contemporary experience. I possess the most valuable experience, the experience of the race, for in spite of going to college I've managed to pick up a good education.'

'You talk glibly.'

'It's not all rubbish,' cried Amory passionately. 'This is the first time in my life I've argued Socialism. It's the only panacea I know. I'm restless. My whole generation is restless. I'm sick of a system where the richest man gets the most beautiful girl if he wants her, where the artist without an income has to sell his talents to a button manufacturer. Even if I had no talents I'd not be content to work ten years, condemned either to celibacy or a furtive indulgence, to give some man's son an automobile.'

'But, if you're not sure – '

'That doesn't matter,' exclaimed Amory. 'My position couldn't be worse. A social revolution might land me on top. Of course I'm selfish. It seems to me I've been a fish out of water in too many outworn systems. I was probably one of the two dozen men in my class at college who got a decent education; still they'd let any well-tutored flathead play football and *I* was ineligible, because some silly old men thought we should *all* profit by conic sections. I loathed the army. I loathed business. I'm in love with change and I've killed my conscience – '

'So you'll go along crying that we must go faster.'

'That, at least, is true,' Amory insisted. 'Reform won't catch up to the needs of civilisation unless it's made to. A *laissez-faire* policy is like spoiling a child by saying he'll turn out all right in the end. He will – if he's made to.'

'But you don't believe all this Socialist patter you talk.'

'I don't know. Until I talked to you I hadn't thought seriously about it. I wasn't sure of half of what I said.'

'You puzzle me,' said the big man, 'but you're all alike. They say Bernard Shaw, in spite of his doctrines, is the most exacting of all dramatists about his royalties. To the last farthing.'

'Well,' said Amory, 'I simply state that I'm a product of a versatile mind in a restless generation – with every reason to throw my mind and pen in with the radicals. Even if, deep in my heart, I thought we were all blind atoms in a world as limited as a stroke of a pendulum, I and my sort would struggle against tradition; try, at least, to displace old cants with new ones. I've thought I was right about life at various times, but faith is difficult. One thing I know. If living isn't a seeking for the grail it may be a damned amusing game.'

For a minute neither spoke and then the big man asked: 'What was your university?'

'Princeton.'

The big man became suddenly interested; the expression of his goggles altered slightly.

'I sent my son to Princeton.'

'Did you?'

'Perhaps you knew him. His name was Jesse Ferrenby. He was killed last year in France.'

'I knew him very well. In fact, he was one of my particular friends.'

'He was – a – quite a fine boy. We were very close.'

Amory began to perceive a resemblance between the father and the dead son and he told himself that there had been all along a sense of familiarity. Jesse Ferrenby, the man who in college had borne off the crown that he had aspired to. It was all so far away. What little boys they had been, working for blue ribbons –

The car slowed up at the entrance to a great estate, ringed around by a huge hedge and a tall iron fence.

'Won't you come in for lunch?'

Amory shook his head.

'Thank you, Mr Ferrenby, but I've got to get on.'

The big man held out his hand. Amory saw that the fact that he had known Jesse more than outweighed any disfavour he had created by his opinions. What ghosts were people with which to work! Even the little man insisted on shaking hands.

'Goodbye!' shouted Mr Ferrenby, as the car turned the corner and started up the drive. 'Good luck to you and bad luck to your theories.'

'Same to you, sir,' cried Amory, smiling and waving his hand.

'OUT OF THE FIRE, OUT OF THE LITTLE ROOM'[167]

Eight hours from Princeton Amory sat down by the Jersey roadside and looked at the frost-bitten country. Nature as a rather coarse phenomenon composed largely of flowers that, when closely inspected, appeared moth-eaten, and of ants that endlessly traversed blades of grass, was always disillusioning; nature represented by skies and waters and far horizons was more likable. Frost and the promise of winter thrilled him now, made him think of a wild battle between St Regis's and Groton, ages ago, seven years ago – and of an autumn day in France twelve months before when he had lain in tall grass, his platoon flattened down close around him, waiting to tap the shoulders of a Lewis gunner.[168] He saw the two pictures together with somewhat the same primitive exaltation – two games he had played, differing in quality of acerbity, linked in a way that differed them from Rosalind or the subject of labyrinths which were, after all, the business of life.

'I am selfish,' he thought.

'This is not a quality that will change when I "see human suffering" or "lose my parents" or "help others".

'This selfishness is not only part of me. It is the most living part.

'It is by somehow transcending rather than by avoiding that selfishness that I can bring poise and balance into my life.

'There is no virtue of unselfishness that I cannot use. I can make sacrifices, be charitable, give to a friend, endure for a friend, lay down my life for a friend – all because these things may be the best possible expression of myself; yet I have not one drop of the milk of human kindness.'

The problem of evil had solidified for Amory into the problem of sex. He was beginning to identify evil with the strong phallic worship in Brooke and the early Wells. Inseparably linked with evil was beauty – beauty, still a constant rising tumult; soft in Eleanor's voice, in an old song at night, rioting deliriously through life like super-imposed waterfalls, half rhythm, half darkness. Amory knew that every time he had reached towards it longingly it had leered out at him with the grotesque face of evil. Beauty of great art, beauty of all joy, most of all the beauty of women.

After all, it had too many associations with licence and indulgence. Weak things were often beautiful, weak things were never good. And in this new loneness of his that had been selected for what greatness he might achieve, beauty must be relative or, itself a harmony, it would make only a discord.

In a sense this gradual renunciation of beauty was the second step after his disillusion had been made complete. He felt that he was leaving behind him his chance of being a certain type of artist. It seemed so much more important to be a certain sort of man.

His mind turned a corner suddenly and he found himself thinking of the Catholic Church. The idea was strong in him that there was a certain intrinsic lack in those to whom orthodox religion was necessary, and religion to Amory meant the Church of Rome. Quite conceivably it was an empty ritual but it was seemingly the only assimilative, traditionary bulwark against the decay of morals. Until the great mobs could be educated into a moral sense someone must cry: 'Thou shalt not!' Yet any acceptance was, for the present, impossible. He wanted time and the absence of ulterior pressure. He wanted to keep the tree without ornaments, realise fully the direction and momentum of this new start.

The afternoon waned from the purging good of three o'clock to the golden beauty of four. Afterwards he walked through the dull ache of a setting sun when even the clouds seemed bleeding and at twilight he came to a graveyard. There was a dusky, dreamy smell of flowers and the ghost of a new moon in the sky and shadows everywhere. On an impulse he considered trying to open the door of a rusty iron vault built into the side of a hill; a vault washed clean and covered with late-blooming, weepy watery-blue flowers that might have grown from dead eyes, sticky to the touch with a sickening odour.

Amory wanted to *feel* 'William Dayfield, 1864'.

He wondered that graves ever made people consider life in vain. Somehow he could find nothing hopeless in having lived. All the broken columns and clasped hands and doves and angels meant romances. He fancied that in a hundred years he would like having young people speculate as to whether his eyes were brown or blue, and he hoped quite passionately that his grave would have about it an air of many, many years ago. It seemed strange that out of a row of Union soldiers two or three made him think of dead loves and dead lovers, when they were exactly like the rest, even to the yellowish moss.

Long after midnight the towers and spires of Princeton were visible, with here and there a late-burning light – and suddenly out of the clear darkness the sound of bells. As an endless dream it went on; the spirit of the past brooding over a new generation, the chosen youth from the muddled, unchastened world, still fed romantically on the mistakes and half-forgotten dreams of dead statesmen and poets. Here was a new generation, shouting the old cries, learning the old creeds, through a reverie of long days and nights; destined finally to go out into that dirty grey turmoil to follow love and pride; a new generation dedicated more than the last to the fear of poverty and the worship of success; grown up to find all gods dead, all wars fought, all faiths in man shaken . . .

Amory, sorry for them, was still not sorry for himself – art, politics, religion, whatever his medium should be, he knew he was safe now, free from all hysteria – he could accept what was acceptable, roam, grow, rebel, sleep deep through many nights . . .

There was no God in his heart, he knew; his ideas were still in riot; there was ever the pain of memory; the regret for his lost youth – yet the waters of disillusion had left a deposit on his soul, responsibility and a love of life, the faint stirring of old ambitions and unrealised dreams. But – oh, Rosalind! Rosalind! . . .

'It's all a poor substitute at best,' he said sadly.

And he could not tell why the struggle was worth while, why he had determined to use to the utmost himself and his heritage from the personalities he had passed . . .

He stretched out his arms to the crystalline, radiant sky.

'I know myself,' he cried, 'but that is all.'

The Beautiful and Damned

◆

F. Scott Fitzgerald

The victor belongs to the spoils.

ANTHONY PATCH

TO

SHANE LESLIE, GEORGE JEAN NATHAN
AND MAXWELL PERKINS[169]

in appreciation of much literary
help and encouragement

Contents

BOOK ONE

CHAPTER I

Anthony Patch

In 1913, when Anthony Patch was twenty-five, two years were already gone since irony, the Holy Ghost of this later day, had, theoretically at least, descended upon him. Irony was the final polish of the shoe, the ultimate dab of the clothes-brush, a sort of intellectual 'There!' – yet at the brink of this story he has as yet gone no further than the conscious stage. As you first see him he wonders frequently whether he is not without honour and slightly mad, a shameful and obscene thinness glistening on the surface of the world like oil on a clean pond, these occasions being varied, of course, with those in which he thinks himself rather an exceptional young man, thoroughly sophisticated, well adjusted to his environment, and somewhat more significant than anyone else he knows.

This was his healthy state and it made him cheerful, pleasant, and very attractive to intelligent men and to all women. In this state he considered that he would one day accomplish some quiet subtle thing that the elect would deem worthy and, passing on, would join the dimmer stars in a nebulous, indeterminate heaven halfway between death and immortality. Until the time came for this effort he would be Anthony Patch – not a portrait of a man but a distinct and dynamic personality, opinionated, contemptuous, functioning from within outwards – a man who was aware that there could be no honour and yet had honour, who knew the sophistry of courage and yet was brave.

A WORTHY MAN AND HIS GIFTED SON

Anthony drew as much consciousness of social security from being the grandson of Adam J. Patch as he would have had from tracing his line over the sea to the Crusaders. This is inevitable; Virginians and Bostonians to the contrary notwithstanding, an aristocracy founded sheerly on money postulates wealth in the particular.

Now Adam J. Patch, more familiarly known as 'Cross Patch', left his father's farm in Tarrytown[170] early in sixty-one to join a New York cavalry regiment. He came home from the war a major, charged into Wall Street, and amid much fuss, fume, applause and ill will he gathered to himself some seventy-five million dollars.

This occupied his energies until he was fifty-seven years old. It was then that he determined, after a severe attack of sclerosis, to consecrate the remainder of his life to the moral regeneration of the world. He became a reformer among reformers. Emulating the magnificent efforts of Anthony Comstock,[171] after whom his grandson was named, he levelled a varied assortment of uppercuts and body-blows at liquor, literature, vice, art, patent medicines and Sunday theatres. His mind, under the influence of that insidious mildew which eventually forms on all but the few, gave itself up furiously to every indignation of the age. From an armchair in the office of his Tarrytown estate he directed against the enormous hypothetical enemy, unrighteousness, a campaign which went on through fifteen years, during which he displayed himself a rabid monomaniac, an unqualified nuisance and an intolerable bore. The year in which this story opens found him wearying; his campaign had grown desultory; 1861 was creeping up slowly on 1895; his thoughts ran a great deal on the Civil War, somewhat on his dead wife and son, almost infinitesimally on his grandson Anthony.

Early in his career Adam Patch had married an anaemic lady of thirty, Alicia Withers, who brought him one hundred thousand dollars and an impeccable entré into the banking circles of New York. Immediately and rather spunkily she had borne him a son and, as if completely devitalised by the magnificence of this performance, she had thenceforth effaced herself within the shadowy dimensions of the nursery. The boy, Adam Ulysses Patch, became an inveterate joiner of clubs, connoisseur of good form and driver of tandems – at the astonishing age of twenty-six he began his memoirs under the title *New York Society as I Have Seen It*. On the rumour of its conception this work was eagerly bid for among publishers, but as it proved after his death to be immoderately verbose and overpoweringly dull, it never obtained even a private printing.

This Fifth Avenue Chesterfield[172] married at twenty-two. His wife was Henrietta Lebrune, the Boston 'Society Contralto', and the single child of the union was, at the request of his grandfather, christened Anthony Comstock Patch. When he went to Harvard, the Comstock dropped out of his name to a nether hell of oblivion and was never heard of thereafter.

Young Anthony had one picture of his father and mother together – so often had it faced his eyes in childhood that it had acquired the impersonality of furniture, but everyone who came into his bedroom regarded it with interest. It showed a dandy of the nineties, spare and handsome, standing beside a tall dark lady with a muff and the suggestion of a bustle. Between them was a little boy with long brown curls, dressed in a velvet Lord Fauntleroy suit.[173] This was Anthony at five, the year of his mother's death.

His memories of the Boston Society Contralto were nebulous and musical. She was a lady who sang, sang, sang, in the music room of their house on Washington Square[174] – sometimes with guests scattered all about her, the men with their arms folded, balanced breathlessly on the edges of sofas, the women with their hands in their laps, occasionally making little whispers to the men and always clapping very briskly and uttering cooing cries after each song – and often she sang to Anthony alone, in Italian or French or in a strange and terrible dialect which she imagined to be the speech of the Southern Negro.

His recollections of the gallant Ulysses, the first man in America to roll the lapels of his coat, were much more vivid. After Henrietta Lebrune Patch had 'joined another choir', as her widower huskily remarked from time to time, father and son lived up at grampa's in Tarrytown, and Ulysses came daily to Anthony's nursery and expelled pleasant, thick-smelling words for sometimes as much as an hour. He was continually promising Anthony hunting trips and fishing trips and excursions to Atlantic City,[175] 'oh, sometime soon now'; but none of them ever materialised. One trip they did take; when Anthony was eleven they went abroad, to England and Switzerland, and there in the best hotel in Lucerne his father died with much sweating and grunting and crying aloud for air. In a panic of despair and terror Anthony was brought back to America, wedded to a vague melancholy that was to stay beside him through the rest of his life.

PAST AND PERSON OF THE HERO

At eleven he had a horror of death. Within six impressionable years his parents had died and his grandmother had faded off almost imperceptibly, until, for the first time since her marriage, her person held for one day an unquestioned supremacy over her own drawing-room. So to Anthony life was a struggle against death, that waited at every corner. It was as a concession to his hypochondriacal imagination that he formed the habit of reading in bed – it soothed him. He read until he was tired and often fell asleep with the lights still on.

His favourite diversion until he was fourteen was his stamp collection; enormous, as nearly exhaustive as a boy's could be – his grandfather considered fatuously that it was teaching him geography. So Anthony kept up a correspondence with a half-dozen 'Stamp and Coin' companies and it was rare that the mail failed to bring him new stamp-books or packages of glittering approval sheets – there was a mysterious fascination in transferring his acquisitions interminably from one book to another. His stamps were his greatest happiness and he bestowed impatient frowns on anyone who interrupted him at play with them; they devoured his allowance every month, and he lay awake at night musing untiringly on their variety and many-coloured splendour.

At sixteen he had lived almost entirely within himself, an inarticulate boy, thoroughly un-American, and politely bewildered by his contemporaries. The two preceding years had been spent in Europe with a private tutor, who persuaded him that Harvard was the thing; it would 'open doors', it would be a tremendous tonic, it would give him innumerable self-sacrificing and devoted friends. So he went to Harvard – there was no other logical thing to be done with him.

Oblivious to the social system, he lived for a while alone and unsought in a high room in Beck Hall[176] – a slim dark boy of medium height with a shy sensitive mouth. His allowance was more than liberal. He laid the foundations for a library by purchasing from a wandering bibliophile first editions of Swinburne, Meredith and Hardy, and a yellowed illegible autograph letter of Keats's, finding later that he had been amazingly overcharged. He became an exquisite dandy, amassed a rather pathetic collection of silk pyjamas, brocaded dressing-gowns, and neckties too flamboyant to wear; in this secret finery he would parade before a mirror in his room or lie stretched in satin along his window-seat looking down on the yard and realising dimly this clamour, breathless and immediate, in which it seemed he was never to have a part.

Curiously enough he found in senior year that he had acquired a position in his class. He learned that he was looked upon as a rather romantic figure, a scholar, a recluse, a tower of erudition. This amused him but secretly pleased him – he began going out, at first a little and then a great deal. He made the Pudding.[177] He drank – quietly and in the proper tradition. It was said of him that had he not come to college so young he might have 'done extremely well'. In 1909, when he graduated, he was only twenty years old.

Then abroad again – to Rome this time, where he dallied with architecture and painting in turn, took up the violin, and wrote some ghastly Italian sonnets, supposedly the ruminations of a thirteenth-century monk on the joys of the contemplative life. It became established among his Harvard intimates that he was in Rome, and those of them who were abroad that year looked him up and discovered with him, on many moonlight excursions, much in the city that was older than the Renaissance or indeed than the republic. Maury Noble, from Philadelphia, for instance, remained two months, and together they realised the peculiar charm of Latin women and had a delightful sense of being very young and free in a civilisation that was very old and free. Not a few acquaintances of his grandfather's called on him, and had he so desired he might have been *persona grata* with the diplomatic set – indeed, he found that his inclinations tended more and more towards conviviality, but that long adolescent aloofness and consequent shyness still dictated to his conduct.

He returned to America in 1912 because of one of his grandfather's sudden illnesses, and after an excessively tiresome talk with the perpetually convalescent old man he decided to put off until his grandfather's death the idea of living permanently abroad. After a prolonged search he took an apartment on Fifty-Second Street and to all appearances settled down.

In 1913 Anthony Patch's adjustment of himself to the universe was in process of consummation. Physically, he had improved since his undergraduate days – he was still too thin but his shoulders had widened and his brunette face had lost the frightened look of his freshman year. He was secretly orderly and in person spick and span – his friends declared that they had never seen his hair rumpled. His nose was too sharp; his mouth was one of those unfortunate mirrors of mood inclined to droop perceptibly in moments of unhappiness, but his blue eyes were charming, whether alert with intelligence or half closed in an expression of melancholy humour.

One of those men devoid of the symmetry of feature essential to the Aryan ideal, he was yet, here and there, considered handsome – moreover, he was very clean, in appearance and in reality, with that especial cleanness borrowed from beauty.

THE REPROACHLESS APARTMENT

Fifth and Sixth Avenues, it seemed to Anthony, were the uprights of a gigantic ladder stretching from Washington Square to Central Park.[178] Coming uptown on top of a bus towards Fifty-Second Street invariably gave him the sensation of hoisting himself hand by hand on a series of treacherous rungs, and when the bus jolted to a stop at his own rung he found something akin to relief as he descended the reckless metal steps to the sidewalk.

After that, he had but to walk down Fifty-Second Street half a block, pass a stodgy family of brownstone houses – and then in a jiffy he was under the high ceilings of his great front room. This was entirely satisfactory. Here, after all, life began. Here he slept, breakfasted, read and entertained.

The house itself was of murky material, built in the late nineties; in response to the steadily growing need for small apartments each floor had been thoroughly remodelled and rented individually. Of the four apartments Anthony's, on the second floor, was the most desirable.

The front room had fine high ceilings and three large windows that loomed down pleasantly upon Fifty-Second Street. In its appointments it escaped by a safe margin being of any particular period; it escaped stiffness, stuffiness, bareness and decadence. It smelt neither of smoke nor of incense – it was tall and faintly blue. There was a deep lounge of the softest brown leather with somnolence drifting about it like a haze. There was a high screen of Chinese lacquer chiefly concerned with geometrical fishermen and huntsmen in black and gold; this made a corner alcove for a voluminous chair guarded by an orange-coloured standing lamp. Deep in the fireplace a quartered shield was burned to a murky black.

Passing through the dining-room, which, as Anthony took only breakfast at home, was merely a magnificent potentiality, and down a comparatively long hall, one came to the heart and core of the apartment – Anthony's bedroom and bath.

Both of them were immense. Under the ceilings of the former even the great canopied bed seemed of only average size. On the floor an exotic rug of crimson velvet was soft as fleece on his bare feet. His bathroom, in contrast to the rather portentous character of his bedroom, was gay, bright, extremely habitable and even faintly facetious. Framed around the walls were photographs of four celebrated thespian beauties of the day: Julia Sanderson as

'The Sunshine Girl', Ina Claire as 'The Quaker Girl', Billie Burke as 'The Mind-the-Paint Girl', and Hazel Dawn as 'The Pink Lady'. Between Billie Burke and Hazel Dawn hung a print representing a great stretch of snow presided over by a cold and formidable sun – this, claimed Anthony, symbolised the cold shower.

The bathtub, equipped with an ingenious bookholder, was low and large. Beside it a wall wardrobe bulged with sufficient linen for three men and with a generation of neckties. There was no skimpy glorified towel of a carpet – instead, a rich rug, like the one in his bedroom a miracle of softness, that seemed almost to massage the wet foot emerging from the tub . . .

All in all a room to conjure with – it was easy to see that Anthony dressed there, arranged his immaculate hair there, in fact did everything but sleep and eat there. It was his pride, this bathroom. He felt that if he had a love he would have hung her picture just facing the tub so that, lost in the soothing steamings of the hot water, he might lie and look up at her and muse warmly and sensuously on her beauty.

NOR DOES HE SPIN

The apartment was kept clean by an English servant with the singularly, almost theatrically, appropriate name of Bounds, whose technique was marred only by the fact that he wore a soft collar. Had he been entirely Anthony's Bounds this defect would have been summarily remedied, but he was also the Bounds of two other gentlemen in the neighbourhood. From eight until eleven in the morning he was entirely Anthony's. He arrived with the mail and cooked breakfast. At nine-thirty he pulled the edge of Anthony's blanket and spoke a few terse words – Anthony never remembered clearly what they were and rather suspected they were deprecative; then he served breakfast on a card-table in the front room, made the bed and, after asking with some hostility if there was anything else, withdrew.

In the mornings, at least once a week, Anthony went to see his broker. His income was slightly under seven thousand a year, the interest on money inherited from his mother. His grandfather, who had never allowed his own son to graduate from a very liberal allowance, judged that this sum was sufficient for young Anthony's needs. Every Christmas he sent him a five-hundred-dollar bond, which Anthony usually sold, if possible, as he was always a little, not very, hard up.

The visits to his broker varied from semi-social chats to discussions of the safety of eight-per-cent investments, and Anthony always enjoyed them. The big trust-company building seemed to link him definitively to the great fortunes whose solidarity he respected and to assure him that he was adequately chaperoned by the hierarchy of finance. From these hurried men he derived the same sense of safety that he had in contemplating his grandfather's money – even more, for the latter appeared, vaguely, a demand loan made by the world to Adam Patch's own moral righteousness, while this money downtown seemed rather to have been grasped and held by sheer indomitable strengths and tremendous feats of will; in addition, it seemed more definitely and explicitly – money.

Closely as Anthony trod on the heels of his income, he considered it to be enough. Some golden day, of course, he would have many millions; meanwhile he possessed a *raison d'être* in the theoretical creation of essays on the popes of the Renaissance. This flashes back to the conversation with his grandfather immediately upon his return from Rome.

He had hoped to find his grandfather dead, but had learned by telephoning from the pier that Adam Patch was comparatively well again – the next day he had concealed his disappointment and gone out to Tarrytown. Five miles from the station his taxicab entered an elaborately groomed drive that threaded a veritable maze of walls and wire fences guarding the estate – this, said the public, was because it was definitely known that if the Socialists had their way, one of the first men they'd assassinate would be old Cross Patch.

Anthony was late and the venerable philanthropist was awaiting him in a glass-walled sun parlour, where he was glancing through the morning papers for the second time. His secretary, Edward Shuttleworth – who before his regeneration had been gambler, saloon-keeper and general reprobate – ushered Anthony into the room, exhibiting his redeemer and benefactor as though he were displaying a treasure of immense value.

They shook hands gravely. 'I'm awfully glad to hear you're better,' Anthony said.

The senior Patch, with an air of having seen his grandson only last week, pulled out his watch.

'Train late?' he asked mildly.

It had irritated him to wait for Anthony. He was under the delusion not only that in his youth he had handled his practical affairs with the utmost scrupulousness, even to keeping every engagement on the dot, but also that this was the direct and primary cause of his success.

'It's been late a good deal this month,' he remarked with a shade of meek accusation in his voice – and then after a long sigh, 'Sit down.'

Anthony surveyed his grandfather with that tacit amazement which always attended the sight. That this feeble, unintelligent old man was possessed of such power that, yellow journals to the contrary, the men in the republic whose souls he could not have bought directly or indirectly would scarcely have populated White Plains, seemed as impossible to believe as that he had once been a pink-and-white baby.

The span of his seventy-five years had acted as a magic bellows – the first quarter-century had blown him full with life, and the last had sucked it all back. It had sucked in the cheeks and the chest and the girth of arm and leg. It had tyrannously demanded his teeth, one by one, suspended his small eyes in dark-bluish sacks, tweeked out his hairs, changed him from grey to white in some places, from pink to yellow in others – callously transposing his colours like a child trying over a paintbox. Then through his body and his soul it had attacked his brain. It had sent him night-sweats and tears and unfounded dreads. It had split his intense normality into credulity and suspicion. Out of the coarse material of his enthusiasm it had cut dozens of meek but petulant obsessions; his energy was shrunk to the bad temper of a spoiled child, and for his will to power was substituted a fatuous puerile desire for a land of harps and canticles on earth.

The amenities having been gingerly touched upon, Anthony felt that he was expected to outline his intentions – and simultaneously a glimmer in the old man's eye warned him against broaching, for the present, his desire to live abroad. He wished that Shuttleworth would have tact enough to leave the room – he detested Shuttleworth – but the secretary had settled blandly in a rocker and was dividing between the two Patches the glances of his faded eyes.

'Now that you're here you ought to *do* something,' said his grandfather softly, 'accomplish something.'

Anthony waited for him to speak of 'leaving something done when you pass on'.

Then he made a suggestion: 'I thought – it seemed to me that perhaps I'm best qualified to write – '

Adam Patch winced, visualising a family poet with long hair and three mistresses.

' – history,' finished Anthony.

'History? History of what? The Civil War? The Revolution?'

'Why – no, sir. A history of the Middle Ages.' Simultaneously an idea was born for a history of the Renaissance popes, written from some novel angle. Still, he was glad he had said 'Middle Ages'.

'Middle Ages? Why not your own country? Something you know about?'

'Well, you see I've lived so much abroad – '

'Why you should write about the Middle Ages, I don't know. Dark Ages, we used to call 'em. Nobody knows what happened, and nobody cares, except that they're over now.' He continued for some minutes on the uselessness of such information, touching, naturally, on the Spanish Inquisition and the 'corruption of the monasteries'. Then: 'Do you think you'll be able to do any work in New York – or do you really intend to work at all?' This last with soft, almost imperceptible, cynicism.

'Why, yes, I do, sir.'

'When'll you be done?'

'Well, there'll be an outline, you see – and a lot of preliminary reading.'

'I should think you'd have done enough of that already.'

The conversation worked itself jerkily towards a rather abrupt conclusion, when Anthony rose, looked at his watch, and remarked that he had an engagement with his broker that afternoon. He had intended to stay a few days with his grandfather, but he was tired and irritated from a rough crossing, and quite unwilling to stand a subtle and sanctimonious browbeating. He would come out again in a few days, he said.

Nevertheless, it was due to this encounter that work had come into his life as a permanent idea. During the year that had passed since then, he had made several lists of authorities, he had even experimented with chapter titles and the division of his work into periods, but not one line of actual writing existed at present, or seemed likely ever to exist. He did nothing – and contrary to the most accredited copybook logic, he managed to divert himself with more than average content.

AFTERNOON

It was October in 1913, midway in a week of pleasant days, with the sunshine loitering in the cross-streets and the atmosphere so languid as to seem weighted with ghostly falling leaves. It was pleasant to sit lazily by the open window finishing a chapter of *Erewhon*.[179] It was pleasant to yawn about five, toss the book on a table, and saunter humming along the hall to his bath.

'To . . . you . . . beaut-if-ul lady,'

he was singing as he turned on the tap.

'I raise . . . my . . . eyes;
To . . . you . . . beaut-if-ul la-a-dy
My . . . heart . . . cries – '

He raised his voice to compete with the flood of water pouring into the tub, and as he looked at the picture of Hazel Dawn upon the wall he put an imaginary violin to his shoulder and softly caressed it with a phantom bow. Through his closed lips he made a humming noise, which he vaguely imagined resembled the sound of a violin. After a moment his hands ceased their gyrations and wandered to his shirt, which he began to unfasten. Stripped, and adopting an athletic posture like the tiger-skin man in the advertisement, he regarded himself with some satisfaction in the mirror, breaking off to dabble a tentative foot in the tub. Readjusting a faucet and indulging in a few preliminary grunts, he slid in.

Once accustomed to the temperature of the water he relaxed into a state of drowsy content. When he finished his bath he would dress leisurely and walk down Fifth Avenue to the Ritz, where he had an appointment for dinner with his two most frequent companions, Dick Caramel and Maury Noble. Afterwards he and Maury were going to the theatre – Caramel would probably trot home and work on his book, which ought to be finished pretty soon.

Anthony was glad *he* wasn't going to work on *his* book. The notion of sitting down and conjuring up, not only words in which to clothe thoughts but thoughts worthy of being clothed – the whole thing was absurdly beyond his desires.

Emerging from his bath he polished himself with the meticulous attention of a bootblack. Then he wandered into the bedroom, and whistling the while a weird, uncertain melody, strolled here and there buttoning, adjusting, and enjoying the warmth of the thick carpet on his feet.

He lit a cigarette, tossed the match out the open top of the window, then paused in his tracks with the cigarette two inches from his mouth – which fell faintly ajar. His eyes were focused upon a spot of brilliant colour on the roof of a house farther down the alley.

It was a girl in a red négligé, silk surely, drying her hair by the still hot sun of late afternoon. His whistle died upon the stiff air of the room; he walked cautiously another step nearer the window with a sudden impression that she was beautiful. Sitting on the stone parapet beside her was a cushion the same colour as her garment and she was leaning both arms upon it as she looked down into the sunny area-way, where Anthony could hear children playing.

He watched her for several minutes. Something was stirred in him, something not accounted for by the warm smell of the afternoon or the triumphant vividness of red. He felt persistently that the girl was beautiful – then of a sudden he understood: it was her distance, not a rare and precious distance of soul but still distance, if only in terrestrial yards. The autumn air was between them, and the roofs and the blurred voices. Yet for a not altogether explained second, posing perversely in time, his emotion had been nearer to adoration than in the deepest kiss he had ever known.

He finished his dressing, found a black bow tie and adjusted it carefully by the three-sided mirror in the bathroom. Then yielding to an impulse he walked quickly into the bedroom and again looked out the window. The woman was standing up now; she had tossed her hair back and he had a full view of her. She was fat, full thirty-five, utterly undistinguished. Making a clicking noise with his mouth he returned to the bathroom and reparted his hair.

'To . . . you . . . beaut-if-ul lady,'

he sang lightly,

'I raise . . . my . . . eyes – '

Then with a last soothing brush that left an iridescent surface of sheer gloss he left his bathroom and his apartment and walked down Fifth Avenue to the Ritz-Carlton.

THREE MEN

At seven Anthony and his friend Maury Noble are sitting at a corner table on the cool roof. Maury Noble is like nothing so much as a large slender and imposing cat. His eyes are narrow and full of incessant, protracted blinks. His hair is smooth and flat, as though it has been licked by a possible – and, if so, Herculean – mother-cat. During Anthony's time at Harvard he had been considered the most unique figure in his class, the most brilliant, the most original – smart, quiet and among the saved.

This is the man whom Anthony considers his best friend. This is the only man of all his acquaintance whom he admires and, to a bigger extent than he likes to admit to himself, envies.

They are glad to see each other now – their eyes are full of kindness as each feels the full effect of novelty after a short separation. They are drawing a relaxation from each other's presence, a new serenity; Maury Noble behind that fine and absurdly catlike face is all but purring. And Anthony, nervous as a will-o'-the-wisp, restless – he is at rest now.

They are engaged in one of those easy short-speech conversations that only men under thirty or men under great stress indulge in.

ANTHONY: Seven o'clock. Where's the Caramel? (*impatiently*) I wish he'd finish that interminable novel. I've spent more time hungry –

MAURY: He's got a new name for it. *The Demon Lover* – not bad, eh?

ANTHONY (*interested*): *The Demon Lover*? Oh 'woman wailing'[180] – No – not a bit bad! Not bad at all – d'you think?

MAURY: Rather good. What time did you say?

ANTHONY: Seven.

MAURY (*his eyes narrowing – not unpleasantly, but to express a faint disapproval*): Drove me crazy the other day.

ANTHONY: How?

MAURY: That habit of taking notes.

ANTHONY: Me, too. Seems I'd said something night before that he considered material but he'd forgotten it – so he had at me. He'd say, 'Can't you try to concentrate?' And I'd say, 'You bore me to tears. How do I remember?'

(MAURY *laughs noiselessly, by a sort of bland and appreciative widening of his features.*)

MAURY: Dick doesn't necessarily see more than anyone else. He merely can put down a larger proportion of what he sees.

ANTHONY: That rather impressive talent –

MAURY: Oh, yes. Impressive!

ANTHONY: And energy – ambitious, well-directed energy. He's so entertaining – he's so tremendously stimulating and exciting. Often there's something breathless in being with him.

MAURY: Oh, yes. (*Silence reigns briefly,*)

ANTHONY (*with his thin, somewhat uncertain face at its most convinced*): But not indomitable energy. Some day, bit by bit, it'll blow away, and his rather impressive talent with it, and leave only a wisp of a man, fretful and egotistic and garrulous.

MAURY (*with laughter*): Here we sit vowing to each other that little Dick sees less deeply into things than we do. And I'll bet he feels a measure of superiority on his side – creative mind over merely critical mind and all that.

ANTHONY: Oh, yes. But he's wrong. He's inclined to fall for a million silly enthusiasms. If it wasn't that he's absorbed in realism and therefore has to adopt the garments of the cynic he'd be – he'd be credulous as a college religious leader. He's an idealist. Oh, yes. He thinks he's not, because he's rejected Christianity. Remember him in college? Just swallowed every writer whole, one after another, ideas, technique and characters, Chesterton, Shaw, Wells,[181] each one as easily as the last.

MAURY (*still considering his own last observation*): I remember.

ANTHONY: It's true. Natural born fetish-worshipper. Take art –

MAURY: Let's order. He'll be –

ANTHONY: Sure. Let's order. I told him –

MAURY: Here he comes. Look – he's going to bump that waiter. (*He lifts his finger as a signal – lifts it as though it were a soft and friendly claw.*) Here y'are, Caramel.

A NEW VOICE (*fiercely*): Hello, Maury. Hello, Anthony Comstock Patch. How is old Adam's grandson? Débutantes still after you, eh?

(*In person* RICHARD CARAMEL *is short and fair – he is to be bald at thirty-five. He has yellowish eyes – one of them startlingly clear, the other opaque as a muddy pool – and a bulging brow like a funny-paper baby. He bulges in other places – his paunch bulges, prophetically, his words have an air of bulging from his mouth, even his dinner-coat pockets bulge, as though from contamination, with a dog-eared collection of timetables, programmes and miscellaneous scraps – on these he takes his notes with great screwings up of his unmatched yellow eyes and motions of silence with his disengaged left hand.*

When he reaches the table he shakes hands with ANTHONY *and* MAURY. *He is one of those men who invariably shake hands, even with people whom they have seen an hour before.*)

ANTHONY: Hello, Caramel. Glad you're here. We needed a comic relief.

MAURY: You're late. Been racing the postman down the block? We've been clawing over your character.

DICK (*fixing* ANTHONY *eagerly with the bright eye*): What'd you say? Tell me and I'll write it down. Cut three thousand words out of Part One this afternoon.

MAURY: Noble aesthete. And I poured alcohol into my stomach.

DICK: I don't doubt it. I bet you two have been sitting here for an hour talking about liquor.

ANTHONY: We never pass out, my beardless boy.

MAURY: We never go home with ladies we meet when we're lit.

ANTHONY: All in all our parties are characterised by a certain haughty distinction.

DICK: The particularly silly sort who boast about being 'tanks'! Trouble is you're both in the eighteenth century. School of the Old English Squire. Drink quietly until you roll under the table. Never have a good time. Oh, no, that isn't done at all.

ANTHONY: This from Chapter Six, I'll bet.

DICK: Going to the theatre?

MAURY: Yes. We intend to spend the evening doing some deep thinking over life's problems. The thing is tersely called *The Woman*.[182] I presume that she will 'pay'.

ANTHONY: My God! Is that what it is? Let's go to the Follies[183] again.

MAURY: I'm tired of it. I've seen it three times. (*To* DICK): The first time, we went out after Act One and found a most amazing bar. When we came back we entered the wrong theatre.

ANTHONY: Had a protracted dispute with a scared young couple we thought were in our seats.

DICK (*as though talking to himself*): I think – that when I've done another novel and a play, and maybe a book of short stories, I'll do a musical comedy.

MAURY: I know – with intellectual lyrics that no one will listen to. And all the critics will groan and grunt about 'dear old *Pinafore*'.[184] And I shall go on shining as a brilliantly meaningless figure in a meaningless world.

DICK (*pompously*): Art isn't meaningless.

MAURY: It is in itself. It isn't in that it tries to make life less so.

ANTHONY: In other words, Dick, you're playing before a grandstand peopled with ghosts.

MAURY: Give a good show anyhow.

ANTHONY (*to* MAURY): On the contrary, I'd feel, it being a meaningless world, why write? The very attempt to give it purpose is purposeless.

DICK: Well, even admitting all that, be a decent pragmatist and grant a poor man the instinct to live. Would you want everyone to accept that sophistic rot?

ANTHONY: Yeah, I suppose so.

MAURY: No, sir! I believe that everyone in America but a selected
thousand should be compelled to accept a very rigid system of
morals – Roman Catholicism, for instance. I don't complain of
conventional morality. I complain rather of the mediocre heretics
who seize upon the findings of sophistication and adopt the pose
of a moral freedom to which they are by no means entitled by
their intelligences.

(*Here the soup arrives and what* MAURY *might have gone on to say is
lost for all time.*)

NIGHT

Afterwards they visited a ticket speculator and, at a price, obtained
seats for a new musical comedy called *High Jinks.*[185] In the foyer of
the theatre they waited a few moments to see the first-night crowd
come in. There were opera cloaks, stitched of myriad, many-
coloured silks, and furs; there were jewels dripping from arms and
throats and ear-tips of white and rose; there were innumerable broad
shimmers down the middles of innumerable silk hats; there were
shoes of gold and bronze and red and shining black; there were the
high-piled, tight-packed coiffures of many women and the slick,
watered hair of well-kept men – most of all there was the ebbing,
flowing, chattering, chuckling, foaming, slow-rolling wave effect of
this cheerful sea of people as tonight it poured its glittering torrent
into the artificial lake of laughter . . .

After the play they parted – Maury was going to a dance at
Sherry's,[186] Anthony homeward and to bed.

He found his way slowly over the jostled evening mass of Times
Square,[187] which the chariot race and its thousand satellites made
rarely beautiful and bright and intimate with carnival. Faces swirled
about him, a kaleidoscope of girls, ugly, ugly as sin – too fat, too
lean, yet floating upon this autumn air as upon their own warm and
passionate breaths poured out into the night. Here, for all their
vulgarity, he thought, they were faintly and subtly mysterious. He
inhaled carefully, swallowing into his lungs perfume and the not
unpleasant scent of many cigarettes. He caught the glance of a dark
young beauty sitting alone in a closed taxicab. Her eyes in the half-
light suggested night and violets, and for a moment he stirred again
to that half-forgotten remoteness of the afternoon.

Two young Jewish men passed him, talking in loud voices and
craning their necks here and there in fatuous supercilious glances.

They were dressed in suits of the exaggerated tightness then semi-fashionable; their turned over collars were notched at the Adam's apple; they wore grey spats and carried grey gloves on their cane handles.

Passed a bewildered old lady borne along like a basket of eggs between two men who exclaimed to her of the wonders of Times Square – explained them so quickly that the old lady, trying to be impartially interested, waved her head here and there like a piece of wind-worried old orange-peel. Anthony heard a snatch of their conversation: 'There's the Astor,[188] mama!'

'Look! See the chariot race sign – '

'There's where we were today. No, *there*!'

'Good gracious! . . . '

'You should worry and grow thin like a dime.' He recognised the current witticism of the year as it issued stridently from one of the pairs at his elbow.

'And I says to him, I says – '

The soft rush of taxis by him, and laughter, laughter hoarse as a crow's, incessant and loud, with the rumble of the subways underneath – and over all, the revolutions of light, the growings and recedings of light – light dividing like pearls – forming and reforming in glittering bars and circles and monstrous grotesque figures cut amazingly on the sky.

He turned thankfully down the hush that blew like a dark wind out of a cross-street, passed a bakery-restaurant in whose windows a dozen roast chickens turned over and over on an automatic spit. From the door came a smell that was hot, doughy and pink. A drugstore next, exhaling medicines, spilt soda water and a pleasant undertone from the cosmetic counter; then a Chinese laundry, still open, steamy and stifling, smelling folded and vaguely yellow. All these depressed him; reaching Sixth Avenue he stopped at a corner cigar store and emerged feeling better – the cigar store was cheerful, humanity in a navy blue mist, buying a luxury . . .

Once in his apartment he smoked a last cigarette, sitting in the dark by his open front window. For the first time in over a year he found himself thoroughly enjoying New York. There was a rare pungency in it certainly, a quality almost Southern. A lonesome town, though. He who had grown up alone had lately learned to avoid solitude. During the past several months he had been careful, when he had no engagement for the evening, to hurry to one of his clubs and find someone. Oh, there was a loneliness here –

His cigarette, its smoke bordering the thin folds of curtain with rims of faint white spray, glowed on until the clock in St Anne's down the street struck one with a querulous fashionable beauty. The elevated, half a quiet block away, sounded a rumble of drums – and should he lean from his window he would see the train, like an angry eagle, breasting the dark curve at the corner. He was reminded of a fantastic romance he had lately read in which cities had been bombed from aerial trains, and for a moment he fancied that Washington Square had declared war on Central Park and that this was a north-bound menace loaded with battle and sudden death. But as it passed the illusion faded; it diminished to the faintest of drums – then to a faraway droning eagle.

There were the bells and the continued low blur of auto horns from Fifth Avenue, but his own street was silent and he was safe in here from all the threat of life, for there was his door and the long hall and his guardian bedroom – safe, safe! The arc-light shining into his window seemed for this hour like the moon, only brighter and more beautiful than the moon.

A FLASHBACK IN PARADISE

Beauty, who was born anew every hundred years, sat in a sort of outdoor waiting-room through which blew gusts of white wind and occasionally a breathless hurried star. The stars winked at her intimately as they went by and the winds made a soft incessant flurry in her hair. She was incomprehensible, for, in her, soul and spirit were one – the beauty of her body was the essence of her soul. She was that unity sought for by philosophers through many centuries. In this outdoor waiting-room of winds and stars she had been sitting for a hundred years, at peace in the contemplation of herself.

It became known to her, at length, that she was to be born again. Sighing, she began a long conversation with a voice that was in the white wind, a conversation that took many hours and of which I can give only a fragment here.

BEAUTY (*her lips scarcely stirring, her eyes turned, as always, inward upon herself*): Whither shall I journey now?

THE VOICE: To a new country – a land you have never seen before.

BEAUTY (*petulantly*): I loathe breaking into these new civilisations. How long a stay this time?

THE VOICE: Fifteen years.

BEAUTY: And what's the name of the place?

THE VOICE: It is the most opulent, most gorgeous land on earth – a land whose wisest are but little wiser than its dullest; a land where the rulers have minds like little children and the law-givers believe in Santa Claus; where ugly women control strong men –

BEAUTY (*in astonishment*): What?

THE VOICE (*very much depressed*): Yes, it is truly a melancholy spectacle. Women with receding chins and shapeless noses go about in broad daylight saying, 'Do this!' and, 'Do that!' and all the men, even those of great wealth, obey implicitly their women to whom they refer sonorously either as 'Mrs So-and-so' or as 'the wife'.

BEAUTY: But this can't be true! I can understand, of course, their obedience to women of charm – but to fat women? to bony women? to women with scrawny cheeks?

THE VOICE: Even so.

BEAUTY: What of me? What chance shall I have?

THE VOICE: It will be 'harder going', if I may borrow a phrase.

BEAUTY (*after a dissatisfied pause*): Why not the old lands, the land of grapes and soft-tongued men or the land of ships and seas?

THE VOICE: It's expected that they'll be very busy shortly.

BEAUTY: Oh!

THE VOICE: Your life on earth will be, as always, the interval between two significant glances in a mundane mirror.

BEAUTY: What will I be? Tell me?

THE VOICE: At first it was thought that you would go this time as an actress in the motion pictures but, after all, it's not advisable. You will be disguised during your fifteen years as what is called a 'susciety gurl'.

BEAUTY: What's that?

(*There is a new sound in the wind which must for our purposes be interpreted as* THE VOICE *scratching its head.*)

THE VOICE (*at length*): It's a sort of bogus aristocrat.

BEAUTY: Bogus? What is bogus?

THE VOICE: That, too, you will discover in this land. You will find much that is bogus. Also, you will do much that is bogus.

BEAUTY (*placidly*): It all sounds so vulgar.

THE VOICE: Not half as vulgar as it is. You will be known during your fifteen years as a ragtime kid, a flapper, a jazz-baby and a baby vamp. You will dance new dances neither more nor less gracefully than you danced the old ones.

BEAUTY (*in a whisper*): Will I be paid?

THE VOICE: Yes, as usual – in love.

BEAUTY (*with a faint laugh which disturbs only momentarily the immobility of her lips*): And will I like being called a jazz-baby?

THE VOICE (*soberly*): You will love it . . .

(*The dialogue ends here, with* BEAUTY *still sitting quietly, the stars pausing in an ecstasy of appreciation, the wind, white and gusty, blowing through her hair.*

All this took place seven years before ANTHONY *sat by the front windows of his apartment and listened to the chimes of St Anne's.*)

CHAPTER 2

Portrait of a Siren

Crispness folded down upon New York a month later, bringing November and the three big football games and a great fluttering of furs along Fifth Avenue. It brought, also, a sense of tension to the city, and suppressed excitement. Every morning now there were invitations in Anthony's mail. Three dozen virtuous females of the first layer were proclaiming their fitness, if not their specific willingness, to bear children unto three dozen millionaires. Five dozen virtuous females of the second layer were proclaiming not only this fitness, but in addition a tremendous undaunted ambition towards the first three dozen young men, who were of course invited to each of the ninety-six parties – as were the young lady's group of family friends, acquaintances, college boys, and eager young outsiders. To continue, there was a third layer from the skirts of the city, from Newark and the Jersey suburbs up to bitter Connecticut and the ineligible sections of Long Island – and doubtless contiguous layers down to the city's shoes: Jewesses were coming out into a society of Jewish men and women, from Riverside[189] to the Bronx,[190] and looking forward to a rising young broker or jeweller and a kosher wedding; Irish girls were casting their eyes, with licence at last to do so, upon a society of young Tammany politicians, pious undertakers and grown-up choirboys.

And, naturally, the city caught the contagious air of entrée – the working girls, poor ugly souls, wrapping soap in the factories and showing finery in the big stores, dreamed that perhaps in the spectacular excitement of this winter they might obtain for themselves the coveted male – as in a muddled carnival crowd an inefficient pickpocket may consider his chances increased. And the chimneys commenced to smoke and the subway's foulness was freshened. And the actresses came out in new plays and the publishers came out with new books and the Castles[191] came out with new dances. And the railroads came out with new schedules containing new mistakes instead of the old ones that the commuters had grown used to . . .

The City was coming out!

Anthony, walking along Forty-Second Street one afternoon under a steel-grey sky, ran unexpectedly into Richard Caramel emerging from the Manhattan Hotel[192] barbershop. It was a cold day, the first definitely cold day, and Caramel had on one of those knee-length, sheep-lined coats, long worn by the working men of the Middle West, that were just coming into fashionable approval. His soft hat was of a discreet dark brown, and from under it his clear eye flamed like a topaz. He stopped Anthony enthusiastically, slapping him on the arms more from a desire to keep himself warm than from playfulness, and, after his inevitable hand shake, exploded into sound.

'Cold as the devil – Good Lord, I've been working like the deuce all day till my room got so cold I thought I'd get pneumonia. Darn landlady economising on coal came up when I yelled over the stairs for her for half an hour. Began explaining why and all. God! First she drove me crazy, then I began to think she was sort of a character, and took notes while she talked – so she couldn't see me, you know, just as though I were writing casually – '

He had seized Anthony's arm and was walking him briskly up Madison Avenue.

'Where to?'

'Nowhere in particular.'

'Well, then what's the use?' demanded Anthony.

They stopped and stared at each other, and Anthony wondered if the cold made his own face as repellent as Dick Caramel's, whose nose was crimson, whose bulging brow was blue, whose yellow unmatched eyes were red and watery at the rims. After a moment they began walking again.

'Done some good work on my novel.' Dick was looking and talking emphatically at the sidewalk. 'But I have to get out once in a while.' He glanced at Anthony apologetically, as though craving encouragement.

'I have to talk. I guess very few people ever really *think*, I mean sit down and ponder and have ideas in sequence. I do my thinking in writing or conversation. You've got to have a start, sort of – something to defend or contradict – don't you think?'

Anthony grunted and withdrew his arm gently.

'I don't mind carrying you, Dick, but with that coat – '

'I mean,' continued Richard Caramel gravely, 'that on paper your first paragraph contains the idea you're going to damn or enlarge on. In conversation you've got your vis-à-vis's last statement – but when you simply *ponder*, why, your ideas just succeed each other like magic-lantern pictures and each one forces out the last.'

They passed Forty-Fifth Street and slowed down slightly. Both of

them lit cigarettes and blew tremendous clouds of smoke and frosted
breath into the air.

'Let's walk up to the Plaza[193] and have an egg-nog,' suggested
Anthony. 'Do you good. Air'll get the rotten nicotine out of your
lungs. Come on – I'll let you talk about your book all the way.'

'I don't want to if it bores you. I mean you needn't do it as a
favour.' The words tumbled out in haste, and though he tried to
keep his face casual it screwed up uncertainly. Anthony was compelled to protest: 'Bore me? I should say not!'

'Got a cousin – ' began Dick, but Anthony interrupted by stretching
out his arms and breathing forth a low cry of exultation.

'Good weather!' he exclaimed, 'isn't it? Makes me feel about ten.
I mean it makes me feel as I should have felt when I was ten.
Murderous! Oh, God! one minute it's my world, and the next I'm
the world's fool. Today it's my world and everything's easy, easy.
Even Nothing is easy!'

'Got a cousin up at the Plaza. Famous girl. We can go up and meet
her. She lives there in the winter – has lately anyway – with her
mother and father.'

'Didn't know you had cousins in New York.'

'Her name's Gloria. She's from home – Kansas City. Her mother's
a practising Bilphist,[194] and her father's quite dull but a perfect
gentleman.'

'What are they? Literary material?'

'They try to be. All the old man does is tell me he just met the
most wonderful character for a novel. Then he tells me about some
idiotic friend of his and then he says: "*There's* a character for you!
Why don't you write him up? Everybody'd be interested in *him*." Or
else he tells me about Japan or Paris, or some other very obvious
place, and says: "Why don't you write a story about that place?
That'd be a wonderful setting for a story!" '

'How about the girl?' enquired Anthony casually, 'Gloria – Gloria
what?'

'Gilbert. Oh, you've heard of her – Gloria Gilbert. Goes to dances
at colleges – all that sort of thing.'

'I've heard her name.'

'Good-looking – in fact damned attractive.'

They reached Fiftieth Street and turned over towards the Avenue.

'I don't care for young girls as a rule,' said Anthony, frowning.

This was not strictly true. While it seemed to him that the average
débutante spent every hour of her day thinking and talking about

what the great world had mapped out for her to do during the next hour, any girl who made a living directly on her prettiness interested him enormously.

'Gloria's darn nice – not a brain in her head.'

Anthony laughed in a one-syllabled snort.

'By that you mean that she hasn't a line of literary patter.'

'No, I don't.'

'Dick, you know what passes as brains in a girl for you. Earnest young women who sit with you in a corner and talk earnestly about life. The kind who when they were sixteen argued with grave faces as to whether kissing was right or wrong – and whether it was immoral for freshmen to drink beer.'

Richard Caramel was offended. His scowl crinkled like crushed paper.

'No – ' he began, but Anthony interrupted ruthlessly.

'Oh, yes; kind who just at present sit in corners and confer on the latest Scandinavian Dante available in English translation.'

Dick turned to him, a curious falling in his whole countenance. His question was almost an appeal.

'What's the matter with you and Maury? You talk sometimes as though I were a sort of inferior.'

Anthony was confused, but he was also cold and a little uncomfortable, so he took refuge in attack.

'I don't think your brains matter, Dick.'

'Of course they matter!' exclaimed Dick angrily. 'What do you mean? Why don't they matter?'

'You might know too much for your pen.'

'I couldn't possibly.'

'I can imagine,' insisted Anthony, 'a man knowing too much for his talent to express. Like me. Suppose, for instance, I have more wisdom than you, and less talent. It would tend to make me inarticulate. You, on the contrary, have enough water to fill the pail and a big enough pail to hold the water.'

'I don't follow you at all,' complained Dick in a crestfallen tone. Infinitely dismayed, he seemed to bulge in protest. He was staring intently at Anthony and caroming off a succession of passers-by, who reproached him with fierce, resentful glances.

'I simply mean that a talent like Wells's could carry the intelligence of a Spencer.[195] But an inferior talent can only be graceful when it's carrying inferior ideas. And the more narrowly you can look at a thing the more entertaining you can be about it.'

Dick considered, unable to decide the exact degree of criticism intended by Anthony's remarks. But Anthony, with that facility which seemed so frequently to flow from him, continued, his dark eyes gleaming in his thin face, his chin raised, his voice raised, his whole physical being raised: 'Say I am proud and sane and wise – an Athenian among Greeks. Well, I might fail where a lesser man would succeed. He could imitate, he could adorn, he could be enthusiastic, he could be hopefully constructive. But this hypothetical me would be too proud to imitate, too sane to be enthusiastic, too sophisticated to be Utopian, too Grecian to adorn.'

'Then you don't think the artist works from his intelligence?'

'No. He goes on improving, if he can, what he imitates in the way of style, and choosing from his own interpretation of the things around him what constitutes material. But after all every writer writes because it's his mode of living. Don't tell me you like this "Divine Function of the Artist" business?'

'I'm not accustomed even to refer to myself as an artist.'

'Dick,' said Anthony, changing his tone, 'I want to beg your pardon.'

'Why?'

'For that outburst. I'm honestly sorry. I was talking for effect.'

Somewhat mollified, Dick rejoined: 'I've often said you were a Philistine at heart.'

It was a crackling dusk when they turned in under the white façade of the Plaza and tasted slowly the foam and yellow thickness of an egg-nog. Anthony looked at his companion. Richard Caramel's nose and brow were slowly approaching a like pigmentation; the red was leaving the one, the blue deserting the other. Glancing in a mirror, Anthony was glad to find that his own skin had not discoloured. On the contrary, a faint glow had kindled in his cheeks – he fancied that he had never looked so well.

'Enough for me,' said Dick, his tone that of an athlete in training. 'I want to go up and see the Gilberts. Won't you come?'

'Why – yes. If you don't dedicate me to the parents and dash off in the corner with Dora.'

'Not Dora – Gloria.'

A clerk announced them over the phone, and ascending to the tenth floor they followed a winding corridor and knocked at 1088. The door was answered by a middle-aged lady – Mrs Gilbert herself.

'How do you do?' She spoke in the conventional American lady-lady language. 'Well, I'm *aw*fully glad to see you – '

Hasty interjections by Dick, and then: 'Mr Pats? Well, do come in, and leave your coat there.' She pointed to a chair and changed her inflection to a deprecatory laugh full of minute gasps. 'This is really lovely – lovely. Why, Richard, you haven't been here for *so* long – no! – no!' The latter monosyllables served half as responses, half as periods, to some vague starts from Dick. 'Well, do sit down and tell me what you've been doing.'

One crossed and recrossed; one stood and bowed ever so gently; one smiled again and again with helpless stupidity; one wondered if she would ever sit down – at length one slid thankfully into a chair and settled for a pleasant call.

'I suppose it's because you've been busy – as much as anything else,' smiled Mrs Gilbert somewhat ambiguously. The 'as much as anything else' she used to balance all her more rickety sentences. She had two other ones: 'at least that's the way I look at it' and 'pure and simple' – these three, alternated, gave each of her remarks an air of being a general reflection on life, as though she had calculated all causes and, at length, put her finger on the ultimate one.

Richard Caramel's face, Anthony saw, was now quite normal. The brow and cheeks were of a flesh colour, the nose politely inconspicuous. He had fixed his aunt with the bright-yellow eye, giving her that acute and exaggerated attention that young males are accustomed to render to all females who are of no further value.

'Are you a writer too, Mr Pats? . . . Well, perhaps we can all bask in Richard's fame.' – Gentle laughter led by Mrs Gilbert.

'Gloria's out,' she said, with an air of laying down an axiom from which she would proceed to derive results. 'She's dancing somewhere. Gloria goes, goes, goes. I tell her I don't see how she stands it. She dances all afternoon and all night, until I think she's going to wear herself to a shadow. Her father is very worried about her.'

She smiled from one to the other. They both smiled.

She was composed, Anthony perceived, of a succession of semi-circles and parabolas, like those figures that gifted folk make on the typewriter: head, arms, bust, hips, thighs and ankles were in a bewildering tier of roundnesses. Well ordered and clean she was, with hair of an artificially rich grey; her large face sheltered weather-beaten blue eyes and was adorned with just the faintest white moustache.

'I always say,' she remarked to Anthony, 'that Richard is an ancient soul.'

In the tense pause that followed, Anthony considered a pun – something about Dick having been much walked upon.

'We all have souls of different ages,' continued Mrs Gilbert radiantly; 'at least that's what I say.'

'Perhaps so,' agreed Anthony with an air of quickening to a hopeful idea.

The voice bubbled on: 'Gloria has a very young soul – irresponsible, as much as anything else. She has no sense of responsibility.'

'She's sparkling, Aunt Catherine,' said Richard pleasantly. 'A sense of responsibility would spoil her. She's too pretty.'

'Well,' confessed Mrs Gilbert, 'all I know is that she goes and goes and goes – '

The number of goings to Gloria's discredit was lost in the rattle of the doorknob as it turned to admit Mr Gilbert.

He was a short man with a moustache resting like a small white cloud beneath his undistinguished nose. He had reached the stage where his value as a social creature was a black and imponderable negative. His ideas were the popular delusions of twenty years before; his mind steered a wobbly and anaemic course in the wake of the daily newspaper editorials. After graduating from a small but terrifying Western university, he had entered the celluloid business, and as this required only the minute measure of intelligence he brought to it, he did well for several years – in fact until about 1911, when he began exchanging contracts for vague agreements with the moving-picture industry. The moving-picture industry had decided about 1912 to gobble him up, and at this time he was, so to speak, delicately balanced on its tongue. Meanwhile he was supervising manager of the Associated Midwestern Film Materials Company, spending six months of each year in New York and the remainder in Kansas City and St Louis. He felt credulously that there was a good thing coming to him – and his wife thought so, and his daughter thought so too.

He disapproved of Gloria: she stayed out late, she never ate her meals, she was always in a mix-up – he had irritated her once and she had used towards him words that he had not thought were part of her vocabulary. His wife was easier. After fifteen years of incessant guerrilla warfare he had conquered her – it was a war of muddled optimism against organised dullness, and something in the number of yeses with which he could poison a conversation had won him the victory.

'Yes-yes-yes-yes,' he would say, 'yes-yes-yes-yes. Let me see. That was the summer of – let me see – ninety-one or ninety-two – Yes-yes-yes-yes – '

Fifteen years of yeses had beaten Mrs Gilbert. Fifteen further years of that incessant unaffirmative affirmative, accompanied by the perpetual flicking of ash-mushrooms from thirty-two thousand cigars, had broken her. To this husband of hers she made the last concession of married life, which is more complete, more irrevocable, than the first – she listened to him. She told herself that the years had brought her tolerance – actually they had slain what measure she had ever possessed of moral courage.

She introduced him to Anthony.

'This is Mr Pats,' she said.

The young man and the old touched flesh; Mr Gilbert's hand was soft, worn away to the pulpy semblance of a squeezed grapefruit. Then husband and wife exchanged greetings – he told her it had grown colder out; he said he had walked down to a news-stand on Forty-Fourth Street for a Kansas City paper. He had intended to ride back in the bus but he had found it too cold, yes, yes, yes, yes, too cold.

Mrs Gilbert added flavour to his adventure by being impressed with his courage in braving the harsh air.

'Well, you *are* spunky!' she exclaimed admiringly. 'You *are* spunky. I wouldn't have gone out for anything.'

Mr Gilbert with true masculine impassivity disregarded the awe he had excited in his wife. He turned to the two young men and triumphantly routed them on the subject of the weather. Richard Caramel was called on to remember the month of November in Kansas. No sooner had the theme been pushed towards him, however, than it was violently fished back to be lingered over, pawed over, elongated, and generally devitalised by its sponsor.

The immemorial thesis that the days somewhere were warm but the nights very pleasant was successfully propounded and they decided the exact distance on an obscure railroad between two points that Dick had inadvertently mentioned. Anthony fixed Mr Gilbert with a steady stare and went into a trance through which, after a moment, Mrs Gilbert's smiling voice penetrated: 'It seems as though the cold were damper here – it seems to eat into my bones.'

As this remark, adequately yessed, had been on the tip of Mr Gilbert's tongue, he could not be blamed for rather abruptly changing the subject.

'Where's Gloria?'

'She ought to be here any minute.'

'Have you met my daughter, Mr – ?'

'Haven't had the pleasure. I've heard Dick speak of her often.'

'She and Richard are cousins.'

'Yes?' Anthony smiled with some effort. He was not used to the society of his seniors, and his mouth was stiff from superfluous cheerfulness. It was such a pleasant thought about Gloria and Dick being cousins. He managed within the next minute to throw an agonised glance at his friend.

Richard Caramel was afraid they'd have to toddle off.

Mrs Gilbert was tremendously sorry.

Mr Gilbert thought it was too bad.

Mrs Gilbert had a further idea – something about being glad they'd come, anyhow, even if they'd only seen an old lady 'way too old to flirt with them. Anthony and Dick evidently considered this a sly sally, for they laughed one bar in three-four time.

Would they come again soon?

'Oh, yes.'

Gloria would be *aw*fully sorry!

'Goodbye – '

'Goodbye – '

Smiles!

Smiles!

Bang!

Two disconsolate young men walking down the tenth-floor corridor of the Plaza in the direction of the elevator.

A LADY'S LEGS

Behind Maury Noble's attractive indolence, his irrelevance and his easy mockery, lay a surprising and relentless maturity of purpose. His intention, as he stated it in college, had been to use three years in travel, three years in utter leisure – and then to become immensely rich as quickly as possible.

His three years of travel were over. He had accomplished the globe with an intensity and curiosity that in anyone else would have seemed pedantic, without redeeming spontaneity, almost the self-editing of a human Baedeker;[196] but, in this case, it assumed an air of mysterious purpose and significant design – as though Maury Noble were some predestined anti-Christ, urged by a preordination to go everywhere there was to go along the earth and to see all the billions of humans who bred and wept and slew each other here and there upon it.

Back in America, he was sallying into the search for amusement with the same consistent absorption. He who had never taken more than a few cocktails or a pint of wine at a sitting, taught himself to drink as he would have taught himself Greek – like Greek it would be the gateway to a wealth of new sensations, new psychic states, new reactions in joy or misery.

His habits were a matter for esoteric speculation. He had three rooms in a bachelor apartment on Forty-Forth Street, but he was seldom to be found there. The telephone girl had received the most positive instructions that no one should even have his ear without first giving a name to be passed on. She had a list of half a dozen people to whom he was never at home, and of the same number to whom he was always at home. Foremost on the latter list were Anthony Patch and Richard Caramel.

Maury's mother lived with her married son in Philadelphia, and there Maury went usually for the weekends, so one Saturday night when Anthony, prowling the chilly streets in a fit of utter boredom, dropped in at the Molton Arms he was overjoyed to find that Mr Noble was at home.

His spirits soared faster than the flying elevator. This was so good, so extremely good, to be about to talk to Maury – who would be equally happy at seeing him. They would look at each other with a deep affection just behind their eyes which both would conceal beneath some attenuated raillery. Had it been summer they would have gone out together and indolently sipped two long Tom Collinses, as they wilted their collars and watched the faintly diverting round of some lazy August cabaret. But it was cold outside, with wind around the edges of the tall buildings and December just up the street, so better far an evening together under the soft lamplight and a drink or two of Bushmill's, or a thimbleful of Maury's Grand Marnier, with the books gleaming like ornaments against the walls, and Maury radiating a divine inertia as he rested, large and catlike, in his favourite chair.

There he was! The room closed about Anthony, warmed him. The glow of that strong persuasive mind, that temperament almost Oriental in its outward impassivity, warmed Anthony's restless soul and brought him a peace that could be likened only to the peace a stupid woman gives. One must understand all – else one must take all for granted. Maury filled the room, tigerlike, godlike. The winds outside were stilled; the brass candlesticks on the mantel glowed like tapers before an altar.

'What keeps you here today?' Anthony spread himself over a yielding sofa and made an elbow-rest among the pillows.

'Just been here an hour. Tea dance – and I stayed so late I missed my train to Philadelphia.'

'Strange to stay so long,' commented Anthony curiously.

'Rather. What'd you do?'

'Geraldine. Little usher at Keith's.[197] I told you about her.'

'Oh!'

'Paid me a call about three and stayed till five. Peculiar little soul – she gets me. She's so utterly stupid.'

Maury was silent.

'Strange as it may seem,' continued Anthony, 'so far as I'm concerned, and even so far as I know, Geraldine is a paragon of virtue.'

He had known her a month, a girl of nondescript and nomadic habits. Someone had casually passed her on to Anthony, who considered her amusing and rather liked the chaste and fairylike kisses she had given him on the third night of their acquaintance, when they had driven in a taxi through the Park. She had a vague family – a shadowy aunt and uncle who shared with her an apartment in the labyrinthine hundreds. She was company, familiar and faintly intimate and restful. Further than that he did not care to experiment – not from any moral compunction, but from a dread of allowing any entanglement to disturb what he felt was the growing serenity of his life.

'She has two stunts,' he informed Maury; 'one of them is to get her hair over her eyes some way and then blow it out, and the other is to say "You cra-a-azy!" when someone makes a remark that's over her head. It fascinates me. I sit there hour after hour, completely intrigued by the maniacal symptoms she finds in my imagination.'

Maury stirred in his chair and spoke.

'Remarkable that a person can comprehend so little and yet live in such a complex civilisation. A woman like that actually takes the whole universe in the most matter-of-fact way. From the influence of Rousseau[198] to the bearing of the tariff rates on her dinner, the whole phenomenon is utterly strange to her. She's just been carried along from an age of spearheads and plunked down here with the equipment of an archer for going into a pistol duel. You could sweep away the entire crust of history and she'd never know the difference.'

'I wish our Richard would write about her.'

'Anthony, surely you don't think she's worth writing about.'

'As much as anybody,' he answered, yawning. 'You know I was thinking today that I have a great confidence in Dick. So long as he sticks to people and not to ideas, and as long as his inspirations come from life and not from art, and always granting a normal growth, I believe he'll be a big man.'

'I should think the appearance of the black notebook would prove that he's going to life.'

Anthony raised himself on his elbow and answered eagerly: 'He tries to go to life. So does every author except the very worst, but after all most of them live on predigested food. The incident or character may be from life, but the writer usually interprets it in terms of the last book he read. For instance, suppose he meets a sea captain and thinks he's an original character. The truth is that he sees the resemblance between the sea captain and the last sea captain Dana[199] created, or whoever creates sea captains, and therefore he knows how to set this sea captain on paper. Dick, of course, can set down any consciously picturesque, character-like character, but could he accurately transcribe his own sister?'

Then they were off for half an hour on literature.

'A classic,' suggested Anthony, 'is a successful book that has survived the reaction of the next period or generation. Then it's safe, like a style in architecture or furniture. It's acquired a picturesque dignity to take the place of its fashion . . .'

After a time the subject temporarily lost its tang. The interest of the two young men was not particularly technical. They were in love with generalities. Anthony had recently discovered Samuel Butler and the brisk aphorisms in the *Notebooks* seemed to him the quintessence of criticism. Maury, his whole mind so thoroughly mellowed by the very hardness of his scheme of life, seemed inevitably the wiser of the two, yet in the actual stuff of their intelligences they were not, it seemed, fundamentally different.

They drifted from letters to the curiosities of each other's day.

'Whose tea was it?'

'People named Abercrombie.'

'Why'd you stay late? Meet a luscious débutante?'

'Yes.'

'Did you really?' Anthony's voice lifted in surprise.

'Not a débutante exactly. Said she came out two winters ago in Kansas City.'

'Sort of left over?'

'No,' answered Maury with some amusement, 'I think that's the last thing I'd say about her. She seemed – well, somehow the youngest person there.'

'Not too young to make you miss a train.'

'Young enough. Beautiful child.'

Anthony chuckled in his one-syllable snort.

'Oh, Maury, you're in your second childhood. What do you mean by beautiful?'

Maury gazed helplessly into space.

'Well, I can't describe her exactly – except to say that she was beautiful. She was – tremendously alive. She was eating gumdrops.'

'What!'

'It was a sort of attenuated vice. She's a nervous kind – said she always ate gumdrops at teas because she had to stand around so long in one place.'

'What'd you talk about – Bergson?[200] Bilphism? Whether the one-step[201] is immoral?'

Maury was unruffled; his fur seemed to run all ways.

'As a matter of fact we did talk on Bilphism. Seems her mother's a Bilphist. Mostly, though, we talked about legs.'

Anthony rocked in glee.

'My God! Whose legs?'

'Hers. She talked a lot about hers. As though they were a sort of choice bric-à-brac. She aroused a great desire to see them.'

'What is she – a dancer?'

'No, I found she was a cousin of Dick's.'

Anthony sat upright so suddenly that the pillow he released stood on end like a live thing and dived to the floor.

'Name's Gloria Gilbert?' he cried.

'Yes. Isn't she remarkable?'

'I'm sure I don't know – but for sheer dullness her father – '

'Well,' interrupted Maury with implacable conviction, 'her family may be as sad as professional mourners but I'm inclined to think that she's a quite authentic and original character. The outer signs of the cut-and-dried Yale prom girl and all that – but different, very emphatically different.'

'Go on, go on!' urged Anthony. 'Soon as Dick told me she didn't have a brain in her head I knew she must be pretty good.'

'Did he say that?'

'Swore to it,' said Anthony with another snorting laugh.

'Well, what he means by brains in a woman is – '

'I know,' interrupted Anthony eagerly, 'he means a smattering of literary misinformation.'

'That's it. The kind who believes that the annual moral let-down of the country is a very good thing or the kind who believes it's a very ominous thing. Either pince-nez or postures. Well, this girl talked about legs. She talked about skin too – her own skin. Always her own. She told me the sort of tan she'd like to get in the summer and how closely she usually approximated it.'

'You sat enraptured by her low alto?'

'By her low alto! No, by tan! I began thinking about tan. I began to think what colour I turned when I made my last exposure about two years ago. I did use to get a pretty good tan. I used to get a sort of bronze, if I remember rightly.'

Anthony retired into the cushions, shaken with laughter.

'She's got you going – oh, Maury! Maury the Connecticut life-saver. The human nutmeg. Extra! Heiress elopes with coastguard because of his luscious pigmentation! Afterwards found to be Tasmanian strain in his family!'

Maury sighed; rising he walked to the window and raised the shade. 'Snowing hard.'

Anthony, still laughing quietly to himself, made no answer.

'Another winter.' Maury's voice from the window was almost a whisper. 'We're growing old, Anthony. I'm twenty-seven, by God! Three years to thirty, and then I'm what an undergraduate calls a middle-aged man.'

Anthony was silent for a moment.

'You *are* old, Maury,' he agreed at length. 'The first signs of a very dissolute and wobbly senescence – you have spent the afternoon talking about tan and a lady's legs.'

Maury pulled down the shade with a sudden harsh snap.

'Idiot!' he cried, 'that from you! Here I sit, young Anthony, as I'll sit for a generation or more and watch such gay souls as you and Dick and Gloria Gilbert go past me, dancing and singing and loving and hating one another and being moved, being eternally moved. And I am moved only by my lack of emotion. I shall sit and the snow will come – oh, for a Caramel to take notes – and another winter and I shall be thirty and you and Dick and Gloria will go on being eternally moved and dancing by me and singing. But after you've all gone I'll be saying things for new Dicks to write down, and listening to the disillusions and cynicisms and emotions of new Anthonys – yes, and talking to new Glorias about the tans of summers yet to come.'

The firelight flurried up on the hearth. Maury left the window, stirred the blaze with a poker, and dropped a log upon the andirons. Then he sat back in his chair and the remnants of his voice faded in the new fire that spit red and yellow along the bark.

'After all, Anthony, it's you who are very romantic and young. It's you who are infinitely more susceptible and afraid of your calm being broken. It's me who tries again and again to be moved – let myself go a thousand times and I'm always me. Nothing – quite – stirs me.

'Yet,' he murmured after another long pause, 'there was something about that little girl with her absurd tan that was eternally old – like me.'

TURBULENCE

Anthony turned over sleepily in his bed, greeting a patch of cold sun on his counterpane, criss-crossed with the shadows of the leaded window. The room was full of morning. The carved chest in the corner, the ancient and inscrutable wardrobe, stood about the room like dark symbols of the obliviousness of matter; only the rug was beckoning and perishable to his perishable feet, and Bounds, horribly inappropriate in his soft collar, was of stuff as fading as the gauze of frozen breath he uttered. He was close to the bed, his hand still lowered where he had been jerking at the upper blanket, his dark-brown eyes fixed imperturbably upon his master.

'Bows!' muttered the drowsy god. 'Thachew, Bows?'

'It's I, sir.'

Anthony moved his head, forced his eyes wide, and blinked triumphantly.

'Bounds.'

'Yes, sir?'

'Can you get off – yeow-ow-oh-oh-oh God! – ' Anthony yawned insufferably and the contents of his brain seemed to fall together in a dense hash. He made a fresh start.

'Can you come around about four and serve some tea and sandwiches or something?'

'Yes, sir.'

Anthony considered with chilling lack of inspiration. 'Some sandwiches,' he repeated helplessly, 'oh, some cheese sandwiches and jelly ones and chicken and olive, I guess. Never mind breakfast.'

The strain of invention was too much. He shut his eyes wearily, let his head roll to rest inertly, and quickly relaxed what he had regained of muscular control. Out of a crevice of his mind crept the vague but inevitable spectre of the night before – but it proved in this case to be nothing but a seemingly interminable conversation with Richard Caramel, who had called on him at midnight; they had drunk four bottles of beer and munched dry crusts of bread while Anthony listened to a reading of the first part of *The Demon Lover*.

– Came a voice now after many hours. Anthony disregarded it, as sleep closed over him, folded down upon him, crept up into the byways of his mind.

Suddenly he was awake, saying: 'What?'

'For how many, sir?' It was still Bounds, standing patient and motionless at the foot of the bed – Bounds who divided his manner among three gentlemen.

'How many what?'

'I think, sir, I'd better know how many are coming. I'll have to plan for the sandwiches, sir.'

'Two,' muttered Anthony huskily; 'lady and a gentleman.'

Bounds said, 'Thank you, sir,' and moved away, bearing with him his humiliating reproachful soft collar, reproachful to each of the three gentlemen, who only demanded of him a third.

After a long time Anthony arose and drew an opalescent dressing grown of brown and blue over his slim pleasant figure. With a last yawn he went into the bathroom, and turning on the dresser light (the bathroom had no outside exposure) he contemplated himself in the mirror with some interest. A wretched apparition, he thought; he usually thought so in the morning – sleep made his face unnaturally pale. He lit a cigarette and glanced through several letters and the morning *Tribune*.[202]

An hour later, shaven and dressed, he was sitting at his desk looking at a small piece of paper he had taken out of his wallet. It was scrawled with semi-legible memoranda: 'See Mr Howland at five. Get haircut. See about Rivers' bill. Go bookstore.'

– And under the last: 'Cash in bank, $690 [crossed out], $612 [crossed out], $607.'

Finally, down at the bottom and in a hurried scrawl: 'Dick and Gloria Gilbert for tea.'

This last item brought him obvious satisfaction. His day, usually a jellylike creature, a shapeless, spineless thing, had attained Mesozoic structure. It was marching along surely, even jauntily, towards a climax, as a play should, as a day should. He dreaded the moment when the backbone of the day should be broken, when he should have met the girl at last, talked to her, and then bowed her laughter out the door, returning only to the melancholy dregs in the teacups and the gathering staleness of the uneaten sandwiches.

There was a growing lack of colour in Anthony's days. He felt it constantly and sometimes traced it to a talk he had had with Maury Noble a month before. That anything so ingenuous, so priggish, as a sense of waste should oppress him was absurd, but there was no denying the fact that some unwelcome survival of a fetish had drawn him three weeks before down to the public library, where, by the token of Richard Caramel's card, he had drawn out half a dozen books on the Italian Renaissance. That these books were still piled on his desk in the original order of carriage, that they were daily increasing his liabilities by twelve cents, was no mitigation of their testimony. They were cloth and morocco witnesses to the fact of his defection. Anthony had had several hours of acute and startling panic.

In justification of his manner of living there was first, of course, The Meaninglessness of Life. As aides and ministers, pages and squires, butlers and lackeys to this great Khan there were a thousand books glowing on his shelves, there was his apartment and all the money that was to be his when the old man up the river should choke on his last morality. From a world fraught with the menace of débutantes and the stupidity of many Geraldines he was thankfully delivered – rather should he emulate the feline immobility of Maury and wear proudly the culminative wisdom of the numbered generations.

Over and against these things was something which his brain persistently analysed and dealt with as a tiresome complex but which, though logically disposed of and bravely trampled under foot, had sent him out through the soft slush of late November to a library which had none of the books he most wanted. It is fair to analyse Anthony as far as he could analyse himself; further than that it is, of course, presumption. He found in himself a growing horror and loneliness. The idea of eating alone frightened him; in preference he dined often with men he detested. Travel, which had once charmed him, seemed at length, unendurable, a business of colour without substance, a phantom chase after his own dream's shadow.

– If I am essentially weak, he thought, I need work to do, work to do. It worried him to think that he was, after all, a facile mediocrity, with neither the poise of Maury nor the enthusiasm of Dick. It seemed a tragedy to want nothing – and yet he wanted something, something. He knew in flashes what it was – some path of hope to lead him towards what he thought was an imminent and ominous old age.

After cocktails and luncheon at the University Club[203] Anthony felt better. He had run into two men from his class at Harvard, and in contrast to the grey heaviness of their conversation his life assumed colour. Both of them were married: one spent his coffee time in sketching an extra-nuptial adventure to the bland and appreciative smiles of the other. Both of them, he thought, were Mr Gilberts in embryo; the number of their yeses would have to be quadrupled, their natures crabbed by twenty years – then they would be no more than obsolete and broken machines, pseudo-wise and valueless, nursed to an utter senility by the women they had broken.

Ah, he was more than that, as he paced the long carpet in the lounge after dinner, pausing at the window to look into the harried street. He was Anthony Patch, brilliant, magnetic, the heir of many years and many men. This was his world now – and that last strong irony he craved lay in the offing.

With a stray boyishness he saw himself a power upon the earth; with his grandfather's money he might build his own pedestal and be a Talleyrand,[204] a Lord Verulam.[205] The clarity of his mind, its sophistication, its versatile intelligence, all at their maturity and dominated by some purpose yet to be born would find him work to do. On this minor his dream faded – work to do: he tried to imagine himself in Congress rooting around in the litter of that incredible pigsty with the narrow and porcine brows he saw pictured sometimes in the rotogravure[206] sections of the Sunday newspapers, those glorified proletarians babbling blandly to the nation the ideas of high-school seniors! Little men with copybook ambitions who by mediocrity had thought to emerge from mediocrity into the lustreless and unromantic heaven of a government by the people – and the best, the dozen shrewd men at the top, egotistic and cynical, were content to lead this choir of white ties and wire collar-buttons in a discordant and amazing hymn, compounded of a vague confusion between wealth as a reward of virtue and wealth as a proof of vice, and continued cheers for God, the Constitution and the Rocky Mountains!

Lord Verulam! Talleyrand!

Back in his apartment the greyness returned. His cocktails had died, making him sleepy, somewhat befogged and inclined to be

surly, Lord Verulam – he? The very thought was bitter. Anthony
Patch with no record of achievement, without courage, without
strength to be satisfied with truth when it was given him. Oh, he was
a pretentious fool, making careers out of cocktails and meanwhile
regretting, weakly and secretly, the collapse of an insufficient and
wretched idealism. He had garnished his soul in the subtlest taste
and now he longed for the old rubbish. He was empty, it seemed,
empty as an old bottle –

The buzzer rang at the door. Anthony sprang up and lifted the
tube to his ear. It was Richard Caramel's voice, stilted and facetious:
'Announcing Miss Gloria Gilbert.'

'How do you do?' he said, smiling and holding the door ajar.

Dick bowed.

'Gloria, this is Anthony.'

'Well!' she cried, holding out a little gloved hand. Under her fur
coat her dress was Alice-blue,[207] with white lace crinkled stiffly about
her throat.

'Let me take your things.'

Anthony stretched out his arms and the brown mass of fur tumbled
into them.

'Thanks.'

'What do you think of her, Anthony?' Richard Caramel demanded
barbarously. 'Isn't she beautiful?'

'Well!' cried the girl defiantly – withal unmoved.

She was dazzling – alight; it was agony to comprehend her beauty
in a glance. Her hair, full of a heavenly glamour, was gay against the
winter colour of the room.

Anthony moved about, magician-like, turning the mushroom lamp
into an orange glory. The stirred fire burnished the copper andirons
on the hearth –

'I'm a solid block of ice,' murmured Gloria casually, glancing
around with eyes whose irises were of the most delicate and transparent bluish white. 'What a slick fire! We found a place where you
could stand on an iron-bar grating, sort of, and it blew warm air up
at you – but Dick wouldn't wait there with me. I told him to go on
alone and let me be happy.'

Conventional enough this. She seemed talking for her own
pleasure, without effort. Anthony, sitting at one end of the sofa,
examined her profile against the foreground of the lamp: the
exquisite regularity of nose and upper lip, the chin, faintly decided,
balanced beautifully on a rather short neck. On a photograph she

must have been completely classical, almost cold – but the glow of her hair and cheeks, at once flushed and fragile, made her the most living person he had ever seen.

' . . . Think you've got the best name I've heard,' she was saying, still apparently to herself; her glance rested on him a moment and then flitted past him – to the Italian bracket-lamps clinging like luminous yellow turtles at intervals along the walls, to the books row upon row, then to her cousin on the other side. 'Anthony Patch. Only you ought to look sort of like a horse, with a long narrow face – and you ought to be in tatters.'

'That's all the Patch part, though. How should Anthony look?'

'You look like Anthony,' she assured him seriously – he thought she had scarcely seen him – 'rather majestic,' she continued, 'and solemn.'

Anthony indulged in a disconcerted smile.

'Only I like alliterative names,' she went on, 'all except mine. Mine's too flamboyant. I used to know two girls named Jinks, though, and just think if they'd been named anything except what they were named – Judy Jinks and Jerry Jinks. Cute, what? Don't you think?' Her childish mouth was parted, awaiting a rejoinder.

'Everybody in the next generation,' suggested Dick, 'will be named Peter or Barbara – because at present all the piquant literary characters are named Peter or Barbara.'

Anthony continued the prophecy: 'Of course Gladys and Eleanor, having graced the last generation of heroines and being at present in their social prime, will be passed on to the next generation of shop-girls – '

'Displacing Ella and Stella,' interrupted Dick.

'And Pearl and Jewel,' Gloria added cordially, 'and Earl and Elmer and Minnie.'

'And then I'll come along,' remarked Dick, 'and picking up the obsolete name, Jewel, I'll attach it to some quaint and attractive character and it'll start its career all over again.'

Her voice took up the thread of subject and wove along with faintly upturning, half-humorous intonations for sentence ends – as though defying interruption – and intervals of shadowy laughter. Dick had told her that Anthony's man was named Bounds – she thought that was wonderful! Dick had made some sad pun about Bounds doing patchwork, but if there was one thing worse than a pun, she said, it was a person who, as the inevitable come-back to a pun, gave the perpetrator a mock-reproachful look.

'Where are you from?' enquired Anthony. He knew, but beauty had rendered him thoughtless.

'Kansas City, Missouri.'

'They put her out the same time they barred cigarettes.'

'Did they bar cigarettes? I see the hand of my holy grandfather.'

'He's a reformer or something, isn't he?'

'I blush for him.'

'So do I,' she confessed. 'I detest reformers, especially the sort who try to reform me.'

'Are there many of those?'

'Dozens. It's, "Oh, Gloria, if you smoke so many cigarettes you'll lose your pretty complexion!' and, "Oh, Gloria, why don't you marry and settle down?" '

Anthony agreed emphatically while he wondered who had had the temerity to speak thus to such a personage.

'And then,' she continued, 'there are all the subtle reformers who tell you the wild stories they've heard about you and how they've been sticking up for you.'

He saw, at length, that her eyes were grey, very level and cool, and when they rested on him he understood what Maury had meant by saying she was very young and very old. She talked always about herself as a very charming child might talk, and her comments on her tastes and distastes were unaffected and spontaneous.

'I must confess,' said Anthony gravely, 'that even *I*'ve heard one thing about you.'

Alert at once, she sat up straight. Those eyes, with the greyness and eternity of a cliff of soft granite, caught his.

'Tell me. I'll believe it. I always believe anything anyone tells me about myself – don't you?'

'Invariably!' agreed the two men in unison.

'Well, tell me.'

'I'm not sure that I ought to,' teased Anthony, smiling unwillingly. She was so obviously interested, in a state of almost laughable self-absorption.

'He means your nickname,' said her cousin.

'What name?' enquired Anthony, politely puzzled.

Instantly she was shy – then she laughed, rolled back against the cushions, and turned her eyes up as she spoke: 'Coast-to-Coast Gloria.' Her voice was full of laughter, laughter undefined as the varying shadows playing between fire and lamp upon her hair. 'O Lord!'

Still Anthony was puzzled.

'What do you mean?'

'*Me*, I mean. That's what some silly boys coined for *me*.'

'Don't you see, Anthony,' explained Dick, 'traveller of a nation-wide notoriety and all that. Isn't that what you've heard? She's been called that for years – since she was seventeen.'

Anthony's eyes became sad and humorous.

'Who's this female Methuselah you've brought in here, Caramel?'

She disregarded this, possibly rather resented it, for she switched back to the main topic.

'What *have* you heard of me?'

'Something about your physique.'

'Oh,' she said, coolly disappointed, 'that all?'

'Your tan.'

'My tan?' She was puzzled. Her hand rose to her throat, rested there an instant as though the fingers were feeling variants of colour.

'Do you remember Maury Noble? Man you met about a month ago. You made a great impression.'

She thought a moment.

'I remember – but he didn't call me up.'

'He was afraid to, I don't doubt.'

It was black dark without now and Anthony wondered that his apartment had ever seemed grey – so warm and friendly were the books and pictures on the walls and the good Bounds offering tea from a respectful shadow and the three nice people giving out waves of interest and laughter back and forth across the happy fire.

DISSATISFACTION

On Thursday afternoon Gloria and Anthony had tea together in the grill room at the Plaza. Her fur-trimmed suit was grey – 'because with grey you *have* to wear a lot of paint,' she explained – and a small toque sat rakishly on her head, allowing yellow ripples of hair to wave out in jaunty glory. In the higher light it seemed to Anthony that her personality was infinitely softer – she seemed so young, scarcely eighteen; her form under the tight sheath, known then as a hobble-skirt, was amazingly supple and slender, and her hands, neither 'artistic' nor stubby, were small as a child's hands should be.

As they entered, the orchestra were sounding the preliminary whimpers to a maxixe,[208] a tune full of castanets and facile faintly languorous violin harmonies, appropriate to the crowded winter grill teeming with an excited college crowd, high-spirited at the approach of the holidays. Carefully, Gloria considered several locations, and rather to Anthony's annoyance paraded him circuitously to a table for two at the far side of the room. Reaching it she again considered. Would she sit on the right or on the left? Her beautiful eyes and lips were very grave as she made her choice, and Anthony thought again how naïve was her every gesture; she took all the things of life for hers to choose from and apportion, as though she were continually picking out presents for herself from an inexhaustible counter.

Abstractedly she watched the dancers for a few moments, commenting murmurously as a couple eddied near.

'There's a pretty girl in blue' – and as Anthony looked obediently – 'there! No. behind you – there!'

'Yes,' he agreed helplessly.

'You didn't see her.'

'I'd rather look at you.'

'I know, but she was pretty. Except that she had big ankles.'

'Was she? – I mean, did she?' he said indifferently.

A girl's salutation came from a couple dancing close to them.

'Hello, Gloria! O Gloria!'

'Hello there.'

'Who's that?' he demanded.

'I don't know. Somebody.' She caught sight of another face. 'Hello, Muriel!' Then to Anthony: 'There's Muriel Kane. Now I think she's attractive, 'cept not very.'

Anthony chuckled appreciatively.

' "Attractive, 'cept not very",' he repeated.

She smiled – was interested immediately.

'Why is that funny?' Her tone was pathetically intent.

'It just was.'

'Do you want to dance?'

'Do you?'

'Sort of. But let's sit,' she decided.

'And talk about you? You love to talk about you, don't you?'

'Yes.' Caught in a vanity, she laughed.

'I imagine your autobiography would be a classic.'

'Dick says I haven't got one.'

'Dick!' he exclaimed. 'What does he know about you?'

'Nothing. But he says the biography of every woman begins with the first kiss that counts, and ends when her last child is laid in her arms.'

'He's talking from his book.'

'He says unloved women have no biographies – they have histories.'

Anthony laughed again.

'Surely you don't claim to be unloved!'

'Well, I suppose not.'

'Then why haven't you a biography? Haven't you ever had a kiss that counted?' As the words left his lips he drew in his breath sharply as though to suck them back. This *baby*!

'I don't know what you mean "counts",' she objected.

'I wish you'd tell me how old you are.'

'Twenty-two,' she said, meeting his eyes gravely. 'How old did you think?'

'About eighteen.'

'I'm going to start being that. I don't like being twenty-two. I hate it more than anything in the world.'

'Being twenty-two?'

'No. Getting old and everything. Getting married.'

'Don't you ever want to marry?'

'I don't want to have responsibility and a lot of children to take care of.'

Evidently she did not doubt that on her lips all things were good. He waited rather breathlessly for her next remark, expecting it to follow up her last. She was smiling, without amusement but pleasantly, and after an interval half a dozen words fell into the space between them: 'I wish I had some gumdrops.'

'You shall!' He beckoned to a waiter and sent him to the cigar counter.

'D'you mind? I love gumdrops. Everybody kids me about it because I'm always whacking away at one – whenever my daddy's not around.'

'Not at all. – Who are all these children?' he asked suddenly. 'Do you know them all?'

'Why – no, but they're from – oh, from everywhere, I suppose. Don't you ever come here?'

'Very seldom. I don't care particularly for "nice girls".'

Immediately he had her attention. She turned a definite shoulder to the dancers, relaxed in her chair, and demanded: 'What *do* you do with yourself?'

Thanks to a cocktail Anthony welcomed the question. In a mood to talk, he wanted, moreover, to impress this girl whose interest seemed so tantalisingly elusive – she stopped to browse in unexpected pastures, hurried quickly over the inobviously obvious. He wanted to pose. He wanted to appear suddenly to her in novel and heroic colours. He wanted to stir her from that casualness she showed towards everything except herself.

'I do nothing,' he began, realising simultaneously that his words were to lack the debonair grace he craved for them. 'I do nothing, for there's nothing I can do that's worth doing.'

'Well?' He had neither surprised her nor even held her, yet she had certainly understood him, if indeed he had said aught worth understanding.

'Don't you approve of lazy men?'

She nodded.

'I suppose so, if they're gracefully lazy. Is that possible for an American?'

'Why not?' he demanded, discomfited.

But her mind had left the subject and wandered up ten floors.

'My daddy's mad at me,' she observed dispassionately.

'Why? But I want to know just why it's impossible for an American to be gracefully idle' – his words gathered conviction – 'it astonishes me. It – it – I don't understand why people think that every young man ought to go downtown and work ten hours a day for the best twenty years of his life at dull, unimaginative work, certainly not altruistic work.'

He broke off. She watched him inscrutably. He waited for her to agree or disagree, but she did neither.

'Don't you ever form judgements on things?' he asked with some exasperation.

She shook her head and her eyes wandered back to the dancers as she answered: 'I don't know. I don't know anything about – what you should do, or what anybody should do.'

She confused him and hindered the flow of his ideas. Self-expression had never seemed at once so desirable and so impossible.

'Well,' he admitted apologetically, 'neither do I, of course, but – '

'I just think of people,' she continued, 'whether they seem right where they are and fit into the picture. I don't mind if they don't do anything. I don't see why they should; in fact it always astonishes me when anybody does anything.'

'You don't want to do anything?'

'I want to sleep.'

For a second he was startled, almost as though she had meant this literally.

'Sleep?'

'Sort of. I want to just be lazy and I want some of the people around me to be doing things, because that makes me feel comfortable and safe – and I want some of them to be doing nothing at all, because they can be graceful and companionable for me. But I never want to change people or get excited over them.'

'You're a quaint little determinist,' laughed Anthony. 'It's your world, isn't it?'

'Well – ' she said with a quick upward glance, 'isn't it? As long as I'm – young.'

She had paused slightly before the last word and Anthony suspected that she had started to say 'beautiful'. It was undeniably what she had intended.

Her eyes brightened and he waited for her to enlarge on the theme. He had drawn her out, at any rate – he bent forward slightly to catch the words.

But 'Let's dance!' was all she said.

That winter afternoon at the Plaza was the first of a succession of 'dates' Anthony made with her in the blurred and stimulating days before Christmas. Invariably she was busy. What particular strata of the city's social life claimed her he was a long time finding out. It seemed to matter very little. She attended the semi-public charity dances at the big hotels; he saw her several times at dinner parties in Sherry's, and once, as he waited for her to dress, Mrs Gilbert, apropos of her daughter's habit of 'going', rattled off an amazing holiday programme that included half a dozen dances to which Anthony had received cards.

He made engagements with her several times for lunch and tea – the former were hurried and, to him at least, rather unsatisfactory occasions, for she was sleepy-eyed and casual, incapable of concentrating upon anything or of giving consecutive attention to his remarks. When after two of these sallow meals he accused her of tendering him the skin and bones of the day she laughed and gave him a tea-time three days off. This was infinitely more satisfactory.

One Sunday afternoon just before Christmas he called up and found her in the lull directly after some important but mysterious quarrel: she informed him in a tone of mingled wrath and amusement that she had sent a man out of her apartment – here Anthony speculated violently – and that the man had been giving a little dinner for her that very night and that of course she wasn't going. So Anthony took her to supper.

'Let's go to something!' she proposed as they went down in the elevator. 'I want to see a show, don't you?'

Enquiry at the hotel ticket desk disclosed only two Sunday night 'concerts'.

'They're always the same,' she complained unhappily, 'same old Yiddish comedians. Oh, let's go somewhere!'

To conceal a guilty suspicion that he should have arranged a performance of some kind for her approval Anthony affected a knowing cheerfulness.

'We'll go to a good cabaret.'

'I've seen every one in town.'

'Well, we'll find a new one.'

She was in wretched humour; that was evident. Her grey eyes were granite now indeed. When she wasn't speaking she stared straight in front of her as if at some distasteful abstraction in the lobby.

'Well, come on, then.'

He followed her, a graceful girl even in her enveloping fur, out to a taxicab, and, with an air of having a definite place in mind, instructed the driver to go over to Broadway and then turn south. He made several casual attempts at conversation but as she adopted an impenetrable armour of silence and answered him in sentences as morose as the cold darkness of the taxicab he gave up, and assuming a like mood fell into a dim gloom.

A dozen blocks down Broadway Anthony's eyes were caught by a large and unfamiliar electric sign spelling 'Marathon' in glorious yellow script, adorned with electrical leaves and flowers that alternately vanished and beamed upon the wet and glistening street. He leaned and rapped on the taxi-window and in a moment was receiving information from a coloured doorman: Yes, this was a cabaret. Fine cabaret. Bes' showina city!

'Shall we try it?'

With a sigh Gloria tossed her cigarette out the open door and prepared to follow it; then they had passed under the screaming sign, under the wide portal, and up by a stuffy elevator into this unsung palace of pleasure.

The gay habitats of the very rich and the very poor, the very dashing and the very criminal, not to mention the lately exploited very Bohemian, are made known to the awed high-school girls of Augusta, Georgia, and Redwing, Minnesota, not only through the bepictured and entrancing spreads of the Sunday theatrical supplements but through the shocked and alarmful eyes of Mr Rupert

Hughes[209] and other chroniclers of the mad pace of America. But the excursions of Harlem on to Broadway, the deviltries of the dull and the revelries of the respectable are a matter of esoteric knowledge only to the participants themselves.

A tip circulates – and in the place knowingly mentioned, gather the lower moral-classes on Saturday and Sunday nights – the little troubled men who are pictured in the comics as 'the Consumer' or 'the Public'. They have made sure that the place has three qualifications: it is cheap; it imitates with a sort of shoddy and mechanical wistfulness the glittering antics of the great cafés in the theatre district; and – this, above all, important – it is a place where they can 'take a nice girl', which means, of course, that everyone has become equally harmless, timid and uninteresting through lack of money and imagination.

There on Sunday nights gather the credulous, sentimental, underpaid, overworked people with hyphenated occupations – book-keepers, ticket-sellers, office-managers, sales-men – and, most of all, clerks – clerks of the express, of the mail, of the grocery, of the brokerage, of the bank. With them are their giggling, over-gestured, pathetically pretentious women, who grow fat with them, bear them too many babies, and float helpless and uncontent in a colourless sea of drudgery and broken hopes.

They name these brummagem cabarets after Pullman cars. The 'Marathon'! Not for them the salacious similes borrowed from the cafés of Paris! This is where their docile patrons bring their 'nice women', whose starved fancies are only too willing to believe that the scene is comparatively gay and joyous, and even faintly immoral. This is life! Who cares for the morrow?

Abandoned people!

Anthony and Gloria, seated, looked about them. At the next table a party of four were in process of being joined by a party of three, two men and a girl, who were evidently late – and the manner of the girl was a study in national sociology. She was meeting some new men – and she was pretending desperately. By gesture she was pretending and by words and by the scarcely perceptible motionings of her eyelids that she belonged to a class a little superior to the class with which she now had to do, that a while ago she had been, and presently would again be, in a higher, rarer air. She was almost painfully refined – she wore a last year's hat covered with violets no more yearningly pretentious and palpably artificial than herself.

Fascinated, Anthony and Gloria watched the girl sit down and radiate the impression that she was only condescendingly present. For *me*, her eyes said, this is practically a slumming expedition, to be cloaked with belittling laughter and semi-apologetics.

– And the other women passionately poured out the impression that though they were in the crowd they were not of it. This was not the sort of place to which they were accustomed; they had dropped in because it was near by and convenient – every party in the restaurant poured out that impression . . . who knew? They were forever changing class, all of them – the women often marrying above their opportunities, the men striking suddenly a magnificent opulence: a sufficiently preposterous advertising scheme, a celestialised ice-cream cone. Meanwhile, they met here to eat, closing their eyes to the economy displayed in infrequent changings of tablecloths, in the casualness of the cabaret performers, most of all in the colloquial carelessness and familiarity of the waiters. One was sure that these waiters were not impressed by their patrons. One expected that presently they would sit at the tables . . .

'Do you object to this?' enquired Anthony.

Gloria's face warmed and for the first time that evening she smiled. 'I love it,' she said frankly. It was impossible to doubt her. Her grey eyes roved here and there, drowsing, idle or alert, on each group, passing to the next with unconcealed enjoyment, and to Anthony were made plain the different values of her profile, the wonderfully alive expressions of her mouth, and the authentic distinction of face and form and manner that made her like a single flower amidst a collection of cheap bric-à-brac. At her happiness, a gorgeous sentiment welled into his eyes, choked him up, set his nerves a-tingle, and filled his throat with husky and vibrant emotion. There was a hush upon the room. The careless violins and saxophones, the shrill rasping complaint of a child near by, the voice of the violet-hatted girl at the next table, all moved slowly out, receded, and fell away like shadowy reflections on the shining floor – and they two, it seemed to him, were alone and infinitely remote, quiet. Surely the freshness of her cheeks was a gossamer projection from a land of delicate and undiscovered shades; her hand gleaming on the stained tablecloth was a shell from some far and wildly virginal sea . . .

Then the illusion snapped like a nest of threads; the room grouped itself around him, voices, faces, movement; the garish shimmer of the lights overhead became real, became portentous; breath began, the slow respiration that she and he took in time with this docile hundred, the rise and fall of bosoms, the eternal meaningless play and interplay and tossing and reiterating of word and phrase – all these wrenched his senses open to the suffocating pressure of life – and then her voice came at him, cool as the suspended dream he had left behind.

'I belong here,' she murmured, 'I'm like these people.'

For an instant this seemed a sardonic and unnecessary paradox hurled at him across the impassable distances she created about herself. Her entrancement had increased – her eyes rested upon a Semitic violinist who swayed his shoulders to the rhythm of the year's mellowest foxtrot:

> Something – goes
> Ring-a-ting-a-ling-a-ling
> Right in-your ear – ' [210]

Again she spoke, from the centre of this pervasive illusion of her own. It amazed him. It was like blasphemy from the mouth of a child.

'I'm like they are – like Japanese lanterns and crêpe paper, and the music of that orchestra.'

'You're a young idiot!' he insisted wildly. She shook her blonde head.

'No, I'm not. I *am* like them . . . You ought to see . . . You don't know me.' She hesitated and her eyes came back to him, rested abruptly on his, as though surprised at the last to see him there. 'I've got a streak of what you'd call cheapness. I don't know where I get it but it's – oh, things like this and bright colours and gaudy vulgarity. I seem to belong here. These people could appreciate me and take me for granted, and these men would fall in love with me and admire me, whereas the clever men I meet would just analyse me and tell me I'm this because of this or that because of that.'

– Anthony for the moment wanted fiercely to paint her, to set her down *now*, as she was, as with each relentless second she could never be again.

'What were you thinking?' she asked.

'Just that I'm not a realist,' he said, and then: 'No, only the romanticist preserves the things worth preserving.'

Out of the deep sophistication of Anthony an understanding formed, nothing atavistic or obscure, indeed scarcely physical at all, an understanding remembered from the romancings of many generations of minds that as she talked and caught his eyes and turned her lovely head, she moved him as he had never been moved before. The sheath that held her soul had assumed significance – that was all. She was a sun, radiant, growing, gathering light and storing it – then after an eternity pouring it forth in a glance, the fragment of a sentence, to that part of him that cherished all beauty and all illusion.

CHAPTER 3

The Connoisseur of Kisses

From his undergraduate days as editor of the *Harvard Crimson*[211] Richard Caramel had desired to write. But as a senior he had picked up the glorified illusion that certain men were set aside for 'service' and, going into the world, were to accomplish a vague yearnful something which would react either in eternal reward or, at the least, in the personal satisfaction of having striven for the greatest good of the greatest number.

This spirit has long rocked the colleges in America. It begins, as a rule, during the immaturities and facile impressions of freshman year – sometimes back in preparatory school. Prosperous apostles known for their emotional acting go the rounds of the universities and, by frightening the amiable sheep and dulling the quickening of interest and intellectual curiosity which is the purpose of all education, distil a mysterious conviction of sin, harking back to childhood crimes and to the ever-present menace of 'women'. To these lectures go the wicked youths to cheer and joke and the timid to swallow the tasty pills, which would be harmless if administered to farmers' wives and pious drug-clerks but are rather dangerous medicine for these 'future leaders of men'.

This octopus was strong enough to wind a sinuous tentacle about Richard Caramel. The year after his graduation it called him into the slums of New York to muck about with bewildered Italians as secretary to an 'Alien Young Men's Rescue Association'. He laboured at it over a year before the monotony began to weary him. The aliens kept coming inexhaustibly – Italians, Poles, Scandinavians, Czechs, Armenians – with the same wrongs, the same exceptionally ugly faces and very much the same smells, though he fancied that these grew more profuse and diverse as the months passed. His eventual conclusions about the expediency of service were vague, but concerning his own relation to it they were abrupt and decisive. Any amiable young man, his head ringing with the latest crusade, could accomplish as much as he could with the débris of Europe – and it was time for him to write.

He had been living in a downtown YMCA, but when he quit the task of making sow-ear purses out of sows' ears, he moved uptown and went to work immediately as a reporter for the *Sun*.[212] He kept at this for a year, doing desultory writing on the side, with little success, and then one day an infelicitous incident peremptorily closed his newspaper career. On a February afternoon he was assigned to report a parade of Squadron A. Snow threatening, he went to sleep instead before a hot fire, and when he woke up did a smooth column about the muffled beats of the horses' hoofs in the snow . . . This he handed in. Next morning a marked copy of the paper was sent down to the City Editor with a scrawled note: 'Fire the man who wrote this.' It seemed that Squadron A had also seen the snow threatening – and had postponed the parade until another day.

A week later he had begun *The Demon Lover* . . .

In January, the Monday of the months, Richard Caramel's nose was blue constantly, a sardonic blue, vaguely suggestive of the flames licking around a sinner. His book was nearly ready, and as it grew in completeness it seemed to grow also in its demands, sapping him, overpowering him, until he walked haggard and conquered in its shadow. Not only to Anthony and Maury did he pour out his hopes and boasts and indecisions, but to anyone who could be prevailed upon to listen. He called on polite but bewildered publishers, he discussed it with his casual vis-à-vis at the Harvard Club;[213] it was even claimed by Anthony that he had been discovered, one Sunday night, debating the transposition of Chapter Two with a literary ticket-collector in the chill and dismal recesses of a Harlem subway station. And latest among his confidantes was Mrs Gilbert, who sat with him by the hour and alternated between Bilphism and literature in an intense cross-fire.

'Shakespeare was a Bilphist,' she assured him through a fixed smile. 'Oh, yes! He was a Bilphist. It's been proved.'

At this Dick would look a bit blank.

'If you've read *Hamlet* you can't help but see.'

'Well, he – he lived in a more credulous age – a more religious age.'

But she demanded the whole loaf: 'Oh, yes, but you see Bilphism isn't a religion. It's the science of all religions.' She smiled defiantly at him. This was the *bon mot* of her belief. There was something in the arrangement of words which grasped her mind so definitely that the statement became superior to any obligation to define itself. It is not unlikely that she would have accepted any idea encased in this radiant formula – which was perhaps not a formula; it was the *reductio ad absurdum* of all formulas.

Then eventually, but gorgeously, would come Dick's turn.

'You've heard of the new poetry movement. You haven't? Well, it's a lot of young poets that are breaking away from the old forms and doing a lot of good. Well, what I was going to say was that my book is going to start a new prose movement, a sort of renaissance.'

'I'm sure it will,' beamed Mrs Gilbert. 'I'm *sure* it will. I went to Jenny Martin last Tuesday, the palmist, you know, that everyone's *mad* about. I told her my nephew was engaged upon a work and she said she knew I'd be glad to hear that his success would be *extraordinary*. But she'd never seen you or known anything about you – not even your *name*.'

Having made the proper noises to express his amazement at this astounding phenomenon, Dick waved her theme by him as though he were an arbitrary traffic policeman, and, so to speak, beckoned forward his own traffic.

'I'm absorbed, Aunt Catherine,' he assured her, 'I really am. All my friends are joshing me – oh, I see the humour in it and I don't care. I think a person ought to be able to take joshing. But I've got a sort of conviction,' he concluded gloomily.

'You're an ancient soul, I always say.'

'Maybe I am.' Dick had reached the stage where he no longer fought, but submitted. He *must* be an ancient soul, he fancied grotesquely; so old as to be absolutely rotten. However, the reiteration of the phrase still somewhat embarrassed him and sent uncomfortable shivers up his back. He changed the subject.

'Where is my distinguished cousin Gloria?'

'She's on the go somewhere, with someone.'

Dick paused, considered, and then, screwing up his face into what was evidently begun as a smile but ended as a terrifying frown, delivered a comment.

'I think my friend Anthony Patch is in love with her.'

Mrs Gilbert started, beamed half a second too late, and breathed her 'Really?' in the tone of a detective-play whisper.

'I *think* so,' corrected Dick gravely. 'She's the first girl I've ever seen him with, so much.'

'Well, of course,' said Mrs Gilbert with meticulous carelessness, 'Gloria never makes me her confidante. She's very secretive. Between you and me' – she bent forward cautiously, obviously determined that only heaven and her nephew should share her confession – 'between you and me, I'd like to see her settle down.'

Dick arose and paced the floor earnestly, a small, active, already rotund young man, his hands thrust unnaturally into his bulging pockets.

'I'm not claiming I'm right, mind you,' he assured the infinitely-of-the-hotel steel-engraving which smirked respectably back at him. 'I'm saying nothing that I'd want Gloria to know. But I think Mad Anthony is interested – tremendously so. He talks about her constantly. In anyone else that'd be a bad sign.'

'Gloria is a very young soul – ' began Mrs Gilbert eagerly, but her nephew interrupted with a hurried sentence: 'Gloria'd be a very young nut not to marry him.' He stopped and faced her, his expression a battle map of lines and dimples, squeezed and strained to its ultimate show of intensity – this as if to make up by his sincerity for any indiscretion in his words. 'Gloria's a wild one, Aunt Catherine. She's uncontrollable. How she's done it I don't know, but lately she's picked up a lot of the funniest friends. She doesn't seem to care. And the men she used to go with around New York were – ' He paused for breath.

'Yes-yes-yes,' interjected Mrs Gilbert, with an anaemic attempt to hide the immense interest with which she listened.

'Well,' continued Richard Caramel gravely, 'there it is. I mean that the men she went with and the people she went with used to be first rate. Now they aren't.'

Mrs Gilbert blinked very fast – her bosom trembled, inflated, remained so for an instant, and with the exhalation her words flowed out in a torrent.

She knew, she cried in a whisper; oh, yes, mothers see these things. But what could she do? He knew Gloria. He'd seen enough of Gloria to know how hopeless it was to try to deal with her. Gloria had been so spoiled – in a rather complete and unusual way. She had been suckled until she was three, for instance, when she could probably have chewed sticks. Perhaps – one never knew – it was this that had given that health and *hardiness* to her whole personality. And then ever since she was twelve years old she'd had boys about her so thick – oh, so thick one couldn't *move*. At sixteen she began going to dances at preparatory schools, and then came the colleges; and everywhere she went, boys, boys, boys. At first, oh, until she was eighteen there had been so many that it never seemed one any more than the others, but then she began to single them out.

She knew there had been a string of affairs spread over about three years, perhaps a dozen of them altogether. Sometimes the men were undergraduates, sometimes just out of college – they lasted on an average of several months each, with short attractions in between. Once or twice they had endured longer and her mother had hoped she would be engaged, but always a new one came – a new one –

The men? Oh, she made them miserable, literally! There was only one who had kept any sort of dignity, and he had been a mere child, young Carter Kirby, of Kansas City, who was so conceited anyway that he just sailed out on his vanity one afternoon and left for Europe next day with his father. The others had been – wretched. They never seemed to know when she was tired of them, and Gloria had seldom been deliberately unkind. They would keep phoning, writing letters to her, trying to see her, making long trips after her around the country. Some of them had confided in Mrs Gilbert, told her with tears in their eyes that they would never get over Gloria . . . at least two of them had since married, though . . . But Gloria, it seemed, struck to kill – to this day Mr Carstairs called up once a week, and sent her flowers which she no longer bothered to refuse.

Several times, twice, at least, Mrs Gilbert knew it had gone as far as a private engagement – with Tudor Baird and that Holcome boy at Pasadena. She was sure it had, because – this must go no further – she had come in unexpectedly and found Gloria acting, well, very much engaged indeed. She had not spoken to her daughter, of course. She had had a certain sense of delicacy and, besides, each time she had expected an announcement in a few weeks. But the announcement never came; instead, a new man came.

Scenes! Young men walking up and down the library like caged tigers! Young men glaring at each other in the hall as one came and the other left! Young men calling up on the telephone and being hung up upon in desperation! Young men threatening South America! . . . Young men writing the most pathetic letters! (She said nothing to this effect, but Dick fancied that Mrs Gilbert's eyes had seen some of these letters.)

. . . And Gloria, between tears and laughter, sorry, glad, out of love and in love, miserable, nervous, cool, amidst a great returning of presents, substitution of pictures in immemorial frames, and taking of hot baths and beginning again – with the next.

That state of things continued, assumed an air of permanency. Nothing harmed Gloria or changed her or moved her. And then out of a clear sky one day she informed her mother that undergraduates wearied her. She was absolutely going to no more college dances.

This had begun the change – not so much in her actual habits, for she danced, and had as many 'dates' as ever – but they were dates in a different spirit. Previously it had been a sort of pride, a matter of her own vainglory. She had been, probably, the most celebrated and sought-after young beauty in the country. Gloria Gilbert of Kansas City! She had fed on it ruthlessly – enjoying the crowds around her, the manner in which the most desirable men singled her out; enjoying the fierce jealousy of other girls; enjoying the fabulous, not to say scandalous, and, her mother was glad to say, entirely unfounded rumours about her – for instance, that she had gone in the Yale swimming-pool one night in a chiffon evening dress.

And from loving it with a vanity that was almost masculine – it had been in the nature of a triumphant and dazzling career – she became suddenly anaesthetic to it. She retired. She who had dominated countless parties, who had blown fragrantly through many ballrooms to the tender tribute of many eyes, seemed to care no longer. He who fell in love with her now was dismissed utterly, almost angrily. She went listlessly with the most indifferent men. She continually broke engagements, not as in the past from a cool assurance that she was irreproachable, that the man she insulted would return like a domestic animal – but indifferently, without contempt or pride. She rarely stormed at men any more – she yawned at them. She seemed – and it was so strange – she seemed to her mother to be growing cold.

Richard Caramel listened. At first he had remained standing, but as his aunt's discourse waxed in content – it stands here pruned by half, of all side references to the youth of Gloria's soul and to Mrs Gilbert's own mental distresses – he drew a chair up and attended rigorously as she floated, between tears and plaintive helplessness, down the long story of Gloria's life. When she came to the tale of this last year, a tale of the ends of cigarettes left all over New York in little trays marked 'Midnight Frolic' and 'Justine Johnson's Little Club',[214] he began nodding his head slowly, then faster and faster, until, as she finished on a staccato note, it was bobbing briskly up and down, absurdly like a doll's wired head, expressing – almost anything.

In a sense Gloria's past was an old story to him. He had followed it with the eyes of a journalist, for he was going to write a book about her someday. But his interests, just at present, were family interests. He wanted to know, in particular, who was this Joseph Bloeckman that he had seen her with several times; and those two girls she was with constantly, 'this' Rachael Jerryl and 'this' Miss Kane – surely Miss Kane wasn't exactly the sort one would associate with Gloria!

But the moment had passed. Mrs Gilbert having climbed the hill of exposition was about to glide swiftly down the ski-jump of collapse. Her eyes were like a blue sky seen through two round, red window-casements. The flesh about her mouth was trembling.

And at that moment the door opened, admitting into the room Gloria and the two young ladies lately mentioned.

TWO YOUNG WOMEN

'Well!'

'How do you do, Mrs Gilbert!'

Miss Kane and Miss Jerryl are presented to Mr Richard Caramel. 'This is Dick' (laughter).

'I've heard so much about you,' says Miss Kane between a giggle and a shout.

'How do you do,' says Miss Jerryl shyly.

Richard Caramel tries to move about as if his figure were better. He is torn between his innate cordiality and the fact that he considers these girls rather common – not at all the Farmover type.

Gloria has disappeared into the bedroom.

'Do sit down,' beams Mrs Gilbert, who is by now quite herself. 'Take off your things.' Dick is afraid she will make some remark about the age of his soul, but he forgets his qualms in completing a conscientious, novelist's examination of the two young women.

Muriel Kane had originated in a rising family of East Orange.[215] She was short rather than small, and hovered audaciously between plumpness and width. Her hair was black and elaborately arranged. This, in conjunction with her handsome, rather bovine eyes, and her over-red lips, combined to make her resemble Theda Bara, the prominent motion-picture actress. People told her constantly that she was a 'vampire', and she believed them. She suspected hopefully that they were afraid of her, and she did her utmost under all circumstances to give the impression of danger. An imaginative man could see the red flag that she constantly carried, waving it wildly, beseechingly – and, alas, to little spectacular avail. She was also tremendously timely: she knew the latest songs, all the latest songs – when one of them was played on the phonograph she would rise to her feet and rock her shoulders back and forth and snap her fingers, and if there was no music she would accompany herself by humming.

Her conversation was also timely: 'I don't care,' she would say, 'I should worry and lose my figure' – and again: 'I can't make my feet behave when I hear that tune. Oh, baby!'

Her fingernails were too long and ornate, polished to a pink and unnatural fever. Her clothes were too tight, too stylish, too vivid, her eyes too roguish, her smile too coy. She was almost pitifully overemphasised from head to foot.

The other girl was obviously a more subtle personality. She was an exquisitely dressed Jewess with dark hair and a lovely milky pallor. She seemed shy and vague, and these two qualities accentuated a rather delicate charm that floated about her. Her family were 'Episcopalians', owned three smart women's shops along Fifth Avenue, and lived in a magnificent apartment on Riverside Drive. It seemed to Dick, after a few moments, that she was attempting to imitate Gloria – he wondered that people invariably chose inimitable people to imitate.

'We had the most *hectic* time!' Muriel was exclaiming enthusiastically. 'There was a crazy woman behind us on the bus. She was absitively, posolutely *nutty*! She kept talking to herself about something she'd like to do to somebody or something. I was *pet*rified, but Gloria simply *wouldn't* get off.'

Mrs Gilbert opened her mouth, properly awed.

'Really?'

'Oh, she was crazy. But we should worry, she didn't hurt us. Ugly! Gracious! The man across from us said her face ought to be on a night-nurse in a home for the blind, and we all *howled*, naturally, so the man tried to pick us up.'

Presently Gloria emerged from her bedroom and in unison every eye turned on her. The two girls receded into a shadowy background, unperceived, unmissed.

'We've been talking about you,' said Dick quickly, ' – your mother and I.'

'Well,' said Gloria.

A pause – Muriel turned to Dick.

'You're a great writer, aren't you?'

'I'm a writer,' he confessed sheepishly.

'I always say,' said Muriel earnestly, 'that if I ever had time to write down all my experiences it'd make a wonderful book.'

Rachael giggled sympathetically; Richard Caramel's bow was almost stately. Muriel continued: 'But I don't see how you can sit down and do it. And poetry! Lordy, I can't make two lines rhyme. Well, I should worry!'

Richard Caramel with difficulty restrained a shout of laughter. Gloria was chewing an amazing gum-drop and staring moodily out the window. Mrs Gilbert cleared her throat and beamed.

'But you see,' she said in a sort of universal exposition, 'you're not an ancient soul – like Richard.'

The Ancient Soul breathed a gasp of relief – it was out at last.

Then as if she had been considering it for five minutes, Gloria made a sudden announcement: 'I'm going to give a party.'

'Oh, can I come?' cried Muriel with facetious daring.

'A dinner. Seven people: Muriel and Rachael and I, and you, Dick, and Anthony, and that man named Noble – I liked him – and Bloeckman.'

Muriel and Rachael went into soft and purring ecstasies of enthusiasm. Mrs Gilbert blinked and beamed. With an air of casualness Dick broke in with a question: 'Who is this fellow Bloeckman, Gloria?'

Scenting a faint hostility, Gloria turned to him.

'Joseph Bloeckman? He's the moving-picture man. Vice-president of Films Par Excellence. He and father do a lot of business.'

'Oh!'

'Well, will you all come?'

They would all come. A date was arranged within the week. Dick rose, adjusted hat, coat and muffler, and gave out a general smile.

'Bye-bye,' said Muriel, waving her hand gaily, 'call me up sometime.'

Richard Caramel blushed for her.

DEPLORABLE END OF THE CHEVALIER O'KEEFE

It was Monday and Anthony took Geraldine Burke to luncheon at the Beaux Arts[216] – afterwards they went up to his apartment and he wheeled out the little rolling-table that held his supply of liquor, selecting vermouth, gin and absinthe for a proper stimulant.

Geraldine Burke, usher at Keith's, had been an amusement of several months. She demanded so little that he liked her, for since a lamentable affair with a débutante the preceding summer, when he had discovered that after half a dozen kisses a proposal was expected, he had been wary of girls of his own class. It was only too easy to turn a critical eye on their imperfections – some physical harshness or a general lack of personal delicacy – but a girl who was usher at Keith's was approached with a different attitude. One could tolerate qualities in an intimate valet that would be unforgivable in a mere acquaintance on one's social level.

Geraldine, curled up at the foot of the lounge, considered him with narrow slanting eyes.

'You drink all the time, don't you?' she said suddenly.

'Why, I suppose so,' replied Anthony in some surprise. 'Don't you?'

'Nope. I go on parties sometimes – you know, about once a week, but I only take two or three drinks. You and your friends keep on drinking all the time. I should think you'd ruin your health.'

Anthony was somewhat touched.

'Why, aren't you sweet to worry about me!'

'Well, I do.'

'I don't drink so very much,' he declared. 'Last month I didn't touch a drop for three weeks. And I only get really tight about once a week.'

'But you have something to drink every day and you're only twenty-five. Haven't you any ambition? Think what you'll be at forty?'

'I sincerely trust that I won't live that long.'

She clicked her teeth with her tongue.

'You cra-azy!' she said as he mixed another cocktail – and then: 'Are you any relation to Adam Patch?'

'Yes, he's my grandfather.'

'Really?' She was obviously thrilled.

'Absolutely.'

'That's funny. My daddy used to work for him.'

'He's a queer old man.'

'Is he nice?' she demanded.

'Well, in private life he's seldom unnecessarily disagreeable.'

'Tell us about him.'

'Why,' Anthony considered ' – he's all shrunken up and he's got the remains of some grey hair that always looks as though the wind were in it. He's very moral.'

'He's done a lot of good,' said Geraldine with intense gravity.

'Rot!' scoffed Anthony. 'He's a pious ass – a chicken-brain.'

Her mind left the subject and flitted on.

'Why don't you live with him?'

'Why don't I board in a Methodist parsonage?'

'You cra-azy!'

Again she made a little clicking sound to express disapproval. Anthony thought how moral was this little waif at heart – how completely moral she would still be after the inevitable wave came that would wash her off the sands of respectability.

'Do you hate him?'

'I wonder. I never liked him. You never like people who do things for you.'

'Does he hate you?'

'My dear Geraldine,' protested Anthony, frowning humorously, 'do have another cocktail. I annoy him. If I smoke a cigarette he comes into the room sniffing. He's a prig, a bore and something of a hypocrite. I probably wouldn't be telling you this if I hadn't had a few drinks, but I don't suppose it matters.'

Geraldine was persistently interested. She held her glass, untasted, between finger and thumb and regarded him with eyes in which there was a touch of awe.

'How do you mean a hypocrite?'

'Well,' said Anthony impatiently, 'maybe he's not. But he doesn't like the things that I like, and so, as far as I'm concerned, he's uninteresting.'

'Hm.' Her curiosity seemed, at length, satisfied. She sank back into the sofa and sipped her cocktail.

'You're a funny one,' she commented thoughtfully. 'Does everybody want to marry you because your grandfather is rich?'

'They don't – but I shouldn't blame them if they did. Still, you see, I never intend to marry.'

She scorned this.

'You'll fall in love someday. Oh, you will – I know.' She nodded wisely.

'It'd be idiotic to be overconfident. That's what ruined the Chevalier O'Keefe.'

'Who was he?'

'A creature of my splendid mind. He's my one creation, the Chevalier.'

'Cra-a-azy!' she murmured pleasantly, using the clumsy rope-ladder with which she bridged all gaps and climbed after her mental superiors. Subconsciously she felt that it eliminated distances and brought the person whose imagination had eluded her back within range.

'Oh, no!' objected Anthony, 'oh, no, Geraldine. You mustn't play the alienist upon the Chevalier. If you feel yourself unable to understand him I won't bring him in. Besides, I should feel a certain uneasiness because of his regrettable reputation.'

'I guess I can understand anything that's got any sense to it,' answered Geraldine a bit testily.

'In that case there are various episodes in the life of the Chevalier which might prove diverting.'

'Well?'

'It was his untimely end that caused me to think of him and made him apropos in the conversation. I hate to introduce him end foremost, but it seems inevitable that the Chevalier must back into your life.'

'Well, what about him? Did he die?'

'He did! In this manner. He was an Irishman, Geraldine, a semi-fictional Irishman – the wild sort with a genteel brogue and "reddish hair". He was exiled from Erin in the late days of chivalry and, of course, crossed over to France. Now the Chevalier O'Keefe, Geraldine, had, like me, one weakness. He was enormously susceptible to all sorts and conditions of women. Besides being a sentimentalist he was a romantic, a vain fellow, a man of wild passions, a little blind in one eye and almost stone-blind in the other. Now a male roaming the world in this condition is as helpless as a lion without teeth, and in consequence the Chevalier was made utterly miserable for twenty years by a series of women who hated him, used him, bored him, aggravated him, sickened him, spent his money, made a fool of him – in brief, as the world has it, loved him.

'This was bad, Geraldine, and as the Chevalier, save for this one weakness, this exceeding susceptibility, was a man of penetration, he decided that he would rescue himself once and for all from these drains upon him. With this purpose he went to a very famous monastery in Champagne called – well, anachronistically known as St Voltaire's. It was the rule at St Voltaire's that no monk could descend to the ground storey of the monastery so long as he lived, but should exist engaged in prayer and contemplation in one of the four towers, which were called after the four commandments of the monastery rule: Poverty, Chastity, Obedience and Silence.

'When the day came that was to witness the Chevalier's farewell to the world he was utterly happy. He gave all his Greek books to his landlady, and his sword he sent in a golden sheath to the King of France, and all his mementos of Ireland he gave to the young Huguenot who sold fish in the street where he lived.

'Then he rode out to St Voltaire's, slew his horse at the door, and presented the carcass to the monastery cook.

'At five o'clock that night he felt, for the first time, free – for ever free from sex. No woman could enter the monastery; no monk could descend below the second storey. So as he climbed the winding stair that led to his cell at the very top of the Tower of Chastity he paused for a moment by an open window which looked down fifty feet on to a road below. It was all so beautiful, he thought, this world that he was leaving, the golden shower of sun beating down upon the long fields, the spray of trees in the distance, the vineyards, quiet and green, freshening wide miles before him. He leaned his elbows on the window casement and gazed at the winding road.

'Now, as it happened, Thérèse, a peasant girl of sixteen from a neighbouring village, was at that moment passing along this same road that ran in front of the monastery. Five minutes before, the little piece of ribbon which held up the stocking on her pretty left leg had worn through and broken. Being a girl of rare modesty she had thought to wait until she arrived home before repairing it, but it had bothered her to such an extent that she felt she could endure it no longer. So, as she passed the Tower of Chastity, she stopped and with a pretty gesture lifted her skirt – as little as possible, be it said to her credit – to adjust her garter.

'Up in the tower the newest arrival in the ancient monastery of St Voltaire, as though pulled forward by a gigantic and irresistible hand, leaned from the window. Farther he leaned and farther until suddenly one of the stones loosened under his weight, broke from its cement with a soft powdery sound – and, first headlong, then head over heels, finally in a vast and impressive revolution tumbled the Chevalier O'Keefe, bound for the hard earth and eternal damnation.

'Thérèse was so much upset by the occurrence that she ran all the way home and for ten years spent an hour a day in secret prayer for the soul of the monk whose neck and vows were simultaneously broken on that unfortunate Sunday afternoon.

'And the Chevalier O'Keefe, being suspected of suicide, was not buried in consecrated ground, but tumbled into a field near by, where he doubtless improved the quality of the soil for many years afterwards. Such was the untimely end of a very brave and gallant gentleman. What do you think, Geraldine?'

But Geraldine, lost long before, could only smile roguishly, wave her first finger at him, and repeat her bridge-all, her explain-all: 'Crazy!' she said, 'you cra-a-azy!'

His thin face was kindly, she thought, and his eyes quite gentle. She liked him because he was arrogant without being conceited, and because, unlike the men she met about the theatre, he had a horror of being conspicuous. What an odd, pointless story! But she had enjoyed the part about the stocking!

After the fifth cocktail he kissed her, and between laughter and bantering caresses and a half-stifled flare of passion they passed an hour. At four-thirty she claimed an engagement, and going into the bathroom she rearranged her hair. Refusing to let him order her a taxi she stood for a moment in the doorway.

'You *will* get married,' she was insisting, 'you wait and see.'

Anthony was playing with an ancient tennis ball, and he bounced it carefully on the floor several times before he answered with a soupçon of acidity: 'You're a little idiot, Geraldine.'

She smiled provokingly.

'Oh, I am, am I? Want to bet?'

'That'd be silly too.'

'Oh, it would, would it? Well, I'll just bet you'll marry somebody inside of a year.'

Anthony bounced the tennis ball very hard. This was one of his handsome days, she thought; a sort of intensity had displaced the melancholy in his dark eyes.

'Geraldine,' he said, at length, 'in the first place I have no one I want to marry; in the second place I haven't enough money to support two people; in the third place I am entirely opposed to marriage for people of my type; in the fourth place I have a strong distaste for even the abstract consideration of it.'

But Geraldine only narrowed her eyes knowingly, made her clicking sound, and said she must be going. It was late.

'Call me up soon,' she reminded him as he kissed her goodbye, 'you haven't for three weeks, you know.'

'I will,' he promised fervently.

He shut the door and coming back into the room stood for a moment lost in thought with the tennis ball still clasped in his hand. There was one of his lonelinesses coming, one of those times when he walked the streets or sat, aimless and depressed, biting a pencil at his desk. It was a self-absorption with no comfort, a demand for expression with no outlet, a sense of time rushing by, ceaselessly and wastefully – assuaged only by that conviction that there was nothing to waste, because all efforts and attainments were equally valueless.

He thought with emotion – aloud, ejaculative, for he was hurt and confused.

'No *idea* of getting married, by *God*!'

Of a sudden he hurled the tennis ball violently across the room, where it barely missed the lamp, and, rebounding here and there for a moment, lay still upon the floor.

SIGNLIGHT AND MOONLIGHT

For her dinner Gloria had taken a table in the Cascades at the Biltmore,[217] and when the men met in the hall outside, a little after eight, 'that person Bloeckman' was the target of six masculine eyes. He was a stoutening, ruddy Jew of about thirty-five, with an expressive face under smooth sandy hair – and, no doubt, in most business gatherings his personality would have been considered ingratiating. He sauntered up to the three younger men, who stood in a group smoking as they waited for their hostess, and introduced himself with a little too evident assurance – nevertheless it is to be doubted whether he received the intended impression of faint and ironic chill: there was no hint of understanding in his manner.

'You related to Adam J. Patch?' he enquired of Anthony, emitting two slender strings of smoke from nostrils over-wide.

Anthony admitted it with the ghost of a smile.

'He's a fine man,' pronounced Bloeckman profoundly. 'He's a fine example of an American.'

'Yes,' agreed Anthony, 'he certainly is.'

– I detest these underdone men, he thought coldly. Boiled looking! Ought to be shoved back in the oven; just one more minute would do it.

Bloeckman squinted at his watch.

'Time these girls were showing up . . . '

– Anthony waited breathlessly; it came –

' . . . but then,' with a widening smile, 'you know how women are.'

The three young men nodded; Bloeckman looked casually about him, his eyes resting critically on the ceiling and then passing lower. His expression combined that of a Middle-Western farmer appraising his wheat crop and that of an actor wondering whether he is observed – the public manner of all good Americans. As he finished his survey he turned back quickly to the reticent trio, determined to strike to their very heart and core.

'You college men? . . . Harvard, eh. I see the Princeton boys beat you fellows in hockey.'

Unfortunate man. He had drawn another blank. They had been three years out and heeded only the big football games. Whether, after the failure of this sally, Mr Bloeckman would have perceived himself to be in a cynical atmosphere is problematical, for –

Gloria arrived. Muriel arrived. Rachael arrived. After a hurried, 'Hello, people!' uttered by Gloria and echoed by the other two, the three swept by into the dressing-room.

A moment later Muriel appeared in a state of elaborate undress and *crept* towards them. She was in her element: her ebony hair was slicked straight back on her head; her eyes were artificially darkened; she reeked of insistent perfume. She was got up to the best of her ability as a siren, more popularly a 'vamp' – a picker up and thrower away of men, an unscrupulous and fundamentally unmoved toyer with affections. Something in the exhaustiveness of her attempt fascinated Maury at first sight – a woman with wide hips affecting a panther-like litheness! As they waited the extra three minutes for Gloria, and, by polite assumption, for Rachael, he was unable to take his eyes from her. She would turn her head away, lowering her eyelashes and biting her nether lip in an amazing exhibition of coyness. She would rest her hands on her hips and sway from side to side in tune to the music, saying: 'Did you ever hear such perfect ragtime? I just can't make my shoulders behave when I hear that.'

Mr Bloeckman clapped his hands gallantly.

'You ought to be on the stage.'

'I'd like to be!' cried Muriel; 'will you back me?'

'I sure will.'

With becoming modesty Muriel ceased her motions and turned to Maury, asking what he had 'seen' this year. He interpreted this as referring to the dramatic world, and they had a gay and exhilarating exchange of titles, after this manner.

MURIEL: Have you seen *Peg o' My Heart*? [218]

MAURY: No, I haven't.

MURIEL (*eagerly*): It's wonderful! You want to see it.

MAURY: Have you seen *Omar, the Tentmaker*? [219]

MURIEL: No, but I hear it's wonderful. I'm very anxious to see it. Have you seen *Fair and Warmer*? [220]

MAURY (*hopefully*): Yes.

MURIEL: I don't think it's very good. It's trashy.

MAURY (*faintly*): Yes, that's true.

MURIEL: But I went to *Within the Law* [221] last night and I thought it was fine. Have you seen *The Little Café*? . . . [222]

This continued until they ran out of plays. Dick, meanwhile, turned to Mr Bloeckman, determined to extract what gold he could from this unpromising load.

'I hear all the new novels are sold to the moving pictures as soon as they come out.'

'That's true. Of course the main thing in a moving picture is a strong story.'

'Yes, I suppose so.'

'So many novels are all full of talk and psychology. Of course those aren't as valuable to us. It's impossible to make much of that interesting on the screen.'

'You want plots first,' said Richard brilliantly.

'Of course. Plots first – ' He paused, shifted his gaze. His pause spread, included the others with all the authority of a warning finger. Gloria followed by Rachael was coming out of the dressing-room.

Among other things it developed during dinner that Joseph Bloeckman never danced, but spent the music time watching the others with the bored tolerance of an elder among children. He was a dignified man and a proud one. Born in Munich he had begun his American career as a peanut vender with a travelling circus. At eighteen he was a sideshow ballyhoo; later, the manager of the sideshow; and, soon after, the proprietor of a second-class vaudeville house. Just when the moving picture had passed out of the stage of a curiosity and become a promising industry he was an ambitious young man of twenty-six with some money to invest, nagging financial ambitions and a good working knowledge of the popular show business. That had been nine years before. The moving-picture industry had borne him up with it where it threw off dozens of men with more financial ability, more imagination and more practical ideas . . . and now he sat here and contemplated the immortal Gloria for whom young Stuart Holcome had gone from New York to Pasadena – watched her, and knew that presently she would cease dancing and come back to sit on his left hand.

He hoped she would hurry. The oysters had been standing some minutes.

Meanwhile Anthony, who had been placed on Gloria's left hand, was dancing with her, always in a certain fourth of the floor. This, had there been stags, would have been a delicate tribute to the girl, meaning, 'Damn you, don't cut in!' It was very consciously intimate.

'Well,' he began, looking down at her, 'you look mighty sweet tonight.'

She met his eyes over the horizontal half foot that separated them.

'Thank you – Anthony.'

'In fact you're uncomfortably beautiful,' he added. There was no smile this time.

'And you're very charming.'

'Isn't this nice?' he laughed. 'We actually approve of each other.'

'Don't you, usually?' She had caught quickly at his remark, as she always did at any unexplained allusion to herself, however faint.

He lowered his voice, and when he spoke there was in it no more than a wisp of badinage.

'Does a priest approve the Pope?'

'I don't know – but that's probably the vaguest compliment I ever received.'

'Perhaps I can muster a few bromides.'

'Well, I wouldn't have you strain yourself. Look at Muriel! Right here next to us.'

He glanced over his shoulder. Muriel was resting her brilliant cheek against the lapel of Maury Noble's dinner-coat and her powdered left arm was apparently twisted around his head. One was impelled to wonder why she failed to seize the nape of his neck with her hand. Her eyes, turned ceiling-ward, rolled largely back and forth; her hips swayed, and as she danced she kept up a constant low singing. This at first seemed to be a translation of the song into some foreign tongue but became eventually apparent as an attempt to fill out the metre of the song with the only words she knew – the words of the title –

> He's a rag-picker,
> A rag-picker;
> A ragtime picking man,
> Rag-picking, picking, pick, pick,
> Rag-pick, pick, pick.[223]

– and so on, into phrases still more strange and barbaric. When she caught the amused glances of Anthony and Gloria she acknowledged them only with a faint smile and a half-closing of her eyes, to indicate that the music entering into her soul had put her into an ecstatic and exceedingly seductive trance.

The music ended and they returned to their table, whose solitary but dignified occupant arose and tendered each of them a smile so ingratiating that it was as if he were shaking their hands and congratulating them on a brilliant performance.

'Blockhead never will dance! I think he has a wooden leg,' remarked

Gloria to the table at large. The three young men started and the gentleman referred to winced perceptibly.

This was the one rough spot in the course of Bloeckman's acquaintance with Gloria. She relentlessly punned on his name. First it had been 'Blockhouse'. Lately, the more invidious 'Blockhead'. He had requested with a strong undertone of irony that she use his first name, and this she had done obediently several times – before slipping, helpless, repentant but dissolved in laughter, back into 'Blockhead'.

It was a very sad and thoughtless thing.

'I'm afraid Mr Bloeckman thinks we're a frivolous crowd,' sighed Muriel, waving a balanced oyster in his direction.

'He has that air,' murmured Rachael. Anthony tried to remember whether she had said anything before. He thought not. It was her initial remark.

Mr Bloeckman suddenly cleared his throat and said in a loud, distinct voice: 'On the contrary. When a man speaks he's merely tradition. He has at best a few thousand years back of him. But woman, why, she is the miraculous mouthpiece of posterity.'

In the stunned pause that followed this astounding remark, Anthony choked suddenly on an oyster and hurried his napkin to his face. Rachael and Muriel raised a mild if somewhat surprised laugh, in which Dick and Maury joined, both of them red in the face and restraining uproariousness with the most apparent difficulty.

' – My God!' thought Anthony. 'It's a subtitle from one of his movies. The man's memorised it!'

Gloria alone made no sound. She fixed Mr Bloeckman with a glance of silent reproach.

'Well, for the love of heaven! Where on earth did you dig that up?'

Bloeckman looked at her uncertainly, not sure of her intention. But in a moment he recovered his poise and assumed the bland and consciously tolerant smile of an intellectual among spoiled and callow youth.

The soup came up from the kitchen – but simultaneously the orchestra leader came up from the bar, where he had absorbed the tone colour inherent in a seidel[224] of beer. So the soup was left to cool during the delivery of a ballad entitled 'Everything's At Home Except Your Wife'.[225]

Then the champagne – and the party assumed more amusing proportions. The men, except Richard Caramel, drank freely; Gloria and Muriel sipped a glass apiece; Rachael Jerryl took none. They sat out the waltzes but danced to everything else – all except Gloria, who seemed to tire after a while and preferred to sit smoking at the table, her eyes now lazy, now eager, according to whether she listened to Bloeckman or watched a pretty woman among the dancers. Several times Anthony wondered what Bloeckman was telling her. He was chewing a cigar back and forth in his mouth, and had expanded after dinner to the extent of violent gestures.

Ten o'clock found Gloria and Anthony beginning a dance. Just as they were out of earshot of the table she said in a low voice: 'Dance over by the door. I want to go down to the drugstore.'

Obediently Anthony guided her through the crowd in the designated direction; in the hall she left him for a moment, to reappear with a cloak over her arm.

'I want some gumdrops,' she said, humorously apologetic; 'you can't guess what for this time. It's just that I want to bite my fingernails, and I will if I don't get some gumdrops.' She sighed, and resumed as they stepped into the empty elevator: 'I've been biting 'em all day. A bit nervous, you see. Excuse the pun. It was unintentional – the words just arranged themselves. Gloria Gilbert, the female wag.'

Reaching the ground floor they naïvely avoided the hotel candy counter, descended the wide front staircase, and walking through several corridors found a drugstore in the Grand Central Station.[226] After an intense examination of the perfume counter she made her purchase. Then on some mutual unmentioned impulse they strolled, arm in arm, not in the direction from which they had come, but out into Forty-Third Street.

The night was alive with thaw; it was so nearly warm that a breeze drifting low along the sidewalk brought to Anthony a vision of an unhoped-for hyacinthine spring. Above in the blue oblong of sky, around them in the caress of the drifting air, the illusion of a new season carried relief from the stiff and breathed-over atmosphere they had left, and for a hushed moment the traffic sounds and the murmur of water flowing in the gutters seemed an illusive and rarefied prolongation of that music to which they had lately danced. When Anthony spoke it was with surety that his words came from something breathless and desirous that the night had conceived in their two hearts.

'Let's take a taxi and ride around a bit!' he suggested, without looking at her.

Oh, Gloria, Gloria!

A cab yawned at the curb. As it moved off like a boat on a labyrinthine ocean and lost itself among the inchoate night masses of the great buildings, among the now stilled, now strident, cries and clangings, Anthony put his arm around the girl, drew her over to him and kissed her damp, childish mouth.

She was silent. She turned her face up to him, pale under the wisps and patches of light that trailed in like moonshine through foliage. Her eyes were gleaming ripples in the white lake of her face; the shadows of her hair bordered the brow with a persuasive unintimate dusk. No love was there, surely; nor the imprint of any love. Her beauty was cool as this damp breeze, as the moist softness of her own lips.

'You're such a swan in this light,' he whispered after a moment. There were silences as murmurous as sound. There were pauses that seemed about to shatter and were only to be snatched back to oblivion by the tightening of his arms about her and the sense that she was resting there as a caught, gossamer feather, drifted in out of the dark. Anthony laughed, noiselessly and exultantly, turning his face up and away from her, half in an overpowering rush of triumph, half lest her sight of him should spoil the splendid immobility of her expression. Such a kiss – it was a flower held against the face, never to be described, scarcely to be remembered; as though her beauty were giving off emanations of itself which settled transiently and already dissolving upon his heart.

. . . The buildings fell away in melted shadows; this was the Park now, and after a long while the great white ghost of the Metropolitan Museum[227] moved majestically past, echoing sonorously to the rush of the cab.

'Why, Gloria! Why, Gloria!'

Her eyes appeared to regard him out of many thousand years: all emotion she might have felt, all words she might have uttered, would have seemed inadequate beside the adequacy of her silence, ineloquent against the eloquence of her beauty – and of her body, close to him, slender and cool.

'Tell him to turn around,' she murmured, 'and drive pretty fast going back . . . '

Up in the supper room the air was hot. The table, littered with napkins and ashtrays, was old and stale. It was between dances as they entered, and Muriel Kane looked up with roguishness extraordinary.

'Well, where have *you* been?'

'To call up mother,' answered Gloria coolly. 'I promised her I would. Did we miss a dance?'

Then followed an incident that though slight in itself Anthony had cause to reflect on many years afterwards. Joseph Bloeckman, leaning well back in his chair, fixed him with a peculiar glance, in which several emotions were curiously and inextricably mingled. He did not greet Gloria except by rising, and he immediately resumed a conversation with Richard Caramel about the influence of literature on the moving pictures.

MAGIC

The stark and unexpected miracle of a night fades out with the lingering death of the last stars and the premature birth of the first newsboys. The flame retreats to some remote and platonic fire; the white heat has gone from the iron and the glow from the coal.

Along the shelves of Anthony's library, filling a wall amply, crept a chill and insolent pencil of sunlight touching with frigid disapproval Thérèse of France[228] and Ann the Superwoman,[229] Jenny of the Orient Ballet[230] and Zuleika the Conjurer[231] – and Hoosier Cora[232] – then down a shelf and into the years, resting pityingly on the over-invoked shades of Helen,[233] Thaïs,[234] Salome[235] and Cleopatra.

Anthony, shaved and bathed, sat in his most deeply cushioned chair and watched it until at the steady rising of the sun it lay glinting for a moment on the silk ends of the rug – and went out.

It was ten o'clock. The *Sunday Times*, scattered about his feet, proclaimed by rotogravure and editorial, by social revelation and sporting sheet, that the world had been tremendously engrossed during the past week in the business of moving towards some splendid if somewhat indeterminate goal. For his part Anthony had been once to his grandfather's, twice to his broker's and three times to his tailor's – and in the last hour of the week's last day he had kissed a very beautiful and charming girl.

When he reached home his imagination had been teeming with high-pitched, unfamiliar dreams. There was suddenly no question on his mind, no eternal problem for a solution and resolution. He had experienced an emotion that was neither mental nor physical, nor merely a mixture of the two, and the love of life absorbed him for the present to the exclusion of all else. He was content to let the experiment remain isolated and unique. Almost impersonally he was convinced that no woman he had ever met compared in any way with

Gloria. She was deeply herself; she was immeasurably sincere – of these things he was certain. Beside her the two dozen schoolgirls and débutantes, young married women and waifs and strays whom he had known were so many *females*, in the word's most contemptuous sense, breeders and bearers, exuding still that faintly odorous atmosphere of the cave and the nursery.

So far as he could see, she had neither submitted to any will of his nor caressed his vanity – except as her pleasure in his company was a caress. Indeed he had no reason for thinking she had given him aught that she did not give to others. This was as it should be. The idea of an entanglement growing out of the evening was as remote as it would have been repugnant. And she had disclaimed and buried the incident with a decisive untruth. Here were two young people with fancy enough to distinguish a game from its reality – who by the very casualness with which they met and passed on would proclaim themselves unharmed.

Having decided this he went to the phone and called up the Plaza Hotel.

Gloria was out. Her mother knew neither where she had gone nor when she would return.

It was somehow at this point that the first wrongness in the case asserted itself. There was an element of callousness, almost of indecency, in Gloria's absence from home. He suspected that by going out she had intrigued him into a disadvantage. Returning she would find his name, and smile. Most discreetly! He should have waited a few hours in order to drive home the utter inconsequence with which he regarded the incident. What an asinine blunder! She would think he considered himself particularly favoured. She would think he was reacting with the most inept intimacy to a quite trivial episode.

He remembered that during the previous month his janitor, to whom he had delivered a rather muddled lecture on the 'brother-hoo've man', had come up next day and, on the basis of what had happened the night before, seated himself in the window seat for a cordial and chatty half-hour. Anthony wondered in horror if Gloria would regard him as he had regarded that man. Him – Anthony Patch! Horror!

It never occurred to him that he was a passive thing, acted upon by an influence above and beyond Gloria, that he was merely the sensitive plate on which the photograph was made. Some gargantuan photographer had focused the camera on Gloria and *snap*! – the poor plate could but develop, confined like all things to its nature.

But Anthony, lying upon his couch and staring at the orange lamp, passed his thin fingers incessantly through his dark hair and made new symbols for the hours. She was in a shop now, it seemed, moving lithely among the velvets and the furs, her own dress making, as she walked, a debonair rustle in that world of silken rustles and cool soprano laughter and scents of many slain but living flowers. The Minnies and Pearls and Jewels and Jennies would gather round her like courtiers, bearing wispy frailties of georgette crêpe, delicate chiffon to echo her cheeks in faint pastel, milky lace to rest in pale disarray against her neck – damask was used but to cover priests and divans in these days, and cloth of Samarkand[236] was remembered only by the romantic poets.

She would go elsewhere after a while, tilting her head a hundred ways under a hundred bonnets, seeking in vain for mock cherries to match her lips or plumes that were graceful as her own supple body.

Noon would come – she would hurry along Fifth Avenue, a Nordic Ganymede,[237] her fur coat swinging fashionably with her steps, her cheeks redder by a stroke of the wind's brush, her breath a delightful mist upon the bracing air – and the doors of the Ritz would revolve, the crowd would divide, fifty masculine eyes would start, stare, as she gave back forgotten dreams to the husbands of many obese and comic women.

One o'clock. With her fork she would tantalise the heart of an adoring artichoke, while her escort served himself up in the thick, dripping sentences of an enraptured man.

Four o'clock: her little feet moving to melody, her face distinct in the crowd, her partner happy as a petted puppy and mad as the immemorial hatter . . . Then – then night would come drifting down and perhaps another damp. The signs would spill their light into the street. Who knew? No wiser than he, they haply sought to recapture that picture done in cream and shadow they had seen on the hushed Avenue the night before. And they might, ah, they might! A thousand taxis would yawn at a thousand corners, and only to him was that kiss for ever lost and done. In a thousand guises Thaïs would hail a cab and turn up her face for loving. And her pallor would be virginal and lovely, and her kiss chaste as the moon . . .

He sprang excitedly to his feet. How inappropriate that she should be out! He had realised at last what he wanted – to kiss her again, to find rest in her great immobility. She was the end of all restlessness, all malcontent.

Anthony dressed and went out, as he should have done long

before, and down to Richard Caramel's room to hear the last revision of the last chapter of *The Demon Lover*. He did not call Gloria again until six. He did not find her in until eight and – oh, climax of anticlimaxes! – she could give him no engagement until Tuesday afternoon. A broken piece of gutta-percha[238] clattered to the floor as he banged up the phone.

BLACK MAGIC

Tuesday was freezing cold. He called at a bleak two o'clock and as they shook hands he wondered confusedly whether he had ever kissed her; it was almost unbelievable – he seriously doubted if she remembered it.

'I called you four times on Sunday,' he told her.

'Did you?'

There was surprise in her voice and interest in her expression. Silently he cursed himself for having told her. He might have known her pride did not deal in such petty triumphs. Even then he had not guessed at the truth – that never having had to worry about men she had seldom used the wary subterfuges, the playings out and haulings in, that were the stock in trade of her sisterhood. When she liked a man, that was trick enough. Did she think she loved him – there was an ultimate and fatal thrust. Her charm endlessly preserved itself.

'I was anxious to see you,' he said simply. 'I want to talk to you – I mean really talk, somewhere where we can be alone. May I?'

'What do you mean?'

He swallowed a sudden lump of panic. He felt that she knew what he wanted.

'I mean, not at a tea-table,' he said.

'Well, all right, but not today. I want to get some exercise. Let's walk!'

It was bitter and raw. All the evil hate in the mad heart of February was wrought into the forlorn and icy wind that cut its way cruelly across Central Park and down along Fifth Avenue. It was almost impossible to talk, and discomfort made him distracted, so much so that he turned at Sixty-First Street to find that she was no longer beside him. He looked around. She was forty feet in the rear standing motionless, her face half hidden in her fur-coat collar, moved either by anger or laughter – he could not determine which. He started back.

'Don't let me interrupt your walk!' she called.

'I'm mighty sorry,' he answered in confusion. 'Did I go too fast?'

'I'm cold,' she announced. 'I want to go home. And you walk too fast.'

'I'm very sorry.'

Side by side they started for the Plaza. He wished he could see her face.

'Men don't usually get so absorbed in themselves when they're with me.'

'I'm sorry.'

'That's very interesting.'

'It *is* rather too cold to walk,' he said, briskly, to hide his annoyance.

She made no answer and he wondered if she would dismiss him at the hotel entrance. She walked in without speaking, however, and to the elevator, throwing him a single remark as she entered it: 'You'd better come up.'

He hesitated for the fraction of a moment.

'Perhaps I'd better call some other time.'

'Just as you say.' Her words were murmured as an aside. The main concern of life was the adjusting of some stray wisps of hair in the elevator mirror. Her cheeks were brilliant, her eyes sparkled – she had never seemed so lovely, so exquisitely to be desired.

Despising himself, he found that he was walking down the tenth-floor corridor a subservient foot behind her; was in the sitting-room while she disappeared to shed her furs. Something had gone wrong – in his own eyes he had lost a shred of dignity; in an unpremeditated yet significant encounter he had been completely defeated.

However, by the time she reappeared in the sitting-room he had explained himself to himself with sophistic satisfaction. After all he had done the strongest thing, he thought. He had wanted to come up, he had come. Yet what happened later on that afternoon must be traced to the indignity he had experienced in the elevator; the girl was worrying him intolerably, so much so that when she came out he involuntarily drifted into criticism.

'Who's this Bloeckman, Gloria?'

'A business friend of father's.'

'Odd sort of fellow!'

'He doesn't like you either,' she said with a sudden smile.

Anthony laughed.

'I'm flattered at his notice. He evidently considers me a – ' He broke off with, 'Is he in love with you?'

'I don't know.'

'The deuce you don't,' he insisted. 'Of course he is. I remember the look he gave me when we got back to the table. He'd probably have had me quietly assaulted by a delegation of movie supes[239] if you hadn't invented that phone call.'

'He didn't mind. I told him afterwards what really happened.'

'You told him!'

'He asked me.'

'I don't like that very well,' he remonstrated.

She laughed again.

'Oh, you don't?'

'What business is it of his?'

'None. That's why I told him.'

Anthony in a turmoil bit savagely at his mouth.

'Why should I lie?' she demanded directly. 'I'm not ashamed of anything I do. It happened to interest him to know that I kissed you, and I happened to be in a good humour, so I satisfied his curiosity by a simple and precise "yes". Being rather a sensible man, after his fashion, he dropped the subject.'

'Except to say that he hated me.'

'Oh, it worries you? Well, if you must probe this stupendous matter to its depths he didn't say he hated you. I simply know he does.'

'It doesn't wor –'

'Oh, let's drop it!' she cried spiritedly. 'It's a most uninteresting matter to me.'

With a tremendous effort Anthony made his acquiescence a twist of subject, and they drifted into an ancient question-and-answer game concerned with each other's pasts, gradually warming as they discovered the age-old, immemorial resemblances in tastes and ideas. They said things that were more revealing than they intended – but each pretended to accept the other at face, or rather word, value.

The growth of intimacy is like that. First one gives off his best picture, the bright and finished product mended with bluff and falsehood and humour. Then more details are required and one paints a second portrait, and a third – before long the best lines cancel out – and the secret is exposed at last; the planes of the pictures have intermingled and given us away, and though we paint and paint we can no longer sell a picture. We must be satisfied with hoping that such fatuous accounts of ourselves as we make to our wives and children and business associates are accepted as true.

'It seems to me,' Anthony was saying earnestly, 'that the position of a man with neither necessity nor ambition is unfortunate. Heaven knows it'd be pathetic of me to be sorry for myself – yet, sometimes I envy Dick.'

Her silence was encouragement. It was as near as she ever came to an intentional lure.

' – And there used to be dignified occupations for a gentleman who had leisure, things a little more constructive than filling up the landscape with smoke or juggling someone else's money. There's science, of course: sometimes I wish I'd taken a good foundation, say at Boston Tech. But now, by golly, I'd have to sit down for two years and struggle through the fundamentals of physics and chemistry.'

She yawned.

'I've told you I don't know what anybody ought to do,' she said ungraciously, and at her indifference his rancour was born again.

'Aren't you interested in anything except yourself?'

'Not much.'

He glared; his growing enjoyment in the conversation was ripped to shreds. She had been irritable and vindictive all day, and it seemed to him that for this moment he hated her hard selfishness. He stared morosely at the fire.

Then a strange thing happened. She turned to him and smiled, and as he saw her smile every rag of anger and hurt vanity dropped from him – as though his very moods were but the outer ripples of her own, as though emotion rose no longer in his breast unless she saw fit to pull an omnipotent controlling thread.

He moved closer and taking her hand pulled her ever so gently towards him until she half lay against his shoulder. She smiled up at him as he kissed her.

'Gloria,' he whispered very softly. Again she had made a magic, subtle and pervading as a spilt perfume, irresistible and sweet.

Afterwards, neither the next day nor after many years, could he remember the important things of that afternoon. Had she been moved? In his arms had she spoken a little – or at all? What measure of enjoyment had she taken in his kisses? And had she at any time lost herself ever so little?

Oh, for him there was no doubt. He had risen and paced the floor in sheer ecstasy. That such a girl should be; should poise curled in a corner of the couch like a swallow newly landed from a clean swift flight, watching him with inscrutable eyes. He would stop his pacing and, half shy each time at first, drop his arm around her and find her kiss.

She was fascinating, he told her. He had never met anyone like her before. He besought her jauntily but earnestly to send him away; he didn't want to fall in love. He wasn't coming to see her any more – already she had haunted too many of his ways.

What delicious romance! His true reaction was neither fear nor sorrow – only this deep delight in being with her that coloured the banality of his words and made the mawkish seem sad and the posturing seem wise. He *would* come back – eternally. He should have known!

'This is all. It's been very rare to have known you, very strange and wonderful. But this wouldn't do – and wouldn't last.' As he spoke there was in his heart that tremulousness that we take for sincerity in ourselves.

Afterwards he remembered one reply of hers to something he had asked her. He remembered it in this form – perhaps he had unconsciously arranged and polished it: 'A woman should be able to kiss a man beautifully and romantically without any desire to be either his wife or his mistress.'

As always when he was with her she seemed to grow gradually older until at the end ruminations too deep for words would be wintering in her eyes.

An hour passed, and the fire leaped up in little ecstasies as though its fading life was sweet. It was five now, and the clock over the mantel became articulate in sound. Then as if a brutish sensibility in him was reminded by those thin, tinny beats that the petals were falling from the flowered afternoon, Anthony pulled her quickly to her feet and held her helpless, without breath, in a kiss that was neither a game nor a tribute.

Her arms fell to her side. In an instant she was free.

'Don't!' she said quietly. 'I don't want that.'

She sat down on the far side of the lounge and gazed straight before her. A frown had gathered between her eyes. Anthony sank down beside her and closed his hand over hers. It was lifeless and unresponsive.

'Why, Gloria!' He made a motion as if to put his arm about her but she drew away.

'I don't want that,' she repeated.

'I'm very sorry,' he said, a little impatiently. 'I – I didn't know you made such fine distinctions.'

She did not answer.

'Won't you kiss me, Gloria?'

'I don't want to.' It seemed to him she had not moved for hours.

'A sudden change, isn't it?' Annoyance was growing in his voice.

'Is it?' She appeared uninterested. It was almost as though she were looking at someone else.

'Perhaps I'd better go.'

No reply. He rose and regarded her angrily, uncertainly. Again he sat down.

'Gloria, Gloria, won't you kiss me?'

'No.' Her lips, parting for the word, had just faintly stirred.

Again he got to his feet, this time with less decision, less confidence.

'Then I'll go.'

Silence.

'All right – I'll go.'

He was aware of a certain irremediable lack of originality in his remarks. Indeed he felt that the whole atmosphere had grown oppressive. He wished she would speak, rail at him, cry out upon him, anything but this pervasive and chilling silence. He cursed himself for a weak fool; his clearest desire was to move her, to hurt her, to see her wince. Helplessly, involuntarily, he erred again.

'If you're tired of kissing me I'd better go.'

He saw her lips curl slightly and his last dignity left him. She spoke, at length: 'I believe you've made that remark several times before.'

He looked about him immediately, saw his hat and coat on a chair – blundered into them, during an intolerable moment. Looking again at the couch he perceived that she had not turned, not even moved. With a shaken, immediately regretted 'goodbye' he went quickly but without dignity from the room.

For over a moment Gloria made no sound. Her lips were still curled; her glance was straight, proud, remote. Then her eyes blurred a little, and she murmured three words half aloud to the death-bound fire: 'Goodbye, you ass!' she said.

PANIC

The man had had the hardest blow of his life. He knew at last what he wanted, but in finding it out it seemed that he had put it for ever beyond his grasp. He reached home in misery, dropped into an armchair without even removing his overcoat, and sat there for over an hour, his mind racing the paths of fruitless and wretched self-absorption. She had sent him away! That was the reiterated burden of his despair. Instead of seizing the girl and holding her by sheer strength until she became passive to his desire, instead of beating down her will by the force of his own, he had walked, defeated and powerless, from her door, with the corners of his mouth drooping and what force there might have been in his grief and rage hidden behind the manner of a whipped schoolboy. At one minute she had liked him tremendously – ah, she had nearly loved him. In the next he had become a thing of indifference to her, an insolent and efficiently humiliated man.

He had no great self-reproach – some, of course, but there were other things dominant in him now, far more urgent. He was not so much in love with Gloria as mad for her. Unless he could have her near him again, kiss her, hold her close and acquiescent, he wanted nothing more from life. By her three minutes of utter unwavering indifference the girl had lifted herself from a high but somehow casual position in his mind, to be instead his complete preoccupation. However much his wild thoughts varied between a passionate desire for her kisses and an equally passionate craving to hurt and mar her, the residue of his mind craved in finer fashion to possess the triumphant soul that had shone through those three minutes. She was beautiful – but especially she was without mercy. He must own that strength that could send him away.

At present no such analysis was possible to Anthony. His clarity of mind, all those endless resources which he thought his irony had brought him were swept aside. Not only for that night but for the days and weeks that followed his books were to be but furniture and his friends only people who lived and walked in a nebulous outer world from which he was trying to escape – that world was cold and full of bleak wind, and for a little while he had seen into a warm house where fires shone.

About midnight he began to realise that he was hungry. He went down into Fifty-Second Street, where it was so cold that he could scarcely see; the moisture froze on his lashes and in the corners of his lips. Everywhere dreariness had come down from the north, settling upon the thin and cheerless street, where black bundled figures blacker still against the night, moved stumbling along the sidewalk through the shrieking wind, sliding their feet cautiously ahead as though they were on skis. Anthony turned over towards Sixth Avenue, so absorbed in his thoughts as not to notice that several passers-by had stared at him. His overcoat was wide open, and the wind was biting in, hard and full of merciless death.

. . . After a while a waitress spoke to him, a fat waitress with black-rimmed eye-glasses from which dangled a long black cord.

'Order, please!'

Her voice, he considered, was unnecessarily loud. He looked up resentfully.

'You wanna order or doncha?'

'Of course,' he protested.

'Well, I ast you three times. This ain't no rest-room.'

He glanced at the big clock and discovered with a start that it was after two. He was down around Thirtieth Street somewhere, and after a moment he found and translated the

CHILD'S [240]

in a white semicircle of letters upon the glass front. The place was inhabited sparsely by three or four bleak and half-frozen night-hawks.

'Give me some bacon and eggs and coffee, please.'

The waitress bent upon him a last disgusted glance and, looking ludicrously intellectual in her corded glasses, hurried away.

God! Gloria's kisses had been such flowers. He remembered as though it had been years ago the low freshness of her voice, the beautiful lines of her body shining through her clothes, her face lily-coloured under the lamps of the street – under the lamps.

Misery struck at him again, piling a sort of terror upon the ache and yearning. He had lost her. It was true – no denying it, no softening it. But a new idea had seared his sky – what of Bloeckman! What would happen now? There was a wealthy man, middle-aged enough to be tolerant with a beautiful wife, to baby her whims and indulge her unreason, to wear her as she perhaps wished to be worn – a bright flower in his buttonhole, safe and secure from the things she feared. He felt that she had been playing with the idea of marrying Bloeckman, and it was well possible that this disappointment in Anthony might throw her on sudden impulse into Bloeckman's arms.

The idea drove him childishly frantic. He wanted to kill Bloeckman and make him suffer for his hideous presumption. He was saying this over and over to himself with his teeth tight shut, and a perfect orgy of hate and fright in his eyes.

But, behind this obscene jealousy, Anthony was in love at last, profoundly and truly in love, as the word goes between man and woman.

His coffee appeared at his elbow and gave off for a certain time a gradually diminishing wisp of steam. The night manager, seated at his desk, glanced at the motionless figure alone at the last table, and then with a sigh moved down upon him just as the hour hand crossed the figure three on the big clock.

WISDOM

After another day the turmoil subsided and Anthony began to exercise a measure of reason. He was in love – he cried it passionately to himself. The things that a week before would have seemed insuperable obstacles, his limited income, his desire to be irresponsible and independent, had in this forty hours become the merest chaff before the wind of his infatuation. If he did not marry her his life would be a feeble parody on his own adolescence. To be able to face people and to endure the constant reminder of Gloria that all existence had become, it was necessary for him to have hope. So he built hope desperately and tenaciously out of the stuff of his dream, a hope flimsy enough, to be sure, a hope that was cracked and dissipated a dozen times a day, a hope mothered by mockery, but, nevertheless, a hope that would be brawn and sinew to his self-respect.

Out of this developed a spark of wisdom, a true perception of his own from out the effortless past.

'Memory is short,' he thought.

So very short. At the crucial point the Trust President is on the stand, a potential criminal needing but one push to be a jailbird, scorned by the upright for leagues around. Let him be acquitted – and in a year all is forgotten. 'Yes, he did have some trouble once, just a technicality, I believe.' Oh, memory is very short!

Anthony had seen Gloria altogether about a dozen times, say two dozen hours. Supposing he left her alone for a month, made no attempt to see her or speak to her, and avoided every place where she might possibly be. Wasn't it possible, the more possible because she had never loved him, that at the end of that time the rush of events would efface his personality from her conscious mind, and with his personality his offence and humiliation? She would forget, for there would be other men. He winced. The implication struck out at him – other men. Two months – God! Better three weeks, two weeks –

He thought this the second evening after the catastrophe when he was undressing, and at this point he threw himself down on the bed and lay there, trembling very slightly and looking at the top of the canopy.

Two weeks – that was worse than no time at all. In two weeks he would approach her much as he would have to now, without personality or confidence – remaining still the man who had gone too far and then for a period that in time was but a moment but in fact an eternity, whined. No, two weeks was too short a time. Whatever poignancy there had been for her in that afternoon must have time to dull. He must give her a period when the incident should fade, and then a new period when she should gradually begin to think of him, no matter how dimly, with a true perspective that would remember his pleasantness as well as his humiliation.

He fixed, finally, on six weeks as approximately the interval best suited to his purpose, and on a desk calendar he marked the days off, finding that it would fall on the ninth of April. Very well, on that day he would phone and ask her if he might call. Until then – silence.

After his decision a gradual improvement was manifest. He had taken at least a step in the direction to which hope pointed, and he realised that the less he brooded upon her the better he would be able to give the desired impression when they met.

In another hour he fell into a deep sleep.

THE INTERVAL

Nevertheless, though, as the days passed, the glory of her hair dimmed perceptibly for him and in a year of separation might have departed completely, the six weeks held many abominable days. He dreaded the sight of Dick and Maury, imagining wildly that they knew all – but when the three met it was Richard Caramel and not Anthony who was the centre of attention; *The Demon Lover* had been accepted for immediate publication. Anthony felt that from now on he moved apart. He no longer craved the warmth and security of Maury's society which had cheered him no further back than November. Only Gloria could give that now and no one else ever again. So Dick's success rejoiced him only casually and worried him not a little. It meant that the world was going ahead – writing and reading and publishing – and living. And he wanted the world to wait motionless and breathless for six weeks – while Gloria forgot.

TWO ENCOUNTERS

His greatest satisfaction was in Geraldine's company. He took her once to dinner and the theatre and entertained her several times in his apartment. When he was with her she absorbed him, not as Gloria had, but quieting those erotic sensibilities in him that worried over Gloria. It didn't matter how he kissed Geraldine. A kiss was a kiss – to be enjoyed to the utmost for its short moment. To Geraldine things belonged in definite pigeon-holes: a kiss was one thing, anyhing further was quite another; a kiss was all right; the other things were 'bad'.

When half the interval was up two incidents occurred on successive days that upset his increasing calm and caused a temporary relapse.

The first was – he saw Gloria. It was a short meeting. Both bowed. Both spoke, yet neither heard the other. But when it was over Anthony read down a column of the *Sun* three times in succession without understanding a single sentence.

One would have thought Sixth Avenue a safe street! Having forsworn his barber at the Plaza he went around the corner one morning to be shaved, and while waiting his turn he took off coat and vest, and with his soft collar open at the neck stood near the front of the shop. The day was an oasis in the cold desert of March and the sidewalk was cheerful with a population of strolling sun-worshippers. A stout woman upholstered in velvet, her flabby cheeks too much massaged, swirled by with her poodle straining at its leash – the effect being given of a tug bringing in an ocean liner. Just behind them a man in a striped blue suit, walking slue-footed in white-spatted feet, grinned at the sight and catching Anthony's eye, winked through the glass. Anthony laughed, thrown immediately into that humour in which men and women were graceless and absurd phantasms, grotesquely curved and rounded in a rectangular world of their own building. They inspired the same sensations in him as did those strange and monstrous fish who inhabit the esoteric world of green in the aquarium.

Two more strollers caught his eye casually, a man and a girl – then in a horrified instant the girl resolved herself into Gloria. He stood there powerless; they came nearer and Gloria, glancing in, saw him. Her eyes widened and she smiled politely. Her lips moved. She was less than five feet away.

'How do you do?' he muttered inanely.

Gloria, happy, beautiful, and young – with a man he had never seen before!

It was then that the barber's chair was vacated and he read down the newspaper column three times in succession.

The second incident took place the next day. Going into the Manhattan bar about seven he was confronted with Bloeckman. As it happened, the room was nearly deserted, and before the mutual recognition he had stationed himself within a foot of the older man and ordered his drink, so it was inevitable that they should converse.

'Hello, Mr Patch,' said Bloeckman amiably enough.

Anthony took the proffered hand and exchanged a few aphorisms on the fluctuations of the mercury.

'Do you come in here much?' enquired Bloeckman.

'No, very seldom.' He omitted to add that the Plaza bar had, until lately, been his favourite.

'Nice bar. One of the best bars in town.'

Anthony nodded. Bloeckman emptied his glass and picked up his cane. He was in evening dress.

'Well, I'll be hurrying on. I'm going to dinner with Miss Gilbert.'

Death looked suddenly out at him from two blue eyes. Had he announced himself as his vis-à-vis's prospective murderer he could not have struck a more vital blow at Anthony. The younger man must have reddened visibly, for his every nerve was in instant clamour. With tremendous effort he mustered a rigid – oh, so rigid – smile, and said a conventional goodbye. But that night he lay awake until after four, half wild with grief and fear and abominable imaginings.

WEAKNESS

And one day in the fifth week he called her up. He had been sitting in his apartment trying to read *L'Éducation sentimentale*,[241] and something in the book had sent his thoughts racing in the direction that, set free, they always took, like horses racing for a home stable. With suddenly quickened breath he walked to the telephone. When he gave the number it seemed to him that his voice faltered and broke like a schoolboy's. The Central[242] must have heard the pounding of his heart. The sound of the receiver being taken up at the other end was a crack of doom, and Mrs Gilbert's voice, soft as maple syrup running into a glass container, had for him a quality of horror in its single 'Hello-o-ah?'

'Miss Gloria's not feeling well. She's lying down, asleep. Who shall I say called?'

'Nobody!' he shouted.

In a wild panic he slammed down the receiver; collapsed into his armchair in the cold sweat of breathless relief.

SERENADE

The first thing he said to her was: 'Why, you've bobbed your hair!' and she answered: 'Yes, isn't it gorgeous?'

It was not fashionable then. It was to be fashionable in five or six years. At that time it was considered extremely daring.

'It's all sunshine outdoors,' he said gravely. 'Don't you want to take a walk?'

She put on a light coat and a quaintly piquant Napoleon-hat of Alice-blue, and they walked along the Avenue and into the Zoo, where they properly admired the grandeur of the elephant and the collar-height of the giraffe, but did not visit the monkey house because Gloria said that monkeys smelt so bad.

Then they returned towards the Plaza, talking about nothing, but glad for the spring singing in the air and for the warm balm that lay upon the suddenly golden city. To their right was the Park, while at the left a great bulk of granite and marble muttered dully a millionaire's chaotic message to whosoever would listen: something about, 'I worked and I saved and I was sharper than all Adam and here I sit, by golly, by golly!'

All the newest and most beautiful designs in automobiles were out on Fifth Avenue, and ahead of them the Plaza loomed up rather unusually white and attractive. The supple, indolent Gloria walked a short shadow's length ahead of him, pouring out lazy casual comments that floated a moment on the dazzling air before they reached his ear.

'Oh!' she cried, 'I want to go south to Hot Springs![243] I want to get out in the air and just roll around on the new grass and forget there's ever been any winter.'

'Don't you, though!'

'I want to hear a million robins making a frightful racket. I sort of like birds.'

'All women *are* birds,' he ventured.

'What kind am I?' – quick and eager.

'A swallow, I think, and sometimes a bird of paradise. Most girls are sparrows, of course – see that row of nursemaids over there? They're sparrows – or are they magpies? And of course you've met canary girls – and robin girls.'

'And swan girls and parrot girls. All grown women are hawks, I think, or owls.'

'What am I – a buzzard?'

She laughed and shook her head.

'Oh, no, you're not a bird at all, do you think? You're a Russian wolfhound.'

Anthony remembered that they were white and always looked unnaturally hungry. But then they were usually photographed with dukes and princesses, so he was properly flattered.

'Dick's a fox terrier, a trick fox terrier,' she continued.

'And Maury's a cat.' Simultaneously it occurred to him how like Bloeckman was to a robust and offensive hog. But he preserved a discreet silence.

Later, as they parted, Anthony asked when he might see her again.

'Don't you ever make long engagements,' he pleaded, 'even if it's a week ahead? I think it'd be fun to spend a whole day together, morning and afternoon both.'

'It would be, wouldn't it?' She thought for a moment. 'Let's do it next Sunday.'

'All right. I'll map out a programme that'll take up every minute.'

He did. He even figured to a nicety what would happen in the two hours when she would come to his apartment for tea: how the good Bounds would have the windows wide to let in the fresh breeze – but a fire going also lest there be chill in the air – and how there would be clusters of flowers about in big cool bowls that he would buy for the occasion. They would sit on the lounge.

And when the day came they did sit upon the lounge. After a while Anthony kissed her because it came about quite naturally; he found sweetness sleeping still upon her lips, and felt that he had never been away. The fire was bright and the breeze sighing in through the curtains brought a mellow damp, promising May and a world of summer. His soul thrilled to remote harmonies; he heard the strum of far guitars and waters lapping on a warm Mediterranean shore – for he was young now as he would never be again, and more triumphant than death.

Six o'clock stole down too soon and rang the querulous melody of St Anne's chimes on the corner. Through the gathering dusk they strolled to the Avenue, where the crowds, like prisoners released, were walking with elastic step at last after the long winter, and the tops of the buses were thronged with congenial kings and the shops full of fine soft things for the summer, the rare summer, the gay promising summer that seemed for love what the winter was for money. Life was singing for his supper on the corner! Life was handing round cocktails in the street! Old women there were in that crowd who felt that they could have run and won a hundred-yard dash!

In bed that night with the lights out and the cool room swimming with moonlight, Anthony lay awake and played with every minute of the day like a child playing in turn with each one of a pile of long-wanted Christmas toys. He had told her gently, almost in the middle of a kiss, that he loved her, and she had smiled and held him closer and murmured, 'I'm glad,' looking into his eyes. There had been a new quality in her attitude, a new growth of sheer physical attraction towards him and a strange emotional tenseness that was enough to make him clench his hands and draw in his breath at the recollection. He had felt nearer to her than ever before. In a rare delight he cried aloud to the room that he loved her.

He phoned next morning – no hesitation now, no uncertainty – instead a delirious excitement that doubled and trebled when he heard her voice: 'Good-morning – Gloria.'

'Good-morning.'

'That's all I called you up to say – dear.'

'I'm glad you did.'

'I wish I could see you.'

'You will, tomorrow night.'

'That's a long time, isn't it?'

'Yes – ' Her voice was reluctant. His hand tightened on the receiver.

'Couldn't I come tonight?' He dared anything in the glory and revelation of that almost whispered 'yes'.

'I have a date.'

'Oh – '

'But I might – I might be able to break it.'

'Oh!' – a sheer cry, a rhapsody. 'Gloria?'

'What?'

'I love you.'

Another pause and then: 'I – I'm glad.'

Happiness, remarked Maury Noble one day, is only the first hour after the alleviation of some especially intense misery. But oh,

Anthony's face as he walked down the tenth-floor corridor of the Plaza that night! His dark eyes were gleaming – around his mouth were lines it was a kindness to see. He was handsome then if never before, bound for one of those immortal moments which come so radiantly that their remembered light is enough to see by for years.

He knocked and, at a word, entered. Gloria, dressed in simple pink, starched and fresh as a flower, was across the room, standing very still, and looking at him wide-eyed.

As he closed the door behind him she gave a little cry and moved swiftly over the intervening space, her arms rising in a premature caress as she came near. Together they crushed out the stiff folds of her dress in one triumphant and enduring embrace.

BOOK TWO

CHAPTER I

The Radiant Hour

After a fortnight Anthony and Gloria began to indulge in 'practical discussions', as they called those sessions when under the guise of severe realism they walked in an eternal moonlight.

'Not as much as I do you,' the critic of *belles-lettres* would insist. 'If you really loved me you'd want everyone to know it.'

'I do,' she protested; 'I want to stand on the street corner like a sandwich man, informing all the passers-by.'

'Then tell me all the reasons why you're going to marry me in June.'

'Well, because you're so clean. You're sort of blowy clean, like I am. There's two sorts, you know. One's like Dick: he's clean like polished pans. You and I are clean like streams and winds. I can tell whenever I see a person whether he is clean, and if so, which kind of clean he is.'

'We're twins.'

Ecstatic thought!

'Mother says' – she hesitated uncertainly – 'mother says that two souls are sometimes created together and – and in love before they're born.'

Bilphism gained its easiest convert . . . After a while he lifted up his head and laughed soundlessly towards the ceiling. When his eyes came back to her he saw that she was angry.

'Why did you laugh?' she cried, 'you've done that twice before. There's nothing funny about our relation to each other. I don't mind playing the fool, and I don't mind having you do it, but I can't stand it when we're together.'

'I'm sorry.'

'Oh, don't say you're sorry! If you can't think of anything better than that, just keep quiet!'

'I love you.'

'I don't care.'

There was a pause. Anthony was depressed . . . At length Gloria murmured: 'I'm sorry I was mean.'

'You weren't. I was the one.'

Peace was restored – the ensuing moments were so much more sweet and sharp and poignant. They were stars on this stage, each playing to an audience of two: the passion of their pretence created the actuality. Here, finally, was the quintessence of self-expression – yet it was probable that for the most part their love expressed Gloria rather than Anthony. He felt often like a scarcely tolerated guest at a party she was giving.

Telling Mrs Gilbert had been an embarrassed matter. She sat stuffed into a small chair and listened with an intense and very blinky sort of concentration. She must have known it – for three weeks Gloria had seen no one else – and she must have noticed that this time there was an authentic difference in her daughter's attitude. She had been given special deliveries to post; she had heeded, as all mothers seem to heed, the hither end of telephone conversations, disguised but still rather warm –

– Yet she had delicately professed surprise and declared herself immensely pleased; she doubtless was; so were the geranium plants blossoming in the window-boxes, and so were the cabbies when the lovers sought the romantic privacy of hansom cabs – quaint device – and the staid bills of fare on which they scribbled 'you know I do', pushing it over for the other to see.

But between kisses Anthony and this golden girl quarrelled incessantly.

'Now, Gloria,' he would cry, 'please let me explain!'

'Don't explain. Kiss me.'

'I don't think that's right. If I hurt your feelings we ought to discuss it. I don't like this kiss-and-forget.'

'But I don't want to argue. I think it's wonderful that we *can* kiss and forget, and when we can't it'll be time to argue.'

At one time some gossamer difference attained such bulk that Anthony arose and punched himself into his overcoat – for a moment it appeared that the scene of the preceding February was to be repeated, but knowing how deeply she was moved he retained his dignity with his pride, and in a moment Gloria was sobbing in his arms, her lovely face miserable as a frightened little girl's.

Meanwhile they kept unfolding to each other, unwillingly, by curious reactions and evasions, by distastes and prejudices and unintended hints of the past. The girl was proudly incapable of jealousy and, because he was extremely jealous, this virtue piqued him. He told her recondite incidents of his own life on purpose to arouse some spark of it, but to no avail. She possessed him now – nor did she desire the dead years.

'Oh, Anthony,' she would say, 'always when I'm mean to you I'm sorry afterwards. I'd give my right hand to save you one little moment's pain.'

And in that instant her eyes were brimming and she was not aware that she was voicing an illusion. Yet Anthony knew that there were days when they hurt each other purposely – taking almost a delight in the thrust. Incessantly she puzzled him: one hour so intimate and charming, striving desperately towards an unguessed, transcendent union; the next, silent and cold, apparently unmoved by any consideration of their love or anything he could say. Often he would eventually trace these portentous reticences to some physical discomfort – of these she never complained until they were over – or to some carelessness or presumption in him, or to an unsatisfactory dish at dinner, but even then the means by which she created the infinite distances she spread about herself were a mystery, buried somewhere back in those twenty-two years of unwavering pride.

'Why do you like Muriel?' he demanded one day.

'I don't very much.'

'Then why do you go with her?'

'Just for someone to go with. They're no exertion, those girls. They sort of believe everything I tell them – but I rather like Rachael. I think she's cute – and so clean and slick, don't you? I used to have other friends – in Kansas City and at school – casual, all of them, girls who just flitted into my range and out of it for no more reason than that boys took us places together. They didn't interest me after environment stopped throwing us together. Now they're mostly married. What does it matter – they were all just people.'

'You like men better, don't you?'

'Oh, much better. I've got a man's mind.'

'You've got a mind like mine. Not strongly gendered either way.'

Later she told him about the beginnings of her friendship with Bloeckman. One day in Delmonico's,[244] Gloria and Rachael had come upon Bloeckman and Mr Gilbert having luncheon and curiosity had impelled her to make it a party of four. She had liked him – rather. He was a relief from younger men, satisfied as he was with so little. He humoured her and he laughed, whether he understood her or not. She met him several times, despite the open disapproval of her parents, and within a month he had asked her to marry him, tendering her everything from a villa in Italy to a brilliant career on the screen. She had laughed in his face – and he had laughed too.

But he had not given up. To the time of Anthony's arrival in the arena he had been making steady progress. She treated him rather well – except that she had called him always by an invidious nick-name – perceiving, meanwhile, that he was figuratively following along beside her as she walked the fence, ready to catch her if she should fall.

The night before the engagement was announced she told Bloeck-man. It was a heavy blow. She did not enlighten Anthony as to the details, but she implied that he had not hesitated to argue with her. Anthony gathered that the interview had terminated on a stormy note, with Gloria very cool and unmoved lying in her corner of the sofa and Joseph Bloeckman of 'Films Par Excellence' pacing the carpet with eyes narrowed and head bowed. Gloria had been sorry for him but she had judged it best not to show it. In a final burst of kindness she had tried to make him hate her, there at the last. But Anthony, understanding that Gloria's indifference was her strongest appeal, judged how futile this must have been. He wondered, often but quite casually, about Bloeckman – finally he forgot him entirely.

HEYDAY

One afternoon they found front seats on the sunny roof of a bus and rode for hours from the fading Square up along the sullied river, and then, as the stray beams fled the westward streets, sailed down the turgid Avenue, darkening with ominous bees from the department stores. The traffic was clotted and gripped in a patternless jam; the buses were packed four deep like platforms above the crowd as they waited for the moan of the traffic whistle.

'Isn't it good!' cried Gloria. 'Look!'

A miller's wagon, stark white with flour, driven by a powdery clown, passed in front of them behind a white horse and his black team-mate.

'What a pity!' she complained; 'they'd look so beautiful in the dusk if only both horses were white. I'm mighty happy just this minute, in this city.'

Anthony shook his head in disagreement.

'I think the city's a mountebank. Always struggling to approach the tremendous and impressive urbanity ascribed to it. Trying to be romantically metropolitan.'

'I don't. I think it is impressive.'

'Momentarily. But it's really a transparent, artificial sort of spectacle. It's got its press-agented stars and its flimsy, unenduring stage settings, and, I'll admit, the greatest army of supers ever assembled – ' He paused, laughed shortly, and added: 'Technically excellent, perhaps, but not convincing.'

'I'll bet policemen think people are fools,' said Gloria thoughtfully, as she watched a large but cowardly lady being helped across the street. 'He always sees them frightened and inefficient and old – they are,' she added. And then: 'We'd better get off. I told mother I'd have an early supper and go to bed. She says I look tired, damn it.'

'I wish we were married,' he muttered soberly; 'there'll be no good-night then and we can do just as we want.'

'Won't it be good! I think we ought to travel a lot. I want to go to the Mediterranean and Italy. And I'd like to go on the stage some time – say for about a year.'

'You bet. I'll write a play for you.'

'Won't that be good! And I'll act in it. And then sometime when we have more money' – old Adam's death was always thus tactfully alluded to – 'we'll build a magnificent estate, won't we?'

'Oh, yes, with private swimming pools.'

'Dozens of them. And private rivers. Oh, I wish it were now.'

Odd coincidence – he had just been wishing that very thing. They plunged like divers into the dark eddying crowd and emerging in the cool Fifties sauntered indolently homeward, infinitely romantic to each other . . . both were walking alone in a dispassionate garden with a ghost found in a dream.

Halcyon days like boats drifting along slow-moving rivers; spring evenings full of a plaintive melancholy that made the past beautiful and bitter, bidding them look back and see that the loves of other summers long gone were dead with the forgotten waltzes of their years. Always the most poignant moments were when some artificial barrier kept them apart: in the theatre their hands would steal together, join, give and return gentle pressures through the long dark; in crowded rooms they would form words with their lips for each other's eyes – not knowing that they were but following in the footsteps of dusty generations but comprehending dimly that if truth is the end of life, happiness is a mode of it, to be cherished in its brief and tremulous moment. And then, one fairy night, May became June. Sixteen days now – fifteen – fourteen –

THREE DIGRESSIONS

Just before the engagement was announced Anthony had gone up to Tarrytown to see his grandfather, who, a little more wizened and grizzly as time played its ultimate chuckling tricks, greeted the news with profound cynicism.

'Oh, you're going to get married, are you?' He said this with such a dubious mildness and shook his head up and down so many times that Anthony was not a little depressed. While he was unaware of his grandfather's intentions he presumed that a large part of the money would come to him. A good deal would go in charities, of course; a good deal to carry on the business of reform.

'Are you going to work?'

'Why – ' temporised Anthony, somewhat disconcerted. 'I *am* working. You know – '

'Ah, I mean work,' said Adam Patch dispassionately.

'I'm not quite sure yet what I'll do. I'm not exactly a beggar, grampa,' he asserted with some spirit.

The old man considered this with eyes half closed. Then almost apologetically he asked: 'How much do you save a year?'

'Nothing so far – '

'And so after just managing to get along on your money you've decided that by some miracle two of you can get along on it.'

'Gloria has some money of her own. Enough to buy clothes.'

'How much?'

Without considering this question impertinent, Anthony answered it. 'About a hundred a month.'

'That's altogether about seventy-five hundred a year.' Then he added softly: 'It ought to be plenty. If you have any sense it ought to be plenty. But the question is whether you have any or not.'

'I suppose it is.' It was shameful to be compelled to endure this pious browbeating from the old man, and his next words were stiffened with vanity. 'I can manage very well. You seem convinced that I'm utterly worthless. At any rate I came up here simply to tell you that I'm getting married in June. Goodbye, sir.' With this he turned away and headed for the door, unaware that in that instant his grandfather, for the first time, rather liked him.

'Wait!' called Adam Patch, 'I want to talk to you.'

Anthony faced about.

'Well, sir?'

'Sit down. Stay all night.'

Somewhat mollified, Anthony resumed his seat.

'I'm sorry, sir, but I'm going to see Gloria tonight.'

'What's her name?'

'Gloria Gilbert.'

'New York girl? Someone you know?'

'She's from the Middle West.'

'What business is her father in?'

'In a celluloid corporation or trust or something. They're from Kansas City.'

'You going to be married out there?'

'Why, no, sir. We thought we'd be married in New York – rather quietly.'

'Like to have the wedding out here?'

Anthony hesitated. The suggestion made no appeal to him, but it was certainly the part of wisdom to give the old man, if possible, a proprietary interest in his married life. In addition Anthony was a little touched.

'That's very kind of you, grampa, but wouldn't it be a lot of trouble?'

'Everything's a lot of trouble. Your father was married here – but in the old house.'

'Why – I thought he was married in Boston.'

Adam Patch considered.

'That's true. He *was* married in Boston.'

Anthony felt a moment's embarrassment at having made the correction, and he covered it up with words.

'Well, I'll speak to Gloria about it. Personally I'd like to, but of course it's up to the Gilberts, you see.'

His grandfather drew a long sigh, half closed his eyes, and sank back in his chair.

'In a hurry?' he asked in a different tone.

'Not especially.'

'I wonder,' began Adam Patch, looking out with a mild, kindly glance at the lilac bushes that rustled against the windows, 'I wonder if you ever think about the afterlife.'

'Why – sometimes.'

'I think a great deal about the afterlife.' His eyes were dim but his voice was confident and clear. 'I was sitting here today thinking about what's lying in wait for us, and somehow I began to remember an afternoon nearly sixty-five years ago, when I was playing with my little sister Annie, down where that summer-house is now.' He pointed out into the long flower-garden, his eyes trembling with tears, his voice shaking.

'I began thinking – and it seemed to me that *you* ought to think a little more about the afterlife. You ought to be – steadier' – he paused and seemed to grope about for the right word – 'more industrious – why – '

Then his expression altered, his entire personality seemed to snap together like a trap, and when he continued the softness had gone from his voice.

' – Why, when I was just two years older than you,' he rasped with a cunning chuckle, 'I sent three members of the firm of Wrenn and Hunt to the poorhouse.'

Anthony started with embarrassment.

'Well, goodbye,' added his grandfather suddenly, 'you'll miss your train.'

Anthony left the house unusually elated, and strangely sorry for the old man; not because his wealth could buy him 'neither youth nor digestion' but because he had asked Anthony to be married there, and because he had forgotten something about his son's wedding that he should have remembered.

Richard Caramel, who was one of the ushers, caused Anthony and Gloria much distress in the last few weeks by continually stealing the rays of their spotlight. *The Demon Lover* had been published in April, and it interrupted the love affair as it may be said to have interrupted everything its author came in contact with. It was a highly original, rather over-written piece of sustained description concerned with a Don Juan of the New York slums. As Maury and Anthony had said before, as the more hospitable critics were saying then, there was no writer in America with such power to describe the atavistic and unsubtle reactions of that section of society.

The book hesitated and then suddenly 'went'. Editions, small at first, then larger, crowded each other week by week. A spokesman of the Salvation Army denounced it as a cynical misrepresentation of all the uplift taking place in the underworld. Clever press-agenting spread the unfounded rumour that 'Gypsy' Smith[245] was beginning a libel suit because one of the principal characters was a burlesque of himself. It was barred from the public library of Burlington, Iowa, and a Midwestern columnist announced by innuendo that Richard Caramel was in a sanatorium with delirium tremens.

The author, indeed, spent his days in a state of pleasant madness. The book was in his conversation three-fourths of the time – he wanted to know if one had heard 'the latest'; he would go into a store and in a loud voice order books to be charged to him, in order to catch a chance morsel of recognition from clerk or customer. He knew to a town in what sections of the country it was selling best; he knew exactly what he cleared on each edition, and when he met anyone who had not read it, or, as it happened only too often, had not heard of it, he succumbed to moody depression.

So it was natural for Anthony and Gloria to decide, in their jealousy, that he was so swollen with conceit as to be a bore. To Dick's great annoyance Gloria publicly boasted that she had never read *The Demon Lover*, and didn't intend to until everyone stopped talking about it. As a matter of fact, she had no time to read now, for the presents were pouring in – first a scattering, then an avalanche, varying from the bric-à-brac of forgotten family friends to the photographs of forgotten poor relations.

Maury gave them an elaborate 'drinking set', which included silver goblets, cocktail shaker and bottle-openers. The extortion from Dick was more conventional – a tea-set from Tiffany's.[246] From Joseph Bloeckman came a simple and exquisite travelling clock, with his card. There was even a cigarette-holder from Bounds; this touched Anthony and made him want to weep – indeed, any emotion short of hysteria seemed natural in the half-dozen people who were swept up by this tremendous sacrifice to convention. The room set aside in the Plaza bulged with offerings sent by Harvard friends and by associates of his grandfather, with remembrances of Gloria's Farmover days, and with rather pathetic trophies from her former beaux, which last arrived with esoteric, melancholy messages, written on cards tucked carefully inside, beginning 'I little thought when – ' or 'I'm sure I wish you all the happiness – ' or even 'When you get this I shall be on my way to – '

The most munificent gift was simultaneously the most disappointing. It was a concession of Adam Patch's – a check for five thousand dollars.

To most of the presents Anthony was cold. It seemed to him that they would necessitate keeping a chart of the marital status of all their acquaintances during the next half-century. But Gloria exulted in each one, tearing at the tissue-paper and excelsior with the rapaciousness of a dog digging for a bone, breathlessly seizing a ribbon or an edge of metal and finally bringing to light the whole article and holding it up critically, no emotion except rapt interest in her unsmiling face.

'Look, Anthony!'

'Darn nice, isn't it!'

No answer until an hour later when she would give him a careful account of her precise reaction to the gift, whether it would have been improved by being smaller or larger, whether she was surprised at getting it, and, if so, just how much surprised.

Mrs Gilbert arranged and rearranged a hypothetical house, distributing the gifts among the different rooms, tabulating articles as 'second-best clock' or 'silver to use *every* day', and embarrassing Anthony and Gloria by semi-facetious references to a room she called the nursery. She was pleased by old Adam's gift and thereafter had it that he was a very ancient soul, 'as much as anything else'. As Adam Patch never quite decided whether she referred to the advancing senility of his mind or to some private and psychic schema of her own, it cannot be said to have pleased him. Indeed he always spoke of her to Anthony as 'that old woman, the mother', as though she were a character in a comedy he had seen staged many times before. Concerning Gloria he was unable to make up his mind. She attracted him but, as she herself told Anthony, he had decided that she was frivolous and was afraid to approve of her.

Five days! – A dancing platform was being erected on the lawn at Tarrytown. Four days! – A special train was chartered to convey the guests to and from New York. Three days! –

THE DIARY

She was dressed in blue silk pyjamas and standing by her bed with her hand on the light to put the room in darkness, when she changed her mind and opening a table drawer brought out a little black book – a 'line-a-day' diary. This she had kept for seven years. Many of the pencil entries were almost illegible and there were notes and references to nights and afternoons long since forgotten, for it was not an intimate diary, even though it began with the immemorial, 'I am going to keep a diary for my children.' Yet as she thumbed over the pages the eyes of many men seemed to look out at her from their half-obliterated names. With one she had gone to New Haven[247] for the first time – in 1908, when she was sixteen and padded shoulders were fashionable at Yale – she had been flattered because 'Touchdown' Michaud had 'rushed' her all evening. She sighed, remembering the grown-up satin dress she had been so proud of and the orchestra playing 'Yama-Yama, My Yama Man'[248] and 'Jungle-Town'.[249] So long ago! – the names: Eltynge Reardon, Jim Parsons, 'Curly' McGregor, Kenneth Cowan, 'Fish-Eye' Fry (whom she had liked for being so ugly), Carter Kirby – he had sent her a present; so had Tudor Baird; – Marty Reffer, the first man she had been in love with for more than a day, and Stuart Holcome, who had run away with her in his automobile and tried to make her marry him by force. And Larry Fenwick, whom she had always admired because he had told her one night that if she wouldn't kiss him she could get out of his car and walk home. What a list!

... And, after all, an obsolete list. She was in love now, set for the eternal romance that was to be the synthesis of all romance, yet sad for these men and these moonlights and for the 'thrills' she had had – and the kisses. The past – her past, oh, what a joy! She had been exuberantly happy.

Turning over the pages her eyes rested idly on the scattered entries of the past four months. She read the last few carefully.

April 1st – I know Bill Carstairs hates me because I was so disagreeable, but I hate to be sentimentalised over sometimes. We drove out to the Rockyear Country Club and the most wonderful moon kept shining through the trees. My silver dress is getting tarnished. Funny how one forgets the other nights at Rockyear – with Kenneth Cowan when I loved him so!

April 3rd – After two hours of Schroeder who, they inform me, has millions, I've decided that this matter of sticking to things wears one out, particularly when the things concerned are men. There's nothing so often overdone and from today I swear to be amused. We talked about 'love' – how banal! With how many men have I talked about love?

April 11th – Patch actually called up today! and when he forswore me about a month ago he fairly raged out the door. I'm gradually losing faith in any man being susceptible to fatal injuries.

April 20th – Spent the day with Anthony. Maybe I'll marry him sometime. I kind of like his ideas – he stimulates all the originality in me. Blockhead came around about ten in his new car and took me out to Riverside Drive. I liked him tonight: he's so considerate. He knew I didn't want to talk so he was quiet all during the ride.

April 21st – Woke up thinking of Anthony and sure enough he called and sounded sweet on the phone – so I broke a date for him. Today I feel I'd break anything for him, including the ten commandments and my neck. He's coming at eight and I shall wear pink and look very fresh and starched –

She paused here, remembering that after he had gone that night she had undressed with the shivering April air streaming in the windows. Yet it seemed she had not felt the cold, warmed by the profound banalities burning in her heart.

The next entry occurred a few days later:

April 24th – I want to marry Anthony, because husbands are so often 'husbands' and I must marry a lover.

There are four general types of husbands.

(1) The husband who always wants to stay in in the evening, has no vices and works for a salary. Totally undesirable!

(2) The atavistic master whose mistress one is, to wait on his pleasure. This sort always considers every pretty woman 'shallow', a sort of peacock with arrested development.

(3) Next comes the worshipper, the idolater of his wife and all that is his, to the utter oblivion of everything else. This sort demands an emotional actress for a wife. God! it must be an exertion to be thought righteous.

(4) And Anthony – a temporarily passionate lover with wisdom enough to realise when it has flown and that it must fly. And I want to get married to Anthony.

What grubworms women are to crawl on their bellies through colourless marriages! Marriage was created not to be a background but to need one. Mine is going to be outstanding. It can't, shan't be the setting – it's going to be the performance, the live, lovely, glamorous performance, and the world shall be the scenery. I refuse to dedicate my life to posterity. Surely one owes as much to the current generation as to one's unwanted children. What a fate – to grow rotund and unseemly, to lose my self-love, to think in terms of milk, oatmeal, nurse, diapers . . . Dear dream children, how much more beautiful you are, dazzling little creatures who flutter (all dream children must flutter) on golden, golden wings –

Such children, however, poor dear babies, have little in common with the wedded state.

June 7th – Moral question: Was it wrong to make Bloeckman love me? Because I did really make him. He was almost sweetly sad tonight. How opportune it was that my throat is swollen plunk together and tears were easy to muster. But he's just the past – buried already in my plentiful lavender.

June 8th – And today I've promised not to chew my mouth. Well, I won't, I suppose – but if he'd only asked me not to eat!

Blowing bubbles – that's what we're doing, Anthony and me. And we blew such beautiful ones today, and they'll explode and then we'll blow more and more, I guess – bubbles just as big and just as beautiful, until all the soap and water is used up.

On this note the diary ended. Her eyes wandered up the page, over the June 8ths of 1912, 1910, 1907. The earliest entry was scrawled in the plump, bulbous hand of a sixteen-year-old girl – it was the name, Bob Lamar, and a word she could not decipher. Then she knew what it was – and, knowing, she found her eyes misty with tears. There in a greying blur was the record of her first kiss, faded as its intimate afternoon, on a rainy veranda seven years before. She seemed to remember something one of them had said that day and yet she could not remember. Her tears came faster, until she could scarcely see the page. She was crying, she told herself, because she could remember only the rain and the wet flowers in the yard and the smell of the damp grass.

. . . After a moment she found a pencil and holding it unsteadily drew three parallel lines beneath the last entry. Then she printed FINIS in large capitals, put the book back in the drawer, and crept into bed.

BREATH OF THE CAVE

Back in his apartment after the bridal dinner, Anthony snapped out his lights and, feeling impersonal and fragile as a piece of china waiting on a serving-table, got into bed. It was a warm night – a sheet was enough for comfort – and through his wide-open windows came sound, evanescent and summery, alive with remote anticipation. He was thinking that the young years behind him, hollow and colourful, had been lived in facile and vacillating cynicism upon the recorded emotions of men long dust. And there was something beyond that; he knew now. There was the union of his soul with Gloria's, whose radiant fire and freshness was the living material of which the dead beauty of books was made.

From the night into his high-walled room there came, persistently, that evanescent and dissolving sound – something the city was tossing up and calling back again, like a child playing with a ball. In Harlem, the Bronx, Gramercy Park[250] and along the waterfronts, in little parlours or on pebble-strewn, moon-flooded roofs, a thousand lovers were making this sound, crying little fragments of it into the air. All the city was playing with this sound out there in the blue summer dark, throwing it up and calling it back, promising that, in a little while, life would be beautiful as a story, promising happiness – and by that promise giving it. It gave love hope in its own survival. It could do no more.

It was then that a new note separated itself jarringly from the soft crying of the night. It was a noise from an area-way within a hundred feet from his rear window, the noise of a woman's laughter. It began low, incessant and whining – some servant-maid with her fellow, he thought – and then it grew in volume and became hysterical, until it reminded him of a girl he had seen overcome with nervous laughter at a vaudeville performance. Then it sank, receded, only to rise again and include words – a coarse joke, some bit of obscure horseplay he could not distinguish. It would break off for a moment and he would just catch the low rumble of a man's voice, then begin again – interminably; at first annoying, then strangely terrible. He shivered, and getting up out of bed went to the window. It had reached a high point, tensed and stifled, almost the quality of a scream – then it ceased and left behind it a silence empty and menacing as the greater silence overhead. Anthony stood by the window a moment longer before he returned to his bed. He found himself upset and shaken. Try as he might to strangle his reaction, some animal quality in that unrestrained laughter had grasped at his imagination, and for the first time in four months aroused his old aversion and horror towards all the business of life. The room had grown smothery. He wanted to be out in some cool and bitter breeze, miles above the cities, and to live serene and detached back in the corners of his mind. Life was that sound out there, that ghastly reiterated female sound.

'Oh, my *God*!' he cried, drawing in his breath sharply.

Burying his face in the pillows he tried in vain to concentrate upon the details of the next day.

MORNING

In the grey light he found that it was only five o'clock. He regretted nervously that he had awakened so early – he would appear fagged at the wedding. He envied Gloria who could hide her fatigue with careful pigmentation.

In his bathroom he contemplated himself in the mirror and saw that he was unusually white – half a dozen small imperfections stood out against the morning pallor of his complexion, and overnight he had grown the faint stubble of a beard – the general effect, he fancied, was unprepossessing, haggard, half unwell.

On his dressing-table were spread a number of articles which he told over carefully with suddenly fumbling fingers – their tickets to California, the book of traveller's checks, his watch, set to the half-minute, the key to his apartment, which he must not forget to give to Maury, and, most important of all, the ring. It was of platinum set around with small emeralds; Gloria had insisted on this; she had always wanted an emerald wedding ring, she said.

It was the third present he had given her; first had come the engagement ring, and then a little gold cigarette-case. He would be giving her many things now – clothes and jewels and friends and excitement. It seemed absurd that from now on he would pay for all her meals. It was going to cost: he wondered if he had not underestimated for this trip, and if he had not better cash a larger cheque. The question worried him.

Then the breathless impendency of the event swept his mind clear of details. This was the day – unsought, unsuspected six months before, but now breaking in yellow light through his east window, dancing along the carpet as though the sun were smiling at some ancient and reiterated gag of his own.

Anthony laughed in a nervous one-syllable snort.

'By God!' he muttered to himself, 'I'm as good as married!'

THE USHERS

Six young men in CROSS PATCH'S *library growing more and more cheery under the influence of Mumm's Extra Dry,*[251] *set surreptitiously in cold pails by the bookcases.*

THE FIRST YOUNG MAN: By golly! Believe me, in my next book I'm going to do a wedding scene that'll knock 'em cold!

THE SECOND YOUNG MAN: Met a débutante th'other day said she

thought your book was powerful. As a rule young girls cry for this primitive business.

THE THIRD YOUNG MAN: Where's Anthony?

THE FOURTH YOUNG MAN: Walking up and down outside talking to himself.

SECOND YOUNG MAN: Lord! Did you see the minister? Most peculiar looking teeth.

FIFTH YOUNG MAN: Think they're natural. Funny thing people having gold teeth.

SIXTH YOUNG MAN: They say they love 'em. My dentist told me once a woman came to him and insisted on having two of her teeth covered with gold. No reason at all. All right the way they were.

FOURTH YOUNG MAN: Hear you got out a book, Dicky. 'Gratulations!

DICK (*stiffly*): Thanks.

FOURTH YOUNG MAN (*innocently*): What is it? College stories?

DICK (*more stiffly*): No. Not college stories.

FOURTH YOUNG MAN: Pity! Hasn't been a good book about Harvard for years.

DICK (*touchily*): Why don't you supply the lack?

THIRD YOUNG MAN: I think I saw a squad of guests turn the drive in a Packard just now.

SIXTH YOUNG MAN: Might open a couple more bottles on the strength of that.

THIRD YOUNG MAN: It was the shock of my life when I heard the old man was going to have a wet wedding.[252] Rabid Prohibitionist, you know.

FOURTH YOUNG MAN (*snapping his fingers excitedly*): By gad! I knew I'd forgotten something. Kept thinking it was my vest.

DICK: What was it?

FOURTH YOUNG MAN: By gad! By gad!

SIXTH YOUNG MAN: Here! Here! Why the tragedy?

SECOND YOUNG MAN: What'd you forget? The way home?

DICK (*maliciously*): He forgot the plot for his book of Harvard stories.

FOURTH YOUNG MAN: No, sir, I forgot the present, by George! I forgot to buy old Anthony a present. I kept putting it off and putting it off, and by gad I've forgotten it! What'll they think?

SIXTH YOUNG MAN (*facetiously*): That's probably what's been holding up the wedding.

(THE FOURTH YOUNG MAN *looks nervously at his watch. Laughter.*)

FOURTH YOUNG MAN: By gad! What an ass I am!

SECOND YOUNG MAN: What d'you make of the bridesmaid who thinks she's Nora Bayes?[253] Kept telling me she wished this was a ragtime wedding. Name's Haines or Hampton.

DICK (*hurriedly spurring his imagination*): Kane, you mean, Muriel Kane. She's a sort of debt of honour, I believe. Once saved Gloria from drowning, or something of the sort.

SECOND YOUNG MAN: I didn't think she could stop that perpetual swaying long enough to swim. Fill up my glass, will you? Old man and I had a long talk about the weather just now.

MAURY: Who? Old Adam?

SECOND YOUNG MAN: No, the bride's father. He must be with a weather bureau.

DICK: He's my uncle, Otis.

OTIS: Well, it's an honourable profession. (*Laughter.*)

SIXTH YOUNG MAN: Bride your cousin, isn't she?

DICK: Yes, Cable, she is.

CABLE: She certainly is a beauty. Not like you, Dicky. Bet she brings old Anthony to terms.

MAURY: Why are all grooms given the title of 'old'? I think marriage is an error of youth.

DICK: Maury, the professional cynic.

MAURY: Why, you intellectual faker!

FIFTH YOUNG MAN: Battle of the highbrows here, Otis. Pick up what crumbs you can.

DICK: Faker yourself! What do *you* know?

MAURY: What do *you* know?

DICK: Ask me anything. Any branch of knowledge.

MAURY: All right. What's the fundamental principle of biology?

DICK: You don't know yourself.

MAURY: Don't hedge!

DICK: Well, natural selection?

MAURY: Wrong.

DICK: I give it up.

MAURY: Ontogeny recapitulates phyllogeny.

FIFTH YOUNG MAN: Take your base!

MAURY: Ask you another. What's the influence of mice on the clover crop? (*Laughter.*)

FOURTH YOUNG MAN: What's the influence of rats on the Decalogue?

MAURY: Shut up, you saphead. There *is* a connection.

DICK: What is it then?

MAURY (*pausing a moment in growing disconcertion*): Why, let's see. I seem to have forgotten exactly. Something about the bees eating the clover.

FOURTH YOUNG MAN: And the clover eating the mice! Haw! Haw!

MAURY (*frowning*): Let me just think a minute.

DICK (*sitting up suddenly*): Listen!

(*A volley of chatter explodes in the adjoining room. The six young men arise, feeling at their neckties.*)

DICK (*weightily*): We'd better join the firing squad. They're going to take the picture, I guess. No, that's afterwards.

OTIS: Cable, you take the ragtime bridesmaid.

FOURTH YOUNG MAN: I wish to God I'd sent that present.

MAURY: If you'll give me another minute I'll think of that about the mice.

OTIS: I was usher last month for old Charlie McIntyre and –

(*They move slowly towards the door as the chatter becomes a babel and the practising preliminary to the overture issues in long pious groans from* ADAM PATCH'*s organ.*)

ANTHONY

There were five hundred eyes boring through the back of his cutaway and the sun glinting on the clergyman's inappropriately bourgeois teeth. With difficulty he restrained a laugh. Gloria was saying something in a clear proud voice and he tried to think that the affair was irrevocable, that every second was significant, that his life was being slashed into two periods and that the face of the world was changing before him. He tried to recapture that ecstatic sensation of ten weeks before. All these emotions eluded him, he did not even feel the physical nervousness of that very morning – it was all one gigantic aftermath. And those gold teeth! He wondered if the clergyman were married; he wondered perversely if a clergyman could perform his own marriage service . . .

But as he took Gloria into his arms he was conscious of a strong reaction. The blood was moving in his veins now. A languorous and pleasant content settled like a weight upon him, bringing responsibility and possession. He was married.

GLORIA

So many, such mingled emotions, that no one of them was separable from the others! She could have wept for her mother, who was crying quietly back there ten feet, and for the loveliness of the June sunlight flooding in at the windows. She was beyond all conscious perceptions. Only a sense, coloured with delirious wild excitement, that the ultimately important was happening – and a trust, fierce and passionate, burning in her like a prayer, that in a moment she would be for ever and securely safe.

Late one night they arrived in Santa Barbara,[254] where the night clerk at the Hotel Lafcadio refused to admit them, on the grounds that they were not married.

The clerk thought that Gloria was beautiful. He did not think that anything so beautiful as Gloria could be moral.

'CON AMORE'

That first half-year – the trip West, the long months' loiter along the California coast and the grey house near Greenwich[255] where they lived until late autumn made the country dreary – those days, those places, saw the enraptured hours. The breathless idyl of their engagement gave way, first, to the intense romance of the more passionate relationship. The breathless idyl left them, fled on to other lovers; they looked around one day and it was gone, how they scarcely knew. Had either of them lost the other in the days of the idyl, the love lost would have been ever to the loser that dim desire without fulfilment which stands back of all life. But magic must hurry on, and the lovers remain . . .

The idyl passed, bearing with it its extortion of youth. Came a day when Gloria found that other men no longer bored her; came a day when Anthony discovered that he could sit again late into the evening, talking with Dick of those tremendous abstractions that had once occupied his world. But, knowing they had had the best of love, they clung to what remained. Love lingered – by way of long conversations at night into those stark hours when the mind thins and sharpens and the borrowings from dreams become the stuff of all life, by way of deep and intimate kindnesses they developed towards each other, by way of their laughing at the same absurdities and thinking the same things noble and the same things sad.

It was, first of all, a time of discovery. The things they found in each other were so diverse, so intermixed and, moreover, so sugared with love as to seem at the time not so much discoveries as isolated phenomena – to be allowed for, and to be forgotten. Anthony found that he was living with a girl of tremendous nervous tension and of the most high-handed selfishness. Gloria knew within a month that her husband was an utter coward towards any one of a million phantasms created by his imagination. Her perception was intermittent, for this cowardice sprang out, became almost obscenely evident, then faded and vanished as though it had been only a creation of her own mind. Her reactions to it were not those attributed to her sex – it roused her neither to disgust nor to a premature feeling of motherhood. Herself almost completely without physical fear, she was unable to understand, and so she made the most of what she felt to be his fear's redeeming feature, which was that though he was a coward under a shock and a coward under a strain – when his imagination was given play – he had yet a sort of dashing recklessness that moved her on its brief occasions almost to admiration, and a pride that usually steadied him when he thought he was observed.

The trait first showed itself in a dozen incidents of little more than nervousness – his warning to a taxi-driver against fast driving, in Chicago; his refusal to take her to a certain tough café she had always wished to visit; these of course admitted the conventional interpretation – that it was of her he had been thinking; nevertheless, their cumulative weight disturbed her. But something that occurred in a San Francisco hotel, when they had been married a week, gave the matter certainty.

It was after midnight and pitch dark in their room. Gloria was dozing off and Anthony's even breathing beside her made her suppose that he was asleep, when suddenly she saw him raise himself on his elbow and stare at the window.

'What is it, dearest?' she murmured.

'Nothing' – he had relaxed to his pillow and turned towards her – 'nothing, my darling wife.'

'Don't say "wife". I'm your mistress. Wife's such an ugly word. Your "permanent mistress" is so much more tangible and desirable . . . Come into my arms,' she added in a rush of tenderness; 'I can sleep so well, so well with you in my arms.'

Coming into Gloria's arms had a quite definite meaning. It required that he should slide one arm under her shoulder, lock both arms about her, and arrange himself as nearly as possible as a sort of three-sided crib for her luxurious ease. Anthony, who tossed, whose arms went tinglingly to sleep after half an hour of that position, would wait until she was asleep and roll her gently over to her side of the bed – then, left to his own devices, he would curl himself into his usual knots.

Gloria, having attained sentimental comfort, retired into her doze. Five minutes ticked away on Bloeckman's travelling clock; silence lay all about the room, over the unfamiliar, impersonal furniture and the half-oppressive ceiling that melted imperceptibly into invisible walls on both sides. Then there was suddenly a rattling flutter at the window, staccato and loud upon the hushed, pent air.

With a leap Anthony was out of the bed and standing tense beside it.

'Who's there?' he cried in an awful voice.

Gloria lay very still, wide awake now and engrossed not so much in the rattling as in the rigid breathless figure whose voice had reached from the bedside into that ominous dark.

The sound stopped; the room was quiet as before – then Anthony pouring words in at the telephone.

'Someone just tried to get into the room! . . . There's someone at the window!' His voice was emphatic now, faintly terrified. 'All right! Hurry!' He hung up the receiver; stood motionless.

. . . There was a rush and commotion at the door, a knocking – Anthony went to open it upon an excited night clerk with three bellboys grouped staring behind him. Between thumb and finger the night clerk held a wet pen with the threat of a weapon; one of the bellboys had seized a telephone directory and was looking at it sheepishly. Simultaneously the group was joined by the hastily summoned house-detective, and as one man they surged into the room.

Lights sprang on with a click. Gathering a piece of sheet about her Gloria dived away from sight, shutting her eyes to keep out the horror of this unpremeditated visitation. There was no vestige of an idea in her stricken sensibilities save that her Anthony was at grievous fault.

. . . The night clerk was speaking from the window, his tone half of the servant, half of the teacher reproving a schoolboy.

'Nobody out there,' he declared conclusively; 'my golly, nobody *could* be out there. This here's a sheer fall to the street of fifty feet. It was the wind you heard, tugging at the blind.'

'Oh.'

Then she was sorry for him. She wanted only to comfort him and draw him back tenderly into her arms, to tell them to go away because the thing their presence connotated was odious. Yet she could not raise her head for shame. She heard a broken sentence, apologies, conventions of the employee and one unrestrained snicker from a bellboy.

'I've been nervous as the devil all evening,' Anthony was saying; 'somehow that noise just shook me – I was only about half awake.'

'Sure, I understand,' said the night clerk with comfortable tact; 'been that way myself.'

The door closed; the lights snapped out; Anthony crossed the floor quietly and crept into bed. Gloria, feigning to be heavy with sleep, gave a quiet little sigh and slipped into his arms.

'What was it, dear?'

'Nothing,' he answered, his voice still shaken; 'I thought there was somebody at the window, so I looked out, but I couldn't see anyone and the noise kept up, so I phoned downstairs. Sorry if I disturbed you, but I'm awfully darn nervous tonight.'

Catching the lie, she gave an interior start – he had not gone to the window, nor near the window. He had stood by the bed and then sent in his call of fear.

'Oh,' she said – and then: 'I'm so sleepy.'

For an hour they lay awake side by side, Gloria with her eyes shut so tight that blue moons formed and revolved against backgrounds of deepest mauve, Anthony staring blindly into the darkness overhead.

After many weeks it came gradually out into the light, to be laughed and joked at. They made a tradition to fit over it – whenever that overpowering terror of the night attacked Anthony, she would put her arms about him and croon, soft as a song: 'I'll protect my Anthony. Oh, nobody's ever going to harm my Anthony!'

He would laugh as though it were a jest they played for their mutual amusement, but to Gloria it was never quite a jest. It was, at first, a keen disappointment; later, it was one of the times when she controlled her temper.

The management of Gloria's temper, whether it was aroused by a lack of hot water for her bath or by a skirmish with her husband, became almost the primary duty of Anthony's day. It must be done just so – by this much silence, by that much pressure, by this much yielding, by that much force. It was in her angers with their attendant cruelties that her inordinate egotism chiefly displayed itself. Because she was brave, because she was 'spoiled', because of her outrageous and commendable independence of judgement, and finally because of her arrogant consciousness that she had never seen a girl as beautiful as herself, Gloria had developed into a consistent, practising Nietzschean. This, of course, with overtones of profound sentiment.

There was, for example, her stomach. She was used to certain dishes, and she had a strong conviction that she could not possibly eat anything else. There must be a lemonade and a tomato sandwich late in the morning, then a light lunch with a stuffed tomato. Not only did she require food from a selection of a dozen dishes, but in addition this food must be prepared in just a certain way. One of the most annoying half-hours of the first fortnight occurred in Los Angeles, when an unhappy waiter brought her a tomato stuffed with chicken salad instead of celery.

'We always serve it that way, madame,' he quavered to the grey eyes that regarded him wrathfully.

Gloria made no answer, but when the waiter had turned discreetly away she banged both fists upon the table until the china and silver rattled.

'Poor Gloria!' laughed Anthony unwittingly, 'you can't get what you want ever, can you?'

'I can't eat *stuff*!' she flared up.

'I'll call back the waiter.'

'I don't want you to! He doesn't know anything, the darn *fool*!'

'Well, it isn't the hotel's fault. Either send it back, forget it, or be a sport and eat it.'

'Shut up!' she said succinctly.

'Why take it out on me?'

'Oh, I'm *not*,' she wailed, 'but I simply *can't* eat it.'

Anthony subsided helplessly.

'We'll go somewhere else,' he suggested.

'I don't *want* to go anywhere else. I'm tired of being trotted around to a dozen cafés and not getting one thing fit to eat.'

'When did we go around to a dozen cafés?'

'You'd *have* to in *this* town,' insisted Gloria with ready sophistry.

Anthony, bewildered, tried another tack.

'Why don't you try to eat it? It can't be as bad as you think.'

'Just – because – I – don't – like – chicken!'

She picked up her fork and began poking contemptuously at the tomato, and Anthony expected her to begin flinging the stuffings in all directions. He was sure that she was approximately as angry as she had ever been – for an instant he had detected a spark of hate directed as much towards him as towards anyone else – and Gloria angry was, for the present, unapproachable.

Then, surprisingly, he saw that she had tentatively raised the fork to her lips and tasted the chicken salad. Her frown had not abated and he stared at her anxiously, making no comment and daring scarcely to breathe. She tasted another forkful – in another moment she was eating. With difficulty Anthony restrained a chuckle; when at length he spoke his words had no possible connection with chicken salad.

This incident, with variations, ran like a lugubrious fugue through the first year of marriage; always it left Anthony baffled, irritated, and depressed. But another rough brushing of temperaments, a question of laundry-bags, he found even more annoying as it ended inevitably in a decisive defeat for him.

One afternoon in Coronado,[256] where they made the longest stay of their trip, more than three weeks, Gloria was arraying herself brilliantly for tea. Anthony, who had been downstairs listening to the latest rumour bulletins of war in Europe, entered the room, kissed the back of her powdered neck, and went to his dresser. After a great pulling out and pushing in of drawers, evidently unsatisfactory, he turned around to the Unfinished Masterpiece.

'Got any handkerchiefs, Gloria?' he asked. Gloria shook her golden head.

'Not a one. I'm using one of yours.'

'The last one, I deduce.' He laughed dryly.

'Is it?' She applied an emphatic though very delicate contour to her lips.

'Isn't the laundry back?'

'I don't know.'

Anthony hesitated – then, with sudden discernment, opened the closet door. His suspicions were verified. On the hook provided hung the blue bag furnished by the hotel. This was full of his clothes – he had put them there himself. The floor beneath it was littered with an astonishing mass of finery – lingerie, stockings, dresses, nightgowns and pyjamas – most of it scarcely worn but all of it coming indubitably under the general heading of Gloria's laundry.

He stood holding the closet door open.

'Why, Gloria!'

'What?'

The lip-line was being erased and corrected according to some mysterious perspective; not a finger trembled as she manipulated the lipstick, not a glance wavered in his direction. It was a triumph of concentration.

'Haven't you ever sent out the laundry?'

'Is it there?'

'It most certainly is.'

'Well, I guess I haven't, then.'

'Gloria,' began Anthony, sitting down on the bed and trying to catch her mirrored eyes, 'you're a nice fellow, you are! I've sent it out every time it's been sent since we left New York, and over a week ago you promised you'd do it for a change. All you'd have to do would be to cram your own junk into that bag and ring for the chambermaid.'

'Oh, why fuss about the laundry?' exclaimed Gloria petulantly, 'I'll take care of it.'

'I haven't fussed about it. I'd just as soon divide the bother with you, but when we run out of handkerchiefs it's darn near time something's done.'

Anthony considered that he was being extraordinarily logical. But Gloria, unimpressed, put away her cosmetics and casually offered him her back.

'Hook me up,' she suggested; 'Anthony, dearest, I forgot all about it. I meant to, honestly, and I will today. Don't be cross with your sweetheart.'

What could Anthony do then but draw her down upon his knee and kiss a shade of colour from her lips.

'But I don't mind,' she murmured with a smile, radiant and magnanimous. 'You can kiss all the paint off my lips any time you want.'

They went down to tea. They bought some handkerchiefs in a notion store near by. All was forgotten.

But two days later Anthony looked in the closet and saw the bag still hung limp upon its hook and that the gay and vivid pile on the floor had increased surprisingly in height.

'Gloria!' he cried.

'Oh – ' Her voice was full of real distress. Despairingly Anthony went to the phone and called the chambermaid.

'It seems to me,' he said impatiently, 'that you expect me to be some sort of French valet to you.'

Gloria laughed, so infectiously that Anthony was unwise enough to smile. Unfortunate man! In some intangible manner his smile made her mistress of the situation – with an air of injured righteousness she went emphatically to the closet and began pushing her laundry violently into the bag. Anthony watched her – ashamed of himself.

'There!' she said, implying that her fingers had been worked to the bone by a brutal taskmaster.

He considered, nevertheless, that he had given her an object-lesson and that the matter was closed, but on the contrary it was merely beginning. Laundry pile followed laundry pile – at long intervals; dearth of handkerchief followed dearth of handkerchief – at short ones; not to mention dearth of sock, of shirt, of everything. And Anthony found at length that either he must send it out himself or go through the increasingly unpleasant ordeal of a verbal battle with Gloria.

GLORIA AND GENERAL LEE

On their way East they stopped two days in Washington, strolling about with some hostility towards its atmosphere of harsh repellent light, of distance without freedom, of pomp without splendour – it seemed a pasty-pale and self-conscious city. The second day they made an ill-advised trip to General Lee's [257] old home at Arlington.

The bus which bore them was crowded with hot, unprosperous people, and Anthony, intimate to Gloria, felt a storm brewing. It broke at the Zoo, where the party stopped for ten minutes. The Zoo, it seemed, smelt of monkeys. Anthony laughed; Gloria called down the curse of heaven upon monkeys, including in her malevolence all the passengers of the bus and their perspiring offspring who had hied themselves monkey-ward.

Eventually the bus moved on to Arlington. There it met other buses and immediately a swarm of women and children were leaving a trail of peanut-shells through the halls of General Lee and crowding at length into the room where he was married. On the wall of this room a pleasing sign announced in large red letters 'Ladies' Toilet'. At this final blow Gloria broke down.

'I think it's perfectly terrible!' she said furiously, 'the idea of letting these people come here! And of encouraging them by making these houses show-places.'

'Well,' objected Anthony, 'if they weren't kept up they'd go to pieces.'

'What if they did!' she exclaimed as they sought the wide pillared porch. 'Do you think they've left a breath of 1860 here? This has become a thing of 1914.'

'Don't you want to preserve old things?'

'But you *can't*, Anthony. Beautiful things grow to a certain height and then they fail and fade off, breathing out memories as they decay. And just as any period decays in our minds, the things of that period should decay too, and in that way they're preserved for a while in the few hearts like mine that react to them. That graveyard at Tarrytown, for instance. The asses who give money to preserve things have spoiled that too. Sleepy Hollow's [258] gone; Washington Irving's dead and his books are rotting in our estimation year by year – then let the graveyard rot too, as it should, as all things should. Trying to preserve a century by keeping its relics up to date is like keeping a dying man alive by stimulants.'

'So you think that just as a time goes to pieces its houses ought to go too?'

'Of course! Would you value your Keats letter if the signature was traced over to make it last longer? It's just because I love the past that I want this house to look back on its glamorous moment of youth and beauty, and I want its stairs to creak as if to the footsteps of women with hoop skirts and men in boots and spurs. But they've made it into a blondined, rouged-up old woman of sixty. It hasn't any right to look so prosperous. It might care enough for Lee to drop a brick now and then. How many of these – these *animals*' – she waved her hand around – 'get anything from this, for all the histories and guidebooks and restorations in existence? How many of them who think that, at best, appreciation is talking in undertones and walking on tiptoes would even come here if it was any trouble? I want it to smell of magnolias instead of peanuts and I want my shoes to crunch on the same gravel that Lee's boots crunched on. There's no beauty without poignancy and there's no poignancy without the feeling that it's going, men, names, books, houses – bound for dust – mortal – '

A small boy appeared beside them and, swinging a handful of banana-peels, flung them valiantly in the direction of the Potomac.

SENTIMENT

Simultaneously with the fall of Liège,[259] Anthony and Gloria arrived in New York. In retrospect the six weeks seemed miraculously happy. They had found to a great extent, as most young couples find in some measure, that they possessed in common many fixed ideas and curiosities and odd quirks of mind; they were essentially companionable.

But it had been a struggle to keep many of their conversations on the level of discussions. Arguments were fatal to Gloria's disposition. She had all her life been associated either with her mental inferiors or with men who, under the almost hostile intimidation of her beauty, had not dared to contradict her; naturally, then, it irritated her when Anthony emerged from the state in which her pronouncements were an infallible and ultimate decision.

He failed to realise, at first, that this was the result partly of her 'female' education and partly of her beauty, and he was inclined to include her with her entire sex as curiously and definitely limited. It maddened him to find she had no sense of justice. But he discovered that, when a subject did interest her, her brain tired less quickly than his. What he chiefly missed in her mind was the pedantic teleology – the sense of order and accuracy, the sense of life as a mysteriously correlated piece of patchwork, but he understood after a while that such a quality in her would have been incongruous.

Of the things they possessed in common, greatest of all was their almost uncanny pull at each other's hearts. The day they left the hotel in Coronado she sat down on one of the beds while they were packing, and began to weep bitterly.

'Dearest – ' His arms were around her; he pulled her head down upon his shoulder. 'What is it, my own Gloria? Tell me.'

'We're going away,' she sobbed. 'Oh, Anthony, it's sort of the first place we've lived together. Our two little beds here – side by side – they'll be always waiting for us, and we're never coming back to 'em any more.'

She was tearing at his heart as she always could. Sentiment came over him, rushed into his eyes.

'Gloria, why, we're going on to another room. And two other little beds. We're going to be together all our lives.'

Words flooded from her in a low husky voice.

'But it won't be – like our two beds – ever again. Everywhere we go and move on and change, something's lost – something's left behind. You can't ever quite repeat anything, and I've been so yours, here – '

He held her passionately near, discerning, far beyond any criticism of her sentiment, a wise grasping of the minute, if only an indulgence of her desire to cry – Gloria the idler, caresser of her own dreams, extracting poignancy from the memorable things of life and youth.

Later in the afternoon when he returned from the station with the tickets he found her asleep on one of the beds, her arm curled about a black object which he could not at first identify. Coming closer he found it was one of his shoes, not a particularly new one, nor clean one, but her face, tear-stained, was pressed against it, and he understood her ancient and most honourable message. There was almost ecstasy in waking her and seeing her smile at him, shy but well aware of her own nicety of imagination.

With no appraisal of the worth or dross of these two things, it seemed to Anthony that they lay somewhere near the heart of love.

THE GREY HOUSE

It is in the twenties that the actual momentum of life begins to slacken, and it is a simple soul indeed to whom as many things are significant and meaningful at thirty as at ten years before. At thirty an organ-grinder is a more or less moth-eaten man who grinds an organ – and once he was an organ-grinder! The unmistakable stigma of humanity touches all those impersonal and beautiful things that only youth ever grasps in their impersonal glory. A brilliant ball, gay with light romantic laughter, wears through its own silks and satins to show the bare framework of a man-made thing – oh, that eternal hand! – a play, most tragic and most divine, becomes merely a succession of speeches, sweated over by the eternal plagiarist in the clammy hours and acted by men subject to cramps, cowardice, and manly sentiment.

And this time with Gloria and Anthony came in this first year of marriage, and the grey house caught them in that stage when the organ-grinder was slowly undergoing his inevitable metamorphosis. She was twenty-three; he was twenty-six.

The grey house was, at first, of sheerly pastoral intent. They lived impatiently in Anthony's apartment for the first fortnight after the return from California, in a stifled atmosphere of open trunks, too many callers, and the eternal laundry-bags. They discussed with their friends the stupendous problem of their future. Dick and Maury would sit with them agreeing solemnly, almost thoughtfully, as Anthony ran through his list of what they 'ought' to do, and where they 'ought' to live.

'I'd like to take Gloria abroad,' he complained, 'except for this damn war – and next to that I'd sort of like to have a place in the country, somewhere near New York, of course, where I could write – or whatever I decide to do.'

Gloria laughed.

'Isn't he cute?' she required of Maury. ' "Whatever he decides to do!" But what am *I* going to do if he works? Maury, will you take me around if Anthony works?'

'Anyway, I'm not going to work yet,' said Anthony quickly.

It was vaguely understood between them that on some misty day he would enter a sort of glorified diplomatic service and be envied by princes and prime ministers for his beautiful wife.

'Well,' said Gloria helplessly, 'I'm sure I don't know. We talk and talk and never get anywhere, and we ask all our friends and they just answer the way we want 'em to. I wish somebody'd take care of us.'

'Why don't you go out to – out to Greenwich or something?' suggested Richard Caramel.

'I'd like that,' said Gloria, brightening. 'Do you think we could get a house there?'

Dick shrugged his shoulders and Maury laughed.

'You two amuse me,' he said. 'Of all the unpractical people! As soon as a place is mentioned you expect us to pull great piles of photographs out of our pockets showing the different styles of architecture available in bungalows.'

'That's just what I don't want,' wailed Gloria, 'a hot stuffy bungalow, with a lot of babies next door and their father cutting the grass in his shirt sleeves – '

'For heaven's sake, Gloria,' interrupted Maury, 'nobody wants to lock you up in a bungalow. Who in God's name brought bungalows into the conversation? But you'll never get a place anywhere unless you go out and hunt for it.'

'Go where? You say "go out and hunt for it", but where?'

With dignity Maury waved his hand paw-like about the room.

'Out anywhere. Out in the country. There're lots of places.'

'Thanks.'

'Look here!' Richard Caramel brought his yellow eye rakishly into play. 'The trouble with you two is that you're all disorganised. Do you know anything about New York State? Shut up, Anthony, I'm talking to Gloria.'

'Well,' she admitted finally, 'I've been to two or three house parties in Portchester and around in Connecticut – but, of course, that isn't in New York State, is it? And neither is Morristown,'[260] she finished with drowsy irrelevance.

There was a shout of laughter.

'Oh, Lord!' cried Dick, 'neither is Morristown! No, and neither is Santa Barbara, Gloria. Now listen. To begin with, unless you have a

fortune there's no use considering any place like Newport or South-
ampton or Tuxedo. They're out of the question.'

They all agreed to this solemnly.

'And personally I hate New Jersey. Then, of course, there's upper
New York, above Tuxedo.'

'Too cold,' said Gloria briefly. 'I was there once in an automobile.'

'Well, it seems to me there're a lot of towns like Rye between New
York and Greenwich where you could buy a little grey house of
some – '

Gloria leaped at the phrase triumphantly. For the first time since
their return East she knew what she wanted.

'Oh, yes!' she cried. 'Oh, yes! that's it: a little grey house with sort
of white around and a whole lot of swamp maples just as brown and
gold as an October picture in a gallery. Where can we find one?'

'Unfortunately, I've mislaid my list of little grey houses with
swamp maples around them – but I'll try to find it. Meanwhile you
take a piece of paper and write down the names of seven possible
towns. And every day this week you take a trip to one of those
towns.'

'Oh, gosh!' protested Gloria, collapsing mentally, 'why won't you
do it for us? I hate trains.'

'Well, hire a car, and – '

Gloria yawned.

'I'm tired of discussing it. Seems to me all we do is talk about
where to live.'

'My exquisite wife wearies of thought,' remarked Anthony
ironically. 'She must have a tomato sandwich to stimulate her jaded
nerves. Let's go out to tea.'

As the unfortunate upshot of this conversation, they took Dick's
advice literally, and two days later went out to Rye, where they
wandered around with an irritated real-estate agent, like bewildered
babes in the wood. They were shown houses at a hundred a month
which closely adjoined other houses at a hundred a month; they were
shown isolated houses to which they invariably took violent dislikes,
though they submitted weakly to the agent's desire that they 'look at
that stove – some stove!' and to a great shaking of doorposts and
tapping of walls, intended evidently to show that the house would
not immediately collapse, no matter how convincingly it gave that
impression. They gazed through windows into interiors furnished
either 'commercially' with slab-like chairs and unyielding settees, or
'homelike' with the melancholy bric-à-brac of other summers –

crossed tennis rackets, fit-form couches, and depressing Gibson Girls.[261] With a feeling of guilt they looked at a few really nice houses, aloof, dignified and cool – at three hundred a month. They went away from Rye thanking the real-estate agent very much indeed.

On the crowded train back to New York the seat behind was occupied by a super-respirating Latin whose last few meals had obviously been composed entirely of garlic. They reached the apartment gratefully, almost hysterically, and Gloria rushed for a hot bath in the reproachless bathroom. So far as the question of a future abode was concerned both of them were incapacitated for a week.

The matter eventually worked itself out with unhoped-for romance. Anthony ran into the living-room one afternoon fairly radiating 'the idea'.

'I've got it,' he was exclaiming as though he had just caught a mouse. 'We'll get a car.'

'Gee whiz! Haven't we got troubles enough taking care of ourselves?'

'Give me a second to explain, can't you? just let's leave our stuff with Dick and just pile a couple of suitcases in our car, the one we're going to buy – we'll have to have one in the country anyway – and just start out in the direction of New Haven. You see, as we get out of commuting distance from New York, the rents'll get cheaper, and as soon as we find a house we want we'll just settle down.'

By his frequent and soothing interpolation of the word 'just' he aroused her lethargic enthusiasm. Strutting violently about the room, he simulated a dynamic and irresistible efficiency. 'We'll buy a car tomorrow.'

Life, limping after imagination's ten-league boots, saw them out of town a week later in a cheap but sparkling new roadster, saw them through the chaotic unintelligible Bronx, then over a wide murky district which alternated cheerless blue-green wastes with suburbs of tremendous and sordid activity. They left New York at eleven and it was well past a hot and beatific noon when they moved rakishly through Pelham.

'These aren't towns,' said Gloria scornfully, 'these are just city blocks plumped down coldly into waste acres. I imagine all the men here have their moustaches stained from drinking their coffee too quickly in the morning.'

'And play pinochle[262] on the commuting trains.'

'What's pinochle?'

'Don't be so literal. How should I know? But it sounds as though they ought to play it.'

'I like it. It sounds as if it were something where you sort of cracked your knuckles or something . . . Let me drive.'

Anthony looked at her suspiciously.

'You swear you're a good driver?'

'Since I was fourteen.'

He stopped the car cautiously at the side of the road and they changed seats. Then with a horrible grinding noise the car was put in gear, Gloria adding an accompaniment of laughter which seemed to Anthony disquieting and in the worst possible taste.

'Here we go!' she yelled. 'Whoo-oop!'

Their heads snapped back like marionettes on a single wire as the car leaped ahead and curved retchingly about a standing milk-wagon, whose driver stood up on his seat and bellowed after them. In the immemorial tradition of the road, Anthony retorted with a few brief epigrams as to the grossness of the milk-delivering profession. He cut his remarks short, however, and turned to Gloria with the growing conviction that he had made a grave mistake in relinquishing control and that Gloria was a driver of many eccentricities and of infinite carelessness.

'Remember now!' he warned her nervously, 'the man said we oughtn't to go over twenty miles an hour for the first five thousand miles.'

She nodded briefly, but evidently intending to accomplish the prohibitive distance as quickly as possible, slightly increased her speed. A moment later he made another attempt.

'See that sign? Do you want to get us pinched?'

'Oh, for heaven's sake,' cried Gloria in exasperation, 'you *always* exaggerate things so!'

'Well, I don't want to get arrested.'

'Who's arresting you? You're so persistent – just like you were about my cough medicine last night.'

'It was for your own good.'

'Ha! I might as well be living with mama.'

'What a thing to say to me!'

A standing policeman swerved into view, was hastily passed.

'See him?' demanded Anthony.

'Oh, you drive me crazy! He didn't arrest us, did he?'

'When he does it'll be too late,' countered Anthony brilliantly.

Her reply was scornful, almost injured.

'Why, this old thing won't *go* over thirty-five.'

'It isn't old.'

'It is in spirit.'

That afternoon the car joined the laundry-bags and Gloria's appetite as one of the trinity of contention. He warned her of railroad tracks; he pointed out approaching automobiles; finally he insisted on taking the wheel and a furious, insulted Gloria sat silently beside him between the towns of Larchmont and Rye.

But it was due to this furious silence of hers that the grey house materialised from its abstraction, for just beyond Rye he surrendered gloomily to it and re-relinquished the wheel. Mutely he beseeched her and Gloria, instantly cheered, vowed to be more careful. But because a discourteous street-car persisted callously in remaining upon its track Gloria ducked down a side-street – and thereafter that afternoon was never able to find her way back to the Post Road. The street they finally mistook for it lost its Post-Road aspect when it had gone five miles from Cos Cob. Its macadam became gravel, then dirt – moreover, it narrowed and developed a border of maple trees, through which filtered the westering sun, making its endless experiments with shadow designs upon the long grass.

'We're lost now,' complained Anthony.

'Read that sign!'

' "Marietta – Five Miles". What's Marietta?'

'Never heard of it, but let's go on. We can't turn here and there's probably a detour back to the Post Road.'

The way became scarred with deepening ruts and insidious shoulders of stone. Three farmhouses faced them momentarily, slid by. A town sprang up in a cluster of dull roofs around a white tall steeple.

Then Gloria, hesitating between two approaches, and making her choice too late, drove over a fire-hydrant and ripped the transmission violently from the car.

It was dark when the real-estate agent of Marietta showed them the grey house. They came upon it just west of the village, where it rested against a sky that was a warm blue cloak buttoned with tiny stars. The grey house had been there when women who kept cats were probably witches, when Paul Revere made false teeth in Boston preparatory to arousing the great commercial people, when our ancestors were gloriously deserting Washington in droves. Since those days the house had been bolstered up in a feeble corner, considerably repartitioned and newly plastered inside, amplified by a kitchen and added to by a side-porch – but, save for where some jovial oaf had roofed the new kitchen with red tin, Colonial it defiantly remained.

'How did you happen to come to Marietta?' demanded the real-estate agent in a tone that was first cousin to suspicion. He was showing them through four spacious and airy bedrooms.

'We broke down,' explained Gloria. 'I drove over a fire-hydrant and we had ourselves towed to the garage and then we saw your sign.'

The man nodded, unable to follow such a sally of spontaneity. There was something subtly immoral in doing anything without several months' consideration.

They signed a lease that night and, in the agent's car, returned jubilantly to the somnolent and dilapidated Marietta Inn, which was too broken for even the chance immoralities and consequent gaieties of a country road house. Half the night they lay awake planning the things they were to do there. Anthony was going to work at an astounding pace on his history and thus ingratiate himself with his cynical grandfather . . . When the car was repaired they would explore the country and join the nearest 'really nice' club, where Gloria would play golf 'or something' while Anthony wrote. This, of course, was Anthony's idea – Gloria was sure she wanted but to read and dream and be fed tomato sandwiches and lemonades by some angelic servant still in a shadowy hinterland. Between paragraphs Anthony would come and kiss her as she lay indolently in the hammock . . . The hammock! a host of new dreams in tune to its imagined rhythm, while the wind stirred it and waves of sun undulated over the shadows of blown wheat, or the dusty road freckled and darkened with quiet summer rain . . .

And guests – here they had a long argument, both of them trying to be extraordinarily mature and far-sighted. Anthony claimed that they would need people at least every other weekend 'as a sort of change'. This provoked an involved and extremely sentimental conversation as to whether Anthony did not consider Gloria change enough. Though he assured her that he did, she insisted upon doubting him . . . Eventually the conversation assumed its eternal monotone: 'What then? Oh, what'll we do then?'

'Well, we'll have a dog,' suggested Anthony.

'I don't want one. I want a kitty.' She went thoroughly and with great enthusiasm into the history, habits and tastes of a cat she had once possessed. Anthony considered that it must have been a horrible character with neither personal magnetism nor a loyal heart.

Later they slept, to wake an hour before dawn with the grey house dancing in phantom glory before their dazzled eyes.

THE SOUL OF GLORIA

For that autumn the grey house welcomed them with a rush of sentiment that falsified its cynical old age. True, there were the laundry-bags, there was Gloria's appetite, there was Anthony's tendency to brood and his imaginative 'nervousness', but there were intervals also of an unhoped-for serenity. Close together on the porch they would wait for the moon to stream across the silver acres of farmland, jump a thick wood and tumble waves of radiance at their feet. In such a moonlight Gloria's face was of a pervading, reminiscent white, and with a modicum of effort they would slip off the blinders of custom and each would find in the other almost the quintessential romance of the vanished June.

One night while her head lay upon his heart and their cigarettes glowed in swerving buttons of light through the dome of darkness over the bed, she spoke for the first time and fragmentarily of the men who had hung for brief moments on her beauty.

'Do you ever think of them?' he asked her.

'Only occasionally – when something happens that recalls a particular man.'

'What do you remember – their kisses?'

'All sorts of things . . . Men are different with women.'

'Different in what way?'

'Oh, entirely – and quite inexpressibly. Men who had the most firmly rooted reputation for being this way or that would sometimes be surprisingly inconsistent with me. Brutal men were tender, negligible men were astonishingly loyal and lovable, and, often, honourable men took attitudes that were anything but honourable.'

'For instance?'

'Well, there was a boy named Percy Wolcott from Cornell who was quite a hero in college, a great athlete, and saved a lot of people from a fire or something like that. But I soon found he was stupid in a rather dangerous way.'

'What way?'

'It seems he had some naïve conception of a woman "fit to be his wife", a particular conception that I used to run into a lot and that always drove me wild. He demanded a girl who'd never been kissed and who liked to sew and sit at home and pay tribute to his self-esteem. And I'll bet a hat if he's got an idiot to sit and be stupid with him he's tearing out on the side with some much speedier lady.'

'I'd be sorry for his wife.'

'I wouldn't. Think what an ass she'd be not to realise it before she married him. He's the sort whose idea of honouring and respecting a woman would be never to give her any excitement. With the best intentions, he was deep in the Dark Ages.'

'What was his attitude towards you?'

'I'm coming to that. As I told you – or did I tell you? – he was mighty good-looking: big brown honest eyes and one of those smiles that guarantee the heart behind it is twenty-carat gold. Being young and credulous, I thought he had some discretion, so I kissed him fervently one night when we were riding around after a dance at the Homestead at Hot Springs. It had been a wonderful week, I remember – with the most luscious trees spread like green lather, sort of, all over the valley and a mist rising out of them on October mornings like bonfires lit to turn them brown – '

'How about your friend with the ideals?' interrupted Anthony.

'It seems that when he kissed me he began to think that perhaps he could get away with a little more, that I needn't be "respected" like this Beatrice Fairfax[263] glad-girl of his imagination.'

'What'd he do?'

'Not much. I pushed him off a sixteen-foot embankment before he was well started.'

'Hurt him?' enquired Anthony with a laugh.

'Broke his arm and sprained his ankle. He told the story all over Hot Springs, and when his arm healed a man named Barley who liked me fought him and broke it over again. Oh, it was all an awful mess. He threatened to sue Barley, and Barley – he was from Georgia – was seen buying a gun in town. But before that mama had dragged me North again, much against my will, so I never did find out all that happened – though I saw Barley once in the Vanderbilt lobby.'[264]

Anthony laughed long and loud.

'What a career! I suppose I ought to be furious because you've kissed so many men. I'm not, though.'

At this she sat up in bed.

'It's funny, but I'm so sure that those kisses left no mark on me –

no taint of promiscuity, I mean – even though a man once told me in all seriousness that he hated to think I'd been a public drinking glass.'

'He had his nerve.'

'I just laughed and told him to think of me rather as a loving-cup that goes from hand to hand but should be valued none the less.'

'Somehow it doesn't bother me – on the other hand it would, of course, if you'd done any more than kiss them. But I believe *you* are absolutely incapable of jealousy except as hurt vanity. Why don't you care what I've done? Wouldn't you prefer it if I'd been absolutely innocent?'

'It's all in the impression it might have made on you. *My* kisses were because the man was good-looking, or because there was a slick moon, or even because I've felt vaguely sentimental and a little stirred. But that's all – it's had utterly no effect on me. But you'd remember and let memories haunt you and worry you.'

'Haven't you ever kissed anyone like you've kissed me?'

'No,' she answered simply. 'As I've told you, men have tried – oh, lots of things. Any pretty girl has that experience . . . You see,' she resumed, 'it doesn't matter to me how many women you've stayed with in the past, so long as it was merely a physical satisfaction, but I don't believe I could endure the idea of your ever having lived with another woman for a protracted period or even having wanted to marry some possible girl. It's different somehow. There'd be all the little intimacies remembered – and they'd dull that freshness that after all is the most precious part of love.'

Rapturously he pulled her down beside him on the pillow.

'Oh, my darling,' he whispered, 'as if I remembered anything but your dear kisses.'

Then Gloria, in a very mild voice: 'Anthony, did I hear anybody say they were thirsty?'

Anthony laughed abruptly and with a sheepish and amused grin got out of bed.

'With just a *little* piece of ice in the water,' she added. 'Do you suppose I could have that?'

Gloria used the adjective 'little' whenever she asked a favour – it made the favour sound less arduous. But Anthony laughed again – whether she wanted a cake of ice or a marble of it, he must go downstairs to the kitchen . . . Her voice followed him through the hall: 'And just a *little* cracker with just a *little* marmalade on it . . . '

'Oh, gosh!' sighed Anthony in rapturous slang, 'she's wonderful, that girl! She *has* it!'

'When we have a baby,' she began one day – this, it had already been decided, was to be after three years – 'I want it to look like you.'

'Except its legs,' he insinuated slyly.

'Oh, yes, except his legs. He's got to have my legs. But the rest of him can be you.'

'My nose?'

Gloria hesitated.

'Well, perhaps my nose. But certainly your eyes – and my mouth, and I guess my shape of the face. I wonder; I think he'd be sort of cute if he had my hair.'

'My dear Gloria, you've appropriated the whole baby.'

'Well, I didn't mean to,' she apologised cheerfully.

'Let him have my neck at least,' he urged, regarding himself gravely in the glass. 'You've often said you liked my neck because the Adam's apple doesn't show, and, besides, your neck's too short.'

'Why, it is *not*!' she cried indignantly, turning to the mirror, 'it's just right. I don't believe I've ever seen a better neck.'

'It's too short,' he repeated teasingly.

'Short?' Her tone expressed exasperated wonder. 'Short? You're crazy!' She elongated and contracted it to convince herself of its reptilian sinuousness. 'Do you call *that* a short neck?'

'One of the shortest I've ever seen.'

For the first time in weeks tears started from Gloria's eyes and the look she gave him had a quality of real pain.

'Oh, Anthony – '

'My Lord, Gloria!' He approached her in bewilderment and took her elbows in his hands. 'Don't cry, *please*! Didn't you know I was only kidding? Gloria, look at me! Why, dearest, you've got the longest neck I've ever seen. Honestly.'

Her tears dissolved in a twisted smile.

'Well – you shouldn't have said that, then. Let's talk about the b-baby.'

Anthony paced the floor and spoke as though rehearsing for a debate.

'To put it briefly, there are two babies we could have, two distinct and logical babies, utterly differentiated. There's the baby that's the combination of the best of both of us. Your body, my eyes, my mind, your intelligence – and then there is the baby which is our worst – my body, your disposition, and my irresolution.'

'I like that second baby,' she said.

'What I'd really like,' continued Anthony, 'would be to have two sets of triplets one year apart and then experiment with the six boys – '

'Poor me,' she interjected.

' – I'd educate them each in a different country and by a different system and when they were twenty-three I'd call them together and see what they were like.'

'Let's have 'em all with my neck,' suggested Gloria.

THE END OF A CHAPTER

The car was at length repaired and with a deliberate vengeance took up where it left off the business of causing infinite dissension. Who should drive? How fast should Gloria go? These two questions and the eternal recriminations involved ran through the days. They motored to the Post-Road towns, Rye, Portchester and Greenwich, and called on a dozen friends, mostly Gloria's, who all seemed to be in different stages of having babies and in this respect as well as in others bored her to a point of nervous distraction. For an hour after each visit she would bite her fingers furiously and be inclined to take out her rancour on Anthony.

'I loathe women,' she cried in a mild temper. 'What on earth can you say to them – except talk "lady-lady"? I've enthused over a dozen babies that I've wanted only to choke. And every one of those girls is either incipiently jealous and suspicious of her husband if he's charming or beginning to be bored with him if he isn't.'

'Don't you ever intend to see any women?'

'I don't know. They never seem clean to me – never – never. Except just a few. Constance Shaw – you know, the Mrs Merriam who came over to see us last Tuesday – is almost the only one. She's so tall and fresh-looking and stately.'

'I don't like them so tall.'

Though they went to several dinner dances at various country clubs, they decided that the autumn was too nearly over for them to 'go out' on any scale, even had they been so inclined. He hated golf; Gloria liked it only mildly, and though she enjoyed a violent rush that some undergraduates gave her one night and was glad that Anthony should be proud of her beauty, she also perceived that their hostess for the evening, a Mrs Granby, was somewhat disquieted by the fact that Anthony's classmate, Alec Granby, joined with enthusiasm in the rush. The Granbys never phoned again, and though Gloria laughed, it piqued her not a little.

'You see,' she explained to Anthony, 'if I wasn't married it wouldn't worry her – but she's been to the movies in her day and she thinks I may be a vampire. But the point is that placating such people requires an effort that I'm simply unwilling to make . . . And those cute little freshmen making eyes at me and paying me idiotic compliments! I've grown up, Anthony.'

Marietta itself offered little social life. Half a dozen farm-estates formed a hexagon around it, but these belonged to ancient men who displayed themselves only as inert, grey-thatched lumps in the back of limousines on their way to the station, whither they were sometimes accompanied by equally ancient and doubly massive wives. The townspeople were a particularly uninteresting type – unmarried females were predominant for the most part – with school-festival horizons and souls bleak as the forbidding white architecture of the three churches. The only native with whom they came into close contact was the broad-hipped, broad-shouldered Swedish girl who came every day to do their work. She was silent and efficient, and Gloria, after finding her weeping violently into her bowed arms upon the kitchen table, developed an uncanny fear of her and stopped complaining about the food. Because of her untold and esoteric grief the girl stayed on.

Gloria's penchant for premonitions and her bursts of vague supernaturalism were a surprise to Anthony. Either some complex, properly and scientifically inhibited in the early years with her Bilphistic mother, or some inherited hypersensitiveness, made her susceptible to any suggestion of the psychic, and, far from gullible about the motives of people, she was inclined to credit any extraordinary happening attributed to the whimsical perambulations of the buried. The desperate squeakings about the old house on windy nights that to Anthony were burglars with revolvers ready in hand represented to Gloria the auras, evil and restive, of dead generations, expiating the inexpiable upon the ancient and romantic hearth. One night, because of two swift bangs downstairs, which Anthony fearfully but unavailingly investigated, they lay awake nearly until dawn asking each other examination-paper questions about the history of the world.

In October Muriel came out for a two weeks' visit. Gloria had called her on long-distance, and Miss Kane ended the conversation characteristically by saying 'All-ll-ll righty. I'll be there with bells!' She arrived with a dozen popular songs under her arm.

'You ought to have a phonograph out here in the country,' she said, 'just a little Vic [265] – they don't cost much. Then whenever you're lonesome you can have Caruso [266] or Al Jolson [267] right at your door.'

She worried Anthony to distraction by telling him that 'he was the first clever man she had ever known and she got so tired of shallow people'. He wondered that people fell in love with such women. Yet he supposed that under a certain impassioned glance even she might take on a softness and promise.

But Gloria, violently showing off her love for Anthony, was diverted into a state of purring content.

Finally Richard Caramel arrived for a garrulous and to Gloria painfully literary weekend, during which he discussed himself with Anthony long after she lay in childlike sleep upstairs.

'It's been mighty funny, this success and all,' said Dick. 'Just before the novel appeared I'd been trying, without success, to sell some short stories. Then, after my book came out, I polished up three and had them accepted by one of the magazines that had rejected them before. I've done a lot of them since; publishers don't pay me for my book till this winter.'

'Don't let the victor belong to the spoils.'

'You mean write trash?' He considered. 'If you mean deliberately injecting a slushy fade-out into each one, I'm not. But I don't suppose I'm being so careful. I'm certainly writing faster and I don't seem to be thinking as much as I used to. Perhaps it's because I don't get any conversation, now that you're married and Maury's gone to Philadelphia. Haven't the old urge and ambition. Early success and all that.'

'Doesn't it worry you?'

'Frantically. I get a thing I call sentence-fever that must be like buck-fever – it's a sort of intense literary self-consciousness that comes when I try to force myself. But the really awful days aren't when I think I can't write. They're when I wonder whether any writing is worth while at all – I mean whether I'm not a sort of glorified buffoon.'

'I like to hear you talk that way,' said Anthony with a touch of his old patronising insolence. 'I was afraid you'd got a bit idiotic over your work. Read the damnedest interview you gave out – '

Dick interrupted with an agonised expression.

'Good Lord! Don't mention it. Young lady wrote it – most admiring young lady. Kept telling me my work was "strong", and

I sort of lost my head and made a lot of strange pronouncements. Some of it was good, though, don't you think?'

'Oh, yes; that part about the wise writer writing for the youth of his generation, the critic of the next, and the schoolmaster of ever afterwards.'

'Oh, I believe a lot of it,' admitted Richard Caramel with a faint beam. 'It simply was a mistake to give it out.'

In November they moved into Anthony's apartment, from which they sallied triumphantly to the Yale–Harvard and Harvard–Princeton football games, to the St Nicholas ice-skating rink,[268] to a thorough round of the theatres and to a miscellany of entertainments – from small, staid dances to the great affairs that Gloria loved, held in those few houses where lackeys with powdered wigs scurried around in magnificent Anglomania under the direction of gigantic major-domos. Their intention was to go abroad the first of the year or, at any rate, when the war was over. Anthony had actually completed a Chestertonian essay on the twelfth century by way of introduction to his proposed book and Gloria had done some extensive research work on the question of Russian sable coats – in fact the winter was approaching quite comfortably, when the Bilphistic demiurge decided suddenly in mid-December that Mrs Gilbert's soul had aged sufficiently in its present incarnation. In consequence Anthony took a miserable and hysterical Gloria out to Kansas City, where, in the fashion of mankind, they paid the terrible and mind-shaking deference to the dead.

Mr Gilbert became, for the first and last time in his life, a truly pathetic figure. That woman he had broken to wait upon his body and play congregation to his mind had ironically deserted him – just when he could not much longer have supported her. Never again would he be able so satisfactorily to bore and bully a human soul.

CHAPTER 2

Symposium

Gloria had lulled Anthony's mind to sleep. She, who seemed of all women the wisest and the finest, hung like a brilliant curtain across his doorways, shutting out the light of the sun. In those first years what he believed bore invariably the stamp of Gloria; he saw the sun always through the pattern of the curtain.

It was a sort of lassitude that brought them back to Marietta for another summer. Through a golden enervating spring they had loitered, restive and lazily extravagant, along the California coast, joining other parties intermittently and drifting from Pasadena to Coronado, from Coronado to Santa Barbara, with no purpose more apparent than Gloria's desire to dance to different music or catch some infinitesimal variant among the changing colours of the sea. Out of the Pacific there rose to greet them savage rocklands and equally barbaric hostelries built that at tea-time one might drowse into a languid wicker bazaar glorified by the polo costumes of Southhampton and Lake Forest and Newport and Palm Beach. And, as the waves met and splashed and glittered in the most placid of the bays, so they joined this group and that, and with them shifted stations, murmuring ever of those strange unsubstantial gaieties in wait just over the next green and fruitful valley.

A simple healthy leisure class it was – the best of the men not unpleasantly undergraduate – they seemed to be on a perpetual candidates list for some etherealised 'Porcellian'[269] or 'Skull and Bones'[270] extended out indefinitely into the world; the women, of more than average beauty, fragilely athletic, somewhat idiotic as hostesses but charming and infinitely decorative as guests. Sedately and gracefully they danced the steps of their selection in the balmy tea hours, accomplishing with a certain dignity the movements so horribly burlesqued by clerk and chorus girl the country over. It seemed ironic that in this lone and discredited offspring of the arts Americans should excel, unquestionably.

Having danced and splashed through a lavish spring, Anthony and Gloria found that they had spent too much money and for this must go into retirement for a certain period. There was Anthony's 'work', they said. Almost before they knew it they were back in the grey house, more aware now that other lovers had slept there, other names had been called over the banisters, other couples had sat upon the porch steps watching the grey-green fields and the black bulk of woods beyond.

It was the same Anthony, more restless, inclined to quicken only under the stimulus of several highballs, faintly, almost imperceptibly, apathetic towards Gloria. But Gloria – she would be twenty-four in August and was in an attractive but sincere panic about it. Six years to thirty! Had she been less in love with Anthony her sense of the flight of time would have expressed itself in a reawakened interest in other men, in a deliberate intention of extracting a transient gleam of romance from every potential lover who glanced at her with lowered brows over a shining dinner table. She said to Anthony one day: 'How I feel is that if I wanted anything I'd take it. That's what I've always thought all my life. But it happens that I want you, and so I just haven't room for any other desires.'

They were bound eastward through a parched and lifeless Indiana, and she had looked up from one of her beloved moving-picture magazines to find a casual conversation suddenly turned grave.

Anthony frowned out of the car window. As the track crossed a country road a farmer appeared momentarily in his wagon; he was chewing on a straw and was apparently the same farmer they had passed a dozen times before, sitting in silent and malignant symbolism. As Anthony turned to Gloria his frown intensified.

'You worry me,' he objected; 'I can imagine *wanting* another woman under certain transitory circumstances, but I can't imagine taking her.'

'But I don't feel that way, Anthony. I can't be bothered resisting things I want. My way is not to want them – to want nobody but you.'

'Yet when I think that if you just happened to take a fancy to someone – '

'Oh, don't be an idiot!' she exclaimed. 'There'd be nothing casual about it. And I can't even imagine the possibility.'

This emphatically closed the conversation. Anthony's unfailing appreciation made her happier in his company than in anyone's else. She definitely enjoyed him – she loved him. So the summer began very much as had the one before.

There was, however, one radical change in the *ménage*. The icy-hearted Scandinavian, whose austere cooking and sardonic manner of waiting on table had so depressed Gloria, gave way to an exceedingly efficient Japanese whose name was Tanalahaka, but who confessed that he heeded any summons which included the dissyllable 'Tana'.

Tana was unusually small even for a Japanese, and displayed a somewhat naïve conception of himself as a man of the world. On the day of his arrival from 'R. Gugimoniki, Japanese Reliable Employment Agency', he called Anthony into his room to see the treasures of his trunk. These included a large collection of Japanese postcards, which he was all for explaining to his employer at once, individually and at great length. Among them were half a dozen of pornographic intent and plainly of American origin, though the makers had modestly omitted both their names and the form for mailing. He next brought out some of his own handiwork – a pair of American pants, which he had made himself, and two suits of solid silk underwear. He informed Anthony confidentially as to the purpose for which these latter were reserved. The next exhibit was a rather good copy of an etching of Abraham Lincoln, to whose face he had given an unmistakable Japanese cast. Last came a flute; he had made it himself but it was broken: he was going to fix it soon.

After these polite formalities, which Anthony conjectured must be native to Japan, Tana delivered a long harangue in splintered English on the relation of master and servant from which Anthony gathered that he had worked on large estates but had always quarrelled with the other servants because they were not honest. They had a great time over the word 'honest', and in fact became rather irritated with each other, because Anthony persisted stubbornly that Tana was trying to say 'hornets', and even went to the extent of buzzing in the manner of a bee and flapping his arms to imitate wings.

After three-quarters of an hour Anthony was released with the warm assurance that they would have other nice chats in which Tana would tell 'how we do in my countree'.

Such was Tana's garrulous première in the grey house – and he fulfilled its promise. Though he was conscientious and honourable, he was unquestionably a terrific bore. He seemed unable to control his tongue, sometimes continuing from paragraph to paragraph with a look akin to pain in his small brown eyes.

Sunday and Monday afternoons he read the comic sections of the newspapers. One cartoon which contained a facetious Japanese butler diverted him enormously, though he claimed that the protagonist, who to Anthony appeared clearly Oriental, had really an American face. The difficulty with the funny paper was that when, aided by

Anthony, he had spelled out the last three pictures and assimilated their context with a concentration surely adequate for Kant's *Critique*,[271] he had entirely forgotten what the first pictures were about.

In the middle of June, Anthony and Gloria celebrated their first anniversary by having a 'date'. Anthony knocked at the door and she ran to let him in. Then they sat together on the couch calling over those names they had made for each other, new combinations of endearments ages old. Yet to this 'date' was appended no attenuated good-night with its ecstasy of regret.

Later in June horror leered out at Gloria, struck at her and frightened her bright soul back half a generation. Then slowly it faded out, faded back into that impenetrable darkness whence it had come – taking relentlessly its modicum of youth.

With an infallible sense of the dramatic it chose a little railroad station in a wretched village near Portchester. The station platform lay all day bare as a prairie, exposed to the dusty yellow sun and to the glance of that most obnoxious type of countryman who lives near a metropolis and has attained its cheap smartness without its urbanity. A dozen of these yokels, red-eyed, cheerless as scarecrows, saw the incident. Dimly it passed across their confused and un-comprehending minds, taken at its broadest for a coarse joke, at its subtlest for a 'shame'. Meanwhile there upon the platform a measure of brightness faded from the world.

With Eric Merriam, Anthony had been sitting over a decanter of Scotch all the hot summer afternoon, while Gloria and Constance Merriam swam and sunned themselves at the Beach Club, the latter under a striped parasol-awning, Gloria stretched sensuously upon the soft hot sand, tanning her inevitable legs. Later they had all four played with inconsequential sandwiches; then Gloria had risen, tapping Anthony's knee with her parasol to get his attention.

'We've got to go, dear.'

'Now?' He looked at her unwillingly. At that moment nothing seemed of more importance than to idle on that shady porch drinking mellowed Scotch, while his host reminisced interminably on the by-play of some forgotten political campaign.

'We've really got to go,' repeated Gloria. 'We can get a taxi to the station . . . Come on, Anthony!' she commanded a bit more imperiously.

'Now see here – ' Merriam, his yarn cut off, made conventional objections, meanwhile provocatively filling his guest's glass with a highball that should have been sipped through ten minutes. But at Gloria's annoyed, 'We really *must*!' Anthony drank it off, got to his feet and made an elaborate bow to his hostess.

'It seems we "must",' he said, with little grace.

In a minute he was following Gloria down a garden-walk between tall rose bushes, her parasol brushing gently the June-blooming leaves. Most inconsiderate, he thought, as they reached the road. He felt with injured naïvety that Gloria should not have interrupted such innocent and harmless enjoyment. The whiskey had both soothed and clarified the restless things in his mind. It occurred to him that she had taken this same attitude several times before. Was he always to retreat from pleasant episodes at a touch of her parasol or a flicker of her eye? His unwillingness blurred to ill will, which rose within him like a resistless bubble. He kept silent, perversely inhibiting a desire to reproach her. They found a taxi in front of the Inn; rode silently to the little station . . .

Then Anthony knew what he wanted – to assert his will against this cool and impervious girl, to obtain with one magnificent effort a mastery that seemed infinitely desirable.

'Let's go over to see the Barneses,' he said without looking at her. 'I don't feel like going home.'

– Mrs Barnes, née Rachael Jerryl, had a summer place several miles from Redgate.

'We went there day before yesterday,' she answered shortly.

'I'm sure they'd be glad to see us.' He felt that that was not a strong enough note, braced himself stubbornly, and added: 'I want to see the Barneses. I haven't any desire to go home.'

'Well, I haven't any desire to go to the Barneses.'

Suddenly they stared at each other.

'Why, Anthony,' she said with annoyance, 'this is Sunday night and they probably have guests for supper. Why we should go in at this hour – '

'Then why couldn't we have stayed at the Merriams'?' he burst out. 'Why go home when we were having a perfectly decent time? They asked us to supper.'

'They had to. Give me the money and I'll get the railroad tickets.'

'I certainly will not! I'm in no humour for a ride in that damn hot train.'

Gloria stamped her foot on the platform.

'Anthony, you act as if you're tight!'

'On the contrary, I'm perfectly sober.'

But his voice had slipped into a husky key and she knew with certainty that this was untrue.

'If you're sober you'll give me the money for the tickets.'

But it was too late to talk to him that way. In his mind was but one idea – that Gloria was being selfish, that she was always being selfish and would continue to be unless here and now he asserted himself as her master. This was the occasion of all occasions, since for a whim she had deprived him of a pleasure. His determination solidified, approached momentarily a dull and sullen hate.

'I won't go in the train,' he said, his voice trembling a little with anger. 'We're going to the Barneses.'

'I'm not!' she cried. 'If you go, I'm going home alone.'

'Go on, then.'

Without a word she turned towards the ticket office; simultaneously he remembered that she had some money with her and that this was not the sort of victory he wanted, the sort he must have. He took a step after her and seized her arm.

'See here!' he muttered, 'you're *not* going alone!'

'I certainly am – why, Anthony!' This exclamation as she tried to pull away from him and he only tightened his grasp.

He looked at her with narrowed and malicious eyes.

'Let go!' Her cry had a quality of fierceness. 'If you have *any* decency you'll let go.'

'Why?' He knew why. But he took a confused and not quite confident pride in holding her there.

'I'm going home, do you understand? And you're going to let me go!'

'No, I'm not.'

Her eyes were burning now.

'Are you going to make a scene here?'

'I say you're not going! I'm tired of your eternal selfishness!'

'I only want to go home.' Two wrathful tears started from her eyes.

'This time you're going to do what *I* say.'

Slowly her body straightened: her head went back in a gesture of infinite scorn.

'I hate you!' Her low words were expelled like venom through her clenched teeth. 'Oh, *let* me go! Oh, I *hate* you!' She tried to jerk herself away but he only grasped the other arm. 'I hate you! I hate you!'

At Gloria's fury his uncertainty returned, but he felt that now he had gone too far to give in. It seemed that he had always given in and that in her heart she had despised him for it. Ah, she might hate him now, but afterwards she would admire him for his dominance.

The approaching train gave out a premonitory siren that tumbled melodramatically towards them down the glistening blue tracks. Gloria tugged and strained to free herself, and words older than the Book of Genesis came to her lips.

'Oh, you brute!' she sobbed. 'Oh, you brute! Oh, I hate you! Oh, you brute! Oh – '

On the station platform other prospective passengers were beginning to turn and stare; the drone of the train was audible, it increased to a clamour. Gloria's efforts redoubled, then ceased altogether, and she stood there trembling and hot-eyed at this helpless humiliation, as the engine roared and thundered into the station.

Low, below the flood of steam and the grinding of the brakes came her voice: 'Oh, if there was one *man* here you couldn't do this! You couldn't do this! You coward! You coward, oh, you coward!'

Anthony, silent, trembling himself, gripped her rigidly, aware that faces, dozens of them, curiously unmoved, shadows of a dream, were regarding him. Then the bells distilled metallic crashes that were like physical pain, the smoke-stacks volleyed in slow acceleration at the sky, and in a moment of noise and grey gaseous turbulence the line of faces ran by, moved off, became indistinct – until suddenly there was only the sun slanting east across the tracks and a volume of sound decreasing far off like a train made out of tin thunder. He dropped her arms. He had won.

Now, if he wished, he might laugh. The test was done and he had sustained his will with violence. Let leniency walk in the wake of victory.

'We'll hire a car here and drive back to Marietta,' he said with fine reserve.

For answer Gloria seized his hand with both of hers and raising it to her mouth bit deeply into his thumb. He scarcely noticed the pain; seeing the blood spurt, he absent-mindedly drew out his handkerchief and wrapped the wound. That too was part of the triumph he supposed – it was inevitable that defeat should thus be resented – and as such was beneath notice.

She was sobbing, almost without tears, profoundly and bitterly.

'I won't go! I won't go! You – can't – make – me – go! You've – you've killed any love I ever had for you, and any respect. But all that's left in me would die before I'd move from this place. Oh, if I'd thought *you'd* lay your hands on me – '

'You're going with me,' he said brutally, 'if I have to carry you.'

He turned, beckoned to a taxicab, told the driver to go to Marietta. The man dismounted and swung the door open. Anthony faced his wife and said between his clenched teeth: 'Will you get in? – or will I *put* you in?'

With a subdued cry of infinite pain and despair she yielded herself up and got into the car.

All the long ride, through the increasing dark of twilight, she sat huddled in her side of the car, her silence broken by an occasional dry and solitary sob. Anthony stared out the window, his mind working dully on the slowly changing significance of what had occurred. Something was wrong – that last cry of Gloria's had struck a chord which echoed posthumously and with incongruous disquiet in his heart. He must be right – yet, she seemed such a pathetic little thing now, broken and dispirited, humiliated beyond the measure of her lot to bear. The sleeves of her dress were torn; her parasol was gone, forgotten on the platform. It was a new costume, he remembered, and she had been so proud of it that very morning when they had left the house . . . He began wondering if anyone they knew had seen the incident. And persistently there recurred to him her cry: 'All that's left in me would die – '

This gave him a confused and increasing worry. It fitted so well with the Gloria who lay in the corner – no longer a proud Gloria, nor any Gloria he had known. He asked himself if it were possible. While he did not believe she would cease to love him – this, of course, was unthinkable – it was yet problematical whether Gloria without her arrogance, her independence, her virginal confidence and courage, would be the girl of his glory, the radiant woman who was precious and charming because she was ineffably, triumphantly herself.

He was very drunk even then, so drunk as not to realise his own drunkenness. When they reached the grey house he went to his own room and, his mind still wrestling helplessly and sombrely with what he had done, fell into a deep stupor on his bed.

It was after one o'clock and the hall seemed extraordinarily quiet when Gloria, wide-eyed and sleepless, traversed it and pushed open the door of his room. He had been too befuddled to open the windows and the air was stale and thick with whiskey. She stood for a moment by his bed, a slender, exquisitely graceful figure in her boyish silk pyjamas – then with abandon she flung herself upon him, half waking him in the frantic emotion of her embrace, dropping her warm tears upon his throat.

'Oh, Anthony!' she cried passionately, 'oh, my darling, you don't know what you did!'

Yet in the morning, coming early into her room, he knelt down by her bed and cried like a little boy, as though it was his heart that had been broken.

'It seemed, last night,' she said gravely, her fingers playing in his hair, 'that all the part of me you loved, the part that was worth knowing, all the pride and fire, was gone. I knew that what was left of me would always love you, but never in quite the same way.'

Nevertheless, she was aware even then that she would forget in time and that it is the manner of life seldom to strike but always to wear away. After that morning the incident was never mentioned and its deep wound healed with Anthony's hand – and if there was triumph some darker force than theirs possessed it, possessed the knowledge and the victory.

Gloria's independence, like all sincere and profound qualities, had begun unconsciously, but, once brought to her attention by Anthony's fascinated discovery of it, it assumed more nearly the proportions of a formal code. From her conversation it might be assumed that all her energy and vitality went into a violent affirmation of the negative principle 'Never give a damn.'

'Not for anything or anybody,' she said, 'except myself and, by implication, for Anthony. That's the rule of all life and if it weren't I'd be that way anyhow. Nobody'd do anything for me if it didn't gratify them to, and I'd do as little for them.'

She was on the front porch of the nicest lady in Marietta when she said this, and as she finished she gave a curious little cry and sank in a dead faint to the porch floor.

The lady brought her to and drove her home in her car. It had occurred to the estimable Gloria that she was probably with child.

She lay upon the long lounge downstairs. Day was slipping warmly out of the window, touching the late roses on the porch pillars.

'All I think of ever is that I love you,' she wailed. 'I value my body because you think it's beautiful. And this body of mine – of yours –

to have it grow ugly and shapeless? It's simply intolerable. Oh, Anthony, I'm not afraid of the pain.'

He consoled her desperately – but in vain. She continued: 'And then afterwards I might have wide hips and be pale, with all my freshness gone and no radiance in my hair.'

He paced the floor with his hands in his pockets, asking: 'Is it certain?'

'*I* don't know anything. I've always hated obstrics, or whatever you call them. I thought I'd have a child sometime. But not now.'

'Well, for God's sake don't lie there and go to pieces.'

Her sobs lapsed. She drew down a merciful silence from the twilight which filled the room. 'Turn on the lights,' she pleaded. 'These days seem so short – June seemed – to – have – longer days when I was a little girl.'

The lights snapped on and it was as though blue drapes of softest silk had been dropped behind the windows and the door. Her pallor, her immobility, without grief now, or joy, awoke his sympathy.

'Do you want me to have it?' she asked listlessly.

'I'm indifferent. That is, I'm neutral. If you have it I'll probably be glad. If you don't – well, that's all right too.'

'I wish you'd make up your mind one way or the other!'

'Suppose you make up *your* mind.'

She looked at him contemptuously, scorning to answer.

'You'd think you'd been singled out of all the women in the world for this crowning indignity.'

'What if I do!' she cried angrily. 'It isn't an indignity for them. It's their one excuse for living. It's the one thing they're good for. It *is* an indignity for *me*.

'See here, Gloria, I'm with you whatever you do, but for God's sake be a sport about it.'

'Oh, don't *fuss* at me!' she wailed.

They exchanged a mute look of no particular significance but of much stress. Then Anthony took a book from the shelf and dropped into a chair.

Half an hour later her voice came out of the intense stillness that pervaded the room and hung like incense on the air.

'I'll drive over and see Constance Merriam tomorrow.'

'All right. And I'll go to Tarrytown and see grampa.'

' – You see,' she added, 'it isn't that I'm afraid – of this or anything else. I'm being true to me, you know.'

'I know,' he agreed.

THE PRACTICAL MEN

Adam Patch, in a pious rage against the Germans, subsisted on the war news. Pin-maps plastered his walls; atlases were piled deep on tables convenient to his hand together with 'Photographic Histories of the World War', official Explain-alls, and the 'Personal Impressions' of war correspondents and of Privates X, Y and Z. Several times during Anthony's visit his grandfather's secretary, Edward Shuttleworth, the one-time 'accomplished gin-physician' of 'Pat's Place' in Hoboken,[272] now shod with righteous indignation, would appear with an extra. The old man attacked each paper with untiring fury, tearing out those columns which appeared to him of sufficient pregnancy for preservation and thrusting them into one of his already bulging files.

'Well, what have you been doing?' he asked Anthony blandly. 'Nothing? Well, I thought so. I've been intending to drive over and see you, all summer.'

'I've been writing. Don't you remember the essay I sent you – the one I sold to *The Florentine* last winter?'

'Essay? You never sent *me* any essay.'

'Oh, yes, I did. We talked about it.'

Adam Patch shook his head mildly.

'Oh, no. You never sent *me* any essay. You may have thought you sent it but it never reached me.'

'Why, you read it, grampa,' insisted Anthony, somewhat exasperated, 'you read it and disagreed with it.'

The old man suddenly remembered, but this was made apparent only by a partial falling open of his mouth, displaying rows of grey gums. Eying Anthony with a green and ancient stare he hesitated between confessing his error and covering it up.

'So you're writing,' he said quickly. 'Well, why don't you go over and write about these Germans? Write something real, something about what's going on, something people can read.'

'Anybody can't be a war correspondent,' objected Anthony. 'You have to have some newspaper willing to buy your stuff. And I can't spare the money to go over as a freelance.'

'I'll send you over,' suggested his grandfather surprisingly. 'I'll get you over as an authorised correspondent of any newspaper you pick out.'

Anthony recoiled from the idea – almost simultaneously he bounded towards it.

'I – don't – know – '

He would have to leave Gloria, whose whole life yearned towards him and enfolded him. Gloria was in trouble. Oh, the thing wasn't feasible – yet; he saw himself in khaki, leaning, as all war correspondents lean, upon a heavy stick, portfolio at shoulder – trying to look like an Englishman. 'I'd like to think it over,' he, confessed. 'It's certainly very kind of you. I'll think it over and I'll let you know.'

Thinking it over absorbed him on the journey to New York. He had had one of those sudden flashes of illumination vouchsafed to all men who are dominated by a strong and beloved woman, which show them a world of harder men, more fiercely trained and grappling with the abstractions of thought and war. In that world the arms of Gloria would exist only as the hot embrace of a chance mistress, coolly sought and quickly forgotten . . .

These unfamiliar phantoms were crowding closely about him when he boarded his train for Marietta, in the Grand Central Station. The car was crowded; he secured the last vacant seat and it was only after several minutes that he gave even a casual glance to the man beside him. When he did he saw a heavy lay of jaw and nose, a curved chin and small, puffed-under eyes. In a moment he recognised Joseph Bloeckman.

Simultaneously they both half rose, were half embarrassed, and exchanged what amounted to a half handshake. Then, as though to complete the matter, they both half laughed.

'Well,' remarked Anthony without inspiration, 'I haven't seen you for a long time.' Immediately he regretted his words and started to add: 'I didn't know you lived out this way.' But Bloeckman anticipated him by asking pleasantly: 'How's your wife? . . . '

'She's very well. How've you been?'

'Excellent.' His tone amplified the grandeur of the word.

It seemed to Anthony that during the last year Bloeckman had grown tremendously in dignity. The boiled look was gone, he seemed 'done' at last. In addition he was no longer overdressed. The inappropriate facetiousness he had affected in ties had given way to a sturdy dark pattern, and his right hand, which had formerly displayed two heavy rings, was now innocent of ornament and even without the raw glow of a manicure.

This dignity appeared also in his personality. The last aura of the successful travelling-man had faded from him, that deliberate ingratiation of which the lowest form is the bawdy joke in the Pullman smoker.[273] One imagined that, having been fawned upon financially, he had attained aloofness; having been snubbed socially, he had acquired reticence. But whatever had given him weight instead of bulk, Anthony no longer felt a correct superiority in his presence.

'D'you remember Caramel, Richard Caramel? I believe you met him one night.'

'I remember. He was writing a book.'

'Well, he sold it to the movies. Then they had some scenario man named Jordan work on it. Well, Dick subscribes to a clipping bureau and he's furious because about half the movie reviewers speak of the "power and strength of William Jordan's *Demon Lover*". Didn't mention old Dick at all. You'd think this fellow Jordan had actually conceived and developed the thing.'

Bloeckman nodded comprehensively.

'Most of the contracts state that the original writer's name goes into all the paid publicity. Is Caramel still writing?'

'Oh, yes. Writing hard. Short stories.'

'Well, that's fine, that's fine . . . You on this train often?'

'About once a week. We live in Marietta.'

'Is that so? Well, well! I live near Cos Cob myself. Bought a place there only recently. We're only five miles apart.'

'You'll have to come and see us.' Anthony was surprised at his own courtesy. 'I'm sure Gloria'd be delighted to see an old friend. Anybody'll tell you where the house is – it's our second season there.'

'Thank you.' Then, as though returning a complementary politeness: 'How is your grandfather?'

'He's been well. I had lunch with him today.'

'A great character,' said Bloeckman severely. 'A fine example of an American.'

THE TRIUMPH OF LETHARGY

Anthony found his wife deep in the porch hammock voluptuously engaged with a lemonade and a tomato sandwich and carrying on an apparently cheery conversation with Tana upon one of Tana's complicated themes.

'In my countree,' Anthony recognised his invariable preface, 'all time – peoples – eat rice – because haven't got. Cannot eat what no have got.' Had his nationality not been desperately apparent one would have thought he had acquired his knowledge of his native land from American primary-school geographies.

When the Oriental had been squelched and dismissed to the kitchen, Anthony turned questioningly to Gloria: 'It's all right,' she announced, smiling broadly. 'And it surprised me more than it does you.'

'There's no doubt?'

'None! Couldn't be!'

They rejoiced happily, gay again with reborn irresponsibility. Then he told her of his opportunity to go abroad, and that he was almost ashamed to reject it.

'What do *you* think? Just tell me frankly.'

'Why, Anthony!' Her eyes were startled. 'Do you want to go? Without me?'

His face fell – yet he knew, with his wife's question, that it was too late. Her arms, sweet and strangling, were around him, for he had made all such choices back in that room in the Plaza the year before. This was an anachronism from an age of such dreams.

'Gloria,' he lied, in a great burst of comprehension, 'of course I don't. I was thinking you might go as a nurse or something.' He wondered dully if his grandfather would consider this.

As she smiled he realised again how beautiful she was, a gorgeous girl of miraculous freshness and sheerly honourable eyes. She embraced his suggestion with luxurious intensity, holding it aloft like a sun of her own making and basking in its beams. She strung together an amazing synopsis for an extravaganza of martial adventure.

After supper, surfeited with the subject, she yawned. She wanted not to talk but only to read *Penrod*,[274] stretched upon the lounge until at midnight she fell asleep. But Anthony, after he had carried her romantically up the stairs, stayed awake to brood upon the day, vaguely angry with her, vaguely dissatisfied.

'What am I going to do?' he began at breakfast. 'Here we've been married a year and we've just worried around without even being efficient people of leisure.'

'Yes, you ought to do something,' she admitted, being in an agreeable and loquacious humour. This was not the first of these discussions, but as they usually developed Anthony in the role of protagonist, she had come to avoid them.

'It's not that I have any moral compunctions about work,' he continued, 'but grampa may die tomorrow and he may live for ten years. Meanwhile we're living above our income and all we've got to show for it is a farmer's car and a few clothes. We keep an apartment that we've only lived in three months and a little old house way off in nowhere. We're frequently bored and yet we won't make any effort to know anyone except the same crowd who drift around California all summer wearing sports clothes and waiting for their families to die.'

'How you've changed!' remarked Gloria. 'Once you told me you didn't see why an American couldn't loaf gracefully.'

'Well, damn it, I wasn't married. And the old mind was working at top speed and now it's going round and round like a cog-wheel with nothing to catch it. As a matter of fact I think that if I hadn't met you I *would* have done something. But you make leisure so subtly attractive – '

'Oh, it's all my fault – '

'I didn't mean that, and you know I didn't. But here I'm almost twenty-seven and – '

'Oh,' she interrupted in vexation, 'you make me tired! Talking as though I were objecting or hindering you!'

'I was just discussing it, Gloria. Can't I discuss – '

'I should think you'd be strong enough to settle – '

' – something with you without – '

' – your own problems without coming to me. You *talk* a lot about going to work. I could use more money very easily, but *I'm* not complaining. Whether you work or not I love you.' Her last words were gentle as fine snow upon hard ground. But for the moment neither was attending to the other – they were each engaged in polishing and perfecting their own attitude.

'I have worked – some.' This by Anthony was an imprudent bringing up of raw reserves. Gloria laughed, torn between delight and derision; she resented his sophistry as at the same time she admired his nonchalance. She would never blame him for being the ineffectual idler so long as he did it sincerely, from the attitude that nothing much was worth doing.

'Work!' she scoffed. 'Oh, you sad bird! You bluffer! Work – that means a great arranging of the desk and the lights, a great sharpening of pencils, and "Gloria, don't sing!" and "Please keep that damn Tana away from me", and "Let me read you my opening sentence", and "I won't be through for a long time, Gloria, so don't stay up for me", and a tremendous consumption of tea or coffee. And that's all. In just about an hour I hear the old pencil stop scratching and look over. You've got out a book and you're "looking up" something. Then you're reading. Then yawns – then bed and a great tossing about because you're all full of caffeine and can't sleep. Two weeks later the whole performance over again.'

With much difficulty Anthony retained a scanty breech-clout of dignity.

'Now that's a *slight* exaggeration. You know *darn well* I sold an essay to *The Florentine* – and it attracted a lot of attention considering the circulation of *The Florentine*. And what's more, Gloria, you know I sat up till five o'clock in the morning finishing it.'

She lapsed into silence, giving him rope. And if he had not hanged himself he had certainly come to the end of it.

'At least,' he concluded feebly, 'I'm perfectly willing to be a war correspondent.'

But so was Gloria. They were both willing – anxious; they assured each other of it. The evening ended on a note of tremendous sentiment, the majesty of leisure, the ill health of Adam Patch, love at any cost.

'Anthony!' she called over the bannister one afternoon a week later, 'there's someone at the door.' Anthony, who had been lolling in the hammock on the sun-speckled south porch, strolled around to the front of the house. A foreign car, large and impressive, crouched like an immense and saturnine bug at the foot of the path. A man in a soft pongee suit, with cap to match, hailed him.

'Hello there, Patch. Ran over to call on you.'

It was Bloeckman; as always, infinitesimally improved, of subtler intonation, of more convincing ease.

'I'm awfully glad you did.' Anthony raised his voice to a vine-covered window: 'Glor-i-*a*! We've got a visitor!'

'I'm in the tub,' wailed Gloria politely.

With a smile the two men acknowledged the triumph of her alibi.

'She'll be down. Come round here on the side-porch. Like a drink? Gloria's always in the tub – good third of every day.'

'Pity she doesn't live on the Sound.'

'Can't afford it.'

As coming from Adam Patch's grandson, Bloeckman took this as a form of pleasantry. After fifteen minutes filled with estimable brilliancies, Gloria appeared, fresh in starched yellow, bringing atmosphere and an increase of vitality.

'I want to be a successful sensation in the movies,' she announced. 'I hear that Mary Pickford[275] makes a million dollars annually.'

'You could, you know,' said Bloeckman. 'I think you'd film very well.'

'Would you let me, Anthony? If I only play unsophisticated roles?'

As the conversation continued in stilted commas, Anthony wondered that to him and Bloeckman both this girl had once been the most stimulating, the most tonic personality they had ever known – and now the three sat like over-oiled machines, without conflict, without fear, without elation, heavily enamelled little figures secure beyond enjoyment in a world where death and war, dull emotion and noble savagery were covering a continent with the smoke of terror.

In a moment he would call Tana and they would pour into themselves a gay and delicate poison which would restore them momentarily to the pleasurable excitement of childhood, when every face in a crowd had carried its suggestion of splendid and significant transactions taking place somewhere to some magnificent and illimitable purpose . . . Life was no more than this summer afternoon; a faint wind stirring the lace collar of Gloria's dress; the slow baking drowsiness of the veranda . . . Intolerably unmoved they all seemed, removed from any romantic iminency of action. Even Gloria's beauty needed wild emotions, needed poignancy, needed death . . .

' . . . Any day next week,' Bloeckman was saying to Gloria. 'Here – take this card. What they do is to give you a test of about three hundred feet of film, and they can tell pretty accurately from that.'

'How about Wednesday?'

'Wednesday's fine. Just phone me and I'll go around with you – '

He was on his feet, shaking hands briskly – then his car was a wraith of dust down the road. Anthony turned to his wife in bewilderment.

'Why, Gloria!'

'You don't mind if I have a trial, Anthony. Just a trial? I've got to go to town Wednesday, *any*how.'

'But it's so silly! You don't want to go into the movies – moon around a studio all day with a lot of cheap chorus people.'

'Lot of mooning around Mary Pickford does!'

'Everybody isn't a Mary Pickford.'

'Well, I can't see how you'd object to my *try*ing.'

'I do, though. I hate actors.'

'Oh, you make me tired. Do you imagine I have a very thrilling time dozing on this damn porch?'

'You wouldn't mind if you loved me.'

'Of course I love you,' she said impatiently, making out a quick case for herself. 'It's just because I do that I hate to see you go to pieces by just lying around and saying you ought to work. Perhaps if I *did* go into this for a while it'd stir you up so you'd do something.'

'It's just your craving for excitement, that's all it is.'

'Maybe it is! It's a perfectly natural craving, isn't it?'

'Well, I'll tell you one thing. If you go into the movies I'm going to Europe.'

'Well, go on then! *I'm* not stopping you!'

To show she was not stopping him she melted into melancholy tears. Together they marshalled the armies of sentiment – words, kisses, endearments, self-reproaches. They attained nothing. Inevitably they attained nothing. Finally, in a burst of gargantuan emotion each of them sat down and wrote a letter. Anthony's was to his grandfather; Gloria's was to Joseph Bloeckman. It was a triumph of lethargy.

One day early in July Anthony, returned from an afternoon in New York, called upstairs to Gloria. Receiving no answer he guessed she was asleep and so went into the pantry for one of the little sandwiches that were always prepared for them. He found Tana seated at the kitchen table before a miscellaneous assortment of odds and ends – cigar-boxes, knives, pencils, the tops of cans, and some scraps of paper covered with elaborate figures and diagrams.

'What the devil you doing?' demanded Anthony curiously.

Tana politely grinned.

'I show you,' he exclaimed enthusiastically. 'I tell – '

'You making a dog-house?'

'No, sa.' Tana grinned again. 'Make typewutta.'

'Typewriter?'

'Yes, sa. I think, oh all time I think, lie in bed think 'bout typewutta.'

'So you thought you'd make one, eh?'

'Wait. I tell.'

Anthony, munching a sandwich, leaned leisurely against the sink.

Tana opened and closed his mouth several times as though testing its capacity for action. Then with a rush he began: 'I been think – typewutta – has, oh, many many many many *thing*. Oh many many many many.'

'Many keys. I see.'

'No-o? *Yes* – key! Many many many many lettah. Like so a-b-c.'

'Yes, you're right.'

'Wait. I tell.' He screwed his face up in a tremendous effort to express himself: 'I been think – many words – end same. Like e-n-g.'

'You bet. A whole raft of them.'

'So – I make – typewutta – quick. Not so many lettah – '

'That's a great idea, Tana. Save time. You'll make a fortune. Press one key and there's "ing". Hope you work it out.'

Tana laughed disparagingly. 'Wait. I tell – '

'Where's Mrs Patch?'

'She out. Wait, I tell – ' Again he screwed up his face for action. '*My* typewutta – '

'Where is she?'

'Here – I make.' He pointed to the miscellany of junk on the table.

'I mean Mrs Patch.'

'She out.' Tana reassured him. 'She be back five o'clock, she say.'

'Down in the village?'

'No. Went off before lunch. She go Mr Bloeckman.'

Anthony started.

'Went out with Mr Bloeckman?'

'She be back five.'

Without a word Anthony left the kitchen with Tana's disconsolate 'I tell' trailing after him. So this was Gloria's idea of excitement, by God! His fists were clenched; within a moment he had worked himself up to a tremendous pitch of indignation. He went to the door and looked out; there was no car in sight and his watch stood at four minutes of five. With furious energy he dashed down to the end of the path – as far as the bend of the road a mile off he could see no car – except – but it was a farmer's flivver. Then, in an undignified pursuit of dignity, he rushed back to the shelter of the house as quickly as he had rushed out.

Pacing up and down the living-room he began an angry rehearsal of the speech he would make to her when she came in –

'So this is love!' he would begin – or no, it sounded too much like the popular phrase 'So this is Paris!' He must be dignified, hurt, grieved. Anyhow – 'So this is what *you* do when I have to go up and trot all day around the hot city on business. No wonder I can't write! No wonder I don't dare let you out of my sight!' He was expanding now, warming to his subject. 'I'll tell you,' he continued, 'I'll tell you – ' He paused, catching a familiar ring in the words – then he realised – it was Tana's 'I tell'.

Yet Anthony neither laughed nor seemed absurd to himself. To his frantic imagination it was already six – seven – eight, and she was never coming! Bloeckman finding her bored and unhappy had persuaded her to go to California with him . . .

– There was a great to-do out in front, a joyous, 'Yoho, Anthony!'

and he rose trembling, weakly happy to see her fluttering up the path. Bloeckman was following, cap in hand.

'Dearest!' she cried. 'We've been for the best jaunt – all over New York State.'

'I'll have to be starting home,' said Bloeckman, almost immediately. 'Wish you'd both been here when I came.'

'I'm sorry I wasn't,' answered Anthony dryly. When he had departed Anthony hesitated. The fear was gone from his heart, yet he felt that some protest was ethically apropos. Gloria resolved his uncertainty.

'I knew you wouldn't mind. He came just before lunch and said he had to go to Garrison on business and wouldn't I go with him. He looked so lonesome, Anthony. And I drove his car all the way.'

Listlessly Anthony dropped into a chair, his mind tired – tired with nothing, tired with everything, with the world's weight he had never chosen to bear. He was ineffectual and vaguely helpless here as he had always been. One of those personalities who, in spite of all their words, are inarticulate, he seemed to have inherited only the vast tradition of human failure – that, and the sense of death.

'I suppose I don't care,' he answered.

One must be broad about these things, and Gloria being young, being beautiful, must have reasonable privileges. Yet it wearied him that he failed to understand.

WINTER

She rolled over on her back and lay still for a moment in the great bed watching the February sun suffer one last attenuated refinement in its passage through the leaded panes into the room. For a time she had no accurate sense of her whereabouts or of the events of the day before, or the day before that; then, like a suspended pendulum, memory began to beat out its story, releasing with each swing a burdened quota of time until her life was given back to her.

She could hear, now, Anthony's troubled breathing beside her; she could smell whiskey and cigarette smoke. She noticed that she lacked complete muscular control; when she moved it was not a sinuous motion with the resultant strain distributed easily over her body – it was a tremendous effort of her nervous system as though each time she were hypnotising herself into performing an impossible action . . .

She was in the bathroom, brushing her teeth to get rid of that intolerable taste; then back by the bedside listening to the rattle of Bounds's key in the outer door.

'Wake up, Anthony!' she said sharply.

She climbed into bed beside him and closed her eyes. Almost the last thing she remembered was a conversation with Mr and Mrs Lacy. Mrs Lacy had said, 'Sure you don't want us to get you a taxi?' and Anthony had replied that he guessed they could walk over to Fifth all right. Then they had both attempted, imprudently, to bow – and collapsed absurdly into a battalion of empty milk bottles just outside the door. There must have been two dozen milk bottles standing open-mouthed in the dark. She could conceive of no plausible explanation for those milk bottles. Perhaps they had been attracted by the singing in the Lacy house and had hurried over agape with wonder to see the fun. Well, they'd had the worst of it – though it seemed that she and Anthony never would get up, the perverse things rolled so . . .

Still, they had found a taxi. 'My meter's broken and it'll cost you a dollar and a half to get home,' said the taxi driver. 'Well,' said Anthony, 'I'm young Packy McFarland[276] and if you'll come down here I'll beat you till you can't stand up' . . . At that point the man had driven off without them. They must have found another taxi, for they were in the apartment . . .

'What time is it?' Anthony was sitting up in bed, staring at her with owlish precision.

This was obviously a rhetorical question. Gloria could think of no reason why she should be expected to know the time.

'Golly, I feel like the devil!' muttered Anthony dispassionately. Relaxing, he tumbled back upon his pillow. 'Bring on your grim reaper!'

'Anthony, how'd we finally get home last night?'

'Taxi.'

'Oh!' Then, after a pause: 'Did you put me to bed?'

'I don't know. Seems to me you put *me* to bed. What day is it?'

'Tuesday.'

'Tuesday? I hope so. If it's Wednesday, I've got to start work at that idiotic place. Supposed to be down at nine or some such ungodly hour.'

'Ask Bounds,' suggested Gloria feebly.

'Bounds!' he called.

Sprightly, sober – a voice from a world that it seemed in the past two days they had left for ever, Bounds sprang in short steps down the hall and appeared in the half-darkness of the door.

'What day, Bounds?'

'February the twenty-second, I think, sir.'

'I mean day of the week.'

'Tuesday, sir.'

'Thanks.'

After a pause: 'Are you ready for breakfast, sir?'

'Yes, and Bounds, before you get it, will you make a pitcher of water, and set it here beside the bed? I'm a little thirsty.'

'Yes, sir.'

Bounds retreated in sober dignity down the hallway.

'Lincoln's birthday,' affirmed Anthony without enthusiasm, 'or St Valentine's or somebody's. When did we start on this insane party?'

'Sunday night.'

'After prayers?' he suggested sardonically.

'We raced all over town in those hansoms and Maury sat up with his driver, don't you remember? Then we came home and he tried to cook some bacon – came out of the pantry with a few blackened remains, insisting it was "fried to the proverbial crisp".'

Both of them laughed, spontaneously but with some difficulty, and lying there side by side reviewed the chain of events that had ended in this rusty and chaotic dawn.

They had been in New York for almost four months, since the country had grown too cool in late October. They had given up California this year, partly because of lack of funds, partly with the idea of going abroad should this interminable war, persisting now into its second year, end during the winter. Of late their income had lost elasticity; no longer did it stretch to cover gay whims and pleasant extravagances, and Anthony had spent many puzzled and unsatisfactory hours over a densely figured pad, making remarkable budgets that left huge margins for 'amusements, trips, etc.', and trying to apportion, even approximately, their past expenditures.

He remembered a time when in going on a 'party' with his two best friends, he and Maury had invariably paid more than their share of the expenses. They would buy the tickets for the theatre or squabble between themselves for the dinner check. It had seemed fitting; Dick, with his naïvety and his astonishing fund of information about himself, had been a diverting, almost juvenile, figure – court jester to their royalty. But this was no longer true. It was Dick who always had money; it was Anthony who entertained within limitations –

always excepting occasional wild, wine-inspired, cheque-cashing parties – and it was Anthony who was solemn about it next morning and told the scornful and disgusted Gloria that they'd have to be 'more careful next time'.

In the two years since the publication of *The Demon Lover*, Dick had made over twenty-five thousand dollars, most of it lately, when the reward of the author of fiction had begun to swell unprecedentedly as a result of the voracious hunger of the motion pictures for plots. He received seven hundred dollars for every story, at that time a large emolument for such a young man – he was not quite thirty – and for every one that contained enough 'action' (kissing, shooting and sacrificing) for the movies, he obtained an additional thousand. His stories varied; there was a measure of vitality and a sort of instinctive technique in all of them, but none attained the personality of *The Demon Lover*, and there were several that Anthony considered downright cheap. These, Dick explained severely, were to widen his audience. Wasn't it true that men who had attained real permanence from Shakespeare to Mark Twain had appealed to the many as well as to the elect?

Though Anthony and Maury disagreed, Gloria told him to go ahead and make as much money as he could – that was the only thing that counted anyhow . . .

Maury, a little stouter, faintly mellower, and more complaisant, had gone to work in Philadelphia. He came to New York once or twice a month and on such occasions the four of them travelled the popular routes from dinner to the theatre, thence to the Frolic or, perhaps, at the urging of the ever-curious Gloria, to one of the cellars of Greenwich Village, notorious through the furious but short-lived vogue of the 'new poetry movement'.

In January, after many monologues directed at his reticent wife, Anthony determined to 'get something to do', for the winter at any rate. He wanted to please his grandfather and even, in a measure, to see how he liked it himself. He discovered during several tentative semi-social calls that employers were not interested in a young man who was only going to 'try it for a few months or so'. As the grandson of Adam Patch he was received everywhere with marked courtesy, but the old man was a back number now – the heyday of his fame as first an 'oppressor' and then an uplifter of the people had been during the twenty years preceding his retirement. Anthony even found several of the younger men who were under the impression that Adam Patch had been dead for some years.

Eventually Anthony went to his grandfather and asked his advice, which turned out to be that he should enter the bond business as a salesman, a tedious suggestion to Anthony, but one that in the end he determined to follow. Sheer money in deft manipulation had fascinations under all circumstances, while almost any side of manufacturing would be insufferably dull. He considered newspaper work but decided that the hours were not ordered for a married man. And he lingered over pleasant fancies of himself either as editor of a brilliant weekly of opinion, an American *Mercure de France*,[277] or as scintillant producer of satiric comedy and Parisian musical revue. However, the approaches to these latter guilds seemed to be guarded by professional secrets. Men drifted into them by the devious highways of writing and acting. It was palpably impossible to get on a magazine unless you had been on one before.

So in the end he entered, by way of his grandfather's letter, that Sanctum Americanum where sat the president of Wilson, Hiemer and Hardy at his 'cleared desk', and issued therefrom employed. He was to begin work on the twenty-third of February.

In tribute to the momentous occasion this two-day revel had been planned, since, he said, after he began working he'd have to get to bed early during the week. Maury Noble had arrived from Philadelphia on a trip that had to do with seeing some man in Wall Street (whom, incidentally, he failed to see), and Richard Caramel had been half persuaded, half tricked into joining them. They had condescended to a wet and fashionable wedding on Monday afternoon, and in the evening had occurred the dénouement: Gloria, going beyond her accustomed limit of four precisely timed cocktails, led them on as gay and joyous a bacchanal as they had ever known, disclosing an astonishing knowledge of ballet steps, and singing songs which she confessed had been taught her by her cook when she was innocent and seventeen. She repeated these by request at intervals throughout the evening with such frank conviviality that Anthony, far from being annoyed, was gratified at this fresh source of entertainment. The occasion was memorable in other ways – a long conversation between Maury and a defunct crab, which he was dragging around on the end of a string, as to whether the crab was fully conversant with the applications of the binomial theorem, and the aforementioned race in two hansom cabs with the sedate and impressive shadows of Fifth Avenue for audience, ending in a labyrinthine escape into the darkness of Central Park. Finally Anthony and Gloria had paid a call on some wild young married people – the Lacys – and collapsed in the empty milk bottles.

Morning now – theirs to add up the cheques cashed here and there in clubs, stores, restaurants. Theirs to air the dank staleness of wine and cigarettes out of the tall blue front room, to pick up the broken glass and brush at the stained fabric of chairs and sofas; to give Bounds suits and dresses for the cleaners; finally, to take their smothery half-feverish bodies and faded depressed spirits out into the chill air of February, that life might go on and Wilson, Hiemer and Hardy obtain the services of a vigorous man at nine next morning.

'Do you remember,' called Anthony from the bathroom, 'when Maury got out at the corner of One Hundred and Tenth Street and acted as a traffic cop, beckoning cars forward and motioning them back? They must have thought he was a private detective.'

After each reminiscence they both laughed inordinately, their overwrought nerves responding as acutely and janglingly to mirth as to depression.

Gloria at the mirror was wondering at the splendid colour and freshness of her face – it seemed that she had never looked so well, though her stomach hurt her and her head was aching furiously.

The day passed slowly. Anthony, riding in a taxi to his broker's to borrow money on a bond, found that he had only two dollars in his pocket. The fare would cost all of that, but he felt that on this particular afternoon he could not have endured the subway. When the taximetre reached his limit he must get out and walk.

With this his mind drifted off into one of its characteristic day-dreams . . . In this dream he discovered that the metre was going too fast – the driver had dishonestly adjusted it. Calmly he reached his destination and then nonchalantly handed the man what he justly owed him. The man showed fight, but almost before his hands were up Anthony had knocked him down with one terrific blow. And when he rose Anthony quickly sidestepped and floored him definitively with a crack to the temple.

. . . He was in court now. The judge had fined him five dollars and he had no money. Would the court take his cheque? Ah, but the court did not know him. Well, he could identify himself by having them call his apartment.

. . . They did so. Yes, it was Mrs Anthony Patch speaking – but how did she know that this man was her husband? How could she know? Let the police sergeant ask her if she remembered the milk bottles . . .

He leaned forward hurriedly and tapped at the glass. The taxi was only at Brooklyn Bridge, but the metre showed a dollar and eighty cents, and Anthony would never have omitted the ten-per-cent tip.

Later in the afternoon he returned to the apartment. Gloria had also been out – shopping – and was asleep, curled in a corner of the sofa with her purchase locked securely in her arms. Her face was as untroubled as a little girl's, and the bundle that she pressed tightly to her bosom was a child's doll, a profound and infinitely healing balm to her disturbed and childish heart.

DESTINY

It was with this party, more especially with Gloria's part in it, that a decided change began to come over their way of living. The magnificent attitude of not giving a damn altered overnight; from being a mere tenet of Gloria's it became the entire solace and justification for what they chose to do and what consequence it brought. Not to be sorry, not to loose one cry of regret, to live according to a clear code of honour towards each other, and to seek the moment's happiness as fervently and persistently as possible.

'No one cares about us but ourselves, Anthony,' she said one day. 'It'd be ridiculous for me to go about pretending I felt any obligations towards the world, and as for worrying what people think about me, I simply *don't*, that's all. Since I was a little girl in dancing-school I've been criticised by the mothers of all the little girls who weren't as popular as I was, and I've always looked on criticism as a sort of envious tribute.'

This was because of a party in the Boul' Mich' one night, where Constance Merriam had seen her as one of a highly stimulated party of four. Constance Merriam, 'as an old school friend', had gone to the trouble of inviting her to lunch next day in order to inform her how terrible it was.

'I told her I couldn't see it,' Gloria told Anthony. 'Eric Merriam is a sort of sublimated Percy Wolcott – you remember that man in Hot Springs I told you about – his idea of respecting Constance is to leave her at home with her sewing and her baby and her book, and such innocuous amusements, whenever he's going on a party that promises to be anything but deathly dull.'

'Did you tell her that?'

'I certainly did. And I told her that what she really objected to was that I was having a better time than she was.'

Anthony applauded her. He was tremendously proud of Gloria, proud that she never failed to eclipse whatever other women might be in the party, proud that men were always glad to revel with her in great rowdy groups, without any attempt to do more than enjoy her beauty and the warmth of her vitality.

These 'parties' gradually became their chief source of entertainment. Still in love, still enormously interested in each other, they yet found as spring drew near that staying at home in the evening palled on them; books were unreal; the old magic of being alone had long since vanished – instead they preferred to be bored by a stupid musical comedy, or to go to dinner with the most uninteresting of their acquaintances, so long as there would be enough cocktails to keep the conversation from becoming utterly intolerable. A scattering of younger married people who had been their friends in school or college, as well as a varied assortment of single men, began to think instinctively of them whenever colour and excitement were needed, so there was scarcely a day without its phone call, its, 'Wondered what you were doing this evening.' Wives, as a rule, were afraid of Gloria – her facile attainment of the centre of the stage, her innocent but nevertheless disturbing way of becoming a favourite with husbands – these things drove them instinctively into an attitude of profound distrust, heightened by the fact that Gloria was largely unresponsive to any intimacy shown her by a woman.

On the appointed Wednesday in February Anthony had gone to the imposing offices of Wilson, Hiemer and Hardy and listened to many vague instructions delivered by an energetic young man of about his own age, named Kahler, who wore a defiant yellow pompadour, and in announcing himself as an assistant secretary gave the impression that it was a tribute to exceptional ability.

'There's two kinds of men here, you'll find,' he said. 'There's the man who gets to be an assistant secretary or treasurer, gets his name on our folder here, before he's thirty, and there's the man who gets his name there at forty-five. The man who gets his name there at forty-five stays there the rest of his life.'

'How about the man who gets it there at thirty?' enquired Anthony politely.

'Why, he gets up here, you see.' He pointed to a list of assistant vice-presidents upon the folder. 'Or maybe he gets to be president or secretary or treasurer.'

'And what about these over here?'

'Those? Oh, those are the trustees – the men with capital.'

'I see.'

'Now some people,' continued Kahler, 'think that whether a man gets started early or late depends on whether he's got a college education. But they're wrong.'

'I see.'

'I had one; I was Buckleigh, class of nineteen-eleven, but when I came down to the Street I soon found that the things that would help me here weren't the fancy things I learned in college. In fact, I had to get a lot of fancy stuff out of my head.'

Anthony could not help wondering what possible 'fancy stuff' he had learned at Buckleigh in nineteen-eleven. An irrepressible idea that it was some sort of needlework recurred to him throughout the rest of the conversation.

'See that fellow over there?' Kahler pointed to a youngish-looking man with handsome grey hair, sitting at a desk inside a mahogany railing. 'That's Mr Ellinger, the first vice-president. Been every-where, seen everything; got a fine education.'

In vain did Anthony try to open his mind to the romance of finance; he could think of Mr Ellinger only as one of the buyers of the handsome leather sets of Thackeray,[278] Balzac,[279] Hugo[280] and Gibbon[281] that lined the walls of the big bookstores.

Through the damp and uninspiring month of March he was prepared for salesmanship. Lacking enthusiasm he was capable of viewing the turmoil and bustle that surrounded him only as a fruitless circumambient striving towards an incomprehensible goal, tangibly evidenced only by the rival mansions of Mr Frick and Mr Carnegie on Fifth Avenue.[282] That these portentous vice-presidents and trustees should be actually the fathers of the 'best men' he had known at Harvard seemed to him incongruous.

He ate in an employees' lunch-room upstairs with an uneasy sus-picion that he was being uplifted, wondering through that first week if the dozens of young clerks, some of them alert and immaculate, and just out of college, lived in flamboyant hope of crowding on to that narrow slip of cardboard before the catastrophic thirties. The conversation that interwove with the pattern of the day's work was all much of a piece. One discussed how Mr Wilson had made his money, what method Mr Hiemer had employed and the means resorted to by Mr Hardy. One related age-old but eternally breath-less anecdotes of the fortunes stumbled on precipitously in the Street by a 'butcher' or a 'bartender', or 'a darn *mess*enger boy, by golly!'

and then one talked of the current gambles, and whether it was best to go out for a hundred thousand a year or be content with twenty. During the preceding year one of the assistant secretaries had invested all his savings in Bethlehem Steel. The story of his spectacular magnificence, of his haughty resignation in January, and of the triumphal palace he was now building in California, was the favourite office subject. The man's very name had acquired a magic significance, symbolising as he did the aspirations of all good Americans. Anecdotes were told about him – how one of the vice-presidents had advised him to sell, by golly, but he had hung on, even bought on margin, 'and *now* look where he is!'

Such, obviously, was the stuff of life – a dizzy triumph dazzling the eyes of all of them, a gypsy siren to content them with meagre wage and with the arithmetical improbability of their eventual success.

To Anthony the notion became appalling. He felt that to succeed here the idea of success must grasp and limit his mind. It seemed to him that the essential element in these men at the top was their faith that their affairs were the very core of life. All other things being equal, self-assurance and opportunism won out over technical knowledge; it was obvious that the more expert work went on near the bottom – so, with appropriate efficiency, the technical experts were kept there.

His determination to stay in at night during the week did not survive, and a good half of the time he came to work with a splitting, sickish headache and the crowded horror of the morning subway ringing in his ears like an echo of hell.

Then, abruptly, he quit. He had remained in bed all one Monday, and late in the evening, overcome by one of those attacks of moody despair to which he periodically succumbed, he wrote and mailed a letter to Mr Wilson, confessing that he considered himself ill adapted to the work. Gloria, coming in from the theatre with Richard Caramel, found him on the lounge, silently staring at the high ceiling, more depressed and discouraged than he had been at any time since their marriage.

She wanted him to whine. If he had she would have reproached him bitterly, for she was not a little annoyed, but he only lay there so utterly miserable that she felt sorry for him, and kneeling down she stroked his head, saying how little it mattered, how little anything mattered so long as they loved each other. It was like their first year, and Anthony, reacting to her cool hand, to her voice that was soft as breath itself upon his ear, became almost cheerful, and talked with her of his future plans. He even regretted, silently, before he went to bed that he had so hastily mailed his resignation.

'Even when everything seems rotten you can't trust that judgement,' Gloria had said. 'It's the sum of all your judgements that counts.'

In mid-April came a letter from the real-estate agent in Marietta, encouraging them to take the grey house for another year at a slightly increased rental, and enclosing a lease made out for their signatures. For a week lease and letter lay carelessly neglected on Anthony's desk. They had no intention of returning to Marietta. They were weary of the place, and had been bored most of the preceding summer. Besides, their car had deteriorated to a rattling mass of hypochondriacal metal, and a new one was financially inadvisable.

But because of another wild revel, enduring through four days and participated in, at one time or another, by more than a dozen people, they did sign the lease; to their utter horror they signed it and sent it, and immediately it seemed as though they heard the grey house, drably malevolent at last, licking its white chops and waiting to devour them.

'Anthony, where's that lease?' she called in high alarm one Sunday morning, sick and sober to reality. 'Where did you leave it? It was here!'

Then she knew where it was. She remembered the house party they had planned on the crest of their exuberance; she remembered a room full of men to whose less exhilarated moments she and Anthony were of no importance, and Anthony's boast of the transcendent merit and seclusion of the grey house, that it was so isolated that it didn't matter how much noise went on there. Then Dick, who had visited them, cried enthusiastically that it was the best little house imaginable, and that they were idiotic not to take it for another summer. It had been easy to work themselves up to a sense of how hot and deserted the city was getting, of how cool and ambrosial were the charms of Marietta. Anthony had picked up the lease and waved it wildly, found Gloria happily acquiescent, and with one last burst of garrulous decision during which all the men agreed with solemn handshakes that they would come out for a visit . . .

'Anthony,' she cried, 'we've signed and sent it!'

'What?'

'The lease!'

'What the devil!'

'Oh, *An*thony!' There was utter misery in her voice. For the summer, for eternity, they had built themselves a prison. It seemed to strike at the last roots of their stability. Anthony thought they might arrange it with the real-estate agent. They could no longer afford the double rent, and going to Marietta meant giving up his apartment, his reproachless apartment with the exquisite bath and the rooms for which he had bought his furniture and hangings – it was the closest to a home that he had ever had – familiar with memories of four colourful years.

But it was not arranged with the real-estate agent, nor was it arranged at all. Dispiritedly, without even any talk of making the best of it, without even Gloria's all-suffing 'I don't care', they went back to the house that they now knew heeded neither youth nor love – only those austere and incommunicable memories that they could never share.

THE SINISTER SUMMER

There was a horror in the house that summer. It came with them and settled itself over the place like a sombre pall, pervasive through the lower rooms, gradually spreading and climbing up the narrow stairs until it oppressed their very sleep. Anthony and Gloria grew to hate being there alone. Her bedroom, which had seemed so pink and young and delicate, appropriate to her pastel-shaded lingerie tossed here and there on chair and bed, seemed now to whisper with its rustling curtains: 'Ah, my beautiful young lady, yours is not the first daintiness and delicacy that has faded here under the summer suns . . . generations of unloved women have adorned themselves by that glass for rustic lovers who paid no heed . . . Youth has come into this room in palest blue and left it in the grey cerements of despair, and through long nights many girls have lain awake where that bed stands pouring out waves of misery into the darkness.'

Gloria finally tumbled all her clothes and unguents ingloriously out of it, declaring that she had come to live with Anthony, and making the excuse that one of her screens was rotten and admitted bugs. So her room was abandoned to insensitive guests, and they dressed and slept in her husband's chamber, which Gloria considered somehow 'good', as though Anthony's presence there had acted as exterminator of any uneasy shadows of the past that might have hovered about its walls.

The distinction between 'good' and 'bad', ordered early and

summarily out of both their lives, had been reinstated in another form. Gloria insisted that anyone invited to the grey house must be 'good', which, in the case of a girl, meant that she must be either simple and reproachless or, if otherwise, must possess a certain solidity and strength. Always intensely sceptical of her sex, her judgements were now concerned with the question of whether women were or were not clean. By uncleanliness she meant a variety of things, a lack of pride, a slackness in fibre and, most of all, the unmistakable aura of promiscuity.

'Women soil easily,' she said, 'far more easily than men. Unless a girl's very young and brave it's almost impossible for her to go downhill without a certain hysterical animality, the cunning, dirty sort of animality. A man's different – and I suppose that's why one of the commonest characters of romance is a man going gallantly to the devil.'

She was disposed to like many men, preferably those who gave her frank homage and unfailing entertainment – but often with a flash of insight she told Anthony that some one of his friends was merely using him, and consequently had best be left alone. Anthony customarily demurred, insisting that the accused was a 'good one', but he found that his judgement was more fallible than hers, memorably when, as it happened on several occasions, he was left with a succession of restaurant checks for which to render a solitary account.

More from their fear of solitude than from any desire to go through the fuss and bother of entertaining, they filled the house with guests every weekend, and often on through the week. The weekend parties were much the same. When the three or four men invited had arrived, drinking was more or less in order, followed by a hilarious dinner and a ride to the Cradle Beach Country Club, which they had joined because it was inexpensive, lively if not fashionable, and almost a necessity for just such occasions as these. Moreover, it was of no great moment what one did there, and so long as the Patch party were reasonably inaudible, it mattered little whether or not the social dictators of Cradle Beach saw the gay Gloria imbibing cocktails in the supper room at frequent intervals during the evening.

Saturday ended, generally, in a glamorous confusion – it proving often necessary to assist a muddled guest to bed. Sunday brought the New York papers and a quiet morning of recuperating on the porch – and Sunday afternoon meant goodbye to the one or two guests who must return to the city, and a great revival of drinking among the one or two who remained until next day, concluding in a convivial if not hilarious evening.

The faithful Tana, pedagogue by nature and man of all work by profession, had returned with them. Among their more frequent guests a tradition had sprung up about him. Maury Noble remarked one afternoon that his real name was Tannenbaum, and that he was a German agent kept in this country to disseminate Teutonic propaganda through Westchester County, and, after that, mysterious letters began to arrive from Philadelphia addressed to the bewildered Oriental as 'Lieutenant Emile Tannenbaum', containing a few cryptic messages signed 'General Staff', and adorned with an atmospheric double column of facetious Japanese. Anthony always handed them to Tana without a smile; hours afterwards the recipient could be found puzzling over them in the kitchen and declaring earnestly that the perpendicular symbols were not Japanese, nor anything resembling Japanese.

Gloria had taken a strong dislike to the man ever since the day when, returning unexpectedly from the village, she had discovered him reclining on Anthony's bed, puzzling out a newspaper. It was the instinct of all servants to be fond of Anthony and to detest Gloria, and Tana was no exception to the rule. But he was thoroughly afraid of her and made plain his aversion only in his moodier moments by subtly addressing Anthony with remarks intended for her ear: 'What Miz Pats want dinner?' he would say, looking at his master. Or else he would comment about the bitter selfishness of ' 'Merican peoples' in such manner that there was no doubt who were the 'peoples' referred to.

But they dared not dismiss him. Such a step would have been abhorrent to their inertia. They endured Tana as they endured ill weather and sickness of the body and the estimable Will of God – as they endured all things, even themselves.

IN DARKNESS

One sultry afternoon late in July Richard Caramel telephoned from New York that he and Maury were coming out, bringing a friend with them. They arrived about five, a little drunk, accompanied by a small, stocky man of thirty-five, whom they introduced as Mr Joe Hull, one of the best fellows that Anthony and Gloria would ever meet.

Joe Hull had a yellow beard continually fighting through his skin and a low voice which varied between *basso profundo* and a husky whisper. Anthony, carrying Maury's suitcase upstairs, followed him into the room and carefully closed the door.

'Who is this fellow?' he demanded.

Maury chuckled enthusiastically.

'Who, Hull? Oh, *he's* all right. He's a good one.'

'Yes, but who is he?'

'Hull? He's just a good fellow. He's a prince.' His laughter redoubled, culminating in a succession of pleasant catlike grins.

Anthony hesitated between a smile and a frown. 'He looks sort of funny to me. Weird-looking clothes' – he paused – 'I've got a sneaking suspicion you two picked him up somewhere last night.'

'Ridiculous,' declared Maury. 'Why, I've known him all my life.' However, as he capped this statement with another series of chuckles, Anthony was impelled to remark: 'The devil you have!'

Later, just before dinner, while Maury and Dick were conversing uproariously, with Joe Hull listening in silence as he sipped his drink, Gloria drew Anthony into the dining-room: 'I don't like this man Hull,' she said. 'I wish he'd use Tana's bathtub.'

'I can't very well ask him to.'

'Well, I don't want him in ours.'

'He seems to be a simple soul.'

'He's got on white shoes that look like gloves. I can see his toes right through them. Uh! Who is he, anyway?'

'You've got me.'

'Well, I think they've got their nerve to bring him out here. This isn't a Sailor's Rescue Home!'

'They were tight when they phoned. Maury said they've been on a party since yesterday afternoon.'

Gloria shook her head angrily, and saying no more returned to the porch. Anthony saw that she was trying to forget her uncertainty and devote herself to enjoying the evening.

It had been a tropical day, and even into late twilight the heat-waves emanating from the dry road were quivering faintly like undulating panes of isinglass. The sky was cloudless, but far beyond the woods in the direction of the Sound [283] a faint and persistent rolling had commenced. When Tana announced dinner the men, at a word from Gloria, remained coatless and went inside.

Maury began a song, which they accomplished in harmony during the first course. It had two lines and was sung to a popular air called Daisy Dear. The lines were:

The – pan-ic – has – come – over us,
So *ha-a-as* – the moral de*cline!*'

Each rendition was greeted with bursts of enthusiasm and prolonged applause.

'Cheer up, Gloria!' suggested Maury. 'You seem the least bit depressed.'

'I'm not,' she lied.

'Here, Tannenbaum!' he called over his shoulder. 'I've filled you a drink. Come on!'

Gloria tried to stay his arm.

'Please don't, Maury!'

'Why not? Maybe he'll play the flute for us after dinner. Here, Tana.'

Tana, grinning, bore the glass away to the kitchen. In a few moments Maury gave him another.

'Cheer up, Gloria!' he cried. 'For heaven's sakes everybody, cheer up Gloria.'

'Dearest, have another drink,' counselled Anthony.

'Do, please!'

'Cheer up, Gloria,' said Joe Hull easily.

Gloria winced at this uncalled-for use of her first name, and glanced around to see if anyone else had noticed it. The word coming so glibly from the lips of a man to whom she had taken an inordinate dislike repelled her. A moment later she noticed that Joe Hull had given Tana another drink, and her anger increased, heightened somewhat from the effects of the alcohol.

' – and once,' Maury was saying, 'Peter Granby and I went into a Turkish bath in Boston, about two o'clock at night. There was no one there but the proprietor, and we jammed him into a closet and locked the door. Then a fella came in and wanted a Turkish bath. Thought we were the rubbers, by golly! Well, we just picked him up and tossed him into the pool with all his clothes on. Then we dragged him out and laid him on a slab and slapped him until he was black and blue. "Not so rough, fellows!" he'd say in a little squeaky voice, "please! . . . " '

– Was this Maury? thought Gloria. From anyone else the story would have amused her, but from Maury, the infinitely appreciative, the apotheosis of tact and consideration . . .

The – pan-ic – has – come – over us,
So *ha-a-as* – '

A drum of thunder from outside drowned out the rest of the song; Gloria shivered and tried to empty her glass, but the first taste nauseated her, and she set it down. Dinner was over and they all marched into the big room, bearing several bottles and decanters. Someone had closed the porch door to keep out the wind, and in consequence circular tentacles of cigar smoke were twisting already upon the heavy air.

'Paging Lieutenant Tannenbaum!' Again it was the changeling Maury. 'Bring us the flute!'

Anthony and Maury rushed into the kitchen; Richard Caramel started the phonograph and approached Gloria.

'Dance with your well-known cousin.'

'I don't want to dance.'

'Then I'm going to carry you around.'

As though he were doing something of overpowering importance, he picked her up in his fat little arms and started trotting gravely about the room.

'Set me down, Dick! I'm dizzy!' she insisted.

He dumped her in a bouncing bundle on the couch, and rushed off to the kitchen, shouting 'Tana! Tana!'

Then, without warning, she felt other arms around her, felt herself lifted from the lounge. Joe Hull had picked her up and was trying, drunkenly, to imitate Dick.

'Put me down!' she said sharply.

His maudlin laugh, and the sight of that prickly yellow jaw close to her face stirred her to intolerable disgust.

'At once!'

'The – pan-ic – ' he began, but got no further, for Gloria's hand swung around swiftly and caught him on the cheek. At this he all at once let go of her, and she fell to the floor, her shoulder hitting the table a glancing blow in transit . . .

Then the room seemed full of men and smoke. There was Tana in his white coat reeling about supported by Maury. Into his flute he was blowing a weird blend of sound that was known, cried Anthony, as the Japanese train-song. Joe Hull had found a box of candles and was juggling them, yelling 'One down!' every time he missed, and Dick was dancing by himself in a fascinated whirl around and about the room. It appeared to her that everything in the room was staggering in grotesque fourth-dimensional gyrations through intersecting planes of hazy blue.

Outside, the storm had come up amazingly – the lulls within were filled with the scrape of the tall bushes against the house and the roaring of the rain on the tin roof of the kitchen. The lightning was interminable, letting down thick drips of thunder like pig iron from the heart of a white-hot furnace. Gloria could see that the rain was spitting in at three of the windows – but she could not move to shut them . . .

. . . She was in the hall. She had said good-night but no one had heard or heeded her. It seemed for an instant as though something had looked down over the head of the bannister, but she could not have gone back into the living-room – better madness than the madness of that clamour . . . Upstairs she fumbled for the electric switch and missed it in the darkness; a roomful of lightning showed her the button plainly on the wall. But when the impenetrable black shut down, it again eluded her fumbling fingers, so she slipped off her dress and petticoat and threw herself weakly on the dry side of the half-drenched bed.

She shut her eyes. From downstairs arose the babel of the drinkers, punctured suddenly by a tinkling shiver of broken glass, and then another, and by a soaring fragment of unsteady, irregular song . . .

She lay there for something over two hours – so she calculated afterwards, sheerly by piecing together the bits of time. She was conscious, even aware, after a long while that the noise downstairs had lessened, and that the storm was moving off westward, throwing back lingering showers of sound that fell, heavy and lifeless as her soul, into the soggy fields. This was succeeded by a slow, reluctant scattering of the rain and wind, until there was nothing outside her windows but a gentle dripping and the swishing play of a cluster of wet vine against the sill. She was in a state halfway between sleeping and waking, with neither condition predominant . . . and she was harassed by a desire to rid herself of a weight pressing down upon her breast. She felt that if she could cry the weight would be lifted, and forcing the lids of her eyes together she tried to raise a lump in her throat . . . to no avail . . .

Drip! Drip! Drip! The sound was not unpleasant – like spring, like a cool rain of her childhood, that made cheerful mud in her backyard and watered the tiny garden she had dug with miniature rake and spade and hoe. Drip – dri-ip! It was like days when the rain came out of yellow skies that melted just before twilight and shot one radiant shaft of sunlight diagonally down the heavens into the damp green trees. So cool, so clear and clean – and her mother there at the centre of the world, at the centre of the rain, safe and dry and strong. She wanted her mother now, and her mother was dead, beyond sight and touch for ever. And this weight was pressing on her, pressing on her – oh, it pressed on her so!

She became rigid. Someone had come to the door and was standing regarding her, very quiet except for a slight swaying motion. She could see the outline of his figure distinct against some indistinguishable light. There was no sound anywhere, only a great persuasive silence – even the dripping had ceased . . . only this figure, swaying, swaying in the doorway, an indiscernible and subtly menacing terror, a personality filthy under its varnish, like smallpox spots under a layer of powder. Yet her tired heart, beating until it shook her breasts, made her sure that there was still life in her, desperately shaken, threatened . . .

The minute or succession of minutes prolonged itself interminably, and a swimming blur began to form before her eyes, which tried with childish persistence to pierce the gloom in the direction of the door. In another instant it seemed that some unimaginable force would shatter her out of existence . . . and then the figure in the doorway – it was Hull, she saw, Hull – turned deliberately and, still slightly swaying, moved back and off, as if absorbed into that incomprehensible light that had given him dimension.

Blood rushed back into her limbs, blood and life together. With a start of energy she sat upright, shifting her body until her feet touched the floor over the side of the bed. She knew what she must do – now, now, before it was too late. She must go out into this cool damp, out, away, to feel the wet swish of the grass around her feet and the fresh moisture on her forehead. Mechanically she struggled into her clothes, groping in the dark of the closet for a hat. She must go from this house where the thing hovered that pressed upon her bosom, or else made itself into stray, swaying figures in the gloom.

In a panic she fumbled clumsily at her coat, found the sleeve just as she heard Anthony's footsteps on the lower stair. She dared not wait; he might not let her go, and even Anthony was part of this weight, part of this evil house and the sombre darkness that was growing up about it . . .

Through the hall then . . . and down the back stairs, hearing Anthony's voice in the bedroom she had just left –

'Gloria! Gloria!'

But she had reached the kitchen now, passed out through the doorway into the night. A hundred drops, startled by a flare of wind from a dripping tree, scattered on her and she pressed them gladly to her face with hot hands.

'Gloria! Gloria!'

The voice was infinitely remote, muffled and made plaintive by the walls she had just left. She rounded the house and started down the front path towards the road, almost exultant as she turned into it, and followed the carpet of short grass alongside, moving with caution in the intense darkness.

'Gloria!'

She broke into a run, stumbled over the segment of a branch twisted off by the wind. The voice was outside the house now. Anthony, finding the bedroom deserted, had come on to the porch. But this thing was driving her forward; it was back there with Anthony, and she must go on in her flight under this dim and oppressive heaven, forcing herself through the silence ahead as though it were a tangible barrier before her.

She had gone some distance along the barely discernible road, probably half a mile, passed a single deserted barn that loomed up, black and foreboding, the only building of any sort between the grey house and Marietta; then she turned the fork, where the road entered the wood and ran between two high walls of leaves and branches that nearly touched overhead. She noticed suddenly a thin, longitudinal gleam of silver upon the road before her, like a bright sword half embedded in the mud. As she came closer she gave a little cry of satisfaction – it was a wagon-rut full of water, and glancing heavenward she saw a light rift of sky and knew that the moon was out.

'Gloria!'

She started violently. Anthony was not two hundred feet behind her.

'Gloria, wait for me!'

She shut her lips tightly to keep from screaming, and increased her gait. Before she had gone another hundred yards the woods disappeared, rolling back like a dark stocking from the leg of the road. Three minutes' walk ahead of her, suspended in the now high and limitless air, she saw a thin interlacing of attenuated gleams and glitters, centred in a regular undulation on some one invisible point. Abruptly she knew where she would go. That was the great cascade of wires that rose high over the river, like the legs of a gigantic spider whose eye was the little green light in the switch-house, and ran with the railroad bridge in the direction of the station. The station! There would be the train to take her away.

'Gloria, it's me! It's Anthony! Gloria, I won't try to stop you! For God's sake, where are you?'

She made no answer but began to run, keeping on the high side of the road and leaping the gleaming puddles – dimensionless pools of thin, unsubstantial gold. Turning sharply to the left, she followed a narrow wagon road, swerving to avoid a dark body on the ground. She looked up as an owl hooted mournfully from a solitary tree. Just ahead of her she could see the trestle that led to the railroad bridge and the steps mounting up to it. The station lay across the river.

Another sound startled her, the melancholy siren of an approaching train, and almost simultaneously, a repeated call, thin now and far away.

'Gloria! Gloria!'

Anthony must have followed the main road. She laughed with a sort of malicious cunning at having eluded him; she could spare the time to wait until the train went by.

The siren soared again, closer at hand, and then, with no anticipatory roar and clamour, a dark and sinuous body curved into view against the shadows far down the high-banked track, and with no sound but the rush of the cleft wind and the clocklike tick of the rails, moved towards the bridge – it was an electric train. Above the engine two vivid blurs of blue light formed incessantly a radiant crackling bar between them, which, like a spluttering flame in a lamp beside a corpse, lit for an instant the successive rows of trees and caused Gloria to draw back instinctively to the far side of the road. The light was tepid, the temperature of warm blood . . . The clicking blended suddenly with itself in a rush of even sound, and then, elongating in sombre elasticity, the thing roared blindly by her and thundered on to the bridge, racing the lurid shaft of fire it cast into the solemn river alongside. Then it contracted swiftly, sucking in its sound until it left only a reverberant echo, which died upon the farther bank.

Silence crept down again over the wet country; the faint dripping resumed, and suddenly a great shower of drops tumbled upon Gloria stirring her out of the trance-like torpor which the passage of the train had wrought. She ran swiftly down a descending level to the bank and began climbing the iron stairway to the bridge, remembering that it was something she had always wanted to do, and that she would have the added excitement of traversing the yard-wide plank that ran beside the tracks over the river.

There! This was better. She was at the top now and could see the lands about her as successive sweeps of open country, cold under the moon, coarsely patched and seamed with thin rows and heavy clumps of trees. To her right, half a mile down the river, which trailed away behind the light like the shiny, slimy path of a snail, winked the scattered lights of Marietta. Not two hundred yards away at the end of the bridge squatted the station, marked by a sullen lantern. The oppression was lifted now – the tree-tops below her were rocking the young starlight to a haunted doze. She stretched out her arms with a gesture of freedom. This was what she had wanted, to stand alone where it was high and cool.

'Gloria!'

Like a startled child she scurried along the plank, hopping, skipping, jumping, with an ecstatic sense of her own physical lightness. Let him come now – she no longer feared that, only she must first reach the station, because that was part of the game. She was happy. Her hat, snatched off, was clutched tightly in her hand, and her short curled hair bobbed up and down about her ears. She had thought she would never feel so young again, but this was her night, her world. Triumphantly she laughed as she left the plank and reaching the wooden platform flung herself down happily beside an iron roof-post.

'Here I am!' she called, gay as the dawn in her elation. 'Here I am, Anthony, dear – old, worried Anthony.'

'Gloria!' He reached the platform, ran towards her. 'Are you all right?' Coming up he knelt and took her in his arms.

'Yes.'

'What was the matter? Why did you leave?' he queried anxiously.

'I had to – there was something' – she paused and a flicker of uneasiness lashed at her mind – 'there was something sitting on me – here.' She put her hand on her breast. 'I had to go out and get away from it.'

'What do you mean by "something"?'

'I don't know – that man Hull – '

'Did he bother you?'

'He came to my door, drunk. I think I'd got sort of crazy by that time.'

'Gloria, dearest – '

Wearily she laid her head upon his shoulder.

'Let's go back,' he suggested.

She shivered.

'Uh! No, I couldn't. It'd come and sit on me again.' Her voice rose to a cry that hung plaintive on the darkness. 'That thing – '

'There – there,' he soothed her, pulling her close to him. 'We won't do anything you don't want to do. What do you want to do? Just sit here?'

'I want – I want to go away.'

'Where?'

'Oh – anywhere.'

'By golly, Gloria,' he cried, 'you're still tight!'

'No, I'm not. I haven't been, all evening. I went upstairs about, oh, I don't know, about half an hour after dinner . . . Ouch!'

He had inadvertently touched her right shoulder.

'It hurts me. I hurt it some way. I don't know – somebody picked me up and dropped me.'

'Gloria, come home. It's late and damp.'

'I can't,' she wailed. 'Oh, Anthony, don't ask me to! I will tomorrow. You go home and I'll wait here for a train. I'll go to a hotel – '

'I'll go with you.'

'No, I don't want you with me. I want to be alone. I want to sleep – oh, I want to sleep. And then tomorrow, when you've got all the smell of whiskey and cigarettes out of the house, and everything straight, and Hull is gone, then I'll come home. If I went now, that thing – oh – !' She covered her eyes with her hand; Anthony saw the futility of trying to persuade her.

'I was all sober when you left,' he said. 'Dick was asleep on the lounge and Maury and I were having a discussion. That fellow Hull had wandered off somewhere. Then I began to realise I hadn't seen you for several hours, so I went upstairs – '

He broke off as a salutatory, 'Hello, there!' boomed suddenly out of the darkness. Gloria sprang to her feet and he did likewise.

'It's Maury's voice,' she cried excitedly. 'If it's Hull with him, keep them away, keep them away!'

'Who's there?' Anthony called.

'Just Dick and Maury,' returned two voices reassuringly.

'Where's Hull?'

'He's in bed. Passed out.'

Their figures appeared dimly on the platform.

'What the devil are you and Gloria doing here?' enquired Richard Caramel with sleepy bewilderment.

'What are *you* two doing here?'

Maury laughed.

'Damned if I know. We followed you, and had the deuce of a time doing it. I heard you out on the porch yelling for Gloria, so I woke up the Caramel here and got it through his head, with some difficulty, that if there was a search-party we'd better be on it. He slowed me up by sitting down in the road at intervals and asking me what it was all about. We tracked you by the pleasant scent of Canadian Club.'

There was a rattle of nervous laughter under the low train-shed.

'How did you track us, really?'

'Well, we followed along down the road and then we suddenly lost you. Seems you turned off at a wagon-trail. After a while somebody hailed us and asked us if we were looking for a young girl. Well, we came up and found it was a little shivering old man, sitting on a fallen tree like somebody in a fairy tale. "She turned down here," he said, "and most steppud on me, goin' somewhere in an awful hustle, and then a fella in short golfin' pants come runnin' along and went after her. He throwed me this." The old fellow had a dollar bill he was waving around – '

'Oh, the poor old man!' ejaculated Gloria, moved.

'I threw him another and we went on, though he asked us to stay and tell him what it was all about.'

'Poor old man,' repeated Gloria dismally.

Dick sat down sleepily on a box.

'And now what?' he enquired in the tone of stoic resignation.

'Gloria's upset,' explained Anthony. 'She and I are going to the city by the next train.'

Maury in the darkness had pulled a timetable from his pocket.

'Strike a match.'

A tiny flare leaped out of the opaque background illuminating the four faces, grotesque and unfamiliar here in the open night.

'Let's see. Two, two-thirty – no, that's evening. By gad, you won't get a train till five-thirty.'

Anthony hesitated.

'Well,' he muttered uncertainly, 'we've decided to stay here and wait for it. You two might as well go back and sleep.'

'You go, too, Anthony,' urged Gloria; 'I want you to have some sleep, dear. You've been as pale as a ghost all day.'

'Why, you little idiot!'

Dick yawned.

'Very well. You stay, we stay.'

He walked out from under the shed and surveyed the heavens.

'Rather a nice night, after all. Stars are out and everything. Exceptionally tasty assortment of them.'

'Let's see.' Gloria moved after him and the other two followed her. 'Let's sit out here,' she suggested. 'I like it much better.'

Anthony and Dick converted a long box into a back-rest and found a board dry enough for Gloria to sit on. Anthony dropped down beside her and with some effort Dick hoisted himself on to an apple-barrel near them.

'Tana went to sleep in the porch hammock,' he remarked. 'We carried him in and left him next to the kitchen stove to dry. He was drenched to the skin.'

'That awful little man!' sighed Gloria.

'How do you do!' The voice, sonorous and funereal, had come from above, and they looked up startled to find that in some manner Maury had climbed to the roof of the shed, where he sat dangling his feet over the edge, outlined as a shadowy and fantastic gargoyle against the now brilliant sky.

'It must be for such occasions as this,' he began softly, his words having the effect of floating down from an immense height and settling softly upon his auditors, 'that the righteous of the land decorate the railroads with billboards asserting in red and yellow that "Jesus Christ is God", placing them, appropriately enough, next to announcements that "Gunter's Whiskey is Good".'

There was gentle laughter and the three below kept their heads tilted upward.

'I think I shall tell you the story of my education,' continued Maury, 'under these sardonic constellations.'

'Do! Please!'

'Shall I, really?'

They waited expectantly while he directed a ruminative yawn towards the white smiling moon.

'Well,' he began, 'as an infant I prayed. I stored up prayers against future wickedness. One year I stored up nineteen hundred "Now I lay me"s.'

'Throw down a cigarette,' murmured someone.

A small package reached the platform simultaneously with the stentorian command: 'Silence! I am about to unburden myself of many memorable remarks reserved for the darkness of such earths and the brilliance of such skies.'

Below, a lighted match was passed from cigarette to cigarette. The voice resumed: 'I was adept at fooling the deity. I prayed immediately after all crimes until eventually prayer and crime became indistinguishable to me. I believed that because a man cried out "My God!" when a safe fell on him, it proved that belief was rooted deep in the human breast. Then I went to school. For fourteen years half a hundred earnest men pointed to ancient flintlocks and cried to me: "There's the real thing. These new rifles are only shallow, superficial imitations." They damned the books I read and the things I thought by calling them immoral; later the fashion changed, and they damned things by calling them "clever".

'And so I turned, canny for my years, from the professors to the poets, listening – to the lyric tenor of Swinburne and the tenor *robusto* of Shelley, to Shakespeare with his first bass and his fine range, to Tennyson with his second bass and his occasional falsetto, to Milton and Marlow, *bassos profundos*. I gave ear to Browning chatting, Byron declaiming and Wordsworth droning. This, at least, did me no harm. I learned a little of beauty – enough to know that it had nothing to do with truth – and I found, moreover, that there was no great literary tradition; there was only the tradition of the eventual death of every literary tradition . . .

'Then I grew up, and the beauty of succulent illusions fell away from me. The fibre of my mind coarsened and my eyes grew miserably keen. Life rose around my island like a sea, and presently I was swimming.

'The transition was subtle – the thing had lain in wait for me for some time. It has its insidious, seemingly innocuous trap for everyone. With me? No – I didn't try to seduce the janitor's wife – nor did I run through the streets unclothed, proclaiming my virility. It is never quite passion that does the business – it is the dress that passion wears. I became bored – that was all. Boredom, which is another name and a frequent disguise for vitality, became the unconscious motive of all my acts. Beauty was behind me, do you understand? – I was grown.' He paused. 'End of school and college period. Opening of Part Two.'

Three quietly active points of light showed the location of his listeners. Gloria was now half sitting, half lying, in Anthony's lap. His arm was around her so tightly that she could hear the beating of his heart. Richard Caramel, perched on the apple-barrel, from time to time stirred and gave off a faint grunt.

'I grew up then, into this land of jazz, and fell immediately into a state of almost audible confusion. Life stood over me like an immoral schoolmistress, editing my ordered thoughts. But, with a mistaken faith in intelligence, I plodded on. I read Smith, who laughed at charity and insisted that the sneer was the highest form of self-expression – but Smith himself replaced charity as an obscurer of the light. I read Jones, who neatly disposed of individualism – and behold! Jones was still in my way. I did not think – I was a battle-ground for the thoughts of many men; rather was I one of those desirable but impotent countries over which the great powers surge back and forth.

'I reached maturity under the impression that I was gathering the experience to order my life for happiness. Indeed, I accomplished the not unusual feat of solving each question in my mind long before it presented itself to me in life – and of being beaten and bewildered just the same.

'But after a few tastes of this latter dish I had had enough. Here! I said, Experience is not worth the getting. It's not a thing that happens pleasantly to a passive you – it's a wall that an active you runs up against. So I wrapped myself in what I thought was my invulnerable scepticism and decided that my education was complete. But it was too late. Protect myself as I might by making no new ties with tragic and predestined humanity, I was lost with the rest. I had traded the fight against love for the fight against loneliness, the fight against life for the fight against death.'

He broke off to give emphasis to his last observation – after a moment he yawned and resumed.

'I suppose that the beginning of the second phase of my education was a ghastly dissatisfaction at being used in spite of myself for some inscrutable purpose of whose ultimate goal I was unaware – if, indeed, there *was* an ultimate goal. It was a difficult choice. The schoolmistress seemed to be saying, "We're going to play football and nothing but football. If you don't want to play football you can't play at all – "

'What was I to do – the playtime was so short!

'You see, I felt that we were even denied what consolation there might have been in being a figment of a corporate man rising from his knees. Do you think that I leaped at this pessimism, grasped it as a sweetly smug superior thing, no more depressing really than, say, a grey autumn day before a fire? – I don't think I did that. I was a great deal too warm for that, and too alive.

'For it seemed to me that there was no ultimate goal for man. Man was beginning a grotesque and bewildered fight with nature – nature, that by the divine and magnificent accident had brought us to where we could fly in her face. She had invented ways to rid the race of the inferior and thus give the remainder strength to fill her higher – or, let us say, her more amusing – though still unconscious and accidental intentions. And, actuated by the highest gifts of the enlightenment, we were seeking to circumvent her. In this republic I saw the black beginning to mingle with the white – in Europe there was taking place an economic catastrophe to save three or four diseased and wretchedly governed races from the one mastery that might organise them for material prosperity.

'We produce a Christ who can raise up the leper – and presently the breed of the leper is the salt of the earth. If anyone can find any lesson in that, let him stand forth.'

'There's only one lesson to be learned from life, anyway,' interrupted Gloria, not in contradiction but in a sort of melancholy agreement.

'What's that?' demanded Maury sharply.

'That there's no lesson to be learned from life.'

After a short silence Maury said: 'Young Gloria, the beautiful and merciless lady, first looked at the world with the fundamental sophistication I have struggled to attain, that Anthony never will attain, that Dick will never fully understand.'

There was a disgusted groan from the apple-barrel. Anthony, grown accustomed to the dark, could see plainly the flash of Richard Caramel's yellow eye and the look of resentment on his face as he cried: 'You're crazy! By your own statement I should have attained some experience by trying.'

'Trying what?' cried Maury fiercely. 'Trying to pierce the darkness of political idealism with some wild, despairing urge towards truth? Sitting day after day supine in a rigid chair and infinitely removed from life staring at the tip of a steeple through the trees, trying to separate, definitely and for all time, the knowable from the unknowable? Trying to take a piece of actuality and give it glamour from your own soul to make up for that inexpressible quality it possessed in life and lost in transit to paper or canvas? Struggling in a laboratory through weary years for one iota of relative truth in a mass of wheels or a test tube – '

'Have you?'

Maury paused, and in his answer, when it came, there was a measure of weariness, a bitter over-note that lingered for a moment in those three minds before it floated up and off like a bubble bound for the moon.

'Not I,' he said softly. 'I was born tired – but with the quality of mother wit, the gift of women like Gloria – to that, for all my talking and listening, my waiting in vain for the eternal generality that seems to lie just beyond every argument and every speculation, to that I have added not one jot.'

In the distance a deep sound that had been audible for some moments identified itself by a plaintive mooing like that of a gigantic cow and by the pearly spot of a headlight apparent half a mile away. It was a steam-driven train this time, rumbling and groaning, and as it tumbled by with a monstrous complaint it sent a shower of sparks and cinders over the platform.

'Not one jot!' Again Maury's voice dropped down to them as from a great height. 'What a feeble thing intelligence is, with its short steps, its waverings, its pacings back and forth, its disastrous retreats! Intelligence is a mere instrument of circumstances. There are people who say that intelligence must have built the universe – why, intelligence never built a steam engine! Circumstances built a steam engine. Intelligence is little more than a short foot-rule by which we measure the infinite achievements of Circumstances.

'I could quote you the philosophy of the hour – but, for all we know, fifty years may see a complete reversal of this abnegation that's absorbing the intellectuals today, the triumph of Christ over Anatole France [284] – ' He hesitated, and then added: 'But all I know – the tremendous importance of myself to me, and the necessity of acknowledging that importance to myself – these things the wise and lovely Gloria was born knowing, these things and the painful futility of trying to know anything else.

'Well, I started to tell you of my education, didn't I? But I learned nothing, you see, very little even about myself. And if I had I should die with my lips shut and the guard on my fountain pen – as the wisest men have done since – oh, since the failure of a certain matter – a strange matter, by the way. It concerned some sceptics who thought they were far-sighted, just as you and I. Let me tell you about them by way of an evening prayer before you all drop off to sleep.

'Once upon a time all the men of mind and genius in the world became of one belief – that is to say, of no belief. But it wearied them to think that within a few years after their death many cults and systems and prognostications would be ascribed to them which they had never meditated nor intended. So they said to one another:
' "Let's join together and make a great book that will last for ever to

mock the credulity of man. Let's persuade our more erotic poets to write about the delights of the flesh, and induce some of our robust journalists to contribute stories of famous amours. We'll include all the most preposterous old wives' tales now current. We'll choose the keenest satirist alive to compile a deity from all the deities worshipped by mankind, a deity who will be more magnificent than any of them, and yet so weakly human that he'll become a byword for laughter the world over – and we'll ascribe to him all sorts of jokes and vanities and rages, in which he'll be supposed to indulge for his own diversion, so that the people will read our book and ponder it, and there'll be no more nonsense in the world.

' "Finally, let us take care that the book possesses all the virtues of style, so that it may last for ever as a witness to our profound scepticism and our universal irony."

'So the men did, and they died.

'But the book lived always, so beautifully had it been written, and so astounding the quality of imagination with which these men of mind and genius had endowed it. They had neglected to give it a name, but after they were dead it became known as the Bible.'

When he concluded there was no comment. Some damp languor sleeping on the air of night seemed to have bewitched them all.

'As I said, I started on the story of my education. But my highballs are dead and the night's almost over, and soon there'll be an awful jabbering going on everywhere, in the trees and the houses, and the two little stores over there behind the station, and there'll be a great running up and down upon the earth for a few hours – Well,' he concluded with a laugh, 'thank God we four can all pass to our eternal rest knowing we've left the world a little better for having lived in it.'

A breeze sprang up, blowing with it faint wisps of life which flattened against the sky.

'Your remarks grow rambling and inconclusive,' said Anthony sleepily. 'You expected one of those miracles of illumination by which you say your most brilliant and pregnant things in exactly the setting that should provoke the ideal symposium. Meanwhile Gloria has shown her far-sighted detachment by falling asleep – I can tell that by the fact that she has managed to concentrate her entire weight upon my broken body.'

'Have I bored you?' enquired Maury, looking down with some concern.

'No, you have disappointed us. You've shot a lot of arrows but did you shoot any birds?'

'I leave the birds to Dick,' said Maury hurriedly. 'I speak erratically, in disassociated fragments.'

'You can get no rise from me,' muttered Dick. 'My mind is full of any number of material things. I want a warm bath too much to worry about the importance of my work or what proportion of us are pathetic figures.'

Dawn made itself felt in a gathering whiteness eastward over the river and an intermittent cheeping in the nearby trees.

'Quarter to five,' sighed Dick; 'almost another hour to wait. Look! Two gone.' He was pointing to Anthony, whose lids had sagged over his eyes. 'Sleep of the Patch family – '

But in another five minutes, despite the amplifying cheeps and chirrups, his own head had fallen forward, nodded down twice, thrice . . .

Only Maury Noble remained awake, seated upon the station roof, his eyes wide open and fixed with fatigued intensity upon the distant nucleus of morning. He was wondering at the unreality of ideas, at the fading radiance of existence, and at the little absorptions that were creeping avidly into his life, like rats into a ruined house. He was sorry for no one now – on Monday morning there would be his business, and later there would be a girl of another class whose whole life he was; these were the things nearest his heart. In the strangeness of the brightening day it seemed presumptuous that with this feeble, broken instrument of his mind he had ever tried to think.

There was the sun, letting down great glowing masses of heat; there was life, active and snarling, moving about them like a fly swarm – the dark pants of smoke from the engine, a crisp 'All aboard!' and a bell ringing. Confusedly Maury saw eyes in the milk-train staring curiously up at him, heard Gloria and Anthony in quick controversy as to whether he should go to the city with her, then another clamour and she was gone and the three men, pale as ghosts, were standing alone upon the platform while a grimy coal-heaver went down the road on top of a motor truck, carolling hoarsely at the summer morning.

CHAPTER 3

The Broken Lute

It is seven-thirty of an August evening. The windows in the living-room of the grey house are wide open, patiently exchanging the tainted inner atmosphere of liquor and smoke for the fresh drowsiness of the late hot dusk. There are dying flower scents upon the air, so thin, so fragile, as to hint already of a summer laid away in time. But August is still proclaimed relentlessly by a thousand crickets around the side-porch, and by one who has broken into the house and concealed himself confidently behind a bookcase, from time to time shrieking of his cleverness and his indomitable will.

The room itself is in messy disorder. On the table is a dish of fruit, which is real but appears artificial. Around it are grouped an ominous assortment of decanters, glasses and heaped ashtrays, the latter still raising wavy smoke-ladders into the stale air, the effect on the whole needing but a skull to resemble that venerable chromo,[285] once a fixture in every 'den', which presents the appendages to the life of pleasure with delightful and awe-inspiring sentiment.

After a while the sprightly solo of the super-cricket is interrupted rather than joined by a new sound – the melancholy wail of an erratically fingered flute. It is obvious that the musician is practising rather than performing, for from time to time the gnarled strain breaks off and, after an interval of indistinct mutterings, recommences.

Just prior to the seventh false start a third sound contributes to the subdued discord. It is a taxi outside. A minute's silence, then the taxi again, its boisterous retreat almost obliterating the scrape of footsteps on the cinder walk. The doorbell shrieks alarmingly through the house.

From the kitchen enters a small, fatigued Japanese, hastily buttoning a servant's coat of white duck. He opens the front screen-door and admits a handsome young man of thirty, clad in the sort of well-intentioned clothes peculiar to those who serve mankind. To his whole personality clings a well-intentioned air: his glance about the room is compounded of curiosity and a determined optimism; when he looks at Tana the entire burden of uplifting the godless Oriental is in his eyes. His name is FREDERICK E. PARAMORE. *He was at Harvard with* ANTHONY, *where because of the initials of their surnames they were constantly placed next to each other in classes. A fragmentary acquaintance developed – but since that time they have never met.*

Nevertheless, PARAMORE *enters the room with a certain air of arriving for the evening.*

Tana is answering a question.

TANA (*grinning with ingratiation*): Gone to Inn for dinnah. Be back half-hour. Gone since ha' past six.

PARAMORE (*regarding the glasses on the table*): Have they company?

TANA: Yes. Company. Mistah Caramel, Mistah and Missays Barnes, Miss Kane, all stay here.

PARAMORE: I see. (*kindly*) They've been having a spree, I see.

TANA: I no un'stan'.

PARAMORE: They've been having a fling.

TANA: Yes, they have drink. Oh, many, many, many drink.

PARAMORE (*receding delicately from the subject*): Didn't I hear the sounds of music as I approached the house?

TANA (*with a spasmodic giggle*): Yes, I play.

PARAMORE: One of the Japanese instruments.

(*He is quite obviously a subscriber to the* National Geographic Magazine.)

TANA: I play flu-u-ute, Japanese flu-u-ute.

PARAMORE: What song were you playing? One of your Japanese melodies?

TANA (*his brow undergoing preposterous contraction*): I play train-song. How you call? – railroad song. So call in my countree. Like train. It go so-o-o; that mean whistle; train start. Then go so-o-o; that mean train go. Go like that. Vera nice song in my countree. Children song.

PARAMORE: It sounded very nice. (*It is apparent at this point that only a gigantic effort at control restrains Tana from rushing upstairs for his postcards, including the six made in America.*)

TANA: I fix highball for gentleman?

PARAMORE: No, thanks. I don't use it. (*He smiles.*)

(TANA *withdraws into the kitchen, leaving the intervening door slightly ajar. From the crevice there suddenly issues again the melody of the Japanese train song – this time not a practice, surely, but a performance, a lusty, spirited performance.*

The phone rings. TANA, *absorbed in his harmonics, gives no heed, so* PARAMORE *takes up the receiver.*)

PARAMORE: Hello . . . Yes . . . No, he's not here now, but he'll be back any moment . . . Butterworth? Hello, I didn't quite catch the name . . . Hello, hello, hello. Hello! . . . Huh!

(*The phone obstinately refuses to yield up any more sound.* PARAMORE *replaces the receiver.*

At this point the taxi motif re-enters, wafting with it a second young man; he carries a suitcase and opens the front door without ringing the bell.)

MAURY (*in the hall*): Oh, Anthony! Yoho! (*He comes into the large room and sees* PARAMORE.) How do?

PARAMORE (*gazing at him with gathering intensity*): Is this – is this Maury Noble?

MAURY: That's it. (*He advances, smiling and holding out his hand.*) How are you, old boy? Haven't seen you for years.

(*He has vaguely associated the face with Harvard, but is not even positive about that. The name, if he ever knew it, he has long since forgotten. However, with a fine sensitiveness and an equally commendable charity* PARAMORE *recognises the fact and tactfully relieves the situation.*)

PARAMORE: You've forgotten Fred Paramore? We were both in old Unc Robert's history class.

MAURY: No, I haven't, Unc – I mean Fred. Fred was – I mean Unc was a great old fellow, wasn't he?

PARAMORE (*nodding his head humorously several times*): Great old character. Great old character.

MAURY (*after a short pause*): Yes – he was. Where's Anthony?

PARAMORE: The Japanese servant told me he was at some inn. Having dinner, I suppose.

MAURY (*looking at his watch*): Gone long?

PARAMORE: I guess so. The Japanese told me they'd be back shortly.

MAURY: Suppose we have a drink.

PARAMORE: No, thanks. I don't use it. (*He smiles.*)

MAURY: Mind if I do? (*yawning as he helps himself from a bottle*) What have you been doing since you left college?

PARAMORE: Oh, many things. I've led a very active life. Knocked about here and there. (*His tone implies anything from lion-stalking to organised crime.*)

MAURY: Oh, been over to Europe?

PARAMORE: No, I haven't – unfortunately.

MAURY: I guess we'll all go over before long.

PARAMORE: Do you really think so?

MAURY: Sure! Country's been fed on sensationalism for more than two years. Everybody getting restless. Want to have some fun.

PARAMORE: Then you don't believe any ideals are at stake?

MAURY: Nothing of much importance. People want excitement every so often.

PARAMORE (*intently*): It's very interesting to hear you say that. Now I was talking to a man who'd been over there –

(*During the ensuing testament, left to be filled in by the reader with such phrases as 'Saw with his own eyes', 'Splendid spirit of France' and 'Salvation of civilisation', MAURY sits with lowered eyelids, dispassionately bored.*)

MAURY (*at the first available opportunity*): By the way, do you happen to know that there's a German agent in this very house?

PARAMORE (*smiling cautiously*): Are you serious?

MAURY: Absolutely. Feel it my duty to warn you.

PARAMORE (*convinced*): A governess?

MAURY (*in a whisper, indicating the kitchen with his thumb*): Tana! That's not his real name. I understand he constantly gets mail addressed to Lieutenant Emile Tannenbaum.

PARAMORE (*laughing with hearty tolerance*): You're kidding me.

MAURY: I may be accusing him falsely. But, you haven't told me what you've been doing.

PARAMORE: For one thing – writing.

MAURY: Fiction?

PARAMORE: No. Non-fiction.

MAURY: What's that? A sort of literature that's half fiction and half fact?

PARAMORE: Oh, I've confined myself to fact. I've been doing a good deal of social-service work.

MAURY: Oh!

(*An immediate glow of suspicion leaps into his eyes. It is as though PARAMORE had announced himself as an amateur pickpocket.*)

PARAMORE: At present I'm doing service work in Stamford. Only last week someone told me that Anthony Patch lived so near.

(*They are interrupted by a clamour outside, unmistakable as that of two sexes in conversation and laughter. Then there enter the room in a body ANTHONY, GLORIA, RICHARD CARAMEL, MURIEL KANE, RACHAEL BARNES and RODMAN BARNES, her husband. They surge about MAURY, illogically replying, 'Fine!' to his general, 'Hello.' . . . ANTHONY, meanwhile, approaches his other guest.*)

ANTHONY: Well, I'll be darned. How are you? Mighty glad to see you.

PARAMORE: It's good to see you, Anthony. I'm stationed in Stamford, so I thought I'd run over. (*roguishly*) We have to work to beat the devil most of the time, so we're entitled to a few hours' vacation. (*In an agony of concentration* ANTHONY *tries to recall the name. After a struggle of parturition his memory gives up the fragment 'Fred', around which he hastily builds the sentence, 'Glad you did, Fred!' Meanwhile the slight hush prefatory to an introduction has fallen upon the company.* MAURY, *who could help, prefers to look on in malicious enjoyment.*)

ANTHONY (*in desperation*): Ladies and gentlemen, this is – this is Fred.

MURIEL (*with obliging levity*): Hello, Fred!

(RICHARD CARAMEL *and* PARAMORE *greet each other intimately by their first names, the latter recollecting that* DICK *was one of the men in his class who had never before troubled to speak to him.* DICK *fatuously imagines that* PARAMORE *is someone he has previously met in* ANTHONY'S *house.*

The three young women go upstairs.)

MAURY (*in an undertone to* DICK): Haven't seen Muriel since Anthony's wedding.

DICK: She's now in her prime. Her latest is, 'I'll say so!'

(ANTHONY *struggles for a while with* PARAMORE *and at length attempts to make the conversation general by asking everyone to have a drink.*)

MAURY: I've done pretty well on this bottle. I've gone from 'Proof' down to 'Distillery'. (*He indicates the words on the label.*)

ANTHONY (*to* PARAMORE): Never can tell when these two will turn up. Said goodbye to them one afternoon at five and darned if they didn't appear about two in the morning. A big hired touring-car from New York drove up to the door and out they stepped, drunk as lords, of course.

(*In an ecstasy of consideration* PARAMORE *regards the cover of a book which he holds in his hand.* MAURY *and* DICK *exchange a glance.*)

DICK (*innocently, to* PARAMORE): You work here in town?

PARAMORE: No, I'm in the Laird Street Settlement in Stamford. (*To* ANTHONY): You have no idea of the amount of poverty in these small Connecticut towns. Italians and other immigrants. Catholics mostly, you know, so it's very hard to reach them.

ANTHONY (*politely*): Lot of crime?

PARAMORE: Not so much crime as ignorance and dirt.

MAURY: That's my theory: immediate electrocution of all ignorant and dirty people. I'm all for the criminals – give colour to life. Trouble is if you started to punish ignorance you'd have to begin in the first families, then you could take up the moving-picture people, and finally Congress and the clergy.

PARAMORE (*smiling uneasily*): I was speaking of the more fundamental ignorance – of even our language.

MAURY (*thoughtfully*): I suppose it is rather hard. Can't even keep up with the new poetry.

PARAMORE: It's only when the settlement work has gone on for months that one realises how bad things are. As our secretary said to me, your fingernails never seem dirty until you wash your hands. Of course we're already attracting much attention.

MAURY (*rudely*): As your secretary might say, if you stuff paper into a grate it'll burn brightly for a moment.

(*At this point* GLORIA, *freshly tinted and lustful of admiration and entertainment, rejoins the party, followed by her two friends. For several moments the conversation becomes entirely fragmentary.* GLORIA *calls* ANTHONY *aside.*)

GLORIA: Please don't drink much, Anthony.

ANTHONY: Why?

GLORIA: Because you're so simple when you're drunk.

ANTHONY: Good Lord! What's the matter now?

GLORIA (*after a pause during which her eyes gaze coolly into his*): Several things. In the first place, why do you insist on paying for everything? Both those men have more money than you!

ANTHONY: Why, Gloria! They're my guests!

GLORIA: That's no reason why you should pay for a bottle of champagne Rachael Barnes smashed. Dick tried to fix that second taxi bill, and you wouldn't let him.

ANTHONY: Why, Gloria –

GLORIA: When we have to keep selling bonds even to pay our bills, it's time to cut down on excess generosities. Moreover, I wouldn't be quite so attentive to Rachael Barnes. Her husband doesn't like it any more than I do!

ANTHONY: Why, Gloria –

GLORIA (*mimicking him sharply*): 'Why, Gloria!' But that's happened a little too often this summer – with every pretty woman you meet. It's grown to be a sort of habit, and I'm *not* going to stand it! If you can play around, I can, too. (*then, as an afterthought*) By the way, this Fred person isn't a second Joe Hull, is he?

ANTHONY: Heavens, no! He probably came up to get me to wheedle some money out of my grandfather for his flock.

(GLORIA *turns away from a very depressed* ANTHONY *and returns to her guests.*

By nine o'clock these can be divided into two classes – those who have

*been drinking consistently and those who have taken little or nothing.
In the second group are the* BARNESES, MURIEL *and* FREDERICK E.
PARAMORE.)

MURIEL: I wish I could write. I get these ideas but I never seem to be
able to put them in words.

DICK: As Goliath said, he understood how David felt, but he couldn't
express himself. The remark was immediately adopted for a motto
by the Philistines.

MURIEL: I don't get you. I must be getting stupid in my old age.

GLORIA (*weaving unsteadily among the company like an exhilarated angel*):
If anyone's hungry there's some French pastry on the dining-
room table.

MAURY: Can't tolerate those Victorian designs it comes in.

MURIEL (*violently amused*): I'd say you're tight, Maury.

(*Her bosom is still a pavement that she offers to the hoofs of many
passing stallions, hoping that their iron shoes may strike even a spark of
romance in the darkness . . .*

Messrs BARNES *and* PARAMORE *have been engaged in conversation
upon some wholesome subject, a subject so wholesome that* MR BARNES *has
been trying for several moments to creep into the more tainted air around
the central lounge. Whether* PARAMORE *is lingering in the grey house out
of politeness or curiosity, or in order at some future time to make a
sociological report on the decadence of American life, is problematical.*)

MAURY: Fred, I imagined you were very broad-minded.

PARAMORE: I am.

MURIEL: Me, too. I believe one religion's as good as another and
everything.

PARAMORE: There's some good in all religions.

MURIEL: I'm a Catholic but, as I always say, I'm not working at it.

PARAMORE (*with a tremendous burst of tolerance*): The Catholic religion
is a very – a very powerful religion.

MAURY: Well, such a broad-minded man should consider the raised
plane of sensation and the stimulated optimism contained in this
cocktail.

PARAMORE (*taking the drink, rather defiantly*): Thanks, I'll try – one.

MAURY: One? Outrageous! Here we have a class-of-nineteen-ten
reunion, and you refuse to be even a little pickled. Come on!

> Here's a health to King Charles,
> Here's a health to King Charles,
> Bring the bowl that you boast –

(PARAMORE *joins in with a hearty voice.*)

MAURY: Fill the cup, Frederick. You know everything's subordinated to nature's purposes with us, and her purpose with you is to make you a rip-roaring tippler.

PARAMORE: If a fellow can drink like a gentleman –

MAURY: What is a gentleman, anyway?

ANTHONY: A man who never has pins under his coat lapel.

MAURY: Nonsense! A man's social rank is determined by the amount of bread he eats in a sandwich.

DICK: He's a man who prefers the first edition of a book to the last edition of a newspaper.

RACHAEL : A man who never gives an impersonation of a dope-fiend.

MAURY: An American who can fool an English butler into thinking he's one.

MURIEL: A man who comes from a good family and went to Yale or Harvard or Princeton, and has money and dances well, and all that.

MAURY: At last – the perfect definition! Cardinal Newman's is now a back number.[286]

PARAMORE: I think we ought to look on the question more broad-mindedly. Was it Abraham Lincoln who said that a gentleman is one who never inflicts pain?

MAURY: It's attributed, I believe, to General Ludendorff.[287]

PARAMORE: Surely you're joking.

MAURY: Have another drink.

PARAMORE: I oughtn't to. (*lowering his voice for* MAURY's *ear alone*) What if I were to tell you this is the third drink I've ever taken in my life?

(DICK *starts the phonograph, which provokes* MURIEL *to rise and sway from side to side, her elbows against her ribs, her forearms perpendicular to her body and out like fins.*)

MURIEL: Oh, let's take up the rugs and dance!

(*This suggestion is received by* ANTHONY *and* GLORIA *with interior groans and sickly smiles of acquiescence.*)

MURIEL: Come on, you lazybones. Get up and move the furniture back.

DICK: Wait till I finish my drink.

MAURY (*intent on his purpose towards* PARAMORE): I'll tell you what. Let's each fill one glass, drink it off and then we'll dance.

(*A wave of protest breaks against the rock of* MAURY's *insistence.*)

MURIEL: My head is simply going *round* now.

RACHAEL (*in an undertone to* ANTHONY): Did Gloria tell you to stay away from me?

ANTHONY (*confused*): Why, certainly not. Of course not.

(RACHAEL *smiles at him inscrutably. Two years have given her a sort of hard, well-groomed beauty.*)

MAURY (*holding up his glass*): Here's to the defeat of democracy and the fall of Christianity.

MURIEL: Now really!

(*She flashes a mock-reproachful glance at* MAURY *and then drinks. They all drink, with varying degrees of difficulty.*)

MURIEL: Clear the floor!

(*It seems inevitable that this process is to be gone through, so* ANTHONY *and* GLORIA *join in the great moving of tables, piling of chairs, rolling of carpets, and breaking of lamps. When the furniture has been stacked in ugly masses at the sides, there appears a space about eight feet square.*)

MURIEL: Oh, let's have music!

MAURY: Tana will render the love song of an eye, ear, nose and throat specialist.

(*Amid some confusion due to the fact that* TANA *has retired for the night, preparations are made for the performance. The pyjamaed Japanese, flute in hand, is wrapped in a comforter and placed in a chair atop one of the tables, where he makes a ludicrous and grotesque spectacle.* PARAMORE *is perceptibly drunk and so enraptured with the notion that he increases the effect by simulating funny-paper staggers and even venturing on an occasional hiccup.*)

PARAMORE (*to* GLORIA): Want to dance with me?

GLORIA: No, sir! Want to do the swan dance. Can you do it?

PARAMORE: Sure. Do them all.

GLORIA: All right. You start from that side of the room and I'll start from this.

MURIEL: Let's go!

(*Then Bedlam creeps screaming out of the bottles:* TANA *plunges into the recondite mazes of the train-song, the plaintive 'tootle toot-toot' blending its melancholy cadences with the 'Poor Butter-fly* [288] [*tink-atink*]*, by the blossoms waiting' of the phonograph.* MURIEL *is too weak with laughter to do more than cling desperately to* BARNES, *who, dancing with the ominous rigidity of an army officer, tramps without humour around the small space.* ANTHONY *is trying to hear* RACHAEL'*s whisper – without attracting* GLORIA'*s attention . . .*

But the grotesque, the unbelievable, the histrionic incident is about to occur, one of those incidents in which life seems set upon the passionate imitation of the lowest forms of literature. PARAMORE *has been trying to emulate* GLORIA, *and as the commotion reaches its height he begins to spin round and round, more and more dizzily – he staggers, recovers, staggers again and then falls in the direction of the hall . . . almost into the arms of old* ADAM PATCH, *whose approach has been rendered inaudible by the pandemonium in the room.*

ADAM PATCH *is very white. He leans upon a stick. The man with him is* EDWARD SHUTTLEWORTH, *and it is he who seizes* PARAMORE *by the shoulder and deflects the course of his fall away from the venerable philanthropist.*

The time required for quiet to descend upon the room like a monstrous pall may be estimated at two minutes, though for a short period after that the phonograph gags and the notes of the Japanese train-song dribble from the end of TANA's *flute. Of the nine people only* BARNES, PARAMORE *and* TANA *are unaware of the late-comer's identity. Of the nine not one is aware that* ADAM PATCH *has that morning made a contribution of fifty thousand dollars to the cause of national Prohibition.*

It is given to PARAMORE *to break the gathering silence; the high tide of his life's depravity is reached in his incredible remark.*)

PARAMORE (*crawling rapidly towards the kitchen on his hands and knees*): I'm not a guest here – I work here.

(*Again silence falls – so deep now, so weighted with intolerably contagious apprehension, that* RACHAEL *gives a nervous little giggle, and* DICK *finds himself telling over and over a line from Swinburne, grotesquely appropriate to the scene:*

'One gaunt bleak blossom of scentless breath.'[289]

. . . Out of the hush the voice of ANTHONY, *sober and strained, saying something to* ADAM PATCH; *then this, too, dies away.*)

SHUTTLEWORTH (*passionately*): Your grandfather thought he would motor over to see your house. I phoned from Rye and left a message. (*A series of little gasps, emanating, apparently, from nowhere, from no one, fall into the next pause.* ANTHONY *is the colour of chalk.* GLORIA's *lips are parted and her level gaze at the old man is tense and frightened. There is not one smile in the room. Not one? Or does* CROSS PATCH's *drawn mouth tremble slightly open, to expose the even rows of his thin teeth? He speaks – five mild and simple words.*)

ADAM PATCH: We'll go back now, Shuttleworth – (*And that is all. He turns, and assisted by his cane goes out through the hall, through the front door, and with hellish portentousness his uncertain footsteps crunch on the gravel path under the August moon.*)

RETROSPECT

In this extremity they were like two goldfish in a bowl from which all the water had been drawn; they could not even swim across to each other.

Gloria would be twenty-six in May. There was nothing, she had said, that she wanted, except to be young and beautiful for a long time, to be gay and happy, and to have money and love. She wanted what most women want, but she wanted it much more fiercely and passionately. She had been married over two years. At first there had been days of serene understanding, rising to ecstasies of proprietorship and pride. Alternating with these periods had occurred sporadic hates, enduring a short hour, and forgetfulnesses lasting no longer than an afternoon. That had been for half a year.

Then the serenity, the content, had become less jubilant, had become, grey – very rarely, with the spur of jealousy or forced separation, the ancient ecstasies returned, the apparent communion of soul and soul, the emotional excitement. It was possible for her to hate Anthony for as much as a full day, to be carelessly incensed at him for as long as a week. Recrimination had displaced affection as an indulgence, almost as an entertainment, and there were nights when they would go to sleep trying to remember who was angry and who should be reserved next morning. And as the second year waned there had entered two new elements. Gloria realised that Anthony had become capable of utter indifference towards her, a temporary indifference, more than half lethargic, but one from which she could no longer stir him by a whispered word, or a certain intimate smile. There were days when her caresses affected him as a sort of suffocation. She was conscious of these things; she never entirely admitted them to herself.

It was only recently that she perceived that in spite of her adoration of him, her jealousy, her servitude, her pride, she fundamentally despised him – and her contempt blended indistinguishably with her other emotions . . . All this was her love – the vital and feminine illusion that had directed itself towards him one April night, many months before.

On Anthony's part she was, in spite of these qualifications, his sole preoccupation. Had he lost her he would have been a broken man, wretchedly and sentimentally absorbed in her memory for the remainder of life. He seldom took pleasure in an entire day spent alone with her – except on occasions he preferred to have a third person with them. There were times when he felt that if he were not left absolutely alone he would go mad – there were a few times when he definitely hated her. In his cups he was capable of short attractions towards other women, the hitherto-suppressed outcroppings of an experimental temperament.

That spring, that summer, they had speculated upon future happiness – how they were to travel from summer land to summer land, returning eventually to a gorgeous estate and possible idyllic children, then entering diplomacy or politics, to accomplish, for a while, beautiful and important things, until finally as a white-haired (beautifully, silkily, white-haired) couple they were to loll about in serene glory, worshipped by the bourgeoisie of the land . . . These times were to begin 'when we get our money'; it was on such dreams rather than on any satisfaction with their increasingly irregular, increasingly dissipated life that their hope rested. On grey mornings when the jests of the night before had shrunk to ribaldries without wit or dignity, they could, after a fashion, bring out this batch of common hopes and count them over, then smile at each other and repeat, by way of clinching the matter, the terse yet sincere Nietzscheanism of Gloria's defiant 'I don't care!'

Things had been slipping perceptibly. There was the money question, increasingly annoying, increasingly ominous; there was the realisation that liquor had become a practical necessity to their amuse-ment – not an uncommon phenomenon in the British aristocracy of a hundred years ago, but a somewhat alarming one in a civilisation steadily becoming more temperate and more circumspect. Moreover, both of them seemed vaguely weaker in fibre, not so much in what they did as in their subtle reactions to the civilisation about them. In Gloria had been born something that she had hitherto never needed – the skeleton, incomplete but nevertheless unmistakable, of her ancient abhorrence, a conscience. This admission to herself was coincidental with the slow decline of her physical courage.

Then, on the August morning after Adam Patch's unexpected call, they awoke, nauseated and tired, dispirited with life, capable only of one pervasive emotion – fear.

PANIC

'Well?' Anthony sat up in bed and looked down at her. The corners of his lips were drooping with depression, his voice was strained and hollow.

Her reply was to raise her hand to her mouth and begin a slow, precise nibbling at her finger.

'We've done it,' he said after a pause; then, as she was still silent, he became exasperated. 'Why don't you say something?'

'What on earth do you want me to say?'

'What are you thinking?'

'Nothing.'

'Then stop biting your finger!'

Ensued a short confused discussion of whether or not she had been thinking. It seemed essential to Anthony that she should muse aloud upon last night's disaster. Her silence was a method of settling the responsibility on him. For her part she saw no necessity for speech – the moment required that she should gnaw at her finger like a nervous child.

'I've got to fix up this damn mess with my grandfather,' he said with uneasy conviction. A faint newborn respect was indicated by his use of 'my grandfather' instead of 'grampa'.

'You can't,' she affirmed abruptly. 'You can't – *ever*. He'll never forgive you as long as he lives.'

'Perhaps not,' agreed Anthony miserably. 'Still – I might possibly square myself by some sort of reformation and all that sort of thing – '

'He looked sick,' she interrupted, 'pale as flour.'

'He *is* sick. I told you that three months ago.'

'I wish he'd died last week!' she said petulantly. 'Inconsiderate old fool!'

Neither of them laughed.

'But just let me say,' she added quietly, 'the next time I see you acting with any woman like you did with Rachael Barnes last night, I'll leave you – *just – like – that*! I'm simply *not* going to stand it!'

Anthony quailed. 'Oh, don't be absurd,' he protested. 'You know there's no woman in the world for me except you – none, dearest.'

His attempt at a tender note failed miserably – the more imminent danger stalked back into the foreground.

'If I went to him,' suggested Anthony, 'and said with appropriate biblical quotations that I'd walked too long in the way of unrighteousness and at last seen the light – ' He broke off and glanced with a whimsical expression at his wife. 'I wonder what he'd do?'

'I don't know.'

She was speculating as to whether or not their guests would have the acumen to leave directly after breakfast.

Not for a week did Anthony muster the courage to go to Tarry-town. The prospect was revolting and left alone he would have been incapable of making the trip – but if his will had deteriorated in these past three years, so had his power to resist urging. Gloria compelled him to go. It was all very well to wait a week, she said, for that would give his grandfather's violent animosity time to cool – but to wait longer would be an error – it would give it a chance to harden.

He went, in trepidation . . . and vainly. Adam Patch was not well, said Shuttleworth indignantly. Positive instructions had been given that no one was to see him. Before the ex-gin-physician's vindictive eye Anthony's front wilted. He walked out to his taxicab with what was almost a slink – recovering only a little of his self-respect as he boarded the train; glad to escape, boylike, to the wonder palaces of consolation that still rose and glittered in his own mind.

Gloria was scornful when he returned to Marietta. Why had he not forced his way in? That was what she would have done!

Between them they drafted a letter to the old man, and after considerable revision sent it off. It was half an apology, half a manufactured explanation. The letter was not answered.

Came a day in September, a day slashed with alternate sun and rain, sun without warmth, rain without freshness. On that day they left the grey house, which had seen the flower of their love. Four trunks and three monstrous crates were piled in the dismantled room where, two years before, they had sprawled lazily, thinking in terms of dreams, remote, languorous, content. The room echoed with emptiness. Gloria, in a new brown dress edged with fur, sat upon a trunk in silence, and Anthony walked nervously to and fro smoking, as they waited for the truck that would take their things to the city.

'What are those?' she demanded, pointing to some books piled upon one of the crates.

'That's my old stamp collection,' he confessed sheepishly. 'I forgot to pack it.'

'Anthony, it's so silly to carry it around.'

'Well, I was looking through it the day we left the apartment last spring, and I decided not to store it.'

'Can't you sell it? Haven't we enough junk?'

'I'm sorry,' he said humbly.

With a thunderous rattling the truck rolled up to the door. Gloria shook her fist defiantly at the four walls. 'I'm so glad to go!' she cried, 'so glad. Oh, my God, how I hate this house!'

So the brilliant and beautiful lady went up with her husband to New York. On the very train that bore them away they quarrelled – her bitter words had the frequency, the regularity, the inevitability of the stations they passed.

'Don't be cross,' begged Anthony piteously. 'We've got nothing but each other, after all.'

'We haven't even that, most of the time,' cried Gloria.

'When haven't we?'

'A lot of times – beginning with one occasion on the station platform at Redgate.'

'You don't mean to say that – '

'No,' she interrupted coolly, 'I don't brood over it. It came and went – and when it went it took something with it.'

She finished abruptly. Anthony sat in silence, confused, depressed. The drab visions of train-side Mamaroneck, Larchmont, Rye, Pelham Manor, succeeded each other with intervals of bleak and shoddy wastes posing ineffectually as country. He found himself remembering how on one summer morning they two had started from New York in search of happiness. They had never expected to find it, perhaps, yet in itself that quest had been happier than anything he expected for ever more. Life, it seemed, must be a setting up of props around one – otherwise it was disaster. There was no rest, no quiet. He had been futile in longing to drift and dream; no one drifted except to maelstroms, no one dreamed without his dreams becoming fantastic nightmares of indecision and regret.

Pelham! They had quarrelled in Pelham because Gloria must drive. And when she set her little foot on the accelerator the car had jumped off spunkily, and their two heads had jerked back like marionettes worked by a single string.

The Bronx – the houses gathering and gleaming in the sun, which was falling now through wide refulgent skies and tumbling caravans of light down into the streets. New York, he supposed, was home – the city of luxury and mystery, of preposterous hopes and exotic dreams. Here on the outskirts absurd stucco palaces reared themselves in the cool sunset, poised for an instant in cool unreality, glided off far away, succeeded by the mazed confusion of the Harlem River. The train moved in through the deepening twilight, above and past half a hundred cheerful sweating streets of the upper East Side, each one passing the car window like the space between the spokes of a gigantic wheel, each one with its vigorous colourful revelation of poor children swarming in feverish activity like vivid ants in alleys of red sand. From the tenement windows leaned rotund, moon-shaped mothers, as constellations of this sordid heaven; women like dark imperfect jewels, women like vegetables, women like great bags of abominably dirty laundry.

'I like these streets,' observed Anthony aloud. 'I always feel as though it's a performance being staged for me; as though the second I've passed they'll all stop leaping and laughing and, instead, grow very sad, remembering how poor they are, and retreat with bowed heads into their houses. You often get that effect abroad, but seldom in this country.'

Down in a tall busy street he read a dozen Jewish names on a line of stores; in the door of each stood a dark little man watching the passers-by from intent eyes – eyes gleaming with suspicion, with pride, with clarity, with cupidity, with comprehension. New York – he could not dissociate it now from the slow, upward creep of this people – the little stores, growing, expanding, consolidating, moving, watched over with a hawk's eyes and a bee's attention to detail – they slathered out on all sides. It was impressive – in perspective it was tremendous.

Gloria's voice broke in with strange appropriateness upon his thoughts.

'I wonder where Bloeckman's been this summer.'

THE APARTMENT

After the sureties of youth there sets in a period of intense and intolerable complexity. With the soda-jerker this period is so short as to be almost negligible. Men higher in the scale hold out longer in the attempt to preserve the ultimate niceties of relationship, to retain 'impractical' ideas of integrity. But by the late twenties the business has grown too intricate, and what has hitherto been imminent and confusing has become gradually remote and dim. Routine comes down like twilight on a harsh landscape, softening it until it is tolerable. The complexity is too subtle, too varied; the values are changing utterly with each lesion of vitality; it has begun to appear that we can learn nothing from the past with which to face the future – so we cease to be impulsive, convincible men, interested in what is ethically true by fine margins, we substitute rules of conduct for ideas of integrity, we value safety above romance, we become, quite unconsciously, pragmatic. It is left to the few to be persistently concerned with the nuances of relationships – and even this few only in certain hours especially set aside for the task.

Anthony Patch had ceased to be an individual of mental adventure, of curiosity, and had become an individual of bias and prejudice, with a longing to be emotionally undisturbed. This gradual change had taken place through the past several years, accelerated by a succession of anxieties preying on his mind. There was, first of all, the sense of waste, always dormant in his heart, now awakened by the circumstances of his position. In his moments of insecurity he was haunted by the suggestion that life might be, after all, significant. In his early twenties the conviction of the futility of effort, of the wisdom of abnegation, had been confirmed by the philosophies he had admired as well as by his association with Maury Noble, and later with his wife. Yet there had been occasions – just before his first meeting with Gloria, for example, and when his grandfather had suggested that he should go abroad as a war correspondent – upon which his dissatisfaction had driven him almost to a positive step.

One day just before they left Marietta for the last time, in carelessly turning over the pages of a *Harvard Alumni Bulletin*, he had found a column which told him what his contemporaries had been about in this six years since graduation. Most of them were in business, it was true, and several were converting the heathen of China or America to a nebulous Protestantism; but a few, he found, were working constructively at jobs that were neither sinecures nor routines. There was Calvin Boyd, for instance, who, though barely out of medical school, had discovered a new treatment for typhus, had shipped abroad and was mitigating some of the civilisation that the Great Powers had brought to Servia; there was Eugene Bronson, whose articles in the *New Democracy* were stamping him as a man with ideas transcending both vulgar timeliness and popular hysteria; there was a man named Daly who had been suspended from the faculty of a righteous university for preaching Marxian doctrines in the class-room: in art, science, politics, he saw the authentic personalities of his time emerging – there was even Severance, the quarter-back, who had given up his life rather neatly and gracefully with the Foreign Legion on the Aisne.

He laid down the magazine and thought for a while about these diverse men. In the days of his integrity he would have defended his attitude to the last – an Epicurus in Nirvana, he would have cried that to struggle was to believe, to believe was to limit. He would as soon have become a churchgoer because the prospect of immortality gratified him as he would have considered entering the leather business because the intensity of the competition would have kept him from unhappiness. But at present he had no such delicate scruples. This autumn, as his twenty-ninth year began, he was inclined to close his mind to many things, to avoid prying deeply into motive and first causes, and mostly to long passionately for security from the world and from himself. He hated to be alone, as has been said he often dreaded being alone with Gloria.

Because of the chasm which his grandfather's visit had opened before him, and the consequent revulsion from his late mode of life, it was inevitable that he should look around in this suddenly hostile city for the friends and environments that had once seemed the warmest and most secure. His first step was a desperate attempt to get back his old apartment.

In the spring of 1912 he had signed a four-year lease at seventeen hundred a year, with an option of renewal. This lease had expired the previous May. When he had first rented the rooms they had been mere potentialities, scarcely to be discerned as that, but Anthony had seen into these potentialities and arranged in the lease that he and the landlord should each spend a certain amount in improvements. Rents had gone up in the past four years, and last spring when Anthony had waived his option the landlord, a Mr Sohenberg, had realised that he could get a much bigger price for what was now a prepossessing apartment. Accordingly, when Anthony approached him on the subject in September he was met with Sohenberg's offer of a three-year lease at twenty-five hundred a year. This, it seemed to Anthony, was outrageous. It meant that well over a third of their income would be consumed in rent. In vain he argued that his own money, his own ideas on the repartitioning, had made the rooms attractive.

In vain he offered two thousand dollars – twenty-two hundred, though they could ill afford it: Mr Sohenberg was obdurate. It seemed that two other gentlemen were considering it; just that sort of an apartment was in demand at the moment, and it would scarcely be business to *give* it to Mr Patch. Besides, though he had never mentioned it before, several of the other tenants had complained of noise during the previous winter – singing and dancing late at night, that sort of thing.

Internally raging, Anthony hurried back to the Ritz to report his discomfiture to Gloria.

'I can just see you,' she stormed, 'letting him back you down!'

'What could I say?'

'You could have told him what he *was*. I wouldn't have *stood* it. No other man in the world would have stood it! You just let people order you around and cheat you and bully you and take advantage of you as if you were a silly little boy. It's absurd!'

'Oh, for heaven's sake, don't lose your temper.'

'I know, Anthony, but you *are* such an ass!'

'Well, possibly. Anyway, we can't afford that apartment. But we can afford it better than living here at the Ritz.'

'You were the one who insisted on coming here.'

'Yes, because I knew you'd be miserable in a cheap hotel.'

'Of course I would!'

'At any rate we've got to find a place to live.'

'How much can we pay?' she demanded.

'Well, we can pay even his price if we sell more bonds, but we agreed last night that until I had found something definite to do we – '

'Oh, I know all that. I asked you how much we can pay out of just our income.'

'They say you ought not to pay more than a fourth.'

'How much is a fourth?'

'One hundred and fifty a month.'

'Do you mean to say we've got only six hundred dollars coming in every month?' A subdued note crept into her voice.

'Of course!' he answered angrily. 'Do you think we've gone on spending more than twelve thousand a year without cutting way into our capital?'

'I knew we'd sold bonds, but – have we spent that much a year? How did we?' Her awe increased.

'Oh, I'll look in those careful account-books we kept,' he remarked ironically, and then added: 'Two rents a good part of the time, clothes, travel – why, each of those springs in California cost about four thousand dollars. That darn car was an expense from start to finish. And parties and amusements and – oh, one thing or another.'

They were both excited now and inordinately depressed. The situation seemed worse in the actual telling Gloria than it had when he had first made the discovery himself.

'You've got to make some money,' she said suddenly.

'I know it.'

'And you've got to make another attempt to see your grandfather.'

'I will.'

'When?'

'When we get settled.'

This eventuality occurred a week later. They rented a small apartment on Fifty-Seventh Street at one hundred and fifty a month. It included bedroom, living-room, kitchenette and bath, in a thin, white-stone apartment house, and though the rooms were too small to display Anthony's best furniture, they were clean, new and, in a blonde and sanitary way, not unattractive. Bounds had gone abroad to enlist in the British army, and in his place they tolerated rather than enjoyed the services of a gaunt, big-boned Irishwoman, whom Gloria loathed because she discussed the glories of Sinn Fein as she served breakfast. But they vowed they would have no more Japanese, and English servants were for the present hard to obtain. Like Bounds, the woman prepared only breakfast. Their other meals they took at restaurants and hotels.

What finally drove Anthony post-haste up to Tarrytown was an announcement in several New York papers that Adam Patch, the multimillionaire, the philanthropist, the venerable uplifter, was seriously ill and not expected to recover.

THE KITTEN

Anthony could not see him. The doctors' instructions were that he was to talk to no one, said Mr Shuttleworth – who offered kindly to take any message that Anthony might care to entrust with him, and deliver it to Adam Patch when his condition permitted. But by obvious innuendo he confirmed Anthony's melancholy inference that the prodigal grandson would be particularly unwelcome at the bedside. At one point in the conversation Anthony, with Gloria's positive instructions in mind, made a move as though to brush by the secretary, but Shuttleworth with a smile squared his brawny shoulders, and Anthony saw how futile such an attempt would be.

Miserably intimidated, he returned to New York, where husband and wife passed a restless week. A little incident that occurred one evening indicated to what tension their nerves were drawn.

Walking home along a cross-street after dinner, Anthony noticed a night-bound cat prowling near a railing.

'I always have an instinct to kick a cat,' he said idly.

'I like them.'

'I yielded to it once.'

'When?'

'Oh, years ago; before I met you. One night between the acts of a show. Cold night, like this, and I was a little tight – one of the first times I was ever tight,' he added. 'The poor little beggar was looking for a place to sleep, I guess, and I was in a mean mood, so it took my fancy to kick it – '

'Oh, the poor kitty!' cried Gloria, sincerely moved. Inspired with the narrative instinct, Anthony enlarged on the theme.

'It was pretty bad,' he admitted. 'The poor little beast turned around and looked at me rather plaintively as though hoping I'd pick him up and be kind to him – he was really just a kitten – and before he knew it a big foot launched out at him and caught his little back – '

'Oh!' Gloria's cry was full of anguish.

'It was such a cold night,' he continued, perversely, keeping his voice upon a melancholy note. 'I guess it expected kindness from somebody, and it got only pain – '

He broke off suddenly – Gloria was sobbing. They had reached home, and when they entered the apartment she threw herself upon the lounge, crying as though he had struck at her very soul.

'Oh, the poor little kitty!' she repeated piteously, 'the poor little kitty. So cold – '

'Gloria'

'Don't come near me! Please, don't come near me. You killed the soft little kitty.'

Touched, Anthony knelt beside her.

'Dear,' he said. 'Oh, Gloria, darling. It isn't true. I invented it – every word of it.'

But she would not believe him. There had been something in the details he had chosen to describe that made her cry herself asleep that night, for the kitten, for Anthony, for herself, for the pain and bitterness and cruelty of all the world.

THE PASSING OF AN AMERICAN MORALIST

Old Adam died on a midnight of late November with a pious compliment to his God on his thin lips. He, who had been flattered so much, faded out flattering the Omnipotent Abstraction which he fancied he might have angered in the more lascivious moments of his youth. It was announced that he had arranged some sort of an armistice with the deity, the terms of which were not made public, though they were thought to have included a large cash payment. All the newspapers printed his biography, and two of them ran short editorials on his sterling worth, and his part in the drama of industrialism, with which he had grown up. They referred guardedly to the reforms he had sponsored and financed. The memories of Comstock and Cato the Censor[290] were resuscitated and paraded like gaunt ghosts through the columns.

Every newspaper remarked that he was survived by a single grandson, Anthony Comstock Patch, of New York.

The burial took place in the family plot at Tarrytown. Anthony and Gloria rode in the first carriage, too worried to feel grotesque, both trying desperately to glean presage of fortune from the faces of retainers who had been with him at the end.

They waited a frantic week for decency, and then, having received no notification of any kind, Anthony called up his grandfather's lawyer. Mr Brett was not in – he was expected back in an hour. Anthony left his telephone number.

It was the last day of November, cool and crackling outside, with a lustreless sun peering bleakly in at the windows. While they waited for the call, ostensibly engaged in reading, the atmosphere, within and without, seemed pervaded with a deliberate rendition of the pathetic fallacy. After an interminable while, the bell jingled, and Anthony, starting violently, took up the receiver.

'Hello . . . ' His voice was strained and hollow. 'Yes – I did leave word. Who is this, please? . . . Yes . . . Why, it was about the estate. Naturally I'm interested, and I've received no word about the reading of the will – I thought you might not have my address . . . What? . . . Yes . . . '

Gloria fell on her knees. The intervals between Anthony's speeches were like tourniquets winding on her heart. She found herself helplessly twisting the large buttons from a velvet cushion. Then: 'That's – that's very, very odd – that's very odd – that's very odd. Not even any – ah – mention or any – ah – reason?'

His voice sounded faint and far away. She uttered a little sound, half gasp, half cry.

'Yes, I'll see . . . All right, thanks . . . thanks . . . '

The phone clicked. Her eyes looking along the floor saw his feet cut the pattern of a patch of sunlight on the carpet. She arose and faced him with a grey, level glance just as his arms folded about her.

'My dearest,' he whispered huskily. 'He did it, goddamn him!'

'Who are the heirs?' asked Mr Haight. 'You see when you can tell me so little about it – '

Mr Haight was tall and bent and beetle-browed. He had been recommended to Anthony as an astute and tenacious lawyer.

'I only know vaguely,' answered Anthony. 'A man named Shuttleworth, who was a sort of pet of his, has the whole thing in charge as administrator or trustee or something – all except the direct bequests to charity and the provisions for servants and for those two cousins in Idaho.'

'How distant are the cousins?'

'Oh, third or fourth, anyway. I never even heard of them.'

Mr Haight nodded comprehensively.

'And you want to contest a provision of the will?'

'I guess so,' admitted Anthony helplessly. 'I want to do what sounds most hopeful – that's what I want you to tell me.'

'You want them to refuse probate to the will?'

Anthony shook his head.

'You've got me. I haven't any idea what "probate" is. I want a share of the estate.'

'Suppose you tell me some more details. For instance, do you know why the testator disinherited you?'

'Why – yes,' began Anthony. 'You see he was always a sucker for moral reform, and all that – '

'I know,' interjected Mr Haight humourlessly.

' – and I don't suppose he ever thought I was much good. I didn't go into business, you see. But I feel certain that up to last summer I was one of the beneficiaries. We had a house out in Marietta, and one night grandfather got the notion he'd come over and see us. It just happened that there was a rather gay party going on and he arrived without any warning. Well, he took one look, he and this fellow Shuttleworth, and then turned around and tore right back to Tarrytown. After that he never answered my letters or even let me see him.'

'He was a Prohibitionist, wasn't he?'

'He was everything – regular religious maniac.'

'How long before his death was the will made that disinherited you?'

'Recently – I mean since August.'

'And you think that the direct reason for his not leaving you the majority of the estate was his displeasure with your recent actions?'

'Yes.'

Mr Haight considered. Upon what grounds was Anthony thinking of contesting the will?

'Why, isn't there something about evil influence?'

'Undue influence is one ground – but it's the most difficult. You would have to show that such pressure was brought to bear so that the deceased was in a condition where he disposed of his property contrary to his intentions – '

'Well, suppose this fellow Shuttleworth dragged him over to Marietta just when he thought some sort of a celebration was probably going on?'

'That wouldn't have any bearing on the case. There's a strong division between advice and influence. You'd have to prove that the secretary had a sinister intention. I'd suggest some other grounds. A will is automatically refused probate in case of insanity, drunkenness' – here Anthony smiled – 'or feeble-mindedness through premature old age.'

'But,' objected Anthony, 'his private physician, being one of the beneficiaries, would testify that he wasn't feeble-minded. And he wasn't. As a matter of fact he probably did just what he intended to with his money – it was perfectly consistent with everything he'd ever done in his life – '

'Well, you see, feeble-mindedness is a great deal like undue influence – it implies that the property wasn't disposed of as originally intended. The most common ground is duress – physical pressure.'

Anthony shook his head.

'Not much chance on that, I'm afraid. Undue influence sounds best to me.'

After more discussion, so technical as to be largely unintelligible to Anthony, he retained Mr Haight as counsel. The lawyer proposed an interview with Shuttleworth, who, jointly with Wilson, Hiemer and Hardy, was executor of the will. Anthony was to come back later in the week.

It transpired that the estate consisted of approximately forty million dollars. The largest bequest to an individual was of one million, to Edward Shuttleworth, who received in addition thirty thousand a year salary as administrator of the thirty-million-dollar trust fund, left to be doled out to various charities and reform societies practically at his own discretion. The remaining nine millions were proportioned among the two cousins in Idaho and about twenty-five other beneficiaries: friends, secretaries, servants

and employees, who had, at one time or another, earned the seal of
Adam Patch's approval.

At the end of another fortnight Mr Haight, on a retainer's fee of
fifteen thousand dollars, had begun preparations for contesting the
will.

THE WINTER OF DISCONTENT

Before they had been two months in the little apartment on Fifty-
Seventh Street, it had assumed for both of them the same indefinable
but almost material taint that had impregnated the grey house in
Marietta. There was the odour of tobacco always – both of
them smoked incessantly; it was in their clothes, their blankets, the
curtains and the ash-littered carpets. Added to this was the wretched
aura of stale wine, with its inevitable suggestion of beauty gone foul
and revelry remembered in disgust. About a particular set of glass
goblets on the sideboard the odour was particularly noticeable, and
in the main room the mahogany table was ringed with white circles
where glasses had been set down upon it. There had been many
parties – people broke things; people became sick in Gloria's bathroom; people spilled wine; people made unbelievable messes of the
kitchenette.

These things were a regular part of their existence. Despite
the resolutions of many Mondays it was tacitly understood as the
weekend approached that it should be observed with some sort of
unholy excitement. When Saturday came they would not discuss
the matter, but would call up this person or that from among their
circle of sufficiently irresponsible friends, and suggest a rendezvous.
Only after the friends had gathered and Anthony had set out
decanters, would he murmur casually, 'I guess I'll have just one
highball myself – '

Then they were off for two days – realising on a wintry dawn that
they had been the noisiest and most conspicuous members of the
noisiest and most conspicuous party at the Boul' Mich', or the Club
Ramée, or at other resorts much less particular about the hilarity of
their clientèle. They would find that they had, somehow, squandered
eighty or ninety dollars, how, they never knew; they customarily
attributed it to the general penury of the 'friends' who had accompanied them.

It began to be not unusual for the more sincere of their friends to
remonstrate with them, in the very course of a party, and to predict

a sombre end for them in the loss of Gloria's 'looks' and Anthony's 'constitution'.

The story of the summarily interrupted revel in Marietta had, of course, leaked out in detail – 'Muriel doesn't mean to tell everyone she knows,' said Gloria to Anthony, 'but she thinks everyone she tells is the only one she's going to tell' – and, diaphanously veiled, the tale had been given a conspicuous place in *Town Tattle*.[291] When the terms of Adam Patch's will were made public and the newspapers printed items concerning Anthony's suit, the story was beautifully rounded out – to Anthony's infinite disparagement. They began to hear rumours about themselves from all quarters, rumours founded usually on a soupçon of truth, but overlaid with preposterous and sinister detail.

Outwardly they showed no signs of deterioration. Gloria at twenty-six was still the Gloria of twenty; her complexion a fresh damp setting for her candid eyes; her hair still a childish glory, darkening slowly from corn colour to a deep russet gold; her slender body suggesting ever a nymph running and dancing through Orphic groves. Masculine eyes, dozens of them, followed her with a fascinated stare when she walked through a hotel lobby or down the aisle of a theatre. Men asked to be introduced to her, fell into prolonged states of sincere admiration, made definite love to her – for she was still a thing of exquisite and unbelievable beauty. And for his part Anthony had rather gained than lost in appearance; his face had taken on a certain intangible air of tragedy, romantically contrasted with his trim and immaculate person.

Early in the winter, when all conversation turned on the probability of America's going into the war, when Anthony was making a desperate and sincere attempt to write, Muriel Kane arrived in New York and came immediately to see them. Like Gloria, she seemed never to change. She knew the latest slang, danced the latest dances, and talked of the latest songs and plays with all the fervour of her first season as a New York drifter. Her coyness was eternally new, eternally ineffectual; her clothes were extreme; her black hair was bobbed, now, like Gloria's.

'I've come up for the midwinter prom at New Haven,' she announced, imparting her delightful secret. Though she must have been older then than any of the boys in college, she managed always to secure some sort of invitation, imagining vaguely that at the next party would occur the flirtation which was to end at the romantic altar.

'Where've you been?' enquired Anthony, unfailingly amused.

'I've been at Hot Springs. It's been slick and peppy this fall – more *men*!'

'Are you in love, Muriel?'

'What do you mean "love"?' This was the rhetorical question of the year. 'I'm going to tell you something,' she said, switching the subject abruptly. 'I suppose it's none of my business, but I think it's time for you two to settle down.'

'Why, we are settled down.'

'Yes, you are!' she scoffed archly. 'Everywhere I go I hear stories of your escapades. Let me tell you, I have an awful time sticking up for you.'

'You needn't bother,' said Gloria coldly.

'Now, Gloria,' she protested, 'you know I'm one of your best friends.'

Gloria was silent. Muriel continued: 'It's not so much the idea of a woman drinking, but Gloria's so pretty, and so many people know her by sight all around, that it's naturally conspicuous – '

'What have you heard recently?' demanded Gloria, her dignity going down before her curiosity.

'Well, for instance, that that party in Marietta *killed* Anthony's grandfather.'

Instantly husband and wife were tense with annoyance.

'Why, I think that's outrageous.'

'That's what they say,' persisted Muriel stubbornly.

Anthony paced the room. 'It's preposterous!' he declared. 'The very people we take on parties shout the story around as a great joke – and eventually it gets back to us in some such form as this.'

Gloria began running her finger through a stray reddish curl. Muriel licked her veil as she considered her next remark.

'You ought to have a baby.'

Gloria looked up wearily.

'We can't afford it.'

'All the people in the slums have them,' said Muriel triumphantly.

Anthony and Gloria exchanged a smile. They had reached the stage of violent quarrels that were never made up, quarrels that smouldered and broke out again at intervals or died away from sheer indifference – but this visit of Muriel's drew them temporarily together. When the discomfort under which they were living was remarked upon by a third party, it gave them the impetus to face this hostile world together. It was very seldom, now, that the impulse towards reunion sprang from within.

Anthony found himself associating his own existence with that of the apartment's night-elevator man, a pale, scraggly bearded person of about sixty, with an air of being somewhat above his station. It was probably because of this quality that he had secured the position; it made him a pathetic and memorable figure of failure. Anthony recollected, without humour, a hoary jest about the elevator man's career being a matter of ups and downs – it was, at any rate, an enclosed life of infinite dreariness. Each time Anthony stepped into the car he waited breathlessly for the old man's, 'Well, I guess we're going to have some sunshine today.' Anthony thought how little rain or sunshine he would enjoy shut into that close little cage in the smoke-coloured, windowless hall.

A darkling figure, he attained tragedy in leaving the life that had used him so shabbily. Three young gunmen came in one night, tied him up and left him on a pile of coal in the cellar while they went through the trunk room. When the janitor found him next morning he had collapsed from chill. He died of pneumonia four days later.

He was replaced by a glib Martinique Negro, with an incongruous British accent and a tendency to be surly, whom Anthony detested. The passing of the old man had approximately the same effect on him that the kitten story had had on Gloria. He was reminded of the cruelty of all life and, in consequence, of the increasing bitterness of his own.

He was writing – and in earnest at last. He had gone to Dick and listened for a tense hour to an elucidation of those minutiae of procedure which hitherto he had rather scornfully looked down upon. He needed money immediately – he was selling bonds every month to pay their bills. Dick was frank and explicit: 'So far as articles on literary subjects in these obscure magazines go, you couldn't make enough to pay your rent. Of course if a man has the gift of humour, or a chance at a big biography, or some specialised knowledge, he may strike it rich. But for you, fiction's the only thing. You say you need money right away?'

'I certainly do.'

'Well, it'd be a year and a half before you'd make any money out of a novel. Try some popular short stories. And, by the way, unless they're exceptionally brilliant they have to be cheerful and on the side of the heaviest artillery to make you any money.'

Anthony thought of Dick's recent output, which had been appearing in a well-known monthly. It was concerned chiefly with the preposterous actions of a class of sawdust effigies who, one was assured, were New York society people, and it turned, as a rule, upon questions of the heroine's technical purity, with mock-sociological overtones about the 'mad antics of the four hundred'.[292]

'But your stories – ' exclaimed Anthony aloud, almost involuntarily.

'Oh, that's different,' Dick asserted astoundingly. 'I have a reputation, you see, so I'm expected to deal with strong themes.'

Anthony gave an interior start, realising with this remark how much Richard Caramel had fallen off. Did he actually think that these amazing latter productions were as good as his first novel?

Anthony went back to the apartment and set to work. He found that the business of optimism was no mean task. After half a dozen futile starts he went to the public library and for a week investigated the files of a popular magazine. Then, better equipped, he accomplished his first story, 'The Dictaphone of Fate'. It was founded upon one of his few remaining impressions of that six weeks in Wall Street the year before. It purported to be the sunny tale of an office boy who, quite by accident, hummed a wonderful melody into the dictaphone. The cylinder was discovered by the boss's brother, a well-known producer of musical comedy – and then immediately lost. The body of the story was concerned with the pursuit of the missing cylinder and the eventual marriage of the noble office boy (now a successful composer) to Miss Rooney, the virtuous stenographer, who was half Joan of Arc and half Florence Nightingale.

He had gathered that this was what the magazines wanted. He offered, in his protagonists, the customary denizens of the pink-and-blue literary world, immersing them in a saccharine plot that would offend not a single stomach in Marietta. He had it typed in double space – this last as advised by a booklet, *Success as a Writer Made Easy*, by R. Meggs Widdlestien, which assured the ambitious plumber of the futility of perspiration, since after a six-lesson course he could make at least a thousand dollars a month.

After reading it to a bored Gloria and coaxing from her the immemorial remark that it was 'better than a lot of stuff that gets published', he satirically affixed the *nom de plume* of 'Gilles de Sade', enclosed the proper return envelope, and sent it off.

Following the gigantic labour of conception he decided to wait until he heard from the first story before beginning another. Dick had told him that he might get as much as two hundred dollars. If by any chance it did happen to be unsuited, the editor's letter would, no doubt, give him an idea of what changes should be made.

'It is, without question, the most abominable piece of writing in existence,' said Anthony.

The editor quite conceivably agreed with him. He returned the manuscript with a rejection slip. Anthony sent it off elsewhere and began another story. The second one was called 'The Little Open Doors'; it was written in three days. It concerned the occult: an estranged couple were brought together by a medium in a vaudeville show.

There were six altogether, six wretched and pitiable efforts to 'write down' by a man who had never before made a consistent effort to write at all. Not one of them contained a spark of vitality, and their total yield of grace and felicity was less than that of an average newspaper column. During their circulation they collected, all told, thirty-one rejection slips, headstones for the packages that he would find lying like dead bodies at his door.

In mid-January Gloria's father died, and they went again to Kansas City – a miserable trip, for Gloria brooded interminably, not upon her father's death, but on her mother's. Russel Gilbert's affairs having been cleared up, they came into possession of about three thousand dollars, and a great amount of furniture. This was in storage, for he had spent his last days in a small hotel. It was due to his death that Anthony made a new discovery concerning Gloria. On the journey East she disclosed herself, astonishingly, as a Bilphist.

'Why, Gloria,' he cried, 'you don't mean to tell me you believe that stuff.'

'Well,' she said defiantly, 'why not?'

'Because it's – it's fantastic. You know that in every sense of the word you're an agnostic. You'd laugh at any orthodox form of Christianity – and then you come out with the statement that you believe in some silly rule of reincarnation.'

'What if I do? I've heard you and Maury, and everyone else for whose intellect I have the slightest respect, agree that life as it appears is utterly meaningless. But it's always seemed to me that if I were unconsciously learning something here it might not be so meaningless.'

'You're not learning anything – you're just getting tired. And if you must have a faith to soften things, take up one that appeals to the reason of someone beside a lot of hysterical women. A person like you oughtn't to accept anything unless it's decently demonstrable.'

'I don't care about truth. I want some happiness.'

'Well, if you've got a decent mind the second has got to be qualified by the first. Any simple soul can delude himself with mental garbage.'

'I don't care,' she held out stoutly, 'and, what's more, I'm not propounding any doctrine.'

The argument faded off, but reoccurred to Anthony several times thereafter. It was disturbing to find this old belief, evidently assimilated from her mother, inserting itself again under its immemorial disguise as an innate idea.

They reached New York in March after an expensive and ill-advised week spent in Hot Springs, and Anthony resumed his abortive attempts at fiction. As it became plainer to both of them that escape did not lie in the way of popular literature, there was a further slipping of their mutual confidence and courage. A complicated struggle went on incessantly between them. All efforts to keep down expenses died away from sheer inertia, and by March they were again using any pretext as an excuse for a 'party'. With an assumption of recklessness Gloria tossed out the suggestion that they should take all their money and go on a real spree while it lasted – anything seemed better than to see it go in unsatisfactory driblets.

'Gloria, you want parties as much as I do.'

'It doesn't matter about me. Everything I do is in accordance with my ideas: to use every minute of these years, when I'm young, in having the best time I possibly can.'

'How about after that?'

'After that I won't care.'

'Yes, you will.'

'Well, I may – but I won't be able to do anything about it. And I'll have had my good time.'

'You'll be the same then. After a fashion, we *have* had our good time, raised the devil, and we're in the state of paying for it.'

Nevertheless, the money kept going. There would be two days of gaiety, two days of moroseness – an endless, almost invariable round. The sharp pull-ups, when they occurred, resulted usually in a spurt of work for Anthony, while Gloria, nervous and bored, remained in bed or else chewed abstractedly at her fingers. After a day or so of this, they would make an engagement, and then – Oh, what did it matter? This night, this glow, the cessation of anxiety and the sense that if living was not purposeful it was, at any rate, essentially romantic! Wine gave a sort of gallantry to their own failure.

Meanwhile the suit progressed slowly, with interminable examinations of witnesses and marshallings of evidence. The preliminary proceedings of settling the estate were finished. Mr Haight saw no reason why the case should not come up for trial before summer.

Bloeckman appeared in New York late in March; he had been in England for nearly a year on matters concerned with 'Films Par Excellence'. The process of general refinement was still in progress – always he dressed a little better, his intonation was mellower, and in his manner there was perceptibly more assurance that the fine things of the world were his by a natural and inalienable right. He called at the apartment, remained only an hour, during which he talked chiefly of the war, and left telling them he was coming again. On his second visit Anthony was not at home, but an absorbed and excited Gloria greeted her husband later in the afternoon.

'Anthony,' she began, 'would you still object if I went in the movies?'

His whole heart hardened against the idea. As she seemed to recede from him, if only in threat, her presence became again not so much precious as desperately necessary.

'Oh, Gloria – !'

'Blockhead said he'd put me in – only if I'm ever going to do anything I'll have to start now. They only want young women. Think of the money, Anthony!'

'For you – yes. But how about me?'

'Don't you know that anything I have is yours too?'

'It's such a hell of a career!' he burst out, the moral, the infinitely circumspect Anthony, 'and such a hell of a bunch. And I'm so utterly tired of that fellow Bloeckman coming here and interfering. I hate theatrical things.'

'It isn't theatrical! It's utterly different.'

'What am I supposed to do? Chase you all over the country? Live on your money?'

'Then make some yourself.'

The conversation developed into one of the most violent quarrels they had ever had. After the ensuing reconciliation and the inevitable period of moral inertia, she realised that he had taken the life out of the project. Neither of them ever mentioned the probability that Bloeckman was by no means disinterested, but they both knew that it lay behind Anthony's objection.

In April war was declared with Germany. Wilson and his cabinet –

a cabinet that in its lack of distinction was strangely reminiscent of the twelve apostles – let loose the carefully starved dogs of war, and the press began to whoop hysterically against the sinister morals, sinister philosophy and sinister music produced by the Teutonic temperament. Those who fancied themselves particularly broad-minded made the exquisite distinction that it was only the German government which aroused them to hysteria; the rest were worked up to a condition of retching indecency. Any song which contained the word 'mother' and the word 'kaiser' was assured of a tremendous success. At last everyone had something to talk about – and almost everyone fully enjoyed it, as though they had been cast for parts in a sombre and romantic play.

Anthony, Maury and Dick sent in their applications for officers' training-camps and the two latter went about feeling strangely exalted and reproachless; they chattered to each other, like college boys, of war's being the one excuse for, and justification of, the aristocrat, and conjured up an impossible caste of officers, to be composed, it appeared, chiefly of the more attractive alumni of three or four Eastern colleges. It seemed to Gloria that in this huge red light streaming across the nation even Anthony took on a new glamour.

The Tenth Infantry, arriving in New York from Panama, were escorted from saloon to saloon by patriotic citizens, to their great bewilderment. West Pointers began to be noticed for the first time in years, and the general impression was that everything was glorious, but not half so glorious as it was going to be pretty soon, and that everybody was a fine fellow, and every race a great race – always excepting the Germans – and in every strata of society outcasts and scapegoats had but to appear in uniform to be forgiven, cheered, and wept over by relatives, ex-friends and utter strangers.

Unfortunately, a small and precise doctor decided that there was something the matter with Anthony's blood-pressure. He could not conscientiously pass him for an officers' training-camp.

THE BROKEN LUTE

Their third anniversary passed, uncelebrated, unnoticed. The season warmed in thaw, melted into hotter summer, simmered and boiled away. In July the will was offered for probate, and upon the contest-ation was assigned by the surrogate to trial term for trial. The matter was prolonged into September – there was difficulty in empanelling an unbiassed jury because of the moral sentiments involved. To Anthony's disappointment a verdict was finally returned in favour of the testator, whereupon Mr Haight caused a notice of appeal to be served upon Edward Shuttleworth.

As the summer waned Anthony and Gloria talked of the things they were to do when the money was theirs, and of the places they were to go to after the war, when they would 'agree on things again', for both of them looked forward to a time when love, springing like the phoenix from its own ashes, should be born again in its mysterious and unfathomable haunts.

He was drafted early in the fall, and the examining doctor made no mention of low blood-pressure. It was all very purposeless and sad when Anthony told Gloria one night that he wanted, above all things, to be killed. But, as always, they were sorry for each other for the wrong things at the wrong times . . .

They decided that for the present she was not to go with him to the Southern camp where his contingent was ordered. She would remain in New York to 'use the apartment', to save money, and to watch the progress of the case – which was pending now in the Appellate Division, of which the calendar, Mr Haight told them, was far behind.

Almost their last conversation was a senseless quarrel about the proper division of the income – at a word either would have given it all to the other. It was typical of the muddle and confusion of their lives that on the October night when Anthony reported at the Grand Central Station for the journey to camp, she arrived only in time to catch his eye over the anxious heads of a gathered crowd. Through the dark light of the enclosed train-sheds their glances stretched across a hysterical area, foul with yellow sobbing and the smells of poor women. They must have pondered upon what they had done to one another, and they must each have accused themselves of drawing this sombre pattern through which they were tracing tragically and obscurely. At the last they were too far away for either to see the other's tears.

BOOK THREE

CHAPTER I

A Matter of Civilisation

At a frantic command from some invisible source, Anthony groped his way inside. He was thinking that for the first time in more than three years he was to remain longer than a night away from Gloria. The finality of it appealed to him drearily. It was his clean and lovely girl that he was leaving.

They had arrived, he thought, at the most practical financial settlement: she was to have three hundred and seventy-five dollars a month – not too much considering that over half of that would go in rent – and he was taking fifty to supplement his pay. He saw no need for more: food, clothes and quarters would be provided – there were no social obligations for a private.

The car was crowded and already thick with breath. It was one of the type known as 'tourist' cars, a sort of brummagem Pullman, with a bare floor, and straw seats that needed cleaning. Nevertheless, Anthony greeted it with relief. He had vaguely expected that the trip South would be made in a freight-car, in one end of which would stand eight horses and in the other forty men. He had heard the 'hommes 40, chevaux 8' [293] story so often that it had become confused and ominous.

As he rocked down the aisle with his barrack-bag slung at his shoulder like a monstrous blue sausage, he saw no vacant seats, but after a moment his eye fell on a single space at present occupied by the feet of a short swarthy Sicilian, who, with his hat drawn over his eyes, hunched defiantly in the corner. As Anthony stopped beside him he stared up with a scowl, evidently intended to be intimidating; he must have adopted it as a defence against this entire gigantic equation. At Anthony's sharp, 'That seat taken?' he very slowly lifted the feet as though they were a breakable package, and placed them with some care upon the floor. His eyes remained on Anthony, who meanwhile sat down and unbuttoned the uniform coat issued him at Camp Upton [294] the day before. It chafed him under the arms.

Before Anthony could scrutinise the other occupants of the section a young second lieutenant blew in at the upper end of the car and wafted airily down the aisle, announcing in a voice of appalling acerbity: 'There will be no smoking in this car! No smoking! Don't smoke, men, in this car!'

As he sailed out at the other end a dozen little clouds of expostulation arose on all sides.

'Oh, cripe!'

'Jeese!'

'No *smokin'*?'

'Hey, come back here, fella!'

'What's 'ee idea?'

Two or three cigarettes were shot out through the open windows. Others were retained inside, though kept sketchily away from view. From here and there in accents of bravado, of mockery, of submissive humour, a few remarks were dropped that soon melted into the listless and pervasive silence.

The fourth occupant of Anthony's section spoke up suddenly.

'G'by, liberty,' he said sullenly. 'G'by, everything except bein' an officer's dog.'

Anthony looked at him. He was a tall Irishman with an expression moulded of indifference and utter disdain. His eyes fell on Anthony, as though he expected an answer, and then upon the others. Receiving only a defiant stare from the Italian he groaned and spat noisily on the floor by way of a dignified transition back into taciturnity.

A few minutes later the door opened again and the second lieutenant was borne in upon his customary official zephyr, this time singing out a different tiding: 'All right, men, smoke if you want to! My mistake, men! It's all right, men! Go on and smoke – my mistake!'

This time Anthony had a good look at him. He was young, thin, already faded; he was like his own moustache; he was like a great piece of shiny straw. His chin receded, faintly; this was offset by a magnificent and unconvincing scowl, a scowl that Anthony was to connect with the faces of many young officers during the ensuing year.

Immediately everyone smoked – whether they had previously desired to or not. Anthony's cigarette contributed to the hazy oxidation which seemed to roll back and forth in opalescent clouds with every motion of the train. The conversation, which had lapsed between the two impressive visits of the young officer, now revived tepidly; the men across the aisle began making clumsy experiments with their straw seats' capacity for comparative comfort; two card games, half-heartedly begun, soon drew several spectators to sitting positions on the arms of seats. In a few minutes Anthony became aware of a persistently obnoxious sound – the small, defiant Sicilian had fallen audibly asleep. It was wearisome to contemplate that animate protoplasm, reasonable by courtesy only, shut up in a car by an incomprehensible civilisation, taken somewhere, to do a vague something without aim or significance or consequence. Anthony sighed, opened a newspaper which he had no recollection of buying, and began to read by the dim yellow light.

Ten o'clock bumped stuffily into eleven; the hours clogged and caught and slowed down. Amazingly the train halted along the dark countryside, from time to time indulging in short, deceitful movements backwards or forwards, and whistling harsh paeans into the high October night. Having read his newspaper through, editorials, cartoons and war-poems, his eye fell on a half-column headed 'Shakespeareville, Kansas'. It seemed that the Shakespeareville Chamber of Commerce had recently held an enthusiastic debate as to whether the American soldiers should be known as 'Sammies' or 'Battling Christians'. The thought gagged him. He dropped the newspaper, yawned, and let his mind drift off at a tangent. He wondered why Gloria had been late. It seemed so long ago already – he had a pang of illusive loneliness. He tried to imagine from what angle she would regard her new position, what place in her considerations he would continue to hold. The thought acted as a further depressant – he opened his paper and began to read again.

The members of the Chamber of Commerce in Shakespeareville had decided upon 'Liberty Lads'.

For two nights and two days they rattled southward, making mysterious inexplicable stops in what were apparently arid wastes, and then rushing through large cities with a pompous air of hurry. The whimsicalities of this train foreshadowed for Anthony the whimsicalities of all army administration.

In the arid wastes they were served from the baggage-car with beans and bacon that at first he was unable to eat – he dined scantily on some milk chocolate distributed by a village canteen. But on the second day the baggage-car's output began to appear surprisingly palatable. On the third morning the rumour was passed along that within the hour they would arrive at their destination, Camp Hooker.

It had become intolerably hot in the car, and the men were all in shirt sleeves. The sun came in through the windows, a tired and ancient sun, yellow as parchment and stretched out of shape in transit. It tried to enter in triumphant squares and produced only warped splotches – but it was appallingly steady; so much so that it disturbed Anthony not to be the pivot of all the inconsequential sawmills and trees and telegraph poles that were turning around him so fast. Outside it played its heavy tremolo over olive roads and fallow cotton-fields, back of which ran a ragged line of woods broken with eminences of grey rock. The foreground was dotted sparsely with wretched, ill-patched shanties, among which there would flash by, now and then, a specimen of the languid yokelry of South Carolina, or else a strolling darky with sullen and bewildered eyes.

Then the woods moved off and they rolled into a broad space like the baked top of a gigantic cake, sugared with an infinity of tents arranged in geometric figures over its surface. The train came to an uncertain stop, and the sun and the poles and the trees faded, and his universe rocked itself slowly back to its old usualness, with Anthony Patch in the centre. As the men, weary and perspiring, crowded out of the car, he smelt that unforgettable aroma that impregnates all permanent camps – the odour of garbage.

Camp Hooker was an astonishing and spectacular growth, suggesting 'A Mining Town in 1870 – The Second Week'. It was a thing of wooden shacks and whitish-grey tents, connected by a pattern of roads, with hard tan drill-grounds fringed with trees. Here and there stood green YMCA houses, unpromising oases, with their muggy odour of wet flannels and closed telephone-booths – and across from each of them there was usually a canteen, swarming with life, presided over indolently by an officer who, with the aid of a side-car, usually managed to make his detail a pleasant and chatty sinecure.

Up and down the dusty roads sped the soldiers of the quarter-master corps, also in side-cars. Up and down drove the generals in their government automobiles, stopping now and then to bring unalert details to attention, to frown heavily upon captains marching at the heads of companies, to set the pompous pace in that gorgeous game of showing off which was taking place triumphantly over the entire area.

The first week after the arrival of Anthony's draft was filled with a series of interminable inoculations and physical examinations, and with the preliminary drilling. The days left him desperately tired. He had been issued the wrong-size shoes by a popular, easy-going supply-sergeant, and in consequence his feet were so swollen that the last hours of the afternoon were an acute torture. For the first time in his life he could throw himself down on his cot between dinner and afternoon drill-call, and seeming to sink with each moment deeper into a bottomless bed, drop off immediately to sleep, while the noise and laughter around him faded to a pleasant drone of drowsy summer sound. In the morning he awoke stiff and aching, hollow as a ghost, and hurried forth to meet the other ghostly figures who swarmed in the wan company streets, while a harsh bugle shrieked and spluttered at the grey heavens.

He was in a skeleton infantry company of about a hundred men. After the invariable breakfast of fatty bacon, cold toast and cereal, the entire hundred would rush for the latrines, which, however well-policed, seemed always intolerable, like the lavatories in cheap hotels. Out on the field, then, in ragged order – the lame man on his left grotesquely marring Anthony's listless efforts to keep in step, the platoon sergeants either showing off violently to impress the officers and recruits, or else quietly lurking in close to the line of march, avoiding both labour and unnecessary visibility.

When they reached the field, work began immediately – they peeled off their shirts for calisthenics. This was the only part of the day that Anthony enjoyed. Lieutenant Kretching, who presided at the antics, was sinewy and muscular, and Anthony followed his movements faithfully, with a feeling that he was doing something of positive value to himself. The other officers and sergeants walked about among the men with the malice of schoolboys, grouping here and there around some unfortunate who lacked muscular control, giving him confused instructions and commands. When they discovered a particularly forlorn, ill-nourished specimen, they would linger the full half-hour making cutting remarks and snickering among themselves.

One little officer named Hopkins, who had been a sergeant in the regular army, was particularly annoying. He took the war as a gift of revenge from the high gods to himself, and the constant burden of his harangues was that these rookies did not appreciate the full gravity and responsibility of 'the service'. He considered that by a combination of foresight and dauntless efficiency he had raised himself to his current magnificence. He aped the particular tyrannies of every officer under whom he had served in times gone by. His frown was frozen on his brow – before giving a private a pass to go to town he would ponderously weigh the effect of such an absence upon the company, the army, and the welfare of the military profession the world over.

Lieutenant Kretching, blond, dull and phlegmatic, introduced Anthony ponderously to the problems of attention, right face, about face, and at ease. His principal defect was his forgetfulness. He often kept the company straining and aching at attention for five minutes while he stood out in front and explained a new movement; as a result only the men in the centre knew what it was all about – those on both flanks had been too emphatically impressed with the necessity of staring straight ahead.

The drill continued until noon. It consisted of stressing a succession of infinitely remote details, and though Anthony perceived that this was consistent with the logic of war, it none the less irritated him. That the same faulty blood-pressure which would have been indecent in an officer did not interfere with the duties of a private was a preposterous incongruity. Sometimes, after listening to a sustained invective concerned with a dull and, on the face of it, absurd subject known as military 'courtesy', he suspected that the dim purpose of the war was to let the regular army officers – men with the mentality and aspirations of schoolboys – have their fling with some real slaughter. He was being grotesquely sacrificed to the twenty-year patience of a Hopkins!

Of his three tent-mates – a flat-faced, conscientious objector from Tennessee, a big, scared Pole, and the disdainful Celt whom he had sat beside on the train – the two former spent the evenings in writing eternal letters home, while the Irishman sat in the tent door whistling over and over to himself half a dozen shrill and monotonous bird-calls. It was rather to avoid an hour of their company than with any hope of diversion that, when the quarantine was lifted at the end of the week, he went into town. He caught one of the swarm of jitneys that overran the camp each evening, and in half an hour was set down in front of the Stonewall Hotel on the hot and drowsy main street.

Under the gathering twilight the town was unexpectedly attractive. The sidewalks were peopled by vividly dressed, over-painted girls, who chattered volubly in low, lazy voices, by dozens of taxi-drivers who assailed passing officers with, 'Take y' anywheh, *Lieu*tenant,' and by an intermittent procession of ragged, shuffling, subservient Negroes. Anthony, loitering along through the warm dusk, felt for the first time in years the slow, erotic breath of the South, imminent in the hot softness of the air, in the pervasive lull of thought and time.

He had gone about a block when he was arrested suddenly by a harsh command at his elbow.

'Haven't you been taught to salute officers?'

He looked dumbly at the man who addressed him, a stout, black-haired captain, who fixed him menacingly with brown pop-eyes.

'*Come to attention!*' The words were literally thundered. A few pedestrians near by stopped and stared. A soft-eyed girl in a lilac dress tittered to her companion.

Anthony came to attention.

'What's your regiment and company?'

Anthony told him.

'After this when you pass an officer on the street you straighten up and salute!'

'All right!'

'Say, "Yes, sir!" '

'Yes, sir.'

The stout officer grunted, turned sharply, and marched down the street. After a moment Anthony moved on; the town was no longer indolent and exotic; the magic was suddenly gone out of the dusk. His eyes were turned precipitately inward upon the indignity of his position. He hated that officer, every officer – life was unendurable.

After he had gone half a block he realised that the girl in the lilac dress who had giggled at his discomfiture was walking with her friend about ten paces ahead of him. Several times she had turned and stared at Anthony, with cheerful laughter in the large eyes that seemed the same colour as her gown.

At the corner she and her companion visibly slackened their pace – he must make his choice between joining them and passing obliviously by. He passed, hesitated, then slowed down. In a moment the pair were abreast of him again, dissolved in laughter now – not such strident mirth as he would have expected in the North from actresses in this familiar comedy, but a soft, low rippling, like the overflow from some subtle joke, into which he had inadvertently blundered.

'How do you do?' he said.

Her eyes were soft as shadows. Were they violet, or was it their blue darkness mingling with the grey hues of dusk?

'Pleasant evening,' ventured Anthony uncertainly.

'Sure is,' said the second girl.

'Hasn't been a very pleasant evening for you,' sighed the girl in lilac. Her voice seemed as much a part of the night as the drowsy breeze stirring the wide brim of her hat.

'He had to have a chance to show off,' said Anthony with a scornful laugh.

'Reckon so,' she agreed.

They turned the corner and moved lackadaisically up a side street, as if following a drifting cable to which they were attached. In this town it seemed entirely natural to turn corners like that, it seemed natural to be bound nowhere in particular, to be thinking nothing . . . The side street was dark, a sudden offshoot into a district of wild rose hedges and little quiet houses set far back from the street.

'Where're you going?' he enquired politely.

'Just goin'.' The answer was an apology, a question, an explanation.

'Can I stroll along with you?'

'Reckon so.'

It was an advantage that her accent was different. He could not have determined the social status of a Southerner from her talk – in New York a girl of a lower class would have been raucous, unendurable – except through the rosy spectacles of intoxication.

Dark was creeping down. Talking little – Anthony in careless, casual questions, the other two with provincial economy of phrase and burden – they sauntered past another corner, and another. In the middle of a block they stopped beneath a lamp-post.

'I live near here,' explained the other girl.

'I live around the block,' said the girl in lilac.

'Can I see you home?'

'To the corner, if you want to.'

The other girl took a few steps backwards. Anthony removed his hat.

'You're supposed to salute,' said the girl in lilac with a laugh. 'All the soldiers salute.'

'I'll learn,' he responded soberly.

The other girl said, 'Well – ' hesitated, then added, 'call me up tomorrow, Dot,' and retreated from the yellow circle of the street-lamp. Then, in silence, Anthony and the girl in lilac walked the three blocks to the small rickety house which was her home. Outside the wooden gate she hesitated.

'Well – thanks.'

'Must you go in so soon?'

'I ought to.'

'Can't you stroll around a little longer?'

She regarded him dispassionately. 'I don't even know you.'

Anthony laughed. 'It's not too late.'

'I reckon I better go in.'

'I thought we might walk down and see a movie.'

'I'd like to.'

'Then I could bring you home. I'd have just enough time. I've got to be in camp by eleven.'

It was so dark that he could scarcely see her now. She was a dress swayed infinitesimally by the wind, two limpid, reckless eyes . . .

'Why don't you come – Dot? Don't you like movies? Better come.'

She shook her head.

'I oughtn't to.'

He liked her, realising that she was temporising for the effect on him. He came closer and took her hand.

'If we get back by ten, can't you? Just to the movies?'

'Well – I reckon so – '

Hand in hand they walked back towards downtown, along a hazy, dusky street where a Negro newsboy was calling an extra in the cadence of the local venders' tradition, a cadence that was as musical as song.

Dot

Anthony's affair with Dorothy Raycroft was an inevitable result of his increasing carelessness about himself. He did not go to her desiring to possess the desirable, nor did he fall before a personality more vital, more compelling than his own, as he had done with Gloria four years before. He merely slid into the matter through his inability to make definite judgements. He could say 'No!' neither to man nor woman; borrower and temptress alike found him tender-minded and pliable. Indeed he seldom made decisions at all, and when he did they were but half-hysterical resolves formed in the panic of some aghast and irreparable awakening.

The particular weakness he indulged on this occasion was his need for excitement and stimulus from without. He felt that for the first time in four years he could express and interpret himself anew. The girl promised rest; the hours in her company each evening alleviated the morbid and inevitably futile poundings of his imagination. He had become a coward in earnest – completely the slave of a hundred disordered and prowling thoughts which were released by the collapse of the authentic devotion to Gloria that had been the chief jailer of his insufficiency.

On that first night, as they stood by the gate, he kissed Dorothy and made an engagement to meet her the following Saturday. Then he went out to camp, and with the light burning lawlessly in his tent, he wrote a long letter to Gloria, a glowing letter, full of the sentimental dark, full of the remembered breath of flowers, full of a true and exceeding tenderness – these things he had learned again for a moment in a kiss given and taken under a rich warm moonlight just an hour before.

When Saturday night came he found Dot waiting at the entrance of the Bijou Moving Picture Theatre. She was dressed as on the preceding Wednesday in her lilac gown of frailest organdy, but it had evidently been washed and starched since then, for it was fresh and unrumpled. Daylight confirmed the impression he had received that in a sketchy, faulty way she was lovely. She was clean, her features were small, irregular, but eloquent and appropriate to each other. She was a dark, unenduring little flower – yet he thought he detected in her some quality of spiritual reticence, of strength drawn from her passive acceptance of all things. In this he was mistaken.

Dorothy Raycroft was nineteen. Her father had kept a small, un-prosperous corner store, and she had graduated from high school in the lowest fourth of her class two days before he died. At high school she had enjoyed a rather unsavoury reputation. As a matter of fact her behaviour at the class picnic, where the rumours started, had been merely indiscreet – she had retained her technical purity until over a year later. The boy had been a clerk in a store on Jackson Street, and on the day after the incident he departed unexpectedly to New York. He had been intending to leave for some time, but had tarried for the consummation of his amorous enterprise.

After a while she confided the adventure to a girl friend, and later, as she watched her friend disappear down the sleepy street of dusty sunshine she knew in a flash of intuition that her story was going out into the world. Yet after telling it she felt much better, and a little bitter, and made as near an approach to character as she was capable of by walking in another direction and meeting another man with the honest intention of gratifying herself again. As a rule things happened to Dot. She was not weak, because there was nothing in her to tell her she was being weak. She was not strong, because she never knew that some of the things she did were brave. She neither defied nor conformed nor compromised.

She had no sense of humour, but, to take its place, a happy dis-position that made her laugh at the proper times when she was with men. She had no definite intentions – sometimes she regretted vaguely that her reputation precluded what chance she had ever had for security. There had been no open discovery: her mother was interested only in starting her off on time each morning for the jewellery store where she earned fourteen dollars a week. But some of the boys she had known in high school now looked the other way when they were walking with 'nice girls', and these incidents hurt her feelings. When they occurred she went home and cried.

Besides the Jackson Street clerk there had been two other men, of whom the first was a naval officer, who passed through town during the early days of the war. He had stayed over a night to make a connection, and was leaning idly against one of the pillars of the Stonewall Hotel when she passed by. He remained in town four days. She thought she loved him – lavished on him that first hysteria of passion that would have gone to the pusillanimous clerk. The naval officer's uniform – there were few of them in those days – had made the magic. He left with vague promises on his lips, and, once on the train, rejoiced that he had not told her his real name.

Her resultant depression had thrown her into the arms of Cyrus Fielding, the son of a local clothier, who had hailed her from his roadster one day as she passed along the sidewalk. She had always known him by name. Had she been born to a higher stratum he would have known her before. She had descended a little lower – so he met her after all. After a month he had gone away to training-camp, a little afraid of the intimacy, a little relieved in perceiving that she had not cared deeply for him, and that she was not the sort who would ever make trouble. Dot romanticised this affair and conceded to her vanity that the war had taken these men away from her. She told herself that she could have married the naval officer. Nevertheless, it worried her that within eight months there had been three men in her life. She thought with more fear than wonder in her heart that she would soon be like those 'bad girls' on Jackson Street at whom she and her gum-chewing, giggling friends had stared with fascinated glances three years before.

For a while she attempted to be more careful. She let men 'pick her up'; she let them kiss her, and even allowed certain other liberties to be forced upon her, but she did not add to her trio. After several months the strength of her resolution – or rather the poignant expediency of her fears – was worn away. She grew restless drowsing there out of life and time while the summer months faded. The soldiers she met were either obviously below her or, less obviously, above her – in which case they desired only to use her; they were Yankees, harsh and ungracious; they swarmed in large crowds . . . And then she met Anthony.

On that first evening he had been little more than a pleasantly unhappy face, a voice, the means with which to pass an hour, but when she kept her engagement with him on Saturday she regarded him with consideration. She liked him. Unknowingly she saw her own tragedies mirrored in his face.

Again they went to the movies, again they wandered along the shadowy, scented streets, hand in hand this time, speaking a little in hushed voices. They passed through the gate – up towards the little porch –

'I can stay a while, can't I?'

'Sh!' she whispered, 'we've got to be very quiet. Mother sits up reading *Snappy Stories*.'[295] In confirmation he heard the faint crackling inside as a page was turned. The open-shutter slits emitted horizontal rods of light that fell in thin parallels across Dorothy's skirt. The street was silent save for a group on the steps of a house across the way, who, from time to time, raised their voices in a soft, bantering song.

> ' – When you wa-ake
> You shall ha-ave
> All the pretty little hawsiz – '[296]

Then, as though it had been waiting on a nearby roof for their arrival, the moon came slanting suddenly through the vines and turned the girl's face to the colour of white roses.

Anthony had a start of memory, so vivid that before his closed eyes there formed a picture, distinct as a flashback on a screen – a spring night of thaw set out of time in a half-forgotten winter five years before – another face, radiant, flower-like, upturned to lights as transforming as the stars –

Ah, *la belle dame sans merci*[297] who lived in his heart, made known to him in transitory fading splendour by dark eyes in the Ritz-Carlton, by a shadowy glance from a passing carriage in the Bois de Boulogne![298] But those nights were only part of a song, a remembered glory – here again were the faint winds, the illusions, the eternal present with its promise of romance.

'Oh,' she whispered, 'do you love me? Do you love me?'

The spell was broken – the drifted fragments of the stars became only light, the singing down the street diminished to a monotone, to the whimper of locusts in the grass. With almost a sigh he kissed her fervent mouth, while her arms crept up about his shoulders.

THE MAN-AT-ARMS

As the weeks dried up and blew away, the range of Anthony's travels extended until he grew to comprehend the camp and its environment. For the first time in his life he was in constant personal contact with the waiters to whom he had given tips, the chauffeurs who had touched their hats to him, the carpenters, plumbers, barbers and farmers who had previously been remarkable only in the subservience of their professional genuflections. During his first two months in camp he did not hold ten minutes' consecutive conversation with a single man.

On the service record his occupation stood as 'student'; on the original questionnaire he had prematurely written 'author'; but when men in his company asked his business he commonly gave it as bank clerk – had he told the truth, that he did no work, they would have been suspicious of him as a member of the leisure class.

His platoon sergeant, Pop Donnelly, was a scraggly 'old soldier', worn thin with drink. In the past he had spent unnumbered weeks in the guardhouse, but recently, thanks to the drill-master famine, he had been elevated to his present pinnacle. His complexion was full of shell-holes – it bore an unmistakable resemblance to those aerial photographs of 'the battlefield at Blank'. Once a week he got drunk downtown on white liquor, returned quietly to camp and collapsed upon his bunk, joining the company at reveille looking more than ever like a white mask of death.

He nursed the astounding delusion that he was astutely 'slipping it over' on the government – he had spent eighteen years in its service at a minute wage, and he was soon to retire (here he usually winked) on the impressive income of fifty-five dollars a month. He looked upon it as a gorgeous joke that he had played upon the dozens who had bullied and scorned him since he was a Georgia country boy of nineteen.

At present there were but two lieutenants – Hopkins and the popular Kretching. The latter was considered a good fellow and a fine leader, until a year later, when he disappeared with a mess fund of eleven hundred dollars and, like so many leaders, proved exceedingly difficult to follow.

Eventually there was Captain Dunning, god of this brief but self-sufficing microcosm. He was a reserve officer, nervous, energetic and enthusiastic. This latter quality, indeed, often took material form and was visible as fine froth in the corners of his mouth. Like most executives he saw his charges strictly from the front, and to his hopeful eyes his command seemed just such an excellent unit as such an excellent war deserved. For all his anxiety and absorption he was having the time of his life.

Baptiste, the little Sicilian of the train, fell foul of him the second week of drill. The captain had several times ordered the men to be clean-shaven when they fell in each morning. One day there was disclosed an alarming breech of this rule, surely a case of Teutonic connivance – during the night four men had grown hair upon their faces. The fact that three of the four understood a minimum of English made a practical object-lesson only the more necessary, so Captain Dunning resolutely sent a volunteer barber back to the company street for a razor. Whereupon for the safety of democracy a half-ounce of hair was scraped dry from the cheeks of three Italians and one Pole.

Outside the world of the company there appeared, from time to time, the colonel, a heavy man with snarling teeth, who circum-navigated the battalion drill-field upon a handsome black horse. He was a West Pointer, and, mimetically, a gentleman. He had a dowdy wife and a dowdy mind, and spent much of his time in town taking advantage of the army's lately exalted social position. Last of all was the general, who traversed the roads of the camp preceded by his flag – a figure so austere, so removed, so magnificent, as to be scarcely comprehensible.

December. Cool winds at night now, and damp, chilly mornings on the drill-grounds. As the heat faded, Anthony found himself increasingly glad to be alive. Renewed strangely through his body, he worried little and existed in the present with a sort of animal content. It was not that Gloria or the life that Gloria represented was less often in his thoughts – it was simply that she became, day by day, less real, less vivid. For a week they had corresponded passionately, almost hysterically – then by an unwritten agreement they had ceased to write more than twice, and then once, a week. She was bored, she said; if his brigade was to be there a long time she was coming down to join him. Mr Haight was going to be able to submit a stronger brief than he had expected, but doubted that the appealed case would come up until late spring. Muriel was in the city doing Red Cross work, and they went out together rather often. What would Anthony think if *she* went into the Red Cross? Trouble was she had heard that she might have to bathe Negroes in alcohol, and after that she hadn't felt so patriotic. The city was full of soldiers and she'd seen a lot of boys she hadn't laid eyes on for years . . .

Anthony did not want her to come South. He told himself that this was for many reasons – he needed a rest from her and she from him. She would be bored beyond measure in town, and she would be able to see Anthony for only a few hours each day. But in his heart he feared that it was because he was attracted to Dorothy. As a matter of fact he lived in terror that Gloria should learn by some chance or intention of the relation he had formed. By the end of a fortnight the entanglement began to give him moments of misery at his own faithlessness. Nevertheless, as each day ended he was unable to withstand the lure that would draw him irresistibly out of his tent and over to the telephone at the YMCA.

'Dot.'

'Yes?'

'I may be able to get in tonight.'

'I'm so glad.'

'Do you want to listen to my splendid eloquence for a few starry hours?'

'Oh, you funny – ' For an instant he had a memory of five years before – of Geraldine. Then –

'I'll arrive about eight.'

At seven he would be in a jitney bound for the city, where hundreds of little Southern girls were waiting on moonlit porches for their lovers. He would be excited already for her warm retarded kisses, for the amazed quietude of the glances she gave him – glances nearer to worship than any he had ever inspired. Gloria and he had been equals, giving without thought of thanks or obligation. To this girl his very caresses were an inestimable boon. Crying quietly she had confessed to him that he was not the first man in her life; there had been one other – he gathered that the affair had no sooner commenced than it had been over.

Indeed, so far as she was concerned, she spoke the truth. She had forgotten the clerk, the naval officer, the clothier's son, forgotten her vividness of emotion, which is true forgetting. She knew that in some opaque and shadowy existence someone had taken her – it was as though it had occurred in sleep.

Almost every night Anthony came to town. It was too cool now for the porch, so her mother surrendered to them the tiny sitting-room, with its dozens of cheaply framed chromos, its yard upon yard of decorative fringe, and its thick atmosphere of several decades in the proximity of the kitchen. They would build a fire – then, happily, inexhaustibly, she would go about the business of love. Each evening at ten she would walk with him to the door, her black hair in disarray, her face pale without cosmetics, paler still under the whiteness of the moon. As a rule it would be bright and silver outside; now and then there was a slow warm rain, too indolent, almost, to reach the ground.

'Say you love me,' she would whisper.

'Why, of course, you sweet baby.'

'Am I a baby?' This almost wistfully.

'Just a little baby.'

She knew vaguely of Gloria. It gave her pain to think of it, so she imagined her to be haughty and proud and cold. She had decided that Gloria must be older than Anthony, and that there was no love between husband and wife. Sometimes she let herself dream that after the war Anthony would get a divorce and they would be married – but she never mentioned this to Anthony, she scarcely knew why. She shared his company's idea that he was a sort of bank clerk – she thought that he was respectable and poor. She would say: 'If I had some money, darlin', I'd give ev'y bit of it to you . . . I'd like to have about fifty thousand dollars.'

'I suppose that'd be plenty,' agreed Anthony.

– In her letter that day Gloria had written: 'I suppose if we *could* settle for a million it would be better to tell Mr Haight to go ahead and settle. But it'd seem a pity . . .'

. . . 'We could have an automobile,' exclaimed Dot, in a final burst of triumph.

AN IMPRESSIVE OCCASION

Captain Dunning prided himself on being a great reader of character. Half an hour after meeting a man he was accustomed to place him in one of a number of astonishing categories – fine man, good man, smart fellow, theoriser, poet and 'worthless'. One day early in February he caused Anthony to be summoned to his presence in the orderly tent.

'Patch,' he said sententiously, 'I've had my eye on you for several weeks.'

Anthony stood erect and motionless.

'And I think you've got the makings of a good soldier.'

He waited for the warm glow, which this would naturally arouse, to cool – and then continued: 'This is no child's play,' he said, narrowing his brows.

Anthony agreed with a melancholy 'No, sir.'

'It's a man's game – and we need leaders.' Then the climax, swift, sure and electric: 'Patch, I'm going to make you a corporal.'

At this point Anthony should have staggered slightly backward, overwhelmed. He was to be one of the quarter million selected for that consummate trust. He was going to be able to shout the technical phrase, 'Follow me!' to seven other frightened men.

'You seem to be a man of some education,' said Captain Dunning.

'Yes, sir.'

'That's good, that's good. Education's a great thing, but don't let it go to your head. Keep on the way you're doing and you'll be a good soldier.'

With these parting words lingering in his ears, Corporal Patch saluted, executed a right about face, and left the tent.

Though the conversation amused Anthony, it did generate the idea that life would be more amusing as a sergeant or, should he find a less exacting medical examiner, as an officer. He was little interested in the work, which seemed to belie the army's boasted gallantry. At the inspections one did not dress up to look well, one dressed up to keep from looking badly.

But as winter wore away – the short, snowless winter marked by damp nights and cool, rainy days – he marvelled at how quickly the system had grasped him. He was a soldier – all who were not soldiers were civilians. The world was divided primarily into those two classifications.

It occurred to him that all strongly accentuated classes, such as the military, divided men into two kinds: their own kind – and those without. To the clergyman there were clergy and laity, to the Catholic there were Catholics and non-Catholics, to the Negro there were blacks and whites, to the prisoner there were the imprisoned and the free, and to the sick man there were the sick and the well . . . So, without thinking of it once in his lifetime, he had been a civilian, a layman, a non-Catholic, a Gentile, white, free and well . . .

As the American troops were poured into the French and British trenches he began to find the names of many Harvard men among the casualties recorded in the *Army and Navy Journal*. But for all the sweat and blood the situation appeared unchanged, and he saw no prospect of the war's ending in the perceptible future. In the old chronicles the right wing of one army always defeated the left wing of the other, the left wing being, meanwhile, vanquished by the enemy's right. After that the mercenaries fled. It had been so simple, in those days, almost as if prearranged . . .

Gloria wrote that she was reading a great deal. What a mess they had made of their affairs, she said. She had so little to do now that she spent her time imagining how differently things might have turned out. Her whole environment appeared insecure – and a few years back she had seemed to hold all the strings in her own little hand . . .

In June her letters grew hurried and less frequent. She suddenly ceased to write about coming South.

DEFEAT

March in the country around was rare with jasmine and jonquils and patches of violets in the warming grass. Afterwards he remembered especially one afternoon of such a fresh and magic glamour that as he stood in the rifle-pit marking targets he recited 'Atalanta in Calydon'[299] to an uncomprehending Pole, his voice mingling with the rip, sing, and splatter of the bullets overhead.

' "When the hounds of spring . . . " '

Spang!

' "Are on winter's traces . . . " '

Whirr-r-r-r! . . .

' "The mother of months . . . " '

'*Hey!* Come to! Mark three-e-e! . . . '

In town the streets were in a sleepy dream again, and together Anthony and Dot idled in their own tracks of the previous autumn until he began to feel a drowsy attachment for this South – a South, it seemed, more of Algiers than of Italy, with faded aspirations pointing back over innumerable generations to some warm, primitive Nirvana, without hope or care. Here there was an inflection of cordiality, of comprehension, in every voice. 'Life plays the same lovely and agonising joke on all of us,' they seemed to say in their plaintive pleasant cadence, in the rising inflection terminating on an unresolved minor.

He liked his barbershop where he was 'Hi, corporal!' to a pale, emaciated young man, who shaved him and pushed a cool vibrating machine endlessly over his insatiable head. He liked 'Johnston's Gardens' where they danced, where a tragic Negro made yearning, aching music on a saxophone until the garish hall became an enchanted jungle of barbaric rhythms and smoky laughter, where to forget the uneventful passage of time upon Dorothy's soft sighs and tender whisperings was the consummation of all aspiration, of all content.

There was an undertone of sadness in her character, a conscious evasion of all except the pleasurable minutiae of life. Her violet eyes would remain for hours apparently insensate as, thoughtless and reckless, she basked like a cat in the sun. He wondered what the tired, spiritless mother thought of them, and whether in her moments of uttermost cynicism she ever guessed at their relationship.

On Sunday afternoons they walked along the countryside, resting at intervals on the dry moss in the outskirts of a wood. Here the birds had gathered and the clusters of violets and white dogwood; here the hoar trees shone crystalline and cool, oblivious to the intoxicating heat that waited outside; here he would talk, intermittently, in a sleepy monologue, in a conversation of no significance, of no replies.

July came scorching down. Captain Dunning was ordered to detail one of his men to learn blacksmithing. The regiment was filling up to war strength, and he needed most of his veterans for drill-masters, so he selected the little Italian, Baptiste, whom he could most easily spare. Little Baptiste had never had anything to do with horses. His fear made matters worse. He reappeared in the orderly room one day and told Captain Dunning that he wanted to die if he couldn't be relieved. The horses kicked at him, he said; he was no good at the work. Finally he fell on his knees and besought Captain Dunning, in a mixture of broken English and scriptural Italian, to get him out of it. He had not slept for three days; monstrous stallions reared and cavorted through his dreams.

Captain Dunning reproved the company clerk (who had burst out laughing), and told Baptiste he would do what he could. But when he thought it over he decided that he couldn't spare a better man. Little Baptiste went from bad to worse. The horses seemed to divine his fear and take every advantage of it. Two weeks later a great black mare crushed his skull in with her hoofs while he was trying to lead her from her stall.

In mid-July came rumours, and then orders, that concerned a change of camp. The brigade was to move to an empty cantonment, a hundred miles farther south, there to be expanded into a division. At first the men thought they were departing for the trenches, and all evening little groups jabbered in the company street, shouting to each other in swaggering exclamations: 'Su-u-ure we are!' When the truth leaked out, it was rejected indignantly as a blind to conceal their real destination. They revelled in their own importance. That night they told their girls in town that they were 'going to get the Germans'. Anthony circulated for a while among the groups – then, stopping a jitney, rode down to tell Dot that he was going away.

She was waiting on the dark veranda in a cheap white dress that accentuated the youth and softness of her face.

'Oh,' she whispered, 'I've wanted you so, honey. All this day.'

'I have something to tell you.'

She drew him down beside her on the swinging seat, not noticing his ominous tone.

'Tell me.'

'We're leaving next week.'

Her arms seeking his shoulders remained poised upon the dark air, her chin tipped up. When she spoke the softness was gone from her voice.

'Leaving for France?'

'No. Less luck than that. Leaving for some darn camp in Mississippi.'

She shut her eyes and he could see that the lids were trembling.

'Dear little Dot, life is so damned hard.'

She was crying upon his shoulder.

'So damned hard, so damned hard,' he repeated aimlessly; 'it just hurts people and hurts people, until finally it hurts them so that they can't be hurt ever any more. That's the last and worst thing it does.'

Frantic, wild with anguish, she strained him to her breast.

'Oh, God!' she whispered brokenly, 'you can't go way from me. I'd die.'

He was finding it impossible to pass off his departure as a common, impersonal blow. He was too near to her to do more than repeat, 'Poor little Dot. Poor little Dot.'

'And then what?' she demanded wearily.

'What do you mean?'

'You're my whole life, that's all. I'd die for you right now if you said so. I'd get a knife and kill myself. You can't leave me here.'

Her tone frightened him.

'These things happen,' he said evenly.

'Then I'm going with you.' Tears were streaming down her cheeks. Her mouth was trembling in an ecstasy of grief and fear.

'Sweet,' he muttered sentimentally, 'sweet little girl. Don't you see we'd just be putting off what's bound to happen? I'll be going to France in a few months – '

She leaned away from him and clenching her fists lifted her face towards the sky.

'I want to die,' she said, as if moulding each word carefully in her heart.

'Dot,' he whispered uncomfortably, 'you'll forget. Things are sweeter when they're lost. I know – because once I wanted something and got it. It was the only thing I ever wanted badly, Dot. And when I got it it turned to dust in my hands.'

'All right.'

Absorbed in himself, he continued: 'I've often thought that if I hadn't got what I wanted things might have been different with me. I might have found something in my mind and enjoyed putting it in circulation. I might have been content with the work of it, and had some sweet vanity out of the success. I suppose that at one time I could have had anything I wanted, within reason, but that was the only thing I ever wanted with any fervour. God! And that taught me you can't have *any*thing, you can't have anything at *all*. Because desire just cheats you. It's like a sunbeam skipping here and there about a room. It stops and gilds some inconsequential object, and we poor fools try to grasp it – but when we do the sunbeam moves on to something else, and you've got the inconsequential part, but the glitter that made you want it is gone – ' He broke off uneasily. She had risen and was standing, dry-eyed, picking little leaves from a dark vine.

'Dot – '

'Go way,' she said coldly.

'What? Why?'

'I don't want just words. If that's all you have for me you'd better go.'

'Why, Dot – '

'What's death to me is just a lot of words to you. You put 'em together so pretty.'

'I'm sorry. I was talking about you, Dot.'

'Go way from here.'

He approached her with arms outstretched, but she held him away.

'You don't want me to go with you,' she said evenly; 'maybe you're going to meet that – that girl – ' She could not bring herself to say wife. 'How do I know? Well, then, I reckon you're not my fellow any more. So go way.'

For a moment, while conflicting warnings and desires prompted Anthony, it seemed one of those rare times when he would take a step prompted from within. He hesitated. Then a wave of weariness broke against him. It was too late – everything was too late. For years now he had dreamed the world away, basing his decisions upon emotions unstable as water. The little girl in the white dress dominated him, as she approached beauty in the hard symmetry of her desire. The fire blazing in her dark and injured heart seemed to glow around her like a flame. With some profound and uncharted pride she had made herself remote and so achieved her purpose.

'I didn't – mean to seem so callous, Dot.'

'It don't matter.'

The fire rolled over Anthony. Something wrenched at his bowels, and he stood there helpless and beaten.

'Come with me, Dot – little loving Dot. Oh, come with me. I couldn't leave you now – '

With a sob she wound her arms around him and let him support her weight while the moon, at its perennial labour of covering the bad complexion of the world, showered its illicit honey over the drowsy street.

THE CATASTROPHE

Early September in Camp Boone, Mississippi. The darkness, alive with insects, beat in upon the mosquito-netting, beneath the shelter of which Anthony was trying to write a letter. An intermittent chatter over a poker game was going on in the next tent, and outside a man was strolling up the company street singing a current bit of doggerel about 'K-K-K-Katy'.[300]

With an effort Anthony hoisted himself to his elbow and, pencil in hand, looked down at his blank sheet of paper. Then, omitting any heading, he began:

> I can't imagine what the matter is, Gloria. I haven't had a line from you for two weeks and it's only natural to be worried –

He threw this away with a disturbed grunt and began again:

I don't know what to think, Gloria. Your last letter, short, cold, without a word of affection or even a decent account of what you've been doing, came two weeks ago. It's only natural that I should wonder. If your love for me isn't absolutely dead it seems that you'd at least keep me from worry –

Again he crumpled the page and tossed it angrily through a tear in the tent wall, realising simultaneously that he would have to pick it up in the morning. He felt disinclined to try again. He could get no warmth into the lines – only a persistent jealousy and suspicion. Since midsummer these discrepancies in Gloria's correspondence had grown more and more noticeable. At first he had scarcely perceived them. He was so inured to the perfunctory 'dearests' and 'darlings' scattered through her letters that he was oblivious to their presence or absence. But in this last fortnight he had become increasingly aware that there was something amiss.

He had sent her a night-letter saying that he had passed his examinations for an officers' training-camp, and expected to leave for Georgia shortly. She had not answered. He had wired again – when he received no word he imagined that she might be out of town. But it occurred and recurred to him that she was not out of town, and a series of distraught imaginings began to plague him. Supposing Gloria, bored and restless, had found someone, even as he had. The thought terrified him with its possibility – it was chiefly because he had been so sure of her personal integrity that he had considered her so sparingly during the year. And now, as a doubt was born, the old angers, the rages of possession, swarmed back a thousandfold. What more natural than that she should be in love again?

He remembered the Gloria who promised that should she ever want anything, she would take it, insisting that since she would act entirely for her own satisfaction she could go through such an affair unsmirched – it was only the effect on a person's mind that counted, anyhow, she said, and her reaction would be the masculine one, of satiation and faint dislike.

But that had been when they were first married. Later, with the discovery that she could be jealous of Anthony, she had, outwardly at least, changed her mind. There were no other men in the world for her. This he had known only too surely. Perceiving that a certain fastidiousness would restrain her, he had grown lax in preserving the completeness of her love – which, after all, was the keystone of the entire structure.

Meanwhile all through the summer he had been maintaining Dot in a boarding-house downtown. To do this it had been necessary to write to his broker for money. Dot had covered her journey south by leaving her house a day before the brigade broke camp, informing her mother in a note that she had gone to New York. On the evening following Anthony had called as though to see her. Mrs Raycroft was in a state of collapse and there was a policeman in the parlour. A questionnaire had ensued, from which Anthony had extricated himself with some difficulty.

In September, with his suspicions of Gloria, the company of Dot had become tedious, then almost intolerable. He was nervous and irritable from lack of sleep; his heart was sick and afraid. Three days ago he had gone to Captain Dunning and asked for a furlough, only to be met with benignant procrastination. The division was starting overseas, while Anthony was going to an officers' training-camp; what furloughs could be given must go to the men who were leaving the country.

Upon this refusal Anthony had started to the telegraph office intending to wire Gloria to come South – he reached the door and receded despairingly, seeing the utter impracticability of such a move. Then he had spent the evening quarrelling irritably with Dot, and returned to camp morose and angry with the world. There had been a disagreeable scene, in the midst of which he had precipitately departed. What was to be done with her did not seem to concern him vitally at present – he was completely absorbed in the disheartening silence of his wife . . .

The flap of the tent made a sudden triangle back upon itself, and a dark head appeared against the night.

'Sergeant Patch?' The accent was Italian, and Anthony saw by the belt that the man was a headquarters orderly.

'Want me?'

'Lady call up headquarters ten minutes ago. Say she have speak with you. Ver' important.'

Anthony swept aside the mosquito-netting and stood up. It might be a wire from Gloria telephoned over.

'She say to get you. She call again ten o'clock.'

'All right, thanks.' He picked up his hat and in a moment was striding beside the orderly through the hot, almost suffocating, darkness. Over in the headquarters shack he saluted a dozing night-service officer.

'Sit down and wait,' suggested the lieutenant nonchalantly. 'Girl seemed awful anxious to speak to you.'

Anthony's hopes fell away.

'Thank you very much, sir.' And as the phone squeaked on the side-wall he knew who was calling.

'This is Dot,' came an unsteady voice, 'I've got to see you.'

'Dot, I told you I couldn't get down for several days.'

'I've got to see you tonight. It's important.'

'It's too late,' he said coldly; 'it's ten o'clock, and I have to be in camp at eleven.'

'All right.' There was so much wretchedness compressed into the two words that Anthony felt a measure of compunction.

'What's the matter?'

'I want to tell you goodbye.

'Oh, don't be a little idiot!' he exclaimed. But his spirits rose. What luck if she should leave town this very night! What a burden from his soul. But he said: 'You can't possibly leave before tomorrow.'

Out of the corner of his eye he saw the night-service officer regarding him quizzically. Then, startlingly, came Dot's next words: 'I don't mean "leave" that way.'

Anthony's hand clutched the receiver fiercely. He felt his nerves turning cold as if the heat was leaving his body.

'What?'

Then quickly in a wild broken voice he heard: 'Goodbye – oh, goodbye!'

Cul-*lup*! She had hung up the receiver. With a sound that was half a gasp, half a cry, Anthony hurried from the headquarters building. Outside, under the stars that dripped like silver tassels through the trees of the little grove, he stood motionless, hesitating. Had she meant to kill herself? – oh, the little fool! He was filled with bitter hate towards her. In this dénouement he found it impossible to realise that he had ever begun such an entanglement, such a mess, a sordid *mélange* of worry and pain.

He found himself walking slowly away, repeating over and over that it was futile to worry. He had best go back to his tent and sleep. He needed sleep. God! Would he ever sleep again? His mind was in a vast clamour and confusion; as he reached the road he turned around in a panic and began running, not towards his company but away from it. Men were returning now – he could find a taxicab. After a minute two yellow eyes appeared around a bend. Desperately he ran towards them.

'Jitney! Jitney!' . . . It was an empty Ford . . . 'I want to go to town.'

'Cost you a dollar.'

'All right. If you'll just hurry – '

After an interminable time, he ran up the steps of a dark ram-shackle little house and through the door, almost knocking over an immense Negress who was walking, candle in hand, along the hall.

'Where's my wife?' he cried wildly.

'She gone to bed.'

Up the stairs three at a time, down the creaking passage. The room was dark and silent, and with trembling fingers he struck a match. Two wide eyes looked up at him from a wretched ball of clothes on the bed.

'Ah, I knew you'd come,' she murmured brokenly.

Anthony grew cold with anger.

'So it was just a plan to get me down here, get me in trouble!' he said. 'Goddamn it, you've shouted "wolf" once too often!'

She regarded him pitifully.

'I had to see you. I couldn't have lived. Oh, I had to see you – '

He sat down on the side of the bed and slowly shook his head.

'You're no good,' he said decisively, talking unconsciously as Gloria might have talked to him. 'This sort of thing isn't fair to me, you know.'

'Come closer.' Whatever he might say Dot was happy now. He cared for her. She had brought him to her side.

'Oh, God,' said Anthony hopelessly. As weariness rolled along its inevitable wave his anger subsided, receded, vanished. He collapsed suddenly, fell sobbing beside her on the bed.

'Oh, my darling,' she begged him, 'don't cry! Oh, don't cry!'

She took his head upon her breast and soothed him, mingled her happy tears with the bitterness of his. Her hand played gently with his dark hair.

'I'm such a little fool,' she murmured brokenly, 'but I love you, and when you're cold to me it seems as if it isn't worth while to go on livin'.'

After all, this was peace – the quiet room with the mingled scent of women's powder and perfume, Dot's hand soft as a warm wind upon his hair, the rise and fall of her bosom as she took breath – for a moment it was as though it were Gloria there, as though he were at rest in some sweeter and safer home than he had ever known.

An hour passed. A clock began to chime in the hall. He jumped to his feet and looked at the phosphorescent hands of his wristwatch. It was twelve o'clock.

He had trouble in finding a taxi that would take him out at that hour. As he urged the driver faster along the road he speculated on the best method of entering camp. He had been late several times recently, and he knew that were he caught again his name would probably be stricken from the list of officer candidates. He wondered if he had not better dismiss the taxi and take a chance on passing the sentry in the dark. Still, officers often rode past the sentries after midnight . . .

'Halt!' The monosyllable came from the yellow glare that the headlights dropped upon the changing road. The taxi-driver threw out his clutch and a sentry walked up, carrying his rifle at the port. With him, by an ill chance, was the officer of the guard.

'Out late, sergeant.'

'Yes, sir. Got delayed.'

'Too bad. Have to take your name.'

As the officer waited, notebook and pencil in hand, something not fully intended crowded to Anthony's lips, something born of panic, of muddle, of despair.

'Sergeant R. A. Foley,' he answered breathlessly.

'And the outfit?'

'Company Q, Eighty-Third Infantry.'

'All right. You'll have to walk from here, sergeant.'

Anthony saluted, quickly paid his taxi-driver, and set off at a run towards the regiment he had named. When he was out of sight he changed his course, and with his heart beating wildly, hurried to his company, feeling that he had made a fatal error of judgement.

Two days later the officer who had been in command of the guard recognised him in a barbershop downtown. In charge of a military policeman he was taken back to the camp, where he was reduced to the ranks without trial, and confined for a month to the limits of his company street.

With this blow a spell of utter depression overtook him, and within a week he was again caught downtown, wandering around in a drunken daze, with a pint of bootleg whiskey in his hip pocket. It was because of a sort of craziness in his behaviour at the trial that his sentence to the guardhouse was for only three weeks.

NIGHTMARE

Early in his confinement the conviction took root in him that he was going mad. It was as though there were a quantity of dark yet vivid personalities in his mind, some of them familiar, some of them strange and terrible, held in check by a little monitor, who sat aloft somewhere and looked on. The thing that worried him was that the monitor was sick, and holding out with difficulty. Should he give up, should he falter for a moment, out would rush these intolerable things – only Anthony could know what a state of blackness there would be if the worst of him could roam his consciousness unchecked.

The heat of the day had changed, somehow, until it was a burnished darkness crushing down upon a devastated land. Over his head the blue circles of ominous uncharted suns, of unnumbered centres of fire, revolved interminably before his eyes as though he were lying constantly exposed to the hot light and in a state of feverish coma. At seven in the morning something phantasmal, something almost absurdly unreal that he knew was his mortal body, went out with seven other prisoners and two guards to work on the camp roads. One day they loaded and unloaded quantities of gravel, spread it, raked it – the next day they worked with huge barrels of red-hot tar, flooding the gravel with black shining pools of molten heat. At night, locked up in the guardhouse, he would lie without thought, without courage to compass thought, staring at the irregular beams of the ceiling overhead until about three o'clock, when he would slip into a broken, troubled sleep.

During the work hours he laboured with uneasy haste, attempting, as the day bore towards the sultry Mississippi sunset, to tire himself physically so that in the evening he might sleep deeply from utter exhaustion . . . Then one afternoon in the second week he had a feeling that two eyes were watching him from a place a few feet beyond one of the guards. This aroused him to a sort of terror. He turned his back on the eyes and shovelled feverishly, until it became necessary for him to face about and go for more gravel. Then they entered his vision again, and his already taut nerves tightened up to the breaking-point. The eyes were leering at him. Out of a hot silence he heard his name called in a tragic voice, and the earth tipped absurdly back and forth to a babel of shouting and confusion.

When next he became conscious he was back in the guardhouse, and the other prisoners were throwing him curious glances. The eyes returned no more. It was many days before he realised that the voice must have been Dot's, that she had called out to him and made some sort of disturbance. He decided this just previous to the expiration of his sentence, when the cloud that oppressed him had lifted, leaving him in a deep, dispirited lethargy. As the conscious mediator, the monitor who kept that fearsome *ménage* of horror, grew stronger, Anthony became physically weaker. He was scarcely able to get through the last two days of toil, and when he was released, one rainy afternoon, and returned to his company, he reached his tent only to fall into a heavy doze, from which he awoke before dawn, aching and unrefreshed. Beside his cot were two letters that had been awaiting him in the orderly tent for some time. The first was from Gloria; it was short and cool:

> The case is coming to trial late in November. Can you possibly get leave?
>
> I've tried to write you again and again but it just seems to make things worse. I want to see you about several matters, but you know that you have once prevented me from coming and I am disinclined to try again. In view of a number of things it seems necessary that we have a conference. I'm very glad about your appointment.
>
> GLORIA

He was too tired to try to understand – or to care. Her phrases, her intentions, were all very far away in an incomprehensible past. At the second letter he scarcely glanced; it was from Dot – an incoherent, tear-swollen scrawl, a flood of protest, endearment and grief. After a page he let it slip from his inert hand and drowsed back into a nebulous hinterland of his own. At drill-call he awoke with a high fever and fainted when he tried to leave his tent – at noon he was sent to the base hospital with influenza.

He was aware that this sickness was providential. It saved him from a hysterical relapse – and he recovered in time to entrain on a damp November day for New York, and for the interminable massacre beyond.

When the regiment reached Camp Mills,[301] Long Island, Anthony's single idea was to get into the city and see Gloria as soon as possible. It was now evident that an armistice would be signed within the week, but rumour had it that in any case troops would continue to be shipped to France until the last moment. Anthony was appalled at the notion of the long voyage, of a tedious debarkation at a French port, and of being kept abroad for a year, possibly, to replace the troops who had seen actual fighting.

His intention had been to obtain a two-day furlough, but Camp Mills proved to be under a strict influenza quarantine – it was impossible for even an officer to leave except on official business. For a private it was out of the question.

The camp itself was a dreary muddle, cold, windswept and filthy, with the accumulated dirt incidental to the passage through of many divisions. Their train came in at seven one night, and they waited in line until one while a military tangle was straightened out somewhere ahead. Officers ran up and down ceaselessly, calling orders and making a great uproar. It turned out that the trouble was due to the colonel, who was in a righteous temper because he was a West Pointer, and the war was going to stop before he could get overseas. Had the militant governments realised the number of broken hearts among the older West Pointers during that week, they would indubitably have prolonged the slaughter another month. The thing was pitiable!

Gazing out at the bleak expanse of tents extending for miles over a trodden welter of slush and snow, Anthony saw the impracticability of trudging to a telephone that night. He would call her at the first opportunity in the morning.

Aroused in the chill and bitter dawn, he stood at reveille and listened to a passionate harangue from Captain Dunning: 'You men may think the war is over. Well, let me tell you, it isn't! Those fellows aren't going to sign the armistice. It's another trick, and we'd be crazy to let anything slacken up here in the company, because, let me tell you, we're going to sail from here within a week, and when we do we're going to see some real fighting.'

He paused that they might get the full effect of his pronouncement. And then: 'If you think the war's over, just talk to anyone who's been in it and see if *they* think the Germans are all in. They don't. Nobody does. I've talked to the people that *know*, and they say there'll be, anyways, a year longer of war. *They* don't think it's over. So you men better not get any foolish ideas that it is.'

Doubly stressing this final admonition, he ordered the company dismissed.

At noon Anthony set off at a run for the nearest canteen telephone. As he approached what corresponded to the downtown of the camp, he noticed that many other soldiers were running also, that a man near him had suddenly leaped into the air and clicked his heels together. The tendency to run became general, and from little excited groups here and there came the sounds of cheering. He stopped and listened – over the cold country whistles were blowing and the chimes of the Garden City churches broke suddenly into reverberatory sound.

Anthony began to run again. The cries were clear and distinct now as they rose with clouds of frosted breath into the chilly air: 'Germany's surrendered! Germany's surrendered!'

THE FALSE ARMISTICE

That evening in the opaque gloom of six o'clock Anthony slipped between two freight-cars, and, once over the railroad, followed the track along to Garden City, where he caught an electric train for New York. He stood some chance of apprehension – he knew that the military police were often sent through the cars to ask for passes, but he imagined that tonight the vigilance would be relaxed. But, in any event, he would have tried to slip through, for he had been unable to locate Gloria by telephone, and another day of suspense would have been intolerable.

After inexplicable stops and waits that reminded him of the night he had left New York, over a year before, they drew into the Pennsylvania Station,[302] and he followed the familiar way to the taxi-stand, finding it grotesque and oddly stimulating to give his own address.

Broadway was a riot of light, thronged as he had never seen it with a carnival crowd which swept its glittering way through scraps of paper, piled ankle-deep on the sidewalks. Here and there, elevated upon benches and boxes, soldiers addressed the heedless mass, each face in which was clear cut and distinct under the white glare overhead. Anthony picked out half a dozen figures – a drunken sailor, tipped backwards and supported by two other gobs, was waving his hat and emitting a wild series of roars; a wounded soldier, crutch in hand, was borne along in an eddy on the shoulders of some shrieking civilians; a dark-haired girl sat cross-legged and meditative on top of a parked taxicab. Here surely the victory had come in time, the climax had been scheduled with the uttermost celestial foresight. The great rich nation had made triumphant war, suffered enough for poignancy but not enough for bitterness – hence the carnival, the feasting, the triumph. Under these bright lights glittered the faces of peoples whose glory had long since passed away, whose very civilisations were dead – men whose ancestors had heard the news of victory in Babylon, in Nineveh, in Baghdad, in Tyre, a hundred generations before; men whose ancestors had seen a flower-decked, slave-adorned cortège drift with its wake of captives down the avenues of Imperial Rome . . .

Past the Rialto, the glittering front of the Astor, the jewelled magnificence of Times Square . . . a gorgeous alley of incandescence ahead . . . Then – was it years later? – he was paying the taxi-driver in front of a white building on Fifty-Seventh Street. He was in the hall – ah, there was the Negro boy from Martinique, lazy, indolent, unchanged.

'Is Mrs Patch in?'

'I have just came on, sah,' the man announced with his incongruous British accent.

'Take me up –'

Then the slow drone of the elevator, the three steps to the door, which swung open at the impetus of his knock.

'Gloria!' His voice was trembling. No answer. A faint string of smoke was rising from a cigarette-tray – a number of *Vanity Fair*[303] sat astraddle on the table.

'Gloria!'

He ran into the bedroom, the bath. She was not there. A négligé of robin's-egg blue laid out upon the bed diffused a faint perfume, illusive and familiar. On a chair were a pair of stockings and a street dress; an open powder box yawned upon the bureau. She must just have gone out.

The telephone rang abruptly and he started – answered it with all the sensations of an impostor.

'Hello. Is Mrs Patch there?'

'No, I'm looking for her myself. Who is this?'

'This is Mr Crawford.'

'This is Mr Patch speaking. I've just arrived unexpectedly, and I don't know where to find her.'

'Oh.' Mr Crawford sounded a bit taken aback. 'Why, I imagine she's at the Armistice Ball. I know she intended going, but I didn't think she'd leave so early.'

'Where's the Armistice Ball?'

'At the Astor.'

'Thanks.'

Anthony hung up sharply and rose. Who was Mr Crawford? And who was it that was taking her to the ball? How long had this been going on? All these questions asked and answered themselves a dozen times, a dozen ways. His very proximity to her drove him half frantic.

In a frenzy of suspicion he rushed here and there about the apartment, hunting for some sign of masculine occupation, opening the bathroom cupboard, searching feverishly through the bureau drawers. Then he found something that made him stop suddenly and sit down on one of the twin beds, the corners of his mouth drooping as though he were about to weep. There in a corner of her drawer, tied with a frail blue ribbon, were all the letters and telegrams he had written her during the year past. He was suffused with happy and sentimental shame.

'I'm not fit to touch her,' he cried aloud to the four walls. 'I'm not fit to touch her little hand.'

Nevertheless, he went out to look for her.

In the Astor lobby he was engulfed immediately in a crowd so thick as to make progress almost impossible. He asked the direction of the ballroom from half a dozen people before he could get a sober and intelligible answer. Eventually, after a last long wait, he checked his military overcoat in the hall.

It was only nine but the dance was in full blast. The panorama was incredible. Women, women everywhere – girls gay with wine singing shrilly above the clamour of the dazzling confetti-covered throng; girls set off by the uniforms of a dozen nations; fat females collapsing without dignity upon the floor and retaining self-respect by shouting, 'Hurraw for the Allies!'; three women with white hair dancing hand in hand around a sailor, who revolved in a dizzying spin upon the floor, clasping to his heart an empty bottle of champagne.

Breathlessly Anthony scanned the dancers, scanned the muddled lines trailing in single file in and out among the tables, scanned the horn-blowing, kissing, coughing, laughing, drinking parties under the great full-bosomed flags which leaned in glowing colour over the pageantry and the sound.

Then he saw Gloria. She was sitting at a table for two directly across the room. Her dress was black, and above it her animated face, tinted with the most glamorous rose, made, he thought, a spot of poignant beauty in the room. His heart leaped as though to a new music. He jostled his way towards her and called her name just as the grey eyes looked up and found him. For that instant as their bodies met and melted, the world, the revel, the tumbling whimper of the music faded to an ecstatic monotone hushed as a song of bees.

'Oh, my Gloria!' he cried.

Her kiss was a cool rill flowing from her heart.

CHAPTER 2

A Matter of Aesthetics

On the night when Anthony had left for Camp Hooker one year before, all that was left of the beautiful Gloria Gilbert – her shell, her young and lovely body – moved up the broad marble steps of the Grand Central Station with the rhythm of the engine beating in her ears like a dream, and out on to Vanderbilt Avenue, where the huge bulk of the Biltmore overhung the street and, down at its low, gleaming entrance, sucked in the many-coloured opera-cloaks of gorgeously dressed girls. For a moment she paused by the taxi-stand and watched them – wondering that but a few years before she had been of their number, ever setting out for a radiant Somewhere, always just about to have that ultimate passionate adventure for which the girls' cloaks were delicate and beautifully furred, for which their cheeks were painted and their hearts higher than the transitory dome of pleasure that would engulf them, coiffure, cloak, and all.

It was growing colder and the men passing had flipped up the collars of their overcoats. This change was kind to her. It would have been kinder still had everything changed, weather, streets and people, and had she been whisked away, to wake in some high, fresh-scented room, alone and statuesque within and without, as in her virginal and colourful past.

Inside the taxicab she wept impotent tears. That she had not been happy with Anthony for over a year mattered little. Recently his presence had been no more than what it would awake in her of that memorable June. The Anthony of late, irritable, weak and poor, could do no less than make her irritable in turn – and bored with everything except the fact that in a highly imaginative and eloquent youth they had come together in an ecstatic revel of emotion. Because of this mutually vivid memory she would have done more for Anthony than for any other human – so when she got into the taxicab she wept passionately, and wanted to call his name aloud.

Miserable, lonesome as a forgotten child, she sat in the quiet apartment and wrote him a letter full of confused sentiment:

. . . I can almost look down the tracks and see you going but without you, dearest, dearest, I can't see or hear or feel or think.

Being apart – whatever has happened or will happen to us – is like begging for mercy from a storm, Anthony; it's like growing old. I want to kiss you so – in the back of your neck where your old black hair starts. Because I love you and whatever we do or say to each other, or have done, or have said, you've got to feel how much I do, how inanimate I am when you're gone. I can't even hate the damnable presence of PEOPLE, those people in the station who haven't any right to live – I can't resent them even though they're dirtying up our world, because I'm engrossed in wanting you so.

If you hated me, if you were covered with sores like a leper, if you ran away with another woman or starved me or beat me – how absurd this sounds – I'd still want you, I'd still love you. I *know*, my darling.

It's late – I have all the windows open and the air outside is just as soft as spring, yet, somehow, much more young and frail than spring. Why do they make spring a young girl, why does that illusion dance and yodel its way for three months through the world's preposterous barrenness. Spring is a lean old plough horse with its ribs showing – it's a pile of refuse in a field, parched by the sun and the rain to an ominous cleanliness.

In a few hours you'll wake up, my darling – and you'll be miserable, and disgusted with life. You'll be in Delaware or Carolina or somewhere and so unimportant. I don't believe there's anyone alive who can contemplate themselves as an impermanent institution, as a luxury or an unnecessary evil. Very few of the people who accentuate the futility of life remark the futility of themselves. Perhaps they think that in proclaiming the evil of living they somehow salvage their own worth from the ruin – but they don't, even you and I . . .

. . . Still I can see you. There's blue haze about the trees where you'll be passing, too beautiful to be predominant. No, the fallow squares of earth will be most frequent – they'll be along beside the track like dirty coarse brown sheets drying in the sun, alive, mechanical, abominable. Nature, slovenly old hag, has been sleeping in them with every old farmer or Negro or immigrant who happened to covet her . . .

So you see that now you're gone I've written a letter all full of contempt and despair. And that just means that I love you, Anthony, with all there is to love within your

GLORIA

When she had addressed the letter she went to her twin bed and lay down upon it, clasping Anthony's pillow in her arms as though by sheer force of emotion she could metamorphose it into his warm and living body. Two o'clock saw her dry-eyed, staring with steady persistent grief into the darkness, remembering, remembering unmercifully, blaming herself for a hundred fancied unkindnesses, making a likeness of Anthony akin to some martyred and transfigured Christ. For a time she thought of him as he, in his more sentimental moments, probably thought of himself.

At five she was still awake. A mysterious grinding noise that went on every morning across the area-way told her the hour. She heard an alarm clock ring, and saw a light make a yellow square on an illusory blank wall opposite. With the half-formed resolution of following him South immediately, her sorrow grew remote and unreal, and moved off from her as the dark moved westward. She fell asleep.

When she awoke the sight of the empty bed beside her brought a renewal of misery, dispelled shortly, however, by the inevitable callousness of the bright morning. Though she was not conscious of it, there was relief in eating breakfast without Anthony's tired and worried face opposite her. Now that she was alone she lost all desire to complain about the food. She would change her breakfasts, she thought – have a lemonade and a tomato sandwich instead of the sempiternal bacon and eggs and toast.

Nevertheless, at noon, when she had called up several of her acquaintances, including the martial Muriel, and found each one engaged for lunch, she gave way to a quiet pity for herself and her loneliness. Curled on the bed with pencil and paper she wrote Anthony another letter.

Late in the afternoon arrived a special delivery, mailed from some small New Jersey town, and the familiarity of the phrasing, the almost audible undertone of worry and discontent, were so familiar that they comforted her. Who knew? Perhaps army discipline would harden Anthony and accustom him to the idea of work. She had immutable faith that the war would be over before he was called upon to fight, and meanwhile the suit would be won, and they could begin again, this time on a different basis. The first thing different would be that she would have a child. It was unbearable that she should be so utterly alone.

It was a week before she could stay in the apartment with the probability of remaining dry-eyed. There seemed little in the city that was amusing. Muriel had been shifted to a hospital in New Jersey, from which she took a metropolitan holiday only every other week, and with this defection Gloria grew to realise how few were the friends she had made in all these years of New York. The men she knew were in the army. 'Men she knew'? – she had conceded vaguely to herself that all the men who had ever been in love with her were her friends. Each one of them had at a certain considerable time professed to value her favour above anything in life. But now – where were they? At least two were dead, half a dozen or more were married, the rest scattered from France to the Philippines. She wondered whether any of them thought of her, and how often, and in what respect. Most of them must still picture the little girl of seventeen or so, the adolescent siren of nine years before.

The girls, too, were gone far afield. She had never been popular in school. She had been too beautiful, too lazy, not sufficiently conscious of being a Farmover girl and a 'FUTURE WIFE AND MOTHER' in perpetual capital letters. And girls who had never been kissed hinted, with shocked expressions on their plain but not particularly wholesome faces, that Gloria had. Then these girls had gone east or west or south, married and become 'people', prophesying, if they prophesied about Gloria, that she would come to a bad end – not knowing that no endings were bad, and that they, like her, were by no means the mistresses of their destinies.

Gloria told over to herself the people who had visited them in the grey house at Marietta. It had seemed at the time that they were always having company – she had indulged in an unspoken conviction that each guest was ever afterwards slightly indebted to her. They owed her a sort of moral ten dollars apiece, and should she ever be in need she might, so to speak, borrow from them this visionary currency. But they were gone, scattered like chaff, mysteriously and subtly vanished in essence or in fact.

By Christmas, Gloria's conviction that she should join Anthony had returned, no longer as a sudden emotion, but as a recurrent need. She decided to write him word of her coming, but postponed the announcement upon the advice of Mr Haight, who expected almost weekly that the case was coming up for trial.

One day, early in January, as she was walking on Fifth Avenue, bright now with uniforms and hung with the flags of the virtuous nations, she met Rachael Barnes, whom she had not seen for nearly a year. Even Rachael, whom she had grown to dislike, was a relief from ennui, and together they went to the Ritz for tea.

After a second cocktail they became enthusiastic. They liked each other. They talked about their husbands, Rachael in that tone of public vainglory, with private reservations, in which wives are wont to speak.

'Rodman's abroad in the Quartermaster Corps. He's a captain. He was determined to go, and he didn't think he could get into anything else.'

'Anthony's in the Infantry.' The words in their relation to the cocktail gave Gloria a sort of glow. With each sip she approached a warm and comforting patriotism.

'By the way,' said Rachael half an hour later, as they were leaving, 'can't you come up to dinner tomorrow night? I'm having two awfully sweet officers who are just going overseas. I think we ought to do all we can to make it attractive for them.'

Gloria accepted gladly. She took down the address – recognising by its number a fashionable apartment building on Park Avenue.

'It's been awfully good to have seen you, Rachael.'

'It's been wonderful. I've wanted to.'

With these three sentences a certain night in Marietta two summers before, when Anthony and Rachael had been unnecessarily attentive to each other, was forgiven – Gloria forgave Rachael, Rachael forgave Gloria. Also it was forgiven that Rachael had been witness to the greatest disaster in the lives of Mr and Mrs Anthony Patch –

Compromising with events time moves along.

THE WILES OF CAPTAIN COLLINS

The two officers were captains of the popular craft, machine-gunnery. At dinner they referred to themselves with conscious boredom as members of the 'Suicide Club' – in those days every recondite branch of the service referred to itself as the Suicide Club. One of the captains – Rachael's captain, Gloria observed – was a tall horsy man of thirty with a pleasant moustache and ugly teeth. The other, Captain Collins, was chubby, pink-faced, and inclined to laugh with abandon every time he caught Gloria's eye. He took an immediate fancy to her, and throughout dinner showered her with inane compliments. With her second glass of champagne Gloria decided that for the first time in months she was thoroughly enjoying herself.

After dinner it was suggested that they all go somewhere and dance. The two officers supplied themselves with bottles of liquor from Rachael's sideboard – a law forbade service to the military – and so equipped they went through innumerable foxtrots in several glittering caravanseries along Broadway, faithfully alternating partners – while Gloria became more and more uproarious and more and more amusing to the pink-faced captain, who seldom bothered to remove his genial smile at all.

At eleven o'clock to her great surprise she was in the minority for staying out. The others wanted to return to Rachael's apartment – to get some more liquor, they said. Gloria argued persistently that Captain Collins's flask was half full – she had just seen it – then catching Rachael's eye she received an unmistakable wink. She deduced, confusedly, that her hostess wanted to get rid of the officers and assented to being bundled into a taxicab outside.

Captain Wolf sat on the left with Rachael on his knees. Captain Collins sat in the middle, and as he settled himself he slipped his arm about Gloria's shoulder. It rested there lifelessly for a moment and then tightened like a vice. He leaned over her.

'You're awfully pretty,' he whispered.

'Thank you kindly, sir.' She was neither pleased nor annoyed. Before Anthony came so many arms had done likewise that it had become little more than a gesture, sentimental but without significance.

Up in Rachael's long front room a low fire and two lamps shaded with orange silk gave all the light, so that the corners were full of deep and somnolent shadows. The hostess, moving about in a dark-figured gown of loose chiffon, seemed to accentuate the already sensuous atmosphere. For a while they were all four together, tasting the sandwiches that waited on the tea table – then Gloria found herself alone with Captain Collins on the fireside lounge; Rachael and Captain Wolf had withdrawn to the other side of the room, where they were conversing in subdued voices.

'I wish you weren't married,' said Collins, his face a ludicrous travesty of 'in all seriousness'.

'Why?' She held out her glass to be filled with a highball.

'Don't drink any more,' he urged her, frowning.

'Why not?'

'You'd be nicer – if you didn't.'

Gloria caught suddenly the intended suggestion of the remark, the atmosphere he was attempting to create. She wanted to laugh – yet she realised that there was nothing to laugh at. She had been enjoying the evening, and she had no desire to go home – at the same time it hurt her pride to be flirted with on just that level.

'Pour me another drink,' she insisted.

'Please – '

'Oh, don't be ridiculous!' she cried in exasperation.

'Very well.' He yielded with ill grace.

Then his arm was about her again, and again she made no protest. But when his pink cheek came close she leaned away.

'You're awfully sweet,' he said with an aimless air.

She began to sing softly, wishing now that he would take down his arm. Suddenly her eye fell on an intimate scene across the room – Rachael and Captain Wolf were engrossed in a long kiss. Gloria shivered slightly – she knew not why . . . Pink face approached again.

'You shouldn't look at them,' he whispered.

Almost immediately his other arm was around her . . . his breath was on her cheek. Again absurdity triumphed over disgust, and her laugh was a weapon that needed no edge of words.

'Oh, I thought you were a sport,' he was saying.

'What's a sport?'

'Why, a person that likes to – to enjoy life.'

'Is kissing you generally considered a joyful affair?'

They were interrupted as Rachael and Captain Wolf appeared suddenly before them.

'It's late, Gloria,' said Rachael – she was flushed and her hair was dishevelled. 'You'd better stay here all night.'

For an instant Gloria thought the officers were being dismissed. Then she understood, and, understanding, got to her feet as casually as she was able.

Uncomprehendingly Rachael continued: 'You can have the room just off this one. I can lend you everything you need.'

Collins's eyes implored her like a dog's; Captain Wolf's arm had settled familiarly around Rachael's waist; they were waiting.

But the lure of promiscuity, colourful, various, labyrinthine, and ever a little odorous and stale, had no call or promise for Gloria. Had she so desired she would have remained, without hesitation, without regret; as it was she could face coolly the six hostile and offended eyes that followed her out into the hall with forced politeness and hollow words.

'*He* wasn't even sport enough to try to take me home,' she thought in the taxi, and then with a quick surge of resentment: 'How *utterly* common!'

GALLANTRY

In February she had an experience of quite a different sort. Tudor Baird, an ancient flame, a young man whom at one time she had fully intended to marry, came to New York by way of the Aviation Corps, and called upon her. They went several times to the theatre, and within a week, to her great enjoyment, he was as much in love with her as ever. Quite deliberately she brought it about, realising too late that she had done a mischief. He reached the point of sitting with her in miserable silence whenever they went out together.

A Scroll and Keys [304] man at Yale, he possessed the correct reticences of a 'good egg', the correct notions of chivalry and *noblesse oblige* – and, of course but unfortunately, the correct biases and the correct lack of ideas – all those traits which Anthony had taught her to despise, but which, nevertheless, she rather admired. Unlike the majority of his type, she found that he was not a bore. He was handsome, witty in a light way, and when she was with him she felt that because of some quality he possessed – call it stupidity, loyalty, sentimentality, or something not quite as definite as any of the three – he would have done anything in his power to please her.

He told her this among other things, very correctly and with a ponderous manliness that masked a real suffering. Loving him not at all she grew sorry for him and kissed him sentimentally one night because he was so charming, a relic of a vanishing generation which lived a priggish and graceful illusion and was being replaced by less gallant fools. Afterwards she was glad she had kissed him, for next day when his plane fell fifteen hundred feet at Mineola a piece of a gasolene engine smashed through his heart.

GLORIA ALONE

When Mr Haight told her that the trial would not take place until autumn she decided that without telling Anthony she would go into the movies. When he saw her successful, both histrionically and financially, when he saw that she could have her will of Joseph Bloeckman, yielding nothing in return, he would lose his silly prejudices. She lay awake half one night planning her career and enjoying her successes in anticipation, and the next morning she called up 'Films Par Excellence'. Mr Bloeckman was in Europe.

But the idea had gripped her so strongly this time that she decided to go the rounds of the moving-picture employment agencies. As so often had been the case, her sense of smell worked against her good intentions. The employment agency smelt as though it had been dead a very long time. She waited five minutes inspecting her unprepossessing competitors – then she walked briskly out into the farthest recesses of Central Park and remained so long that she caught a cold. She was trying to air the employment agency out of her walking suit.

In the spring she began to gather from Anthony's letters – not from any one in particular but from their cumulative effect – that he did not want her to come South. Curiously repeated excuses that seemed to haunt him by their very insufficiency occurred with Freudian regularity. He set them down in each letter as though he feared he had forgotten them the last time, as though it were desperately necessary to impress her with them. And the dilutions of his letters with affectionate diminutives began to be mechanical and unspontaneous – almost as though, having completed the letter, he had looked it over and literally stuck them in, like epigrams in an Oscar Wilde play. She jumped to the solution, rejected it, was angry and depressed by turns – finally she shut her mind to it proudly, and allowed an increasing coolness to creep into her end of the correspondence.

Of late she had found a good deal to occupy her attention. Several aviators whom she had met through Tudor Baird came into New York to see her and two other ancient beaux turned up, stationed at Camp Dix. As these men were ordered overseas they, so to speak, handed her down to their friends. But after another rather disagreeable experience with a potential Captain Collins she made it plain that when anyone was introduced to her he should be under no misapprehensions as to her status and personal intentions.

When summer came she learned, like Anthony, to watch the officers' casualty list, taking a sort of melancholy pleasure in hearing of the death of someone with whom she had once danced a german and in identifying by name the younger brothers of former suitors – thinking, as the drive towards Paris progressed, that here at length went the world to inevitable and well-merited destruction.

She was twenty-seven. Her birthday fled by scarcely noticed. Years before it had frightened her when she became twenty, to some extent when she reached twenty-six – but now she looked in the glass with calm self-approval seeing the British freshness of her complexion and her figure boyish and slim as of old.

She tried not to think of Anthony. It was as though she were

writing to a stranger. She told her friends that he had been made a
corporal and was annoyed when they were politely unimpressed.
One night she wept because she was sorry for him – had he
been even slightly responsive she would have gone to him without
hesitation on the first train – whatever he was doing he needed to be
taken care of spiritually, and she felt that now she would be able to
do even that. Recently, without his continual drain upon her moral
strength she found herself wonderfully revived. Before he left she
had been inclined through sheer association to brood on her wasted
opportunities – now she returned to her normal state of
mind, strong, disdainful, existing each day for each day's worth. She
bought a doll and dressed it; one week she wept over *Ethan Frome*;[305]
the next she revelled in some novels of Galsworthy's, whom she
liked for his power of recreating, by spring in darkness, that illusion
of young romantic love to which women look forever forward and
forever back.

In October Anthony's letters multiplied, became almost frantic –
then suddenly ceased. For a worried month it needed all her powers
of control to refrain from leaving immediately for Mississippi. Then
a telegram told her that he had been in the hospital and that she
could expect him in New York within ten days. Like a figure in a
dream he came back into her life across the ballroom on that
November evening – and all through long hours that held familiar
gladness she took him close to her breast, nursing an illusion of
happiness and security she had not thought that she would know
again.

DISCOMFITURE OF THE GENERALS

After a week Anthony's regiment went back to the Mississippi camp
to be discharged. The officers shut themselves up in the compart-
ments on the Pullman cars and drank the whiskey they had bought
in New York, and in the coaches the soldiers got as drunk as possible
also – and pretended whenever the train stopped at a village that
they were just returned from France, where they had practically put
an end to the German army. As they all wore overseas caps and
claimed that they had not had time to have their gold service stripes
sewn on, the yokelry of the seaboard were much impressed and
asked them how they liked the trenches – to which they replied, 'Oh,
boy!' with great smacking of tongues and shaking of heads. Someone
took a piece of chalk and scrawled on the side of the train, 'We won

the war – now we're going home,' and the officers laughed and let it stay. They were all getting what swagger they could out of this ignominious return.

As they rumbled on towards camp, Anthony was uneasy lest he should find Dot awaiting him patiently at the station. To his relief he neither saw nor heard anything of her and thinking that were she still in town she would certainly attempt to communicate with him, he concluded that she had gone – whither he neither knew nor cared. He wanted only to return to Gloria – Gloria reborn and wonderfully alive. When eventually he was discharged he left his company on the rear of a great truck with a crowd who had given tolerant, almost sentimental, cheers for their officers, especially for Captain Dunning. The captain, on his part, had addressed them with tears in his eyes as to the pleasure, etc., and the work, etc., and time not wasted, etc., and duty, etc. It was very dull and human; having given ear to it Anthony, whose mind was freshened by his week in New York, renewed his deep loathing for the military profession and all it connoted. In their childish hearts two out of every three professional officers considered that wars were made for armies and not armies for wars. He rejoiced to see general and field-officers riding desolately about the barren camp deprived of their commands. He rejoiced to hear the men in his company laugh scornfully at the inducements tendered them to remain in the army. They were to attend 'schools'. He knew what these 'schools' were.

Two days later he was with Gloria in New York.

ANOTHER WINTER

Late one February afternoon Anthony came into the apartment and groping through the little hall, pitch-dark in the winter dusk, found Gloria sitting by the window. She turned as he came in.

'What did Mr Haight have to say?' she asked listlessly.

'Nothing,' he answered, 'usual thing. Next month, perhaps.'

She looked at him closely; her ear attuned to his voice caught the slightest thickness in the dissyllable.

'You've been drinking,' she remarked dispassionately.

'Couple glasses.'

'Oh.'

He yawned in the armchair and there was a moment's silence between them. Then she demanded suddenly: 'Did you go to Mr Haight? Tell me the truth.'

'No.' He smiled weakly. 'As a matter of fact I didn't have time.'

'I thought you didn't go . . . He sent for you.'

'I don't give a damn. I'm sick of waiting around his office. You'd think he was doing *me* a favour.' He glanced at Gloria as though expecting moral support, but she had turned back to her contemplation of the dubious and unprepossessing out-of-doors.

'I feel rather weary of life today,' he offered tentatively. Still she was silent. 'I met a fellow and we talked in the Biltmore bar.'

The dusk had suddenly deepened but neither of them made any move to turn on the lights. Lost in heaven knew what contemplation, they sat there until a flurry of snow drew a languid sigh from Gloria.

'What've you been doing?' he asked, finding the silence oppressive.

'Reading a magazine – all full of idiotic articles by prosperous authors about how terrible it is for poor people to buy silk shirts. And while I was reading it I could think of nothing except how I wanted a grey squirrel coat – and how we can't afford one.'

'Yes, we can.'

'Oh, no.'

'Oh, yes! If you want a fur coat you can have one.'

Her voice coming through the dark held an implication of scorn.

'You mean we can sell another bond?'

'If necessary. I don't want to go without things. We have spent a lot, though, since I've been back.'

'Oh, shut up!' she said in irritation.

'Why?'

'Because I'm sick and tired of hearing you talk about what we've spent or what we've done. You came back two months ago and we've been on some sort of a party practically every night since. We've both wanted to go out, and we've gone. Well, you haven't heard me complain, have you? But all you do is whine, whine, whine. I don't care any more what we do or what becomes of us and at least I'm consistent. But I will *not* tolerate your complaining and calamity-howling – '

'You're not very pleasant yourself sometimes, you know.'

'I'm under no obligations to be. You're not making any attempt to make things different.'

'But I am – '

'Huh! Seems to me I've heard that before. This morning you weren't going to touch another thing to drink until you'd got a position. And you didn't even have the spunk to go to Mr Haight when he sent for you about the suit.'

Anthony got to his feet and switched on the lights.

'See here!' he cried, blinking, 'I'm getting sick of that sharp tongue of yours.'

'Well, what are you going to do about it?'

'Do you think *I'm* particularly happy?' he continued, ignoring her question. 'Do you think I don't know we're not living as we ought to?'

In an instant Gloria stood trembling beside him.

'I won't *stand* it!' she burst out. 'I won't be lectured to. You and your suffering! You're just a pitiful weakling and you always have been!'

They faced one another idiotically, each of them unable to impress the other, each of them tremendously, achingly, bored. Then she went into the bedroom and shut the door behind her.

His return had brought into the foreground all their pre-bellum exasperations. Prices had risen alarmingly and in perverse ratio their income had shrunk to a little over half of its original size. There had been the large retainer's fee to Mr Haight; there were stocks bought at one hundred now down to thirty and forty and other investments that were not paying at all. During the previous spring Gloria had been given the alternative of leaving the apartment or of signing a year's lease at two hundred and twenty-five a month. She had signed it. Inevitably as the necessity for economy had increased they found themselves as a pair quite unable to save. The old policy of pre-varication was resorted to. Weary of their incapabilities they chattered of what they would do – oh – tomorrow, of how they would 'stop going on parties' and of how Anthony would go to work. But when dark came down Gloria, accustomed to an engagement every night, would feel the ancient restlessness creeping over her. She would stand in the doorway of the bedroom, chewing furiously at her fingers and sometimes meeting Anthony's eyes as he glanced up from his book. Then the telephone, and her nerves would relax, she would answer it with ill-concealed eagerness. Someone was coming up 'for just a few minutes' – and oh, the weariness of pretence, the appearance of the wine table, the revival of their jaded spirits – and the awakening, like the mid-point of a sleepless night in which they moved.

As the winter passed with the march of the returning troops along Fifth Avenue they became more and more aware that since Anthony's return their relations had entirely changed. After that reflowering of tenderness and passion each of them had returned into some solitary dream unshared by the other and what endearments passed between them passed, it seemed, from empty heart to empty heart, echoing hollowly the departure of what they knew at last was gone.

Anthony had again made the rounds of the metropolitan newspapers and had again been refused encouragement by a motley of office boys, telephone girls and city editors. The word was: 'We're keeping any vacancies open for our own men who are still in France.' Then, late in March, his eye fell on an advertisement in the morning paper and in consequence he found at last the semblance of an occupation.

YOU CAN SELL!!!
Why not earn while you learn?
Our salesmen make $50–$200 weekly.

There followed an address on Madison Avenue, and instructions to appear at one o'clock that afternoon. Gloria, glancing over his shoulder after one of their usual late breakfasts, saw him regarding it idly.

'Why don't you try it?' she suggested.

'Oh – it's one of these crazy schemes.'

'It might not be. At least it'd be experience.'

At her urging he went at one o'clock to the appointed address, where he found himself one of a dense miscellany of men waiting in front of the door. They ranged from a messenger-boy evidently misusing his company's time to an immemorial individual with a gnarled body and a gnarled cane. Some of the men were seedy, with sunken cheeks and puffy pink eyes – others were young, possibly still in high school. After a jostled fifteen minutes during which they all eyed one another with apathetic suspicion there appeared a smart young shepherd clad in a 'waistline' suit and wearing the manner of an assistant rector who herded them upstairs into a large room, which resembled a schoolroom and contained innumerable desks. Here the prospective salesmen sat down – and again waited. After an interval a platform at the end of the hall was clouded with half a dozen sober but sprightly men who, with one exception, took seats in a semicircle facing the audience.

The exception was the man who seemed the soberest, the most sprightly and the youngest of the lot, and who advanced to the front of the platform. The audience scrutinised him hopefully. He was rather small and rather pretty, with the commercial rather than the thespian sort of prettiness. He had straight blond bushy brows and eyes that were almost preposterously honest, and as he reached the edge of his rostrum he seemed to throw these eyes out into the audience, simultaneously extending his arm with two fingers outstretched. Then while he rocked himself to a state of balance an expectant silence settled over the hall. With perfect assurance the young man had taken his listeners in hand and his words when they came were steady and confident and of the school of 'straight from the shoulder'.

'Men!' – he began, and paused. The word died with a prolonged echo at the end of the hall, the faces regarding him, hopefully, cynically, wearily, were alike arrested, engrossed. Six hundred eyes were turned slightly upward. With an even graceless flow that reminded Anthony of the rolling of bowling balls he launched himself into the sea of exposition.

'This bright and sunny morning you picked up your favourite newspaper and you found an advertisement which made the plain, unadorned statement that *you* could sell. That was all it said – it didn't say "what", it didn't say "how", it didn't say "why". It just made one single solitary assertion that *you* and *you* and *you*' – business of pointing – 'could sell. Now my job isn't to make a success of you, because every man is born a success, he makes himself a failure; it's not to teach you how to talk, because each man is a natural orator and only makes himself a clam; my business is to tell you one thing in a way that will make you *know* it – it's to tell you that *you* and *you* and *you* have the heritage of money and prosperity waiting for you to come and claim it.'

At this point an Irishman of saturnine appearance rose from his desk near the rear of the hall and went out.

'That man thinks he'll go look for it in the beer parlour around the corner. [Laughter.] He won't find it there. Once upon a time I looked for it there myself [laughter], but that was before I did what every one of you men no matter how young or how old, how poor or how rich [a faint ripple of satirical laughter], can do. It was before I found – *myself*!

'Now I wonder if any of you men know what a "Heart Talk" is. A "Heart Talk" is a little book in which I started, about five years ago, to write down what I had discovered were the principal reasons for a man's failure and the principal reasons for a man's success – from John D. Rockerfeller back to John D. Napoleon [laughter], and before that, back in the days when Abel sold his birthright for a mess of pottage. There are now one hundred of these "Heart Talks".

Those of you who are sincere, who are interested in our proposition, above all who are dissatisfied with the way things are breaking for you at present will be handed one to take home with you as you go out yonder door this afternoon.

'Now in my own pocket I have four letters just received concerning "Heart Talks". These letters have names signed to them that are familiar in every household in the USA. Listen to this one from Detroit:

> DEAR MR CARELTON – I want to order three thousand more copies of "Heart Talks" for distribution among my salesmen. They have done more for getting work out of the men than any bonus proposition ever considered. I read them myself constantly, and I desire to heartily congratulate you on getting at the roots of the biggest problem that faces our generation today – the problem of salesmanship. The rock bottom on which the country is founded is the problem of salesmanship. With many felicitations I am
> Yours very cordially,
>
> HENRY W. TERRAL'

He brought the name out in three long booming triumphancies – pausing for it to produce its magical effect. Then he read two more letters, one from a manufacturer of vacuum cleaners and one from the president of the Great Northern Doily Company.

'And now,' he continued, 'I'm going to tell you in a few words what the proposition is that's going to *make* those of you who go into it in the right spirit. Simply put, it's this: "Heart Talks" have been incorporated as a company. We're going to put these little pamphlets into the hands of every big business organisation, every salesman, and every man who *knows* – I don't say "thinks", I say "*knows*" – that he can sell! We are offering some of the stock of the "Heart Talks" concern upon the market, and in order that the distribution may be as wide as possible, and in order also that we can furnish a living, concrete, flesh-and-blood example of what salesmanship is, or rather what it may be, we're going to give those of you who are the real thing a chance to sell that stock. Now, I don't care what you've tried to sell before or how you've tried to sell it. It don't matter how old you are or how young you are. I only want to know two things – first, do you *want* success, and, second, will you work for it?

'My name is Sammy Carleton. Not "Mr" Carleton, but just plain Sammy. I'm a regular no-nonsense man with no fancy frills about me. I want you to call me Sammy.

'Now this is all I'm going to say to you today. Tomorrow I want those of you who have thought it over and have read the copy of "Heart Talks" which will be given to you at the door, to come back to this same room at this same time, then we'll go into the proposition further and I'll explain to you what I've found the principles of success to be. I'm going to make you *feel* that *you* and *you* and *you* can sell!'

Mr Carleton's voice echoed for a moment through the hall and then died away. To the stamping of many feet Anthony was pushed and jostled with the crowd out of the room.

FURTHER ADVENTURES WITH 'HEART TALKS'

With an accompaniment of ironic laughter Anthony told Gloria the story of his commercial adventure. But she listened without amusement.

'You're going to give up again?' she demanded coldly.

'Why – you don't expect me to – '

'I never expected anything of you.'

He hesitated.

'Well – I can't see the slightest benefit in laughing myself sick over this sort of affair. If there's anything older than the old story, it's the new twist.'

It required an astonishing amount of moral energy on Gloria's part to intimidate him into returning, and when he reported next day, somewhat depressed from his perusal of the senile bromides skittishly set forth in 'Heart Talks on Ambition', he found only fifty of the original three hundred awaiting the appearance of the vital and compelling Sammy Carleton. Mr Carleton's powers of vitality and compulsion were this time exercised in elucidating that magnificent piece of speculation – how to sell. It seemed that the approved method was to state one's proposition and then to say not, 'And now, will you buy?' – this was not the way – oh, no! – the way was to state one's proposition and then, having reduced one's adversary to a state of exhaustion, to deliver oneself of the categorical imperative: 'Now see here! You've taken up my time explaining this matter to you. You've admitted my points – all I want to ask is how many do you want?'

As Mr Carleton piled assertion upon assertion Anthony began to feel a sort of disgusted confidence in him. The man appeared to know what he was talking about. Obviously prosperous, he had risen to the position of instructing others. It did not occur to Anthony that the type of man who attains commercial success seldom knows how or why, and, as in his grandfather's case, when he ascribes reasons, the reasons are generally inaccurate and absurd.

Anthony noted that of the numerous old men who had answered the original advertisement, only two had returned, and that among the thirty odd who assembled on the third day to get actual selling instructions from Mr Carleton, only one grey head was in evidence. These thirty were eager converts; with their mouths they followed the working of Mr Carleton's mouth; they swayed in their seats with enthusiasm, and in the intervals of his talk they spoke to each other in tense approving whispers. Yet of the chosen few who, in the words of Mr Carleton, 'were determined to get those deserts that rightly and truly belonged to them', less than half a dozen combined even a modicum of personal appearance with that great gift of being a 'pusher'. But they were told that they were all natural pushers – it was merely necessary that they should believe with a sort of savage passion in what they were selling. He even urged each one to buy some stock himself, if possible, in order to increase his own sincerity.

On the fifth day then, Anthony sallied into the street with all the sensations of a man wanted by the police. Acting according to instructions he selected a tall office building in order that he might ride to the top storey and work downward, stopping in every office that had a name on the door. But at the last minute he hesitated. Perhaps it would be more practicable to acclimate himself to the chilly atmosphere which he felt was awaiting him by trying a few offices on, say, Madison Avenue. He went into an arcade that seemed only semi-prosperous, and seeing a sign which read Percy B. Weatherbee, Architect, he opened the door heroically and entered. A starchy young woman looked up questioningly.

'Can I see Mr Weatherbee?' He wondered if his voice sounded tremulous.

She laid her hand tentatively on the telephone-receiver.

'What's the name, please?'

'He wouldn't – ah – know me. He wouldn't know my name.'

'What's your business with him? You an insurance agent?'

'Oh, no, nothing like that!' denied Anthony hurriedly. 'Oh, no. It's a – it's a personal matter.' He wondered if he should have said this. It had all sounded so simple when Mr Carleton had enjoined his flock: 'Don't allow yourself to be kept out! Show them you've made up your mind to talk to them, and they'll listen.'

The girl succumbed to Anthony's pleasant, melancholy face, and in a moment the door to the inner room opened and admitted a tall, splay-footed man with slicked hair. He approached Anthony with ill-concealed impatience.

'You wanted to see me on a personal matter?'

Anthony quailed.

'I wanted to talk to you,' he said defiantly.

'About what?'

'It'll take some time to explain.'

'Well, what's it about?' Mr Weatherbee's voice indicated rising irritation.

Then Anthony, straining at each word, each syllable, began: 'I don't know whether or not you've ever heard of a series of pamphlets called "Heart Talks" – '

'Good grief!' cried Percy B. Weatherbee, Architect, 'are you trying to touch my heart?'

'No, it's business. "Heart Talks" have been incorporated and we're putting some shares on the market – '

His voice faded slowly off, harassed by a fixed and contemptuous stare from his unwilling prey. For another minute he struggled on, increasingly sensitive, entangled in his own words. His confidence oozed from him in great retching emanations that seemed to be sections of his own body. Almost mercifully Percy B. Weatherbee, Architect, terminated the interview: 'Good grief!' he exploded in disgust, 'and you call that a *personal* matter!' He whipped about and strode into his private office, banging the door behind him. Not daring to look at the stenographer, Anthony in some shameful and mysterious way got himself from the room. Perspiring profusely he stood in the hall wondering why they didn't come and arrest him; in every hurried look he discerned infallibly a glance of scorn.

After an hour and with the help of two strong whiskies he brought himself up to another attempt. He walked into a plumber's shop, but when he mentioned his business the plumber began pulling on his coat in a great hurry, gruffly announcing that he had to go to lunch. Anthony remarked politely that it was futile to try to sell a man anything when he was hungry, and the plumber heartily agreed.

This episode encouraged Anthony; he tried to think that had the plumber not been bound for lunch he would at least have listened.

Passing by a few glittering and formidable bazaars he entered a grocery store. A talkative proprietor told him that before buying any stocks he was going to see how the armistice affected the market. To

Anthony this seemed almost unfair. In Mr Carleton's salesman's Utopia the only reason prospective buyers ever gave for not purchasing stock was that they doubted it to be a promising investment. Obviously a man in that state was almost ludicrously easy game, to be brought down merely by the judicious application of the correct selling points. But these men – why, actually they weren't considering buying anything at all.

Anthony took several more drinks before he approached his fourth man, a real-estate agent; nevertheless, he was floored with a coup as decisive as a syllogism. The real-estate agent said that he had three brothers in the investment business. Viewing himself as a breaker-up of homes Anthony apologised and went out.

After another drink he conceived the brilliant plan of selling the stock to the bartenders along Lexington Avenue. This occupied several hours, for it was necessary to take a few drinks in each place in order to get the proprietor in the proper frame of mind to talk business. But the bartenders one and all contended that if they had any money to buy bonds they would not be bartenders. It was as though they had all convened and decided upon that rejoinder. As he approached a dark and soggy five o'clock he found that they were developing a still more annoying tendency to turn him off with a jest.

At five, then, with a tremendous effort at concentration he decided that he must put more variety into his canvassing. He selected a medium-sized delicatessen store, and went in. He felt, illuminatingly, that the thing to do was to cast a spell not only over the storekeeper but over all the customers as well – and perhaps through the psychology of the herd instinct they would buy as an astounded and immediately convinced whole.

'Af'ernoon,' he began in a loud thick voice. 'Ga l'il prop'sition.'

If he had wanted silence he obtained it. A sort of awe descended upon the half-dozen women marketing and upon the grey-haired ancient who in cap and apron was slicing chicken.

Anthony pulled a batch of papers from his flapping briefcase and waved them cheerfully.

'Buy a bon',' he suggested, 'good as liberty bon'!' The phrase pleased him and he elaborated upon it. 'Better'n liberty bon'. Every one these bon's worth *two* liberty bon's.' His mind made a hiatus and skipped to his peroration, which he delivered with appropriate gestures, these being somewhat marred by the necessity of clinging to the counter with one or both hands.

'Now see here. You taken up my time. I don't want know *why* you won't buy. I don't want you say *why*. Want you say *how many*!'

At this point they should have approached him with cheque-books and fountain-pens in hand. Realising that they must have missed a cue Anthony, with the instincts of an actor, went back and repeated his finale.

'Now see here! You taken up my time. You followed prop'sition. You agreed 'th reasonin'? Now, all I want from *you* is, how many lib'ty bon's?'

'See here!' broke in a new voice. A portly man whose face was adorned with symmetrical scrolls of yellow hair had come out of a glass cage in the rear of the store and was bearing down upon Anthony. 'See here, you!'

'How many?' repeated the salesman sternly. 'You taken up my time – '

'Hey, you!' cried the proprietor, 'I'll have you taken up by the police.'

'You mos' cert'nly won't!' returned Anthony with fine defiance. 'All I want know is how many.'

From here and there in the store went up little clouds of comment and expostulation.

'How terrible!'

'He's a raving maniac.'

'He's disgracefully drunk.'

The proprietor grasped Anthony's arm sharply.

'Get out, or I'll call a policeman.'

Some relics of rationality moved Anthony to nod and replace his bonds clumsily in the case.

'How many?' he reiterated doubtfully.

'The whole force if necessary!' thundered his adversary, his yellow moustache trembling fiercely.

'Sell 'em all a bon'.'

With this Anthony turned, bowed gravely to his late auditors, and wobbled from the store. He found a taxicab at the corner and rode home to the apartment. There he fell sound asleep on the sofa, and so Gloria found him, his breath filling the air with an unpleasant pungency, his hand still clutching his open briefcase.

Except when Anthony was drinking, his range of sensation had become less than that of a healthy old man, and when Prohibition came in July he found that, among those who could afford it, there was more drinking than ever before. One's host now brought out a bottle upon the slightest pretext. The tendency to display liquor was a manifestation of the same instinct that led a man to deck his wife with jewels. To have liquor was a boast, almost a badge of respectability.

In the mornings Anthony awoke tired, nervous, and worried. Halcyon summer twilights and the purple chill of morning alike left him unresponsive. Only for a brief moment every day in the warmth and renewed life of a first highball did his mind turn to those opalescent dreams of future pleasure – the mutual heritage of the happy and the damned. But this was only for a little while. As he grew drunker the dreams faded and he became a confused spectre, moving in odd crannies of his own mind, full of unexpected devices, harshly contemptuous at best and reaching sodden and dispirited depths. One night in June he had quarrelled violently with Maury over a matter of the utmost triviality. He remembered dimly next morning that it had been about a broken pint bottle of champagne. Maury had told him to sober up and Anthony's feelings had been hurt, so with an attempted gesture of dignity he had risen from the table and seizing Gloria's arm half led, half shamed her into a taxicab outside, leaving Maury with three dinners ordered and tickets for the opera.

This sort of semi-tragic fiasco had become so usual that when they occurred he was no longer stirred into making amends. If Gloria protested – and of late she was more likely to sink into contemptuous silence – he would either engage in a bitter defence of himself or else stalk dismally from the apartment. Never since the incident on the station platform at Redgate had he laid his hands on her in anger – though he was withheld often only by some instinct that itself made him tremble with rage. Just as he still cared more for her than for any other creature, so did he more intensely and frequently hate her.

So far, the judges of the Appellate Division had failed to hand down a decision, but after another postponement they finally affirmed the decree of the lower court – two justices dissenting. A notice of appeal was served upon Edward Shuttleworth. The case was going to the Court of Last Resort, and they were in for another interminable wait. Six months, perhaps a year. It had grown enormously unreal to them, remote and uncertain as heaven.

Throughout the previous winter one small matter had been a subtle and omnipresent irritant – the question of Gloria's grey fur coat. At that time women enveloped in long squirrel wraps could be seen every few yards along Fifth Avenue. The women were converted to the shape of tops. They seemed porcine and obscene; they resembled kept women in the concealing richness, the feminine animality of the garment. Yet – Gloria wanted a grey squirrel coat.

Discussing the matter – or, rather, arguing it, for even more than in the first year of their marriage did every discussion take the form of bitter debate full of such phrases as 'most certainly', 'utterly outrageous', 'it's so, nevertheless', and the ultra-emphatic 'regardless' – they concluded that they could not afford it. And so gradually it began to stand as a symbol of their growing financial anxiety.

To Gloria the shrinkage of their income was a remarkable phenomenon, without explanation or precedent – that it could happen all within the space of five years seemed almost an intended cruelty, conceived and executed by a sardonic God. When they were married seventy-five hundred a year had seemed ample for a young couple, especially when augmented by the expectation of many millions. Gloria had failed to realise that it was decreasing not only in amount but in purchasing power until the payment of Mr Haight's retaining fee of fifteen thousand dollars made the fact suddenly and startlingly obvious. When Anthony was drafted they had calculated their income at over four hundred a month, with the dollar even then decreasing in value, but on his return to New York they discovered an even more alarming condition of affairs. They were receiving only forty-five hundred a year from their investments. And though the suit over the will moved ahead of them like a persistent mirage and the financial danger-mark loomed up in the near distance they found, nevertheless, that living within their income was impossible.

So Gloria went without the squirrel coat and every day upon Fifth Avenue she was a little more conscious of her well-worn, half-length leopard skin, now hopelessly old-fashioned. Every other month they sold a bond, yet when the bills were paid it left only enough to be gulped down hungrily by their current expenses. Anthony's calculations showed that their capital would last about seven years longer. So Gloria's heart was very bitter, for in one week, on a prolonged hysterical party during which Anthony whimsically divested himself of coat, vest and shirt in a theatre and was assisted out by a posse of ushers, they spent twice what the grey squirrel coat would have cost.

It was November, Indian summer rather, and a warm, warm night – which was unnecessary, for the work of the summer was done. Babe Ruth [306] had smashed the home-run record for the first time and Jack Dempsey [307] had broken Jess Willard's cheekbone out in Ohio. Over in Europe the usual number of children had swollen stomachs from starvation, and the diplomats were at their customary business of making the world safe for new wars. In New York City the proletariat were being 'disciplined', and the odds on Harvard were generally quoted at five to three. Peace had come down in earnest, the beginning of new days.

Up in the bedroom of the apartment on Fifty-Seventh Street Gloria lay upon her bed and tossed from side to side, sitting up at intervals to throw off a superfluous cover and once asking Anthony, who was lying awake beside her, to bring her a glass of ice-water. 'Be sure and put ice in it,' she said with insistence; 'it isn't cold enough the way it comes from the faucet.'

Looking through the frail curtains she could see the rounded moon over the roofs and beyond it on the sky the yellow glow from Times Square – and watching the two incongruous lights, her mind worked over an emotion, or rather an interwoven complex of emotions, that had occupied it through the day, and the day before that and back to the last time when she could remember having thought clearly and consecutively about anything – which must have been while Anthony was in the army.

She would be twenty-nine in February. The month assumed an ominous and inescapable significance – making her wonder, through these nebulous half-fevered hours, whether after all she had not wasted her faintly tired beauty, whether there was such thing as a use for any quality bounded by a harsh and inevitable mortality.

Years before, when she was twenty-one, she had written in her diary: 'Beauty is only to be admired, only to be loved – to be harvested carefully and then flung at a chosen lover like a gift of roses. It seems to me, so far as I can judge clearly at all, that my beauty should be used like that . . .'

And now, all this November day, all this desolate day, under a sky dirty and white, Gloria had been thinking that perhaps she had been wrong. To preserve the integrity of her first gift she had looked no more for love. When the first flame and ecstasy had grown dim, sunk down, departed, she had begun preserving – what? It puzzled her that she no longer knew just what she was preserving – a sentimental memory or some profound and fundamental concept of honour. She was doubting now whether there had been any moral issue involved in her way of life – to walk unworried and unregretful along the gayest of all possible lanes and to keep her pride by being always herself and doing what it seemed beautiful that she should do. From the first little boy in an Eton collar whose 'girl' she had been, down to the latest casual man whose eyes had grown alert and appreciative as they rested upon her, there was needed only that matchless candour she could throw into a look or clothe with an inconsequent clause – for she had talked always in broken clauses – to weave about her immeasurable illusions, immeasurable distances, immeasurable light. To create souls in men, to create fine happiness and fine despair she must remain deeply proud – proud to be inviolate, proud also to be melting, to be passionate and possessed.

She knew that in her breast she had never wanted children. The reality, the earthiness, the intolerable sentiment of child-bearing, the menace to her beauty – had appalled her. She wanted to exist only as a conscious flower, prolonging and preserving itself. Her sentimentality could cling fiercely to her own illusions, but her ironic soul whispered that motherhood was also the privilege of the female baboon. So her dreams were of ghostly children only – the early, the perfect symbols of her early and perfect love for Anthony.

In the end then, her beauty was all that never failed her. She had never seen beauty like her own. What it meant ethically or aesthetically faded before the gorgeous concreteness of her pink-and-white feet, the clean perfectness of her body, and the baby mouth that was like the material symbol of a kiss.

She would be twenty-nine in February. As the long night waned she grew supremely conscious that she and beauty were going to make use of these next three months. At first she was not sure for what, but the problem resolved itself gradually into the old lure of the screen. She was in earnest now. No material want could have moved her as this fear moved her. No matter for Anthony, Anthony the poor in spirit, the weak and broken man with bloodshot eyes, for whom she still had moments of tenderness. No matter. She would be twenty-nine in February – a hundred days, so many days; she would go to Bloeckman tomorrow.

With the decision came relief. It cheered her that in some manner the illusion of beauty could be sustained, or preserved perhaps in celluloid after the reality had vanished. Well – tomorrow.

The next day she felt weak and ill. She tried to go out, and saved herself from collapse only by clinging to a mailbox near the front door. The Martinique elevator boy helped her upstairs, and she waited on the bed for Anthony's return without energy to unhook her brassiere.

For five days she was down with influenza, which, just as the

month turned the corner into winter, ripened into double pneumonia. In the feverish perambulations of her mind she prowled
through a house of bleak unlighted rooms hunting for her mother.
All she wanted was to be a little girl, to be efficiently taken care of by
some yielding yet superior power, stupider and steadier than herself.
It seemed that the only lover she had ever wanted was a lover in a
dream.

'ODI PROFANUM VULGUS'[308]

One day in the midst of Gloria's illness there occurred a curious
incident that puzzled Miss McGovern, the trained nurse, for some
time afterwards. It was noon, but the room in which the patient lay
was dark and quiet.

Miss McGovern was standing near the bed mixing some medicine
when Mrs Patch, who had apparently been sound asleep, sat up and
began to speak vehemently: 'Millions of people,' she said, 'swarming
like rats, chattering like apes, smelling like all hell . . . monkeys! Or
lice, I suppose. For one really exquisite palace . . . on Long Island,
say – or even in Greenwich . . . for one palace full of pictures from
the Old World and exquisite things – with avenues of trees and
green lawns and a view of the blue sea, and lovely people about in
slick dresses . . . I'd sacrifice a hundred thousand of them, a million
of them.' She raised her hand feebly and snapped her fingers. 'I care
nothing for them – understand me?'

The look she bent upon Miss McGovern at the conclusion of this
speech was curiously elfin, curiously intent. Then she gave a short
little laugh, polished with scorn, and tumbling backwards fell off
again to sleep.

Miss McGovern was bewildered. She wondered what were the
hundred thousand things that Mrs Patch would sacrifice for her
palace. Dollars, she supposed – yet it had not sounded exactly like
dollars.

THE MOVIES

It was February, seven days before her birthday, and the great snow
that had filled up the cross-streets as dirt fills the cracks in a floor
had turned to slush and was being escorted to the gutters by the
hoses of the street-cleaning department. The wind, none the less
bitter for being casual, whipped in through the open windows of the

living-room bearing with it the dismal secrets of the area-way and clearing the Patch apartment of stale smoke in its cheerless circulation.

Gloria, wrapped in a warm kimona, came into the chilly room and taking up the telephone receiver called Joseph Bloeckman.

'Do you mean Mr Joseph *Black*?' demanded the telephone girl at 'Films Par Excellence'.

'Bloeckman, Joseph Bloeckman. B-l-o – '

'Mr Joseph Bloeckman has changed his name to Black. Do you want him?'

'Why – yes.' She remembered nervously that she had once called him 'Blockhead' to his face.

His office was reached by courtesy of two additional female voices; the last was a secretary who took her name. Only with the flow through the transmitter of his own familiar but faintly impersonal tone did she realise that it had been three years since they had met. And he had changed his name to Black.

'Can you see me?' she suggested lightly. 'It's on a business matter, really. I'm going into the movies at last – if I can.'

'I'm awfully glad. I've always thought you'd like it.'

'Do you think you can get me a trial?' she demanded with the arrogance peculiar to all beautiful women, to all women who have ever at any time considered themselves beautiful.

He assured her that it was merely a question of when she wanted the trial. Any time? Well, he'd phone later in the day and let her know a convenient hour. The conversation closed with conventional padding on both sides. Then from three o'clock to five she sat close to the telephone – with no result.

But next morning came a note that contented and excited her:

My dear Gloria – Just by luck a matter came to my attention that I think will be just suited to you. I would like to see you start with something that would bring you notice. At the same time if a very beautiful girl of your sort is put directly into a picture next to one of the rather shop-worn stars with which every company is afflicted, tongues would very likely wag. But there is a 'flapper' part in a Percy B. Debris production that I think would be just suited to you and would bring you notice. Willa Sable plays opposite Gaston Mears in a sort of character part and your part I believe would be her younger sister.

Anyway Percy B. Debris who is directing the picture says if

you'll come to the studios day after tomorrow (Thursday) he will run off a test. If ten o'clock is suited to you I will meet you there at that time.

With all good wishes
Ever faithfully,

JOSEPH BLACK

Gloria had decided that Anthony was to know nothing of this until she had obtained a definite position, and accordingly she was dressed and out of the apartment next morning before he awoke. Her mirror had given her, she thought, much the same account as ever. She wondered if there were any lingering traces of her sickness. She was still slightly under weight, and she had fancied, a few days before, that her cheeks were a trifle thinner – but she felt that those were merely transitory conditions and that on this particular day she looked as fresh as ever. She had bought and charged a new hat, and as the day was warm she had left the leopard-skin coat at home.

At the 'Films Par Excellence' studios she was announced over the telephone and told that Mr Black would be down directly. She looked around her. Two girls were being shown about by a little fat man in a slash-pocket coat, and one of them had indicated a stack of thin parcels, piled breast-high against the wall, and extending along for twenty feet.

'That's studio mail,' explained the fat man. 'Pictures of the stars who are with "Films Par Excellence".'

'Oh.'

'Each one's autographed by Florence Kelley or Gaston Mears or Mack Dodge – ' He winked confidentially. 'At least, when Minnie McGlook out in Sauk Center gets the picture she wrote for, she *thinks* it's autographed.'

'Just a stamp?'

'Sure. It'd take 'em a good eight-hour day to autograph half of 'em. They say Mary Pickford's studio mail costs her fifty thousand a year.'

'Say!'

'Sure. Fifty thousand. But it's the best kinda advertising there is – '

They drifted out of earshot and almost immediately Bloeckman appeared – Bloeckman, a dark suave gentleman, gracefully engaged in the middle forties, who greeted her with courteous warmth and told her she had not changed a bit in three years. He led the way into a great hall, as large as an armoury and broken intermittently with busy sets and blinding rows of unfamiliar light. Each piece of scenery was marked in large white letters 'Gaston Mears Company', 'Mack Dodge Company', or simply 'Films Par Excellence'.

'Ever been in a studio before?'

'Never have.'

She liked it. There was no heavy closeness of greasepaint, no scent of soiled and tawdry costumes which years before had revolted her behind the scenes of a musical comedy. This work was done in the clean mornings; the appurtenances seemed rich and gorgeous and new. On a set that was joyous with Manchu hangings a perfect Chinaman was going through a scene according to megaphone directions as the great glittering machine ground out its ancient moral tale for the edification of the national mind.

A red-headed man approached them and spoke with familiar deference to Bloeckman, who answered: 'Hello, Debris. Want you to meet Mrs Patch . . . Mrs Patch wants to go into pictures, as I explained to you . . . All right, now, where do we go?'

Mr Debris – the great Percy B. Debris, thought Gloria – showed them to a set which represented the interior of an office. Some chairs were drawn up around the camera, which stood in front of it, and the three of them sat down.

'Ever been in a studio before?' asked Mr Debris, giving her a glance that was surely the quintessence of keenness. 'No? Well, I'll explain exactly what's going to happen. We're going to take what we call a test in order to see how your features photograph and whether you've got natural stage presence and how you respond to coaching. There's no need to be nervous over it. I'll just have the cameraman take a few hundred feet in an episode I've got marked here in the scenario. We can tell pretty much what we want to from that.'

He produced a typewritten continuity and explained to her the episode she was to enact. It developed that one Barbara Wainwright had been secretly married to the junior partner of the firm whose office was there represented. Entering the deserted office one day by accident she was naturally interested in seeing where her husband worked. The telephone rang and after some hesitation she answered it. She learned that her husband had been struck by an automobile and instantly killed. She was overcome. At first she was unable to realise the truth, but finally she succeeded in comprehending it, and went into a dead faint on the floor.

'Now that's all we want,' concluded Mr Debris. 'I'm going to stand here and tell you approximately what to do, and you're to act as though I wasn't here, and just go on, do it your own way. You needn't be afraid we're going to judge this too severely. We simply want to get a general idea of your screen personality.'

'I see.'

'You'll find make-up in the room in back of the set. Go light on it. Very little red.'

'I see,' repeated Gloria, nodding. She touched her lips nervously with the tip of her tongue.

THE TEST

As she came into the set through the real wooden door and closed it carefully behind her, she found herself inconveniently dissatisfied with her clothes. She should have bought a 'misses' dress for the occasion – she could still wear them, and it might have been a good investment if it had accentuated her airy youth.

Her mind snapped sharply into the momentous present as Mr Debris's voice came from the glare of the white lights in front.

'You look around for your husband . . . Now – you don't see him . . . you're curious about the office . . . '

She became conscious of the regular sound of the camera. It worried her. She glanced towards it involuntarily and wondered if she had made up her face correctly. Then, with a definite effort she forced herself to act – and she had never felt that the gestures of her body were so banal, so awkward, so bereft of grace or distinction. She strolled around the office, picking up articles here and there and looking at them inanely. Then she scrutinised the ceiling, the floor, and thoroughly inspected an inconsequential lead pencil on the desk. Finally, because she could think of nothing else to do, and less than nothing to express, she forced a smile.

'All right. Now the phone rings. Ting-a-ling-a-ling! Hesitate, and then answer it.'

She hesitated – and then, too quickly, she thought, picked up the receiver.

'Hello.'

Her voice was hollow and unreal. The words rang in the empty set like the ineffectualities of a ghost. The absurdities of their requirements appalled her – Did they expect that on an instant's notice she could put herself in the place of this preposterous and unexplained character?

' . . . No . . . no . . . Not yet! Now listen: "John Sumner has just been knocked over by an automobile and instantly killed!" '

Gloria let her baby mouth drop slowly open. Then: 'Now hang up! With a bang!'

She obeyed, clung to the table with her eyes wide and staring. At length she was feeling slightly encouraged and her confidence increased.

'My God!' she cried. Her voice was good, she thought. 'Oh, my God!'

'Now faint.'

She collapsed forward to her knees and throwing her body outwards on the ground lay without breathing.

'All right!' called Mr Debris. 'That's enough, thank you. That's plenty. Get up – that's enough.'

Gloria arose, mustering her dignity and brushing off her skirt.

'Awful!' she remarked with a cool laugh, though her heart was bumping tumultuously. 'Terrible, wasn't it?'

'Did you mind it?' said Mr Debris, smiling blandly. 'Did it seem hard? I can't tell anything about it until I have it run off.'

'Of course not,' she agreed, trying to attach some sort of meaning to his remark – and failing. It was just the sort of thing he would have said had he been trying not to encourage her.

A few moments later she left the studio. Bloeckman had promised that she should hear the result of the test within the next few days. Too proud to force any definite comment she felt a baffling uncertainty and only now when the step had at last been taken did she realise how the possibility of a successful screen career had played in the back of her mind for the past three years. That night she tried to tell over to herself the elements that might decide for or against her. Whether or not she had used enough make-up worried her, and as the part was that of a girl of twenty, she wondered if she had not been just a little too grave. About her acting she was least of all satisfied. Her entrance had been abominable – in fact not until she reached the phone had she displayed a shred of poise – and then the test had been over. If they had only realised! She wished that she could try it again. A mad plan to call up in the morning and ask for a new trial took possession of her, and as suddenly faded. It seemed neither politic nor polite to ask another favour of Bloeckman.

The third day of waiting found her in a highly nervous condition. She had bitten the insides of her mouth until they were raw and smarting, and burnt unbearably when she washed them with Listerine. She had quarrelled so persistently with Anthony that he had left the apartment in a cold fury. But because he was intimidated by her exceptional frigidity, he called up an hour afterwards, apologised and said he was having dinner at the Amsterdam Club, the only one in which he still retained membership.

It was after one o'clock and she had breakfasted at eleven, so, deciding to forgo luncheon, she started for a walk in the Park. At three there would be a mail. She would be back by three.

It was an afternoon of premature spring. Water was drying on the walks and in the Park little girls were gravely wheeling white doll-buggies up and down under the thin trees while behind them followed bored nursery-maids in twos, discussing with each other those tremendous secrets that are peculiar to nursery-maids.

Two o'clock by her little gold watch. She should have a new watch, one made in a platinum oblong and encrusted with diamonds – but those cost even more than squirrel coats and of course they were out of her reach now, like everything else – unless perhaps the right letter was awaiting her . . . in about an hour . . . fifty-eight minutes exactly. Ten to get there left forty-eight . . . forty-seven now . . .

Little girls soberly wheeling their buggies along the damp sunny walks. The nursery-maids chattering in pairs about their inscrutable secrets. Here and there a raggedy man seated upon newspapers spread on a drying bench, related not to the radiant and delightful afternoon but to the dirty snow that slept exhausted in obscure corners, waiting for extermination . . .

Ages later, coming into the dim hall she saw the Martinique elevator boy standing incongruously in the light of the stained-glass window.

'Is there any mail for us?' she asked.

'Up-stays, madame.'

The switchboard squawked abominably and Gloria waited while he ministered to the telephone. She sickened as the elevator groaned its way up – the floors passed like the slow lapse of centuries, each one ominous, accusing, significant. The letter, a white leprous spot, lay upon the dirty tiles of the hall . . .

MY DEAR GLORIA – We had the test run off yesterday afternoon, and Mr Debris seemed to think that for the part he had in mind he needed a younger woman. He said that the acting was not bad, and that there was a small character part supposed to be a very haughty rich widow that he thought you might –

Desolately Gloria raised her glance until it fell out across the area-way. But she found she could not see the opposite wall, for her grey eyes were full of tears. She walked into the bedroom, the letter crinkled tightly in her hand, and sank down upon her knees before the long mirror on the wardrobe floor. This was her twenty-ninth birthday, and the world was melting away before her eyes. She tried to think that it had been the make-up, but her emotions were too profound, too overwhelming for any consolation that the thought conveyed.

She strained to see until she could feel the flesh on her temples pull forward. Yes – the cheeks were ever so faintly thin, the corners of the eyes were lined with tiny wrinkles. The eyes were different. Why, they were different! . . . And then suddenly she knew how tired her eyes were.

'Oh, my pretty face,' she whispered, passionately grieving. 'Oh, my pretty face! Oh, I don't want to live without my pretty face! Oh, what's *happened*?'

Then she slid towards the mirror and, as in the test, sprawled face downwards upon the floor – and lay there sobbing. It was the first awkward movement she had ever made.

CHAPTER 3

No Matter!

Within another year Anthony and Gloria had become like players who had lost their costumes, lacking the pride to continue on the note of tragedy – so that when Mrs and Miss Hulme of Kansas City cut them dead in the Plaza one evening, it was only that Mrs and Miss Hulme, like most people, abominated mirrors of their atavistic selves.

Their new apartment, for which they paid eighty-five dollars a month, was situated on Claremont Avenue,[309] which is two blocks from the Hudson in the dim hundreds. They had lived there a month when Muriel Kane came to see them late one afternoon.

It was a reproachless twilight on the summer side of spring. Anthony lay upon the lounge looking up One Hundred and Twenty-Seventh Street towards the river, near which he could just see a single patch of vivid green trees that guaranteed the brummagem umbrageousness of Riverside Drive. Across the water were the Palisades,[310] crowned by the ugly framework of the amusement park – yet soon it would be dusk and those same iron cobwebs would be a glory against the heavens, an enchanted palace set over the smooth radiance of a tropical canal.

The streets near the apartment, Anthony had found, were streets where children played – streets a little nicer than those he had been used to pass on his way to Marietta, but of the same general sort, with an occasional hand organ or hurdy-gurdy, and in the cool of the evening many pairs of young girls walking down to the corner drugstore for ice cream soda and dreaming unlimited dreams under the low heavens.

Dusk in the streets now, and children playing, shouting up incoherent ecstatic words that faded out close to the open window – and Muriel, who had come to find Gloria, chattering to him from an opaque gloom over across the room.

'Light the lamp, why don't we?' she suggested. 'It's getting *ghostly* in here.'

With a tired movement he arose and obeyed; the grey window-panes vanished. He stretched himself. He was heavier now, his stomach was a limp weight against his belt; his flesh had softened and expanded. He was thirty-two and his mind was a bleak and disordered wreck.

'Have a little drink, Muriel?'

'Not me, thanks. I don't use it any more. What're you doing these days, Anthony?' she asked curiously.

'Well, I've been pretty busy with this lawsuit,' he answered indifferently. 'It's gone to the Court of Appeals – ought to be settled up one way or another by autumn. There's been some objection as to whether the Court of Appeals has jurisdiction over the matter.'

Muriel made a clicking sound with her tongue and cocked her head on one side.

'Well, you tell 'em! I never heard of anything taking so long.'

'Oh, they all do,' he replied listlessly; 'all will cases. They say it's exceptional to have one settled under four or five years.'

'Oh . . .' Muriel daringly changed her tack, 'why don't you go to work, you la-azy!'

'At what?' he demanded abruptly.

'Why, at anything, I suppose. You're still a young man.'

'If that's encouragement, I'm much obliged,' he answered dryly – and then with sudden weariness: 'Does it bother you particularly that I don't want to work?'

'It doesn't bother me – but, it does bother a lot of people who claim – '

'Oh, God!' he said brokenly, 'it seems to me that for three years I've heard nothing about myself but wild stories and virtuous admonitions. I'm tired of it. If you don't want to see us, let us alone. I don't bother my former "friends". But I need no charity calls, and no criticism disguised as good advice – ' Then he added apologetically: 'I'm sorry – but really, Muriel, you mustn't talk like a lady slum-worker even if you are visiting the lower middle classes.' He turned his bloodshot eyes on her reproachfully – eyes that had once been a deep, clear blue, that were weak now, strained, and half-ruined from reading when he was drunk.

'Why do you say such awful things?' she protested. 'You talk as if you and Gloria were in the middle classes.'

'Why pretend we're not? I hate people who claim to be great aristocrats when they can't even keep up the appearances of it.'

'Do you think a person has to have money to be aristocratic?'

Muriel . . . the horrified democrat . . . !

'Why, of course. Aristocracy's only an admission that certain traits which we call fine – courage and honour and beauty and all that sort of thing – can best be developed in a favourable environment, where you don't have the warpings of ignorance and necessity.'

Muriel bit her lower lip and waved her head from side to side.

'Well, all *I* say is that if a person comes from a good family they're always nice people. That's the trouble with you and Gloria. You think that just because things aren't going your way right now all your old friends are trying to avoid you. You're too sensitive – '

'As a matter of fact,' said Anthony, 'you know nothing at all about it. With me it's simply a matter of pride, and for once Gloria's reasonable enough to agree that we oughtn't go where we're not wanted. And people don't want us. We're too much the ideal bad examples.'

'Nonsense! You can't park your pessimism in my little sun-parlour. I think you ought to forget all those morbid speculations and go to work.'

'Here I am, thirty-two. Suppose I did start in at some idiotic business. Perhaps in two years I might rise to fifty dollars a week – with luck. That's *if* I could get a job at all; there's an awful lot of unemployment. Well, suppose I made fifty a week. Do you think I'd be any happier? Do you think that if I don't get this money of my grandfather's life will be *endurable*?'

Muriel smiled complacently.

'Well,' she said, 'that may be clever but it isn't common sense.'

A few minutes later Gloria came in seeming to bring with her into the room some dark colour, indeterminate and rare. In a taciturn way she was happy to see Muriel. She greeted Anthony with a casual 'Hi!'

'I've been talking philosophy with your husband,' cried the irrepressible Miss Kane.

'We took up some fundamental concepts,' said Anthony, a faint smile disturbing his pale cheeks, paler still under two days' growth of beard.

Oblivious to his irony Muriel rehashed her contention. When she had done, Gloria said quietly: 'Anthony's right. It's no fun to go around when you have the sense that people are looking at you in a certain way.'

He broke in plaintively: 'Don't you think that when even Maury Noble, who was my best friend, won't come to see us, it's high time to stop calling people up?' Tears were standing in his eyes.

'That was your fault about Maury Noble,' said Gloria coolly.

'It wasn't.'

'It most certainly was.'

Muriel intervened quickly: 'I met a girl who knew Maury, the other day, and she says he doesn't drink any more. He's getting pretty cagey.'

'Doesn't?'

'Practically not at all. He's making *piles* of money. He's sort of changed since the war. He's going to marry a girl in Philadelphia who has millions, Ceci Larrabee – anyhow, that's what *Town Tattle* said.'

'He's thirty-three,' said Anthony, thinking aloud. 'But it's odd to imagine his getting married. I used to think he was so brilliant.'

'He was,' murmured Gloria, 'in a way.'

'But brilliant people don't settle down in business – or do they? Or what do they do? Or what becomes of everybody you used to know and have so much in common with?'

'You drift apart,' suggested Muriel with the appropriate dreamy look.

'They change,' said Gloria. 'All the qualities that they don't use in their daily lives get cobwebbed up.'

'The last thing he said to me,' recollected Anthony, 'was that he was going to work so as to forget that there was nothing worth working for.'

Muriel caught at this quickly.

'That's what *you* ought to do,' she exclaimed triumphantly. 'Of course I shouldn't think anybody would want to work for nothing. But it'd give you something to do. What do you do with yourselves, anyway? Nobody ever sees you at Montmartre or – or anywhere. Are you economising?'

Gloria laughed scornfully, glancing at Anthony from the corners of her eyes.

'Well,' he demanded, 'what are you laughing at?'

'You know what I'm laughing at,' she answered coldly.

'At that case of whiskey?'

'Yes' – she turned to Muriel – 'he paid seventy-five dollars for a case of whiskey yesterday.'

'What if I did? It's cheaper that way than if you get it by the bottle. You needn't pretend that you won't drink any of it.'

'At least I don't drink in the daytime.'

'That's a fine distinction!' he cried, springing to his feet in a weak rage. 'What's more, I'll be damned if you can hurl that at me every few minutes!'

'It's true.'

'It is *not*! And I'm getting sick of this eternal business of criticising me before visitors!' He had worked himself up to such a state that his arms and shoulders were visibly trembling. 'You'd think everything was my fault. You'd think you hadn't encouraged me to spend money – and spent a lot more on yourself than I ever did by a long shot.'

Now Gloria rose to her feet.

'I *won't* let you talk to me that way!'

'All right, then; by heaven, you don't have to!'

In a sort of rush he left the room. The two women heard his steps in the hall and then the front door banged. Gloria sank back into her chair. Her face was lovely in the lamplight, composed, inscrutable.

'Oh – !' cried Muriel in distress. 'Oh, what *is* the matter?'

'Nothing particularly. He's just drunk.'

'Drunk? Why, he's perfectly sober. He talked – '

Gloria shook her head.

'Oh, no, he doesn't show it any more unless he can hardly stand up, and he talks all right until he gets excited. He talks much better than he does when he's sober. But he's been sitting here all day drinking – except for the time it took him to walk to the corner for a newspaper.'

'Oh, how terrible!' Muriel was sincerely moved. Her eyes filled with tears. 'Has this happened much?'

'Drinking, you mean?'

'No, this – leaving you?'

'Oh, yes. Frequently. He'll come in about midnight – and weep and ask me to forgive him.'

'And do you?'

'I don't know. We just go on.'

The two women sat there in the lamplight and looked at each other, each in a different way helpless before this thing. Gloria was still pretty, as pretty as she would ever be again – her cheeks were flushed and she was wearing a new dress that she had bought – imprudently – for fifty dollars. She had hoped she could persuade Anthony to take her out tonight, to a restaurant or even to one of the great, gorgeous moving-picture palaces where there would be a few people to look at her, at whom she could bear to look in turn. She wanted this because she knew her cheeks were flushed and because her dress was new and becomingly fragile. Only very occasionally, now, did they receive any invitations. But she did not tell these things to Muriel.

'Gloria, dear, I wish we could have dinner together, but I promised a man and it's seven-thirty already. I've got to *tear*.'

'Oh, I couldn't, anyway. In the first place I've been ill all day. I couldn't eat a thing.'

After she had walked with Muriel to the door, Gloria came back into the room, turned out the lamp, and leaning her elbows on the window sill looked out at Palisades Park, where the brilliant revolving circle of the Ferris wheel was like a trembling mirror catching the yellow reflection of the moon. The street was quiet now; the children had gone in – over the way she could see a family at dinner. Pointlessly, ridiculously, they rose and walked about the table; seen thus, all that they did appeared incongruous – it was as though they were being jiggled carelessly and to no purpose by invisible overhead wires.

She looked at her watch – it was eight o'clock. She had been pleased for a part of the day – the early afternoon – in walking along that Broadway of Harlem, One Hundred and Twenty-Fifth Street, with her nostrils alert to many odours, and her mind excited by the extraordinary beauty of some Italian children. It affected her curiously – as Fifth Avenue had affected her once, in the days when, with the placid confidence of beauty, she had known that it was all hers, every shop and all it held, every adult toy glittering in a window, all hers for the asking. Here on One Hundred and Twenty-Fifth Street there were Salvation Army bands and spectrum-shawled old ladies on doorsteps and sugary, sticky candy in the grimy hands of shiny-haired children – and the late sun striking down on the sides of the tall tenements. All very rich and racy and savoury, like a dish by a provident French chef that one could not help enjoying, even though one knew that the ingredients were probably leftovers . . .

Gloria shuddered suddenly as a river siren came moaning over the dusky roofs, and leaning back in till the ghostly curtains fell from her shoulder, she turned on the electric lamp. It was growing late. She knew there was some change in her purse, and she considered whether she would go down and have some coffee and rolls where the liberated subway made a roaring cave of Manhattan Street or eat the devilled ham and bread in the kitchen. Her purse decided for her. It contained a nickel and two pennies.

After an hour the silence of the room had grown unbearable, and she found that her eyes were wandering from her magazine to the ceiling, towards which she stared without thought. Suddenly she stood up, hesitated for a moment, biting at her finger – then she went to the pantry, took down a bottle of whiskey from the shelf and poured herself a drink. She filled up the glass with ginger ale, and returning to her chair finished an article in the magazine. It concerned the last revolutionary widow, who, when a young girl, had married an ancient veteran of the Continental Army and who had died in 1906. It seemed strange and oddly romantic to Gloria that she and this woman had been contemporaries.

She turned a page and learned that a candidate for Congress was being accused of atheism by an opponent. Gloria's surprise vanished when she found that the charges were false. The candidate had merely denied the miracle of the loaves and fishes. He admitted, under pressure, that he gave full credence to the stroll upon the water.

Finishing her first drink, Gloria got herself a second. After slipping on a négligé and making herself comfortable on the lounge, she became conscious that she was miserable and that the tears were rolling down her cheeks. She wondered if they were tears of self-pity, and tried resolutely not to cry, but this existence without hope, without happiness, oppressed her, and she kept shaking her head from side to side, her mouth drawn down tremulously in the corners, as though she were denying an assertion made by someone, somewhere. She did not know that this gesture of hers was years older than history, that, for a hundred generations of men, intolerable and persistent grief has offered that gesture, of denial, of protest, of bewilderment, to something more profound, more powerful than the God made in the image of man, and before which that God, did he exist, would be equally impotent. It is a truth set at the heart of tragedy that this force never explains, never answers – this force intangible as air, more definite than death.

RICHARD CARAMEL

Early in the summer Anthony resigned from his last club, the Amsterdam. He had come to visit it hardly twice a year, and the dues were a recurrent burden. He had joined it on his return from Italy because it had been his grandfather's club and his father's, and because it was a club that, given the opportunity, one indisputably joined – but as a matter of fact he had preferred the Harvard Club, largely because of Dick and Maury. However, with the decline of his fortunes, it had seemed an increasingly desirable bauble to cling to . . . It was relinquished, at the last, with some regret . . .

His companions numbered now a curious dozen. Several of them he had met in a place called 'Sammy's', on Forty-Third Street, where, if one knocked on the door and were favourably passed on from behind a grating, one could sit around a great round table drinking fairly good whiskey. It was here that he encountered a man named Parker Allison, who had been exactly the wrong sort of rounder at Harvard, and who was running through a large 'yeast' fortune as rapidly as possible. Parker Allison's notion of distinction consisted in driving a noisy red-and-yellow racing-car up Broadway with two glittering, hard-eyed girls beside him. He was the sort who dined with two girls rather than with one – his imagination was almost incapable of sustaining a dialogue.

Besides Allison there was Pete Lytell, who wore a grey derby on the side of his head. He always had money and he was customarily cheerful, so Anthony held aimless, long-winded conversation with him through many afternoons of the summer and fall. Lytell, he found, not only talked but reasoned in phrases. His philosophy was a series of them, assimilated here and there through an active, thoughtless life. He had phrases about Socialism – the immemorial ones; he had phrases pertaining to the existence of a personal deity – something about one time when he had been in a railroad accident; and he had phrases about the Irish problem, the sort of woman he respected, and the futility of Prohibition. The only time his conversation ever rose superior to these muddled clauses, with which he interpreted the most rococo happenings in a life that had been more than usually eventful, was when he got down to the detailed discussion of his most animal existence: he knew, to a subtlety, the foods, the liquor, and the women that he preferred.

He was at once the commonest and the most remarkable product of civilisation. He was nine out of ten people that one passes on a city street – and he was a hairless ape with two dozen tricks. He was the hero of a thousand romances of life and art – and he was a virtual moron, performing staidly yet absurdly a series of complicated and infinitely astounding epics over a span of threescore years.

With such men as these two Anthony Patch drank and discussed and drank and argued. He liked them because they knew nothing about him, because they lived in the obvious and had not the faintest conception of the inevitable continuity of life. They sat not before a motion picture with consecutive reels, but at a musty old-fashioned travelogue with all values stark and hence all implications confused. Yet they themselves were not confused, because there was nothing in them to be confused – they changed phrases from month to month as they changed neckties.

Anthony, the courteous, the subtle, the perspicacious, was drunk each day – in Sammy's with these men, in the apartment over a book, some book he knew, and, very rarely, with Gloria, who, in his eyes, had begun to develop the unmistakable outlines of a quarrelsome and unreasonable woman. She was not the Gloria of old, certainly – the Gloria who, had she been sick, would have preferred to inflict misery upon everyone around her, rather than confess that she needed sympathy or assistance. She was not above whining now; she was not above being sorry for herself. Each night when she prepared for bed she smeared her face with some new unguent which she hoped illogically would give back the glow and freshness to her vanishing beauty. When Anthony was drunk he taunted her about this. When he was sober he was polite to her, on occasions even tender; he seemed to show for short hours a trace of that old quality of understanding too well to blame – that quality which was the best of him and had worked swiftly and ceaselessly towards his ruin.

But he hated to be sober. It made him conscious of the people around him, of that air of struggle, of greedy ambition, of hope more sordid than despair, of incessant passage up or down, which in every metropolis is most in evidence through the unstable middle class. Unable to live with the rich he thought that his next choice would have been to live with the very poor. Anything was better than this cup of perspiration and tears.

The sense of the enormous panorama of life, never strong in Anthony, had become dim almost to extinction. At long intervals now some incident, some gesture of Gloria's, would take his fancy – but the grey veils had come down in earnest upon him. As he grew older those things faded – after that there was wine.

There was a kindliness about intoxication – there was that indescribable gloss and glamour it gave, like the memories of ephemeral and faded evenings. After a few highballs there was magic in the tall glowing Arabian night of the Bush Terminal Building[311] – its summit a peak of sheer grandeur, gold and dreaming against the inaccessible sky. And Wall Street, the crass, the banal – again it was the triumph of gold, a gorgeous sentient spectacle; it was where the great kings kept the money for their wars . . .

. . . The fruit of youth or of the grape, the transitory magic of the brief passage from darkness to darkness – the old illusion that truth and beauty were in some way entwined.

As he stood in front of Delmonico's lighting a cigarette one night he saw two hansoms drawn up close to the curb, waiting for a chance drunken fare. The outmoded cabs were worn and dirty – the cracked patent leather wrinkled like an old man's face, the cushions faded to a brownish lavender; the very horses were ancient and weary, and so were the white-haired men who sat aloft, cracking their whips with a grotesque affectation of gallantry. A relic of vanished gaiety!

Anthony Patch walked away in a sudden fit of depression, pondering the bitterness of such survivals. There was nothing, it seemed, that grew stale so soon as pleasure.

On Forty-Second Street one afternoon he met Richard Caramel for the first time in many months, a prosperous, fattening Richard Caramel, whose face was filling out to match the Bostonian brow.

'Just got in this week from the Coast. Was going to call you up, but I didn't know your new address.'

'We've moved.'

Richard Caramel noticed that Anthony was wearing a soiled shirt, that his cuffs were slightly but perceptibly frayed, that his eyes were set in half-moons the colour of cigar smoke.

'So I gathered,' he said, fixing his friend with his bright-yellow eye. 'But where and how is Gloria? My God, Anthony, I've been hearing the dog-gonedest stories about you two even out in California – and when I get back to New York I find you've sunk absolutely out of sight. Why don't you pull yourself together?'

'Now, listen,' chattered Anthony unsteadily, 'I can't stand a long lecture. We've lost money in a dozen ways, and naturally people have talked – on account of the lawsuit, but the thing's coming to a final decision this winter, surely – '

'You're talking so fast that I can't understand you,' interrupted Dick calmly.

'Well, I've said all I'm going to say,' snapped Anthony. 'Come and see us if you like – or don't!'

With this he turned and started to walk off in the crowd, but Dick overtook him immediately and grasped his arm.

'Say, Anthony, don't fly off the handle so easily! You know Gloria's my cousin, and you're one of my oldest friends, so it's natural for me to be interested when I hear that you're going to the dogs – and taking her with you.'

'I don't want to be preached to.'

'Well, then, all right – How about coming up to my apartment and having a drink? I've just got settled. I've bought three cases of Gordon's gin from a revenue officer.'

As they walked along he continued in a burst of exasperation: 'And how about your grandfather's money – you going to get it?'

'Well,' answered Anthony resentfully, 'that old fool Haight seems hopeful, especially because people are tired of reformers right now – you know it might make a slight difference, for instance, if some judge thought that Adam Patch made it harder for him to get liquor.'

'You can't do without money,' said Dick sententiously. 'Have you tried to write any – lately?'

Anthony shook his head silently.

'That's funny,' said Dick. 'I always thought that you and Maury would write someday, and now he's grown to be a sort of tight-fisted aristocrat, and you're – '

'I'm the bad example.'

'I wonder why?'

'You probably think you know,' suggested Anthony, with an effort at concentration. 'The failure and the success both believe in their hearts that they have accurately balanced points of view, the success because he's succeeded, and the failure because he's failed. The successful man tells his son to profit by his father's good fortune, and the failure tells *his* son to profit by his father's mistakes.'

'I don't agree with you,' said the author of *A Shave-Tail* [312] *in France*. 'I used to listen to you and Maury when we were young, and I used to be impressed because you were so consistently cynical, but now – well, after all, by God, which of us three has taken to the – to the intellectual life? I don't want to sound vainglorious, but – it's me, and I've always believed that moral values existed, and I always will.'

'Well,' objected Anthony, who was rather enjoying himself, 'even granting that, you know that in practice life never presents problems as clear cut, does it?'

'It does to me. There's nothing I'd violate certain principles for.'

'But how do you know when you're violating them? You have to guess at things just like most people do. You have to apportion the values when you look back. You finish up the portrait then – paint in the details and shadows.'

Dick shook his head with a lofty stubbornness. 'Same old futile cynic,' he said. 'It's just a mode of being sorry for yourself. You don't do anything – so nothing matters.'

'Oh, I'm quite capable of self-pity,' admitted Anthony, 'nor am I claiming that I'm getting as much fun out of life as you are.'

'You say – at least you used to – that happiness is the only thing worth while in life. Do you think you're any happier for being a pessimist?'

Anthony grunted savagely. His pleasure in the conversation began to wane. He was nervous and craving for a drink.

'My golly!' he cried, 'where do you live? I can't keep walking for ever.'

'Your endurance is all mental, eh?' returned Dick sharply. 'Well, I live right here.'

He turned in at the apartment house on Forty-Ninth Street, and a few minutes later they were in a large new room with an open fireplace and four walls lined with books. A coloured butler served them gin rickeys, and an hour vanished politely with the mellow shortening of their drinks and the glow of a light mid-autumn fire.

'The arts are very old,' said Anthony after a while. With a few glasses the tension of his nerves relaxed and he found that he could think again.

'Which art?'

'All of them. Poetry is dying first. It'll be absorbed into prose sooner or later. For instance, the beautiful word, the coloured and glittering word, and the beautiful simile belong in prose now. To get attention poetry has got to strain for the unusual word, the harsh, earthy word that's never been beautiful before. Beauty, as the sum of several beautiful parts, reached its apotheosis in Swinburne. It can't go any further – except in the novel, perhaps.'

Dick interrupted him impatiently: 'You know these new novels make me tired. My God! Everywhere I go some silly girl asks me if I've read *This Side of Paradise*. Are our girls really like that? If it's true to life, which I don't believe, the next generation is going to the dogs. I'm sick of all this shoddy realism. I think there's a place for the romanticist in literature.'

Anthony tried to remember what he had read lately of Richard Caramel's. There was *A Shave-Tail in France*, a novel called *The Land of Strong Men*, and several dozen short stories, which were even worse. It had become the custom among young and clever reviewers to mention Richard Caramel with a smile of scorn. 'Mr' Richard Caramel, they called him. His corpse was dragged obscenely through every literary supplement. He was accused of making a great fortune by writing trash for the movies. As the fashion in books shifted he was becoming almost a byword of contempt.

While Anthony was thinking this, Dick had got to his feet and seemed to be hesitating at an avowal.

'I've gathered quite a few books,' he said suddenly.

'So I see.'

'I've made an exhaustive collection of good American stuff, old and new. I don't mean the usual Longfellow–Whittier thing[313] – in fact, most of it's modern.'

He stepped to one of the walls and, seeing that it was expected of him, Anthony arose and followed.

'Look!'

Under a printed tag *Americana* he displayed six long rows of books, beautifully bound and, obviously, carefully chosen.

'And here are the contemporary novelists.'

Then Anthony saw the joker. Wedged in between Mark Twain[314] and Dreiser[315] were eight strange and inappropriate volumes, the works of Richard Caramel – *The Demon Lover*, true enough . . . but also seven others that were execrably awful, without sincerity or grace.

Unwillingly Anthony glanced at Dick's face and caught a slight uncertainty there.

'I've put my own books in, of course,' said Richard Caramel hastily, 'though one or two of them are uneven – I'm afraid I wrote a little too fast when I had that magazine contract. But I don't believe in false modesty. Of course some of the critics haven't paid so much attention to me since I've been established – but, after all, it's not the critics that count. They're just sheep.'

For the first time in so long that he could scarcely remember, Anthony felt a touch of the old pleasant contempt for his friend. Richard Caramel continued: 'My publishers, you know, have been advertising me as the Thackeray of America[316] – because of my New York novel.'

'Yes,' Anthony managed to muster, 'I suppose there's a good deal in what you say.'

He knew that his contempt was unreasonable. He knew that he would have changed places with Dick unhesitatingly. He himself had tried his best to write with his tongue in his cheek. Ah, well, then – can a man disparage his life-work so readily? . . .

– And that night while Richard Caramel was hard at toil, with great hittings of the wrong keys and screwings up of his weary, unmatched eyes, labouring over his trash far into those cheerless hours when the fire dies down and the head is swimming from the effect of prolonged concentration – Anthony, abominably drunk, was sprawled across the back seat of a taxi on his way to the flat on Claremont Avenue.

THE BEATING

As winter approached it seemed that a sort of madness seized upon Anthony. He awoke in the morning so nervous that Gloria could feel him trembling in the bed before he could muster enough vitality to stumble into the pantry for a drink. He was intolerable now except under the influence of liquor, and as he seemed to decay and coarsen under her eyes, Gloria's soul and body shrank away from him; when he stayed out all night, as he did several times, she not only failed to be sorry but even felt a measure of relief. Next day he would be faintly repentant, and would remark in a gruff, hang-dog fashion that he guessed he was drinking a little too much.

For hours at a time he would sit in the great armchair that had been in his apartment, lost in a sort of stupor – even his interest in reading his favourite books seemed to have departed, and though an incessant bickering went on between husband and wife, the one subject upon which they ever really conversed was the progress of the will case. What Gloria hoped in the tenebrous depths of her soul, what she expected that great gift of money to bring about, is difficult to imagine. She was being bent by her environment into a grotesque similitude of a housewife. She who until three years before had never made coffee, prepared sometimes three meals a day. She walked a great deal in the afternoons, and in the evenings she read – books, magazines, anything she found at hand. If now she wished for a child, even a child of the Anthony who sought her bed blind drunk, she neither said so nor gave any show or sign of interest in children. It is doubtful if she could have made it clear to anyone what it was she wanted, or indeed what there was to want – a lonely, lovely woman, thirty now, retrenched behind some impregnable inhibition born and coexistent with her beauty.

One afternoon when the snow was dirty again along Riverside Drive, Gloria, who had been to the grocer's, entered the apartment to find Anthony pacing the floor in a state of aggravated nervousness. The feverish eyes he turned on her were traced with tiny pink lines that reminded her of rivers on a map. For a moment she received the impression that he was suddenly and definitely old.

'Have you any money?' he enquired of her precipitately.

'What? What do you mean?'

'Just what I said. Money! Money! Can't you speak English?'

She paid no attention but brushed by him and into the pantry to put the bacon and eggs in the ice-box. When his drinking had been unusually excessive he was invariably in a whining mood. This time he followed her and, standing in the pantry door, persisted in his question.

'You heard what I said. Have you any money?'

She turned about from the ice-box and faced him.

'Why, Anthony, you must be crazy! You know I haven't any money – except a dollar in change.'

He executed an abrupt about-face and returned to the living-room, where he renewed his pacing. It was evident that he had something portentous on his mind – he quite obviously wanted to be asked what was the matter. Joining him a moment later she sat upon the long lounge and began taking down her hair. It was no longer bobbed, and it had changed in the last year from a rich gold dusted with red to an unresplendent light brown. She had bought some shampoo soap and meant to wash it now; she had considered putting a bottle of peroxide into the rinsing water.

' – Well?' she implied silently.

'That darn bank!' he quavered. 'They've had my account for over ten years – ten *years*. Well, it seems they've got some autocratic rule that you have to keep over five hundred dollars there or they won't carry you. They wrote me a letter a few months ago and told me I'd been running too low. Once I gave out two bum cheques – remember? that night in Reisenweber's?[317] – but I made them good the very next day. Well, I promised old Halloran – he's the manager, the greedy Mick – that I'd watch out. And I thought I was going all right; I kept up the stubs in my cheque-book pretty regular. Well, I went in there today to cash a cheque, and Halloran came up and told me they'd have to close my account. Too many bad cheques, he said, and I never had more than five hundred to my credit – and that only for a day or so at a time. And by God! What do you think he said then?'

'What?'

'He said this was a good time to do it because I didn't have a damn penny in there!'

'You didn't?'

'That's what he told me. Seems I'd given these Bedros people a cheque for sixty for that last case of liquor – and I only had forty-five dollars in the bank. Well, the Bedros people deposited fifteen dollars to my account and drew the whole thing out.'

In her ignorance Gloria conjured up a spectre of imprisonment and disgrace.

'Oh, they won't do anything,' he assured her. 'Bootlegging's too risky a business. They'll send me a bill for fifteen dollars and I'll pay it.'

'Oh.' She considered a moment. ' – Well, we can sell another bond.'

He laughed sarcastically.

'Oh, yes, that's always easy. When the few bonds we have that are paying any interest at all are only worth between fifty and eighty cents on the dollar. We lose about half the bond every time we sell.'

'What else can we do?'

'Oh, we'll sell something – as usual. We've got paper worth eighty thousand dollars at par.' Again he laughed unpleasantly. 'Bring about thirty thousand on the open market.'

'I distrusted those ten per cent investments.'

'The deuce you did!' he said. 'You pretended you did, so you could claw at me if they went to pieces, but you wanted to take a chance as much as I did.'

She was silent for a moment as if considering, then: 'Anthony,' she cried suddenly, 'two hundred a month is worse than nothing. Let's sell all the bonds and put the thirty thousand dollars in the bank – and if we lose the case we can live in Italy for three years, and then just die.' In her excitement as she talked she was aware of a faint flush of sentiment, the first she had felt in many days.

'Three years,' he said nervously, 'three years! You're crazy. Mr Haight'll take more than that if we lose. Do you think he's working for charity?'

'I forgot that.'

' – And here it is Saturday,' he continued, 'and I've only got a dollar and some change, and we've got to live till Monday, when I can get to my broker's . . . And not a drink in the house,' he added as a significant afterthought.

'Can't you call up Dick?'

'I did. His man says he's gone down to Princeton to address a literary club or some such thing. Won't be back till Monday.'

'Well, let's see – Don't you know some friend you might go to?'

'I tried a couple of fellows. Couldn't find anybody in. I wish I'd sold that Keats letter like I started to last week.'

'How about those men you play cards with in that Sammy place?'

'Do you think I'd ask *them*?' His voice rang with righteous horror. Gloria winced. He would rather contemplate her active discomfort than feel his own skin crawl at asking an inappropriate favour. 'I thought of Muriel,' he suggested.

'She's in California.'

'Well, how about some of those men who gave you such a good time while I was in the army? You'd think they might be glad to do a little favour for you.'

She looked at him contemptuously, but he took no notice.

'Or how about your old friend Rachael – or Constance Merriam?'

'Constance Merriam's been dead a year, and I wouldn't ask Rachael.'

'Well, how about that gentleman who was so anxious to help you once that he could hardly restrain himself, Bloeckman?'

'Oh – !' He had hurt her at last, and he was not too obtuse or too careless to perceive it.

'Why not him?' he insisted callously.

'Because – he doesn't like me any more,' she said with difficulty, and then as he did not answer but only regarded her cynically: 'If you want to know why, I'll tell you. A year ago I went to Bloeckman – he's changed his name to Black – and asked him to put me into pictures.'

'You went to Bloeckman?'

'Yes.'

'Why didn't you tell me?' he demanded incredulously, the smile fading from his face.

'Because you were probably off drinking somewhere. He had them give me a test, and they decided that I wasn't young enough for anything except a character part.'

'A character part?'

'The "woman of thirty" sort of thing. I wasn't thirty, and I didn't think I – looked thirty.'

'Why, damn him!' cried Anthony, championing her violently with a curious perverseness of emotion, 'why – '

'Well, that's why I can't go to him.'

'Why, the insolence!' insisted Anthony nervously, 'the insolence!'

'Anthony, that doesn't matter now; the thing is we've got to live over Sunday and there's nothing in the house but a loaf of bread and a half-pound of bacon and two eggs for breakfast.' She handed him the contents of her purse. 'There's seventy, eighty, a dollar fifteen. With what you have that makes about two and a half altogether, doesn't it? Anthony, we can get along on that. We can buy lots of food with that – more than we can possibly eat.'

Jingling the change in his hand he shook his head. 'No. I've got to have a drink. I'm so darn nervous that I'm shivering.' A thought struck him. 'Perhaps Sammy'd cash a check. And then Monday I could rush down to the bank with the money.'

'But they've closed your account.'

'That's right, that's right – I'd forgotten. I'll tell you what: I'll go down to Sammy's and I'll find somebody there who'll lend me something. I hate like the devil to ask them, though . . . ' He snapped his fingers suddenly. 'I know what I'll do. I'll hock my watch. I can get twenty dollars on it, and get it back Monday for sixty cents extra. It's been hocked before – when I was at Cambridge.'

He had put on his overcoat, and with a brief goodbye he started down the hall towards the outer door.

Gloria got to her feet. It had suddenly occurred to her where he would probably go first.

'Anthony!' she called after him, 'hadn't you better leave two dollars with me? You'll only need car-fare.'

The outer door slammed – he had pretended not to hear her. She stood for a moment looking after him; then she went into the bathroom among her tragic unguents and began preparations for washing her hair.

Down at Sammy's he found Parker Allison and Pete Lytell sitting alone at a table, drinking whiskey sours. It was just after six o'clock, and Sammy, or Samuele Bendiri, as he had been christened, was sweeping an accumulation of cigarette butts and broken glass into a corner.

'Hi, Tony!' called Parker Allison to Anthony. Sometimes he addressed him as Tony, at other times it was Dan. To him all Anthonys must sail under one of these diminutives.

'Sit down. What'll you have?'

On the subway Anthony had counted his money and found that he had almost four dollars. He could pay for two rounds at fifty cents a drink – which meant that he would have six drinks. Then he would go over to Sixth Avenue and get twenty dollars and a pawn ticket in exchange for his watch.

'Well, rough-necks,' he said jovially, 'how's the life of crime?'

'Pretty good,' said Allison. He winked at Pete Lytell. 'Too bad you're a married man. We've got some pretty good stuff lined up for about eleven o'clock, when the shows let out. Oh, boy! Yes, sir – too bad he's married – isn't it, Pete?'

' 'Sa shame.'

At half-past seven, when they had completed the six rounds, Anthony found that his intentions were giving audience to his desires. He was happy and cheerful now – thoroughly enjoying himself. It seemed to him that the story which Pete had just finished telling was unusually and profoundly humorous – and he decided, as he did every day at about this point, that they were 'damn good fellows, by golly!' who would do a lot more for him than anyone else he knew. The pawnshops would remain open until late Saturday nights, and he felt that if he took just one more drink he would attain a gorgeous rose-coloured exhilaration.

Artfully, he fished in his vest pockets, brought up his two quarters, and stared at them as though in surprise.

'Well, I'll be darned,' he protested in an aggrieved tone, 'here I've come out without my pocketbook.'

'Need some cash?' asked Lytell easily.

'I left my money on the dresser at home. And I wanted to buy you another drink.'

'Oh – knock it.' Lytell waved the suggestion away disparagingly. 'I guess we can blow a good fella to all the drinks he wants. What'll you have – same?'

'I tell you,' suggested Parker Allison, 'suppose we send Sammy across the street for some sandwiches and eat dinner here.'

The other two agreed.

'Good idea.'

'Hey, Sammy, wantcha do somep'm for us . . .'

Just after nine o'clock Anthony staggered to his feet and, bidding them a thick good-night, walked unsteadily to the door, handing Sammy one of his two quarters as he passed out. Once in the street he hesitated uncertainly and then started in the direction of Sixth Avenue, where he remembered frequently to have passed several loan offices. He went by a news-stand and two drugstores – and then he realised that he was standing in front of the place which he sought, and that it was shut and barred. Unperturbed he continued; another one, half a block down, was also closed – so were two more across the street, and a fifth in the square below. Seeing a faint light in the last one, he began to knock on the glass door; he desisted only when a watchman appeared in the back of the shop and motioned him angrily to move on. With growing discouragement, with growing befuddlement, he crossed the street and walked back towards Forty-Third. On the corner near Sammy's he paused undecided – if he went back to the apartment, as he felt his body required, he would lay himself open to bitter reproach; yet, now that the pawnshops were closed, he had no notion where to get the money. He decided finally that he might ask Parker Allison, after all – but he approached Sammy's only to find the door locked and the lights out. He looked at his watch: nine-thirty. He began walking.

Ten minutes later he stopped aimlessly at the corner of Forty-Third Street and Madison Avenue, diagonally across from the bright but nearly deserted entrance to the Biltmore Hotel. Here he stood for a moment, and then sat down heavily on a damp board amid some débris of construction work. He rested there for almost half an hour, his mind a shifting pattern of surface thoughts, chiefest among which were that he must obtain some money and get home before he became too sodden to find his way.

Then, glancing over towards the Biltmore, he saw a man standing directly under the overhead glow of the porte-cochère lamps beside a woman in an ermine coat. As Anthony watched, the couple moved forward and signalled to a taxi. Anthony perceived by the infallible identification that lurks in the walk of a friend that it was Maury Noble.

He rose to his feet.

'Maury!' he shouted.

Maury looked in his direction, then turned back to the girl just as the taxi came up into place. With the chaotic idea of borrowing ten dollars, Anthony began to run as fast as he could across Madison Avenue and along Forty-Third Street.

As he came up Maury was standing beside the yawning door of the taxicab. His companion turned and looked curiously at Anthony.

'Hello, Maury!' he said, holding out his hand. 'How are you?'

'Fine, thank you.'

Their hands dropped and Anthony hesitated. Maury made no move to introduce him, but only stood there regarding him with an inscrutable feline silence.

'I wanted to see you – ' began Anthony uncertainly. He did not feel that he could ask for a loan with the girl not four feet away, so he broke off and made a perceptible motion of his head as if to beckon Maury to one side.

'I'm in rather a big hurry, Anthony.'

'I know – but can you, can you – ' Again he hesitated.

'I'll see you some other time,' said Maury.

'It's important.'

'I'm sorry, Anthony.'

Before Anthony could make up his mind to blurt out his request, Maury had turned coolly to the girl, helped her into the car and, with a polite 'good-evening', stepped in after her. As he nodded from the window it seemed to Anthony that his expression had not changed by a shade or a hair. Then with a fretful clatter the taxi moved off, and Anthony was left standing there alone under the lights.

Anthony went on into the Biltmore, for no reason in particular except that the entrance was at hand, and ascending the wide stair found a seat in an alcove. He was furiously aware that he had been snubbed; he was as hurt and angry as it was possible for him to be when in that condition. Nevertheless, he was stubbornly preoccupied with the necessity of obtaining some money before he went home, and once again he told over on his fingers the acquaintances he might conceivably call on in this emergency. He thought, eventually, that he might approach Mr Howland, his broker, at his home.

After a long wait he found that Mr Howland was out. He returned to the operator, leaning over her desk and fingering his quarter as though loath to leave unsatisfied.

'Call Mr Bloeckman,' he said suddenly. His own words surprised him. The name had come from some crossing of two suggestions in his mind.

'What's the number, please?'

Scarcely conscious of what he did, Anthony looked up Joseph Bloeckman in the telephone directory. He could find no such person, and was about to close the book when it flashed into his mind that Gloria had mentioned a change of name. It was the matter of a minute to find Joseph Black – then he waited in the booth while central called the number.

'Hello-o. Mr Bloeckman – I mean Mr Black in?'

'No, he's out this evening. Is there any message?' The intonation was cockney; it reminded him of the rich vocal deferences of Bounds.

'Where is he?'

'Why, ah, who is this, please, sir?'

'This Mr Patch. Matter of vi'al importance.'

'Why, he's with a party at the Boul' Mich', sir.'

'Thanks.'

Anthony got his five cents change and started for the Boul' Mich', a popular dancing resort on Forty-Fifth Street. It was nearly ten but the streets were dark and sparsely peopled until the theatres should eject their spawn an hour later. Anthony knew the Boul' Mich', for he had been there with Gloria during the year before, and he remembered the existence of a rule that patrons must be in evening dress. Well, he would not go upstairs – he would send a boy up for Bloeckman and wait for him in the lower hall. For a moment he did not doubt that the whole project was entirely natural and graceful. To his distorted imagination Bloeckman had become simply one of his old friends.

The entrance hall of the Boul' Mich' was warm. There were high yellow lights over a thick green carpet, from the centre of which a white stairway rose to the dancing floor.

Anthony spoke to the hallboy: 'I want to see Mr Bloeckman – Mr Black,' he said. 'He's upstairs – have him paged.'

The boy shook his head.

' 'Sagainsa rules to have him paged. You know what table he's at?'

'No. But I've got see him.'

'Wait an' I'll getcha waiter.'

After a short interval a head waiter appeared, bearing a card on which were charted the table reservations. He darted a cynical look at Anthony – which, however, failed of its target. Together they bent over the cardboard and found the table without difficulty – a party of eight, Mr Black's own.

'Tell him Mr Patch. Very, very important.'

Again he waited, leaning against the bannister and listening to the confused harmonies of 'Jazz-Mad' which came floating down the stairs. A check-girl near him was singing:

> 'Out in – the shimmee sanitarium
> The jazz-mad nuts reside.
> Out in – the shimmee sanitarium
> I left my blushing bride.
> She went and shook herself insane,
> So let her shiver back again – '

Then he saw Bloeckman descending the staircase, and took a step forward to meet him and shake hands.

'You wanted to see me?' said the older man coolly.

'Yes,' answered Anthony, nodding, 'personal matter. Can you jus' step over here?'

Regarding him narrowly Bloeckman followed Anthony to a half bend made by the staircase where they were beyond observation or earshot of anyone entering or leaving the restaurant.

'Well?' he enquired.

'Wanted talk to you.'

'What about?'

Anthony only laughed – a silly laugh; he intended it to sound casual.

'What do you want to talk to me about?' repeated Bloeckman.

'Wha's hurry, old man?' He tried to lay his hand in a friendly gesture upon Bloeckman's shoulder, but the latter drew away slightly. 'How've been?'

'Very well, thanks . . . See here, Mr Patch, I've got a party upstairs. They'll think it's rude if I stay away too long. What was it you wanted to see me about?'

For the second time that evening Anthony's mind made an abrupt jump, and what he said was not at all what he had intended to say.

'Un'erstand you kep' my wife out of the movies.'

'What?' Bloeckman's ruddy face darkened in parallel planes of shadows.

'You heard me.'

'Look here, Mr Patch,' said Bloeckman, evenly and without changing his expression, 'you're drunk. You're disgustingly and insultingly drunk.'

'Not too drunk talk to you,' insisted Anthony with a leer. 'Firs' place, my wife wants nothin' whatever do with you. Never did. Un'erstand me?'

'Be quiet!' said the older man angrily. 'I should think you'd respect your wife enough not to bring her into the conversation under these circumstances.'

'Never you min' how I expect my wife. One thing – you leave her alone. You go to hell!'

'See here – I think you're a little crazy!' exclaimed Bloeckman. He took two paces forward as though to pass by, but Anthony stepped in his way.

'Not so fas', you goddam Jew.'

For a moment they stood regarding each other, Anthony swaying gently from side to side, Bloeckman almost trembling with fury.

'Be careful!' he cried in a strained voice.

Anthony might have remembered then a certain look Bloeckman had given him in the Biltmore Hotel years before. But he remembered nothing, nothing –

'I'll say it again, you god – '

Then Bloeckman struck out, with all the strength in the arm of a well-conditioned man of forty-five, struck out and caught Anthony squarely in the mouth. Anthony cracked up against the staircase, recovered himself and made a wild drunken swing at his opponent, but Bloeckman, who took exercise every day and knew something of sparring, blocked it with ease and struck him twice in the face with two swift smashing jabs. Anthony gave a little grunt and toppled over on to the green plush carpet, finding, as he fell, that his mouth was full of blood and seemed oddly loose in front. He struggled to his feet, panting and spitting, and then as he started towards Bloeckman, who stood a few feet away, his fists clenched but not up, two waiters who had appeared from nowhere seized his arms and held him, helpless. In back of them a dozen people had miraculously gathered.

'I'll kill him,' cried Anthony, pitching and straining from side to side. 'Let me kill – '

'Throw him out!' ordered Bloeckman excitedly, just as a small man with a pockmarked face pushed his way hurriedly through the spectators.

'Any trouble, Mr Black?'

'This bum tried to blackmail me!' said Bloeckman, and then, his voice rising to a faintly shrill note of pride: 'He got what was coming to him!'

The little man turned to a waiter.

'Call a policeman!' he commanded.

'Oh, no,' said Bloeckman quickly. 'I can't be bothered. Just throw him out in the street . . . Ugh! What an outrage!' He turned and with conscious dignity walked towards the washroom just as six brawny hands seized upon Anthony and dragged him towards the door. The 'bum' was propelled violently to the sidewalk, where he landed on his hands and knees with a grotesque slapping sound and rolled over slowly on to his side.

The shock stunned him. He lay there for a moment in acute distributed pain. Then his discomfort became centralised in his stomach, and he regained consciousness to discover that a large foot was prodding him.

'You've got to move on, y' bum! Move on!'

It was the bulky doorman speaking. A town car had stopped at the curb and its occupants had disembarked – that is, two of the women were standing on the running-board,[318] waiting in offended delicacy until this obscene obstacle should be removed from their path.

'Move on! Or else I'll *throw* y'on!'

'Here – I'll get him.'

This was a new voice; Anthony imagined that it was somehow

more tolerant, better disposed than the first. Again arms were about him, half lifting, half dragging him into a welcome shadow four doors up the street and propping him against the stone front of a millinery shop.

'Much obliged,' muttered Anthony feebly. Someone pushed his soft hat down upon his head and he winced.

'Just sit still, buddy, and you'll feel better. Those guys sure give you a bump.'

'I'm going back and kill that dirty – ' He tried to get to his feet but collapsed backwards against the wall.

'You can't do nothin' now,' came the voice. 'Get 'em some other time. I'm tellin' you straight, ain't I? I'm helpin' you.'

Anthony nodded.

'An' you better go home. You dropped a tooth tonight, buddy. You know that?'

Anthony explored his mouth with his tongue, verifying the statement. Then with an effort he raised his hand and located the gap.

'I'm agoin' to get you home, friend. Whereabouts do you live – '

'Oh, by God! By God!' interrupted Anthony, clenching his fists passionately. 'I'll show the dirty bunch. You help me show 'em and I'll fix it with you. My grandfather's Adam Patch, of Tarrytown – '

'Who?'

'Adam Patch, by God!'

'You wanna go all the way to Tarrytown?'

'No.'

'Well, you tell me where to go, friend, and I'll get a cab.'

Anthony made out that his Samaritan was a short, broad-shouldered individual, somewhat the worse for wear.

'Where d'you live, hey?'

Sodden and shaken as he was, Anthony felt that his address would be poor collateral for his wild boast about his grandfather.

'Get me a cab,' he commanded, feeling in his pockets.

A taxi drove up. Again Anthony essayed to rise, but his ankle swung loose, as though it were in two sections. The Samaritan must needs help him in – and climb in after him.

'See here, fella,' said he, 'you're soused and you're bunged up, and you won't be able to get in your house 'less somebody carries you in, so I'm going with you, and I know you'll make it all right with me. Where d'you live?'

With some reluctance Anthony gave his address. Then, as the cab moved off, he leaned his head against the man's shoulder and went into a shadowy, painful torpor. When he awoke, the man had lifted him from the cab in front of the apartment on Claremont Avenue and was trying to set him on his feet.

'Can y' walk?'

'Yes – sort of. You better not come in with me.' Again he felt helplessly in his pockets. 'Say,' he continued, apologetically, swaying dangerously on his feet, 'I'm afraid I haven't got a cent.'

'Huh?'

'I'm cleaned out.'

'Sa-a-ay! Didn't I hear you promise you'd fix it with me? Who's goin' to pay the taxi bill?' He turned to the driver for confirmation. 'Didn't you hear him say he'd fix it? All that about his grandfather?'

'Matter of fact,' muttered Anthony imprudently, 'it was you did all the talking; however, if you come round, tomorrow – '

At this point the taxi-driver leaned from his cab and said ferociously: 'Ah, poke him one, the dirty cheapskate. If he wasn't a bum they wouldn'ta throwed him out.'

In answer to this suggestion the fist of the Samaritan shot out like a battering-ram and sent Anthony crashing down against the stone steps of the apartment-house, where he lay without movement, while the tall buildings rocked to and fro above him . . .

After a long while he awoke and was conscious that it had grown much colder. He tried to move himself but his muscles refused to function. He was curiously anxious to know the time, but he reached for his watch only to find the pocket empty. Involuntarily his lips formed an immemorial phrase: 'What a night!'

Strangely enough, he was almost sober. Without moving his head he looked up to where the moon was anchored in mid-sky, shedding light down into Claremont Avenue as into the bottom of a deep and uncharted abyss. There was no sign or sound of life save for the continuous buzzing in his own ears, but after a moment Anthony himself broke the silence with a distinct and peculiar murmur. It was the sound that he had consistently attempted to make back there in the Boul' Mich', when he had been face to face with Bloeckman – the unmistakable sound of ironic laughter. And on his torn and bleeding lips it was like a pitiful retching of the soul.

Three weeks later the trial came to an end. The seemingly endless spool of legal red tape having unrolled over a period of four and a half years, suddenly snapped off. Anthony and Gloria and, on the other side, Edward Shuttleworth and a platoon of beneficiaries testified and lied and ill-behaved generally in varying degrees of greed and desperation. Anthony awoke one morning in March realising that the verdict was to be given at four that afternoon, and at the thought he got up out of his bed and began to dress. With his extreme nervousness there was mingled an unjustified optimism as to the outcome. He believed that the decision of the lower court would be reversed, if only because of the reaction, due to excessive Prohibition, that had recently set in against reforms and reformers. He counted more on the personal attacks that they had levelled at Shuttleworth than on the more sheerly legal aspects of the proceedings.

Dressed, he poured himself a drink of whiskey and then went into Gloria's room, where he found her already wide awake. She had been in bed for a week, humouring herself, Anthony fancied, though the doctor had said that she had best not be disturbed.

'Good-morning,' she murmured, without smiling. Her eyes seemed unusually large and dark.

'How do you feel?' he asked grudgingly. 'Better?'

'Yes.'

'Much?'

'Yes.'

'Do you feel well enough to go down to court with me this afternoon?'

She nodded.

'Yes. I want to. Dick said yesterday that if the weather was nice he was coming up in his car to take me for a ride in Central Park – and look, the room's all full of sunshine.'

Anthony glanced mechanically out of the window and then sat down upon the bed.

'God, I'm nervous!' he exclaimed.

'Please don't sit there,' she said quickly.

'Why not?'

'You smell of whiskey. I can't stand it.'

He got up absent-mindedly and left the room. A little later she called to him and he went out and brought her some potato salad and cold chicken from the delicatessen.

At two o'clock Richard Caramel's car arrived at the door and, when he phoned up, Anthony took Gloria down in the elevator and walked with her to the curb.

She told her cousin that it was sweet of him to take her riding.

'Don't be simple,' Dick replied disparagingly. 'It's nothing.'

But he did not mean that it was nothing and this was a curious thing. Richard Caramel had forgiven many people for many offences.

But he had never forgiven his cousin, Gloria Gilbert, for a statement she had made just prior to her wedding, seven years before. She had said that she did not intend to read his book.

Richard Caramel remembered this – he had remembered it well for seven years.

'What time will I expect you back?' asked Anthony.

'We won't come back,' she answered, 'we'll meet you down there at four.'

'All right,' he muttered, 'I'll meet you.'

Upstairs he found a letter waiting for him. It was a mimeographed notice urging 'the boys' in condescendingly colloquial language to pay the dues of the American Legion. He threw it impatiently into the waste-basket and sat down with his elbows on the window sill, looking down blindly into the sunny street.

Italy – if the verdict was in their favour it meant Italy. The word had become a sort of talisman to him, a land where the intolerable anxieties of life would fall away like an old garment. They would go to the watering-places first and among the bright and colourful crowds forget the grey appendages of despair. Marvellously renewed, he would walk again in the Piazza di Spagna[319] at twilight, moving in that drifting flotsam of dark women and ragged beggars, of austere, barefooted friars. The thought of Italian women stirred him faintly – when his purse hung heavy again even romance might fly back to perch upon it – the romance of blue canals in Venice, of the golden green hills of Fiesole after rain, and of women, women who changed, dissolved, melted into other women and receded from his life, but who were always beautiful and always young.

But it seemed to him that there should be a difference in his attitude. All the distress that he had ever known, the sorrow and the pain, had been because of women. It was something that in different ways they did to him, unconsciously, almost casually – perhaps finding him tender-minded and afraid, they killed the things in him that menaced their absolute sway.

Turning about from the window he faced his reflection in the mirror, contemplating dejectedly the wan, pasty face, the eyes with their criss-cross of lines like shreds of dried blood, the stooped and flabby figure whose very sag was a document in lethargy. He was thirty-three – he looked forty. Well, things would be different.

The doorbell rang abruptly and he started as though he had been dealt a blow. Recovering himself, he went into the hall and opened the outer door. It was Dot.

THE ENCOUNTER

He retreated before her into the living-room, comprehending only a word here and there in the slow flood of sentences that poured from her steadily, one after the other, in a persistent monotone. She was decently and shabbily dressed – a somehow pitiable little hat adorned with pink and blue flowers covered and hid her dark hair. He gathered from her words that several days before she had seen an item in the paper concerning the lawsuit, and had obtained his address from the clerk of the Appellate Division. She had called up the apartment and had been told that Anthony was out by a woman to whom she had refused to give her name.

In the living-room he stood by the door regarding her with a sort of stupefied horror as she rattled on . . . His predominant sensation was that all the civilisation and convention around him was curiously unreal . . . She was in a milliner's shop on Sixth Avenue, she said. It was a lonesome life. She had been sick for a long while after he left for Camp Mills; her mother had come down and taken her home again to Carolina . . . She had come to New York with the idea of finding Anthony.

She was appallingly in earnest. Her violet eyes were red with tears; her soft intonation was ragged with little gasping sobs.

That was all. She had never changed. She wanted him now, and if she couldn't have him she must die . . .

'You'll have to get out,' he said at length, speaking with tortuous intensity. 'Haven't I enough to worry me now without you coming here? My *God*! You'll have to get *out*!'

Sobbing, she sat down in a chair.

'I love you,' she cried; 'I don't care what you say to me! I love you.'

'I don't care!' he almost shrieked; 'get out – oh, get out! Haven't you done me harm enough? Haven't – you – done – *enough*?'

'Hit me!' she implored him – wildly, stupidly. 'Oh, hit me, and I'll kiss the hand you hit me with!'

His voice rose until it was pitched almost at a scream. 'I'll kill you!' he cried. 'If you don't get out I'll kill you, I'll kill you!'

There was madness in his eyes now, but, unintimidated, Dot rose and took a step towards him. 'Anthony! Anthony! – '

He made a little clicking sound with his teeth and drew back as though to spring at her – then, changing his purpose, he looked wildly about him on the floor and wall.

'I'll kill you!' he was muttering in short, broken gasps. 'I'll *kill* you!' He seemed to bite at the word as though to force it into materialisation. Alarmed at last she made no further movement forward, but meeting his frantic eyes took a step back towards the door. Anthony began to race here and there on his side of the room, still giving out his single cursing cry. Then he found what he had been seeking – a stiff oaken chair that stood beside the table. Uttering a harsh, broken shout, he seized it, swung it above his head and let it go with all his raging strength straight at the white, frightened face across the room ... then a thick, impenetrable darkness came down upon him and blotted out thought, rage and madness together – with almost a tangible snapping sound the face of the world changed before his eyes ...

Gloria and Dick came in at five and called his name. There was no answer – they went into the living-room and found a chair with its back smashed lying in the doorway, and they noticed that all about the room there was a sort of disorder – the rugs had slid, the pictures and bric-à-brac were upset upon the centre table. The air was sickly sweet with cheap perfume.

They found Anthony sitting in a patch of sunshine on the floor of his bedroom. Before him, open, were spread his three big stamp-books, and when they entered he was running his hands through a great pile of stamps that he had dumped from the back of one of them. Looking up and seeing Dick and Gloria he put his head critically on one side and motioned them back.

'Anthony!' cried Gloria tensely, 'we've won! They reversed the decision!'

'Don't come in,' he murmured wanly, 'you'll muss them. I'm sorting, and I know you'll step in them. Everything always gets mussed.'

'What are you doing?' demanded Dick in astonishment. 'Going back to childhood? Don't you realise you've won the suit? They've reversed the decision of the lower courts. You're worth thirty millions!'

Anthony only looked at him reproachfully.

'Shut the door when you go out.' He spoke like a pert child.

With a faint horror dawning in her eyes, Gloria gazed at him –

'Anthony!' she cried, 'what is it? What's the matter? Why didn't you come – why, what *is* it?'

'See here,' said Anthony softly, 'you two get out – now, both of you. Or else I'll tell my grandfather.'

He held up a handful of stamps and let them come drifting down about him like leaves, varicoloured and bright, turning and fluttering gaudily upon the sunny air: stamps of England and Ecuador, Venezuela and Spain – Italy . . .

TOGETHER WITH THE SPARROWS

That exquisite heavenly irony which has tabulated the demise of so many generations of sparrows doubtless records the subtlest verbal inflections of the passengers of such ships as the *Berengaria*. And doubtless it was listening when the young man in the plaid cap crossed the deck quickly and spoke to the pretty girl in yellow.

'That's him,' he said, pointing to a bundled figure seated in a wheel-chair near the rail. 'That's Anthony Patch. First time he's been on deck.'

'Oh – that's him?'

'Yes. He's been a little crazy, they say, ever since he got his money, four or five months ago. You see, the other fellow, Shuttleworth, the religious fellow, the one that didn't get the money, he locked himself up in a room in a hotel and shot himself – '

'Oh, he *did* – '

'But I guess Anthony Patch don't care much. He got his thirty million. And he's got his private physician along in case he doesn't feel just right about it. Has *she* been on deck?' he asked.

The pretty girl in yellow looked around cautiously.

'She was here a minute ago. She had on a Russian-sable coat that must have cost a small fortune.' She frowned and then added decisively: 'I can't stand her, you know. She seems sort of – sort of dyed and *unclean*, if you know what I mean. Some people just have that look about them whether they are or not.'

'Sure, I know,' agreed the man with the plaid cap. 'She's not bad-looking, though.' He paused. 'Wonder what he's thinking about – his money, I guess, or maybe he's got remorse about that fellow Shuttleworth.'

'Probably . . . '

But the man in the plaid cap was quite wrong. Anthony Patch, sitting near the rail and looking out at the sea, was not thinking of his money, for he had seldom in his life been really preoccupied with material vainglory, nor of Edward Shuttleworth, for it is best to look on the sunny side of these things. No – he was concerned with a series of reminiscences, much as a general might look back upon a successful campaign and analyse his victories. He was thinking of the hardships, the insufferable tribulations he had gone through. They had tried to penalise him for the mistakes of his youth. He had been exposed to ruthless misery, his very craving for romance had been punished, his friends had deserted him – even Gloria had turned against him. He had been alone, alone – facing it all.

Only a few months before people had been urging him to give in, to submit to mediocrity, to go to work. But he had known that he was justified in his way of life – and he had stuck it out staunchly. Why, the very friends who had been most unkind had come to respect him, to know he had been right all along. Had not the Lacys and the Merediths and the Cartwright-Smiths called on Gloria and him at the Ritz-Carlton just a week before they sailed?

Great tears stood in his eyes, and his voice was tremulous as he whispered to himself.

'I showed them,' he was saying. 'It was a hard fight, but I didn't give up and I came through!'

NOTES ON THE TEXT OF
THIS SIDE OF PARADISE

1   (p. 39) *Well . . . wise*   from the final lines of Brooke's poem 'Tiare Tahiti'. *Experience . . . Wilde*: from Act III of *Lady Windermere's Fan* (1893)

2   (p. 42) *Sigourney Fay*   Father Cyril Sigourney Webster Fay (1875–1919), the model for Monsignor Darcy in this novel. Fay was a Catholic priest Fitzgerald met 1912.

3   (p. 43) *Bar Harbor*   a resort on the coast of Maine

4   (p. 43) *Queen Margherita*   Margherita di Savoia (1851–1926), Queen of Italy from 1878 to 1900 and queen dowager from 1900 to 1926

5   (p. 44) *Coronado*   a resort in southern California, catering to the wealthy

6   (p. 44) *Newport*   a resort in Rhode Island

7   (p. 44) *Do and Dare . . . Frank on the Mississippi*   *Do and Dare* (1884), a novel by Horatio Alger Jr (1834–99); *Frank on the Lower Mississippi* (1867), a novel by Harry Castlemon, a pseudonym for Charles Austin Fosdick

8   (p. 44) *Waldorf*   a fashionable New York hotel, then located at Fifth Avenue and 33rd Street

9   (p. 44) *Bernhardt's*   Sarah Bernhardt, a famous French-born actress (1844–1923)

10   (p. 45) *Fêtes Galantes*   a book of poems (1869) by Paul Verlaine, (1844–96)

11   (p. 45) *Hot Springs*   a fashionable resort in Arkansas

12   (p. 45) *Pasadena to Cape Cod*   Pasadena – a resort in California, Cape Cod – a resort on the Massachusetts coast: fashionable locations of the wealthy

13   (p. 46) *Asheville*   a resort in the western mountains of North Carolina

14   (p. 49) *'trade-lasts'*   the understanding that the giving of a compliment entails one given in return

15   (p. 50) *Arrow-collar*   detachable shirt collar worn by fashionable men of the day

16   (p. 52) *graphophone*   a machine, invented by Alexander Graham Bell (1847–1922), which played music on wax-covered discs through a large horn. Bell invented the telephone.

17 (p. 53) *Arsène Lupin*   a play by Francis de Croisset and Maurice Leblanc, first performed in the USA in 1909, and featuring Leblanc in the role of the title character, a gentleman criminal

18 (p. 53) *McGovern of Minnesota*   John Francis McGovern was, in 1909, the first University of Minnesota football player named to the first-string All-American team.

19 (p. 54) *Three-fingered Brown . . . Christy Mathewson*   Mordecai 'Three-finger' Brown (1876–1948) and Mathewson (1880–1925), famous baseball pitchers, celebrated in baseball's Hall of Fame

20 (p. 54) *For the Honor of the School . . . Gunga Din'*   R. H. Barbour's boys' book *For the Honor of the School* (1900); Louisa May Alcott's novel *Little Women* (1869); Robert Chambers's novel *The Common Law* (1911); Alphonse Daudet's novel *Sappho* (1884); Robert Service's poem 'The Shooting of Dan McGrew' (1907); Jeffery Farnol's novel *The Broad Highway* (1910); Edgar Allan Poe's short story 'The Fall of the House of Usher' (1839); Elinor Glyn's novel *Three Weeks* (1907); Annie Fellows Johnston's novel *Mary Ware* (1908); *The Little Colonel's Chum* in Johnston's *Little Colonel* series; Rudyard Kipling's poem 'Gunga Din' (1892)

21 (p. 54) *The Police Gazette . . . Jim-Jam Jems*   The *Police Gazette* was a periodical that featured sensational crime; *Jim-Jam Gems* was a pocket-sized mass-circulation magazine also featuring sensational crime stories.

22 (p. 54) *Henty biases . . . Rinehart*   G. A. Henty (1832–1902), a British war correspondent and author of numerous historical novels for children, such as *Under Drake's Flag* (1883), *With Clive in India* (1884) and *With Roberts to Pretoria* (1902); Mary Roberts Rinehart (1876–1956), an American writer of mystery novels, including *The Circular Staircase* (1908) and *The Man in Lower Ten* (1909)

23 (p. 56) *Brooks*   Brooks Brothers, a fashionable New York clothing store

24 (p. 56) *'Bull'*   'Bull' Durham Smoking Tobacco, used in rolling one's own cigarettes

25 (p. 59) *a Turner sunset*   the English painter J. M. W. Turner (1775–1851), famous for his paintings of landscapes and sea-scapes featuring sunsets

26 (p. 60) *Bonnie Prince Charlie . . . Hannibal*   two heroes of lost causes. Charles Edward Stuart (1720–88), the last of his family to claim, unsuccessfully, the British throne, became a national hero in Scotland as 'Bonnie Prince Charlie'; Hannibal (247–

*c.*182BC) was a Carthaginian general who unsuccessfully fought against Rome in the Second Punic War (218–201BC).

27 (p. 61) *Parnell and Gladstone and Bismarck* late nineteenth-century European political leaders. Charles Stewart Parnell (1846–91) was leader of the Irish nationalist movement; William Ewart Gladstone (1909–98) was four times prime minister of Britain between 1868 and 1894; Otto von Bismarck (1815–98) was chancellor of Prussia from 1862 to 1890.

28 (p. 61) *Biltmore teas . . . Hot Springs golf-links* tea-dances at New York's Biltmore Hotel and games of golf at the Homestead, a resort in the mountains of Virginia

29 (p. 61) *The Beloved Vagabond . . . Sir Nigel* *The Beloved Vagabond* (1900), a romantic novel by W. J. Locke, and *Sir Nigel* (1906), a romantic novel by Arthur Conan Doyle

30 (p. 64) *The White Company* a romantic historical novel (1891) by Arthur Conan Doyle

31 (p. 64) *the chariot-race sign on Broadway* the climactic scene from Lew Wallace's novel *Ben-Hur* (1880) depicted with simulated movement on a large electric advertising sign

32 (p. 64) *The Little Millionaire* a musical (1911) by George M. Cohan

33 (p. 65) *Roland and Horatius, Sir Nigel and Ted Coy* Roland was the legendary knight of Charlemagne in the medieval French epic *La Chanson de Roland*; Horatius was the legendary sixth-century BC Roman hero who held a bridge against invading Etruscans; Sir Nigel is the hero of Arthur Conan Doyle's novel of 1906, set in the Middle Ages; and Edward H. 'Ted' Coy was an American football star at Yale from 1906 to 1909.

34 (p. 66) *L'Allegro* John Milton's (1608–74) famous pastoral elegy

35 (p. 67) *The Gentleman . . . and Son* Booth Tarkington's novel *The Gentleman from Indiana* (1899); Robert Louis Stevenson's short-story collection *New Arabian Nights* (1882); W. J. Locke's novel *The Morals of Marcus Ordeyne* (1905); G. K. Chesterton's novel *The Man Who Was Thursday* (1908); *Stover at Yale* (1912) by O. M. Johnson; *Dombey and Son* (1848) by Charles Dickens

36 (p. 68) *Robert Chambers . . . Oppenheim* Robert W. Chambers (1865–1933), a popular American novelist who wrote *The King in Yellow* (1895) and *Ashes of Empire* (1897); David Graham Phillips (1867–1911), American novelist and journalist; E. Phillips Oppenheim (1866–1946), a British novelist of tales of

mystery and espionage, including *The Mysterious Mr Sabin* (1901) and *The Double Traitor* (1920)

37 (p. 67) *Harstrum's*   the Harstrum School in Norwalk, Connecticut, a remedial school that prepared students for admission to Yale

38 (p. 67) *Sheff*   Yale's Sheffield Scientific School, a three-year course of study, admission to which was considered easier than to Yale's regular four-year undergraduate programme

39 (p. 67) *locomotor ataxia*   a syphilis of the spinal cord resulting in the loss of motor control and paralysis

40 (p. 69) '*tapped for Skull and Bones*'   the most coveted and secret of the senior societies at Yale.

41 (p. 70) '*Jigger Shop*'   In America, a confectionary shop in which a 'jigger' was a soda-fountain unit of measure.

42 (p. 70) *Gibson girls*   popular pen-and-ink drawings of fashionable young women by the artist Charles Dana Gibson

43 (p. 71) *the freshman cap*   First-year students at many American colleges and universities of the day were required to wear skullcaps for the first term.

44 (p. 71) *tiger pictures*   Princeton's athletic teams are nicknamed the Tigers.

45 (p. 72) '*By The Sea*'   Harold R. Atteridge and Harry Carroll's 1914 song 'By The Beautiful Sea'

46 (p. 74) *blue and crimson lines*   the colours of American football teams, respectively of Yale and Harvard

47 (p. 77) *Fatimas*   Fatima Turkish Blend cigarettes

48 (p. 78) *Golden Treasury*   Francis Turner Palgrave's famous anthology of English poetry, *The Golden Treasury of the Best Songs and Lyrical Poems in the English Language*, first published in 1861 and repeatedly reissued

49 (p. 79) *Farmington . . . Dana Hall*   fashionable private girls' schools of the day

50 (p. 79) *the Twin Cities*   St Paul and Minneapolis, Minnesota

51 (p. 79) *St Timothy*   St Timothy's School for Girls, Catonsville, Maryland

52 (p. 80) *Mrs Warren's Profession*   George Bernard Shaw's controversial play about prostitution, first published in 1893 but not produced until 1905 in the USA and 1925 in England

53 (p. 80) *Marpessa* by Stephen Phillips   an English poet (1868–1915), known for his verse dramas. *Marpessa* was first published in 1900.

54 (p. 80) *'Come into the Garden, Maude'*   the first words of poem XII in Alfred Lord Tennyson's *Maud, and Other Poems* (1855)

55 (p. 81) *a Brentano's clerk*   the name of a famous American book-shop

56 (p. 81) *Patience*   an operetta (1881) by W. S. Gilbert and Arthur Sullivan with a satirical portrayal of Oscar Wilde

57 (p. 81) *The Picture of Dorian Gray*   Oscar Wilde's novel of 1891

58 (p. 81) *'Mystic . . . Merci'*   'Mystic and Sombre Dolores' is an allusion to line 7 of Algernon Charles Swinburne's poem 'Dolores' (1866); 'La Belle Dame Sans Merci' is a poem by John Keats.

59 (p. 81) *'Fingal O'Flahertie'*   Wilde's full name was Oscar Fingal O'Flahertie Wills Wilde

60 (p. 82) *Sudermann, Robert Hugh Benson*   Herman Sudermann (1857–1928) was a German playwright; Robert Hugh Benson (1871–1914) was an English priest and novelist, author of *The Light Invisible* (1903) and *The Lord of the World* (1907).

61 (p. 82) *the Savoy Operas*   operettas by Gilbert and Sullivan, so called because they premièred at London's Savoy Theatre

62 (p. 82) *Lord Dunsany's poems*   Edward John Moreton Drax Plunkett (Lord Dunsany), an Irish poet and playwright (1878–1957)

63 (p. 82) *'Hearts and Flowers'*   a sentimental song of 1899 by Mary D. Brine and Theodore Moses Tobani

64 (p. 82) *'Doctor Johnson and Boswell'*   Samuel Johnson (1709–84), poet, essayist, critic, literary editor and lexicographer; James Boswell (1740–95), author of *The Life of Samuel Johnson* (1791)

65 (p. 83) *'Asleep or waking . . . for a fleck . . . '*   the first stanza of Swinburne's 'Laus Veneris', published in his *Poems and Ballads* (1866)

66 (p. 86) *Elis*   nickname given to Yale students, from the name of Elihu Yale (1649–1721) the early benefactor for whom Yale is named

67 (p. 87) *Midnight Frolic*   the roof garden above New York's New Amsterdam Theatre, owned and operated by the impresario Florenz Ziegfeld

68 (p. 88) *Williams*   Williams College in Williamstown, Massachusetts

69 (p. 89) *Thaïs . . . Carmen*   *Thaïs* is an opera (1894) by Jules Massenet, and *Carmen* is the opera (1875) by Georges Bizet.

70 (p. 94) *Stutzes*   The Stutz bearcat was a fashionable two-seater sports car in the 1910s and 1920s.

71 (p. 95) *'Babes In The Wood'* a popular song by Jerome Kern and Schuyler Greene for their Broadway musical *Very Good Eddie* (1915)

72 (p. 98) *black balls* Election to a Princeton dining club depended on the members, who dropped white or black balls into a box; one black ball would eliminate a candidate.

73 (p. 99) *Deal Beach . . . Asbury Park* Deal Beach was a fashionable resort on the New Jersey coast; Asbury Park is a town in the same area.

74 (pp. 99–100) *'Oh, winter's rains . . . flower of –'* from a speech by the Chorus in stanza 4 of Swinburne's *Atalanta in Calydon* (1865)

75 (p. 101) *Ganymede* cupbearer to Zeus in Greek mythology

76 (p. 103) *'Beaches of Lukanon . . . came'* from the second stanza of Rudyard Kipling's poem 'Lukannon' in *The Jungle Book* (1894)

77 (p. 104) *Corneille and Racine* Pierre Corneille (1606–84) and Jean Racine (1639–99), major French playwrights of the seventeenth century

78 (p. 106) *'Love Moon'* . . . *'Goodbye, Boys, I'm Through'* 'Love Moon' was a song by Anne Caldwell and Evan Caryll from the musical *Chin-Chin* (1914); 'Goodbye Boys' was a 1913 song by Andrew B. Sterling, William Dillon, and Harry von Tilzer.

79 (p. 107) *Franks* a fashionable New York shoe store

80 (p. 108) *'silver snarling trumpet'* from line 31 of Keats's poem 'The Eve of St Agnes' (1820)

81 (p. 112) *All the perfumes . . . little hand* from *Macbeth*, 5, 1

82 (p. 115) *'Each life . . . been happy'* stanza 16 of Robert Browning's 'Youth and Art' from his *Dramatis Personae* (1864)

83 (p. 122) *Lafayette Escadrille* a French fighter squadron in the First World War that included American volunteers

84 (p. 125) *John Fox Jr* an American journalist and author of the *The Little Shepherd of Kingdom Come* (1903) and *The Trail of the Lonesome Pine* (1908)

85 (p. 125) *What Every Middle-Aged Woman . . . of the Yukon* J. M. Barrie's play *What Every Woman Knows* (1918), and Robert Service's poetry collection *The Spell of the Yukon* (1915)

86 (p. 127) *General Booth* William Booth (1829–1912), founder of the Salvation Army in 1878

87 (p. 128) *jitney waiter* a waiter who accepts small tips, derived from the term for a bus or train that charged a small fare

88 (p. 135) *The New Machiavelli* a novel (1911) by H. G. Wells

89 (p. 136) *None Other . . . Research Magnificent*   Robert Hugh Benson's novel *None Other Gods* (1911); Compton Mackenzie's novel *Sinister Street* (1913); H. G. Wells's novel *The Research Magnificent* (1915)

90 (p. 137) *Woodrow*   Woodrow Wilson (1856–1924), president of Princeton during the First World War, tried and failed to abolish the college's dining clubs.

91 (p. 138) *the Masses*   a politically left-wing monthly magazine

92 (p. 139) *Varieties of Religious Experience*   William James's treatise on natural religion published in 1902

93 (p. 139) *Edward Carpenter*   a British writer and social reformer (1844–1929)

94 (p. 139) *Anna Karenina and The Kreutzer Sonata*   Tolstoy's novel *Anna Karenina*, published 1875–7, and his story *The Kreutzer Sonata*, published 1889

95 (p. 139) *claqueurs*   a body of people hired to applaud a given situation or event

96 (p. 139) *Huysmans and Bourget*   Joris Karl Huysmans (1848–1907), the French novelist whose famous decadent novel *À rebours* (*Against Nature*) was published in 1884; Paul Bourget (1852–1935), a French critic and novelist

97 (p. 139) *Ralph Adams Cram*   an American architect (1863–1942) who served as supervising architect at Princeton

98 (p. 145) *Philadelphian Society*   a collegiate religious organisation whose members were often intending to enter the ministry

99 (p. 146) *Savonarola*   the Dominican friar Girolamo Savonarola who ruled Florence after the fall of the Medici family and was known as an enemy of corruption in the clergy

100 (p. 146) *'He who is not with me is against me'*   from St Matthew 12:30

101 (p. 148) *Sir Oliver Lodge*   a British scientist (1851–1940) interested in reconciling science and religion

102 (p. 149) *preceptors*   instructors at Princeton who taught small discussion groups and were generally regarded as among the best teachers on campus

103 (p. 150) *Amelia-like*   Amelia Osborne, the modest widow in Thackeray's novel *Vanity Fair* (1848)

104 (p. 158) *Stephen*   Acts 5–6

105 (p. 159) *Peter the Hermit*   the French priest and military officer (1050–1115) who proposed the First Crusade to Pope Urban II

106 (p. 160) *Germany in 1870* supporters of Germany in the
     Franco-Prussian War

107 (p. 162) *'Poor Butterfly'* a song by John L. Golden and
     Raymond Hubbell from the musical *The Big Show* (1916)

108 (p. 162) *von Hindenburg* Paul von Hindenburg (1847–1934),
     leader of the German military in the First World War

109 (p. 163) *Burr and Light-Horse Harry Lee* probably Aaron Burr
     Sr (1716–57), president of Princeton and father of the vice-
     president of the USA, who was a Princeton graduate; Henry
     'Light-Horse Harry' Lee (1756–1818), another Princeton
     graduate who became a Revolutionary War hero for his daring
     missions

110 (p. 163) *Messalina* Valeria Messalina, the third wife of the
     Roman Emperor Claudius, notorious for her lascivious ways

111 (p. 163) *Heraclitus* the fifth-century-BC Greek philosopher
     who believed the cosmos to be in a ceaseless state of flux

112 (p. 170) *Donald Hankey* a British soldier killed in action in
     October 1916 whose essays were collected in *A Student in Arms*
     (1917) and *A Student in Arms, Second Series* (1917)

113 (p. 171) *'Cherry Ripe' . . . Maxfield Parrish* 'Cherry Ripe' was a
     popular painting of a young girl by Sir John Everett Millais; Sir
     Edwin Henry Landseer (1802–73) was a British artist known
     for his paintings of dogs; Maxfield Parrish (1870–1966) was an
     American artist and illustrator.

114 (p. 178) *Spence* the Spence School for Girls, an exclusive private
     school in New York

115 (p. 180) *Coronas* cigarettes aimed at an upscale market

116 (p. 182) *since the French officers went back* During the First
     World War French officers frequently attended social events in
     New York.

117 (p. 183) *Cocoanut Grove* a fashionable rooftop nightclub above
     the Century Theatre in New York

118 (p. 184) *'Kiss Me Again'* a song (1905) by Henry Blossom and
     Victor Herbert which had a popular revival in 1915

119 (p. 186) *Benvenuto Blaine* an allusion to Benvenuto Cellini
     (1500–71), the Italian sculptor and goldsmith known for his
     arrogant autobiography begun in 1558 but not published until
     1730

120 (p. 187) *Annette Kellerman* an Australian swimmer (1887–1975)
     who became a stage and screen actress and was known as the
     'Million Dollar Mermaid'

121 (p. 188) '*Et tu, Brutus*' the reference is to J. M. Barrie's play *Dear Brutus* (1917)

122 (p. 192) *Sancho* Don Quixote's squire Sancho Panza

123 (p. 192) *Ella Wheeler Wilcox* an American newspaperwoman (1850–1919) and popular poet. The first two lines of her poem 'Solitude' have ensured her posthumous fame: 'Laugh and the world laughs with you, / Weep and you weep alone.'

124 (p. 192) '*For this is wisdom . . . let go*' from Lawrence Hope's (pseudonym of Adela Florence Nicolson) 'The Teak Forest' in her *India's Love Lyrics* (1902)

125 (p. 195) '*Rye . . . Bronx*' A rye highball mixes rye whiskey with either soda water or ginger ale; a Bronx mixes gin, vermouth and orange juice.

126 (p. 197) '*Clair de Lune*' a poem by the French poet Paul Verlaine collected in his *Fêtes Galantes* (1869)

127 (p. 197) '*Tyson's . . . The Jest*' Tyson's was a Broadway ticket agency; a play with 'a four-drink programme' was one with five acts and four intervals; '*The Jest*' was a play (1919) with a medieval setting by the Italian dramatist Sam Binelli.

128 (p. 201) '*After You've Gone*' a song (1918) by Henry Creamer and Turner Layton

129 (p. 203) '*A Portrait of the Artist . . . Undying Fire*' The first American edition of James Joyce's *A Portrait of the Artist as a Young Man* was published in 1916; *Joan and Peter* (1918) and *The Undying Fire* (1919) are two novels by H. G. Wells.

130 (p. 203) '*Vandover . . . Gerhardt*' novels by Frank Norris, Harold Frederic and Theodore Dreiser, published in 1914, 1896 and 1911 respectively

131 (p. 203) *Bennett* the British novelist Arnold Bennett (1867–1931), best known for *Anna of the Five Towns* (1902), *The Old Wives' Tale* (1908) and *Clayhanger* (1910)

132 (p. 203) *the Irish President* Eamon de Valera, president of Ireland's Sinn Fein party, visited the USA in 1919 to seek financial aid and political recognition for the Irish Republic.

133 (p. 204) *Stephen Vincent Benét* Benét (1898–1943) was a student and literary figure of considerable repute at Yale: his later narrative poem *John Brown's Body* (1928) won a Pulitzer Prize for its realistic and sympathetic picture of the American Civil War.

134 (p. 204) *Edward Carson and Justice Cohalon* Edward Carson (1854–1935), an Irish Protestant politician who led opposition

to Irish Home Rule; Daniel Florence Cohalan, a New York Supreme Court judge, who, in support of the Irish revolution, advocated German air raids on England

135 (p. 205) *Montespan's wraith*   Louis XIV's mistress, Madame de Montespan, tried to poison her court rivals and was accused of participating in the Black Mass.

136 (p. 206) *Foch*   Ferdinand Foch (1851–1929), known as Marshal Foch, commanded the Allied Forces in the First World War.

137 (p. 206) *Guynemer . . . Sergeant York . . . Pershing*   During the First World War, Georges Marie Guynemer (1894–1917) was a famous and successful French fighter pilot; Alvin Cullum York (1887–1964), popularly known as Sergeant York, was an American hero; John J. Pershing (1860–1927), a life-long career soldier, led the American army in the First World War offensive of July 1918.

138 (p. 206) *'The Hero as a Big Man'*   The reference is to Thomas Carlyle's *On Heroes, Hero-Worship, and the Heroic in History* (1841).

139 (p. 206) *Wood*   Leonard Wood (1860–1927) was Chief of Staff of the US Army from 1910 to 1914, and was considered as the Republican presidential nominee in 1920.

140 (p. 208) *Gouverneur Morris*   an American novelist (1876–1953), author of *Ellen and Mr Man* (1904) and *The Penalty* (1913)

141 (p. 208) *Fannie Hurst*   an American writer of popular fiction including *Every Soul Hath Its Song* (1916) and *Humoresque: A Laugh on Life with a Tear Behind It* (1920)

142 (p. 208) *Cobb*   An American humorist, short-story writer and dramatist, Irvin Cobb (1876–1944) was author of *Old Judge Priest* (1915) and *The Life of the Party* (1919).

143 (p. 209) *Harold Bell Wright*   an American novelist whose works included *Shepherd of the Hills* (1907) and *The Winning of Barbara Worth* (1911)

144 (p. 209) *Rupert Hughes*   an American journalist, novelist and dramatist, author of *Music Lovers' Cyclopedia* (1914), the novel *What Will People Say?* (1914) and the play *Excuse Me* (1911)

145 (p. 209) *Ernest Poole and Dorothy Canfield*   American novelists: Poole (1880–1950) wrote *The Harbor* (1915) and *His Family* (1917), for which he won the Pulitzer Prize; Canfield (1879–1958) wrote *The Squirrel Cage* (1912) and *The Day of Glory* (1918).

146 (p. 209) '*Boston Bards and Hearst Reviewers*' a reference to Byron's satirical *English Bards and Scotch Reviewers* (1809)

147 (pp. 209–10) '*So . . . collected editions*' a list of poets whose work appeared in *The New Poetry* (1917), edited by Harriet Monroe, editor of the avant-garde magazine *Poetry*. Of the poets listed only Carl Sandburg, Louis Untermeyer and Conrad Aiken are still highly regarded.

148 (p. 210) *James J. Hill* an American railroad tycoon (1838–1916)

149 (p. 215) '*Les Sanglots . . . Monotone*' . . . '*Tout suffocant . . . je pleure*' from Paul Verlaine's 'Chanson d'automne' in his *Poèmes saturniens* (1866)

150 (p. 215) *Manfred* the titular hero of Byron's dramatic poem (1817)

151 (p. 217) *Madeline* a reference to Lade Madeline Usher who returns from the dead in Edgar Allan Poe's story 'The Fall of the House of Usher' (1839)

152 (p. 217) '*And now . . . was born*' from Poe's 'Ulalume: A Ballad' (1847)

153 (p. 219) '*Bind on thy sandals . . . thy feet*' from a speech by the Chorus in Swinburne's *Atalanta in Calydon* (1865)

154 (p. 220) '*Granchester to Waikiki*' a reference to Rupert Brooke's poems 'Waikiki' (1913) and 'The Old Vicarage, Granchester' (1912)

155 (p. 221) '*Is it worth . . . deed forborne?*' from Swinburne's 'The Triumph of Time' in his *Poems and Ballads* (1866)

156 (p. 226) *the sixth and ninth commandments* 'Thou shalt not kill' and 'Thou shalt not bear false witness against thy neighbour'

157 (p. 232) *the Mann Act* Passed by congress in 1910, the Mann Act made it illegal for an individual to assist or participate in the transportation of a woman across state lines 'for immoral purposes': transgressors could receive a prison sentence.

158 (p. 234) *Weep not for me but for thy children* from St Luke 23:28–9

159 (p. 239) *porte-cochère* the roof over the entrance to a theatre.

160 (p. 240) *car cards* advertisements on cards that appeared above the windows in subway (underground) cars

161 (p. 246) *Bernhardi, Bonar Law and Bethmann-Hollweg* Friedrich von Bernhardi (1849–1930), a Prussian general and author of the novel *Germany and the Next War* (1911), in which he asserted Germany's right to wage war; Bonar Law (1858–1923), a British

statesman who formed a coalition government with Lloyd
George during the First World War; Theobald von Bethmann-
Hollweg (1856–1921), chancellor of Germany who encouraged
his country's participation in the First World War as a
distraction from its internal problems

162 (p. 247) *Renan*   the French critic, writer, and scholar Joseph
Ernest Renan (1823–92), whose *La Vie de Jésus* (1863) argued
that Jesus was not the Son of God but a human being divinely
inspired

163 (p. 248) *Requiem aeternam*   the Mass for the dead of the Roman
Catholic faith

164 (p. 249) *Locomobile*   an expensive autombile of the day: it was
open to the air, so that those riding in it wore goggles

165 (p. 254) *Mackays instead of Burlesons*   Clarence Hungerford
Mackay (1874–1938) was a philanthropic Catholic businessman
of the day whose first wife, Katherine Mackay, was a leading
suffragette; Albert Sidney Burleson (1863–1937) was an
American politician and served as Postmaster General during
the First World War and sought to ban from the mail any
material critical of government policy.

166 (p. 254) *McAdoo*   William G. McAdoo (1863–1941) was
Secretary of the Treasury from 1913 to 1918 and director
general of railways from 1917 to 1919.

167 (p. 259) *'Out of the Fire, Out of the Little Room'*   from Rupert
Brooke's 'The Night Journey' in his *1914 and Other Poems*
(1915)

168 (p. 259) *Lewis gunner*   a light machine-gun used by the
American and British forces in the First World War

NOTES ON THE TEXT OF
THE BEAUTIFUL AND DAMNED

169 (p. 264) *Shane Leslie . . . Perkins* Sir John Randolph Leslie (1885–1971), scion of an Anglo-Irish aristocratic family and educated at Eton and Cambridge, was a diplomat and writer; known as Shane Leslie, he lived in America for several years where he knew Fitzgerald who regarded him 'as the most romantic figure I had ever known'. George Jean Nathan (1882–1958) was a drama and social critic, editor, memoirist; Maxwell Perkins (1884–1947) was Fitzgerald's editor at Scribner's.

170 (p. 268) *Tarrytown* a village on the Hudson River north of New York City

171 (p. 268) *Anthony Comstock* Founder of the Society for the Suppression of Vice, Comstock (1844–1915) devoted his life to the enactment and enforcement of laws regulating morality in the USA.

172 (p. 268) *Chesterfield* Philip Dormer Stanhope, 4th Earl of Chesterfield (1694–1773), notorious in British cultural history as the man who failed to keep his promise of financial patronage to Samuel Johnson in the making of Johnson's *A Dictionary of the English Language*

173 (p. 269) *Lord Fauntleroy suit* a velvet suit with lace collar and cuffs, the epitome of inappropriate foppishness in dress for boys. See Frances Hodgson Burnett's novel *Little Lord Fauntleroy* (1886).

174 (p. 269) *Washington Square* a public park in an area of New York south of Fifth Avenue

175 (p. 269) *Atlantic City* a resort in south-east New Jersey on the Atlantic Ocean

176 (p. 270) *Beck Hall* a private dormitory that catered to the sons of the wealthy

177 (p. 271) *Pudding* Harvard University Hasty Pudding Club, devoted to the production of an annual theatrical musical

178 (p. 272) *Central Park* the famous large park in Manhattan

179 (p. 276) *Erewhon* a satire on the concept of utopia (1872), by Samuel Butler (1835–1902). The title is an anagram of 'nowhere'.

180 (p. 279) *The Demon Lover . . . 'woman wailing'* from the second stanza of Samuel Taylor Coleridge's poem 'Kubla Khan' (1798)

181 (p. 280) *Chesterton, Shaw, Wells* G. K. Chesterton (1874–1936), George Bernard Shaw (1856–1950) and H. G. Wells (1886–1946)

182 (p. 281) *The Woman* melodrama by William C. de Mille, starring Mary Nash, which opened in New York on 19 September 1911

183 (p. 281) *Follies* theatrical review presented by Florenz Ziegfeld at the New Amsterdam Theatre, Broadway

184 (p. 281) *'Dear old Pinafore'* HMS *Pinafore* (1878), an operetta by Gilbert and Sullivan

185 (p. 282) *High Jinks* musical farce by Leo Ditrichstein and Otto Hauerbach, music by Rudolf Friml, which opened in New York in December 1913

186 (p. 282) *Sherry's* fashionable restaurant on Fifth Avenue and 44th Street

187 (p. 282) *Times Square* midtown Manhattan with theatres and hotels, on the intersection of Broadway and Seventh Avenue; named after the *New York Times* newspaper building on 43rd Street

188 (p. 283) *Astor* large hotel on Broadway between 44th and 45th Streets

189 (p. 287) *Riverside* Riverside Drive, an area on the West Side of Manhattan.

190 (p. 287) *Bronx* the northernmost borough of New York City

191 (p. 287) *Castles* ballroom dancers Irene (1893–1969) and Vernon Castle (1887–1918)

192 (p. 288) *the Manhattan Hotel* on Madison Avenue between 42nd and 43rd Streets

193 (p. 289) *Plaza* luxury hotel on Fifth Avenue between 58th and 59th Streets

194 (p. 289) *Bilphist* Fitzgerald's coinage: a satirical view of theosophy

195 (p. 290) *Spencer* Herbert Spencer (1820–1903), major nineteenth-century thinker who applied Darwin's theory of evolution to his philosophical ideas and believed in the power of the individual in society and science over religion: he coined the phrase 'survival of the fittest'.

196 (p. 295) *Baedeker* popular guidebooks for tourists, named after their publisher, Karl Baedeker (1801–59)

197 (p. 297) *Keith's* one of a chain of vaudeville theatres owned by B. F. Keith

198 (p. 297) *Rousseau* philosopher Jean Jacques Rousseau (1712–78), who believed that humans were good by nature but had been corrupted by civilisation and society

199 (p. 298) *Dana* Richard Henry Dana (1815–82), author of *Two Years Before the Mast* (1840), autobiographical narrative of a sailor

200 (p. 299) *Bergson* French philosopher Henri Bergson (1859–1941), who believed that evolution was not merely mechanistic and was affected by an *élan vital* (vital impuse) in all life

201 (p. 299) *one-step* a ballroom dance; a version of the foxtrot popularised by Irene and Vernon Castle

202 (p. 302) *Tribune* the *Tribune*, a New York newspaper with Republican leanings

203 (p. 304) *University Club* housed on Fifth Avenue and 54th Street; one of New York's many prestigious clubs

204 (p. 304) *Talleyrand* Charles Maurice de Talleyrand (1754–1838), French statesman during the French Revolution, under Napoleon, during the Bourbon restoration and under King Louis Philippe. He was known for his skills and cunning and his many diplomatic triumphs.

205 (p. 304) *Lord Verulam* Francis Bacon, Viscount St Albans, Baron Verulam (1561–1626), Lord Chancellor of England (1618–21), philosopher, essayist, counsellor to Queen Elizabeth I and King James I. He was known for his wide intellectual gifts as well as his ability as a forceful speaker.

206 (p. 304) *rotogravure* printing process used for newspaper supplements and magazines that reproduced photographs and other illustrations with a full range of tonal values. Thus the word was used for a newspaper section mainly with photographs.

207 (p. 305) *Alice-blue* a shade of blue – pale greenish or greyish blue – named after Alice Roosevelt Longworth, daughter of President Theodore Roosevelt

208 (p. 308) *maxixe* a popular ballroom dance of the time resembling the two-step and related to the tango

209 (p. 313–14) *Rupert Hughes* popular and prolific American author (1872–1956) of fiction and non-fiction, plays and magazine articles

210 (p. 316) '*Something – goes . . . your ear*' 'Ring-A-Ting-A-Ling On The Telephone', music by Jean Schwartz, lyrics by William Jerome, from *Over the River*, which opened in New York on 8 January 1912

211 (p. 318) *Harvard Crimson* Harvard student newspaper

212 (p. 319) *the Sun* New York afternoon politically independent newspaper

213 (p. 319) *Harvard Club* handsome building at 44th Street, between Fifth and Sixth Avenues, noted for its extremely spacious triple-height lounge

214 (p. 323) *Justine Johnson's Little Club* nightclub in the Schubert Theatre Building, West 44th Street, between Broadway and Eighth Avenue

215 (p. 324) *East Orange* a small city in north-east New Jersey, a suburb of Newark

216 (p. 326) *Beaux Art* Cafés des Beaux Arts, a popular after-dinner meeting-place at 40th Street and Sixth Avenue

217 (p. 332) *Cascades at the Biltmore* internationally celebrated summer dining-room at the top of the Biltmore Hotel, Vanderbilt Avenue to Madison Avenue, known for its Italian Renaissance-style architecture

218 (p. 333) *Peg o' My Heart* sentimental comedy by J. Hartley Manners, starring Laurette Taylor, which opened in New York 20 December 1912

219 (p. 333) *Omar, the Tentmaker* melodrama (based on *The Rubáiyát of Omar Khayyám*) by Richard Walton Tully and starring Guy Bates Post, which opened in New York, 13 January 1914

220 (p. 333) *Fair and Warmer* farce by Avery Hopwood, starring Madge Kennedy and Ralph Morgan, which opened in New York on 6 November 1915

221 (p. 333) *Within the Law* melodrama by Bayard Veiller, starring Jane Cowl, which opened in New York 11 September 1912

222 (p. 333) *The Little Café* music by Ivan Caryll, lyrics by C. M. S. McLellan, which opened in New York on 10 November 1913; adapted from *Le Petit Café* by Tristan Bernard

223 (p. 335) *He's a rag-picker . . . pick, pick* song, 'He's A Rag Picker' (1914), by Irving Berlin

224 (p. 336) *seidel* a large glass or mug for beer

225 (p. 336) '*Everything's At Home Except Your Wife*' song, music by Ivan Caryll, lyrics by C. M. S. McLellan, from *Oh! Oh! Delphine*, which opened in New York on 30 September 1912

226 (p. 337) *Grand Central Station*   railway terminal at 42nd Street

227 (p. 338) *the Metropolitan Museum*   the Metropolitan Museum of Art, on Fifth Avenue and 82nd Street

228 (p. 339) *Thérèse of France*   in the novel *Thérèse Raquin* (1867) by Emile Zola

229 (p. 339) *Ann the Superwoman*   Ann Whitfield in George Bernard Shaw's *Man and Superman* (1903)

230 (p. 339) *Jenny of the Orient Ballet*   possibly an allusion to Lady Randolph Churchill (1845–1921). Fitzgerald visited her in May 1921, a month before her death, as well as Shane Leslie, her cousin by marriage.

231 (p. 339) *Zuleika the Conjurer*   in Sir Max Beerbohm's satire *Zuleika Dobson* (1911)

232 (p. 339) *Hoosier Cora*   in Booth Tarkington's play *Clarence* (1919), a comedy

233 (p. 339) *Helen*   Helen of Troy

234 (p. 339) *Thaïs*   Athenian courtesan of the fourth century BC, who, according to legend, induced Alexander the Great to set fire to the palace of the Persian kings at Persepolis. See also Anatole France's novel *Thaïs* (1890).

235 (p. 339) *Salome*   niece of Herod Antipas, who danced for the head of John the Baptist. See St Mark 6:16–28.

236 (p. 341) *cloth of Samarkand*   John Keats in 'The Eve of St Agnes' refers to 'silken Samarcand'.

237 (p. 341) *Ganymede*   in Greek mythology a Trojan boy of great beauty taken by Zeus

238 (p. 342) *gutta-percha*   a hard rubber-like substance; here a piece of the telephone

239 (p. 344) *supes*   supernumeraries, actors in non-speaking roles

240 (p. 349) *Child's*   one of a chain of New York restaurants

241 (p. 353) *L'Éducation sentimentale*   novel (1870) by Gustave Flaubert (1821–80)

242 (p. 353) *Central*   the telephone operator

243 (p. 354) *Hot Springs*   a health resort in Arkansas noted for its thermal springs

244 (p. 361) *Delmonico's*   fashionable restaurant on Fifth Avenue and 44th Street

245 (p. 366) *'Gypsy' Smith*   an evangelist. There were two well-known Gypsy Smiths, both evangelists, in New York in 1921 when Fitzgerald was writing and revising this novel – the English Gypsy Rodney Smith and the Scottish Captain Gypsy

Pat Smith. On 15 October, Captain Gypsy Pat Smith's apology for repeating a false story about New York mayor John Hylan's wife was reported in the *New York Times*; on 20 October the same paper published his letter noting the confusion between the two evangelists.

246 (p. 367) *Tiffany's*   a jewellery store then on Fifth Avenue at 37th Street

247 (p. 368) *New Haven*   Connecticut location of Yale University

248 (p. 369) *'Yama-Yama, My Yama Man'*   'The Yama-Yama Man', music by Karl Hoschna, lyrics by Collin Davis, from *Three Twins*, which opened in New York on 15 June 1908.

249 (p. 369) *'Jungle-Town'*   song (1908) by Walter G. Samuels, Jack Scholl and Leonard Whitcup, from *Jungle Town Review*

250 (p. 372) *Gramercy Park*   a neighbourhood with luxury apartments and town houses on the East Side of Manhattan between 18th and 23rd Streets, with a private park of the same name

251 (p. 373) *Mumm's Extra Dry*   a popular champagne from the House of G. H. Mumm

252 (p. 374) *wet wedding*   wedding at which alcoholic drinks were served during the time of Prohibition

253 (p. 375) *Nora Bayes*   actress and singer (1880–1928)

254 (p. 377) *Santa Barbara*   Californian city on the Pacific Ocean; at the time a seaside resort

255 (p. 377) *Greenwich*   upper-class Connecticut town on Long Island Sound, a body of water between the south shore of Connecticut and the north shore of Long Island

256 (p. 382) *Coronado*   a tourist city in southern California near San Diego

257 (p. 384) *General Lee*   Robert E. Lee (1807–1970), Confederate general in the American Civil War, commander of the army of Northern Virginia

258 (p. 385) *Sleepy Hollow*   locality at North Tarrytown, New York, mentioned in Washington Irving's *The Legend of Sleepy Hollow* (1819–20)

259 (p. 385) *Liège*   city in Belgium invaded by Germany in August 1914

260 (p. 388) *Morristown*   town in northern New Jersey

261 (p. 390) *Gibson girls*   illustrations of attractive women by Charles Dana Gibson (1867–1944)

262 (p. 390) *pinochle*   a card game played with a deck of forty-eight cards

263 (p. 395) *Beatrice Fairfax*   pseudonym of writers of a popular column of the time in Hearst newspapers giving advice on personal problems

264 (p. 395) *Vanderbilt lobby*   lobby of a large hotel on Madison Avenue and 34th Street

265 (p. 400) *Vic*   the Victrola, a generic term for gramophone or phonograph

266 (p. 400) *Caruso*   famous operatic tenor Enrico Caruso (1873–1921)

267 (p. 400) *Al Jolson*   (1886–1950), musical-comedy singer

268 (p. 401) *St Nicholas ice-skating rink*   rink at Columbus Avenue and 66th Street

269 (p. 402) *Porcellian*   exclusive Harvard University students' club

270 (p. 402) *Skull and Bones*   exclusive Yale University students' club

271 (p. 405) *Kant's Critique*   *Critique of Pure Reason* (1781) by Immanuel Kant (1724–1804)

272 (p. 412) *Hoboken*   New Jersey city on the Hudson River opposite Manhattan

273 (p. 413) *Pullman smoker*   a railroad car in which smoking was permitted

274 (p. 415) *Penrod*   a novel (1914) by Booth Tarkington

275 (p. 417) *Mary Pickford*   screen actress (1893–1979)

276 (p. 422) *Packy McFarland*   Patrick Francis McFarland (1888–1936), lightweight boxer

277 (p. 425) *Mercure de France*   a French literary review. Anthony has in mind the second *Mercure de France* founded by symbolist writers in Paris in 1889.

278 (p. 429) *Thackeray*   novelist William Makepeace Thackeray (1811–63)

279 (p. 429) *Balzac*   novelist Honoré de Balzac (1799–1850)

280 (p. 429) *Hugo*   poet, novelist and playwright Victor Hugo (1802–85)

281 (p. 429) *Gibbon*   historian Edward Gibbon (1737–94)

282 (p. 429) *rival mansions of Mr Frick and Mr Carnegie on Fifth Avenue*   wealthy industrialists Henry Clay Frick (1849–1919) and Andrew Carnegie (1835–1919), ex-business partners with a mutual dislike, who both owned mansions on Fifth Avenue

283 (p. 435) *Sound*   Long Island Sound

284 (p. 449) *Anatole France*   French writer (1844–1924)

285 (p. 452) *chromo*   a chromolithograph, a type of picture printed in colour

286 (p. 459) *At last . . . the perfect definition! Cardinal Newman's is now a back number*   In *The Idea of a University* (1873), John Henry, Cardinal Newman wrote: 'It is almost a definition of a gentleman to say he is one who never inflicts pain.'

287 (p. 459) *General Ludendorff*   German general Erich Ludendorff (1865–1937), military strategist and policy maker; chief of staff during the First World War to General Paul von Hindenberg

288 (p. 460) *Poor Butter-fly . . .*   'Poor Butterfly', music by Raymond Hubbell, lyrics by John Golden, from *The Big Show*, which opened in New York, 31 August 1916

289 (p. 461) *One gaunt bleak blossom of scentless breath*   from the fifth stanza of Algernon Charles Swinburne's 'A Forsaken Garden' (1876)

290 (p. 473) *Cato the Censor*   Marcus Porcius Cato (234–149 BC), Roman statesman and moral reformer

291 (p. 477) *Town Tattle*   *Town Topics* was a gossip magazine of the time.

292 (p. 480) *four hundred*   phrase referring to New York City society originated in 1892 by lawyer and social leader Ward McAllister

293 (p. 487) *hommes 40, chevaux 8*   During the First World War in France, the standing troop transport by train was a boxcar with provision for forty men and eight horses.

294 (p. 487) *Camp Upton*   army reception and training centre, Yaphank, Long Island, New York

295 (p. 498) *Snappy Stories*   bi-monthly pulp magazine featuring popular short stories as well as essays, cartoons and film and play reviews

296 (p. 498) *When you wa-ake . . . hawsiz*   from 'All The Pretty Little Horses', a traditional Southern lullaby

297 (p. 498) *la belle dame sans merci*   'The Beautiful Lady without Mercy' was the final rejected title for *The Beautiful and Damned*; one of the title-pages of the manuscript included a stanza from John Keats's 'La Belle Dame Sans Merci: A Ballad' (written 1819):

> 'I saw pale kings, and princes too,
>   Pale warriors, death pale were they all:
> Who cried – "La belle Dame sans Merci
>   Hath thee in thrall!" '

298 (p. 498) *Bois de Boulogne*   a large park in Paris

299 (p. 504) *Atalanta in Calydon*   verse drama (1865) by Algernon Charles Swinburne

300 (p. 508) *K-K-K-Katy*   a popular 'stammering song' (1918), words and music by Geoffrey O'Hara

301 (p. 515) *Camp Mills*   army embarkation camp, Garden City, Long Island, New York

302 (p. 517) *Pennsylvania Station*   railroad station between Seventh and Eighth Avenues

303 (p. 518) *Vanity Fair*   a contemporary American magazine of fashion, the arts, sport and humour

304 (p. 527) *Scroll and Keys*   Scroll and Keys Society, Yale. University, a students' club

305 (p. 529) *Ethan Frome*   novel (1911) by Edith Wharton. The reference here is to Gloria's reaction to this tale of a man trapped in a loveless marriage.

306 (p. 542) *Babe Ruth*   famous baseball player who in 1919 had set a record for the most home runs in a season while playing for the Boston Red Sox

307 (p. 542) *Jack Dempsey*   boxer who won the heavyweight championship by defeating Jess Willard on 4 July 1919 in Toledo, Ohio

308 (p. 545) *'Odi Profanum Vulgus'*   'I hate the common herd' (Horace, Odes, III, i, 1)

309 (p. 553) *Claremont Avenue*   in uptown Manhattan, west of Columbia University

310 (p. 553) *the Palisades*   cliffs along the west side of the Hudson River

311 (p. 561) *Bush Terminal Building*   Bush Terminal Sales Building, 42nd Street, between Fifth and Sixth Avenues, the tallest building in the Times Square area at the time; the upper storeys were designed to look like a Gothic chapel and, at night, strong electric lights were concentrated on the building, thus its popular title, 'The Rajah's Jewel'.

312 (p. 563) *Shave-Tail*   army slang for a young or newly commissioned second lieutenant

313 (p. 565) *the usual Longfellow–Whittier thing*   American poets Henry Wadsworth Longfellow (1807–82) and John Greenleaf Whittier (1807–92) were considered writers of traditional values.

314 (p. 565) *Mark Twain*   pen-name of the American writer Samuel L. Clemens (1835–1910)

315 (p. 565) *Dreiser*   American writer Theodore Dreiser (1871–1945)

316 (p. 565) *Thackeray of America*   Many of Thackeray's novels were famous for scenes set in London: the point here is that Caramel's novel is set in New York.

317 (p. 567) *Reisenweber's*   prestigious restaurant with a dance hall on the roof; at Broadway and Columbus Circle

318 (p. 576) *running-board*   a narrow footboard on the lower side of a motor car

319 (p. 580) *Piazza di Spagna*   a tourist attraction in Rome, a square dominated by the Spanish Steps